# THE HARMONY PARADOX

## VIRTUAL IMMORTALITY BOOK 2

## MATTHEW S. COX

DIVISION ZERO PRESS

The Harmony Paradox
Virtual Immortality Book 2
© 2017 Matthew S. Cox
All rights reserved

ISBN (ebook): 978-1-949174-58-8

ISBN (print): 978-1-949174-59-5

# CONTENTS

# AUTHOR'S NOTE

At times during this story, characters have conversations via cybernetic implants. This form of communication does not project audio to the outside world and can be heard only by the participants. Dialogue indicating conversations over implants are denoted by bracket quotes:

「This is an example of conversation inside the character's head over an implant.」

"This is normal dialogue."

Also, some non-English dialogue (where context does not provide translation) is translated at the end of the book for reference.)

# SEVENTEEN DAYS

**Eight months after the events of *Virtual Immortality*.**

Methodical as always, Nina thought over the operation backward and forward while observing forty-eight-year-old Jerome Drummond in the green-on-green of a night vision scope. Seventeen days ago, GlobeNet sniffer programs tripped on a communication channel to Europe, a network address belonging to the Allied Corporate Council Citizen Management group—their law enforcement. Contents of multiple successive messages detailed the intent for a UCF corporation to purchase eight prisoners, orphaned children of rebel fighters who'd survived a raid on their resistance cell. The only problem was, no one had yet figured out how they'd been smuggled into West City, or where they were.

Nina, as well as many of the people working under her on this case, hadn't slept a full night in seventeen days.

In her crosshairs, the senior vice president of Osiris Biotechnic—chief of R&D —reclined in a massive black chair behind a desk of chrome and glass. He sported a sculpted flattop, white-collar shirt, thin tie, seventy-five thousand credit emerald cufflinks, and an 'I own the world' smile. A holo-panel hovering over his desk bore the image of a stocky, square-jawed man of similar age, though far paler than the dark-skinned Drummond, who shimmered from the light it cast.

*What is it about corporate types? They always leave the lights off when they ignore the law... or human decency.*

For six hours, she lay prone atop the roof of another century tower, one full of office space owned by Halcyon-Ormyr. It took five hours and forty-four minutes of waiting for Drummond to receive the call the network people said he would. The hovercar manufacturer would likely never become aware Division 9 had been there. If anyone happened to notice her, they'd probably decide to mind their own business: her sand brown long coat and clingy black bodysuit screamed government agent. She shifted, attempting to evade an awkward lump pressing into her side. The layer of gel in the ballistic stealth armor could harden in a microsecond to stop bullets, but it didn't do much to protect against a roof covered in egg-sized 'decorative stones.'

Her jet-black bob blew in a wind her body could ignore when she wanted it to; synthetic skin and plastisteel didn't care about cold. She sometimes missed having her hair long. In this body, it didn't grow unless she triggered nanobots to make it longer, and so far, she hadn't seen a reason to beyond sentiment.

A wire connected a port at the back of her neck to a modified UCF-M22A7 assault rifle, allowing its optics to interface with her eyes. Range and windage information appeared in tiny text at the lower right of her vision above a giant numeral '6' indicating the number of rounds remaining. Optical elements in the rifle's boxy outer casing projected a pattern matching the multicolored rocks, creating the illusion the weapon had been made of glass. Her mental command extended the motorized barrel out to its full five-foot length. Lime green crosshairs and a hairline trajectory estimation arc centered on the executive's head as her vision zoomed in enough to perceive particles of dust in the gaps between loaf-shaped segments of cushion behind him. A faint *whirr* in her right ear announced a caseless round sliding into the chamber by her cheek.

*If the intel's good, 12.5mm is too quick.*

For more than two weeks, Nina and her team had been staring at 'arrest photos' of eight young children who'd probably watched their parents die. Grainy images, wide-eyed expressions of anguish and dread had etched in her memory. She, and everyone at Division 9 who'd gotten wind of this operation, wanted to kick down a door or two, but Osiris had five research facilities, three of which they'd tried to hide from the government. They all feared choosing wrong would spook the VP, and a potential rescue operation would become an eight-count murder investigation—if anyone ever managed to find bodies. Normally, Nina preferred delicate operations… but these were children. The waiting had been the second most unbearable thing she'd ever lived through.

Division 9 NetOps owned the Osiris Biotechnic network for the past two weeks. The audio feed patched in via her internal uplink brought her ears virtually into the room as though she stood at Drummond's side.

"I am glad we could come to an arrangement," said the man on the holo-panel —Gamedi Zharkov according to her case notes—a director of citizen management in Minsk. The Allied Corporate Council ran everything, even their military, like another part of a corporation. "My associates tell me the merchandise arrived intact, yet we are still waiting for the payment."

Drummond's eyes flickered with irritation. "There should be no deviation from our deal, Gamedi. Two and a half million per unit. Fifteen percent up front, the rest on delivery. Doctor Rice has yet to confirm that nothing was damaged in transit and none of the petri dishes are contaminated with anything that could render them useless for our purposes. As soon as he tells me everything is as expected, you will get paid."

Gamedi's lips stretched into a wide line, not quite a frown, but not far from it. "We are short seventeen million credits, Mr. Drummond." His Russian accent thickened. "You are aware these castoffs could have been more easily dealt with locally, especially the ones too young to have adopted their parents' radical ideologies. It is a risk for both of us."

"Oh, come now." Drummond reached forward, resting his hand on the desk, one finger tapping the glass. "We both know your people have little regard for non-citizens no matter how old they are, and these were part of your little"—the man failed to conceal all of his condescending amusement—"resistance problem? I am curious, Gamedi, if your society is the superior one, why is it that your very own citizens have taken up arms in secret?"

"Unrest is universal, my friend. Regardless of who is in charge, someone will claim it unjust." Gamedi coughed into his fist. "The vermin are as you requested. Their families *were* criminals. There is no one to ask questions, no trails to cause problems. It is perhaps ironic that your company, within the great and noble UCF, conducts such unseemly business."

Jerome turned his hands upward. "If you find our research so distasteful, why then did you sell them to us? Could it be your stake in the research data? Hmm?"

"Need I remind you the sort of issues you may experience should your, how you say, 'NewsNet' receives certain recordings?" Gamedi smiled. "It would be not so pleasant for Osiris's stock, yes?"

Drummond flinched. "You should have received the funds by now. Perhaps some of them aren't quite as healthy and useful as you claimed?" He waved a hand at his desk, summoning another holo-panel. "Give me a minute."

Forty-one seconds later, an exasperated middle-aged man with short silvery hair swept back over his head appeared on the second screen. A mixture of wailing children, one screaming in anger, and monkey-like whooping came over the new connection.

"I'm very busy now, Drummond, dealing with your rush job. We were supposed to have another two weeks to prepare."

"Why haven't I received a message confirming receipt? Our friends in the east are expecting payment." Drummond had to yell to overpower the noise.

Doctor Rice's irritation deepened. "They're all usable, but it will be a few weeks of waiting for them to get back up to normal weight before we can start any tests. As of now, their systems are too stressed for any useful data collections. The weakest of the samples would likely kill them in hours. However, for purposes of the agreement, they are fine. I sent the confirmation message over twenty minutes ago. Now, if you'll leave me to my work."

⌐ Lieutenant Duchenne, this is DeWinter. Confirm trace on the remote facility. We're kicking the gates down now and securing their network. Physical location should upload to group Navcon in three seconds.⌐

Hardin's virtual face offered a solemn nod. ⌐Duchenne, proceed.⌐

⌐Roger, Ops. Net Team, lights out. One ticket to Miami.⌐ Nina's voice over the comm channel set off a flurry of activity. Her boss shouted at a field squad to move on the lab where eight foreign children were about to face who-knows-what. The Vidphone calls to both Gamedi and Doctor Rice went dark, and a little red dot winked on beside the door of the VP's office as the mechanism locked.

She sent her voice over the GlobeNet to his holo-terminal. "Jerome Drummond, this is Division 9. Have fun in hell."

The man opened his mouth to shout; time dragged to a standstill as Nina's combat boosters kicked in. A handful of electrons raced down the wire into the rifle, setting off the electronic trigger so her finger didn't have to move. A spark tickled the electrode foil at the back end of a caseless block of propellant. Three relative seconds later, a massive 12.5mm slug came spiraling out of the barrel without a trace of muzzle flare. The projectile cruised across the street ninety-seven stories below and kissed the window of Drummond's office.

Bright silver lines raced a zigzag spider web away from the contact point; glittering diamond flakes followed the bullet into the room amid the slow-motion symphony of glass shearing apart. A split second of scream left the VP's throat, a low demonic sound in Nina's accelerated time state, as the spinning bullet struck the cheek ridge below Drummond's right eye.

The window turned white; long, jagged cracks flashed to a near-opaque crisscross of tiny fragments. Streams of blood squirted out of his ears, expelled by a pressure wave traveling through his brain. The majority of solid material within the man's head erupted in a blast of gore, which leapt onto the wall. Like snow, the suspension of glass fragments cascaded down, more than half raining along the side of the building toward the distant street.

She shut off her boosters; time returned to normal.

Drummond slumped in the chair, two vertebrae and a flap of skin all that remained above his shoulders. A cloud of diamond-like glass bits collapsed on the rug, and the door lock turned green. Hardin would probably grumble about speaking to the target, calling it a warning that could've increased the risk of the VP getting away. She didn't care. He had to know *why*. The recording of everything she'd seen and heard over the past twenty minutes went out over a shadow VPN few civilians even knew existed, back to the D9 system.

⌜I'm done here. Tell the site team I'm on the way.⌟

---

DRUMMOND'S CALL TO DOCTOR RICE HAD BEEN LIKE A BRIGHT NEON ROADMAP through the darkness of the GlobeNet, leading the Division 9 NetOps team straight to an unregistered R&D facility in Sector 7904, near the south edge of what had once been called Oregon. The lower-middle-class residential district sat one alley away from the wall on the inland edge of West City, seventy-five meters over an area known four centuries ago as Ashland, according to the archives. It surprised her they hadn't put a project like this out in the Badlands, and she wondered if educated people actually believed in all the stories about technology mysteriously failing out there.

She flicked her thumb at the hovercar's control stick, entertaining an idle memory of Shabundo Ghede moving souls between humans and machines. *I suppose stranger things have been true.*

Her unmarked black patrol craft rounded the corner of a steel-and-glass residence tower; the flight south from the Osiris Biotechnic corporate office had taken nineteen minutes at 618 mph. Sometimes, having a Class 3 doll body and far-beyond-human reflexes came in handy.

Already, a scattering of nondescript black hovercars, two vans, and four blue-and-white Division 1 patrol craft collected around the front.

⌜Network is clear. No automated defenses. Initiating file lockdown,⌟ said DeWinter on a voice-only link.

A virtual holo-panel opened, bearing the face of a woman with short black hair and brown skin in a black Division 9 operator's suit, rubbery material straight up to her jawline. The ID widget under the panel read: Operative [O1] Padilla, R.

「Lieutenant. The facility is located two levels below street. The super says he had no idea it was there. All four elevators reach it, but only with a specific code and ID. You should be able to walk right in. Sanchez must've been sleeping in training. It took him fifteen minutes to get the damn front door open.」

Seconds later, Sergeant Sanchez appeared on a separate virtual window, holding up a middle finger.

Nina eyed the ground; the closest clear landing area offered a longer walk than she wanted to waste time on. 「I'm here. Is the site secure?」

「Yes, lieutenant. No hostiles, but...」 Operative Padilla looked off to the side, somewhere between wanting to cry and scream in rage. A shrieking child and a repetitive *bang, bang, bang* echoed in the background. 「They're... these people. They're not even human.」

Nina's mental impulse caused her virtual avatar to nod. She hurried into a reckless landing between the building and a pair of tech vans, with less than two inches of clearance on all sides. Nothing an unaugmented person would've dared to try. The rapid descent made two Division 1 patrol officers scream and dive for cover, evidently expecting a crash.

She got out and stormed through the building's entrance, six feet from her car. A small group of civilians loitered about, curious at the police presence, but seeming clueless as to the reason for it. Ignoring the questions shouted over the helmets of more patrol officers, Nina headed for the elevator.

NetOps had hacked the touchscreen, adding a destination labeled 'Secret Illegal Research Facility' below the basement. *That's got 'Joey' written all over it.* She whirled to face the door and jabbed a finger into the screen, barely holding back enough not to shatter the glass.

Soon, the elevator doors opened to a lounge-like room with two purple couches, four vendomats, and a wall-mounted holo-screen showing a Gee-ball match. Two mirror-finished disc bots as big as dinner plates scooted back and forth over pristine white tiles, cleaning the floor. The same repetitive *bang, bang, bang* noise she'd heard over the comm link grew louder the farther she walked. She followed the sound of activity into a hallway leading out from the front right corner and strode past five offices and a conference room to a pinned-open double glass sliding security door.

She stopped short at the sight waiting for her.

Four Division 9 field operatives stood around a large room with medium-sized primate cages, four-foot cubes built into the left and right walls, stacked two rows high like tiny jail cells. Rhesus monkeys occupied four of them, as well as a lone black chimpanzee. The remaining non-empty cages contained dirt-smeared human children, ranging in age from around five to maybe ten, all of whom looked malnourished. A plastiboard box on a silver table at the center of the room held a mound of stained, ratty clothing that stank to the point a street vagrant would scoff at it. Next to it sat a pile of police-style zip cuffs, all cut open.

Myofiber muscles in Nina's arms shivered with imperceptible trembles of anger as she imagined the children being carried in, cut free, stripped, and stuffed into cages one after the next like goddamned research monkeys.

In the first cage, left wall top row, a tiny blonde girl of about six lay on her back, stomping both feet against the bars of her cube-shaped prison, while screeching like the animal they'd treated her as. The cage had little reaction to her assault, though a hanging water bottle had already been shaken halfway empty. Next to her in the adjacent enclosure, a girl a year or two older with dark hair cowered, trembling, against the inner wall, back to the room and trying to cover herself as much as she could. The remaining six children were all boys. Some sat like lumps where they'd been dropped, morose expressions of acceptance on their faces; the youngest sobbed, but tried to stay quiet. The oldest, a sandy-brown haired boy of about ten, knelt in the center of his cage, both hands covering his crotch, and stared at the Division 9 team with a look of guarded hostility.

A cabinet on the wall to the left of the kicking girl's cage held sedative autoinjectors and a five-foot pole mount. The scientists likely used it to spear the larger primates in their cages without having to open them, but the mere thought that some labcoat might use that stick to tranquilize a trapped child fighting against whatever they'd try to do to them made her knuckles creak.

She took a second to center herself with the reassurance that they'd prevented the worst-case scenario. *At least they're all still alive.*

One of the Division 9 agents fiddled with a little black device connected by wires to the electronic lock on the angry girl's cage. Nina figured him for Sanchez, even from behind. He seemed frustrated and poked and slapped the component in his hands.

The girl howled louder, pummeling her feet back and forth into the bars. She wheezed and gasped for air, as though she expected to drop dead if she didn't escape in the next thirty seconds.

"Sanchez." Nina walked up to him, catching a whiff of sour awfulness from the box of clothes: sewer, vomit, and urine. She almost considered they'd been stripped to *improve* their comfort, but seeing them all still dirt-smeared made it clear the scientists thought of them only as animals—expendable creatures they could do whatever they wanted with.

Taken by a spike of rage, Nina ripped the tranq cabinet off the wall and smashed it to the floor, sending green autoinjectors scattering across the smooth, shiny metal. The loud *smash* of thin plastisteel stunned the field team in their tracks. The children all went quiet and watched her. The little blonde girl stilled. After a few seconds more of staring, she lowered her feet from the bars and sat up.

Nina's presence, the raw fury wafting from her eyes, caused the kids all to shy away... except for the blonde girl. She scooted closer, grabbed the bars, and pressed her face to them. A boy on the opposite side whispered to his neighbor, speaking Russian. An echo of his words followed in English at the back of her mind.

"Are they going to kill us now?"

The black-haired, maybe eight-year-old boy didn't reply, his gaze locked square on Nina.

"Sorry, lieutenant. I'm trying to get this open as fast as I can, but they've got some serious crypto here. It's separate from the network. Self-contained. You'd think they were teaching the monkeys how to hack security codes..."

As if on cue, the chimpanzee snorted.

The filthy, savage blonde girl kicked the bars again before slapping them a few times and grunting, out of breath. She locked terrified blue eyes with Nina's. Droplets from her battered water bottle fell in trickles down her body, collecting dirt, and dripping black onto the lining pad below the cage floor. The girl looked as though she hadn't had a decent meal in months: her ribs were prominent, her hips and legs bony and bruised. Red marks on her wrists and ankles suggested she hadn't much cared for the plastic zip cuffs. Finger-shaped bruises on both her upper arms filled Nina with the need to hit someone, but those marks could've come from the Citizen Management officers who'd arrested her back in Russia.

Growling, the girl grabbed the bars and tried to rattle the door, but couldn't budge it. She seemed to sense Nina had come to help them, and her wild expression teased at a nervous smile. A whine escaped from her nose, the tone imploring, her expression asked how people could do this to her.

"*Pozhaluysta otkroyte.*" The girl leaned her face between two bars, her voice fell to a pleading whisper. "*Pozhaluysta.*"

The ghostly child voice in the back of her head echoed, "Please open... please."

"Get someone in here with some goddamned blankets, and a medical transport." Nina pushed Sanchez aside, grasped the bars, and switched to Russian. "Back up, sweetie. We will not harm you. I'm going to get you out of there." The language came courtesy of a neuronal chip, a cortical copy of someone else's knowledge that, after so many months, functioned no different from having learned it.

The girl startled, gawking at Nina as if shocked someone could speak. She scooted away, fingers and toes gripping the floor of the cage like a feral thing ready to pounce and sprint at the first chance. Waist-long hair, frizzed up into a lion's mane, added to the effect. The transition in the eyes staring up at her from abject terror to hope made Nina sick, wondering what horrible things the girl had seen back home, and how terrifying it must be to not understand anything one's captors said.

Nina clenched her fingers around the bars. A quick tug snapped the plastisteel door from its hinges with a loud *pank*, and sent a blast of sparks spewing from the electronic lock panel. She rotated left and handed the door to Sanchez, who grabbed it before thinking and staggered to the side as the unexpected weight dragged him down to his knees.

"How did you do that?" whispered the child, crawling up to the open edge. "What are you?"

Three of the boys behind Nina, on the opposite wall, thrust their arms out between the bars of their enclosures, all hollering to be let out next. From what they yelled, some of which consisted of slang her chip missed, they all understood they were to be used for medical tests, and expected to die in their cages, never having been let out again.

Nina reached in and grasped the girl by the armpits, lifting her into a delicate embrace. The child clamped on, trembling. "I was hurt very badly, and they had to give me a new body so I didn't die." She looked around at the other children, struggling to keep her mood out of her voice. "Please stay calm. We are here to help. I know you've all grown up scared of the police, but you are not in Europe anymore. You are safe now."

"I'm not a lab monkey, I'm Elizaveta," murmured the girl. The former ball of rage sniffled. "They were going to be mean to us, yes? To make us sick and see if their medicines work? To test the doctor machines. Treat us like mice in boxes." Her grip tightened. "Thank you for saving us. I don't want to die."

"Don't be frightened, Elizaveta." Nina patted the girl's back in an attempt to be comforting.

A woman in Division 1 armor holding a grey blanket open to receive approached.

Nina found it oddly difficult to want to let go of the girl, and the child's death grip didn't make it easier. "Can you speak any English?"

"No. What will happen to us?"

"It's okay. This woman will keep you safe."

Elizaveta clung tighter and whined. Nina held her for a moment more while the shouting from the boys grew louder and more insistent. The somewhat older girl in the next space kept quiet, staring ashamedly at the floor of her cage.

"Come on, sweetie. I have to get the others out, and I can't do that with you hanging on me."

Elizaveta trembled. After a bit of coaxing, Nina managed to hand her into the blanket-grip of the patrol officer. Burritoed in the warm fabric except for her head, the child peered at her, again seeming fearful. "What will they do to us now?"

"You'll be taken to a *real* doctor who will make sure you are healthy, then given to proper families here. We are not going to send you back to Europe."

Elizaveta bit her lip and rested her head against the armored shoulder of the woman holding her. She stared into Nina's soul as the officer carried her toward the corridor leading to the elevators. A second before they disappeared past the archway, the child raised a hand to wave.

*I'm going to be seeing that poor kid in my dreams for the rest of my life.*

Nina turned back to the next cage and grabbed the bars. The dark-haired girl continued to try to become part of the inner wall. She whimpered, fidgeting and trying to keep herself covered with her arms. At the *pank* of the bolts failing, the child looked over her shoulder, her face bright red with shame. Nina hurled the cage door like a Frisbee, embedding it into a cabinet of electronic equipment.

The second girl remained quiet and still.

"Come on, sweetie," said Nina in Russian. "You don't belong in a cage."

She whimpered and made eye contact, but still didn't move.

"What's your name? I'm Nina. It's all right… you don't have anything to be afraid of anymore."

The perhaps eight-year-old kept staring at her, ignoring Nina's continued attempts to be comforting and coax her out, until a man in blue Division 1 armor brought over a waiting blanket. She inched backward a little and hid her face against her knees, remaining curled in a tight ball as Nina reached in, lifted her out, and handed her to the officer. Her hair reeked with a mixture of mossy earth and sewer.

"You're safe now," whispered Nina in Russian. "No one is going to hurt you."

As soon as the officer closed the blanket around her, the girl seemed to relax a little. She gathered the cloth tight at her chin and whispered, "Polina," before she burst into tears. The man carried the bawling girl out to the elevator lobby.

One by one, Nina tore the doors away from the cages, getting angrier and angrier. The field team scurried to find a place to stand clear of fifty-pound square shuriken flying about. By the fifth broken cage, the boys practically came out clinging to the doors, jumping to freedom as soon as they could fit. Sanchez had disappeared down an interior hallway, muttering something about not being needed here anymore. Nina freed Dimitri, Fedor, Ivan, Josef, and a five-year-old who seemed too terrified to speak. Pavel, the oldest, waited for Nina to clear the door and hopped down from his second-story perch to stand in front of his former prison, fists on his hips in the pose of a conquering hero.

"I am glad I do not have to kill you all." His bravado lasted all of three more seconds before another officer wrapped him in a plain grey police-issue blanket, and the tears came. "The police always lie. A-are you lying again? Are we really free?"

Nina grasped his shoulder and gave him a comforting squeeze. "You're really free."

He reached up and put his hand atop hers. "Thank you."

Operative Padilla approached after the officer carried Pavel out of the room. The chimpanzee screeched and slapped the bars, tilting its head at Nina with an expectant look. She seethed at the box of dingy clothes, a few small moldy sneakers, and one teddy bear that looked as though it had spent months in a sewer. She found herself transfixed on the pathetic stuffed animal.

"What happened to the staff?" asked Nina.

"Lieutenant." Padilla greeted her with a nod, then gestured at one of two hallways going deeper into the facility. "We've detained five individuals. We have two others in a separate conference room who had apparently suffered an attack of conscience. The woman's story is that as soon as they saw their new test subjects were human children and not actual primates, they attempted to stop it. When persuasion failed, it got violent. The woman suffered a non-fatal gunshot wound; the man is still unconscious from being hit over the head with a fire suppression unit."

Nina picked up the bear, staring into its plastic eyes. An air of moldy must exuded from its matted, crusty fur. *Every goddamned day I see something worse than the last. Maybe Shinigami was right... we are all just circling the drain.* ⌈Hardin... are you getting this?⌋

Her immediate superior appeared in a virtual holo-panel courtesy of her electronic eyes. Pasty, but military-hardened face, brown hair of tight curls looking like a dead beaver draped over his head. ⌈I am. Unbelievable. Are you okay?⌋

⌈I want Osiris Biotechnic shut down. If this doesn't warrant a dissolution order, I don't know what would. Fucking *cages*, sir. Like goddamned chimps.⌋

⌈That'll be a month of inquest hearings, but, you're right.⌋ Virtual-Hardin sighed at the mountain of paperwork waiting for him, his expression grim. Brown caterpillar eyebrows rose together. ⌈Oh, there's someone from Zero trying to contact you.⌋

Operative Padilla, unable to hear the back-channel communication, cleared her throat. "Lieutenant? Is everything okay?"

"If you have to ask that, you haven't been looking at what's going on here." Nina tossed the desiccated stuffed animal atop the pile of foul-smelling clothes.

Before Nina could think 'who is it?' back over the head-comm to Hardin, a commotion got her attention from the rear hallway.

Additional field team agents, all clad head to toe in black operator suits, their faces covered, escorted five handcuffed scientists in sky blue lab coats over business casual. A frightened woman in her mid-twenties with tan skin and dark hair kept her head down, mumbling repetitively. In front of her, a somewhat older woman with pale skin and brown hair maintained a haughty look of detachment, as though she expected the company lawyers to sort it all out within the hour. Ahead of the women walked three men, the farthest thirtyish and Chinese, the next a pale, gaunt, dweebish man who couldn't stop trembling. An annoyed fifty-something with a perfect neat coif of white-grey hair led the group in single file. She recognized him from the vid call.

"You're overstepping!" yelled Doctor Rice. "You're interrupting vital research! This is going to harm all of humanity. It is exceedingly unlikely that any of the subjects would have suffered any lasting detriment to their health. I'd be happy to show you the testing documentation if you don't believe me. They will merely be exposed to various pathogens and cured, or used to evaluate surgical techniques that *will* save countless lives once we perfect them. At worst, they'll have some mild scar tissue and perhaps some light nerve damage."

Nina stormed around the large central table and got in the way of the prisoner escort. "You put *children* in cages. Children who'd probably watched the ACC kill everyone they'd known."

Doctor Rice struggled at his handcuffs while trying to stick out his chin, searching for some modicum of dignity. "Yes, yes. Resistance. They should consider themselves fortunate not to have been killed over there. I'm afraid the whole thing came together on short notice and this was the best solution in the interim."

She glared at him, fists tightening.

He offered a shocked blink. "What? Thanks to those bleeding-heart activists, primates have more legal protection than foreign children. Besides, they're a closer analog for the cures we're trying to find. They're about the same size as chimpanzees, so the enclosures have plenty of space. If we tried to use monkeys, we'd have a thousand university students outside at all hours singing and waving little signs at us."

Nina tried to melt one of the empty cages with a stare.

He sighed. "Security is a factor—we can't have them carrying pathogens out into the world—and these conditions *are* better than what they had been living in." He tried to gesture, but the binders clicked. "Think about all we could have done for the advancement of medicine. Our schedule had seventy-four pathogens and fourteen experimental surgical procedures. Is 'ethics' worth tens of thousands of lives? These test subjects would've been shot in the street if not for our purchasing them. Osiris money *saved* them. Surely, you see the benefits far outweigh the negatives? Is it *that* distasteful for a handful of throwaways no one will miss to suffer a few years of discomfort for unimaginable advancements in—"

The man's voice needled Nina's brain beyond rational thought. She grabbed Doctor Rice by the shoulder and jerked him over sideways, slamming him downward with every ounce of anger and strength she could force out of her Myofiber muscles. The edge of the table met him at the neck, causing his skull to stop while the rest of his body continued to the floor. His head liquefied on impact with a dull *whump* that left a crimpled dent in the metal. The decapitated body's arms continued twitching for several seconds, rattling the binders around his wrists.

Operative Padilla, on the other side of the table, wound up covered in a spray of gore. One eyeball with a squiggle of nerve clung to her chest, which she flicked to the side.

"Holy shit," whispered Sergeant Cooper.

"Damn." Sergeant Romero whistled. "I don't think a Narcoderm's gonna dent *that* headache."

Nina glared at the remaining four scientists. "Would anyone else like to attempt to justify what you people were doing?"

The nerdy man and the younger of the two women urinated. The fortyish woman passed out, draping limp in the arms of the field agent escorting her.

"Y-You c-can't do that," stammered the Chinese man. "You k-killed him."

Nina fixated on the dark crimson depression in the mirror-like table. Blood pooled in the indentation, gooping over the side drop by drop. "The only reason I'm not performing a summary execution on all of you is so you can provide testimony about what was going on here during a dissolution inquest. Osiris Biotechnic has forfeited its right to exist." She snapped her gaze to the scientists. "All of you will provide complete and true disclosure of everything that happened and everything that was going to happen to those children." A long blank stare came back at her from the Chinese man. "Or I'll just save everyone the circle jerk and wasted time right now."

He babbled. "But... But..."

"This is a Division 9 investigation. You don't *have* rights. You don't even count as a human fucking being anymore." She grabbed him by the lab coat.

After a half-second of serious consideration to cramming him into a monkey cage, she flung him at the hallway out with enough force to launch him off his feet. He sailed through the air, landed on his chest, and slid for a little farther before his legs hit the ground.

"Get him out of here."

The field team picked him up and hurried away with the other detainees.

Operative Padilla looked down at her dripping suit and back up at Nina. "What about the other two?"

"The dissenters?" Nina clenched a trembling fist for a few seconds until her rage ebbed. "Consider them cooperating witnesses instead of suspects unless they give you a reason to do otherwise." She turned away from Padilla, scowling at the cages before shifting her gaze to Hardin's floating image. 「Sorry... you said something about Zero?」

The chimpanzee slapped the bars and howled. It pointed at her, pointed at the bars, and... smiled.

Four medtechs entered, trailing a pair of hover-gurneys behind them. Pale yellow light spots followed the floating stretchers down the back hallway amid the clatter of boots.

"Heh. He almost seems smart." Nina chuckled to herself.

Hardin's virtual face tinted green from the left side. 「Yes, Zero. That one you worked with on the moon. Agent Wren. She said she has an important message about something you'd asked her to look into.」

The chimpanzee gave her two thumbs up and tapped its head.

She blinked. "Don't tell me you know what I'm saying?"

It nodded, patted the bars, and made a praying gesture with its hands.

Nina twisted around to look at the rhesus monkeys on the other side of the room. They appeared to be acting like rhesus monkeys, oblivious to what went on in the room. Again, she glanced at the chimpanzee. "You understand English." It nodded. *I'm... wow. Whatever.* "Fine. Someone please deal with this... umm... creature." She popped the door off the cage and heaved it aside. It hit the ground with a heavy *thud* that shook the floor.

The chimpanzee lowered itself out of the enclosure, ambled over to the table, and picked up a datapad. Within a few seconds, it had opened a word processing app, and typed, ‹I am Francis. I have extra brain parts. Electronic. I am not dangerous.›

"What will they do next?" Nina shook her head.

Francis flipped the datapad back to look at it, typed, and spun it around for her to see again. ‹Why humans put small humans in cage?›

"Greed."

More typing. ‹Evil. May I leave, too? Do not like this place.›

Nina grabbed a random field operative and glanced at his chest. "Sergeant Cooper, please do something with"—she gestured at the chimpanzee—"Francis. Bring him to the university or something." ⌜Go ahead, sir. Patch her through.⌟

Francis gave a thumbs-up, tucked the datapad under his arm, and reached up with his other hand to hold Cooper's.

She paced around the table twice before needing to get far away from the box of fetid clothes, and headed to the lounge by the elevators. The air hung thick with the smell of 'child,' but none remained, all likely en route to the nearest Amaranth medical building. The more time she spent with Division 9, the less idyllic her view of the UCF became. Things seemed a lot more like the police state the fringers claimed, but at least when it came to children, the government tended to bend over backward and spare no expense. *Coddle the kids and they become loyal citizens, I guess.* Still, police state or not, it beat starving in the sewers of Minsk, or whatever other cities they'd been rounded up in. ACC security forces tended to deal with dissidents in a rather ham-handed fashion. *Damn miracle they'd survived at all.*

She closed her eyes, letting anger and sorrow wash over her. *Maybe I should've listened to Dad. If I knew what kind of shit I'd see in this job... Every damn time it gets worse. Soul-eating.* Nina stared up at flickering overhead lights that cast the lab in a baleful glow as though they drained the life out of everything they touched. *Can something go right for once? Can I feel like I am making some difference?*

⌜Nina!⌟ The smiling blonde, blue-eyed Division 0 agent appeared in another small virtual window, this one dead center in her vision and high. With only a bust to look at, the woman could pass for a young teenager. Her bright expression and naïve idealism didn't help that either. ⌜Sorry if this is a bad time, you look pissed... You, umm, told me to let you know if any ghosts told me about, uhh...⌟

Though on an intellectual level, she knew her 'heart' was a mechanical device circulating blood for her living brain and spinal cord, Nina's body gave her the sense of it racing, pulse pounding in her head. *So easy to forget what I've become sometimes.* ⌜You... found him?⌟

Agent Kirsten Wren, Division 0, I-Ops, bowed her head. ⌜I've got a spirit next to me who says she was killed five weeks ago by a huge aug with a curved blade for a right hand and a giant hammer for a left.⌋

「The Russian.⌋ The walls closed in around her. Nina couldn't stand another instant of being in this place... of not racing off to find the man who'd almost killed her, the man who *had* killed her dreams, and her Vincent. 「Where is he?⌋

「Stardance said he wasn't Russian.⌋ Kirsten glanced left, muttering to someone. 「He was... singing something like Italian.⌋

Nina thought about the case file from the Division 2 detective who'd been killed trying to catch him. The suspect had a thing for classical music. Belted out opera sometimes while eviscerating prostitutes. She shifted her focus to Hardin's panel, her intention limiting outbound to only him. 「I've gotta deal with something.⌋ She opened the channel to Kirsten again. 「He isn't. It's his street name. Hammer and sickle. Real name's Bertrand Foster.⌋

「Nina...⌋ The corner of Hardin's lip tightened to a smirk. 「If you want this disillusion proceeding to hold, we've got to be thorough.⌋ His voice lowered, more 'sympathetic parental figure' than commander. 「I understand what you have to do, and won't stand in your way; if you can get that psycho, go for it... but those kids deserve your full attention first.⌋

「Wren, what's the situation? Can that woman find him at will, or are we looking at a limited window?⌋ Nina shivered with restlessness, but wandered back into the room full of cages.

"It's kids," muttered Sanchez to the blood-soaked Padilla, evidently assuming Nina had left. "All the chick doll operatives get like that with cases like this since they can't have any. Don't take it personally."

"Working on a psych degree in your spare time, Sanchez?" Nina glanced at him. "Maybe you should throw a little more time at your network skills so you can open a basic fucking lock."

Padilla stiffened, unable to make eye contact with her.

The room fell quiet. Sanchez looked down. The field team got back to tearing the place apart file by file, room by room. Beyond the lab, two hallways full of offices and a dorm still waited.

Nina tried not to let her *need* to run off and find Bertrand result in rushing what she had to do here. She opened a playback window; her systems kept a continuous recording of the past two hours, more if she enabled extended logging. From it, she isolated a still close-up of the desperate, pleading face Elizaveta had given her as soon as the girl had realized Nina could speak to her. She left the 'please let me out of here' picture open in the corner of her sight for motivation and to take her mind off Bertrand. 「Ops, send a cleanup team over to the Osiris Biotech tower to scrape up Drummond. I want D1 there in the morning to detain everyone in the building until we find out who exactly was involved with this project.⌋

"Diaz and Simpson," said Padilla, "Do a complete clone process on Price's terminal. Hines, Romero, and Cooper, with me." She headed down the left hallway, deeper into the facility.

「Even their food service people?⌋ asked a man, on a voice-only channel.

「Does *anyone* have a brain? Osiris employees only. Leave the contractors alone.⌋ Nina glowered. Elizaveta's picture kept her from storming out.

The medtechs reappeared, pulling out a semiconscious man and woman hooked up to gel sleeves to perform field-repairs on bullet wounds. Peach-hued goo flowed through clear hoses with a constant, repeating *squish-click-hiss* from small pumps.

Kirsten finished a whispered conversation with thin air. ⌜She says she can find him whenever you want, but she's not the most patient spirit I've met.⌟

Nina patted the nearest medtech on the shoulder. "Thanks." She looked at Kirsten's avatar. ⌜This'll take a while. I'll vid you as soon as I can. Oh, and tell that ghost I know exactly how she feels.⌟

# MAESTRO'S REQUIEM

Four hours later, Nina crossed the main concourse of the Police Administrative Center, heading for the Division 0 wing. Psychobabble rattled around her head about how the communication barrier between the scientists and the non-English-speaking orphans made it easier for them to treat human beings as lab animals. As much as she couldn't sit still anticipating finally tracking down Bertrand after almost two years, she'd ordered a replacement teddy (fluffy and white) and stopped by the Amaranth hospital where the children were under observation. Her guess proved right; the rotting bear had belonged to Elizaveta, who lit up at the sight of its replacement.

Of the eight, only she and Pavel seemed unafraid of her. At first, she'd assumed the others feared she might hurt them after witnessing her display of anger and hurling cage doors, but Elizaveta had whispered the truth—they feared her position as a government police officer. None of them wanted to go back to jail. Despite Nina's best attempt at projecting sincerity while explaining they were safe in the UCF, the children proved slow to trust, so she'd kept her visit short enough to verify they'd all been declared healthy. The doctors wanted to keep them a few days on nutrient-supplement IVs and perform standard psychological evaluations.

In a scary-calm tone, Elizaveta explained she'd seen people shot and die before, and wouldn't be upset if the same thing happened to the 'bad doctors' who'd put her in a cage. Nina had left it at telling her Doctor Rice had a skull-splitting headache. Still, the memory of the child's imploring blue-eyed stare refused to leave her mind. The scrawny six-year-old blonde looked much happier in a clean hospital bed, but couldn't hide her fear at what would happen to her. Being orphaned would've been frightening enough to a girl her age without being sent across the world and treated like an animal for lab testing.

Nina clenched her fists, wanting to kill Dr. Rice all over again.

The squeak of elevator doors brought her thoughts back to the present. Amid a sea of identical black patrol craft with narrow, clear bar lights on the roof, Kirsten stood waiting for her, flanked on either side by faint thermal anomalies. The one closer and on her right registered fifty-two degrees, six colder than the other.

Kirsten pushed away from her car and stood as Nina approached. "Lieutenant."

"Agent." Nina glanced at the exit ramp leading up to street level, five lanes with security booths across. "Thank you. You're sure this is him?"

A faint noise, warbling, hinting at a feminine voice but too weak to form words, caused a sensation like muscles Nina didn't have in her neck tensing.

Kirsten looked at the less intense cold spot. She held her hand as high as she could reach to indicate someone huge, then relaxed and sighed with annoyance. "Sorry I'm short. He's... wow." She nodded at nothing before looking to Nina. "'Bout seven feet tall or so. Two cybernetic arms double the size of a normal person's, chest full of metal, mohawk, sword and a hammer for hands?"

"Wonder how he touches himself." A man's voice picked at the edges of Nina's electronic ears, sounding a hundred yards away yet speaking at a normal tone.

Kirsten's face went bright red. "Dorian!"

Nina couldn't find a scrap of humor under the weight on her heart, synthetic as it may be. "Yeah. That's him."

"Stardance is extremely angry." Kirsten grimaced. "That man... well. Be glad you can't see what he did to her."

Phantom burning pain speared into Nina's lower back. "I can guess. I got a real close look once. Tell her I'm sorry she's dead and I survived."

Ephemeral warbling.

Kirsten shot a scolding look at the non-space to her left. "That's not it at all... Nina called it in. Her backup was already on the way there *before* she got hurt. It's not that she was a cop and you're poor that..." She nodded at something. "Ready? Stardance is angry enough to feel where he is."

"I've been ready for eighteen months." Nina walked around to the passenger side door and got in.

A man's grumbling seemed to pass by her on the way to the back seat.

Kirsten half-smiled, also subdued by the somber topic.

Nina stared off into space, watching images of that night play across her mind as the car rolled up and out of the garage before taking flight. A dark alley lit in shades of metallic blue, the vendomat flying, useless bullets striking a chest covered in two layers of subdermal armor. As long as she'd carried her MCP50, with 15mm slugs more than double the diameter of the 6mm ammo her old Division 1 duty pistol had, she *still* had a mental hang up about guns. Despite the enormity of her Class 6 hand cannon, she expected bullets to bounce off whatever she shot.

Buildings glided by on either side of the car. The occasional feminine murmur in the air came from the back seat. Every so often, a recognizable "left" or "there" came across in whisper.

"I can go in with you if you want." asked Kirsten. "Star's a little angry at me for making her wait for you."

"You know all those rumors you hear about Division 9?"

Kirsten looked over. "Yeah."

"I'm about to live up to them." Nina glanced through her reflection on the video display serving as a window at a decaying skyscraper. "Should've figured he'd be in a disavowed sector. Tell her thank you for waiting."

"She can hear you." A second later, Kirsten mumbled "yeah" at the back seat before glancing once more at Nina. "She understands."

The Navcon display on the dashboard showed the little yellow arrow indicating the patrol craft crossing into a blacked-out area of the map.

"From what Stardance's saying, this guy's more machine than human. I could flatten him with one mind blast." Kirsten cringed, bit her lip, and shrank in on herself. "Oh, crap. I'm sorry…"

"It's okay. I know what you mean." Nina tapped two fingers on the handle above the door in a repetitive motion, trying to be meditative.

Kirsten looked forward and made a sudden descending left that came within a second of more murmuring from behind. "I know how that sounded. Thanks for not being freaked out that I have that power."

Nina spoke in a flat tone, her thoughts frozen on Vincent's last seconds of life. "Right back at you. Most normals look at me like I'm going to twist them in half if they breathe too much of my air."

"Great, so you could both kill each other without any effort. Fantastic." A 'clap' sounded right behind Nina's head.

Nina couldn't help but half-smile. "Heh."

Kirsten looked at her. "Did you just hear Dorian?"

"My ears are digital, remember? And sensitive. Guess that EVP stuff is true. The girl's indecipherable though."

Female murmuring, louder, and tinged with emotion came from the back seat.

"Stardance is a lot younger as a ghost. She said he's in that alley." Kirsten gave her a mournful look. "Are you sure you don't want backup?"

The air by Nina's left shoulder got cooler as the man's voice returned. "She needs to do this."

"You probably won't want to watch." Nina looked out and down. "Which alley?"

Kirsten pointed at a gap between two buildings little more than steel skeletons with nuggets of concrete still clinging in spots. Holes in the floor slabs made it seem possible for someone to fall from the top story to the ground given a few lucky bounces on the way. Old furniture rotted in place, some hidden by tattered plastic sheeting hung by squatters attempting to live out here. A handful of active campfires dotted the upper levels. The sun had gone down only twenty minutes ago.

"Descend to about forty feet, and I'll hop out."

"Okay. I'll hang back here. If you need me, just comm and we'll come running." Kirsten brought the car down to the level of the fourth floor.

Murmuring emanated from the back seat.

"What did she say?" Nina pushed the gull wing door on her side up, letting in a blast of warm, humid, garbage-laden air.

"She said she's going to watch and doesn't care if you don't want her to."

Nina looked at the back seat, focusing in on the warmer of the two cold spots. "No, that's fine with me. Come on. You deserve this, too."

She jumped out, falling thirty-eight feet onto the top of a large boxy trash crusher with a resounding *boom* that echoed up and down the alley. Myofiber muscles in her legs and back absorbed the force of the landing, imparting a slight dent to the surface of the cube. Pigeons exploded from everywhere, and a vagrant emitted a startled, drunken shout.

Nina stood, took one step, and dropped to the plastisteel ground without a noise. The thermal anomaly hovered nearby. "I can't understand you when you talk, but I can see where you're standing because you're cold. Lead the way."

Feminine murmuring lasted three seconds before the amorphous area of chill drifted off into the alley. Nina followed at a brisk walk. A few Frags poked out of garbage piles or plastiboard cartons to give her curious stares. Most of the time, her body looking, feeling, and behaving so close to still-normal human was amazing, the only thing sometimes that kept her going. Two-point-three miles into the center of a black zone however, her slender, athletic looks and 'cute' French nose were the opposite of helpful.

The word 'cute' happened in her thoughts with Joey's voice. He'd used it to describe her nose. She hadn't told him about this side trip yet. He would have tried to talk her out of it, or more likely wanted to come and help. *Damn adrenaline junkie. No, Bertie, you're not killing another man I love.*

Three Frags, one with a cybernetic arm, emerged from the building on her left, assuming her a 'rich bitch' who'd gotten lost. It didn't seem to strike them as strange that she walked *deeper* into the black, and didn't look the least bit afraid. Their expressions (and gleaming blades) promised at best rape/robbery, and at worst, murder.

As soon as the first man got within grabbing distance, Nina spun around and palmed his face in her right hand. She whirled into a kick at Metal-Arm as she hurled the first man headfirst into the ground. His skull burst like a rotten cantaloupe on impact; the other man crumpled over her leg like a bag of jelly and fish bones. The third man had barely registered the event in his expression by the time she'd recovered her stance and faced him.

He managed to suck in a breath to scream before she drove a palm strike into his sternum to avoid putting her fist in him to the elbow. A crunching squish emanated from his torso; he slapped to the ground on his back, legs in the air, and slid thirty feet before vanishing under a mound of debris. The pile of appliances, furniture, and random shit someone threw out of the adjacent skyscraper shifted and collapsed forward, burying him deeper.

*That'll either scare the other eleven watching off, or they'll be back with missiles.* Humanoid thermal signatures in the dark faded out as people scattered.

Nina whirled in search of Stardance's cold spot. It took a moment to find, and she jogged after it once she did. Three quarters of a block down on the left, firelight flickered out of a wide alley strewn with dead cars. Recognizable gouges from a curved vibro blade suggested Bertrand had set them up on their sides as a barricade.

She wandered through the improvised gate and emerged in a section of alley that dead-ended in the hollow of a U-shaped building. The road descended a slight gradient to a loading dock, upon which sat the trappings of a crude 'apartment,' furniture made from scraps of whatever had been salvaged from the nearby towers.

A momentary fit of 'frightened little girl' panic froze her in her tracks at the sight of the man who, eighteen months ago, had killed her. The doctors, her superiors in Division 9, even her mother told her she hadn't died... but they didn't know what she meant. Nina Duchenne, the twenty-five-year-old idealist, died face down in an alley an arm's length away from the man she'd wanted to marry.

Bertrand Foster, seven feet and change tall when he didn't slouch, hovered over a barrel-turned-grill. Legs, big by any male standard, seemed ridiculously thin compared to his augmented torso. A mass of segmented steel tubes descended like dreadlocks from the back of his head, curving around and into the center of his back. Bulbous metal shoulders glinted in the orange firelight. Both of his cybernetic arms hung down to his knees; tiny (normal-human-sized) metal fingers unfolded from the side of the hammer, which had replaced his left hand. Rubberized hoses swayed from it, lines powering the hydraulic ram that could drive the striking head forward to pulverize.

For months, this man had been the star in her nightmares, and despite *knowing* her new body was more than capable of tearing him apart, the sight of him paralyzed her with the need to flee, to get away from him as far and fast as possible.

He painstakingly manipulated a large outdoor grill fork with his clumsy hammer-fist, turning bits of meat over on a grating. Faint music, something ancient and classical, leaked from earphones on either side of a head that sported a ten-inch lime green mohawk. Bertrand waved the fork about like a conductor's baton, leaning back and swaying as the music took him. His body shuddered, arms raised as if the ratty collection of bed, chairs, and small table were a prestigious orchestra giving the performance of their lives.

"Nina..." whispered Vincent out of her memory.

Fear, panic, and terror swirled. Nina looked down at her pale hands, clenched them to fists, and straightened her posture. Confident. Calm. Ready.

*I've wanted to find this piece of shit ever since I finished acclimation training. What am I afraid of?* She sighed out her nose. *I've already seen him. I'm going to have a wonderful dream tonight no matter what I do now.*

She walked up to within twelve paces of the gesticulating homicidal conductor. "Hello, Bertrand."

The man froze. His head tilted a few degrees to the right. For a moment, he stood like a statue, the alley silent save for the muted sound of music coming from his headphones. He stepped back with his left boot, still the same armor-covered, spiked thing she remembered on the ground inches from her nose, and faced her.

His huge chin, wide and square, framed giant, blocky teeth outlined in grey rot. His eyes, crude street-tech cybernetics like old camera lenses, telescoped six inches away from his skull. Each glowed deep orange like the coals of a demon's furnace. They whirred, shortening and lengthening as he focused on her.

"You're a hard man to find."

The same bloodthirsty grin he'd flashed the first time he'd seen her returned. She couldn't be sure, but it seemed a degree or two less wide. Perhaps the old, shorter, cuter Nina had been more 'appetizing.' Being short had made most people regard her as someone in need of protection even if they'd been younger than her. Granted, as a Division 1 cop, she *had* been a total failure.

"Remember me, Bertrand?"

The beginnings of a deep, grating chuckle stalled to a grunt of confusion. He reached behind himself to put the fork on the grill, and took a step closer. The glowing spots at the tips of his eye tubes widened as iris doors expanded inside. "You... I... do remember."

A voice she had so long heard in her restless dreams rattled her; deeper than a man should be, slow, over-enunciating every syllable, it belonged to the monster in the closet waiting to devour the part of her brain that still wanted to cling to Nix, her old stuffed rabbit. She didn't let it show, managing to find an amused smile instead.

Bertrand glanced at his hammer arm.

"That's right. I'm back from the dead to take you with me." Nina shook her head. "You didn't quite finish me off. You lost your arm that night, didn't you, Bertie?"

「Nina, are you okay? It's quiet down there.」 Kirsten's head popped in on a small floating holo-pane.

"I think I remember pieces of you landing on me when the explosive round shredded you. Honestly, I'm impressed you walked away from that." 「I'm fine.」

「Copy. Still up here if you need us.」 Kirsten's panel collapsed to a thin blue line, which shrank to one white pixel and disappeared.

"Finish." Bertrand's blade arm emitted a high-pitched scraping noise as the vibro-inducer came to life. "Smash."

"That's what I had in mind." Nina raised her arms. "I should warn you, I'm not the same helpless little thing you remember, but it won't matter. I don't really care what drove you insane. Whoever you were before, he's long gone."

Bertrand lunged forward, raising his hammer arm. Nina's speedware pushed the world into slow motion as she slipped to the right, grabbed his forearm, and jiu-jitsu flipped him over onto his back. He struck the metal ground with enough force to blast dirt and trash away, forming a clear spot six feet across. Time resumed with Bertrand skidding to a halt a few yards away. He let off a confused grunt and scrambled back to his feet. After a momentary bewildered glance at his arm where she'd grabbed, he charged.

He led with the scythe. Nina ducked to the left, letting the whining blade careen over her head. She grabbed his tattered excuse for an olive-drab jacket in both hands and shoved him into the plastisteel wall. The dull *clank* of his impact echoed up into the night, startling another wave of pigeons to wing. Both tips of his elongated eyes left crescent-shaped dents in the metal. A pair of Nano claws popped out between the knuckles of her left hand, and she sank the ten-inch transparent blades into the small of his back before giving a twist and yanking them loose.

The synthetic diamond held an edge one atom wide. With the strength of a military-grade doll behind them, they sliced implanted armor as easily as if she'd stabbed a block of ballistic gelatin. She meant the strike as a statement, not a kill, and backed away.

Bertrand howled, hooking his sword arm into the building, tearing a three-foot rent with an ear-splitting squelch of hypersonic edge against plastisteel. Roaring in rage, he shoved away from the wall into a spinning backhand with the hammer block. Nina ducked the *whoosh*, and popped back up in time to catch the bladed limb at the wrist.

She kicked at the elbow while pulling with her left hand. Bertrand's cybernetic limb smashed upward, the joint bent and broken past its normal range of motion. While the hit (to her surprise) hadn't torn the limb in half, it brought forth a cry of agony suggesting he'd felt it in his bones where metal grafted to flesh.

"Glorious..." His iris-door-eyes widened as far as they could. "You... I have rebirthed you in perfection."

Nina backed up as he raised one working, and one fused arm skyward.

"I have purged the flesh, and now you are one of us." The orange light in his lenses shifted chromatic. "Yes! *Yes!* You are as I am. The sin of the flesh is lesser with you... daughter."

She let off a furious scream and stomp-kicked him in the chest. Bertrand sailed a few feet back into the wall, denting it. Another tremendous *boom* echoed in the alley, something light and metal clattered to the ground inside the abandoned structure.

"I am *not* your daughter!"

Laughing, Bertrand stumbled into a loping charge and swiped at her with the hammer. She danced back, having little difficulty evading it. As she'd fantasized, this fight played out as one-sided as it had been the last time they met. Only tonight, *she* had all the advantage. She thought about how weak she'd been. Two years and some months as a patrol officer with Division 1, waiting for a transfer to forensics that she'd never get. Caught in some bureaucratic snarl. Killed, her life forever ruined by paperwork.

Bertrand came in again with a backswing. She caught the arm in a braced stance, stopping it cold. After a split-second 'I'm stronger than I look' smile, she spun into a flip and hurled him at the second story wall across the alley. He slapped face-first into false stucco tiles and fell amid a rain of debris that exposed a patch of plastisteel.

His body hit a dumpster with a loud *whump*, amid his grumbling and growling. He dragged himself to the edge and slid headfirst to the ground, rolling onto his back. With visible effort, he forced himself to his feet again.

*Ruined...* She stared at the visage of Bertrand Foster, altered cheeks and jaw so large his face had become a parody of humanity, too wide for the top of his head. Saliva oozed between square teeth as he gasped for breath. *A version of a life I could have had.* She saw Joey smiling at her, reckless idiot he was, and put a hand on her stomach. *Maybe not ruined... but changed.* This body of Myofiber, silicon, and plastisteel would keep her alive and beautiful for as long as her sanity could hold, but it would never offer her the chance to be a mother. They'd supposedly kept her ovaries before cremating the twisted mess Bertrand had left of her body, but she hadn't been able to bring herself to have them checked. Sanchez's taunt had hurt because it rang true. Given the condition she'd been in, she doubted they'd even be viable.

Whatever adoration he'd shown before, his insanity seemed to shift gears back to 'it's got a vagina, kill it.' He wagged his hammer arm in an attempt to grab the submachine gun he no longer carried.

"Lose something?" asked Nina. "That thirty-mil cannon cause brain damage when it took your meat arm? How are you going to pull a trigger with a solid metal brick?"

Bertrand let off a foam-at-the-mouth, head-shaking roar. Veins in his forehead bulged. He spun, trying to pick up the trash crusher he'd landed on, but his scythe arm, now a fused, inflexible bit of metal, couldn't get a grip on it. Snarling, he whirled to face her and charged.

Nina leaned left to avoid a downstroke, and jumped away from a telegraphed side swing. He reared back in slow motion courtesy of her neuralware. The hoses on his arm all twitched, an insectoid muscle readying for a strike. The hammer head lanced forward on a hydraulic piston, straight at her nose.

She evaded with a quarter turn to the right, allowing the metal to pass three inches away from her face. The instant the *shhthonk* of it slamming out to full extension reached her ears, she grabbed the piston near the head; Nano claws sprouted from her left fist as she raked downward, severing the strut where it met the arm. Dark green hydraulic fluid sprayed in arterial spurts from the hole. Bertrand stared at the missing weapon, a look of horror warping his caricature of a face. On a whim, she swung the sparking hammer around with both hands and buried it in his large pauldron of a shoulder.

Blue lightning flickered from the smashed armor sphere; his left arm twitched, jerking out of control as he emitted a snarl of pain. She grabbed him by the chest and pulled him down while driving her knee up into his gut; the strike launched a spray of blood from his mouth. While he wheezed for air, she gave him a light shove that sent him staggering back and flailing to keep his balance.

"Payback's a bitch, Bertie... and her name's Nina." She stomped forward and punched him dead in the nose, knocking him flat to the ground like a plank. He bounced ass over head and slammed against the wall, precipitating another waterfall of smashed tiles.

He grunted.

*Damn. His entire head must be plastisteel.* A momentary switch of vision mode to metallurgical scan painted the world in black and white. A brilliant white skull showed within his head, a sure sign of it being metal. Medium grey bands in his neck highlighted the Myofiber grafts that let him keep it upright with such weight. Wires throughout his body became apparent, as well as the crisscross weave of fibers below the skin, including a flat, featureless groin. A mechanism in his side where urine and waste collected in removable baggies appeared in clear detail a few inches away from an adrenaline/stimulant pump near the kidneys.

Nina switched back to normal sight. While the man's skull might be metal, the brain inside wasn't, and he lay stunned, muttering, and apparently unaware of where he was. She pounced on his chest, grabbed his left arm at the elbow, and curled her right hand into a fist before deploying a pair of Nano claws. As soon as they locked at full extension, she sliced through the bicep. After discarding the severed limb with a casual toss to the side, she severed his smashed vibro-blade arm an inch shy of the shoulder.

"It's a violation of UCF law, Section CI-42 D, for a felon to possess a cybernetic prosthesis with a rating beyond rehabilitative." She chucked the other arm over her shoulder. "Furthermore, it is a violation of Section CI-11 B for a person with diagnosed psychosis to possess any cybernetics with combat capabilities. This includes, but is not limited to strength-enhanced limbs, and"—she punched her hand into his gut, grabbed the adrenal pump along with its nest of tubes, and tore it free—"combat grade boosters. Military spec targeting optics are a no-no as well, even if they're four generations old."

She tossed the bloody box and tubing aside before grasping his lens eyes, one in each hand. Bertrand moaned and squirmed, bloody froth oozing between his teeth.

"I'm afraid I have to confiscate these."

Nina braced a knee against his neck and, with a wrenching twist, snapped both mechanisms away from his skull, yanking a few inches of thin wires out of what he had left of a brain. Bertrand convulsed and drooled even more. He stopped moving, though continued breathing, mouth agape and tongue lolling. She examined the crude optics for a few seconds before heaving one then the other aside.

"By the power vested in me by the United Coalition Front National Police Force, Division 9"—Nina reached under her coat and pulled her MCP50—"I pronounce you guilty of the murder of Officer Vincent Montoya, UCF National Police Force, Division 1"—she put the barrel up to Bertrand's forehead —"Attempted murder of Officer Nina Duchenne, also Division 1." She adjusted her grip on the gun. "I further pronounce you guilty of the murder of a young woman named Stardance, and however many others you've killed, you sick, twisted fuck. For these crimes, you are subject to summary execution."

*Boom.*

Hot splatter rained over Nina's face. Contrary to her expectation, her massive hand cannon left a hole in the artificial forehead and blasted every ounce of bio matter out the back. She stood, took two steps back, and put seven more rounds into his chest. Azure muzzle flash painted the alley in quick snaps, and the echo-back of rapid gunshots combined into rolling thunder. Not that she could've ever used such a giant handgun before having a doll body, but it made her feel a little better to see seven clean holes.

The Division 0 patrol craft landed a short distance away, it's powerful headlights washing over her, casting her silhouette over Bertrand's remains. Four bulges at the corners opened to allow wheels to unfold and make contact with the ground. A few seconds after touchdown, the bright cyan glow of ion engines faded out from under it.

Nina swapped magazines, reloading her pistol, and holstered it under her left arm before walking over to her ride. Two thin bands of static appeared in her vision and disappeared, but an odd eeriness hung in the air behind her.

Kirsten paused with one leg out of the car, her face ashen while staring past Nina.

"Sorry," said Nina. "I told you not to watch."

"Not you. I've seen way worse than that guy." Kirsten bowed her head in reverence. "Did I ever tell you about Harbingers?"

"I don't think so." Nina took a tissue from her coat pocket and wiped some Bertrand off her face. She looked up with a sudden thought. "Is his ghost here?"

"Yeah… sort of." Kirsten twisted to her right and peered over the car, as if watching something drift away down the alley. "Not for long though."

A palpable sense of calmness became profound for a few seconds before fading. Nina blinked. "Did something weird just happen?"

Kirsten took a second to collect herself, having choked up. "Stardance said thank you. She just moved on. You gave her the justice she needed. I couldn't have brought myself to kill him unless my life was in direct danger."

"Oh, don't worry. As soon as he got a good look at you, that would've been true." Nina stared at the traction-coated plastisteel at her feet, trying to stop thinking about her last night as a normal person. "He likes them short, cute, and terrified."

"I don't scare that easy." Kirsten nodded toward the patrol craft. "Want a ride back?"

"…crime scene crew… "

Nina looked at where she assumed Dorian to be. "Seriously? Out here?"

Kirsten grinned. "He said, 'Not like we're going to call a crime scene crew.'"

"Oh." Nina got into the patrol craft. "Right."

# PLUS ONE

Six days later, Nina swayed side to side, amusing herself with how her oversized sweatshirt brushed her knees. Three slabs of hydroponic chicken francese sautéed with a soothing hiss. She frowned at her toes and got into the same old debate about feeling silly painting false nails, no matter how real they looked or felt. A butterfly of nervousness swirled around her gut as she worried at the chicken with a spatula.

Crystalline wind chime sound filled her apartment. Nina glanced to her right at the floor-to-ceiling windows looking out over West City; a jagged skyline of black absorbed the deep reds and oranges of dusk. *Wow... he's actually on time.*

Nina patched in to the house computer, linking to the panel out in the hallway by the door. A virtual window popped up showing the corridor, and a weary-looking Joey in his cowboy hat and black trench coat. He'd let his black hair get frizzy and long, too many late nights in NetOps. She opened the lock and sent her voice out via the speaker. "Hey. I'm in the kitchen. Decided to cook tonight."

"Okay, that works..."

Nina took the pan off the heat and eased the three pieces of chicken onto individual plates. She'd about finished doling out pasta and pouring more of the sauce over it when Joey walked into the kitchen, eyebrow raised, thumb cocked back over his shoulder.

"What's up with the critter on the couch?" He sidled up behind her and threaded his arms around her.

Nina smiled at the food. "Her name is Elizaveta."

"*Privet,*" said a tiny voice from the doorway behind Joey. "*Eto Vash muzh?*"

"Bad case. I picked her up this afternoon. I'll be fostering her... maybe more than that if things work out. She doesn't speak any English yet." She set the pan on a cool burner and turned around to kiss Joey. After, she smiled at the clean, straight-haired girl in a neat white dress and purple-painted toenails, switching to Russian. "I have not married him… yet. Maybe I will." Nina winked.

The girl flashed a conspiratorial grin as she padded into the kitchen.

He took off his hat and coat, giving the child a narrow-eyed stare like a gunfighter about to draw on his nemesis. Long hair and a couple days without shaving left him looking more like a pirate captain than a cowboy. "Is it housebroken?"

Elizaveta climbed into her seat, wide eyed at the food. After a second of staring at her plate, she looked up at Nina. *"Eto vse dlya menya?"*

"Yes it's all yours. Don't hurt yourself, but as much as you can finish," said Nina in Russian before smirking at Joey as she joined them at the table. "I know you're trying to be cute, but… can you skip the animal comparisons for now? You heard about Osiris?"

He cringed and slithered into a chair. "Crap. She's one of *those* kids? Wow, I'm fried. I saw those files… Spent the past week balls-deep in Osiris's neuroprocessor cluster array. Didn't recognize her cleaned up." He watched her eat for a moment before a look of recognition appeared on his face. "Oh yeah, the aggressive little bugger who kept kicking the door." Joey shoveled a forkful of chicken and pasta into his mouth, chewing with exaggerated *mmm* sounds. "Oh, damn. This is great."

"First time trying this… Just simple instructions." She nibbled on hers. "Damn corporations… kidnapping across the ocean. What's next?"

Elizaveta shoveled forkful after forkful in her mouth.

"Their whole system is more akin to the capitalist runaway that occurred in the years leading up to the war. Most of their population is shit poor, but the corporations over there are still concerned about bad PR. Odd to say it, but they'd be *less* likely to do something this scummy." He sighed, staring down. "They'd sooner just kill them and blame the resistance, or I guess they were too small to be thought of as a threat. Probably would've sent them to Mars to bolster a colony."

*ACC Mars…* Nina cringed. *They were safer in the cages. It's a damn mess up there.*

He chuckled under his breath. "So you wanted to keep one? No consult?"

Elizaveta whined, staring at about half a plate of food she seemed too full to eat —but *really* wanted to.

"I saw how you were with Hayley… I thought you'd be okay with—"

"We'll see." He leaned to the side and raised an eyebrow at the girl. When she looked at him, he switched eyebrows. She smiled. "Maybe we can work with this one."

"I have clingy parents. They'd adore watching her whenever we wanted 'us time.'" Nina sat straighter.

Joey forced a smile. "You sure you want to expose her to the creepy twins?"

Nina chuckled. "They're not creepy, and I can't believe Dad. He's warming up to them, even knowing…"

"Yeah." He winced.

Nina smiled. "I think she adopted *me* at first sight. Only one of the lot who wasn't afraid of me."

"Well you are pretty scary when you're mad, or got your mind set on something, or find a giant, knuckle-dragging bastard…"

"Oh." Nina set the fork down on her plate. "You watched my logs, didn't you?"

"Twice. With popcorn." He winked. "Extra butter. About that whole revenge thing... Do you feel better?"

She spent a few seconds watching the child attempt to eat just one more forkful while swaying her feet back and forth. Elizaveta still had a hint of wariness, as though someone might come up behind her and take the food away, but seemed... grateful.

Nina let her mind dwell on the memory of tearing Bertrand Foster's telescoping eyes out of his skull.

"Yeah." She exhaled past a smile. "I do. I think I can finally let myself live."

# 4

# DAY JOB

Uneasy silence pervaded the apartment, save for the occasional pat of a droplet falling in the autoshower tube. Wrapped from armpit to thigh in a plain black towel, Katya leaned on the bathroom sink and stared into the chocolate-brown eyes of a woman she didn't even know anymore. Her reflection seemed to be giving her the 'what the hell are you doing?' face. Of all the random turns her life might've taken, choosing a random exit off the 'could die at any minute' express into something that might almost resemble a normal life hadn't even been at the bottom of her list. It hadn't made it into her thought process at all. She'd expected to die in her sleep or at the end of a desperate—and ultimately futile—effort to flee her former 'employers.'

*What's wrong with me? A kid. Really?*

She sighed.

The cruelest thing Katya imagined anyone could do to a child in this day and age would be to conceive them in the first place. She couldn't count the number of times she'd had sex because of an assignment requiring it. Counting the number of times she'd made love to someone she had feelings for proved easier—zero. Not that it much mattered. Her former owners had given her a cybernetic contraceptive. A similar implant existed here in the UCF, but the owner could turn it on and off via mental command. Hers had no such feature, the switch likely still controlled by someone at *Vertex Investments*. She scoffed at the thought. Vertex existed on paper as a financial firm, but in reality provided a cover for the Office of Operational Intelligence. It made no sense that they should keep the 'cover company,' as the UCF already knew Vertex for what it was. If the 'company' didn't ruin lives on a daily basis, the whole thing would seem like some kind of bizarre game. Both sides know what's going on, but they played along anyway.

Company assets seldom received permission to have kids. Attachments created weakness, not to mention childbirth would've sidelined a useful operator for months. She could've played the game, sucked up to the right person, asked nicely. Maybe a Director would've let her have a baby as a reward for some assignment performed above and beyond. Most women in her position who wanted out attached themselves to men with power or influence, even if they were twenty or thirty years their senior, and became wives.

Katya had never bothered asking. She'd never even thought about it.

*I don't want children. I didn't then either. I still don't. Eve's not a child; she only looks like one.*

She let her head hang and exhaled.

*So why do I feel like I don't want her and can't let her go at the same time?*

Katya pushed off the sink, standing straight, and unwrapped the towel. After draping it over a silver bar mounted to the wall, she stepped once again in the autoshower tube to let another dry cycle finish off her damp hair. The plastic door closed with a *thunk* that echoed loud in the cylindrical chamber. An eight-by-eight inch holo-panel scrolled open in front of her, three-fourths of it covered with cycle and temperature selections, and a tiny NewsNet window in the upper right corner.

The reporter, Kimberly Brightman, rattled on about some mess at an abandoned nuclear power plant, where some kind of 'psionic terrorist' group had been amassing themselves. It seemed no one knew what they wanted, how many of them there'd been, or even where they'd gone off to. As usual, the news played to the paranoia.

With a few finger taps at the holographic control panel, Katya skipped straight to the dry cycle. Warm air swam in a cyclone around her. Head back, she closed her eyes and tried to enjoy the feeling of not needing to worry about assassins.

Less likely than her contemplating finding a regular job and living in an apartment with a legal daughter had been Joey's getting in the door of Division 9. Not only the National Police Force, but their intelligence group. Scary people with scary reach and even more frightening abilities to influence society. For all the rumored talk of the Citizen Management Office being a bunch of fascists, they had nothing on Division 9. The CMOs still cared more about their paycheck and promotions than any sense of national identity or loyalty to a unified government as a concept. No, Division 9 worried her far more. Some of them would do stupid things, like risk their life for the 'greater good,' or some sense of misguided patriotism. A wistful smile teased at her lips. Despite finding the notion romantic in an archaic sort of way, she thought them fools for buying into it.

Somehow, the anti-establishment thrill-seeker had found his ass in a government chair. The irony of it almost made her laugh out loud in the tube. She still couldn't claim to like him, straight-laced or neo-punk. He took too many risks, acted without thinking, didn't respect anything, and either pretended to be or was an unrepentant chauvinist. An association with him would only bring disaster, but something about him kept her from scrubbing him out of her sphere of awareness.

That mess with the AI invading a military production facility had gotten attention. Even Katya's tangential role in the whole thing brought with it an unwelcome amount of scrutiny. Division 9 knew who she was now, though perhaps it had been a small price to pay for peace of mind.

His new connections had proved invaluable. Because of him, Katya Wolf existed as a citizen of the UCF, with no need to worry about anyone from back home coming after her. He'd also set the girl, EAO-106, up with a proper citizen record after she chose the name Eve. No one needed to know her past. With that cruel anti-aging mechanism removed, she had nothing Starpoint Corporation could want, merely an ordinary little girl with special forces training.

The whirring fans died down. Katya pushed the autoshower hatch open and stepped into a bathroom that felt like it had dropped twenty degrees while she'd been in the tube. She slipped into a cream-colored t-shirt and sweat pants before heading out and down the hallway to the living room.

Her apartment, at least according to the building management, sat dead center of 'middle class.' Two bedrooms, a full kitchen, decent sized living room with a dining area, and even a retractable patio/deck—if one could stomach being on a slab of plastisteel sixty-one stories off the ground.

Dark orange threaded among the rectangular forms of century towers across the street. Light from a stream of hovercars eleven stories down shimmered on facing glass, making the distant twilight sky seem darker. Carpet squished underfoot, like walking on a sponge that massaged her soles. She passed the end of the couch and folded her arms, gazing out the window. Small flying bots zipped among the city in view, some delivering merchandise to apartment windows, others chasing down any pedestrian they could find and displaying ads based on some algorithm to calculate needs. Here and there, luminous 'daisies' bloomed and vanished in the dark, wherever petals of holo-panels full of products exploded into being around orb bots.

*Welcome to the UCF.*

She glanced away from the strip of window that covered the entire interior wall of the living room, and shot a wary look past the kitchen to the door. Her apartment had one way in or out, not counting the fire escape tube. They'd been here about eight months, and she still had trouble falling asleep in the Comforgel bed. It had taken her almost seven weeks to stop sleeping in a chair facing the door with a gun in her lap.

Katya rubbed her face and grumbled. *How long is it going to take me to believe they're not coming?*

She flopped on the long black sectional. At her side upon a small black lacquer table, small orbs of white light appeared within a silver lattice frame, an artistic lamp attempting to mimic faeries sitting on the branches of a tree.

"Terminal."

A thirty-inch holo-panel scrolled open in midair nearby. A pinpoint of light near the ceiling gave away its origin, a hidden projector. Katya swiped her hand at the display, paging over screen after screen in her message client, finding nothing new. She couldn't figure out how to get rid of the NewsNet window, but had shrunk it to a six-inch square, as small as the software would let it go.

Two swipes of her hand pulled up her credit account, which displayed a balance of C699,421. Seeing the first digit no longer a seven annoyed and worried her in equal measure. The apartment drained her for C4700 a month, plus whatever power and water she used. A few trickling residual deposits showed from Alex for past jobs, the most significant deposit hit almost nine months ago, the 250 grand from Siege Arms Corporation. Every time she looked at it, she had to laugh. More of Joey's weird sense of humor. To think that the company she'd stolen a truck full of weapons from had paid her a reward for finding and returning them.

Katya moaned into her hand at the thought of Anatoly Nemsky, the general. The man she'd met in that lounge hadn't been real. Could an AI have followed through on its promise of making *Vertex Investments* forget she existed? Joey might've had a surprising amount of influence in the GlobeNet, but no deck jockey could influence minds the way a genocidal military commander with friends in all the right places could.

She shifted her gaze to the contacts section and twirled her finger around Alex's entry. Even as a still image, the mid-twenties blond man in the fancy, shimmery blue suit exuded superiority, but beneath his genteel veneer lurked danger. He represented everything her inexplicable choice needed to stay away from. She couldn't risk herself anymore. It didn't matter as much if a job went south when the brightest future she could hope for was not seeing the assassin coming and dying a painless death. Now she had a child to watch out for. Or at least a small person who needed a little help getting by until her body caught up to her age.

A few more gestures at the intangible screen opened a GlobeNet browser, and she pulled up a search for job ads. The money she'd made spying, stealing, and planting listening devices wouldn't last forever, and she expected Siege Arms might eventually figure things out and quietly take back their reward. Maybe they wouldn't, but she didn't want to let the account dip below 250 grand at least until a few years had passed.

Page after page of boredom scrolled by. She flicked her finger every few seconds, read the title of a post, and moved on. Almost all of the listings involved business, law, or professional training she lacked. Ten-ish years infiltrating companies could let her fake her way through a conversation, perhaps even an interview, but she didn't trust herself to be able to do any of the jobs on the screen.

Human resources, data analytics, programming, medical technician... she stopped on an office manager position and read a few lines: manage conference room allocations, supplies, coordinate meetings, field complaints. *Maybe I could do* —requires four-year degree or equivalent experience. Masters in managerial studies preferred.

"Chort."

She dismissed the terminal with a wave of her arm and reclined on the couch, staring at the dark grey drop ceiling. Memories of disarming explosives, evading sensor grids, climbing narrow places, disabling security systems, and seducing her way into the bed of a man she needed to kill cycled around and around in her mind. *Hmm. Security.* She pondered applying for a job with corporate security. *That* she could probably fake competently enough to hold on to the position until she learned the rest. She sat up and drew a breath to say 'terminal' again, but froze at the continued silence.

Anyone looking at the dark blue rug, neat table and chair set in the adjacent dining room, or numerous small decorative (breakable) objects everywhere would never believe an eight-year-old lived here, even one with an abnormally high level of maturity. Katya twisted the material of her shirt around in her fingers, trying to come up with a good answer as to why she'd gone back to collect the girl rather than let her go into the system like an orphan. Perhaps the similarity in their lives had forged a connection. Katya still had no desire to take care of children, but Eve didn't exactly need the same level of parental monitoring.

After all, the eight-year-old had been alive for twenty years.

She looked up, left, and right. Even a not-child at that age should be making some noise.

"Eve?" After a few breaths of silence, Katya called again in a louder voice. "Eve?"

*Something's wrong.*

Katya got up and jogged into the apartment's only hallway where a dinner-plate sized silver disc bot glided back and forth across the carpet, barely making a sound. She stepped over it and walked past the bathroom, stopping at the point where two bedroom doors faced each other. The tiny closet at the end of the hallway sat open, with a few stacks of folded linens spilled out onto the rug. She brushed her fingers through the air at the sensor on the wall, and the door slid to the left, vanishing into the wall.

"Eve?" Katya peered in.

A small figure lay curled up on the floor between a desk and the Comforgel pad, wearing a cream-colored dress and a thick coating of sweat. Her snow-white hair had grown to shoulder-length since they'd found her, and fanned out in a messy spray upon the carpet. Her senshelmet lay nearby as though it had fallen off her after she collapsed; the Yume-Koujou system displayed a 'game join' screen for *Colony Commando 8 – Scarlet Faction* with an overlay in red text: You have been timed out due to inactivity.

The pseudo-child clasped her hands at her chest and seemed to be hyperventilating, showing no reaction at all to Katya walking in, instead staring glassy-eyed into nothingness.

"Eve?" She knelt nearby and put a hand on the girl's head. "What's wrong?"

Eve twitched, startled, and looked up. Panic weakened with a glimmer of recognition. "It's almost time." She grabbed at her throat, wheezing as if she had to fight to breathe. "It's gonna get me."

Katya pulled the shivering body into her lap. "Almost time?"

Eve exaggerated a slow nod. "The pain..."

"It's not going to get you." Katya wrapped her arms around the girl and held her, scowling at the wall while imagining Joey making fun of her for trying to act like a 'real person with emotions.' "The nanobots are gone."

Eve shivered. "I know." She grasped two fistfuls of Katya's shirt, continuing to tremble. "But I'm still freaking out. Any second now, everything is gonna hurt like I'm burning."

Katya rocked her. "It's not going to happen."

"It's late." Eve squirmed. "I gotta hide. I can't let them find me when it happens, when I'm helpless. Gotta hide."

"You're safe," whispered Katya, struggling to hang on to the squirming girl.

"Gotta hide." Eve strained to escape, pushing and wriggling, her whimpers growing to shrieks.

Katya pinned Eve's wrists together at her chest and trapped the girl's legs between hers. Despite her diminutive size, the child had enough strength that Katya had to work to hold her still. She held on, repeatedly whispering, "The nanobots are gone. The pain is gone."

Eventually, Eve stopped fighting and went limp.

"Breathe slow. Hold it for two seconds, let it out," said Katya.

Eve gasped, sucked in a few rapid gulps of air, and worked on rhythmic breathing. Five minutes later, she seemed to have regained control, so Katya released her grip.

The girl reached up and wiped her face with both hands. "Okay, that was embarrassing."

"Don't be ashamed. What those people did to you…"

Eve sat up with a pensive expression. She squirmed around a little before smiling. "It's getting better. I didn't shit myself this time."

Katya stifled a laugh. "Progress is good." She eyed the dress. "Did you not say you disliked that one because it made you look 'too girly?'"

"I dunno. Figure it'll be less suspicious if I act like a little kid in public." Eve shrugged. "I have to wait until I'm legally eighteen to join the military anyway. Might as well frill it up when I can. They trained us to 'exploit our cuteness.'"

Katya blinked. "What? You *want* to join the military after what they did to you?"

"No." Eve shook her head. "The military didn't do that to us. Starpoint did. The military tried to shut it down once they found out about it." She stood and held her arms out to the sides. "I've got like twelve years of training in special operations tactics, weapons, hand to hand combat techniques—not that this stringbean body is going to do much with it—what else am I going to do when I 'grow up?'"

"You are going to school. You're only in second grade. Study whatever you want when you get older. Don't do something that will get you shot." Katya fussed at the girl's hair. "I didn't take you out of that facility only to get a notice that you've been killed in action."

Eve swatted at Katya's hand, half-grinning. "Overprotective much, *Mom?*"

Katya started to laugh, but wound up sighing. "If I had a second chance like you, the last thing I'd ever want to do is what I've been trained to do."

Eve sat cross-legged. "I doubt your life was as fucked up as mine. What did they do to you?"

"I only have a few memories of being with a family. We were commoners, and they—"

"Poor?" asked Eve.

Katya nodded. "It is a strict system there. 'Commoner' is more official than merely being poor. There is the Board of Directors, who live like royalty. Then you have the Executives who want for nothing. To them, the ACC is the perfect life. Freedom, wealth, political influence." She grumbled. "Citizens come next. They don't have it too bad either. Commoners are the lowest, above only criminals… though the difference is a small one. They treated us like two-legged rats. A necessary evil."

Eve stared down at her hands. For a second, it seemed another panic attack would set in, but she stretched her fingers, smiled, and grasped her knees. "There's lots of poor people here too."

"Yes. I suppose then it is not so different. One day, my parents never came home. I was alone. I never did find out what happened. Perhaps I was six? I lived for a while by myself in our tiny flat until the rent ate up all the credits. I heard the landlord calling the CMO to take me, so I ran."

"CMO?" asked Eve.

"Citizen Management Officers. Like police... Division 1 here, only to them it is like a job. They stop caring when they clock out."

Eve nodded.

"I ran away and lived on the streets for a while. There were communes where the poorest commoners, unable to rent even a flat like my parents had, lived in ruined buildings. No one took me in, but enough felt sorry for me that I didn't starve. I was about ten when my former 'employer' found me. They offered me food and a clean bed, but I had to work for them. At the time, I thought they were asking me. Looking back on it, I didn't have any choice. I was basically abducted."

"They made you work as a little kid?" Eve blinked.

"No... First they poked me with all sorts of needles and machines, trying to make me psionic. It didn't work. I remember being sick and weak for a long time. When I turned twelve, they started to train me on how to infiltrate. What they could not do with psionics, they did with cybernetics as I got older. As a teen, they forced me to do training missions. If I failed or got caught, I would be beaten or..."

Eve tilted her head. "Raped?"

Katya looked away. "It's not so easy to think of you as an adult. I should not discuss such things with a child."

"Yeah. I know. Sometimes I forget too." Eve picked at the rug.

"It was motivation." Katya grumbled. "They would not shoot to kill. That would waste all the money they spent on me, but it hurt. After my training finished, I became a company asset. A slave. The company owned me. When I fled to come to the UCF, they charged me with stealing company property—myself."

Eve gasped. "That's bullshit."

Katya shrugged. "It's legal to them. I owed them for all the money they spent taking care of me as I grew up, all the money they spent training me, and all the value of my enhancements. I was a spy, an assassin, an escort... whatever they needed."

"That's really screwed up." Eve stretched her legs out and tapped her big toes together. "I still think I got ya beat."

"I think so too." Katya leaned forward and ruffled the girl's hair. "I suppose to be fair, up until sixteen, my life was not *so* bad. Strict, yes. Controlled, yes, but I never wanted for food or a warm bed."

"I'm not really a kid mentally, but sometimes it gets the better of me. Like this morning I whacked my foot on the bed and I just couldn't stop crying."

Katya laughed.

Eve glowered. "It's not funny. I was sitting there freaking out why I'm crying over jamming my toe like some little kid, while I'm sitting there screaming my head off."

"Well, your body is still that of a child's, even if you have been conscious for twenty years. Some things might be umm..." Katya waved her hand around in a circle while thinking. "Chemical?"

Eve kept picking at the rug beside her knee. "I'm still surprised I'm not like totally psychotic."

"Probably because your mind was older than a child's when the pain started to get bad."

"The training helped too." Eve stretched. "So, now what?"

Katya fiddled with the drawstring on her sweatpants. "Well, my associate altered records so you're legally eight, and my daughter... How do you want to do this? Am I Mom? Big Sis? Roommate?"

Eve glanced at the ceiling, pursed her lips, and smiled. "Why don't you run with all three depending on where my brain goes at any given moment?"

Katya chuckled.

"I'll act like a normal kid in public. At home..." Eve stared at her, slate-blue eyes giving off too much maturity for the face around them. "I never did have parents. That whole clone thing sucked. If you wanna be my mother, I'm okay with that... but if you try to make me to go bed at eight, we're going to have an issue."

"We'll see about that." Katya winked.

Eve laughed. "So what about you? Guess you need, like, a day job or something."

*Ugh.* Katya slouched forward, head down. "Yeah. I do."

# REHAB

Anxious pacing filled the pristine white hallway with the muted scuff of boots. Kenny Marlon suppressed a cringe every time he glanced up at the gold caduceus on the wall above the Amaranth Medical logo. Eight months his wife Kathy had been in and out of this place—more in than out. He'd never be able to thank Joey enough for finding the files about the shit TMC had gotten her hooked on. The bill had to have gone into the millions of credits by now, but Triton Manufacturing Corporation had agreed to cover it, provided he didn't sue them or talk to the NewsNet.

Of course, he insisted on adding an escape clause: Kathy had to survive detox. Maybe it had been foolish, but he didn't care about punitive money as long as he had her back. He'd leave punitive to the law.

A pair of passing medtechs gave him a disdainful look. They both probably thought his dark brown duster coat had been made of real leather. Or maybe they didn't think he looked like the 'right sort of person' to be in an Amaranth facility. Nerves made the exchange humorous, and he chuckled, a gesture that seemed to further annoy them. He raised two fingers to the brim of his cowboy hat and saluted them.

"Well," he whispered to himself. "Might as well do this."

At his move to approach the plain white door, a panel on the wall chirped. A C-shaped area under a fingerprint reader glowed green without him even touching it, and the door split in half and receded into the walls.

Kathy sat on the room's only Comforgel pad, the soft glow of the luminous mattress tinted the back of her clingy smock orange. He paused after one step, unable to help but stare at her. Frizzy light brown hair hung wild, down to the middle of her back. She had her head bowed slightly forward, hands together at her chest as though she appraised something small. A pile of folded clothes sat to her right, though she hadn't made a move to get dressed.

"Hey," said Kenny. "You almost ready?"

Kathy twisted around to look at him. Her expression of utter frustration gave way to relief. "You're a little early."

He sauntered up to the foot end of the bed, hooking his thumbs in his jean pockets. "Heard a rumor some lady was in need of a ride. And she's in a bit of a hurry."

Kathy laughed. The way her eyes sparkled washed away the past year or so of hell. She'd again become the woman he remembered marrying. "Well, you heard right... only I can't figure out how to get this damn thing off."

"Well now. I think I can help you with that." He rounded the corner of the bed and took her hand. "I've got a little experience in that regard."

A hint of blush appeared in her cheeks. She looked about to laugh at herself, but let her hands fall in her lap with a morose stare at the floor.

"What?" His playfulness gave way to concern. "Is it something the doctors said?"

"No." She picked at her fingernails. "I can't figure out how to open this MolWeave. I've been fighting with it for almost a half hour. How much damage is there? What else will I forget how to do?"

He caressed her cheek for a second before sitting on the edge of the bed at her side. "They didn't detect any memory loss from the time before they got you hooked on that shit."

"I know... but I'm worried." She leaned against him. "I feel like I've been in and out of a dream for months. Sometimes I'm not sure if things I remember really happened or if I had nightmares."

Kenny pulled her tight with one arm while grasping at the grape-sized black lump at the medical smock's collar. He gave it a squeeze, but it didn't do anything. "Ain't you."

"What?" Kathy looked up.

"The MolWeave's broken." He squeezed it again for show. "These things ain't hard to work. Squeeze it and pull. It ain't doin' nothin'."

Kathy covered her mouth and laughed. "I didn't think these things broke."

"Probably a dead battery." He reached for a knife on his belt.

"Wait." Kathy leaned over and hit the call button. "They'll probably charge us ten grand to replace it."

He chuckled.

A moment or so later, a head-sized orb bot glided in. Golden light glowed from its single large lens-eye as well as from seams in its plastisteel shell. "Good afternoon, Kathy Marlon. How may I assist you?"

She pulled the stretchy material an inch off her collarbone and pointed at the MolWeave fastener. "It's broken... I can't get this off."

"Oh. Amaranth Medical apologizes for the inconvenience." The orb glided closer, and projected a small grid of blue laser light over the area. "Indeed. Its micro power cell has run down. I shall replace it for you immediately."

A tiny hatch opened in the orb, from which extended a thin metal arm and a gripper claw. It grasped the plastic egg while inserting the thin prod into the fastener, which detached from the garment with a click. The orb rocketed off, carrying the grape-sized MolWeave pod.

Kathy glanced down at the sheer fabric. "I can't remember being sewn into my clothing before."

He chuckled. "That thing's so tight it may as well be paint."

She blushed. "It'll be good to go home again."

"Your parents aren't too thrilled with that, I bet."

"Oh, not really." She grumbled. "The way Mom's reacting to us *not* getting a divorce, you'd think I'd lost a child… and Dad." A scowl hardened her features. "He thinks you somehow had something to do with giving me the drugs."

Kenny drew in a breath to shout a declaration of innocence, but stalled at her grin.

"He convinced himself you wanted to get rid of me. Both of them wanted me to wind up an exec somewhere… permanently single, like Mom almost did."

"The way those two are always after each other, it's a miracle you exist at all." He chuckled.

"Oh." Kathy shrugged. "It's just stuff she blurts when they argue. I don't really think she regrets her choice, but she wanted me to do what she didn't. I think having them in a permanent state of being disappointed in me and angry with you keeps them on better terms with each other."

Kenny grinned and rendered a half-bow. "I live to please."

The orb shot back in, glided up to Kathy, and clipped a MolWeave onto the material at the smock's neck. As soon as the tiny device snapped shut, it chirped. Two seconds later, it beeped.

"There," said the orb. "That one should work. Again, we apologize for the inconvenience. If you would like me to remain for a moment while you verify that you are now able to change clothing, I shall."

Kathy squeezed the rubbery egg, and it chirped again. She pulled it down her front, and the formerly-solid cloth opened on either side of a trail of thin plastic as nanobots constructed a 'zipper' on the fly. "It's good. Thank you."

The orb glided out as she stood.

Kenny leaned back to appreciate the view. While in the throes of her addiction, Kathy had threatened Alyssa with a knife on more than one occasion. Despite proof that her former employer had gotten her addicted against her knowledge, and the drug had been responsible for her personality changes, it had taken the courts forever to rescind their order that she not share a dwelling with the girl. After yesterday's last round of psychological interviews, they finally accepted that she would not try to kill her daughter again.

Not a second after Kathy stepped out of the garment and stood naked before him, he wrapped his arms around her and held on.

"Ken…" She giggled. "What are you doing? We're in the middle of a hospital."

"I've never been this happy before. Well… okay maybe once." He gave her a brief kiss and let go so she could dress.

"Oh?" She pulled panties on before reaching for the shirt. "And when would that be?"

He waved his hand around, eyes squinting like he had to fight for a memory. "I'm a bit fuzzy on the details. That day I had to wear a suit and say a bunch of stuff in front of a city clerk."

She pulled on the shirt, fluffed her hair out of it, and kissed him again. Her smile faded. "I'm so, so sorry."

"It's not your fault. Please believe me when I say I don't blame you for any of it." He brushed her hair off her face. "It's just so damn good to have you back."

She slipped into a loose pair of grey pants with thigh pockets and a pseudo-military aesthetic. She didn't look up while buttoning them. "How's Alyssa feel about me coming home?"

"Don't worry. She can't wait. She's not the least bit afraid."

Kathy buried her face in her hands and sighed. "I keep seeing that night replay in my dreams. That look she gave me..."

"Hey." He pulled her in close again. "Alyssa's smart like her mother. She understands that wasn't really you."

"I don't deserve this." She stepped into her shoes. "I was so... evil to my family."

"Not you." He folded his arms. "Every day I worried that we'd lose you. You know I never wanted to separate. If they didn't threaten to take Alyssa away, I wouldn't have made you leave."

Kathy crouched long enough to hit the buttons to tighten her shoes before standing again. "It felt like I was inside someone else's life watching, helpless to do anything. I'm sorry I keep apologizing, but it's going to take me a while to forgive myself."

He took her hand. "So. You ready to go *home?*"

She glanced around at the room, and two plastiboard boxes full of the stuff she'd decorated it with. "You have no idea..."

Kenny lifted her chin with one finger, and stared into her eyes. "Bet I do."

---

DRIVING FROM THE AMARANTH MEDICAL FACILITY IN SECTOR 2081 TO THE checkpoint at the city edge in a land vehicle took the better part of two hours. It surprised him that Kathy didn't seem to mind the truck as much as he'd expected her to. Her initial attraction to his whole 'cowboy' affect had waned not too long before the mess began, likely due to their continued disagreements over his going into the Badlands. The truck had become a physical embodiment of his fondness for the place, and she often referred to it as 'the monstrosity.'

*Let a person out of prison, and they won't care what kind of car takes them home.*

Kathy kept quiet for the ride, seemingly enamored with the view of the city from ground level. Her former job had required a long enough ride that a ground car would've been impractical, so she'd gotten a hovercar. No one commutes three hundred miles twice a day without one. Granted, she didn't work for TMC anymore. The basic Alton Mercury her parents had gotten her wouldn't win many style points, but as hovercars went, it had a reputation for being safe and a little on the speedy side. They'd likely hoped keeping her surrounded by modernity would convince her spending time with him had been foolish.

She shrank away from the window as they neared the security station at the top of the ramp that would take them down to the natural earth, off the raised platform of West City. Kenny glanced past her at a crowd of older teens and young twenty-somethings in the trappings of the '24' gang. Though no one could accuse Sector 24 of being even close to a grey zone, the gang had established itself here. The area had mostly warehouses and low-end housing, as few with the means to live elsewhere wanted to be so close to the edge. Doomsday preachers espousing the idea that 'the next big quake' will send the edge plates falling to the ground coupled with the general fear of being 'too close to the Badlands' kept the locals on the poor and desperate side.

"The city looks so different from down here." Kathy scratched at her hair, smoothing it back over her head in a repetitive manner.

He debated one of his usual rambles about 'down here, you see things as they are. Easy to ignore all the bad shit from fifty stories up,' but didn't want to hit her with deep thoughts yet. "Yeah. It's almost a different world."

Seconds after the truck rolled to a stop at the checkpoint, A Division 1 cop in shiny blue armor approached the door. With the lift on the truck, the man had to pull himself up a bit to peer in the window. A faceless mirror-silver visor wrapped around the front of his helmet. "Afternoon."

Kenny nodded. "Howdy."

A faint chirp came from Kenny's NetMini. The officer leaned to his left to peer at Kathy.

"Her 'Mini's in a box in the back. On the way home from Amaranth in 2081."

The cop leaned far to the right, peering into the truck bed. "Damn, that's a ride for wheels."

Kenny chuckled. "Yeah. I kinda like it though."

"Not getting a signal," said the cop.

"I used it too much." Kathy leaned forward and smiled at the cop. "My former employer was paying for treatment so... bare bones. No room terminal. The battery's dead."

The officer stared at her for a few seconds, likely running a facial recognition search on her. "No problem, ma'am. Hope you're feeling better." He glanced at Kenny, back to Kathy, and tilted his head a little to the right. "Are you taking her home, where the minor Alyssa Marlon is residing?"

Kathy squeezed Kenny's arm through his coat.

He exhaled a sigh. "Yes. They cleared the protection order earlier this morning. It should be in the system. All the doctors agreed it wasn't her fault."

"Hmm." The Division 1 officer held up a finger in a 'wait a second' gesture. His body language indicated a conversation, but he made no sound.

Kenny took Kathy's hand in both of his and rubbed her fingers. "It's just a delay. Don't worry."

She forced herself to smile and nod.

"Got it," said the cop. "They hadn't updated the record yet, and we confirmed her 'Mini's been offline for a few hours." He waved them to proceed, and the inner door sank into the ground. "Sorry for the delay. Stay safe down there."

"Thanks." Kenny tipped his hat to the cop.

"Thank you," said Kathy a touch over a whisper.

As soon as the barrier folded flat into the road, Kenny accelerated over it and headed down the long, straight ramp. The sprawl of light brown dirt, scrub brush, and small buildings spread out before him, far below the surface of West City. Most of the structures looked like they'd been standing for centuries, creating the feeling they drove back in time to the days before the Corporate War. Of course, few if any were that old, but everyone who chose to live south of the raised portion of West City seemed to share a common love for 'keeping things sane.'

The rumble of his tires changed tone as the surface went from traction-coated plastisteel to bona fide pavement. Even Kathy seemed to brighten up as they left the colossus of plastisteel and electric lights behind for a bright blue sky over wide-open nature. He pointed at a hawk circling overhead. She leaned out her window to get a better look, and stared up like a fascinated child. As much as her parents refused to believe it, Kathy had a thing for the whole 'western' aesthetic too.

Twenty-three minutes after rubber hit the road, Kenny pulled up in front of their wide one-story ranch house. Monoliths of junk towered over it in the yard out back, full of the trappings of his 'legitimate' job as a salvage and scrap trader.

Kathy sniffed and dabbed her eyes.

"You okay?"

"I'm fine." She smiled. "Just happy."

He shut off the truck's electronics, pushed the door open, and slid out to the ground. It took Kathy a few seconds to decide between going out ass-first or trying the slide. She climbed down and dusted herself off before closing the door with a loud *thunk*. After collecting her boxes from the truck bed, he walked after her to the front door.

Kathy stopped in the middle of the living room, doing a slow turn to look at everything. "It hasn't changed at all."

He put her stuff on the couch and patted her butt. "You haven't been gone all that long."

"I love you." She leapt into a hug so tight it seemed she feared to let go would kill her. "I'm sorry."

He held her for a moment before easing her back enough to make eye contact. "I never gave up on you, and I never will." He pointed at the tip of her nose. "Now, stop blaming yourself."

"Easier said than done, but I'll try." She rubbed her forehead.

"Hey, look... I've been thinkin'." Kenny peeled his coat off and hung it on a peg by the door. He tossed his hat on the next peg. "You never did much care 'bout me runnin' off inta the Badlands. I know we've had words over it in the past, and I mighta—naw, I did say a bunch of stuff I regret. Took me almost losin' you to realize you weren't just decidin' to hate something I liked. You were all kinds a' worried I wouldn't come home."

She looked down. "Yeah. Every time you went out there..."

"Nothing means anything to me without you." Kenny stooped a bit to try and catch eye contact. "I'm willin' ta retire from goin' out there if it'll help you sleep at night. Got enough squirreled away to make do if we're careful with it. With the scrap business, we'll be okay."

Kathy blinked. "Really? But... you love it so much. You're like a giant little boy at Wintermas."

"I'm not as young as I used to be. Sooner or later, maybe I'll be too slow."

"You're thirty-four." Kathy folded her arms. "You are not old." She put her hands on his shoulders and swayed side to side with him. "It's so much of a part of you. I don't want you to resent me for 'making you stop.' You wouldn't be you if you didn't run out there. I'm... you're right. I'm terrified you're going to get hurt one of these days, but that's the man I decided to spend the rest of my life with."

"Well." Kenny kicked the toe of his boot at the carpet. "It'll be a couple years 'fore I *need* to run out there anyway. Got a decent bit of change for that revolver."

Kathy flashed an impish smile. "Maybe next time I'll go with you."

"Your parents would kill me." Kenny laughed.

"I'm serious." She stared into his eyes. "If you feel that itch come back… I'll go with you."

A rush of emotion came over him at the thought of mixing his two greatest loves—Kathy and adventuring in the Badlands. She wasn't half bad with a rifle, and he'd make sure to bring Eldon along, maybe another hired hand if he could swing it… She wouldn't be stuck home worrying about him, and unless they did something crazy like going to Southern Texas, she'd probably be safer with them than home alone.

Motion caught his eye, and he peered over Kathy's shoulder at Alyssa, lurking in the arch where the hallway met the living room. A long plum-colored shirt covered her to the knee, and hot pink paint gleamed from her toenails. She clutched the wall with both hands, staring at Kathy. Dark chestnut hair covered most of the cartoon character on the front of her shirt.

Kenny almost did a double-take at her, certain her chest hadn't been that noticeable only earlier this morning. Visions of chasing would-be boyfriends away with a rifle danced around his mind.

"Ken?" asked Kathy.

"I'll keep that in mind." He winked. "Like I said, I'm not in a hurry to get back out there. Probably not 'til Alyssa's old enough to go with us."

"You're going to bring her into the Badlands?" Kathy blinked.

Alyssa crept into the room, padding up behind her mother. She didn't look at all afraid, which reassured him, though she did seem to be on the verge of a sobby explosion.

Kenny nodded. "She's not fond of staying with the Rodriguezes, and she doesn't want to be home alone. I said I'd consider bringing her with, but I agreed under the expectation my next trip wouldn't be for a couple years."

"So… Umm…" Kathy fidgeted. "Where—"

"Mom," whispered Alyssa.

Kathy spun around.

"Mom…" Alyssa covered her mouth with both hands and started crying. Two seconds later, she wrapped her arms around Kathy and sobbed into her shoulder.

"Liss… I'm so sorry for what I did. I'm never going to forgive myself for going after you with a—" Kathy wept, evidently unable to say the word 'knife.'

Alyssa swayed side to side. "It's okay. I know it was the drugs. Dad said it made you like nuts and stuff. Wasn't really you." She sniffled. "Are they gonna let you stay home?"

"Yeah," mumbled Kathy between sniffles. "I'm home."

Hayley appeared in the arch, also in an oversized t-shirt, only white. She had the same hot-pink polish on her toes and fingers as Alyssa, and held the Nanochroma wand responsible for it. She glanced at the two hugging with an expression that radiated a hint of awkwardness as well as being happy for Alyssa.

"Hey," whispered Kenny, raising an arm.

Hayley crossed the room, climbed over the back of the sofa, and attached herself to Kenny's side.

"Oh, hello," said Kathy. "You must be Hayley."

"Yeah." Hayley looked down.

"You're so thin. Are you feeding her?" Kathy glanced at Kenny. "You said she's twelve. She looks younger."

Hayley shrugged. "I guess. Thanks for letting me stay here."

Kathy gave him a hesitant look before taking her hand. "We're not 'letting you stay here,' Hayley. We're adopting you."

"Wait... we are?" Kenny blinked.

Hayley gasped at him, betrayal all over her face.

Kathy pulled both girls into a hug. "I know it's not official yet, but we wanted to wait until they declared me officially 'not nuts.'"

"I'm teasing." Kenny kissed Hayley atop the head. "You seem happy here. We're thrilled to have you, and if it's okay with you, we want to make you officially part of the family."

Hayley's eyes widened. She pulled Kenny closer so she could hug him as well as Kathy at the same time. "Yes! That's awesome." After a second of laughter, she seemed about to burst into tears, but lapsed into bouncing on her toes.

Alyssa grinned. "Mom's home!"

"Umm." Hayley's enthusiasm waned. "Am I supposed to call you Mom and Dad now?" She fidgeted.

"If you want to," said Kathy.

"Fine with me." Kenny patted her shoulder. "If you are comfortable with it."

"Well... I never really called my actual mother much of anything but 'bitch.'" Hayley smirked. "The woman didn't want me. I guess I can try."

"Mom," whispered Alyssa as she got clingy again. "I'm so glad you're home."

Kenny imagined Eldon making a weak joke about his missing a chance to 'escape his psycho wife' and return to the freedom of being able to do whatever he wanted whenever he wanted. As he stood there watching Kathy soak up Alyssa's relief and joy, and Hayley gradually releasing her awkwardness, it hit him that maybe he ought to grow up a little. The cowboy persona, the running around the Badlands and sleeping under the stars, maybe he *could* live without it.

He chuckled to himself.

Maybe.

# TOMORROW

Masaru Kurotai reclined against the wall of a massive hot tub made of dark stacked stone and surrounded on three sides by bamboo and rice paper. If not for the electric glow of the Miyazaki skyline against the fading deep orange of the setting sun, the décor could have been lifted from a millennia ago. He stretched his arms to either side upon the rough stone, behind the two women who he'd escorted home from the 'event' his father had thrown for his official return to Japan. He pondered the relaxing bath, a vessel so large he could swim laps in it, and amused himself by calculating how many women it could hold. He stopped counting around twenty and let his gaze track a slow-moving advert bot about the size of a PubTran car. Whatever it tried to sell occupied a massive holo-panel it aimed down at street level.

Before he could stop himself, his mind ran away with a cost-benefit analysis of using a single large advertising unit at the seventieth story versus a greater number of smaller units at street level, where potential customers could complete transactions with less effort. With the large bot, they had to see the product, desire the product, then use their personal NetMinis to order it before desire faded. With the personal bots, ordering would be right in front of them with holo-panels. Customers could complete transactions before impulse could fade.

Amid his mental wanderings, the women chatted with each other. Though they sounded civil, their cheer had a false undertone. Masaru lay there somewhat like a deer carcass between a pair of lionesses discussing how best to devour him. Of the eight or nine women who'd been hovering around him at the dinner and after-party, these two wound up in his limo.

Kiyomi worked on her degree in electrical engineering and nanotechnology. She wanted to spend her life making computers and everything that used them smaller, more portable, and more available. Her parents lived in a small town, Daro, west of Miyazaki City in the forested hills. She'd turned twenty last month, and made no secret of her intention to avoid commitments with a man until after she'd established herself career wise. However, she also hadn't been terribly subtle about her willingness to fuck him on the casual. Cozying up to the son of the CEO could only help her.

Sayoko on the other hand had Masaru by two years. At twenty-four, she represented the sort of life his father would have expected of him had he been born female. Her father sat on the board of directors for Kurotai, and she lived the life of the idle rich. The woman's greatest fear wound up somewhere between going out in public in an outfit two days out of fashion and using the wrong formal greeting. Her presence radiated a regal quality, unlike the younger woman who looked and acted like the teenager she barely wasn't.

Both women kept their hair natural black and seemed fascinated by Masaru's orb of snow-white, especially the lime green accent over his left temple. Kiyomi thought it 'killer,' while Sayoko asked how he managed that without creating a furor of impropriety among the company. True, some on the board and perhaps his father frowned upon such a show of irreverence. It made him look more like one of the disaffected youth who congregated around cybernetics shops, and not the second heir to a multi-billion credit empire. Of course, having an older brother shielded him from much of the responsibility and afforded him a degree of latitude.

He glanced from Kiyomi's frizzy pixie cut and wide eyes to Sayoko's long, regal coif and warning stare. Fair bet that she expected to wind up as his wife, little more than another company accessory, and regarded the younger woman as a threat to that future. Kurotai ranked perhaps third or fourth among the Japanese companies in terms of wealth or power. Not exactly White Orchid Corporation, but then again, they also didn't take the anachronism *that* far. It took a special kind of person to tolerate having to live Kabuki Theater.

Masaru chuckled to himself.

Conversation shifted to include him, and he found himself replying to the banal exchanges as a reflex. Faces changed in his memory, hundreds of women he'd been with for only a single night. Perhaps two in ten of whom he'd done more with than relax and drink. He couldn't quite place the moment 'pussy on tap' as Joey had so eloquently phrased it had become boring. Someone with his money and status would've had their pick of women hoping to marry upward in social order even if he'd been unpleasant to look at. He didn't regard his appearance as too far above average, and didn't take the endless compliments from women as anything more than the required pleasantries while worming a hook. Masaru couldn't place the point where he'd gone from feeling like a wolf in the henhouse to being a koi staring up at wild-eyed women dangling barbed offerings in his pond.

Again, Masaru chuckled to himself.

Kiyomi assumed the sudden end to his silence to be in regard to something she said, a comment his conscious mind had barely registered about one of her classmates who'd suffered the misfortune of his latest project failing in front of the professor. The greatest disgrace came in that the nature of the failure proved he had stolen work from another student, who had laid a trap with purposefully non-working designs.

He unthreaded his arms from behind the women and reached at open air. A terminal pane unrolled like a window shade with controls for the bath. He ticked the temperature up two degrees and turned on the bubble massage before sliding forward to sink neck deep. The women followed suit. Kiyomi stretched out under the surface in a most ungainly manner for a woman, and let off a moan of relaxation. Sayoko curled up at his left side, giving the other woman a look critical of her too-casual sprawl, like some farm child who had flopped in a pond to cool off.

The voice of Hideo Kurotai rambled around in the back of Masaru's mind. His father chided him for his lack of focus on the company, and his having become too 'lazy and westernized' during his time in the UCF.

"I think it is wise of you to put your career first, Kiyomi-chan." Sayoko traced her fingers over Masaru's shoulder. "It would be a shame for you to waste your talents."

"Mmm." The spritely woman shrugged underwater. "Oh, I agree. It must be awful to be one of those women who haven't learned any skills and needs to marry to survive. Wouldn't you say?"

A palpable wave of venom washed over him on its way to Kiyomi from Sayoko. He let his head tilt back and closed his eyes, enjoying the continuous massage of bubbles streaming up from below. He intended to tune out the subsequent exchange of sniping, though his companions exercised more restraint than he imagined possible. Since he knew Kiyomi had no aspirations at becoming his wife, he figured she played the game more to annoy Sayoko.

*We're all playing the game.* He focused on the sound of the bubbles to drown out his father's remembered voice. The man had asked him not to make him regret being 'lenient' with him growing up. He had been permitted a relatively normal childhood, including friends beneath his station, games, technology, and even attending university in the west. Of course, he hadn't much applied himself to his classes… he had gone only to please his parents, attended only enough sessions not to get kicked out, and paid others to take his exams.

Masaru sighed, unable to shake the disappointed specter of his father's face hanging against the black of his eyelids. The man trusted him, hoped he would be an asset to the company someday, and he could only claim to be a billionaire's son. A playboy with a bank account rivaling that of some third-world countries, and no real skills other than kenjutsu—but a katana couldn't solve every problem. He considered himself decent with a gun too, mostly due to spending hours playing at the prototype range at the office, testing new laser weapons. *Fun* things he put time into improving. Boring things, not so much… but Kiyomi's words haunted him.

He had not prepared himself to survive in the world of his father's company—except perhaps as an enforcer.

His eyes opened, and he beheld the two nude forms sharing the gargantuan hot tub with him. All three of them 'played the game.' The women he so often brought home cared only for his political power and money.

Kiyomi thought him cute; he thought her interesting, a driven and gifted engineer with the body of a high school senior. So few women had been so blunt with him. Her offer of 'we can fuck if you want' while tossing a maki roll into her mouth had rolled off her tongue so casually she may as well have been talking to some workaday drone rather than a man of his station. She clearly didn't care one way or the other what he thought of her or if he'd pay any attention to her. Neither one of them expected more than casual sex. He found the honesty refreshing.

Sayoko, on the other hand, likely hoped this evening would grow into a formal offer of marriage between their parents. Such things occurred with a matter of routine in the more anachronistic prefectures. Kurotai put on a show of appearing ancient, but the gears that turned under the veneer favored practicality over theatrics. Unlike even Matsushita in Tokyo, the samurai caste could not kill 'peasants.' No right of *kirisute gomen* existed within Miyazaki Prefecture, despite every outward appearance suggesting it should based on the décor.

No—everything about this room, these women, his life, was as artificial as the trappings of feudal Japan laid over the modern world. *Is this the life I want, or the life my father wanted for me? What* do *I want?* Masaru sat for some minutes in silent contemplation. Unable to think of anything, his mind drifted to his friend back in the UCF with a surprising twinge of… jealousy.

Sayoko turned down the heat a touch and whispered at his ear about being too long in the water.

Masaru murmured and nodded. Sayoko stood first, followed a few seconds later by Kiyomi. They stepped over the tub edge, high enough that they gave him quite a view as they raised their legs. The women padded up to half-cylinders embedded in the wall, where a torrent of hot air surrounded them. He stretched and sat forward, draping his arms over his knees, admiring them in the gale of the auto-dryers.

Joey had spent years living in the most distasteful slums imaginable, going for months without seeing the inside of an autoshower tube. His friend had even eaten refuse. The very notion of it made Masaru's skin crawl. He envied the man his freedom and lack of responsibility, but smiled around at his apartment that took up nearly the entire floor of the building. *Perhaps for some things, I can sacrifice a little freedom.* His eyebrow quirked up with a thought of his friend's new occupation. *Joey is not so free of responsibility now. I wonder how long that will last for him.*

He couldn't grasp how his friend could be so content in abject poverty, but then again he had upgraded his living accommodations as soon as he had a steady income. Perhaps 'content' had not been accurate. Tolerant. Masaru entertained a moment of pity at the thought his friend lived poor out of necessity, but he could have sought honest work at any time. Though, the man had appeared to actually enjoy being amid the detritus of society.

When the women finished with the driers and walked naked out into the apartment, Masaru stood and swatted water from his body. He climbed out of the tub and crossed over black tile floor to the left chamber. Basking in a whirl of hot air reminded him of a marketing meeting.

「Hey man,」 said Yoshinori, as a virtual holo-panel opened in his field of vision, showing his university classmate. 「You got a minute?」

Masaru's implant created a smiling version of his face for the other end's terminal, despite his expressionless demeanor in the real world. 「I am presently entertaining company, Oda-san.」

「I'll be quick, man. I saw you're still e-registered for Professor Callo's biz-

three. There's a midterm coming up next week. Just wondering if you want the usual arrangement.」

Masaru smile migrated out of VR, mirroring in reality. 「That is kind of you to offer.」 Again, his father's disapproving countenance regarded him from behind the veil of imagination. An odd idea sprang up, perhaps caused by a ripple of Kiyomi's laughter from the next room. 「I think perhaps this time, I shall attend to the examination myself.」

The hot-air stream shut down.

「Whoa, man. Are you sure? Callo's a perfectionist. You've zoned through about a third of the classes.」

Masaru laughed over the vid call. 「Are you as concerned for my academic success as you are for my usual fee?」

Yoshinori made a finger-gun to his temple and a *pssh* sound. 「Creds are nice, but it's going to set off a shitstorm if you fail. I don't want to get caught in the fallout. Even over here, I'll get some on me.」

Masaru's avatar gave a placating nod. He stepped out of the chamber as the wind shut down, his body dry. He leaned to the side, staring past Yoshinori's floating head at a mirror, and ruffled at his hair. The dryer always left it puffed up like a cat standing too close to a Van-de-Graf. 「I appreciate your concern, Oda-san. I will send along my usual fee as a gesture of thanks.」

「Your funeral, man. I'm here if you need me.」 Yoshinori saluted, and hung up.

The small rectangle collapsed in on itself, leaving Masaru an unobstructed view of his hair as he tried to smooth it down.

"Are you going to join us, Kurotai-sama?" asked Sayoko.

He peered around the doorjamb at the two of them lounging nude on his queen-sized Comforgel pad. The mattress glowed beneath dark violet silk, making their paleness seem luminous. Kiyomi had evidently ordered snacks and plucked wasabi peas from her hand one at a time. The cattiness had evaporated, leaving them both seeming eager for him to join them.

Sayoko sipped from a drink while holding up a cup she'd poured for him. Sake, unfiltered.

"One moment." Masaru opened a GlobeNet browser in his headware, leapt to the university's store page, and purchased a C3300 'Modern Business Strategies II' e-learn. Essentially, the cheap version of the instructor-led course he'd been dodging. A few solid days applying himself should let him catch up. The time compression effect of VR would let him cover a standard semester course in about twelve hours. Three months' worth of hour-and-a-half long classes, five days a week, worked out to about eleven and a quarter hours of VR instruction time. Factoring in coursework, simulation scenarios, and needing to log out for breaks, he figured he could process the course several times over in the week he had left.

Masaru leaned both hands on the black marble countertop and stared at himself. "I shall not disappoint my father."

"We're waiting, Masaru," cooed Kiyomi.

"I shall master this knowledge as I have mastered my sword."

The women giggled.

He smiled. "Tomorrow."

# 7

# MEANIES

Joey deflated into the long beige sofa, letting the smart cushions lift him away with a sense of reclining on a cloud. It took mere seconds for the material to soften or firm up in response to his motion. If he closed his eyes, he could almost dream of flying. When Nina bought it, he'd given her a little attitude about dumping twenty grand on a couch, but in less than five minutes, he'd become a believer.

He glanced down at two paths of long, black hair over his equally black t-shirt. Somehow, months of steady income providing access to real food plus a job where he spent all day sitting hadn't done a thing to his shape. Still, he had the body of a zoom-head holovid star, the kind of guy who never ate because he spent his life too high to remember food existed.

Hands at his hips, he daydreamed about a cowboy style shootout and tossed around ideas for a game. *Can't be all that hard to write one.* Vistas of Old West towns, sunsets behind mesas, and the requisite tumbleweed rolling between two men about to throw down played across the canvas of his mind.

A loud *clank* came from the back hallway, followed a split second later by a child's shrill scream.

"Liz? You okay?" yelled Joey.

Silence.

Seconds before he could find the willpower to get up, the willowy form of Elizaveta appeared at the mouth of the corridor, wearing only a blindingly white pair of brand new underpants. Head bowed, hands clasped in front of her, she peered up at him, fear of getting in trouble plain on her face. She gasped for breath, trembling from whatever had frightened her.

"What happened, kiddo?"

"*Ya ne znayu, chto Vy skazali,*"[1] said the child, in a voice barely past a whisper. "*Ya uronila siden'ye dlya unitaza.*[2]"

Joey sat up with a faint moan and scratched his head. Cushions morphed under him. "Ugh… The least you could do is speak English."

Elizaveta looked down. "*Prostite pozhaluista za shum.*[3]"

"Hey… Hey…" He smiled. "What's wrong?"

She covered her face with her hands and sniffled.

"Aww, dammit."

"*Ya ne khotel!*[4]" Elizaveta's wide blue eyes and apologetic tone made him feel like an ogre and he hadn't even done anything. "*Prosto aekisdent. Ya ne budu bolshe!*[5]"

*Accident?* Joey fished out his NetMini. A few finger taps brought up the translator app. "I'm not angry with you. What happened?"

Elizaveta stared at the device while it repeated his words in Russian. Her worried expression gave way to a faint smile, and she spoke a little louder than whispering. "*Trachnula vot sidenyem – I shumno poluchilos'.*"

"I dropped the toilet seat hard and it made a loud noise," said the NetMini, in an attempt to copy her voice.

"Oh." Joey chuckled, and melted into the sofa with relief. She hadn't done anything wrong or dangerous. "It's okay. I thought you'd hurt yourself or something." As the device repeated his words in Russian, the girl smiled. "My fault for leaving it up. You're okay?"

She glanced from him to the NetMini while it spoke in his voice. "*Da. Shum menya udivil.*" Elizaveta put her hands over her ears. After the NetMini translated, "Yes. The noise surprised me," she whispered "noise" in English, as if testing the word.

"Oh, okay. That's good. You're not hurt then. I'll be right here if you need me."

The child stared at the NetMini until it finished speaking, nodded at him, and walked out of sight.

He set it down on the sofa next to him and reclined once more. Nina hadn't been thrilled about a sudden call sending her on duty after hours, but she'd been far less pleased that the other Division 9 lieutenant she went in to cover for had been nearly killed. Internal affairs investigations always got messy, more so when they involved a Division 5 man suspected of selling impounded cyberware to fringers in a grey zone. Lieutenant Woodring had been investigating him for months. The man had an impressive record and skill set—but no augmented limbs. Trusting Sergeant Hickman to surrender peacefully at the mere mention of Division 9 turned out to be a mistake.

*Poor bastard. Those mil-spec arms aren't gonna help him against Nina.* He entertained an idle daydream of her tearing one of his arms off and clubbing him with it, his brain going total cartoon with the scene.

The toilet flushed.

He caught a glimpse of a shadow drift across the corridor, but the girl didn't come out to the living room again. Joey tapped a finger on the corner of the NetMini while going back over the video he'd watched involving her case, mostly security camera footage from inside the Osiris Biotechnic facility. Elizaveta had been subdued and fearful until she'd been carried in to the primate lab. As soon as she'd seen the cages, she'd gone ballistic. Two of the scientists had to hold her down while a third snipped the zip-ties from her wrists and ankles, peeled her fetid clothing away, and wrestled her into the cage. Now that she'd escaped what she had to have believed to be imminent death, she'd gone back to being quiet.

Hours in the GlobeNet running image match searches had turned up their entry point. A Citycam in Sector 16797 with a view of the ocean captured a small, enclosed boat with angled sides—likely stealth coated—coming in at 2:41 a.m. Within minutes of it touching sand, a hover van landed nearby. A trapezoidal hatch opened on the side of the boat, and three unidentified men carried the zip-tied Russian kids over their shoulders like sacks of concrete to the van. Elizaveta dropped her bear along the way, and much to Joey's surprise, the man carrying her went back for it.

*They weren't total* assholes, *but I still wanna roast them.* He tapped the NetMini harder, the repetitive clicking loud in the otherwise silent apartment. They had to be mercs like the ones who tried to feed him a missile outside the Imperial Hotel. Generic-faced, augmented everymen who could be one of any hundred 'freelancers.' Not all of them took illegal jobs, some just provided extra security for legitimate operations... a fact that made finding these particular three a royal pain in the ass.

At the continued quiet, Joey forced himself to get up from the couch of awesomeness, and crept into the back. He paused at the door to the girl's room and peered in.

Nina had done the space up in a shade somewhere between lavender and pink. Elizaveta had evidently chosen those colors. *Katherine she is not.* Joey fought the instinctual urge to hit something at thinking of his sister. At first, he couldn't find the child, but faint whispering drew his attention to the far side of the Comforgel pad, by the wall. He tapped a knuckle on the door in two light knocks, and stepped in. A few steps later, he peered over the glowing mattress.

Elizaveta hid in the narrow space between the bed and the wall, sitting in the corner by the head end, arms wrapped around her legs, chin on her knees, and still wearing only her underpants. She didn't seem to be in a bad, or even fearful, mood, and glanced up at him with a neutral expression.

"Hey, kiddo. What's up?"

"*Gde tvoy NetMini? Ty zabyl, chto ya ne govoryu po-angliyski?*6"

Joey pointed at her and grinned. "I have no idea what you just said, but I think I know."

She tilted her head at him.

He ran back to the living room to grab the NetMini and returned. She hadn't moved from her spot.

Joey held up the device and asked, "What's up?"

"Spaceships?" said Elizaveta, courtesy of the NetMini.

"Oh. This thing doesn't do idioms well." He thought for a second. "What are you doing?"

She shifted her gaze from the device to his chest. "Sitting in my room. I have never had a room before. I like it. I feel safe here."

He wandered to the small white dresser, which contained two dresses, a few pairs of tights, one skirt, three shirts, and some socks. Joey picked up a folded dress. "You know you're allowed to wear stuff, right?"

Elizaveta nodded. "If I wear it, it will get dirty and my new mother will have to wash it. I do not wish to make more work for her. It is not cold here. She is busy, and I am going to bed soon, so I would take it off again anyway."

Joey waved her over and flicked his hand to unfold the small dress. "It's okay. I'll wash it."

She offered a timid stare, seeming unsure if she'd get in trouble. After a second or two of consideration, she stood and walked around the bed from the narrow space she'd been hiding in... probably for the past few hours. She stopped with her toes inches from his boot and raised her arms straight up, causing her ribs to press outward, glaringly obvious.

*Damn, this kid needs to eat more.* He pulled the hot pink over her and fidgeted it into place. "My sister hated this color. Our grandparents always bought her pink things and she'd scream and throw fits."

"It is nice." Elizaveta brushed her hands down her front. "They made the girls wear pink and carry dolls all the time, but I like it."

"Made?" He raised an eyebrow.

"Yes. The men say we are cuter, so the police will not shoot us."

He stared at her, mouth open for a few seconds. No wonder this kid weathered the Osiris lab without batting an eyelash. How much worse had she seen living with the Russian Resistance? Before his thoughts spiraled down into a black pit, he scooped her up into a hug and carried her to the living room. "Come on, kiddo. You are in serious need of some fun."

She bit her lip, fixing him with a curious stare, but said nothing.

He set her on the couch, fired up the Yume-Koujou system, and plucked a pair of wireless Senshelmets from the stand on the cabinet. He ran down a mental list of his game library: mostly titles no six-year-old girl should even know about, much less play. A Gee-Ball simulation represented the tamest option available, but even that had some blood. *Nothing worse than she's probably seen.*

Joey took a seat next to her and set the thin silver plastic helmet over her head before flipping down the opaque visor over her eyes. She sat for a few seconds before reaching up to lift it so she could see him.

"*Pochemy mi v shlemah? Mi chto, voyevat' idyem?*"

"Uhh." He grabbed the NetMini, which had gone to sleep. As soon as it lit back up, he set it on the cushion between them. "What?"

She repeated the phrase and the NetMini said, "Why are we wearing helmets? Are we going to fight?"

Joey whistled. "Oh... you've never seen these before. Right. It's a game. The helmet lets you see and hear what's happening inside the game. It's not real, but it can look real."

Elizaveta narrowed her eyes with suspicion, but offered a hesitant nod. She reached up and pulled the visor down, covering most of her face except for her mouth and chin. "I can't see anything. How do I work it?"

"When the game starts, it knows what you're thinking so you just need to want to do things."

"Okay."

He scratched his head. The title screen for the Ultimate Gee-Ball 14 came up on a holo-panel projected by the Yume-Koujou base unit. An enormous square-jawed man with black lines painted under his eyes appeared, wearing the uniform of the Manglers pro Gee-Ball team.

The animated player punched his metal-armored fist into his other hand, pointed at the screen, and yelled, "Time to mothafuckin' do this. Manglers gon' own this bitch!"

*Shit.* Joey killed the NetMini before it could translate that, and shot a cheesy smile at Elizaveta. She swished her feet back and forth and turned her head about, showing little reaction to the coarse language. *If she repeats that, Nina's going to kill me.* He turned the translator back on. "Since you've never used one of these before, you should run the calibration first..." *While I download something we can play that won't result in me being hospitalized.*

"*Khorosho.*" Elizaveta smiled as the NetMini repeated "Okay" in her voice.

Joey set her helmet ID up with the calibration routine, which consisted of some simple maze-walking, climbing, object manipulation, and options to set levels for volume, smells, touch, and control sensitivity. Elizaveta's cheeks lit up from the mini-screen embedded in the visor, and soon her legs twitched as if she dreamed about walking.

While she explored a virtual environment to get used to the Senshelmet sending and receiving information directly to her brain, Joey skimmed the download catalog and picked a 'kid-friendly' game based on the Monwyn franchise. He'd never been big on fantasy, preferring games like *Colony Commando*, or the over-the-top scary survival horror ones like *Nocturnus Calling*. He grinned and shivered in equal parts remembering the first time he'd played that one... at eleven. As soon as he'd gone through a doorway and found a demon peeling the skin from a dead, naked woman, he'd simultaneously wet himself and become a permanent fan of the series.

Of course, his parents wouldn't yell at him for playing a 21+ rated game ten years too early anymore.

*Beep.* The NetMini wobbled.

"Incoming call from..." said an electronic female voice, followed by a recording of Joey. "The censorious bloviating cum dumpster."

He slapped his hand over the small black rectangle, hoping to death that Elizaveta hadn't heard that. Ignoring his sister as he usually did would only make her call a few more times, and risk permanently embedding that phrase in Elizaveta's mind. *Dammit. I need to change that announce. Having a kid around is such a pain in the ass.* A mental command linked the NetMini to his headware, and a virtual holo-panel scrolled open in front of him bearing his sister Katherine's head and shoulders. The sight of her dark navy 'lawyer-suit' always got him into an antagonistic mood, but seeing her hair out of its usual severe bun made him hesitate. She wore her hair loose, scraggles of jet-black around her lily-white face.

His sister looked... weary. The last time he'd seen her had been before fleeing Mars with half the UCF government coming after him for trying to steal a file he hadn't even gotten close to. At the time, she'd been Queen of the World, and he hadn't wanted to bother hearing her rattle on and on yet again at how he wasted his life and why couldn't he be more like her.

This version of Katherine fit the way he imagined if he'd ever unloaded on her the way he often fantasized about, an unrestrained network assault that would've crushed her sanctimonious life into ashes. Of course, he'd never quite gotten around to doing it. As much of a holier-than-thou prig as she'd been, she *was* still family.

Elizaveta grabbed empty air in a gesture reminiscent of climbing a ladder. "*Odin, dva, tri...*"

"Well," said Joey, cracking a wry smile. "How have I ruined the world today?"

"Joe." Katherine looked away and a little down. "This isn't easy for me to say."

He smiled. "Hang on. Let me record this for later use."

She frowned at him, but her expression went to one of surprise. "You look... a lot better than I'd expected."

"What do you want?" Joey folded his arms. "You're being civil."

Katherine leaned side to side, peering around his head at the apartment behind him. "Nice place... are you—"

"Squatting? No."

She looked down. "Finally pulled off that big data nab? Got rich?"

"Not exactly." He glanced to his right at Elizaveta who made small hand motions while picking up objects and rearranging them. He pictured the calibration game with the geometric shapes on a table. *At least she's smiling.* "Things haven't exactly gone the way I'd been dreaming about, but I guess I can't complain. So really, what's going on? We've been talking for thirty-four seconds and you haven't said anything that makes me want to put hot sauce in your eye drops."

Katherine winced. "You do know you could've blinded me with that?"

"Oh, sure. What was I, seven? Totally what I wanted to do."

"Look, Joe. I need your help." She pulled a few fingers through her hair and made eye contact again. She'd opted for sapphire blue this week.

He squinted, trying to remember her natural color. "Hold on. Did *you* just ask *moi*"—he touched the fingertips of both hands to his chest—"for help?"

Katherine's lip quivered. She fought her usual habit of scowling at his wiseassery. "Yes."

"Oh." He clapped. "Give me a sec to savor this." He kissed his fingertips and waved his hand as if praising some gourmet chef's latest creation. "Katherine is asking me for help."

"*Chto[7]?*" asked Elizaveta.

"Nothing to worry about." He patted her on the head.

"Who's that voice?" asked Katherine. "Is that a little girl? What are you doing with a little girl? Did you break into someone's apartment?"

Joey laughed. A flick of his eyes threw the call out of his headware to the NetMini, which projected Katherine's bust in hologram. She peered at Elizaveta grasping phantom objects. "That's Elizaveta."

At the sound of her name, the girl swiveled her helmet-covered head toward him and flipped the opaque visor away from her face. She squinted, struggling to perceive the real world with her eyes at the same time the helmet injected the virtual one into her brain. "*Kto ona? Ona vyglyadit ustavshey[8].*"

"Katherine, Elizaveta. Elizaveta, Katherine."

"What did she say?" asked Katherine.

"This"—Joey put an arm around the girl, flashed a big grin, and spoke with a tone like someone might use with a dog after they did a trick—"is my sanctimonious older sister. She thinks everything I do is worthless and I've wasted my education and entire life, unlike her. She's got a big, fancy job with a big, fancy corporation. And now, apparently, the queen of smug wants *moi* to do something for her." He grinned at the holographic head. "What do you think, kiddo? Should I make her beg?"

Elizaveta looked up at him and blinked. *"Vy pridurivayetes'. Vy zhe znayete, ya ne ponymayu[9]."*

"Good point." Joey patted her on the shoulder. "See? She agrees with me."

Katherine's face tinged red around the nose and eyes. That usually meant the screaming would start in seconds. "I'm not sure I want to know why you've got a... what language is that... kid." She paled again. "You're not part of some kidnapping plot are you?"

Joey laughed like a kicked chicken. "Of course, I have to be doing something nefarious."

Elizaveta peered a few seconds more at Katherine before flipping the visor down. *"Ona ne vyglyadit schastlivym.[10]"*

"You have to admit, Joe, you and the law haven't exactly... you and *society* haven't exactly been on the best of terms." She sighed. "And that's why I'm calling you."

He brought his palms together at his chin like a Buddhist monk. "Oh... this I have to hear. Miss Perfection wants me to do something possibly illegal?" At a mental impulse, the hologram dissipated and Katherine reappeared in a virtual window courtesy of his headware. "Okay, I *gotta* hear this."

"I'm serious, Joe." She hung her head. "Look. I know you and I haven't exactly gotten along for a few years, but I really do need your help."

He raised an eyebrow. "Wow. That almost sounded sincere."

"Please..." Katherine added a hint of desperate whine, something she hadn't done since twelve or so. She *hated* not being the one with all the power and advantage. Showing even that smidgen of weakness picked at the dried-up, withered little black nugget of familial loyalty he still had. "I'm in trouble."

"Oh... Mrs. Squeaky Clean finally got caught with her hand in the cookie jar?"

Elizaveta made little grunting noises. The way she twitched suggested running down a virtual hallway. Joey couldn't help but grin at the overload of cute, and became somewhat aware of a female voice nagging at his senses.

"... are you even listening to me?" Katherine sighed.

"Not really. Sorry. Kid was being adorable." He looked at her. "What?"

"Where did you get a child anyway?"

"Oh, she's not mine. I'm babysitting. Well. Okay maybe she's mine partly at least in some weird twisty legal way. The woman I'm seeing is fostering her. This is her place."

"You're seeing a woman?" Katherine blinked. "What did his name used to be?"

Joey picked at his eye with his middle finger. "A masters in law and *that's* the best shot you can come up with?"

"I've got a lot on my mind and I... can't imagine what a woman would see in you to stick around for any length of time."

"I'm wounded." He put a hand over his heart. "At least, I would've been if I gave a flying rat fuck what you thought of me." Joey's eyebrows crept together. "But you do have me intrigued. This is the longest we've spoken without you going banshee. We work together... well, sort of."

"Another net head?"

Elizaveta held her arms up a little for balance and her toes flexed.

"She's not bad, but cyberspace isn't her focus." He grinned to himself and poked Elizaveta in the ribs.

The child squirmed and grabbed his finger. *"Prekrati eto. Most takoi uzkiy! Ya ne khochu upast'."*[11]

"So you've got a job now? *You* a job?" Katherine blinked.

"Yes." He forced the words past his teeth in a tone like he admitted to something horrible. "I, Joey Dillon, have a goddamned day job."

"What?" Katherine leaned closer to the holo cam. "Is it at least something you went to school for?"

"I'm impressed." He scratched above his right eye. "No insult. Yeah. I'm doing white hat work now."

"That's good." The venom seemed to fade from her expression. It seemed so wrong. She almost looked like a human being. "Hope the company's at least reputable."

Joey chuckled. "Ehh… they can get pretty dark sometimes, but at least my crew's got their heads in the right place."

"Any place I've heard of?"

"You wouldn't believe me if I told you, so I'll just skip over that part."

Katherine grumbled. "Look. Grant's gone full asshole."

Joey laughed. "Gone? He's been a prick since day one. Come on, K… 'Grant Williams?' He *sounds* like the rich dickhead bad guy from every single university sex-romp-comedy holo ever made."

She put a hand over her mouth and nibbled on her finger. "You were right. You had this thing with him ever since the two of you met."

"Of course." Joey rolled his eyes. "People who take themselves that seriously get under my skin."

Katherine managed a wistful smile. "You never take yourself seriously. Guess it's like a matter-antimatter reaction."

Elizaveta raised her hands as if holding a gun, aiming at a moving target. *"Eta veselo!"*

Joey glanced at the NetMini screen, which read: "[Russian] This is fun."

He patted her on the helmet. *If I knew she'd spend all night playing in the calibration room, I wouldn't have bothered buying a game.* "Yeah." He stared at Katherine, wondering how long it had been since he could do so without wanting to hit her. Not that he'd ever do it, but their old apartment on Mars had a few dents in the walls. *Probably around the time I started slacking and she started working her ass off… Grade 9?* "Yeah. So what's asshat doing?"

"Grant's seeing another woman. He's afraid to face me in court, so he's sabotaging everything about my life. Bills for things I've never ordered, fake Vidphone calls to my boss… he's even putting naked pictures of me out on the GlobeNet and editing in underage boys." She shivered and ran both hands up and through her hair. "I'm… so stressed out, I'm about to lose my job. The MDF has interviewed me twice about those pictures. I can't concentrate on anything and I think Mr. Forrest is beginning to wonder if some of the bullshit is real. I… Please, Joe. This is me eating crow. Help."

Joey tapped a finger on his chin, thinking of Katya and that creepy not-a-little-girl she took in. *That one might be willing to pose—no. Fuck that. I don't want those images in my head even if she is supposed to be like, twenty.* He scratched his chin.

Setting someone up with fake child porn was a noob's deal anyway. Even though the request for attack had come from *Katherine*, that didn't give him an excuse to play amateur hour.

Katherine or not, he had pride to worry about.

"Download complete. *Alduin's Adventure* is now ready for play," said a digitized female voice.

"Wow. You actually said you need my help." Joey tapped his chin. "Okay. I never did like that asshole anyway. Suppose I can't let him fuck with my sister."

Elizaveta squealed. She flipped the visor up, grabbed both of her feet, and blinked at them.

His sister gave him a suspicious stare. "I can't tell if you're messing with me."

"Probably because I can't either." He chuckled and looked at the girl. "What's wrong?"

"*Eto voda.*" She looked at her feet again, and back to him with the most thoroughly bewildered expression he'd ever seen. "*Ya chuvstvoval chto ya stupil v vodu.*"

"It's water," said Elizaveta's voice from the NetMini. "I felt like I stepped in cold water."

Joey's mental avatar held a 'wait a sec' finger up to Katherine. "That's what the helmet does, sweetie. It sends feelings and stuff into your head. It's not real. Just a game."

Elizaveta stared at the NetMini while it translated. Confusion and fear melted away to wide-eyed eagerness. "*Khorosho!*"

"Okay!" chirped the NetMini.

Joey turned his attention back to his sister. "Okay. Kid's never used a sens before. She's in the woods part of the calibration and got a little freaked out when she stepped in virtual water, her feet got cold."

"Don't do anything to get in trouble at work." Katherine looked down. "I wouldn't even ask, but… it's my job on the line now, and sanity."

"Sanity? When did you ever have that?" He grinned. "Don't worry about my job. They won't mind."

She raised both eyebrows. "That's a pretty open-minded place." Eyebrows down. "Wait… are you self-employed?"

"Nope." He smiled.

"So your company doesn't mind if you skirt the law?"

Joey grinned ear-to-ear and laughed. "Skirting the law *is* my job. Well… The people who make the rules can't exactly break them."

"What are you talking about?" Katherine lowered her voice to a whisper. "Who do you work for?"

He leaned back, lacing his fingers together behind his head. "Got hired by Division 9."

Katherine stared at him for a few seconds before bursting into laughter. "Oh… you had me going there for a sec." She sighed and shook her head. "I almost thought you'd really gotten a job."

Joey rummaged his hip pocket and pulled out his ID badge. He shifted the vid call back to the NetMini and held it up so she could see it. "Funny thing is, I'm not messing with you. Course, I'm in Net Ops… not a field agent, but I'm still technically working for the government."

"That's not funny, Joseph. If they catch you faking that…"

He kept a straight face.

"No… absolutely not. *You* are working for the government? You *hate* all forms of authority. How the hell… Seriously?"

Elizaveta flipped up the visor, rubbed her eyes, and looked up at him with an earnest expression. "*Ya zakonchila testovyy uroven'. Teper' mi mozhem poigrat?*"

He glanced at text on the NetMini's physical screen. ‹[Russian] I've finished the test level. Can we play now?› "Few minutes. Let me get off the vid first."

She listened to his voice repeat from the machine, nodded, and flipped the visor down while muttering. "*Hochu yeshe poigrat' v tu igru gde nado v shariky strelyat.*"

‹Okay. I will play the game where I shoot balls again.› popped up on his NetMini screen.

Elizaveta raised her arms, gripping her virtual gun.

Joey put his ID away and flashed a big shit-eating grin at his sister. "Not kidding. It's real."

"How?" Katherine gawked.

"Oh nothing too extravagant. Just helped one of their people stop a megalomaniacal AI from overrunning West City with rampaging murder machines. None of their Net Ops people have the testicular fortitude to leave the safe confines of the lab. It impressed them I'm not a coward."

"There's a difference between being a coward and an idiot gambling with their life." She frowned. "And testicles have nothing to do with courage."

He rolled his eyes at the ceiling. "It's a figure of speech, not a criticism of your gender."

"It's deeply rooted in the misogynistic vernacular of a society from three centuries ago. You spend too much damn time immersed in that Wild West nonsense."

Joey pursed his lips and narrowed his eyes at her.

"You know I only started shouting at you because I didn't want you to get yourself killed." She let her head sag. "I guess I didn't express it very well, but I am worried about you."

"Yeah. I didn't forget you're a lawyer. As soon as you don't need me for anything, you'll be back to telling me how much of a failure I am and how I've made Mom cry."

Katherine scowled. "Everything I say isn't a lie… and save the lawyer joke. I'm *not* a criminal defense attorney… anymore."

"Chasing MedVans?"

She scoffed. "No, Joseph… I'm splitting my time working inter-corporate lawsuits while trying to get my foot in the door of the Arcadia prosecutor's office."

They stared at each other in silence for a few minutes.

"Hey…" Katherine looked up with a rare shade of vulnerability in her features. "This is gonna sound crazy but…"

Joey flicked a bit of lint from his chest. "You've called me for help. It already does sound crazy."

"I mean it, Joe. I…" She shook her head. "Look, never mind. If you can—"

"What? Come on. Out with it."

Katherine seemed to stare into his soul. "I got a vid from Dad three days ago."

Her lip quivered and tears gathered in her eyes. "At first, I thought it was Grant trying to twist the knife... but Dad said I should vid you, said you could help." She sniffled and wiped her face. "What's going on, Joe?"

He nodded. "There's an AI out there that's basically Dad. It's a long story. You know that thing with the murder machines? Well, the AI that started that whole mess was designed to collate exabytes of data from millions of sources to generate child AIs that capture the essence of a person. I still don't know *why* it picked Dad, but... the entity that called you was an AI version of him."

"Oh, wow." Katherine looked around as if afraid of being spied on. "What does it want?"

A whimsical smile preceded Joey laughing. "Same thing Dad did when he's on vacation. It's just wandering around taking in the sights. It's kinda freaky how much like him it is."

"You're saying an AI made an AI? That's illegal."

"Yeah. Because declaring something illegal stops criminals from doing it." Joey frowned. "I know. Don't worry. I deleted the creator. Dad-AI seemed harmless, so I didn't bother."

"Thanks." Katherine smiled. "I know you can get Grant off my ass. He's really trying to ruin my life... maybe even get me put in jail."

"I got him." Joey winked. *Okay, this is surreal. I'm working* for *the government, and I'm looking at Katherine and I don't want to eat a bullet to make her shut up.* "Hey, since I don't have to worry about getting black-bagged anymore if I set foot on Mars, maybe I'll pop up and visit sometime. How's Mom?"

"Lonely." Katherine folded her arms, staring down. "After Grant left, I was going to have her move in with me, but with all this crap going on now, she doesn't want to terminate her lease and then wind up being out on the street if I lose my place." She lifted her head. "Mom would like to see you again. If the two of us could exist in the same room without trying to kill each other, it'd probably make her year."

"Oh." Joey cracked his knuckles. "This jackass is involving Mom? Consider him dealt with."

"Thanks. I owe you."

"Yes... yes, you do. Don't think I'm not going to expect atonement for the past five years."

Katherine chuckled and wiped a tear. "If you fix this Grant situation, I'll kiss your boots."

He raised an eyebrow. "Are you being literal, like lips to pseudo-leather or metaphorical?"

"Asshole," she muttered.

After two seconds of staring at each other, they laughed.

"I'll vid you back when it's done."

Katherine reached off frame. "Thanks." She started to turn away, but looked at him again. "And sorry."

The call dropped.

"*Gde mama?*" asked Elizaveta.

"I should probably get a Russian chip." Joey glanced at the screen showing ‹Where's mama?› "Working late. It's probably going to happen a lot."

"*Oy. Spasibo, chto ostalsya so mnoy.*" She smiled. "*A shas ty pokazhesh' mne igru?*"

The NetMini spoke in the child's voice, "Oh. Thank you for staying with me. Will you show me the game now?"

"Sure."

Joey picked up the second Senshelmet with the mild cringe and head turn one often used while handling a loaded diaper. The Yume had M3 ports, but plugging direct would give him an unfair advantage. *Damn. I haven't even touched one of these things since I was seventeen.* He eased it down on his head and tried to remember the old routine of relaxing and letting the brain trust the signal. After a momentary tingle spread across the top of his head, the living room melted away to a white-floored room with glowing green and pink energy fields. A virtual slab of glass held a series of commands for the Yume-Koujou system. To his right, a shimmery orb of golden light bobbed up and down, a representation of Elizaveta's presence in the VR world.

"It's pretty in here," said a somewhat-louder English child voice on top of Elizaveta's real-world Russian.

"Oh, that's so handy." Joey smiled. "I had no idea these things did on-the-fly translation."

The girl giggled. "It is funny to hear you talking twice."

"Okay." Joey walked over to the slab and accessed the library. Fortunately, *Alduin's Adventure* sat at the top of the list, so he didn't have to scroll past game covers full of gore with the kid nearby. He poked it.

A few seconds later, the shimmery 'lobby' changed to a stone-floored room. The surroundings resembled a medieval castle rendered in cartoon. Elizaveta's 'presence indicator' had changed from a ball of light to a faerie. Joey looked down at himself and confirmed that he, too, had taken on the outward appearance of a twelve-inch-tall faerie.

"Sigh," he said. "Okay... what's the setup here?"

He perused the information tiles for the game, which unrolled in midair like ancient scrolls. The game differed from most in that the player did not embody their character. *Alduin's Adventure*, while based on the Monwyn RPG, had been simplified and turned into a maze crawl for younger players. The character advancement and skill elements were almost gone, with each of sixteen playable characters having only six 'choice points' where a player could select one of three abilities that would alter how the character played a bit. The player's point of view hovered above and behind the character as they guided them around various levels full of hallways, treasure chests, monsters, and traps. The cartoony/anime appearance of everything reassured him he'd chosen a kid-appropriate game. Hopefully, nothing too graphic would happen.

Elizaveta selected an elf woman with a bow and a dog-sized dragon companion. Joey chuckled to himself. *Well, since we're going cliché, I might as well go full-cliché.* He picked a guy that looked like a knight with a sword and shield.

*Thok.*

An arrow stuck into his character's face. Aside from a sound effect, little happened.

"Why did you do that?" asked Joey.

"Umm." The elf woman bit her lip and shrugged. "Aren't we supposed to fight?"

Joey found it easy to disregard the quiet Russian leaking into his right ear. "No... we work together to fight monsters."

"Oh!" The elf bounced and clapped. The sofa jostled, likely from Elizaveta bobbing in her seat. "That is better."

Despite not being 'in' the character, controlling the knight played much like other games. It moved as he wanted to move, and all he needed to do was think about it. The effect proved wildly disorienting as the disembodied view followed his character from above and behind.

After a few minutes to get used to moving and attacking, Joey walked over to a giant pair of metal-banded wooden doors.

"Is the adventure inside there?" asked Elizaveta.

"Yep." He grasped a large iron ring and pulled.

The doors opened with a slow, groaning creak, revealing a long tunnel.

"Die!" yelled a tiny creature voice.

A three-foot tall grass-green goblin leapt out into the hallway brandishing a small sword. Its huge eyes and floppy ears made Joey want to laugh at it. It raised its pitiful weapon and started to charge at them.

Elizaveta shot it in the chest.

The goblin flew backward, bounced on its head, and landed flat on its chest, giant Xs where its eyes had been.

"I got a meanie," yelled Elizaveta.

Joey chuckled. "You did. Wanna go find more?"

"This is fun!" The elf woman zoomed off into the dungeon.

Joey ran after her, smiling at the gleeful noises coming from the girl next to him. "Hey, wait. You're weak up close. Don't get too far away from me."

"I found a door," echoed from around a corner up ahead.

He ran past several torches and hooked a left not quite a full second before the elf kicked open a pair of double doors.

Dozens of goblins ranging from the size of the one she'd shot moments before to pudgy ones a little shorter than men littered a large, open chamber. Some had been dancing, some eating, some sleeping... but they all froze and turned as one to stare at the two of them.

"Uh oh," said Elizaveta. "That's a lot of meanies."

"Nah." Joey stepped in front of her. "It's just the marketing department."

She blinked at him. "What?"

"Arrows. Put them into goblins." He raised his shield.

The mass of goblins swarmed at them, a tidal wave of green.

# 8

# SANCTUARY

Rotating jets coated Nina with hot water and soap. The metal ring descended inside the autoshower tube to the floor, lingered for a few seconds, and rose again. She held her arms up to expose her sides to the cleansing foam and combed at her hair with her fingers. Pressure from the streams embraced her like a slow massage. The soapy mix washed over her face, but didn't sting her eyes.

She closed them anyway, a few seconds late, trying to avoid the reminder that every part of her aside from her brain and spinal cord had been made in a factory. The military-grade Class 3 doll body fooled even her parents, as well as everyone else who saw her. Even Nina forgot sometimes, but only when something existed for her attention to cling to. Joey's irreverent smile could offer such escape, and apparently so could comforting a terrified orphan who'd snapped awake from a nightmare.

The spray ring descended once more.

Nina ran her hands around her chest and up over her shoulders one after the next. Skin made from high-grade flexible composites had the exact feel and texture of living tissue. Of course, they couldn't cover this body in real skin. As soon as she used her full strength, she'd tear it. When she'd yanked the cage doors from their frames in the Osiris lab, she'd have peeled all the skin off her hands had it been living tissue. When she'd twisted Sergeant Hickman's augmented arm off at the shoulder and knocked him out with it, she'd have sheared her palms off.

Nina narrowed her eyes. *Why did Joey die laughing when I told him about Hickman? That wasn't funny.* She prodded the holo-panel in front of the metal strip where the autoshower tube touched the wall, adding another five minutes to the wash cycle. Even if her body consisted of plastisteel and synthetic materials, a hot shower still *felt* good.

"I'm a brain in a jar. It doesn't know any better. Reality is a product of one's experiences. I'm experiencing a shower, so for all intents and purposes, I am real."

*Beep.* A flashing green dot appeared in the upper left of her vision.

‹Incoming: [D9] Cmdr (O6) Hardin, Harold J›

"He knows I'm going to be late today." Her mental impulse caused her hardware to answer the call.

A panel opened dead center in her vision; her boss floated three feet away, which made him appear to be standing behind a window in the wall. ⌜Good morning, lieutenant.⌟ He smiled. Brown-grey curly hair draped over his scalp like a woodland creature hit by a PubTran bus. ⌜Hope I'm not interrupting anything important. Just a quick heads-up. I thought you'd like to know Lieutenant Woodring's out of the tank and back to his old self.⌟

Nina smiled, both in reality and via her virtual presence on Hardin's terminal. The spray ring again climbed, filling the tube with steam and the scent of lavender. ⌜That's good. I'm going to guess that he wants the case back?⌟

⌜Yeah. He's a little miffed we didn't wait for him to finish his dunk. He wanted to go after Hickman.⌟

⌜I'm sure he did… and he probably would've shot the guy as soon as said 'fuck you,' assuming Hickman didn't disappear before he got out of the tank.⌟

Hardin gave her a solemn nod. ⌜Exactly why we sent you in. He knew we had him, and we figured he'd make a run for Sector 6060. All the parts he'd funneled in for them, his friends there would've protected him.⌟

Nina chuckled. ⌜We should've let him go to the black, sir. Prison's like a four-star hotel by comparison.⌟

⌜Except he could've left the disavowed sector any time he wanted… assuming he remained alive to do so. More risk to citizens that way.⌟

She arched her back and adored the shower on its last up-down pass. ⌜Hickman wasn't expecting me. He actually laughed when I confronted him.⌟ Nina stared down at her hands, fingers splayed, soapy water running in trails over her palms. *So delicate looking. So harmless.* She closed her fingers to fists. *So false.* ⌜He stopped laughing when he hit the floor.⌟

Hardin scratched at the side of his head. ⌜Damn fine of you to leave the man alive.⌟

The dry cycle kicked on; hot air blasted up from the base, creating a tornado in a bottle. Her skin rippled as if she'd gone skydiving nude. ⌜I didn't get the feeling command wanted him on a 'flight to Miami'… even if he did try to tear Woodring's head off.⌟

⌜Well…⌟ Hardin chuckled. ⌜Let's just say no one would've complained if you'd gone that route. I'm half-tempted to ask if you want to talk to someone, but I know you better than that. Most in your position would've killed him.⌟

Nina lifted her gaze to her reflection on the clear tube. A vacant, emotionless face stared back at her. ⌜You're worried I'm having a crisis of humanity, sir? That I can somehow 'be more real' by acting more humane?⌟

⌜The thought had crossed my mind, though I doubt Doctor Rice would call you reluctant to do your job.⌟

⌜Tell me everyone in Division 9 doesn't fight to keep their soul.⌟ Her attention fixated on a droplet of water dangling from the tip of her nose. Gravid, it wobbled, threatening to fall at any second. ⌜I've tasted death, so they worry I hesitate taking life when necessary? Would they rather we solve every problem with expedience, or does some shred of morality still live within this shell of metal and plastic?⌋

⌈Nina... Are you feeling all right?⌋

⌈I suppose. I know I had to have been dead for a little while. That I'm in this body only proves I had to have been beyond help.⌋

⌈You had lost almost all of your blood, and most of your vital organs were mush. The only thing they could do was rig a bypass to your brain to keep it oxygenated; the rest of you had been dead for six minutes by the time you arrived in the procedure room. You seem oddly morbid. What happened?⌋

Nina smiled. ⌈I'm cranky when I oversleep. I think it's the way Hickman looked at me as soon as he realized I was a doll. Panicked like a little boy staring at the closet monster. He was sure I'd kill him. Probably why I didn't. ⌋ She straightened her posture and gathered her hair behind her back. ⌈I'll be okay. Late night, reports, overslept. I think everyone goes through some sort of existential crisis at one point or another. I haven't quite decided if I'm *still* alive or if this is some kind of second chance-slash-'dark Nina rising' situation.⌋

⌈That's fair, but if you want to talk to one of the head-docs, I won't think less of you. Any one of us behind a badge needs to air shit out now and then. No shame in it.⌋

⌈Right. Thanks.⌋

⌈Oh... things look quiet save for some additional paperwork needed for the dissolution process on Osiris, but you can do that from home. Why don't you take the day and get some rest?⌋

⌈Sounds good to me. Been awhile since I had some quiet time. See you Monday.⌋

Hardin nodded, and dropped off the vid.

Nina stepped out of the shower tube into the chilly bathroom air. She spent a minute or so at the sink fussing with her hair. How strange to think that this body generated real hair, modeled on her actual DNA. It had the same texture, and the same tendency to retain 'bedhead' as before most of her consisted of nonliving parts.

*Stop thinking about that.* She pictured Bertrand's gaping skull. Perhaps she'd lied a little to herself. Revenge did make her feel happier, but not *better*. Most of that happiness came from knowing he wouldn't victimize any more innocent women or girls. Sixty-four percent of his victims weren't even eighteen yet. One survivor had been fourteen, the youngest of the prostitutes he'd attacked; that girl had pleaded for her life and told him her age. By some strange twist of whatever psychological disaster he'd become, he didn't feel like killing a girl that young. She'd been so scared by the near miss she'd begged Division 1 to send her to a colony adoption. The girl didn't even want to be on the same planet as Bertrand.

*Maybe I'll send her a message. She'd probably like to know he's dead.*

Nina padded out into the living room, eager to get started on her day of doing nothing but lounging around the house. She froze two steps from her new sofa at the sound of a small sneeze from the corridor behind her.

*Shit. I've got a kid now.* She looked down at her naked self. *I suppose I'll need to get used to wearing clothes around the house again.* After hurrying back to her room to grab a knee-length white t-shirt, she flopped on the sofa and logged in wirelessly to the Division 9 network. At least having a doll body let her carry restricted headware: a direct connection to the secure government system.

Six panels opened in midair over her, email client, reports database, bulletins, and three screens' worth of empty space where various search and monitoring apps would open if she needed them. Two emails from Hardin requested additional details and records on the Osiris case. Thirty-six more contained back-patting from everyone who'd helped work on it, grateful they'd found the kids alive. A bit of a morale boost seemed in order, so she sent the team an hours-old picture of Elizaveta smiling with the note, 'Thank you for helping me' on it.

She took video files Joey'd sent into the master incident report and crosslinked them with the write-ups she'd done, as well as her personal-recorded-video. Any judge, lawyer, or investigator who subsequently needed to refer to the raid on the lab could watch the whole thing from her point-of-view. Of course, they wouldn't be able to feel the blinding rage that came over her as Doctor Rice attempted to justify keeping children in cages and using them for medical experimentation. *Anyone who questions doing a summary on that asshole needs to be tested to make sure they're not an AI.*

The sight of the lab, even a still image on paused video, got her angry all over again. Watching the recording Joey found of the kids being carried over the beach to a van didn't help. Her mind ran away with how terrified they must've been for however long they'd been on the boat, not knowing what future awaited them. She'd done a little digging. The old bastard on the vid hadn't been lying. Much to her astonishment, the ACC *did* tend to remand child detainees taken in anti-resistance operations back to an adoption queue rather than treat them as prisoners, as long as they had no evidence the kid had participated in actual resistance activity. Merely being the child of a traitor wasn't a crime.

She grumbled. *Who knows what happens when the cameras aren't running.*

It took about twenty minutes to finish off the additional details Hardin wanted. She'd be damned if Osiris lawyers would worm their way out. Already, other companies circled like sharks looking to glom onto soon-to-be-former employees, facilities, and equipment. Assuming the judge found in favor of the government, Osiris Biotechnic would cease to exist, and everything it owned would be seized and sold at government auction for perhaps a third of its actual value.

While those children had most of her sympathy, she afforded a little pity for the Osiris employees who had nothing to do with the illegal project. The stigma of being associated with the company might hamper finding new work, not so much for any sense of moral outrage, but more that they feared the government would bring increased scrutiny in their wake.

Nina logged out; all the windows collapsed, leaving her a clear view of her empty—and too quiet—living room. Metal slats outside the amber windows responded to a wireless command, pivoting to mute the glaring morning sun.

"Elizaveta?"

She waited five seconds before standing. Since she'd heard a small sneeze earlier, she headed into the back hallway, and the girl's room. The door had been pushed within two inches of closed. No sound came from within.

"Elizaveta?" asked Nina in a soft tone.

"Yes?" Her chip provided an echo in English after the child's spoken Russian. "I'm here."

Nina walked in, finding the girl sitting in the narrow space between her bed and the wall, curled up in the corner with both arms wrapped around the white bear in her lap. The child didn't look upset, though that she hadn't gotten dressed yet worried her. "Why are you hiding back there?"

"I don't want the soldiers to see me if they find us."

"Come here." Nina sat on the foot of the bed.

Elizaveta stood. Her underpants started to fall, but she caught them and held them up while crawling to sit beside her.

"It's okay if you want to wear something. I don't mind doing laundry."

The girl shrugged. "Joey made me put the dress on. I didn't wanna get it dirty."

Nina put an arm around her. "He told me. It's fine." She smiled for a second until worry gripped her. "Did you get in trouble before for wearing too many clothes?"

Elizaveta shook her head. "No. I only had my shirt and pants and sneakers. I wore them every day until the bad doctors stole them."

Nina's heart sank at the memory of that box of disgusting rags. Maybe she shouldn't push her too much too fast. She'd acclimate eventually, and around the house... let her be comfortable.

"Can I really have this whole room?" Elizaveta looked around. "It's so big."

"Yes, sweetie." Nina brushed blonde strands away from the girl's eyes. "This is your room."

The girl clasped her hands in her lap and stared down at her feet. "I'm sorry for having bad dreams and being afraid of loud noise. I'm trying to get better." She lifted her head with the same pleading look she'd given Nina from inside the cage. "Please don't return me."

"Elizaveta..." Nina gathered the girl's hands and held them. "You're not something I bought. As soon as I saw you in that place, I knew you needed a home. I..." *Don't know what came over me. I'm a couple months away from twenty-six. What am I doing with a kid?* She stifled a sardonic chuckle. *Not like I'm hitting the clubs with Vincent every night anymore.*

Elizaveta leaned in and hugged her. "I'm glad you found us."

"Me too."

"You killed the bad doctor, didn't you?"

Nina glanced at the girl, pursed her lips, and sighed. The kid had probably seen people shot, not to mention who knows what kind of violence in the underground of Minsk, or wherever she'd been taken from. "Yeah. He tried to tell me what he was going to do to you was acceptable."

Elizaveta shivered. "He was bad."

Nina slid her hands under the girl's armpits, picked her up, and set her standing in front of her. "Hold still a moment."

Elizaveta stiffened like a soldier, hands flat against her legs, chin high.

A wireless connection filled Nina's vision with a GlobeNet interface as though she'd opened her NetMini. She navigated to TMC's online store, which sold just about everything a company wouldn't get in legal trouble for selling, and pulled up the kids' clothes section. A few mental button taps later, her cybereyes calculated Elizaveta's dimensions, and she placed an order for an assortment of dresses, sweaters, pajamas, and a few shirts and pants.

"What are you doing?" Elizaveta snuggled her underwear up again.

Nina ordered a ten pack of new ones based on the measurements. "Ordering some stuff."

"Stuff?" She squirmed. "Can I move yet?"

"Yes." Nina grinned, and logged off the GlobeNet. "I'm getting you some more clothes. I've been so busy with that last case I'd only gotten you a few things."

Elizaveta climbed onto the Comforgel pad, crawled to the pillow end, and retrieved her new bear. She carried it back and sat once more at Nina's side, holding it in her lap. Nina watched her for a little while as she spoke to the stuffed animal, telling it how her last bear had kept her safe when things got scary, but now that she wasn't living in a scary place, she would keep him safe instead.

A few minutes later, Nina looked up at a chime from the front door. A quick link to the security system showed a trio of delivery bots hovering in the hallway outside. "Be right back."

She crossed the apartment to the entrance and opened the door. One by one, the floating bots opened hatches, dropped off boxes, and glided off toward the 'bot door' her building had at the end of every hallway on each floor. When she returned to Elizaveta's room and set her haul on the bed, the girl hopped to her feet and stood up on her toes to get a better look.

Nina opened each box in turn, laying out dresses, shirts, pants, leggings, and a few sets of pajamas. The new underwear came in individual plastic packs, which she loaded into the cleaning unit on the wall after removing the stack of slightly-too-large ones. Those, she packed in the closet for future use, once the child had grown a little.

Elizaveta clutched the white bear to her chest, staring at the clothes arranged on her bed, eyes wide with shock.

Nina smiled. "Would you like to wear one of them now?"

The girl looked up at her, back at the clothes, back at her, and collapsed to her knees, sobbing.

*I wasn't expecting that...* Nina sat on the floor nearby, rubbing Elizaveta's back. "What's wrong?"

"It's so much..." She sniffled into the bear's head. "So much clothes."

*She's never seen my closet.* Nina bit her lip. *Is she crying because she's happy?* Nina pulled the girl into her lap and held on.

Elizaveta calmed in a few minutes, looking guilty. "There's still people who only have one thing to wear, like I used to... It's bad for me to have so much."

Nina hugged her and rocked slightly back and forth. "There are people everywhere who are barely hanging on. Even here in the UCF... on the Moon, Mars... We should help when we can, but you shouldn't feel guilty for being safe. You are safe now. No one is going to come and take you."

"I can stay here?" Elizaveta sniffed and wiped at her face. "Not like before?"

"What happened before?" Nina squeezed her.

The girl looked down. "A police man found me begging, and took me to his home. He let me sleep on his sofa for a few days, but then he took me to another place. The man and woman there didn't really like me. They didn't give me as much food as the other kids, and made me clean. If I didn't listen to them, they would hit. I ran away."

Nina shook her head. "Sometimes, police officers will take in an orphan like that until they can find them a better home. I'm sure he didn't know those people would be mean to you. You're not 'crashing on my couch' for a couple days. This is your home now." *I guess I'm doing more than fostering. They'll approve it. I could always ask Dad to make sure. He's got pull.* She ran her hand over the girl's hair, smiling. *Makes sense why she's been hiding in her room. She's afraid she'll lose it.*

Elizaveta blinked, looking shocked. "But you're the police."

"That's right, but I knew the minute I saw you that you needed a good home."

The child beamed, hugged her, and leapt away to pick at the clothes on the bed. She went straight for a white dress with a pink heart on the chest and pulled it on before modeling it for Nina.

"It's pretty!" Nina grinned.

Elizaveta curtseyed. "Thank you."

*Beep.*

Hardin appeared in a floating panel. 「Nina... Sorry to bother you again. Something has come up and I'd like you to take the lead on the investigation.」 He raised a hand. 「Nothing's on fire. Monday's fine.」 He dropped his arm and smiled. 「You could use a weekend to unwind.」

"You're welcome, sweetie." Nina shifted her gaze to Hardin, and chuckled mentally over the comm. 「It can wait 'til Monday? You're not throwing me a softball are you?」

「Doubtful, but no one is in any imminent danger.」

Elizaveta picked up a pair of pajamas with teddy bear feet. "What is this?"

"Pajamas." Nina's avatar nodded. 「Right. See you Monday, sir.」

Hardin returned the nod and hung up.

"What are pajamas?" Elizaveta held them up to herself and looked down at the footies.

"Something to wear to sleep in when it's cold."

"Oh." She set them back on the bed.

Nina stood. "Would you like to watch a holovid?"

Elizaveta tilted her head.

"Don't know what that is?"

"No."

"Come on." Nina reached toward her. "I know a few you'd like. I still have a bunch I liked at your age."

Elizaveta took her hand and beamed. "Okay."

# 9

# ISLANDS

Page after page of employment listings scrolled left within a blue-on-black holo-panel. Katya sat cross-legged on the floor, her back against the sofa, her pale skin tinged azure in the radiant glow of thousands of options she didn't feel qualified for. A search for 'security work' turned up numerous high-risk-shit-pay jobs that involved a lot of ass-in-chair time behind monitoring stations or walking around a facility after-hours and being the first idiot to get shot at by anyone trying to break in.

Her vision of leveraging her experience into corporate security more involved planning, design, and/or management... not being the girl munching donuts behind a desk. While she could do it, the pay wouldn't sustain the apartment—and the boredom wouldn't sustain her sanity. More advanced options always seemed to require eight or more years of experience doing the same job.

*How does anyone get such experience when they all want people to have it already?*

She grumbled, debating asking Joey to fiddle with her public record. A few falsified 'previous employers' might get her in the door. Of course, trying to fit in and 'make nice' with the UCF wouldn't work so well if she got caught. Her cherry-red fingernail glowed as she impaled it in the hologram and dragged left to the next page. *Everyone has to do it. There is no way to get a job without experience, and no way to get experience without the job.*

Frustrated, Katya went to the 'job wizard' area of the listing site, and got to filling out a questionnaire about her skills. Perhaps the software could come up with a better suggestion. Eve walked in from the back wearing tight black shorts that stopped halfway down her thighs, and no top. Katya raised an eyebrow. The not-quite-child went over to a fitness machine by the living room's exterior wall, which consisted of floor-to-ceiling glass from wall to wall. She leapt half her height up to grab a bar, and proceeded to do pull-ups.

"Eve?" asked Katya.

"Morning," said the girl between grunts.

"You don't have to do that anymore."

Eve relaxed and hung on her arms. "I know, but it's fun. I enjoy working out, plus I gotta get used to not having those damn nanobots in me. It's weird getting tired so fast." She resumed doing pull-ups. "I mean, it's weird getting tired in general."

Katya smiled. "All right. As long as you're doing it because you *want* to."

"Did they make you work out when you were a kid?" Eve looked up and muttered, "Thirteen... fourteen..."

"Not so much. Running, acrobatics, gymnastics mostly. They didn't want me looking unfeminine with too much muscle."

Eve scoffed. "Pigs."

"Yes, they are... but it is easy to be offended when you do not face consequences for having an opinion." Katya stared through the hologram, all the words reduced to meaningless shapes as old memories haunted her.

"Twenty... twenty-one," whispered Eve. She stopped, hanging again and breathing hard. "Maybe you should do some pull-ups. A guy can't beat a girl into submission if she can kick his ass."

Katya blinked away the past and swiped a strand of hair off her face. "It is more than one man. The society rewards strength and punishes weakness. Women are expected to be weak. Those who aren't gain a little respect, but are always talked about in vile terms behind their backs." She exhaled contempt. "They tell us the UCF is a police state, where no one has freedom and the government watches everything. *They* watch everything too. This place has many flaws, but at least here I do not feel lesser for being a woman."

Eve growled, her face beet-red as she struggled to complete her thirtieth pull-up. She flailed her legs as if trying to walk up steps that didn't exist; her entire body shuddered with determination. Though she didn't quite go all the way up, she got far enough to count it, and fell to dangle by her hands again. "Most of the people in charge at the facility where you found me were women."

"I thought Welker ran that place." Katya scrolled up and down a list of 'skills' she could claim. She tapped a few: basic electronics, security systems, cybersecurity...

Eve took a few quick breaths and hooked her legs over the bar. She let go with her hands and hung upside down. "Sitting behind a desk and reading emails isn't being in charge." The girl folded her arms over her chest and started doing inverted sit-ups. "Find anything yet?"

Katya grumbled. "Not yet." Her NetMini rang with an incoming call, from Alex Hunter. "*Ovtetit'.*"[1]

The shimmery face of a perpetually mid-twenties man with thick brown hair and a boyish, aristocratic charm appeared. After a second or two, the glowy effect of the hologram stabilized and he looked solid, albeit tiny. Light gleamed from his iridescent blue suit, a garment that probably cost forty thousand credits.

"*Bonjour, mon cher. J'espère que vous allez bien.*" He tapped a finger to his eyebrow and flashed a rogue's smile.

"*J'ai eu des jours meilleurs, mais je l'ai aussi eu bien pire*[2]." She leaned back on the sofa and placed the NetMini on her thigh. "What's the job? Must be good if you're calling me on Sunday."

Eve let out a roar of victory after her fortieth sit up. She went limp again, arms outstretched over her head, her hands still well above the floor. "Who's that?" She straightened her legs and slipped from the bar, landing into a somersault. "He's kinda cute. I'd totally date him"

Alex's expression flickered to a grimace.

Katya let off a genuine laugh. The same laugh that Joey once described as befitting a deranged noblewoman watching peasants suffer beheading for amusement.

Alex gave her a momentary weary look before his smile returned. "I noticed you were trolling for work. It just so happens I have something you would be perfect for."

Katya sighed. "I can't afford to skirt the law, Alex. You know that. Things are different now. They know about me... my background makes them suspicious. I am being watched."

He steepled his fingers before his face. "Yes, yes. All who defect from the ACC are watched for a time."

Eve padded over and sat at the edge of the couch. Sweat ran in trails over her face and chest, which rose and fell with rapid breathing. Katya couldn't help but feel a little proud of her, even if the girl was more 'mooching roommate who can't work' than a true child. Despite having the body of a skinny eight-year-old, she had muscle tone that would put some cops to shame. "So who is this guy?"

"He's an old associate."

"Not friend?" Alex feigned a wounded expression. "I am a man who puts people who have things in need of doing in touch with people who can do things."

"You've got ties to the Syndicate?" Eve gawked.

"He's not Syndicate. He's his own little marketplace." Katya picked at her nails.

Alex examined his fingernails. "This job shouldn't be a problem for your particular paranoia."

"He painted his nails," said Eve. "Peach."

Alex thrust his arm down out of frame, a peevish glint in his eye.

Eve grinned.

*Fuck it. We need money.* "What is it?"

"I've been approached by a senior design engineer from Laughlin-Reed Innovation. She is upset that her employer is giving all the credit for her work to her immediate superior, along with the bonus. I've located a buyer for the information. Your role in this is to get in to LRI's facility and meet her for a physical exchange."

Eve stood, stretched, and headed into the kitchen.

"Why not have Joey go in and get the files?" asked Katya.

The clink of ice chips tumbling into a glass echoed from her right.

"Well..." Alex smiled. "For one thing, his current employer might take issue with this sort of work. For another, the data resides on an island network inaccessible from the GlobeNet. He would have to go onsite to access it."

"Like that's ever stopped him before... The Imperial?"

Eve walked back in, nursing an enormous cup of ice water. She set it on the coffee table before doing a series of stretching exercises.

Alex nodded. "Correct, but in this case, there is no need to *steal* the information as someone on the inside is prepared to hand it over."

"This woman is upset about not getting credit, but if she sells it to a rival company, they can't put her name on it without exposing her." Katya extended her arms out to the sides and rested them along the sofa back.

"True. However, her work is already being stolen by her current employer in a manner of speaking. All you need to do is get into Laughlin-Reed, make contact with our woman, and collect a neural memory stick with the data."

*That doesn't sound too difficult or dangerous. Probably means it's both.* "What's my compensation?"

"A clean drop is worth five percent." Katya started to roll her eyes. "Of thirteen million."

She blinked. "That's…"

"About 650,000 in your account."

Katya stared for a moment at the half-filled-out job search form. *Six fifty for a couple hours of work… this can wait.* She extended a leg and tapped the logout button with her toe. "I'll do it."

"Excellent." Alex's body shifted as he pushed something across his desk. "I'm sending over the particulars. There is a time element involved here, so it would be ideal if you could handle this tomorrow."

The whirr of a treadmill started, accompanied by the soft *thumps* of Eve running.

Katya glanced over the miniature holographic Alex at the small figure bouncing near the windows. *Watching her is making me tired.* The NetMini chimed with an arriving file. "Got it. Tomorrow. Right."

"Talk to you soon."

Alex smiled. *"La fortune sourit aux audacieux, ou la belle.*[3]"

"He's trying too hard," said Eve, at a full sprint.

Katya chuckled, and muttered to herself, *"Mozhet byt' no priyatniy na vid.*[4]"

He seemed hesitant. She caught a subtle glance to the side, likely at a translation. The rogue's grin returned. Alex raised his hand in mock toast, and ended the call.

*Pity. I think Joey is correct in his opinion of the man.* She batted around a short fantasy of an evening with Alex, a rare moment of regarding sex as pleasurable rather than a mechanical task sometimes necessary for whatever mission she had to complete.

"Might as well get started."

Eve slowed to a light jog. "You're going out?"

"Not yet. I've got some setup to do first." She stood and went to the master bedroom closet, from which she retrieved her net deck, a NinTek Phantom IV. It lacked some of the features of her old unit, but anyone logging in with a *Vostochnaya Proizvodstva* machine from inside the UCF territory would set off a pile of red flags.

The NinTek at least supported ghost mode, a trick to mask the user's presence from the pulse detection signal of the net. This approximated to the ability to hide while logged in. Without it, other people in cyberspace could find a user easily with basic utility programs, even in a dark room. The laws of reality took a backseat to the laws of man where money came in to play. Technically speaking, a ghost-enabled deck could get her in trouble with the law, though enough people played RPG style MMOs where 'stealth' became a factor that claiming to be a gamer would often work. The illegality of ghosting functioned more like frangible ammunition. Legal to own, legal to use in most situations, but extra penalties if they caught someone breaking the law with it.

Katya carried the sleek, grey-silver case back to the living room where Eve continued on the treadmill, though only at a walking pace while testing her pulse rate. She set the NinTek on the table, handed the girl her half-finished glass of ice water (earning a grateful smile) and flopped on the cushions once more. After settling into the most comfortable position she could manage, Katya pulled the retractable wire from the deck and slid the asterisk-shaped prong into the port behind her left ear.

The bladed connector seated with a *snap* that rattled her skull. She tapped the silver N in the NinTek logo, and the deck emitted an orchestral chime as it powered up. Eve hopped off the treadmill and rounded the coffee table. She flopped on the couch, more lying down than sitting, and tapped her hands back and forth on her taut stomach while trying to catch her breath.

"I'm going to look like I'm sleeping for a bit."

Eve gave her a-thumbs up. "I know. My team ran a few escort missions when Starpoint sent cyber-operators into hostile installations."

Katya blinked. "They used you kids for real missions?"

"Only a few times... and all out in the Badlands. I think they wanted to make sure we were 'fully operationally capable' or some bullshit like that. It was kinda boring actually. They never told us which companies ran the three sites we hit, but their onsite forces sucked. It was like sending in Special Forces to ambush mall security guards."

"That's beyond evil." Katya wiggled deeper into the cushions. If she could avoid a cramp from being immobile for an hour or two, all the better.

"We weren't kids then... well not by time anyway. We'd been out of the growth tank for at least sixteen years at that point."

"Wait, so you didn't age up to eight?"

Eve shook her head. "No. I've always been this size."

"So you're really twelve, not twenty?"

"No... I've been out of the tank for twenty years four months and change." She stared at herself. "What's it like to have a period?"

Katya coughed. "Uhh. How much did those nanobots hurt?"

Eve stared at her. For a few seconds, any trace of adulthood fled from her expression.

"Sorry." Katya's vision blurred as the deck invaded her vision with its front menu. Spinning silver icons made to look like the inner workings of something like a starship engine gleamed before her mind's eye. "It's different for everyone."

"Sucks that bad?" Eve traced a finger around her abdomen. "I don't even know if everything's gonna work right after so long."

Katya reached over and squeezed the girl's shoulder. "The doctor said everything looked fine. Don't worry about it. Enjoy not having any responsibilities. Sometimes I wish I could do things over again with someone looking out for me."

"That's escapism," said Eve.

"Maybe for me. But you never *had* a childhood to begin with."

Eve's smile turned wistful. "Neither did you… is that why you wanted to look out for me?"

Katya stared at the little one beside her. It seemed none of the parts of having kids she dreaded, the whining, tantrums, arguing, carelessness, like trying to contain a drunken wolverine desperate to destroy everything it came into contact with, applied here. This tiny person had all the physical characteristics of a child but few of the mental ones. *Okay, borderline psychopathic, but we all have our flaws.* In truth, she wanted to save the girl from a life like the one that had been forced on her almost twenty years ago. Her mind found it easy to discard the illogical truth of Eve being chronologically old enough to drink, drive, and vote, and focus on the innocent creature she appeared to be.

"Yeah. Let me get this done and we can do something fun."

"Okay." Eve patted herself on the stomach for a few seconds more before lifting the seam of her stretchy shorts up, peering in, and pointing at her crotch. "If you betray me, I will wound you." She released her grip on the fabric. *Snap.*

Katya laughed. She stared at the login option, green text floating within a darker green window on the side of a giant silver wheel. As soon as she wanted to 'push' it, reality melted away.

Her consciousness seemed to peel forward out of her body and fly face-first down a long spiraling tunnel with black walls. Small boxes of color streaked by, individual at first, they soon became a torrent of rainbow. Two seconds later, with a white flash, Katya found herself standing in a virtual recreation of her apartment, devoid of furniture.

Some people took the time to buy digital replicas of everything they owned in real life. Many opted for more extravagant versions since the cyberspace ones cost a mere fraction of what the genuine items cost. People like Joey sometimes made their own; after all, everything from a simple chair to a motorized, wheeled recliner with built-in massage and coffee maker consisted of program code.

Katya hadn't the inclination or the time to worry about what her virtual apartment looked like. Some part of her, perhaps the Russian mother she never knew, had an itch to collect fine things and decorate the place… but with no regular source of income, comfort had to wait.

She activated a mirror soft and looked at herself. After a few minutes of thought, she reached forward and poked at a series of control icons to the right of the 'reflection.' Her skin darkened to a rich brown. She left her hair black, but made it fluffier. Brown eyes became green, and she tweaked and adjusted her face until she looked nothing like Katya Volkov, or 'Wolf' as the UCF identity file called her. Something like eighty-five percent of the population of UCF Earth had some variation of brownish skin. Most who retained a Caucasian appearance either purchased it from Reinventions or had been born somewhere in Europe… or came from Mars. Then again, Marsborn went beyond Caucasian. They took 'white' as literally as snow. Less chance to stand out looking like the majority. No one would bat an eyelash at her. If everything went according to plan, she'd spend less than half an hour in the Laughlin-Reed building.

"I am Rosalie Hernandez." Katya fiddled with her face a little more until she looked closer to twenty than twenty-eight. "Newly hired lab tech…" She adjusted a little more, making her cyberspace avatar look even younger. "No… Intern. University first year student."

With her appearance done, she traced a box in midair while thinking about her NetMini. A connection opened on a holo-panel, and she accessed the data tile that Alex had sent her. It contained the LRI badge photo of one Tamara Crowley, PhD, a thirty-six-year-old nano-engineer. The woman had a confident smile, frizzy hair, and darker skin. She looked younger in the photo, her poise likely borne from her inexperience with corporate bullshit.

She marked the geo-tag for the LRI building in the deck's navigation client and walked to the patio door. Outside, West City sprawled in its digital glory. Aside from the lack of endless streams of hovercars, it looked little different from reality, even down to the weather and time of day. A faint shiver ran down her spine at the same idle worry she had every time she logged into the GlobeNet. If someone snuck up on her while she slept and plugged her in, she wouldn't know if she existed in the real world or a virtual one. Sometimes she even wondered if what she thought was the real world existed on a computer somewhere in the catacombs below Moscow, her body suspended in a tank of nutrient gel and tended by nanobots.

*What if I'm still ten and the past eighteen years have been the dream?*

She pinched the bridge of her nose.

*Ugh. I've been hanging around Joey too much.*

Katya moved to the edge of the patio deck and climbed up on the railing, peering down sixty-some-odd stories to the road below. At a mental impulse, her NinTek ran a soft called 'Raven,' and a pair of large, feathery wings expanded outward from her back in glowing violet wireframe. Once they reached their full span, twelve feet to either side of her, they filled in solid with black feathers, and stopped glowing.

Perched like a gargoyle, Katya closed her eyes and savored the nonexistent wind across her face. The GlobeNet—especially with these wings—offered a kind of freedom she could never know in the real world. A little girl once plucked from the streets of a commoners' slum had no escape from her corporate masters until she'd tasted flight.

One's sense of location in this world relied on a network of computers all agreeing on where you stood, which in turn caused the interface deck to create the environment it showed to the brain. Going from one place to another could be as simple as changing a pointer in a file, but those who ran the GlobeNet restricted 'teleportation' out of security concerns. Travel within the net took a wide variety of forms from walking to simulations of vehicles to fantastical things like her wings or even 'riding dragons' for people into that sort of thing. Whatever a software engineer could dream up could exist in the net, as long as it didn't break the Sages' rules.

She stretched her wings to their limit and let gravity pull her forward. On some conscious level, Katya knew the human body shouldn't fly. She had no tail to steer with, no proper musculature in the chest to support the tremendous strain of wings, yet in a world of ones and zeroes, that didn't matter.

*I understand how some consider tech a religion. Logic and reason have no place here.*

The Laughlin-Reed Innovation office was located in Sector 13650, almost three hundred miles away from her residential district within Sector 10722. The waypoint indicator she'd previously set floated in the shape of a blue sphere in the distance, about the size of a person's head. She angled toward it. Her desire for speed manifested in a coating of violet energy that sheathed her wings and left glowing trails behind her in midair.

West City raced along below and around her. Wind blasted her hair back, but not nearly with the strength it should have given her simulated speed. The Raven soft had a top speed of 500 mph, making it essentially an aesthetically-altered 'hovercar' program that couldn't support passengers. She banked and swerved among skyscrapers, dodged a handful of advert-bots, and continued pursuing the blue navigation marker ball for a little more than half an hour. The light faded as she slowed back to a speed more believable for a woman with giant raven's wings.

LRI's GlobeNet presence took the form of a 102-story tower in regal silicon grey surrounded by a small park-like area with a handful of trees, an artificial lake, and a biking/jogging trail snaking in and around the miniature nature preserve. Whoever designed it had kept it professional; rather than some outlandish physically-impossible shape, the building would have been a perfect, rectangular bar if not for the northwestern top corner appearing sheared off. A flat corner spanned five stories, with the letters LRI at the center of the inverted triangle. The forty-eighth through fifty-fourth floor contained parking decks for hovercars, and a ground-level ramp on the south facing side hinted at an underground space for land vehicles.

Normally, Katya would spend a week or so checking a place out in the real world before a job, but with Alex wanting this done tomorrow... and Katya wanting it done before any legal backblast could find her, she'd have to settle for exploring via cyberspace. That brought with it another element of risk—she would be relying on their virtual office building mirroring reality. While most companies did that, some went off the deep end in a world where physics didn't apply.

She circled the building in a downward spiral, her left wingtip only a few feet from the corners. When she reached the fifth floor, she diverted away and headed for a section of park with decent tree cover. Leaves rustled and scuffed as she descended amid the branches; the oddity of 'feeling' them touch her wings blanked her mind for a second or two after she landed. They offered an easy means out of virtual buildings, and unlike a vehicle-based travel soft, the system didn't force them to remain persistent in the world. She didn't need to 'leave the car outside' so to speak.

Never before had anything touched them.

Katya curled her wings around herself and wasted a minute or five stroking the soft feathers. She shivered at the inhuman sensation of having feeling in limbs that shouldn't exist. How a human mind coped with such input went beyond her rather limited understanding of psychology or physiology.

*Get on with it.*

Solidity faded from the wings, reducing them to a wireframe drawing of feathers, which retracted into her back. She rolled her shoulders to adjust her bearings to normal and walked along the path to the front door. Being Sunday, the campus had little in the way of activity.

LRI had its hand in biomedical products, research, diagnostic technology, and related software development, nothing the average consumer purchased directly. It seemed unlikely they would have much of a greeter application waiting in the lobby, though she didn't want to attract the attention of a hopeful sales construct mistaking her for a representative of some hospital or private practice.

Stealth in the GlobeNet worked in two ways. A physical barrier such as a tree or wall could prevent a program construct or living user from seeing someone, though only at a casual level. Anti-intrusion systems and defense operators ran programs that effectively let them see through walls. The second order of stealth involved the ghost electronics in her deck. They allowed the interface to disregard background detection, which could—depending on the skill and hardware of the other person—leave her unseen.

For this portion of her mission, Katya needed to avoid detection. She went around the building, ignoring the main lobby, and sprinted across perfect green grass to the access ramp leading to the subterranean parking deck. Pink, red, and yellow splat marks on the walls of the tunnel leading down suggested the employees used the virtual garage as an arena for paintball. Since most 'net gamers used 'real' guns with simulated gore, she assumed HR had a problem with 'violence' and insisted on the use of paintballs.

Fortunately, the designers recreated the real building enough for there to be an access elevator. According to the sign by the door, the parking deck extended five stories down into the city plate, and warned employees that the company would not be responsible for any injury or legal issues that resulted if anyone left the company property while below the surface.

She activated the ghost mode of her NinTek before stepping around the concrete column at the end of the ramp and crossing the open area to the elevators. Instead of parked cars, the space contained an arrangement of obstacles, fortifications, and sniper's nests, all awash with colorful splats.

*Hmm. This might be a fun place to work.* She crept to the elevator and went in. A message appeared in text at the top of her vision, informing her that she had left the public GlobeNet and had entered a private network owned by Laughlin-Reed Innovation. A basic smiley face icon indicated the region as flagged 'public.' Many companies maintained public areas, so prospective customers could visit.

A few mental pokes triggered a scanning routine on the NinTek, and by the time the elevator let her out in a first-floor hallway off the lobby, a small map of the building existed in midair ahead and to the right. She grasped the wireframe tower and turned it about, searching for the human resources department. It took under a minute to find it on the second floor. Another mapping soft sprang to life as she picked at the red square denoting the room as 'nonpublic.' The software analyzed network buffer memory, looking for the route path and destination of the majority of data packets sent out by terminals in HR.

*Where are the servers?*

Pulsing red extended in a thread from that room, snaking down along the second story to a vertical channel in the center of the building, dropped to the first floor, and headed into a large room in the northeast corner.

*Perfect, already on the first.*

She went left, away from the lobby, following the map to an employees-only door with a badge swipe panel. The act of pulling 'lockpicks' out of her pocket triggered a suite of intrusion software. Katya took a knee and stuck her tools into the solid plastic box intended to read RFID badges. Wiggling them around as a gesture of intent set the programs loose on the network. This portion of the network read as a Grade 4, reasonably secure. As much contempt as she had for Joey, she had to acknowledge his skill in the electronic reality. Where she relied mostly on pre-written hack softs that wound up being useless on networks over Grade 5 (and even then proved iffy), he talked about sneaking into Grade 7 networks like he'd been bored. Katya narrowed her eyes as her program ran. Being king of the GlobeNet didn't mean anything when he seemed useless in the physical world.

*Lazy... pampered... fool.*

The thought he'd had the sort of upbringing that offered him the luxury to loaf about got under her skin. She couldn't blame him for what happened to her, but she could hold him in contempt for scoffing at the ease he'd been gifted.

The door chimed and opened along with a digitized voice saying, "Good morning," followed by a distorted buzz where a name should've been.

Katya ducked inside and followed the hallway past a series of small meeting rooms and offices until she could head to the right in the general direction of the data room. According to her map, the corridor sat behind the lobby by a good twenty meters, and crossed into the eastern portion of the building. Two hallways and a left turn later, she approached a small chamber bearing a desk and 'security guard' next to the passageway into the data storage array.

Another soft, Haunt, changed her avatar into a faint transparent version of its usual appearance. While the visual effect did little other than cosmetics, it added another layer of interference to detection protocols, a software backup for the hardware keeping her 'invisible.'

The guard, in actuality a defense program, sat stone-faced, staring into nowhere as she crept past him. Five doors down a narrow, grey hallway, she ducked into the room housing the data nodes the HR terminals always talked to. She sighed at dozens of rows of constructs that took the form of ancient filing cabinets. She knew from her time with Joey that each 'drawer' opened forty or so feet long, laden with innumerable data tiles, silver squares four inches per side and one inch thick. The back and edges looked like mirror chrome, while the face contained a snapshot of the contents.

It took about six minutes of tracing the red trails from the HR workstations to the cabinets before she found the personnel records. She picked a random data tile bearing the face of a man in a lab coat and lifted the tile from the drawer. A gesture like opening a book caused the contents to appear in a floating virtual holo-panel. Katya generated a new blank file by mental command, which appeared as a glass box in her hand. She copied the structure of the employee record over, which animated as pouring a stream of various colored liquid into the empty tile. No longer needing the template, she returned Dr. Emil Shabaz to the drawer, and proceeded to edit in the information about Miss Rosalie Hernandez.

Had she any intention to spend more than an hour in the building for real, she'd probably have gone to West City Biotech University and created a student record too, lest someone cross check, but if anyone suspected her of anything unusual, she'd be out of the building before they could even log in to verify her story. Posing as an intern with little security clearance didn't put her high on the scrutiny list.

She opened Alex's information again to get the location code for the lab in which Dr. Crowley worked, and gave herself security access that would let her walk right in to the secure room. As far as anyone at LRI would know, Miss Hernandez worked as a lab assistant for that team, a college intern doing it for extra credit rather than pay. After embedding an ID photo based on her current net avatar's appearance, she tucked the data tile into the drawer with the rest and closed it.

On the far end of the same room, she found the database that managed the physical security of the building. She wouldn't be able to get into the place in meatspace without a badge, though she could probably make do without a physical one. For the limited time she expected to be there, she only needed to fool doors, not people. If a guard did challenge her, she could play the panicky college student on her first day. They'd probably believe—with a little pheromone help—that someone screwed up and she hadn't been given one yet. Unless that happened, she could use a burner NetMini to fake out the doors.

After copying a few data tiles from the security system, enough to cobble together a 'software badge' that would let her NetMini replicate an access pass, she made her way back out to the elevator hallway. In the solitude of the empty parking deck, a holographic keyboard/terminal window opened in which lines of computer code formed as fast as she could think them. Katya programmed a virtual ID badge, which appeared as soon as she hit the 'compile' button, and hovered before her eyes. She plucked it out of the air and clipped it to her shirt. The identity token should allow her to roam around the building in cyberspace without an issue, provided she kept to areas appropriate for her 'job.' She'd spend a few hours learning the layout of the place, and then pop over to a nearby Citycam repeater for a little trick Joey showed her.

Creating a new PID, or personal identity, generally required a fair amount of skill to do without official access. However, Joey had figured out a way to backdoor it in. The Citycam network shared information with the Department of Official Records. By creating an identity file with specific header information, the Citycam system would treat it as though the DOR sent a records update. That, in turn, would propagate the file across the surveillance grid and ultimately cause it to get 'updated' back into the DOR database. The downsides in the method included taking anywhere from two to four hours for the identity to respond to searches, and it would lack an official creation date. Any live operator at the DOR could tell the entry had been spoofed, but evidently they still hadn't figured out how records entered the system without the create date, a hard-coded requirement. Given that Katya needed Rosalie Hernandez to exist for only one day on the off chance someone at Laughlin-Reed cross checked her, it would suffice.

Katya patted the badge. "Now, let's find that lab."

⸻

BLEARY EYES STARED BACK AT KATYA FROM THE BATHROOM MIRROR. DESPITE HER four-ish hours of exploring the LRI campus in cyberspace occurring while her real body lay inert on her sofa, her muscles ached as though she'd walked herself sore. Or perhaps her brain simply rejected having to obey an alarm clock like the rest of the workaday world after two years of waking up whenever she wanted. Steam drifted in a cloud behind her, seeping out of the autoshower tube.

She tapped her NetMini, which projected the ID photo she'd generated of

'Rosalie Hernandez.' While her CamNano cyberware couldn't alter the physical shape of her face, highlight and shade created illusory contours that could fool the eye in the absence of close scrutiny. Millions of nanobots darkened her skin to match the rich hue of the photo. Bit by bit, mental command added adjustments to her face that made the years peel away. Not that going from twenty-eight to nineteen required a lot of effort. Besides, people kept telling her she looked young for her age. Granted, her former owners had probably done something to her at a genetic level to keep her pretty longer.

Eve traipsed in, threw off the t-shirt she'd slept in, and hopped on the toilet.

Katya, still naked from her shower, glanced back at her with a 'do you mind' look.

"Nice disguise," said Eve. "No need to run screaming, I'm just peeing. Not gonna bomb you out of the room."

Katya blinked. "Umm… I'm not wearing anything. I just got out of the shower."

"Neither am I." Eve's eyebrows scrunched together. "And? Oh… right. Guess I got used to military barracks. No privacy. Open showers." She shrugged. "At least there weren't any boys at the facility."

The irony of that made Katya chuckle. As clinical as her 'owners' had been with her and the other kids they trained up as ghost operators, they provided them with tiny apartments that included private bathrooms. More like being small adults not allowed to leave their place of employment than prisoners or even soldiers.

She forced aside her feelings of awkwardness and kept working on her appearance.

"I could take up a position on the Robertson International building across the quad if you want sniper cover," said Eve. "It's got the best vantage of the front, and since you're going in early in the day the sun will be behind me."

Katya shook her head. "I shouldn't need it. And how are you going to work a sniper rifle? They're taller than you." She made eye contact via the mirror.

"Modular." Eve held her hands up about two feet apart. "The MSR-18 collapses down to a compact AR. It's portable." She shrugged. "'Course you'd have to go buy me one. I don't think they'd sell me a firearm."

"No." Katya laughed. "They most certainly would not."

Eve moved from the toilet (which flushed itself) to the autoshower, pausing at the door. "So… are you going to leave an eight-year-old girl home alone while you go break the law?"

"You're not the average little girl."

With one foot in the tube, Eve put her fists on her hips and struck a superhero pose. "No. I'm better than that."

Katya laughed again, tinged with guilt. If something went south, what would happen to her? Her only real choice would be not to get caught. "This isn't going to be too complicated or dangerous. Walk in; walk out. Meet someone nearby and hand off a neuro-stick."

The autoshower hatch closed with a *thunk*. Eve's voice took on an echoing quality inside the tube. "It's the simple ops that always go to shit."

Katya leaned her weight on the sink, head bowed. "Thanks for the confidence."

"No problem." Eve laughed. After a few *beeps* from the console, the autoshower kicked on. "Guess I'll wait here."

*Only an hour or two.* "I suppose."

"Or you could drop me off at one of those child-sitting places. Naturahealth runs one with this badass climbing wall. But, if you wanna save the money, I'm totally fine being alone."

Katya glanced at the pale blur moving around within foggy plastic cylinder. If she left her here, and the social services people showed up for a 'random check,' the shit might hit the fan. Not like she could tell them Eve was twenty years old. They'd either think Katya'd gone crazy, or if they *did* believe her, whisk the kid off to be poked and prodded. "Okay, you got the address of the place?"

"You sure you don't want sniper cover?" yelled Eve, over the shower.

"Positive."

KATYA WENT OVER AND OVER THE INTERIOR LAYOUT OF THE LAUGHLIN-REED building in her mind as the PubTran Hover brought her to Sector 13650. At C1277 compared to C248 to ride in a ground autocab, it felt like robbery—but she didn't want to spend four hours on the road. Many accused the PubTran cars of being rattletraps, but they had nothing on the terror of the hovercar versions. A tiny ground car barely big enough for four adults with a top speed of about ninety could do only so much damage. Hurtling across the sky at the fiftieth-story level in a vehicle made as cheaply as possible, driven by an AI programed as cheaply as possible, redefined fear.

At 8:51 a.m., the car landed within walking distance of the LRI campus. Katya, rather Rosalie Hernandez, stepped out on wobbly legs. The silver and teal hovercar emitted a pleasant jingle.

"Thank you for using PubTran Prime! We hope your priority travel needs were met with flying colors. Have a great day."

With that, the PubTran car shot off into the sky. At the sight of one of its ion cowls visibly flapping, she put a hand over her mouth to keep from throwing up.

*I'll take the maglev back. Never again.*

She allowed two minutes to set her nerves at ease, and walked across the parklike area around the building to the main entrance. Going for 'college student,' she'd worn a short-sleeved tee with the logo of the 'Screaming Raspberries,' an 'alternative' folksy thrash metal band that the GlobeNet indicated popular among the seventeen-to-twenty-year-old crowd. Plain blue jeans and a new pair of grey sneakers completed the outfit.

The front doors opened as she approached, releasing a blast of sterile processed air. On Monday morning, the lobby buzzed with activity. Voices and the shuffle of footsteps emanated from five different hallways leading deeper into the building, all of which connected to an area behind a massive security station that also served as a reception desk.

*Damn.* She eyed the front counter, where two women and a man in grey security armor with Sentinel Corporation logos sat at tables behind a man and woman in normal office attire. A handful of other security officers stood around by the hallway entrances and the inner end of an enormous scanning machine consisting of five square tunnels, no doubt packed with scanners of various type.

The setup reminded her of the Berlin Starport, even down to the hint of coffee in the air.

Acting too 'lost and new' would attract attention from the security team, but acting too 'I've come here every day for years' might bite her in the ass considering this being Rosalie Hernandez's first day.

With as natural a walk as she could summon, she crossed the lobby and entered one of the scanner tunnels. She hadn't brought a firearm, and her specialty cybernetics had shielding to hide them from scans. Only the upper end of military equipment could pick up enough of an anomaly to raise suspicions. A distant buzz sounded when she reached the midway point, and thin strips of red light appeared in recessed grooves along both black walls.

A spike of fear ran down her spine, as she scrambled to think what might've triggered an alarm. Before she reached the end of the tunnel, a woman in Sentinel Corporation armor stepped in front of her. A compact assault rifle hung on a strap at her side, a rig that would let her bring it to bear in under a second if needed.

Katya put on her best 'confused college student' smile.

"Miss Hernandez," said the woman. "Please step to the side."

*Facial recognition... at least the record held up.* "Is something wrong?" Katya edged left once she exited the scanner, and stopped at the side of the faux-marble counter that surrounded the front station. The three other officers inside each had five holo-panel terminals on front of them, full of security camera feeds.

"You have a NetMini." The officer gave her an expectant look.

Katya blinked. "Well, yeah. Duh. Doesn't everyone?"

"This is your first day, isn't it?" asked the guard.

"Yeah. I'm an intern." Katya smiled. "First day."

The guard looked her up and down. "No badge?"

*Shit. Shit. Shit.* Katya acted annoyed. "Umm. No one gave me one. I just got told to show up and go to Lab 11-B."

The female guard folded her arms and shook her head. "I swear, those people in HR get dumber every damn week. Look, kid. Laughlin-Reed takes security very seriously. We can't allow any personal electronics out of the lobby. You can either leave it in your car or we can put it in a cubby until you check out."

"Cara, this girl's file doesn't say anything about cyberware." One of the male guards looked over.

Katya rolled her eyes. "I told the guy I didn't have anything major. Port, wireless 'net, and a chip board. Like who *doesn't* have the big three?"

Cara, the Sentinel Corporation guard, gave her an unamused frown.

*This is what I get for rushing. I should've made a fake badge.*

"I swear." Cara grumbled and walked around the counter to a small swinging door. She went up behind the man looking at her file. "Why do they even bother having an HR department at all? We wind up having to do everything."

Katya glanced at the main entrance, debating between her odds of fleeing without getting shot or going with the college dare story. When Cara grabbed a plastic card and stuck it into a machine, she couldn't believe her eyes—or her luck. *They're making me an ID badge...*

Cara tapped a few holographic buttons, withdrew the card (which had a holographic still image of Katya's face embedded within) and handed it to her. "NetMini, please."

Katya extricated the device from her front left pocket. "One sec. Gonna tell the girls not to try and vid me."

"No problem," said Cara.

After sending Eve a quick message that she wouldn't have access to her 'mini for a little while, she tapped a fake email app icon, which put the device into 'secure' mode. In a second and a half, the machine switched over to a sandbox OS, which simulated the NetMini environment, linked to the false PID she'd made for Rosalie. If the security people checked it out, the device would appear to belong to a very boring young woman with only a handful of friends and almost no money.

She sent two more quick emails to nonexistent people warning them not to try and vid her, and locked the device. The guard gave her a plastic tag with '1752' on it in exchange. She passed the 'mini to the man behind her, and he took it across the station to a wall of tiny lockers.

"When you're leaving, stop by and give us the tag."

Katya nodded and stuffed the tag in her pocket. "Okay. Gee, I'm glad you mentioned that. I guess I won't bring my LimeTab. Ugh, they never told me. This is gonna suck without music."

"Sorry. No unauthorized electronics past this point. Surprised you're not carrying a weapon." Cara chuckled. "WCBU's not exactly the safest place for a girl with your looks."

"I run fast." Katya laughed nervously. "Really? Hmm. Maybe I should, but I'm kinda scared of guns."

"It's just what I hear." The woman shrugged. "Good luck on your first day."

"Thanks." Katya attached the ID badge to her belt and walked over to the elevators.

Never did she expect the security would actually *help* her infiltrate the place. *So much for the virtual badge program.* She grinned once no one could see her face. The panel emitted a pleasant chime when she swiped the badge past it.

Being seen was bad enough... *interacting* with the guards created a five-pound lump of worry in her gut. *Nothing for it but to go on.* She far preferred 'traditional' sneak jobs. Thermal suit, black, in the middle of the night, no one laying eyes on her at all, hence the term 'ghosts' for people trained like her. When the doors opened, she stepped in and faced out.

Tamara Crowley's lab took up about one-fifth of the eleventh floor, along the middle of the western side of the building, nested in among other labs all around the outer edge of the floorplan. The central portion held break areas, bathrooms, an emergency medical station, storage, and a few conference rooms. As she had a hundred times in virtual reality, Katya headed straight for Lab 11-B. A handful of people, some in white lab coats, some in business attire, gave her odd looks.

As soon as the door for Lab 11-B came into view, a tall blonde woman with a face like a holovid-star coming the other way stepped in her path. The woman looked to be in her late twenties, but something about the set of her jade-green eyes suggested her age was a Reinventions lie.

"What on earth are you doing here?" asked the woman.

Katya blinked, bit her lip, and pointed. "Uhh, I work here. This is my first day. I'm an intern from WCBU." She showed off the badge on her left hip.

The blonde folded her arms, shaking her head. "Did they forget to tell you about dress code? You look like you're on the way to a sorority party. Who are you and who is your supervisor?"

A mental command activated a series of small cybernetic components in her trachea. Nanobots assembled a stress-reducing pheromone, which she began exhaling within a second of wanting to. Katya shrank a little, looking apologetic. "Rosalie Hernandez... I'm supposed to report to Doctor Tamara Crowley." She added a 'kid caught doing something wrong' huff at the end, puffing the air toward the woman's face.

"That's Lab B. I should drag you straight to HR and have you sent home to change, but..." She blinked, seeming light-headed. "I suppose it's not your fault no one told you anything. Make sure you dress appropriately tomorrow... and I will be sending a message to Doctor Crowley." The woman took a breath, blinked again, and smiled with an overwhelming air of peace. Anyone looking at her would assume she'd taken a hit of Flowerbasket. "Go on then. Don't be late."

"Thanks." Katya nodded, and hurried up to the door, which opened at a swipe of her employee badge.

A small area on the other side contained the expected lockers, and she helped herself to the first plain white labcoat she found. An airlock of glass doors separated the changing room from the lab, which hadn't been included in cyberspace. *Hope that thing's automatic.*

The inner door opened at her approach, and closed a few seconds after she'd gone in. Hissing filled the chamber, and a sense of a light mist washed over her. Her Tox filter didn't pick up anything dangerous in the air, so she stayed calm. Forty seconds later, the interior door opened, and a blast of antiseptic smell hit her hard enough to make her eyes water.

Five women and four men stood at various stations in a room with glowing walls composed of three-foot white tiles lit from behind; cobalt blue light shone from the narrow gaps between the squares. Some of the people had their arms elbow-deep in machines, working with substances inside of sealed chambers via robotic grips. Others ran theoretical models on computers. Two of the men flanked a short brown-skinned woman, all three of them engrossed in a conversation about improving the near-field scanning optics of a medical diagnostic device LRI manufactured.

Doctor Crowley had her back turned to the entrance, stooped over the viewport of an enormous electron microscope, though her puffy hair made her recognizable. Katya crept across the room and walked over to her. After going unnoticed for a minute, she cleared her throat.

The woman leaned back from the eyepiece and gave her an imperious look tinged with confusion. "Who are you?"

"Hi, doctor... I'm Rosalie, your new lab assistant."

"What?" Doctor Crowley blinked. "I didn't—"

"You know. *Lab assistant.* In case you needed someone to clean stuff, or perhaps move stuff from one place to another." Katya smiled.

"I don't remember putting in a request for an assistant."

"You must be so busy you forgot." Katya's 'eager new girl' expression sharpened to a pointed stare for two seconds. "Alex in HR said you really needed a hand in here." She glanced around to make sure no one had gotten too close, and whispered, "Shame Dr. Anders is getting all the credit."

"Oh, now I remember." Doctor Crowley laughed. "You're right about that, girl. With everything going on lately, I'd forget my hair if it wasn't attached."

"Awesome," said Katya, adding a bit too much 'teen.' "What should I start with?"

"Well, I'm not sure what you were told to expect. I understand you're studying nanobiology?"

Katya nodded.

"There's going to be mostly boring grunt work... but you'll get some interesting hands on now and then. Come with me."

Doctor Crowley led her across the lab to the back corner, where she swiped her badge at the wall to open a door. Inside, ten rows of shelves held various items, mostly canisters or clear plastic boxes with groups of smaller canisters inside. "Each of these projects has an asset tag, and there's been a lot of complaining that things aren't where they belong. You can start by organizing the sample closet." The doctor handed her a datapad after tapping at the screen for a moment. "This is the room map, asset tags indicated where they belong on the shelves."

Katya took the datapad, giving her an 'are you serious?' look.

After nudging the door closed behind her, Doctor Crowley leaned close and whispered, "I need a few minutes to get things ready. I'm not walking around with it."

*Of course.* "Okay. I'll do my best." She put on a smile worthy of Eager Girl, and stared at the datapad.

Sneaking into LRI as a fake employee and working as an intern wouldn't get her in *too* much trouble, assuming she could come up with a believable answer as to why she did it. Hacker bet seemed like the best excuse, people doing stuff just to see if they could, with no interest in monetary gain or real harm to the company. Such things happened all the time. With that in mind, she set about organizing the shelves so the physical objects matched where the datapad said they should be.

Tamara Crowley, Ph.D. returned after fifty-two mind-numbing minutes. She came down the row of shelves where Katya hunted for a sample but couldn't seem to find it. "How's it going, Miss Hernandez?"

"Good. Umm. CN-185-C seems to be missing. I can't find it anywhere."

Doctor Crowley sighed. "Of course. It's always the cannabinoids that grow legs." She folded her arms and edged closer. A dark, silvery-grey object poked out of her sleeve. It had a rounded nose, looked about four inches long, and an inch thick.

Katya made a show of scratching at her hair in frustration. When her hand came down, she palmed the bizarre thing, and found it spongy. The foam had a sparkling quality, suggesting it contained tiny bits of metal or crystal. A short length of string dangled from the blunter of the two ends. *What the fuck is this? Some kind of space tampon... for a giant?*

"Let me see the chart." Doctor Crowley reached for the datapad.

"I've been around the room twice. I can't find that sample." She handed the pad over.

"Hmm." Crowley made a show of looking annoyed as she brushed the room map aside and opened a note file.

‹They scan for electronic devices leaving the building to prevent exactly what we're about to do. I encased the neurostick in signal-absorbent foam from the EM lab. I'm sorry, but you'll have to put that somewhere uncomfortable to get it out of the building. I don't recommend swallowing it. The foam will react with stomach acid and become toxic. If you get caught with it, we're both screwed. Once you're clear, you can cut the foam away with any standard knife.›

Katya leaned over and typed. ‹Can't I just upload this into my headware?›

"We've had a few things go missing," said Crowley, before typing. ‹Do you have 2.7 petabytes of storage space? Besides, they will probably have you plug in on the way out to scan. If you hesitate, it won't go well.›

*Oh yay. And I thought I finally took a job where I didn't need to use my crotch.* She shivered at the thought of the other option. *Okay, small blessings.* She grumbled. "Damn." ‹No. That's a shitload of data. Guess I feed it to kitty.›

Doctor Crowley chuckled, and erased the text file's contents before closing the app.

Katya nodded and tucked the tampon from hell into her jean pocket. It created a rather noticeable swell that would surely get asked about. "I suppose you'll need to investigate where that sample went. Oh, shit, it's almost two... I've gotta get to class."

"All right. Not bad for a first day. Finding that sample is probably a lost cause. Whoever's doing it keeps disabling the security cameras in here."

Katya raised both eyebrows.

Doctor Crowley nodded. "Damn things haven't worked for months." She winked.

"Some people." Katya rolled her eyes.

The itch to get the hell out of the building as fast as possible proved difficult to resist, but she kept herself at a calm walk across the lab to the airlock. Anxiety made the forty-five second decontamination spray seem more like twenty minutes before the door opened and released her into the outer room. She peeled off the labcoat and stuffed it into the nearest locker before heading out into the hallway and bee-lining for the ladies' room.

She walked to the rearmost stall, locked the door, and dropped her pants. After taking a seat, she fished the reason for the entire trip out of her pocket—thirteen million credits trapped in an elongated foam egg. Katya held it between her thumb and forefinger, staring at it. *I wonder how much Alex is getting for this.*

"I'd make a joke about buying me dinner first, but I suppose you *are* going to technically buy me dinner." *And rent... and whatever else we need.*

To ease her nerves and relax, Katya spent a few minutes fantasizing about Arl Turing, an actor she favored from *Our Final Hours*, a drama series about the crew of an exploration starship stranded on a planet of hostile environments. The crew had been 'hours from death' for fourteen seasons. The magma cave scene came to mind; he'd spent the entire episode shirtless. Eventually, she bit her lip and inserted the Godzilla tampon. She suppressed the need to gasp, and seated it as naturally as one could such an object. *So thoughtful of Crowley to add a string...*

After a flush to keep up the illusion, she fixed her jeans in place, washed her hands, and headed back to the elevator. Whenever she saw someone, she muttered about being late for a class. Hopefully, they would think it normal for an intern to leave in the middle of the work day.

The weight inside her nether regions grew heavier with each floor down. By the time she reached the ground, it had become so ponderous, she expected the foam-encased neural memory stick would drop right out of her, jeans be damned, and hit the floor as a glaring mark of guilt.

It took some effort to ignore the sensation of fullness and walk normally. With each step she took toward the scanning tunnel, the precious cargo grew heavier and more uncomfortable. Any second now, it would shock her, vibrate, beep, or do something to throw off her calm. *No. Otto is dead.* She had faith in the coating the Office of Operational Intelligence put on her cyberware, but who knows what type of foam Crowley found. Would the security people see a black void inside her, or would it diffuse and become invisible while surrounded by biomatter? Her jaw clenched, though she found it easy to look worried. She exited the sensor tunnel at a brisk walk.

A man in Sentinel Armor beckoned her with a wave. "Hang on there, miss. Need to do a port scan."

Between nerves and not being able to think about anything other than carrying millions of credits between her legs, her brain took 'port' the wrong way, and her cheeks warmed. "Uhh... what?"

"You've got an M3." He tapped behind his ear. "Everyone with a port gets scanned on the way out. Company policy."

"Oh." She slouched and approached the counter, grasping the edge with both hands. "Is it going to take long? I'm late for a class."

"Shouldn't." He handed her a standard interface wire. "Go on and connect that."

Katya flicked her hair off her neck and socketed the plug. A screen in front of the guard shifted from dark to pale blue, and he poked a few buttons. She hoped he wouldn't think much of her having a storage module installed, especially since she hadn't declared it on her 'employee record,' but lots of people had them to carry games, movies, or music. That hers happened to be empty at the moment should make it a non-issue.

The word <Connected> appeared floating in front of her face, followed by a small white box with black text:

<Sentinel Corporation SecurScan would like to run a data catalog process. Do you grant permission?>

Yes and No boxes appeared under it. Of course, saying no would probably jump straight to something between guns pointed at her and handcuffs... and police. She stared at the 'yes' button and mentally clicked.

A progress meter appeared and jumped to eighteen percent, where it hesitated. Katya shifted her weight, and tried not to think about standing three feet away from armed security guards while smuggling data valuable enough to put her away for decades. The progress bar crept up at about one percent per second. *I am so glad I didn't wear a skirt.* She kept her smile pleasant and her mind on random things like coffee, white rabbits, sunflowers, and blue skies. When the progress indicator reached twenty-four percent, it zoomed to finished.

"All set." The man smiled and held out his hand.

Katya smiled and disconnected the wire before draping it over his palm. "Sorry to run, but I'm missing class."

He nodded.

"Oh... I almost forgot." She fished out the tag. "My NetMini's in a cubby."

The man took the ticket, and retrieved her device.

Heartbeat pounding in her head, she scurried for the doors. The guard and a teal-haired woman receptionist watched her. Fearing they might've grown suspicious, she smiled back at them.

"Professor Dorran is going to kill me." Katya pointed at the exit. "I'm late for class. They stuck me with a shitty schedule, first class at 2:00 p.m."

The woman gave her a sympathetic look like she'd experienced the same thing.

*Chert voz'mi!* [5] Her heart slowed. *They didn't see it.*

She walked away from the building to the edge of where a curving road cut through the campus grounds, about twenty yards from the doors. A mental nudge opened a call to Alex. His face appeared on a virtual panel, bearing a large smile.

「*Bonjour, mon chéri.* How are you on this fine Monday afternoon?」

「I'm well. What about that blind date you're supposed to set me up with?」

Alex's smile went from pleasant to predatory. 「Excellent. Proceed north 725 meters. There is a sidewalk café, Bruno's Bistro. The agency will send a driver to pick you up. He'll be wearing a blue necktie. To confirm his identity, say 'nice tie.' He will reply with 'go fuck yourself.'」

Katya squirmed. *Already did that.* 「Right. Minimal chance of an accidental correct response.」

Alex chuckled. 「Well, some people *are* that antisocial. Talk soon. *Adieu.*」

She pivoted ninety degrees to her right and walked. A glint of sunlight behind caught her eye. A thirty-ish man in a nice grey suit with a white shirt exited the building, heading her way. He had a strange smile that could've meant any of a thousand things, but Katya read 'I know what you did.'

Old training took over, and she strolled into the light flow of pedestrian traffic, heading north. She made a random right turn past a PubTran obelisk and cut left at the next cross street. The man kept back about twenty meters, but made the same turns. He walked with his right hand in his pocket, his left arm loose, and an amused half-smile on his face.

*Yeah... he's following me. Shit.*

# 10

# THE ONYX STALLION

K enny hovered at the kitchen sink, hand-washing dishes from lunch in flagrant disregard of the machine below the counter. A repetitive thrumming rattled the walls from whatever music Alyssa had on in her room. He smiled to himself, feeling not the slightest inclination to go demand she turn it down. They had a few weeks left before school started up again, and… *shit.* He hung his head. *She's going to be in high school.*

"What's wrong?" asked Kathy, sidling up behind him and threading an arm around his back.

"It just hit me we're the parents of a high schooler." He chuckled.

"Not quite yet." She rested her chin on his shoulder from behind. "Technically, she's still in eighth grade. She's a little girl 'til the end of the summer."

He twisted around and kissed her on the lips. "They're right you know."

"Who is? About what?" She tilted her head.

"Whoever the 'they' is that said 'you don't know what you got 'til it's gone.'" He turned and put his arms around her. "Going out there… that's like Joey rolling the dice with his life by doing stupid shit. It's dangerous fun. I can live without it. I can't live without you."

She stared up at him, guilt simmering in her deep brown eyes. "At first, I thought it was charming and romantic. Some rough and tumble wild man heading off to tame the unknown… then I started wondering if you just wanted time away from me. I can't say I understand that pull you've got, but I know it's part of you." Kathy leaned her head against his shoulder. "Pretty stupid of me, huh? Even before that shit made me paranoid."

"It's not your fault."

"They got me on it without me knowing, but I kept taking it after that. I knew what it was doing to me, but I just couldn't resist it." She leaned back, a shocked look on her face. "I... is that what it's like for you? Feeling like you've just *got* to go back out there or you're going to die?"

Kenny smiled with a wistful chuckle. "Not quite that bad. It's more like sex. Kinda think about it all the time and whenever the opportunity presents itself..."

She jabbed a finger in his side. "You're so bad."

"Am I now?" He wagged his eyebrows. "Isn't that what got you in trouble in the first place?"

"Maybe." Her grin turned coy. "Still wanna try for a son?"

Kenny leaned in and kissed her. They crossed tongues for a minute or two before the faint *pap* of a bare foot hitting the kitchen tile broke the silence.

"Ooo-kay. I'll come back later," said Hayley.

Their kiss slid apart, and they chuckled into each other's shoulders. Kenny lifted his head and caught a trail of blonde beating a hasty retreat back into the house. Not long after she disappeared, the music got louder and dampened again with the soft *thud* of a closing door.

Kathy peered into his eyes, but couldn't keep a straight face, and broke up laughing.

The generic *bing-bong* chime of an electric bell filled the house.

"Oh, come on." Kathy sighed. "Those people are never going to leave me alone."

"You think it's Family Services again?" Kenny stepped past her, walking to the living room and to the door on the far side of it.

Kathy hovered in the archway between dining room and kitchen. "Who else would it be? Your friends always vid you before they show up."

*Unless Joey's dropping off another orphan.* He pulled the door open, revealing a dark haired man in a black suit with a deep tan. A taller, much wider man stood next to a black mini-limo hovercar parked out front, a Halcyon-Ormyr Executive Sedan, easy four million new. His instinctive contempt for those who flaunted wealth flattened his expression.

"Mr. Marlon?" asked the man, his voice soft yet confident, and lacking any trace of a discernible accent.

"Yeah." Kenny hooked his thumbs in his pants pockets. "Somethin' I can help you boys with? This ain't exactly local for ya."

The man made a polite chuckle. "No, you are quite correct. My name is Arthur Polini." He gestured toward the large man behind him with an open hand. "My associate, Marco."

The large man rendered a curt nod while grunting, "Mmm."

"My employer possesses an appreciation for certain exotic artifacts." Arthur offered a clear business card. "It's come to our attention you are one of the more reputable individuals involved in the procurement of such things."

Kenny glanced at the rectangle of plastic. A shimmery rainbow stripe of holographic data underlined the name 'Mr. Jordan A. Ferrero.' Under that, another line read, 'Venture Capital, Art Galleries, Imports.' His chest tightened. *This guy's got Syndicate written all over him.* He shifted his gaze up from the card to Arthur. *Fuck.* "That's right. 'Course things have been a little trying as of late. Family matters."

"Ahh." Arthur clasped his hands in front of himself and bowed his head for a second. "You have my condolences. They look well."

Kenny glanced back, finding Kathy in the living room behind him, Alyssa and

Hayley on either side of her. Both girls had blue t-shirts and bright pink shorts on, small enough to where he made a mental note to have a chat with the girls later. Kathy fidgeted with the front of her blue flannel shirt.

"You've got a beautiful family," said Arthur.

"Thanks." Kenny tapped his trigger finger on his leg.

Arthur lifted his eyebrows a touch. "I mean that sincerely. I assume you are familiar with my employer. Please don't take my words as anything other than a compliment." He smiled.

"What's Mr. Ferrero want?" asked Kenny.

"I was hoping you would ask." Arthur pulled a rolled up plasfilm sheet from his coat pocket and handed it to Kenny. "We think we've found an item of considerable value. An old computer my employer had been restoring—his hobby you see—had some data on it from an insurance company that predates the Corporate War."

Kenny whistled and unrolled the sheet. The top part had an image of a black horse statuette with a gold-plated mane, tail, and hooves, perched on a desk in front of a green lamp. He figured it about fourteen inches from nose to ass. Below the image, a screen capture of a prewar spreadsheet file had one line highlighted in yellow. The image had been zoomed in on a column labeled 'product description,' containing 'Onyx Stallion' next to an insured value of $8,500. "Interesting piece. If that's actual onyx, probably start somewhere 'bout twelve million credits, assuming it's intact."

Arthur smiled. "You live up to your reputation, Mr. Marlon. My employer would like to offer you a finder's fee of four million."

Kenny failed to stifle a cough. Sure, he could probably throw a piece like that on the market through one of his contacts in the art circuit and pocket around eight mil... assuming it sold on the high end and the auction house didn't keep too much. Of course... Syndicate. Four million done deal, no questions asked, no unfortunate accidents. "That's a generous offer, Mr. Polini." He smacked his lips. "Like I said, I got some things I need ta work out. Wife hasn't been takin' too kindly to me goin' out there so much." He thwapped the plasfilm back and forth past his other hand a few times. The urge called to him, manifesting as a twitch of the eye.

Arthur offered another clear card. "Here's my PID. Go on an' think it over. If it sounds like something you'd be interested in, vid me and I'll give you the particulars. We got a reasonably good idea where it is."

"All right." Kenny nodded.

"Ma'am." Arthur nodded to Kathy before heading back to his car.

Marco opened the door for him, revealing a white-leather interior with two facing bench seats and a wet bar done up in wood paneling. Kenny stood, flicking the plasfilm at his open hand as the big guy got in behind the wheel. The mini-limo glided up into the sky, leaving behind a cloud of swirling dust that broke apart into four separate little cyclones. He squinted as the wind met his face, painting his tongue with the flavor of dirt. The soft whine of ion thrusters faded to silence a moment later.

"What was that all about?" asked Kathy.

He walked inside, letting the door slide closed behind him. For the first time he could ever remember, he found it possible to stifle his desire to run off to the

Badlands. He'd only gotten Kathy back home to stay days ago, and the last thing he wanted was an argument, or her believing he could up and run off to 'have fun with the boys' when she needed him. "Umm."

"Someone wants you to go back out there." Kathy didn't add any accusation in her voice, but he felt it anyway. "Right?"

"Yeah." He continued tapping the plasfilm.

"I've never seen you look so guilty before. Usually someone says 'Badlands,' and you're like a five-year-old at Wintermas." She chuckled.

"I want to tell them no." He looked her in the eye.

"So… why didn't you?" asked Hayley.

"Yeah, Dad," said Alyssa. "Why do you look like someone kicked you in the balls?"

"Ken…" Kathy took a breath.

"Syndicate." Kenny held eye contact with her. "What does it mean to you when the Syndicate says 'that's a beautiful family you've got?'"

Kathy put a hand over her mouth.

"They're gonna hurt us?" whispered Alyssa.

Kenny raised his hands. "I… he said he didn't mean it that way, but… shit. I don't need to get into a pissing contest with them."

"How much?" asked Kathy.

The rant building inside Kenny ground to a screeching halt. He quirked an eyebrow at her. "What?"

"How much did they offer you?" Kathy hesitated a few seconds. "Or was it just 'do this or we kill your family'?"

"Four million," said Kenny, head down.

"Holy shit," muttered Alyssa.

"Language," said Kenny.

Alyssa sighed. "I'm fourteen, not four. And it's not like I said f—"

"Liss!" said Kenny, almost shouting.

She stuck her tongue out at him. "Fudge!"

He slouched, chuckling.

"Okay," said Kathy.

"What?" Kenny stared at her.

"I see it in your eyes. Some part of you either wants that money or wants to go out there."

Kenny shook his head. "It's mostly not wanting some guy to show up in the middle of the night and machinegun the house. 'Course that payoff would mean a lot for the girls' future."

Hayley gawked. "Would they really do that?"

He scratched his head. "Over not going out there to grab some statue? Ehh… probably not. Not like it would cost them money. I'm just their top pick apparently."

Kathy grinned and walked into a hug. "Well, you are good at what you do."

"How long are you gonna be gone?" asked Hayley.

"No idea. I haven't told them I'd do it yet, so they haven't told me where the thing is. Standard. They don't want me runnin' out there and grabbin' it on my own. *That* would probably cause a midnight bullet party."

The girls shivered.

"I'll go," said Kathy.

"What?" Kenny shook his head. "Did you just say—?"

"Do it." She squeezed him. "And take me with you."

"What?" He reeled backward as if slapped. "Did you just say…?"

"Take. Me. With. You." She crossed her wrists behind his neck and stared into his eyes. "I used to get all wound up being afraid you wouldn't come back. Going out there is so much a part of you it's in your marrow. I'll go."

"Whoa. They replaced Mom with an alien." Alissa leaned back.

Kathy smirked at her. "I'm serious. If I'm out there with you, I won't have to worry about you disappearing."

"What about them?" Kenny nodded toward the girls.

"Please don't leave me with the Rodriguezes again," whined Alyssa. "They're super nice, but they treat me like I'm a little kid."

"My parents would probably watch them," said Kathy.

"Your parents loathe me. They'd take the girls to Mars and we'd never see them again. What about Joey?"

Hayley fidgeted and gave him an earnest look.

"Uhh, no." Alyssa shook his head. "He's like the cool uncle to hang out with at like parties and stuff, but you shouldn't trust him to be an adult."

Kenny laughed.

"I wanna go, too," said Alyssa.

Kenny stopped laughing and stared at her.

Hayley crept forward, toes gripping the carpet. "I don't want to stay with someone else. Joey's cool, but I'd rather be with my family."

"Oh, dammit." Kenny pinched the bridge of his nose and paced back and forth. "Okay, hold on just a second." He gave the three of them the 'wait' hand. "I need to find out exactly where this is going to go first. There's some places out there that I am never bringing a woman… or girl within fifty miles of."

"Like what?" asked Alyssa.

"You're not getting a reason other than 'because,' until you're at least thirty."

Hayley glanced at Alyssa. "Steel Reavers in the area that used to be Northern Texas would take us as slaves and have sex with us until we died from it."

Kenny stared at her. "Where the hell did you hear that?"

"Net." Hayley looked down. "I guess it's true if you're making that face."

"Holy shit," whispered Alyssa.

"Swear jar," said Kenny and Kathy at the same time.

"Aww." Grumbling, Alyssa stomped into the kitchen and stuck her hand into a giant plastic jar. She stared at the scrap of metal she extracted. "Seriously!? Toilets? When did this go in there?"

"Your twelfth birthday," said Kathy. "You're old enough to clean toilets."

"This is bullshit," muttered Alyssa. Before either of them could say 'swear jar' again, she drew another token. Red-faced anger turned to laughter. "Bathroom floor. At least they're close."

"Okay." Kathy grasped his shoulders. "North Texas is out. I'll stay home with the girls if it's bad, but if it's not… we're all going."

"I'm not taking two kids out there without at least one more rifle along." Kenny stared at Arthur's PID card. "All right. Let me find out where this goes. If I call him, I'm obligating myself to do this. I want to be absolutely sure you're okay with it."

Kathy leaned up and kissed him. "Four million credits and not getting the Syndicate mad at us? How could it be a bad decision?"

He chuckled. "Never ask that." After grabbing his NetMini from a basket on the kitchen counter, he waved the PID card over it. The device chirped as it added the man's contact information. He held it up and muttered, "Vid, Polini, Arthur."

"Calling," said the NetMini, in a generic female voice as a small holo-panel opened.

"Whoa, Dad…" Hayley scooted up next to him. "You're still using the default voice?"

He put an arm around her and squeezed. "Sure. I touch this thing maybe once a month."

Arthur appeared in a six-inch hologram floating above the NetMini. "Mr. Marlon. Good of you to call. I hope your ruminations over our arrangement have turned positive."

"Yeah. I'll do it."

"Excellent." Arthur rendered a slight bow and transmitted a document. "Please review our contract for your services. I will give you all the details once you've signed it."

Kenny read it over, surprised by the apparent honesty and simplicity of it. He scrawled his signature with the tip of his finger and flicked it back across the GlobeNet.

"The insurance company records put the location of the item at… one moment." He reached out of view of the holo-cam and rummaged at something. "Uhh, Chapel Hills Mall in Colorado Springs. The store name is 'Crystal Emporium.' Says here, the item was kept in a safe while they had a photo in the display case. We're hopeful it's still in there."

"What makes you think that?" asked Kenny.

Alyssa crept up, peering at the holographic man.

"The information we've recovered has a shipping receipt for the piece arriving at the store only two weeks before the area experienced a forced evacuation ahead of the war. We couldn't find any other records of it being transferred, so we are assuming it wound up getting left behind in the safe by the owners who expected to be able to go back in a couple days."

"Poor bastards," muttered Kenny.

"Swear jar," sang Alyssa.

"Nice try, but bastard isn't high enough on the meter for a swear jar pull."

She stared up at him. "You made me pull on it."

"You were seven," he said. "There's gradations for age."

"Oh, and BS is too severe for fourteen?" She tapped her foot.

Kenny chuckled. "You swear jarred yourself on that one, hon. Neither of us said a word."

She grumbled.

He pulled her closer and kissed the top of her head. "I'll give you a freebie. Next time you can claim that one already pulled."

"Can't I just toss it back?"

"Not until you finish it." He winked. "Once it's out, it's out."

"Fine." She huffed and headed off to the bathroom.

"Cute kids," said Arthur.

"One thing." Kenny glanced down at the hologram floating over his hand. "What if we get out there and there ain't no horse?"

"Well... record some video of the area so we can confirm the site. Try to get some shots of the safe if you can. No one's making any unreasonable requests here. We're all professionals." Arthur smiled. "Take it a day at a time. No sense worryin' about spilled OmniSoy until it's spilled."

"Fair enough."

"Oh, one more thing." Arthur smiled. "When can we expect to hear from you again?"

Kenny thought. "Trip like that... conservative estimate'd be a week out, week back. Since you haven't said anything about any great rush, I'd like to take this one careful. Gonna take me a few days to gear up first. I 'spect ta leave maybe Wednesday. If that changes, I'll vid."

"I'll pass your timetable along to Mr. Ferrero. He is eager to have this piece among his collection, but he understands the value of a job done the right way." Arthur flashed a smile at Kenny as if chatting with a distant relative he hadn't seen in years. "You be careful out there, and let me know if you need anything."

"Right. Thanks." Kenny tipped the brim of the hat he didn't have on. "Pleasure makin' your acquaintance."

Arthur nodded, and ended the call.

"That guy didn't seem too scary," said Alyssa. "Kinda looks like Mr. Armand, the history teacher I had last year."

"The Syndicate's friendly until they decide not to be," said Hayley.

"Yeah. Something like that." Kenny pulled the girls close, one under each arm.

"So, how bad is it?" Kathy walked over, sipping iced tea. She leaned her hip against the kitchen island counter.

"Well, it's a bit longer of a ride than I'd been hoping for, but the area isn't too bad as Badlands goes. Good amount of settlers and Scrags around there. I need to make a couple arrangements first, but I guess this is turning into a family camping trip."

Kathy nodded with no trace of the worry she should've had.

Alyssa seemed excited and nervous.

Hayley looked at him with fear in her eyes, but also resolve. As unhappy as she seemed about the idea of going out there, being separated from her new family must have been more frightening.

"Have you handled a firearm before?" He gave Hayley's shoulder a squeeze.

"Only in games, but it's not too different in VR."

"You're going to arm an eleven-year-old?" asked Kathy.

"If we're going out there? Yes. All three of you are going to carry a weapon at all times."

"Won't that make people shoot at us?" asked Hayley.

Kenny ruffled her hair. "Anyone who you'd likely wind up having to shoot would probably be trying to kill you anyway, gun or not. And most of the stuff you'd need a gun for can't rightly be called a man anymore."

She trembled.

"Oh, it's not *that* bad. There's a chance we'll go out there and come back and no one will fire a single bullet." He smiled.

"Really?" Kathy raised an eyebrow. "That happens?"

"Yeah." Kenny glanced at her tea and headed for the cabinet to get a glass for himself. "Once."

# FALLING DRAGON

C harts, tables of numbers, and the steady droning voice of the AI instructor swirled in a tornado of delirium around Masaru. He glided in midair, arms and legs splayed out to the sides, floating upon a still ocean. Weightless and peaceful, he found himself muttering responses to the ghostly voice before it even finished asking its questions. Business fundamentals, management concepts, streamlining, optimization of engagement marketing with production capacity, everything swam around and around within his brain. Twice he reached toward a flickering light overhead, struggling to force its way through dense, grey clouds. Some part of his consciousness clung to knowing he'd wound up caught in a cognitive loop, but his exhausted body refused to cooperate.

An enormous koi wrapped in an expensive Yoshida suit, limp sleeves dangling, glided up to him. Masaru lifted his head, blinked at it, and set his head back down, not believing his eyes.

"Kurotai-sama," said the fish.

"Mmmn." Masaru thought about raising a hand to cover his eyes from the sun, which had somehow grown brighter, but the limb didn't move. "You do not exist, fish."

"Kurotai-sama, your father has summoned you." The koi patted him on the cheek with a fin protruding from the end of a formerly-empty sleeve.

"I am busy," moaned Masaru.

"What have you done to yourself?" *Pat pat pat.* "Kurotai-sama. Wake up."

Masaru groaned again. *I am dreaming.*

"Apologies, Kurotai-sama," said the fish.

Cloth brushed past his right ear and a sensation as though ten inches of icepick extracted from his brain scraped in his eardrums. The incessant droning of the instructor ceased. Ponderous charcoal clouds rolled away to reveal not the sun, but harsh LED lights within his bathroom ceiling. A gradual creep of pins and needles climbed his legs, except for his toes, which had gone utterly numb.

"How long have you been like this?" asked a man.

Masaru raised an arm to shield his eyes, and stared at the blurry silhouette until it resolved into the form of Shuji Maeda, his personal assistant. "Maeda-san…"

"Yes, Kurota-sama. When you did not answer your father's vid, he asked me to check on you."

"I see." Masaru looked down at himself, naked upon his toilet, his Kurotai Fire-spirit cyberspace deck perched on a tiny wooden table beside him. Maeda-san had unplugged the wire from his head. "I… must have fallen asleep while online."

Shuji dropped the wire and stood upright, no longer hovering over him. He had a bit of cockiness in his smile, a familiarity more like best friends than executive and employee. "Why did you call me fish?"

"If more people fell asleep while in cyberspace, the world would not need recreational chems." He rubbed his eyes.

"What game was it this time?" Shuji gave him a conspiratorial wink. "Or should I ask what her name was?"

"No. I do not need virtual women." Masaru peered between his legs at the water and winced. He flushed the evidence of a thirty-two hour cyberspace binge. "I have an exam in two days… studying."

Shuji started laughing, but at Masaru's continued serious expression, petered out to a disbelieving open-mouthed stare. "You're serious? You… did your own schoolwork?"

Masaru leaned forward, elbows on his still-dead knees, and held his head in both hands. "I would be laughing along with you if I possessed more than twelve conscious brain cells at the moment. Yes. I've spent the past two days in there."

"Two days?" Shuji blinked. "Your father will be proud of your dedication. How many times did you take the course?"

"Two… and a couple sessions into a third." The disorientation of experiencing almost nine days of time passing in virtual reality with back-to-back classes left him feeling as though he'd separated from the fleshy prison of his body and existed on a plane separate from the rest of the world. Like falling asleep in the middle of the afternoon and waking up hours later not knowing what day it was. Reality didn't seem real anymore.

"Come on, Kurotai-sama." Shuji grabbed his arm and pulled him upright. "They are waiting for you."

Masaru's legs supported him about as well as a pair of giant gummy worms. "Get off…"

Shuji helped him across the bathroom, holding up most of his weight, and packed him into the autoshower tube. While Masaru preferred his enormous bathtub, sometimes luxury had to take a back seat to time constraints.

Masaru's face and chest hit the plastic on the far side with a skull-rattling *thump*. Shuji leaned in, pushed the 'go' button on the holographic panel, and shut the hatch. Masaru slid down to his knees, cheek and pectorals emitting a squeal as they dragged over the tube.

"You look drunk, Kurotai-sama." Shuji shook his head. "The last time I found you this ruined, you had five women littered around your bedroom."

"I require water." Masaru's voice distorted somewhat as his cheek remained mushed against the plastic. "And a Narcoderm... standard headache dose."

"Of course." Shuji exited the bathroom while tapping at his NetMini.

The metal ring descended, spraying him with perfect-temperature water and soap that smelled like the forests of Mount Fuji. Within a minute or so, the numbness in his legs shifted to cramps atop pins and needles. He reached over his head to the handrail and held on. Water streamed over his face and off his nose. Masaru shuddered, stifling the want to scream at the agony gripping his lower body.

His forehead hit the plastic. *I knew this would happen. I did this to myself.* Most of the coursework seemed like incomprehensible babble, everything running together into nonsense. It would take his brain time to categorize and store everything, like a gourmet dessert that needed time to set.

The shower ring descended for the third time while Masaru rubbed his hands up and down his thighs, trying to work feeling back into the muscles. Shuji re-entered long enough to leave a glass of water and a small packet on the sink. Eventually, his legs ceased tingling, though they remained stiff and sore. He pulled himself upright, leaning most of his weight on the handrail.

Masaru weathered the rinse and dry cycles with his eyes closed. Once the machine shut down, he fumbled the hatch open and stick-walked to the sink. Before the tightening knot in the back of his neck could bloom into a crippling headache, he peeled the Narcoderm off its backing plasfilm and affixed it to his forearm. He chugged the water, and leaned on the sink until the painkiller took effect. In a few minutes, the urge to chop both legs off at the hip to stop the pain faded.

Shuji had laid a clean suit out on his giant bed, and from the sound of a rapid-talking female voice in the main room, flipped on the holo-bar to kill time by watching the NSK news feed. A too-cheerful woman detailed the latest events regarding a territorial dispute between Yamamoto Heavy Industries in Miyagi prefecture and Fuji-Noki Corporation in Yamagata Prefecture. Explosions underlined the chipper teen-girl voice as she described Yamamoto hover-tanks gliding down the streets of Funagata, lobbing plasma cannon fire at Fuji-Noki's forces who'd caught them drifting too far west.

Masaru retrieved a clean pair of briefs from the bottom of the white box on his wall, unwrapped the plastic, and put them on. He shook his head at the thought of old, wealthy men gambling large sums on the outcome of the microbattle. His father had done the same before; most of the inner circle around the CEOs had a habit of wagering on things. Sometimes different companies' executives would maintain friendly enough terms to place gentleman's bets when the outcome of conflict did not directly affect either company.

*They do not see it as violence and death, but as a form of market fluctuation. Gains and losses.* Masaru sat on the edge of the bed and pulled his socks on. It had been something that plagued him for years; how had Japan fallen into such a state? Forty-seven individual prefectures with separate military forces. They couldn't even all agree on how far back in time to pretend to be.

Okinawa had taken things to the most extreme end with strict social policies that bordered on insanity. White Orchid Corporation behaved as though only technology had changed since the Edo period—and all technology not destined for export had to be made to *look* like it belonged in the year 1610. They stratified people in social orders, the lowest of which, the Eta, had next to zero rights. Someone of Masaru's stature could slay them on a whim without repercussion.

On the other end of the spectrum, areas like Hokkaidō prefecture had little difference from West City, UCF other than a predominance of Japanese lettering on the signs. Yoshida-Nakano Corporation saw zero purpose in pageantry, favoring practicality.

The rest of Japan fell somewhere between the two, with Kurotai unfortunately leaning a bit ancient-of-center. Nowhere near as rigid as Okinawa, but still a bit too far for Masaru's liking. The board disapproved of his friendliness toward Shuji due to their significant difference in social standing. Of course, Miyazaki Prefecture had no true Eta class. At least not in the same sense as Okinawa. Someone of Shuji's station working for White Orchid would scarcely be permitted to talk to Masaru except as a direct response to questions, despite being his personal assistant.

True they had only met four years and some months ago during Masaru's second year in university, but given the weight of his station, few people acted like human beings around him. Shuji had a similar sort of irreverence to him as Joey, only Masaru never expected a westerner to care who he was. For Shuji to—aside from linguistic nuances showing formal address—behave as more of his peer than subordinate had clicked.

*Perhaps I am not well-suited to take over the company; I shall hope my brother enjoys a long and healthy life. I find only tedium in the endless formality.*

He slipped his suit jacket up over his shoulders and seated it with two tugs on the lapels. The iridescent material shifted between black and metallic grey depending on how the light hit it. Upon the breast pocket perched a thumbnail sized gold disk bearing the stylized 'K' logo of the Kurotai Corporation, with the Kanji in a vertical line down the main spar of the letter.

The woman's voice cut off in the midst of her stating the 'territorial dispute' had claimed thirty-four lives, eleven of which belonged to civilians. Shuji appeared in the doorway between bedroom and hall, shaking his head. Behind him, sunlight lit the Epoxil floor, making the simulated pale wood gleam. Faux rice paper walls divided into neat squares by dark bands caught the light and glowed. His friend and assistant leaned against the doorjamb, a datapad tucked under his left arm.

Masaru froze for a few seconds listening to the distant trills of birds, unable to tell if the sounds came from an ambiance module, or if real birds perched nearby.

"You almost look alive now, Kurotai-sama." Shuji smiled.

Masaru opened a narrow closet door and examined himself in a full-length mirror. His suit was immaculate, though his father would still find something of which to disapprove. "It will have to be enough."

"I'm sure Kurotai-heika will find at least four flaws worthy of seppuku in your attire." Shuji approached, snatching a cloth napkin from a small table by the door, and wrapped it about the datapad like a ceremonial wakizashi. He presented the device and bowed his head.

Masaru chuckled, overacting formality as he accepted the datapad. "What does my father want?"

"He originally sought to have a few moments with you this morning. I neglected to pass along that I found you passed out on your throne." He grinned. "I expressed to his eminence that you had exhausted yourself preparing for an upcoming exam." Shuji folded his arms and tapped a finger to his chin. "You know, I'm not sure he believed me."

"Ironic." Masaru chuckled, tossed the napkin to the bed, and tapped the screen. A Kurotai logo appeared in the center, dark copper on black.

"I showed him the transaction, and explained you had purchased the e-learn for a cram session to prepare."

"Oh?" Masaru raised an eyebrow and swiped his finger across the screen, revealing a message from his father simulating hand-brushed kanji on a scroll.

---

*Masaru-kun,*

*The time has come for you to take a greater role in the affairs of Kurotai Electronics Corporation. I had hoped to discuss matters with you in person, but there is insufficient time remaining. Maeda-san will accompany you along with a member of our legal team and a pair of sales engineers. You will be travelling southwest into Kagoshima Prefecture to meet with representatives of Daiichi-Fuso Corporation.*

*You will lead the contract negotiations to provide the electronic components and control mechanisms for a new line of heavy construction equipment. Ikeda Tadashi is an honorable man. This contract will benefit both companies as well as thousands of citizens down the line.*

*I trust you will make me a proud father.*

*Kurotai Hideo*

---

Unlike the rest of the letter, the characters composing the name at the bottom appeared as dark, smoky glass rather than ink-on-paper. A chromatic shimmer reflected from within, as if the characters had 'bones' of refractive metal. The holographic 'signature' proved the man himself had signed it—or someone with the resources of a national intelligence agency faked it.

A wind-chime noise emanated from the main room.

"Ahh. Coffee is here." Shuji smiled and hurried out.

Masaru tossed the datapad on the Comforgel bed and followed him down the inner hallway to a sun-lit kitchen. "You are too good to me, Maeda-san."

Shuji opened the patio glass and took a pair of coffees from a hovering delivery bot. He handed one to Masaru and sipped from the other.

*Caramel latte. Perhaps the west* has *corrupted me.* He savored the first sip, holding the heat on his tongue for a few seconds before letting it slide down his throat to form a pleasant core of warmth in his chest. "My father's letter implied a lack of time. We shall eat after."

"Heh." Shuji chuckled as he headed into the cavernous living room. "The way you look, I didn't think you'd have been able to eat anyway."

Masaru rubbed his gut. He had swallowed a military 'slow release' ration prior to logging in. A tasteless bright blue gelatin egg that supposedly released nutrients enough to provide for a twenty-four-hour period. That would put him somewhere close to twelve hours late for a meal, but he didn't feel much like eating. Even thinking about it lofted a small burp flavored in caramel plastic. He grimaced. The chemical flavor confirmed at least some of the false egg remained in his stomach.

Perhaps the state of the body while in cyberspace did something to the rate of digestion.

"Indeed," said Masaru.

Shuji crossed to the center of the apartment's main room to a door set in the front of a square-walled section covered in faux bricks and decorated with plastic plants. It stood like a separate tiny house surrounded by a lawn of beige carpet. As his home occupied an entire floor of the high-rise building, his 'front door' consisted of a private elevator that served the top five floors, and expressed to the ground floor lobby.

Masaru diverted to the display case at the center of the north wall. He took his Nano katana from the daisho stand, and affixed it to his belt. Rubberized elements shaped like ancient cloth cording compressed under his grip. He did not consider himself a 'samurai,' nor did most of the more anachronistic prefectures. Among the places where one could be executed for carrying a katana while not of the proper social strata, he would be considered a nobleman, and thus permitted to do so.

He suppressed the urge to roll his eyes, and wondered where it came from. Had he spent too much time in the west, or did all of this genuinely strike him as ridiculous? Too exhausted to continue that line of mental debate, he strode back across the living room and stepped into the elevator behind Shuji.

Waist-high realistic stones surrounded him on three sides. Holo-displays above the stonework created the appearance of standing in a gazebo at the center of a vast Zen garden. Bald men in dark grey haori and black hakama pants raked sand in endless circles. Of course, the 'monks' were little more than program code. Still, the falsehood notwithstanding, he found the ambiance peaceful.

The elevator stopped at the roof, where a limo waited. Two large men wearing serious frowns worthy of an Edo Period samurai stood near the rear of the car. The man on the left had snow white hair like Masaru's, though lacked the green accent at the temple. No one cared if a member of the security team opted for an alternative look. Even Shuji could've gotten away with it without much scrutiny, though his friend kept his appearance traditional—short black hair—as befitting the personal assistant to the third most influential man in the prefecture.

Even the security man with white hair betrayed a hint of disbelief in his expression. While they may think his break from tradition audacious, few would dare say as much to his face. The shorter security man opened the rear door for him, revealing a lush white leather interior where three other men waited, each holding bowl-shaped teacups and saucers.

Masaru offered the security men a nod of acknowledgement before sitting in the front-facing seat next to a grey-haired man with crows' feet. Shuji sat in the rear-facing seat next to two men older than Masaru but perhaps half the age of the grey-haired man. Within a second of the door closing, the fragrance of black tea grew suffocating. Masaru held the coffee to his mouth, inhaling caramel essence.

"Kurotai-sama, it is an honor to be here," said the left-most man in front of him. "I am Sato Akihiro, with sales engineering." He gestured at the man beside him. "This is Himura Toru, also with sales engineering." He bowed at the older man. "And this is Ito Yutaka, from legal."

"Kurotai-sama." Toru bowed.

"Kurotai-sama." Yutaka bowed.

Masaru returned a shallow bow of acknowledgement to the sales engineers, and a slightly deeper one to Yutaka. The man may not have had station over him, but he had to be almost three times his age. Yutaka's eyebrow twitched, betraying his surprise at the gesture of respect.

"I am Maeda Shuji," said Shuji. "Kurotai-sama's personal assistant."

Another round of bowing occurred among them while Masaru sipped coffee.

The huge security men entered via doors at the center of the limo, sitting in a space sectioned off from Masaru's compartment by a bullet-resistant panel. Past them, a lone driver sat at the front. Masaru gazed at the immense teacup in Toru's grip, decorated with a black-line painting of a caricature frowning man standing upon a boat while fishing. The lower third of the cup tinted blue, pale where the ocean lines started to a rich hue at the bottom.

*A man in a tiny boat defies the waves to seek fish in the ocean with a bamboo stick and twine. Does this cup say the man is a fool who attempts a large task with small tools, or is it simple art?*

"Apologies, Kurotai-sama," said a voice from a speaker in the door. "We will arrive in Kagoshima city in approximately twelve minutes."

"Mmm," said Masaru, nodding.

The car lifted off in a graceful sweeping left turn. After climbing away from the high-rises of Miyazaki City, firm acceleration pressed him into the seat and caused the two sales engineers to scramble to contain their tea. A twelve-minute trip to go about eighty miles suggested a direct route.

"Kurota-sama," said Yutaka, "Most of the details of this agreement have been established by our sales team and Daiichi-Fuso's purchasing department. Our meeting today is in large part merely a formal reading of the contract at best, or a last minute opportunity to make adjustments."

Masaru nodded at the elder from legal. Surely, he must have thought Masaru's presence as much pageantry as the rest of it. The old man sent him along on a child's errand. He offered Yutaka a pleasant smile. *No master is born such. There is no shame in learning.*

"I trust in your judgement and would not seek to create the appearance of impropriety while meeting with Daiishi-Fuso," said Yutaka. "If they do make unexpected changes, I will relay my opinion by the position of my hand. Flat on the armrest, I agree or do not think it consequential enough to quibble. A fist indicates caution."

"Thank you, Ito-san."

"There is a low risk involved with this." Toru sipped tea. "We are providing next generation instrumentation and electronic control mechanisms for heavy equipment intended for use in construction and farming. There is little military application for any of it aside from cargo-hauling trucks."

"And our physical proximity to Kagoshima makes a slightly higher price point an irrelevant concern, as shipping from Matsushita would offset the cost." Masaru swirled his coffee around, trying to prevent all the sweet from collecting at the bottom.

The sales engineers smiled.

"Of course," said Toru. "Our systems are superior to Matushita's offering. They are still on a two-year-old design. A few more credits-per-unit is hardly an issue when there is such a vast difference in features and scalability."

*Two years old. Why expend effort to replace that which still performs the function it had been created to do? Matsushita favors reliability over leading edge. The 'Kenja' series units have only been in production for two months. How many flaws remain unseen below the surface? Father has an obsession with being 'first' rather than being 'better.' We should seek to change this. We lose much in reputation and revenue from malfunctions.*

"Matsushita has had time to catch many flaws. Their systems may lack our feature set, but they have a commendable failure rate. Both of our companies have prices considered 'high,' though they charge for reliability while we up-value our products based on performance. For a failure-intolerant application where an expanded feature set offers little consolation when the device ceases functioning, we should consider a lower offer."

Toru looked horrified. "You are suggesting Matsushita superior to us?"

Masaru raised a hand. "I am suggesting that there is no such thing as a one solution fits all cases scenario. For any given situation, the ideal varies."

Yutaka's eyebrows edged upward. A mild frown of impressed respect crossed his lips.

*He expected me to be useless.* Masaru allowed a smug smile, but only after the coffee cup concealed it. The aromatic elixir drained to a mere trace of froth, gone too fast. It would be too impolite and western to walk into a meeting with a beverage, and by the time the meeting ended, they would likely proceed out for the obligatory business lunch. More coffee would have to wait.

"Do you expect them to have made any significant changes?" Masaru glanced at Yutaka.

"It is doubtful." The elder made a face of thought while taking another sip of tea. "If anything, they may request alterations in the timing of shipments to meet their production qu—"

*Boom.*

Yutaka's face blurred past; a violent lurch in the undercarriage of the hover limo kicked Masaru out of his seat. His nerves screamed with the electric rush of activating speedware, an automatic reaction to an unexpected chaotic situation. Hot tea splashed over the right side of his face in slow motion as he careened past the company lawyer. An accelerated perception of time did little to stop him from flying cheek-first into the left side window, though he did manage to get one hand up, absorbing some of the force.

For three-quarters of a second stretched to four, Masaru Kurotai stared down at the ruins of a large city. A radiant pattern of destruction spread out from a point near the city center. Some buildings had toppled and debris scattered directly away from where a 'backpack nuke' had gone off over three hundred years ago. Here and there among the concrete ruins, patches of green appeared where nature had begun to reclaim the land.

*Miyakonojo...*

City slid away, replaced with sky and ground in the wrong place.

The car had rolled upside down. Shrieking wind and a fluttering of metal roared; bits of foam and leather scraps sprayed past him and slipped across the window, carried in a fierce current of air.

Men's screams flew away, distorting as if down a tube. More scalding tea saturated the left leg of his suit.

Masaru's weight continued forward, compressing his skull into the glass as the city came once again into view below. The impact thundered in his ears like a cannon fired underwater. In what seemed an instant, total chaos in drawn-out time gave way to stillness and an incessant beeping. His head throbbed. Trickles of warmth ran down his face. Beyond the fog of his breath on the window lay a ruined street. They had crashed. Yutaka lay under him, unconscious but breathing. One of the sales engineers moaned. Repetitive thuds in the door, likely from the security men kicking their way out of the car, carried into his cheek.

Anger—who would dare attack him—welled up. Who would dare make him late for a meeting? He started to grumble, but his indignation melted to unease when a sharp chattering noise outside smashed the silence.

Gunfire.

# 12

# HECK OF A RIDE

Thousands of lines of bright green program instructions scrolled across a black monolith of holo-panels surrounding Joey's workstation. Four columns of three thirty-inch screens showed the output of auditing routines chewing on the guts of a personal accounting software suite. He scanned a new trouble-ticketing program Teradyne Corporation was about to set up for its internal help desk, and the source code for *The Shade King's Gambit*, the latest game in the Monwyn franchise that wouldn't be released for another three months.

Since the NewsNet hadn't exploded, no one knew Division 9 got into Dreamcraft Entertainment's system and lifted the game. Not that the hack represented any deviation of normal protocols. Division 9 hunted down any significant new program it detected on the net, and ran it through the process unfolding before Joey's eyes. His boss, Major Preema Iyer, had brought him into an anechoic meeting room as if about to let him in on state secrets that could tilt the balance of power of the colonized galaxy—only to assign him the task of auditing a video game.

She knew he didn't subscribe to the vast fandom of the Monwyn franchise, so she trusted him with it—not that the Division 9 network operations servers had much chance of being hacked by an outside operator even if word leaked. Between live personnel and three 'black dragon' AIs, the odds of a successful breach were somewhat less plausible than his successfully talking Nina into twelve-hour rotating-partner marathon sex with her parents plus two randomly selected homeless people and a singing clown.

Joey pinched his nose, wanting that thought out of his mind.

Of course, the lure of Monwyn reached a significant enough point that Preema didn't want him telling anyone else in the room that he had the source code for such an eagerly-awaited game in his little slice of their CPU farm. She didn't worry about an external breach as much as one of his coworkers sneaking it out to play at home, or firing the game up on the Division 9 system.

He chuckled to himself. *She didn't want any reporters dead.* The public might care about the government helping themselves to everyone's software for all of ten minutes before they got distracted by some celebrity trying to marry their dog or the latest 'if you have this in your kitchen, it could kill you' scare story. Okay, so he wouldn't tell anyone. No big deal. He'd run the audit, checking the software for any suspicious routines that could compromise national security. Log it if it passes and delete it, or drop kick the hornet nest if he finds something suspicious.

Hah.

If the program finds something suspicious. He only needed to put ass to chair and watch it churn. Four hours and counting.

Yeah. Monday.

Joey rolled a few inches back and reached for the butterfly valve he'd rigged to the surgical tubing that ran coffee down from the drop ceiling. He expected that to last all of two hours before someone complained of his installing a dedicated java line from the break room to his desk, but only three people noticed. Simon even copied it—the *last* person he'd ever have expected to do something 'unsanctioned.'

His cubicle sat in a circular cluster with four others at the end of a short 'security separator' corridor, an eight-meter-long, narrow passage intended to keep anyone from walking by the cube farm from seeing things they shouldn't. To his right sat the senior of their four-person team, Tech-Four Chris DeWinter. He'd been sitting in the same desk going on fifteen years, straight out of college. Despite being a few years shy of forty, his hair had gone grey. Joey figured stress the culprit, which he knew wouldn't get him. Stress only killed you if you gave a shit what happened.

Abby Brown, Tech Two, sat in the workstation to DeWinter's right. The two of them hadn't gotten off on the best footing. Probably due to the first thing Joey had said to her, which he'd thought hilarious. She'd introduced herself by saying "Abby Brown," and the wiseass in him couldn't help but say, "Yes, apparently she is."

Mindy Wu, the 'wild one' as he'd mentally tagged her, had the next space. Her being twenty-two left Joey the second youngest member of the team by a year. A Tech One like Joey, she always had her belt-length hair done up in vivid colors. For the past few weeks, she wore it in a gradient that faded from white at the ends, progressing past ever-darkening shades of blue to violet at the top of her head. Last month, it had migrated from white through pink to crimson. She shared Joey's utter lack of seriousness, but didn't quite have the nerve to keep up the act whenever Preema could see her. She had laughed at the Abby Brown remark, which almost started a war between the women until she clarified she'd laughed at it being such a stupid thing to say.

Joey couldn't argue with that.

Dan Simon, Tech Three, had the space to Joey's left, and a vampire tap on his coffee artery. His thirtieth birthday approached in two months, and a quiet war of private messages raged across the entire department about how best to 'memorialize' the date. Dan had the kind of personality that brought everyone together—to mess with him. While DeWinter had the unassuming confidence of a man who'd been doing the job forever, Dan suffered from a crippling case of rulebook. Whenever anyone asked him to do anything, if he wasn't completely convinced it followed process, he'd research department policy. Sometimes he'd spend more time trying to figure out if he *should* do something rather than doing it. So far, he'd only found two cases where someone unwittingly asked him to violate policy, and in such minor ways, his effort to 'keep the department ethical' blew up in his face. Preema had been more irritated at the time he'd spent to find out that someone had used the wrong requisition template than she would've been if the person hadn't had clearance to request that information.

Everybody 'loved' Dan.

*The man likes coffee, so he can't be all bad.*

A soft beep came from DeWinter's workstation along with the creak of a chair as the man leaned back. Joey smiled at him, noticing his shirt seemed a little loose. He still rocked a glorious muffin top, but the buttons didn't seem about to pop off and kill someone anymore.

"Got a hit? Anything good?" asked Joey. "Hey… looks like you're losing some weight. Won't be long before you've got Mindy all over you."

DeWinter chuckled and patted his stomach. "Thanks. Trying, and I could be her father."

Mindy's chair chirped as she spun to face Joey. He admired her gothy black skirt, heavy boots, and black-and-white striped leggings and sleeves. "Joseph… you're going to make me go to HR."

He laughed. 'Mindy going to HR' was a running joke. They'd hired her after she'd been arrested for breaking into the Manticore Investments main network as a seventeen-year-old. Evidently, the Division 2 detective who'd brought her in had been a little free with his hands. Days after she'd made the transition from prisoner to employee, someone patted her on the shoulder and she'd threatened to drag him to HR. One of the field agents quipped she'd drag the food reassembler to HR, and Mindy overheard. Ever since, she'd made a joke of it herself.

"Oh, come on, Mindy." Joey grinned. "You know you dream about DeWinter covered in massage oil."

She stared at him, eyes narrowing.

Joey indicated his chest. "Whipped cream on each nipple…"

"Thanks, Joe," said Simon. "Now there's a mental image I'm going to need vodka to get rid of."

"Fuck you all," muttered DeWinter.

Chuckling simmered around the workstations.

A soft beep from Joey's terminal drew his attention. Excitement dawned for a second until he realized it meant nothing interesting. The scan of the finance software ended with a pass. No suspicious code detected.

*Thok!*

His skull rattled inside the skin around it. It took a second for shock to wear off and a tiny point of pain to manifest at the back of his head. He reached up and found a dart, stuck in bone. "Ow." He glanced at Mindy, who had a set of four (now three) darts on her desk.

"Get my point?" She folded her arms.

Joey raised an eyebrow at DeWinter. "I think our relationship has moved to the next stage. Penetration." He grunted and jerked the dart out of his skull, blinked a few times, and tossed it into the dartboard hung to the left of her display panels. "Wow that felt *weird*."

"I'm pretty sure that's not in the handbook," said Simon.

"Neither are my balls in your mouth," said Joey.

Dan Simon cringed. DeWinter chuckled. Abby sputtered and covered her mouth to stop from laughing.

"I'll take myself to HR," said Mindy, before spinning around to face her workstation again.

Simon sighed.

"Besides," said Joey. "Mindy's got it bad for Abby. Even put an upskirt cam under her desk."

Simon's face reddened.

"Aww, why'd you tell her?" said Mindy.

Abby blinked, and peeked under her desk. As soon as she did, Mindy cackled.

"I hate you both," said Abby, in a playful tone.

Silence, save for the bubbly slurp of coffee going into Joey's mouth, pervaded the circular work area for a while, accompanied by the occasional pleasant *beep* of an analysis routine completing. Joey traced his finger around his desk while debating how much some superfan might pay for early access to the Monwyn game on his screens. Of course, no one would be able to play it until the servers went live. Joey grinned at the thought of all the fantasy junk littered around the server admin's office at the Imperial Hotel. *That poor idiot would've sold his mother for a chance like this.*

DeWinter laced his fingers behind his head and yawned. His terminal made a squawking noise, and he leaned forward to read something closer.

"That sounded promising, in a 'someone's doing something they shouldn't' way." Joey stretched back to peek.

"Nah, nothing actionable. I'm scanning the source code for some indy spy game named *Unum*, and the thing got a hit on a few references to 'The Five.'"

"Oh." Joey rolled his eyes and resumed watching letters and numbers grind across his screen. He glanced up and right at a plasfilm printout of a Citycam shot showing him and Nina standing in the street after leaving the Starpoint production facility. An inconvenient plume of smoke blocked the shot at the moment they'd kissed, but them staring into each other's eyes captured the mood even better.

"So you think they exist?" asked DeWinter.

"Huh?" Joey glanced at him.

"The Five."

"Yeah, right," said Mindy.

"Who knows?" Abby twirled hair around her finger. "I could see it. Stranger shit's been known to happen."

Joey admired her for a few seconds. Large eyes and a wide nose with a cute upturned tip coupled with a take-no-shit personality and technical competence would've made for a long, and likely disappointing pursuit if he hadn't already found Nina. Not that he had any intention of messing around on the side or leaving her, but he could at least acknowledge Abby's appeal. "Maybe."

"What?" Simon leaned back. "Five what?"

"Wow…" Joey laughed. "You really do have your head so deep in the P&P you can't see anything."

The women snickered.

"I don't spend every waking minute reading the policy and procedure documentation." Simon folded his arms and stared at Joey. Overhead lights glared off his baldness.

"Conspiracy wonks think there's these five senators that run the entire UCF like some kinda shadow government." Joey slurped another mouthful of coffee.

"I heard they're all supposed to be chosen from high-ranking military officers... usually with intelligence backgrounds." Mindy glanced over her shoulder at them.

"Something like that." DeWinter reached forward to tap a button. "Looks like this game is intended as fiction. It's just tripping the filter for the phrasing."

"Well, there ya go." Joey held up a finger. "If the Colon Expander 3000 flags it, there must be some truth to it."

Simon stared at him. "Colon Expander?"

"I'm getting HR!" said Mindy.

Abby put her head down, muffling laughter with her arm.

"No, no, no." Joey waved him off. "I'm not talking about the thing in your nightstand, I mean the scanning software." Simon gasped. "Oh, and you really should be careful. The power grid around your place is pretty old. You might melt wiring."

"Oh, for the love of..." Simon sighed.

"He's got a point," said DeWinter.

"I do *not* have a sex toy!" yelled Simon.

The entire floor seemed to go quiet.

Simon turned florid crimson.

*Victory is mine,* shouted Joey in his mind.

"That's not what I meant." DeWinter shook his head. "Why would Argos flag it if it didn't mean anything?"

"It wouldn't surprise me if The Five were real." Joey shrugged. "Not like I give a shit honestly. Some people are always going to have power, some people are always going to want it, and the rest of us just hope the sodomy stops before we lose too much blood."

"You have a colorful imagination," said Abby.

Simon smirked. "What is your fixation with that?"

Joey chuckled. "You take everything literally, don't you? I mean the way society gives it to the common schmuck in the ass. Taxes, heavy-handed police, threat of the ACC doing whatever, drudgery jobs, drugs, gangs, society as a whole. There's maybe two people for every ten thousand who can really claim to be happy." He slurped more coffee. "Unless you're like me and Mindy over there and just don't give a fuck. Ride the missile like a horse all the way to the target, laughing on the way in."

"Riding a missile." Simon raised his eyebrows. "You're just one sexual metaphor after another."

Joey leaned back and raised one eyebrow, hoping 'are you for real' appeared across his forehead. "Sometimes riding a missile is literally riding a missile, not a giant pulsating dick. Ever hear 'fiddling while Rome burns?' What are *you* thinking about?"

Simon grumbled and tucked in to his cube, out of sight.

"You don't really seem the type for government work," said DeWinter. "Usually, we get the gung-ho ones."

Joey chuckled. "Probably because I'm not."

DeWinter responded to another 'pass – no suspicious entries detected' notification. "So, why'd you sign up? I know you're not another Mindy scenario."

"Wish I was there for that. She'd look good in cuffs."

Another dart hit him in the back of the head.

"Yow!" he yelled, grabbing the metal shaft sticking out of his skull.

"That asshole detective thought so too." Mindy held out her hand to accept the dart back.

"You take him to HR?" Joey winked.

She grabbed another dart from the rack.

"Hey!" He raised his hands. "Easy…"

Mindy put it down.

"You two are going to give Simon a heart attack," said Abby.

"Which form does he need to fill out to properly submit a crass but humorous comment?" asked DeWinter.

Mindy, Abby, and Joey stared at him in shock.

"He's evolving," whispered Joey. "We have the first signs of a sense of humor."

Joey plucked the dart out, handed it to Mindy, and rubbed the wound. "Signing up was the most dangerous thing I could think of to do at that moment. Plus, I had about forty credits left in the account and I got kind of addicted to the whole food thing."

DeWinter raised one caterpillar-like eyebrow. "As opposed to hooking up with a Class 3 doll? That's gotta be a heck of a ride."

"Heh, yeah." Joey's laugh sounded insincere even to him.

Admitting the storm of emotion that took him as soon as he'd first made eye contact with her in the New Hope center would destroy his persona here, so he went along with DeWinter's shallow humor. It might've been a virtual avatar, but something about her hit him in a place he didn't think he even had. Nina had developed a reputation as a bit of a hardass, the 'new girl with something to prove.' While he couldn't argue she had a moment or two that lived up to that, the overall image people had of her couldn't be further from the person inside. Maybe she'd erected a shield around her emotions too.

*Beep.*

"Oh, big surprise, the Mon—" He coughed. "Monster file passed." *Nice. Cleared my queue and it's only 4:28.* He wrapped up the post-analysis report, entertained another brief daydream about owning some drooling fanboy, and hit the key to send the code off to deep storage. Aside from any future need to reference it should the demands of legal proceedings require, Division 9's copy wouldn't see the light of day again.

"You sound almost disappointed," said Abby. "It's such a headache when something flags."

"That's the fundamental difference between us." Joey smiled. "You see this as work. This is what I do for fun."

Mindy held up a thumb, but didn't look back.

"You people are screwed up. Fun is clear sky, clear oceans, and sixty miles an hour." Abby leaned back, eyes closed, probably dreaming about personal watercraft again.

"I see your point. If I had a body like that, I'd probably want to be in a bathing suit as much as humanly possible." Joey nodded.

Abby shifted around to look at him with an alluring smile. "Honey, I go to the cove off Sector 1041." She winked. "No one wears bathing suits there."

It didn't matter if she'd merely said that to tease him or really did frequent the nude beach. He grinned.

Joey kicked off the cube wall and spun back to face his terminal. Four Grade 9 decks connected in parallel, sleek black rectangular forms that made him think of 'stealth starships,' if such a thing existed. Thin lines of dark blue light along the front edge conjured the image of tiny windows in the side of a massive deep-space battleship. Before he'd been hired, he'd have sold vital body parts to get his hands on hardware like this.

With his queue cleared, he could bug out for the day. Of course, everyone in the room worked on call. If something big hit the fan, they'd all have to come back. But feces to fan blade interaction had been calm as of late. *Unfucking what asshat did to Katherine I can do from here… though retribution might be an issue.* He eyed the wall to his left, picturing Simon slobbering all over a chance to make trouble for him 'using official equipment for illegitimate purposes.' Half of what he wanted to do was legal. The fun part, not so much.

Joey slid his chair close to the desk and reclined. Two wires with interface plugs extended on motorized arms from the back of the headrest and plugged in to his head. Since taking the job, his implants had undergone a few upgrades. He got the multitasker he'd been lusting after, as well as a second jack. Both of his head ports had been upgraded to M6s, which had an advantage over the M3 in that they contained modular sub-processors that took the load of common, mundane tasks off the deck and left more resources open for the happy stuff. They'd also given him a component that could supposedly block a telepath from eavesdropping on his thoughts. Of course, that one they would take back (by force if necessary) if he ever resigned.

He figured taking the job worth it since he got to play with major tech and muck around in places he didn't belong. Sooner or later, he'd have probably wound up like Mindy and been nabbed. Though knowing his mouth, his ass would've been in a black bag.

The plugs snapped home at the same instant and his surroundings shifted in two tenths of a second. He stood in a blank cube of a room with blue grid lines in the gloss black walls. By default, Division 9 techs didn't use custom avatars as much as the same shadow figure, which he assumed inspired by old ghost-hunting shows. Anyone who he allowed to see him would perceive a vaguely person-shaped suspension of jet-black smoke. Division 9 decks operated on a hidden layer of the GlobeNet. Only other Division 9 hardware—or C-Branch—could sense his presence. Any equipment physically located within the UCF had to be compliant.

Economies of production often extended the shroud to servers and networks hosted elsewhere, though any serious target within the ACC or 'non-allied' nations didn't support it, leaving them no more hidden than any other user who didn't belong there. Good thing the Division 9 hardware could smoke most things not made by C-Branch. He swore the military intelligence people must've found some kind of alien technology. The ACC might've had a four-to-one advantage in numbers, but everything they used followed the doctrine of as cheap as possible.

Joey pictured the data relay node at the Edmonson Memorial Starport. The cube room faded away to a huge chamber with a building-sized amethyst CPU crystal in the center. Millions of glowing pink-purple orbs of light swarmed around it like fireflies, occasionally pausing for seconds at a time or darting into the crystal. A dull roar reminiscent of a massive waterfall filled the space, emanating from a thick ray of energy that raced away from the crystal's top point, heading up into the blackness of outer space.

Teleporting around the net didn't carry the same thrill it once had, since as a Division 9 Net Ops agent, he had the authority to do so. Of course, he'd been doing it for years already, so what little excitement he once got from it he found easy to overlook. Joey's shadow body glided upward and grasped a black tube, visible against the backdrop of space only by the absence of stars in its path.

The restricted military link baffled him. They used advanced versions of the civilian relay equipment with half again the bandwidth, but only supported a fraction of the users. While he had no trouble grasping the idea of a private military conduit, all that wasted throughput irked him in the way a blind billionaire owning a six million credit hovercar would irk him.

*Okay. Analogy fail. A billionaire wouldn't remain blind.*

Joey glided across the vastness of space for nineteen seconds before Mars came into view. *Ahh, home shit home.* The last time he'd seen the place, the government wanted him dead. He raised his arms over his head, and laughed like a fool as he flew down toward the planet's surface. Black energy fluttered around him, though no wind met his face.

After landing, he teleported to the primary Mars Defense Force system, Olympus, housed in a server cluster on Tier 1 of Primus City. The network disregarded him entirely. Joey walked down a mirrored steel corridor, sidestepping MDF cybersecurity people going about their day to day. None reacted to him, which had the eerie quality of making him feel like the ghost his avatar resembled.

While hunting about for the files Grant manipulated to mess with Katherine, he pondered those wild stories of actual ghosts trapped wandering in places for decades and decades after death. Nina claimed to have seen one, and Division 0 had some files that either proved ghosts existed or classified eighteen percent of their people as shit nuts.

He went to the citizen records and pulled Katherine's tile. Sure enough, twenty-six entries had all been added within the past month. He traced all but the first two to falsified MDF employee IDs.

"Oh, Grant… you silly little unicorn. Inventing false police officers is naughty."

Joey reached a shadowy hand into his insubstantial chest and extracted a wispy indigo spider with a body as big as his fist. He tossed it to the floor, where it burst into hundreds of copies. They swam out and over the data nodes, replicating until they formed a moving plaque of inky darkness. Each arachnid represented a searcher program sniffing the access logs and buffer memory of every system any connection had taken. That Grant had created, or paid someone else to create, fake MDF officers didn't worry him at all. Compared to Earth, Mars struggled to keep basic things (like breathable air) operational, and didn't have the time or the equipment to really throw at cyberspace. Some of the newer places in Arcadia City or the UCF military bases kept up with technology, but hacking the MDF was no more sporting than beating up the kid on crutches. Joey had managed free access to their system before his fourteenth birthday.

One by one, spiders returned with data tiles in their fangs. He back-traced four different users, all of whom came from a database query as being employees of The Bandau Group, the law firm Grant had made partner with. *Looks like someone's misusing company resources.* Joey chuckled as he collated all the records into an organized log of who accessed Katherine's municipal file when, and changed what. He crosslinked to nine different false MDF officer profiles, cops who never existed, added that to the report, and generated a new data tile. After sliding that into his chest, which transferred the file back down the military uplink to his hardware on Earth, he held up Katherine's tile and clucked his ghostly tongue at it.

Line by line, he flicked his clawed finger to the left, flagging each of the spurious entries as hidden. Only Division 9 (or C-Branch) would see them. He would've deleted them, but since Grant had been stupid enough to spread his net-love to the police network and not just Katherine, it constituted an attack against the Mars Defense Force, which gave jurisdiction to Division 9. Depending on how mightily he wanted to savage Grant, he might need the altered records later for the inquest.

Joey hummed to himself while reading. They'd added false reports of Katherine taking bribes, bribing judges, the underage boy sex thing, trafficking in illegal recreational chems, a few charges of theft via misrouting delivery bots, prostitution... He laughed. *Clearly, they're not trying to get her arrested... though he has that whole 'moral character' thing.* The system showed six pending investigation tags on her record, five of which came from her law firm attempting to verify her claim of being a victim of altered records.

He got a silly grin. At least, he experienced the feeling of one—his shadow person avatar had no facial features. A few mental impulses remapped the investigating agent on each charge to Don Simon. For once in Joey's weird life, he *was* doing something perfectly legal and above board. If he took the investigation himself, a reasonable person would question the conflict of interest of him clearing his sister, regardless of the bogosity of the charges.

For good measure, he copied his evidence tile and shot it down the pipe to Simon's ID. He had all he needed in there to respond to the investigations confirming tampering. And with the investigation closed by Division 9 instead of the Mars Defense Force, that should slam the door in Grant's face.

Going beyond the simple legal record in Katherine's file, he swam into the nest of data about her everything. Finances, job history, medical history, Citycam records of her moving around, PubTran travel logs... heck if he dove deep enough, he could even calculate out how many times a day she used a bathroom. He didn't dwell on any of the actual data, but looked for yellow or red triangles at the edges of each record. Sure enough, Grant's pet hackers messed with her account, causing her bank to show rent paid, but rather than sending the credits to the building management, the money went into a black hole.

They also set worms loose that siphoned credits from her law firm and redirected them to the PID of a nonexistent man, who then sent them to Katherine's account. *Okay, this is a little over the line, but fuck this guy.* Joey made a few tweaks, changing the worm to send things to Grant instead of Katherine. He shifted all the deposits it made to Grant's account, altering the records to appear as though they'd gone straight there. With the firepower of his official login, no one would be able to tell the software hadn't always been feeding Grant's account, nor would they be able to prove any of it had ever been in Katherine's. After that, he moved the 'black hole' credits to her property management company's system to legitimately pay her rent, and created a proper log trail for it.

He scrubbed out thousands of connection records creating the appearance of Katherine spending hours connected to MarsNet interactive porn. Again, the overabundance of making it look like she fancied sims with underage boys screamed amateur. Joey's skin crawled. In VR, such things weren't illegal since a sub-sentient program simulating a child had no legal rights. However, it struck him as only slightly less skeevy than the bottom-feeders who purchased WellTech child dolls and had them modified to be anatomically correct. While the law wouldn't do much about them, society often stepped in to 'make adjustments.'

*This asshole is trying to kill her reputation.* An upwelling of anger almost made him respond in kind, but... not with Division 9 hardware.

It took him another two hours and eighteen minutes to finish cleaning up everything else Grant had done to her record. He logged out at 4:37 p.m., sitting up as the plugs retracted from his head.

"Damn, I love time compression."

"Dillon," said Simon, leaning against the cube wall behind him. "What's this data you sent me?"

Joey swiveled his chair to face Simon, hands up in a gesture of 'trust me.' "My sister's ex is shitting on her life. Swear it's all on the level. That's why I sent it to you. Wouldn't be proper for me to look into that. I wanted to make sure it got done by the book."

Simon squinted at him. "After the nuclear-powered dildo joke, you're asking me to investigate your sister?"

Joey closed his eyes, pinched the bridge of his nose, and raised a hand in a 'stop' gesture. "Please don't put those two images in my head at the same time again. But yeah." He shook off the horrifying thought of his sister and a 'toy' in the same mindspace, and smiled. "Everyone knows I tease you, and I know you're so 'by-the-book' it makes C-Branch synthetics look like party animals. When you look over that data and clear her, no one will question it."

Simons' eyebrows shot up. "Are you asking me to—?"

"I'm asking you to investigate it. The situation is a legit intrusion. Her ex-husband got some of his law firm's network people to mess with her. No favors; just play it straight." Joey stood. "Seriously. They hacked the MDF system and created false identity records for officers. That gives us jurisdiction."

"All right. I don't know what your game is, but..." He stopped leaning on the cube and tapped his foot. "I'll take a look at it."

Joey shut down his workstation and patted Simons on the shoulder as he went out.

HUMMING TO HIMSELF, JOEY HEADED DOWN THE HALLWAY OF HIS APARTMENT building while slurping up ramen noodles from a bowl too large for him to wear as a helmet. Grandpa Sang's noodles might come from a tiny little shop, but they *almost* scratched the itch. Being across the street, and cheap, he'd been overindulging. *I gotta hit the Fu Sheng House again.*

He found it strange to return home to a place not loaded with gangers, drifters, prostitutes, or random homeless cyborgs. He'd gotten an apartment in a building where the hallway's rich blue carpet didn't have holes exposing plasticrete and the elevators worked. He'd almost lost his habit of watching the floor on his way in to avoid tripping over a random stranger passed out drunk or flying high. By 5:12 p.m., Joey stepped into his seventy-fourth floor home, and took a deep breath of air that didn't smell like dead rat.

He did miss Howard, and wondered if the huge cockroach still lived.

No one could call the place extravagant: modest living room, small kitchen, decent-sized bathroom, decent-sized bedroom, and one tiny-ass room he didn't know what to do with catty-corner from his bedroom at the end of the hall. The agent tried to call it a second bedroom, but some prison cells had more space. He regarded it as a huge closet.

The kitchen counter, coffee table, and kitchen table disappeared under a mountain of empty ramen containers and synthbeer cans. Every day, he looked at the trash and figured he'd clean it tomorrow. Maybe he missed living in a grey zone squat, or maybe he really *was* that lazy.

"Fuck it. I'm gonna need the table."

He leaned his ass against the kitchen counter, knocking three month-old ramen containers to the floor and sending plastic chopsticks scattering. After devoting six minutes to finishing off his dinner, he went to the bedroom long enough to hang his hat and duster coat, and returned. Throwing trash at a one-foot-square hole in the wall proved surprisingly challenging, especially when only half looking.

Eventually, he cleared the crap into the disassembler, which rebuilt it at a molecular level into even-sized beige blocks of hard matter. Somewhere in the walls, the trash cubes fell down chutes to a collection bin, and probably got carted off to be made into OmniSoy, plastic utensils, or dildos for all he knew.

"Okay." He stared at his clean kitchen table and clapped. "Now, Grant, thine ass is mine."

He stopped by the bedroom again to change into shorts and a t-shirt, omitting shoes, and grabbed the Nishihama Necromancer deck out of 'mega closet.' Seeing the black slab made him think of Hugo, or Kelly, or whatever he'd become. How a net god like Proscion could walk away from 'the life' never to set foot in the GlobeNet again, all to live as a little girl forever confounded him.

Some of it, he knew, came from jealousy. In his prime, Proscion had been the sort of hacker everyone spoke of in mythic overtones and whispers. Even with all the Division 9 hardware behind him, Joey didn't feel as good as Proscion had been rumored to be. Hell, the man hacked The Silver, not that anyone could prove it… and his soul had somehow wound up inside a synthetic child body… that happened to live with Nina's parents.

*Who keeps playing a game after you beat it?* Joey chuckled.

He couldn't think of any other explanation that made sense. Proscion had 'beat' the GlobeNet. He had nothing else to do on it that wouldn't feel like 'been there done that.' More and more, Proscion—now Kelly—behaved as though the man had never existed. Perhaps in some way *he* had ceased to exist and the little girl had become real.

*I'm not high enough to figure that out.*

Joey ran his fingers back and forth over the four-foot long deck. It had a profile similar to a concert electric piano, only lacking keys. Some musicians still used physical instruments, eschewing holographic interfaces as they didn't 'feel' right.

"Your former owner has moved out to crazy town." He pet the deck like a cat. "It's just you and me now. The master's sword in the hands of the apprentice trying to fill boots too big for him."

Joey carried the Necromancer deck to the kitchen and set it on the table before making a cup of orange herbal tea in the 'sem. He took a seat and meditated, clearing his mind of the laziness Division 9 hardware afforded him. Using this machine, he wouldn't be an automatic ghost. He'd have to work for everything, use his skills, and experience the danger of being detectable. If anything, his new job added a sharper edge to the thrill of 'black work.' Getting caught now could severely bite him in the ass. Division 9 didn't fuck around. If they stopped trusting him, they'd probably 'send him to Miami.'

He grinned; the thrill of it sent a shiver down his arms.

After getting as comfortable as the chair would allow, he grabbed the wire and pulled the plastic guard away from the bladed asterisk-shaped prong. Staring at it triggered a momentary twitch at the memory of Cleopatra's shocker. He still had to pay her back somehow for all that. Of course, given that Cleopatra turned out to be an eleven-year-old girl named Hayley living on her own after her cop father had been murdered... he couldn't get past the guilt of what he'd daydreamed about doing to her. Instead of the vicious retribution he had in mind for the 'woman' who had tormented him for months, he'd have to come up with something more appropriate for a kid... something that would possibly embarrass her, but nothing bad enough to send her into therapy or piss Kenny off.

He didn't have time for a small girl right now.

The plug slid in behind his ear with a *click.*

Joey had a Grant to fuck with.

# 13

# THE PARADOX OF WANT

Nina's parents had fallen in love with Elizaveta at first sight. Neither dolls nor synthetics existed in significant numbers within ACC territory, so it had proved easier to tell her Emily and Kelly were other orphans her parents had agreed to adopt. Kelly, formerly Proscion/Hugo, appeared to have little trace of the person he'd once been and acted so eerily like an ordinary eight-year-old girl that Nina couldn't help but share in Joey's unease. Emily, the doll who had been at Hugo's side for years, could pass for a live ten-year-old—if not an overly mature one. Unless something highly unusual happened and Elizaveta noticed Emily's lack of genitals, there would be no need to explain what a doll was. Though, with Nina for a mother, the question would come up at some point anyway, but that could wait a few years.

She couldn't begin to fathom what had happened out in Louisiana. How Shabundo Ghede had taken Hugo's spirit, soul, ghost, or whatever, and stuffed it into a synthetic body defied everything she thought she'd known about the world. Of course, she had seen Vincent's ghost on the deck of the bayou house. A real ghost, not some electronic fuckery from an insane AI. She had a feeling Emily had that in common with Kelly, though had been a woman prior to whatever fate resulted in her ghost being merged with a doll. Perhaps that explained the oddness Nina sensed in her presence. Without a living body around it, could her 'exposed' brain detect what amounted to a specter possessing a machine?

At least Emily didn't overact the child angle, ever Hugo's protector. Or Kelly, as it seemed 'Hugo' no longer existed in any sense of being. His, rather her, mind had evidently collapsed. None of Nina's training and experience catching liars flagged. Kelly didn't strike her as a man pretending to be a child; she really believed herself to be as she appeared.

As always, Nina's father had been distant, looking at her as one might look at the reanimated corpse of someone he'd once loved. His overt hostility had faded however, though he still refused to make eye contact with her.

*Great. Maybe by the time he's ninety, he'll actually speak to me.*

Elizaveta was everything they had always wanted from Nina, a super-girly granddaughter. Once she managed to convince the child not to feel guilty for owning more than one outfit, the girl had gone straight for the dresses. Nina had warned Mother not to spoil her, given her background. Overindulgence would trigger a storm of guilty tears. Getting the child to tolerate a 'normal' amount of possessions had been a task. Leaving her with the parents at all presented a gamble. Their home in the north could in no way be portrayed as modest. Elizaveta had come from the 'commoner' caste, and they often held a high degree of contempt for the wealthy. Fortunately, at six, perhaps such feelings of resentment hadn't had time to develop yet. She'd either pick up a happy child, or a little ball of anger who didn't realize the woman she'd chosen to adopt came from wealth.

*Ugh.*

Nina drove in hot, aiming for a narrow gap between levels of the parking deck adjacent to the Police Administrative Center. Her reckless landing made her remember Vincent… and darkened her mood further. She left her unmarked black hovercar behind and stormed across the garage to the elevators. She caught herself soon after the doors closed; anyone seeing her would probably roll their eyes and make some comment about 'her reputation' once she'd gotten out of earshot.

*I'm not that woman.* Nina stared at her reflection on the chrome doors. *Am I?*

The giant chip she'd had on her shoulder had a name, Bertrand, and she'd dealt with it. She closed her eyes and pictured Elizaveta smiling, hands clasped to her chest as she accepted the beautiful white dress was hers to keep. The expression of utter joy exuded from her memory and infused her.

By the time the elevator stopped, she smiled.

The lobby of the PAC contained a near-deafening din of activity. Members of every Division, as well as a handful of civilians walked, jogged, and in one case sprinted, across the room. Far left near the Division 0 wing, she caught a glimpse of Kirsten dropping off a small brown-haired boy, probably at the psionic school. He hugged her and ran inside.

Nina headed to the opposite end of the room where a plain white door emblazoned with a giant numeral '9' afforded access to the Division 9 wing. She nodded at the two junior field operatives who'd drawn guard detail and made her way inside and down a series of blue-tinted corridors to the area holding her office. She stopped in only long enough to hang her brown trench coat on a peg. Six steps later, she hooked a left and continued past seven doors to the office of Harold Hardin at the end.

A small waiting area in front held a few chairs and a table full of datapads. The wall separating it from the office proper consisted mostly of soundproof, bullet-resistant resin. He smiled before she got close enough to trigger the door's auto-open feature.

Her boss, a former field operator, gave her a nod of greeting as she walked in. The chestnut brown in his hair fought a stubborn battle against relentless grey that had crept over most of his head. As usual, his frumpy polo shirt and khaki pants made him look more like a high-school history teacher than a spymaster.

*If they didn't force him to fly a desk, he'd still be out there.*

"Morning." He leaned back in his chair. "I hope you had a pleasant weekend. How's the new arrival doing?"

Nina took a seat in a chair facing his desk. "She's gone from fearless to terrified to hesitant normal. Still hides in her room a lot, and there's nightmares... but I think she'll get over them eventually."

"Seems like the arrangement is good for the both of you." He smiled.

She glanced at her knees, where the ceiling lights created a blob of reflected glare on the glossy stealth armor, white on black. "It caught me off guard."

"Off guard?" Hardin's right eyebrow edged up a notch.

"Even with Vincent, I hadn't really given any thought to having kids. My father had always been talking about 'his grandchildren' as though I should've been a married mother of three by the time I was twenty-two. Something about that... I don't know..." She raised and lowered her fingers on the armrests. "I didn't *dislike* children, but I never saw myself wanting them. And the more he talked like it was a foregone conclusion that I would have kids, the more I distanced myself from the idea."

Hardin stood. "Coffee?"

"Sure."

He turned his back to her while operating a small machine on a shelf behind him. "I suppose you prove the old adage about 'whatever you want your child to do, tell them to do the opposite.' Still, I think it's good for you to have her."

"I never thought about it until I saw her in that shithole." Nina scowled, glancing off to the side and down. "That look in her eyes... I almost killed every last one of those bastards for what they did to her... to all of them." She let off a wistful chuckle. "I suppose it's also true you don't want anything until it's out of reach."

"How's that?" Hardin handed her a camouflage green mug with a UCF eagle logo on it before sitting with a steel-grey mug bearing a Siege Arms Corporation logo over a boxy rifle graphic. "What happened to her?"

"Not her. Me. I never wanted kids until I couldn't have them anymore. I guess having the option taken away..." She made eye contact, fighting back the urge to feel sorry for herself. "Don't know what you got 'til it's gone, right?"

"They were able to preserve some of your ovarian tissue." Hardin added the contents of a blue packet to his mug, flicking it with his index finger. The *thwap, thwap, thwap* irritated Nina for no reason she could determine. "It should be possible to have one of your own if you ever feel the need."

*Can a machine form a maternal bond?* "It's something to consider." She sipped hers black.

"Well." Hardin stirred his coffee until a layer of froth appeared. "The dissolution proceedings are grinding on. Osiris lawyers are trying to claim Doctor Rice acted without the approval of their board of directors and ethics committee."

Nina barked a laugh. "They *have* an ethics committee?"

"At least on paper." Hardin chuckled and set the stirrer down. "They allege the R&D group acted on the spur of the moment under Price's misguided influence." He raised the mug to his lips and slurped coffee.

"I suppose people who can treat children like disposable primates don't have much of a problem speaking ill of the dead. I don't regret what happened in there, sir. Even if it did provide them with a convenient scapegoat. A dead man can't refute whatever they try to blame him for."

Hardin smiled. "I'd have done the same." He tilted his head, eyebrows shifting upward. "Well, maybe not the exact same thing. I'd probably have shot him. You and your team did solid work. It's just the usual clusterfuck these things turn into once lawyers get involved."

"Yeah. A necessary tedium."

"Oh?" He took a deeper swig of coffee. "You're not annoyed?"

"They provide a service, like maggots devouring the dead." She cradled her mug in two hands, staring into the wavering pattern of ceiling lights on the surface. "We need the hesitation, the review, the assurance that we're not turning into a society where the moral justifications of a small number of people impose their wants upon the masses."

"So you believe them?"

"No. Nothing with the scope of what Price was doing happens without executives' knowledge. Knowing about it and letting it happen is tantamount to approval. I still think the company should get shut down, but it doesn't bother me if it takes two weeks or two years to get there. The end result is the message. If they want to waste millions trying to fight a pointless battle, let them."

"Interesting." He kept his eyes locked on her as he took another long sip. The mug lowered away from a grin. "The people to most trust with power are those who don't want it."

Nina picked at the side of her mug for a moment, and drank a mouthful. She never wanted to join Division 9.

"If you could go back, would you?" asked Hardin.

"Back, sir?" She swirled the coffee around, inhuman dexterity bringing the fluid within a millimeter of the rim without spilling.

"Back to a biological body. Your old self." He peered at her over his drink, steam wafting past his eyes. "Like it never happened."

Nina stared into the coffee. Vincent's scream echoed in her mind as image after image of that night played a slideshow upon her thoughts. The tug of bullets striking her, the white-hot pain of Bertrand's vibro-blade in her back, and the gritty caress of traction coating on her cheek. "I didn't believe it possible to regrow an entire body. The damage Bertrand did to me was too severe."

Hardin gestured his coffee mug around in a small circle. "I'm just speaking theoretically. A thought experiment. I find myself curious about your headspace."

Her bob drooped forward as her head bowed, framing her vision in a square of black. "If it were possible, I'd probably do things differently. The reason I joined the force was because I wanted to do some good for society, not to be some debutante living in a bubble of indifference. If I could go back and talk to myself, I'd have stayed away. There are plenty of better ways for someone with money to help the 'little guy.' Maybe I wouldn't have studied forensic science. I could've gone into medicine or some engineering path instead. Make things to improve the quality of life. Start charity foundations, that sort of thing." She shook her head and chuckled. "You saw my Division 1 files. I was five-four, the proverbial ninety pounds wet. I had no business being a cop."

"And yet you still joined, and you made it through two years of everyone telling you to go home. If that night had never happened, would you be happy working for Division 2?"

Nina tried to wrap her brain around the thought of never running into Bertrand. Vincent alive, her intact, her transfer approved. She'd have gone from picked-on runt beat cop to science nerd crawling around after all the shooting stopped. The job wouldn't have helped her save lives, but she could've found justice for people. Though in some sense, stopping a killer might save the life of future victims. Of course, then she'd never have met Joey or Elizaveta. He seemed to adore her very being, but what if he'd only been attracted by the adrenaline rush of what she'd become? If Bertrand Foster hadn't mangled her that night, would Elizaveta be dying a slow miserable death in a cage? No, anyone in Division 9 could've run that investigation. She hadn't done anything above and beyond. Someone would've found them.

"Nina?"

"It's a pointless question because I can't go back." She downed three-quarters of a mug of hot coffee in one shot.

"I suppose I expected that non-answer. You're tempted, but you aren't so sure you hate where your life has gone enough to wish it different."

That he'd hit the nail on the proverbial head got under her DuraFib-reinforced skin. "All due respect, sir, 'wishing' never got anyone anywhere."

He mushed his lower lip upward into an appraising frown. "Yeah. I suppose you're right. Might as well get to the new operation." Hardin tapped a button on his holo-panel, which elicited a responding chirp from her NetMini. "Last Friday, the operations manager for Reliant Logistics had a bad day. He evidently had a pleasant breakfast with his wife, then left his apartment and proceeded to ring the doorbells of two neighbors and shoot them dead, before emptying the rest of his handgun's magazine at random into the walls. He injured six more, including two minors before exiting the building and going to his office. Once there, he began work as though nothing strange had occurred."

Nina raised an eyebrow. "This sounds like something you should be sending to Zero."

Hardin raised a hand. "There's more."

She nodded.

"Approximately ten minutes after Mr. Estrada settled in at his desk, before Division 1 had pieced together the identity of the shooter from the apartment, he received a notice to report to the office of Marion Ruiz, the Operations Director, his boss. He's in there for four minutes before he puts one between her eyes. Anyway, D1 eventually shows up and he charges at them."

"Sounds like this case is over already. This guy isn't still alive, is he? How do we fit into this man snapping?"

"The morgue technicians, as part of routine process, plugged him in to see if they could find any black-ware. Within seconds of connection, a data burst went out, which we traced to a chimeric network address in Mexico."

Nina's head (and interest level) perked up. "They suspect him being an ACC infiltrator?" *Tracing that is going to be fun.*

"They were able to determine the destination only generally as Mexico. The transmission didn't sustain long enough to gather enough samples to track it down."

Nina pursed her lips. At the wanting, her headware opened a link to her NetMini, which filled her vision with virtual holo-panels bearing an ID photo of Paul Estrada next to everything the system had about him. Thirty-six years old, born in West City, married Valerie Cortez eleven years ago, no children. Clean police record, no obvious financial troubles, no known enemies. The man looked like such a stereotypical middle-manager it reeked of being fake. "His record is too 'normal.' It's so normal I'm almost tempted to believe it. The Corporates wouldn't make this guy up because he's *too* tame. His blandness would be suspicious."

"Well, there's got to be *some* reason a plain ol' guy with a decent job and decent life winds up sending a postmortem data burst to the Corporates." Hardin set his mug down, leaned back, and laced his fingers behind his head. "What do you make of him being married eleven years and not having any children?"

Nina offered a mild shrug. "Maybe they didn't want any." She looked over his medical records, and pulled up Valerie's as well. "Nothing in their file shows infertility. Not everyone wants kids. It's not unnatural not to have them."

"Normally, I'd agree with you. But factor that in with the demographic trend for people in his income bracket who are married. Add to that the transmission to the ACC... There's a chance they're both operatives and they didn't want attachments."

*Is he trying to say I'm normal for wanting to keep Elizaveta, or is he just assuming humans are broken if they don't want offspring?* She locked stares with the file photo of Valerie Estrada. Mid-thirties, works as a designer for Teradyne Corporation in their 'aesthetics' division. After someone else made the functional guts of a product, her group made it appealing to the eye. "Could be they were both just too busy with work to think about it... but I'll check all angles."

"Good." Hardin brought his hands out from behind his head, and lowered his arms with a healthy pat on the desk. "That's why I'm tossing this one to you. Anyone else would think I'm upset with them and giving them a dead end."

"This isn't payback for pasting Doctor Rice?" Nina stood, chuckling.

Hardin, deadpan serious, said, "Not at all. And I know you know that."

Nina turned halfway to the door. *Another slice of my soul falls away.* She pictured a black mass floating in space, thin sheets separating and falling off to oblivion. Elizaveta ran into the daydream, caught one of the gossamer wafers and reattached it, patting it down like wallpaper. *Maybe I'm not a lost cause yet.*

"Right." She glanced back at him. "Anything else I need to know?"

"The coroner found traces of 'H' in his system."

Nina's eyebrows crept together as she struggled to think of the meaning. "New drug?"

"Yeah. Been on the street for about six months or so. It's basically Placinil, an anti-anxiety medication re-sold on the street under the name 'Harmony.' They think the drug is what caused the rampage, which might've done us a favor. Something tells me he wasn't supposed to go crazy and get himself killed."

"Only to wind up on our network where we caught the transmission going south."

"Right." Hardin went to drink from his empty mug and gave it a dirty look. "If anyone's going to make sense of this one, it's you."

Nina collapsed all the virtual panels with a thought. "On my way."

# 14

# MIYAKONOJO

**P**ings and *cracks* filled the limousine from bullets glancing off. The armor afforded Masaru a reasonable sense of safety, so long as he remained inside. He pushed himself up off Yutaka Ito. The older man bled from the nose and appeared unconscious. The two sales engineers, Toru Himura and Akihiro Sato moaned. Both had been knocked around—hard—and showed little reaction to the car coming under fire.

Shuji had himself pressed up against the passenger-side door; whatever he stared at had reduced his attempts to speak into hyperventilating babble. "They've…. They've…"

Both security men in the middle section pulled combat rifles from a case embedded in the partition between them and the driver.

"There is no need to panic, Kurotai-sama," said the darker-skinned security man. "Their weapons are no threat to us."

"Ryo-san," said Masaru. "If their weapons are no threat to us, why then are we on the ground?"

"M-missile!" shouted Shuji.

A split-second hiss outside preceded a deafening *whump*, and a sensation as though a giant had kicked the nose end of the car. The clear barrier behind the driver flashed opaque red. Evident chunks of flesh oozed downward at varying speeds.

"Go, go, go!" yelled Shuji, while pushing Masaru over Yutaka toward the driver-side door.

"Maeda-san." Masaru grabbed him by the shoulders. "Calm yourself."

The security men exited the limo on the driver's side, as the unknown attackers seemed to be coming from the right and somewhat to the rear. No sooner had the thunder of rifle fire started overhead, than the two sales engineers came around. In their panic, they crammed themselves against

Masaru and Shuji. Unable to push past, they leapt for the passenger-side door.

"Do not!" yelled Masaru.

Toru pushed the door open. He got one foot out before he screamed with blind panic.

A fusillade of bullets tore over him, peppering Akihiro as well. An explosion of fluff and white 'leather' scraps flew from the rear-facing seat. Shuji convulsed in Masaru's grip and his eyes widened. A nip of searing pain cut Masaru's side a hand's width under his left armpit.

"Ma... sa... ru," wheezed Shuji. He coughed up blood, digging his fingers into Masaru's sleeves. "I..."

One of the security men fired a long burst of automatic fire, which drowned out whatever Shuji tried to say. Akihiro rolled back into the car and curled fetal, clutching his arm while howling. Masaru fumbled behind his back for the door handle and dragged Shuji with him as he slid out to the ground beside the limo.

Akihiro's agonized wails continued, though the man made no effort to move.

Masaru pulled Shuji from the wreck and rolled him flat on his back upon an ancient street covered in at least an inch of fine grey silt. To his right, Ryo and Saburo, the security escort, huddled for cover behind the car and traded bullets with people in the distance. On one knee at Shuji's side, Masaru couldn't see their attackers with the car in the way.

"Shit!" shouted Saburo.

Sensing danger, Masaru's speedware activated. He whipped his head around to face the limousine. The big men twisted toward him, their faces contorted from rapid motion, black suit jackets flaring out. The two open rear doors gave him a clean view of a man covered in mismatched scraps of metal and dingy cloth pointing an over-the-shoulder tube straight at him.

In his temporary slow-motion world, a spinning black rocket leapt into the air. Spring-loaded fins snapped out of the back end as a billowing plume of white smoke erupted from behind it, obscuring the man holding the launcher. Since the missile resembled a dark dot embedded in cotton, he knew it came straight for him. With two seconds to react, perhaps one-sixteenth of a second in real time, Masaru flung himself to the side. His hands hit the street at the same instant his foot caught the limo door and kicked it shut.

A spray of metal spalling shot off the outside of the door in time with a bone-jarring *thud*. The inside of the armored car flickered between orange, black, and white for three speedware seconds before fading to dark black. Heavy smoke laced with the stink of burned meat rolled out of the still-open passenger-side door. By some miracle, the armored door contained the detonation within the limo.

He had no doubt Akihiro and Yutaka had perished.

Thunder like mountain giants pounding on Taiko drums the size of buildings melted into automatic gunfire as his speedware shut down. Ryo and Saburo stood a short distance back from the limo, shooting over it.

Masaru flipped around and checked Shuji. The man stared into the clouds with a vacant expression, blood leaking down his cheeks from both corners of his mouth. Masaru tore his friend's suit jacket and shirt open, revealing four holes in his chest big enough to stick a finger in. He flipped open a belt case and yanked a pair of stimpaks out, flicked the safety caps off the ends, and jammed them into

Shuji's chest like sacrificial daggers. Bloody foam swelled out of the bullet holes, but they did not shrink.

*Shuji! You do not have permission to die!* He grasped his hands together and attempted CPR, but pushing down only caused a small geyser of blood to spray up from the man's mouth. He pushed again, harder, and blood squirted out of the chest wound as well, hitting him in the face.

Masaru grunted past clenched teeth. "Shuji! Don't give up!"

Again and again he performed chest compressions, but his friend remained still. Masaru kept trying until no more blood spurted when he pushed. Unconcerned with flying bullets, Masaru bowed his head, slouched over the body of Shuji Maeda, and let off a gurgling wail of anger mixed with sorrow. With great effort, he forced down the rising tide of emotion threatening to rob him of reason, and opened a connection to his NetMini via wireless from his headware.

‹Network Error: No signal found.›

Incoming bullets skittered across the road mere feet to his right, kicking up puffs of grey dust.

"Kurotai-sama!" shouted Saburo. "He is gone. You are in the open." The big man lunged at him, seizing him by the shoulder of his suit jacket and flinging him into the side of the armored limo.

More bullets rained down, causing Shuji's corpse to twitch and Saburo to roar. Disregarding the fresh gout of blood spraying from his left shoulder, the six-foot-and-change security man one-handed his assault rifle, aiming over the limo. Azure muzzle flare belched from the weapon, the relatively slow rate of fire on the large-bore rifle hammered Masaru's ears. Though he couldn't see what happened behind the car, the look of satisfaction on Saburo's face assured him whatever dishonorable wretch had desecrated Shuji's body had paid for his indiscretion.

Masaru glared at the signal error text floating across his field of vision. In a best-case scenario, if he could get his friend's body to a medical center within two minutes, they might be able to revive him. The brain might last for three, but it would take the medtechs some time to start working. Out in the middle of nowhere, with no signal... even if he *had* signal, it would take a MedVan longer than two minutes to reach them.

Masaru slumped, ass on cold pavement, back against hard armor plates, and stared at Shuji's limp body. His hair didn't even stir in the wind, too caked with blood.

His only true friend would stay dead.

Over control mechanisms for construction equipment.

"Fuc—"

*Thump.*

Ryo staggered backward, a thin line of smoke lanced into his chest like a spear, fire sputtering from the point of contact. Before the giant man could even look down, most of his torso exploded in a shower of gore. His upper body and a few inches of smoking spine sailed skyward before careening into a heap a few feet away. Legs and hips fell over backward.

A high-pitched male scream came from the direction of the car, followed by the clank of boots on metal. Saburo swore and hurried to change magazines. Footsteps scuffed up toward the back end of the limo.

Masaru sensed someone about to jump down from the roof. He grasped the handle of his Nano katana and activated his speedware as the first traces of shadow fell over him. A skinny man in rags, bare chest covered by a bandolier made of old power cables and canvas pouches, came drifting downward after jumping off the limo.

"Die!" roared Masaru. He leapt to his feet while drawing his blade into an upward swing.

The gleaming transparent-blue edge caught the man below the left hip, slicing flesh and bone with little resistance before exiting the right side of the neck. Other than a thin red line, the body showed no sign of trauma until his right foot struck the ground, at which point the head, half the torso, and left arm slid apart from the rest of him, pulled down by weight.

Masaru spun to his left at a hint of motion encroaching on his peripheral vision. Two more men in tattered rags rounded the corner of the limo, raising submachine guns in Saburo's direction. They hadn't yet reacted to Masaru's presence, or the separating body of their associate.

He shifted his stance to face them and sprang forward; his sword still high from the first killing strike, he grasped it in both hands and pulled a downstroke into the head of the left attacker. Before any change appeared in the man's expression, Masaru slid to his right and thrust the sword into the chest of the second man. At the instant the tsuba touched skin—the katana rammed as deep as possible—the submachine gun erupted with blue flames. Masaru twisted to the side, glaring down at four slugs passing with the speed of a casually thrown ball. He thrust his shoulder into the vagrant, knocking him off his feet, yanked the katana free, and took the dead man's head before the corpse hit the ground. The thrust to the heart had killed him, but the beheading made a statement.

Sensing no imminent threats, Masaru's speedware cut off to spare his nerves from wireburn.

The bisected man collapsed to the ground with a wet splatter while the attacker nearest Masaru screamed. The downward slash had severed the man's body in half from the top of his skull to a little below the base of the neck. Nano cut so clean, the man survived for two seconds, frantically trying to hold the two halves of his head from sliding apart.

Masaru glared as the man's futile battle succumbed to lost consciousness, and he fell.

Saburo's bellow of, "Bastard sons of unclean dogs," came before the *pop-pop* of a double tap.

Another attacker off in the distance gurgled.

The big man staggered into the side of the limo and held on. The one Masaru beheaded had evidently managed to land a few bullets into Saburo before his body had realized he'd died and stopped moving. His security man shot a moaning figure on the ground again while grumbling curses under his breath.

Masaru shifted, glancing over the limo's roof at a field of smashed buildings. Few survived with more than a single story of piecemeal walls upright, the devastation to the point he couldn't even tell what sort of buildings they had been. At least fourteen dead lay scattered among the rubble they had tried to take cover in. Dark trails of blood ran down smashed concrete walls caked in a thick layer of silt. A massive rifle-shaped weapon lay near a filthy dead man wearing a beige JSDF armored vest.

*Twenty-millimeter rocket rifle...* Masaru's eyebrows furrowed. *Where did these scraps get that from?*

Ryo and Saburo had done themselves proud, killing seven to one, plus whatever had fallen out of sight.

He glanced down at Ryo's corpse... or at least his legs, staring until the pool of red under the bisected man ceased expanding. Masaru's mind refused to process the scene.

"Are you injured, sir?" asked Saburo.

Masaru winced at the pain in his left side, only now aware of it again. "A scratch." He pulled a stimpak from his belt case and took a step toward Saburo, offering it. "You need this far more than I."

The big man shifted to face him, smiling. "You are most gen—"

Saburo's head rocked, the right side blasted open in a sluice of brain and skull fragments.

Masaru dove to the ground as the distant *crack* of a sniper's rifle echoed over the ruined city. He huddled against the car, confident its armor would stop the bullet given the timbre of its rapport. His gaze went from straight ahead down a wide-open street to left at another cluster of ruined buildings. Behind him, more of the same continued into a hazy distance for about seven blocks, after which a standing wall of dust obscured his view.

Of course, he had studied Hiroshima and Nagasaki in grade school. Until the Corporate War of 2092, Japan had been the only nation to suffer a nuclear attack perpetrated by a foreign threat. The Six Minute War, fought five years prior to that, didn't count. The tiny device detonated in Tehran had been set off by the Iranian military, not Israel as they had claimed.

He wondered if this is what it had been like afterward, though neither of those ancient cities had been as grand as Miyakonojo of 2097, when North Korean infiltrators had set off a series of 'backpack nukes.' Compared to the virtual tour his seventh-grade class had taken through the 'ruins of Hiroshima,' this place embodied a deeper melancholia. Perhaps because the modern buildings had resisted to a greater degree and the land hadn't been utterly flattened.

*Sniper...* He tried again to access his NetMini, but received the same signal error. The limo was a lost cause; its only remaining use consisted of being a bulletproof wall. He crawled to where Saburo fell and slid his katana back in the scabbard until it locked in with a *click*. While he hadn't spent much time practicing with firearms, he wasn't about to attempt to take on a sniper with a sword.

"Hold on, friend." He stared at Shuji's corpse. "I will not leave you to rot here. I must deal with this nuisance first."

Masaru examined the rifle, a Daito series chambered in 15mm, as big a slug as handheld firearms took. The ammo counter showed fourteen shots remaining. Near the display, a single rubber button activated a four-by-four inch holo-panel. A few seconds later, he had the weapons' optics linked to his headware over a wireless connection.

He duck-walked closer to the rear of the limo and pushed the rifle up over the trunk near the back window. The video feed appeared in a floating virtual panel, fed into his optic nerves along nanometer-thick platinum wires. Bands of static crawled up and down, distorting the image somewhat, but not so much where he couldn't use it to aim.

Amid the field of ruin stretching out on the passenger side of the limo, only three buildings stood taller than two stories. The nearest, with five floors remaining, ranged at 272 meters. Beyond it, at 304 meters, a slimmer tower that had to have been an office building managed to keep six floors. Chunks of plasticrete dangled on rebar, wobbling as the entire structure shifted in the breeze. *No... too unstable. Only a fool would dare.* He sighted in on the third building, which the rifle indicated at 608 meters. Floor by floor, he swept. On the seventh, he caught an orange glimmer along a patch of pale grey wall. Fire.

Given the length of time since this city had been ashed, the only possible explanation for fire would be more vagrants. Whatever contained the fire sat too far back in the structure to be seen. Masaru found no trace of a sniper in any of the structures, but didn't trust standing.

"Forgive me, Maeda-san. I must wait for dark before I can carry you from this place."

The *crunch* of a footstep brought his attention back to ground level, thirty meters away. Blurry images in the scope window sharpened as the optics refocused.

About twenty rag-clad men and women emerged from the rubble, all carrying either submachine guns or military combat rifles. The closest three figures had at least one cybernetic arm. A man who stooped to pick up the rocket rifle appeared to be made of banded dark blue plastisteel from the waist up. Rather than a human face, he'd opted for a stylized metal skull that made no pretense at anatomical correctness. The center of his plastisteel forehead had an engraving of the kanji for death, 死, filled in with black paint. If not for the man's size—and the rocket-rifle coming to bear—Masaru would've laughed at him for looking like the villain from a child's afternoon holo-vid show.

Of course, laughing at psychotic cyber-freaks usually ended in violence.

Masaru squeezed the trigger and discovered holding a Class 6 rifle up over one's head made for a lousy shooting position. The massive firearm bucked straight out of his grip, though he took some pleasure in the roar of pain that followed. He fell over backward to recover the weapon, and stayed down.

*Sniper... somewhere. Twenty heavily armed augs.* Masaru closed his eyes, debating a last stand to defend what remained of his friend. He doubted Shuji would want him to commit suicide, and he could always return later to recover the body. The augs blocked him off from heading northeast, though walking all the way back to Miyazaki City was hardly necessary. He only needed to travel far enough to find a signal, and could vid back to Kurotai for assistance.

Masaru activated his speedware and sprang to his feet, holding the trigger down as he sprinted to the side. He swept the rifle over the approaching nomads, hitting somewhere between four and nine of them before his weapon went silent —out of ammo. Within a second of his grip releasing to drop the useless thing, a long, pointed bullet spiraled past his face. From the angle, he figured the sniper to be in the middle building, the one he had dismissed as too dangerous a perch.

*They are all insane.*

Masaru flung himself into a sprint, as fast as his neural wiring could force his muscles to contract. Muted detonations of gunfire went off behind him, accented by the occasional whistle of a near miss or the sharp *tap* of a slug hitting rubble somewhere nearby. He headed for the most intact building and jumped the wreckage of a car that had crashed into the doorway. Crouching, he let his speedware rest and peered back over a vehicle made before hover technology existed. Murky figures in the swirling dust approached, spreading out, but all heading toward him.

Fortunately, time and looters had rendered the building he'd chosen a giant open space inside. He dashed across the ground floor, dove through an open window into the street behind it, and headed to the right. After passing the rubble of five structures that didn't even come up to his waist, he crossed to an alley between four-story tall stacks of debris.

An explosion of cats flew out of the debris lining the walls, scrambling to get away from him. Masaru's speedware-boosted sprint pushed him past the cluster of felines before any of their paws caught a grip on the ground. He made a series of random turns, eventually finding cover in an underground area that appeared to have once been a parking garage.

Heat in his arms and legs warned him he needed a break. His Kurotai Daimyo speedware represented close to the best hardware money could buy, but even it had its limits. Only the NSK had better, but the only way to get it without being one of them was to pull it out of a corpse... and fend off the resulting assassination attempts.

Out of breath, muscles burning, Masaru took a seat on the hood of a tiny lime-green compact car. It hadn't moved in so long, weeds encased it in a sarcophagus of vegetation. Barring some quite unusual circumstances, he figured every car in this place had to be about three centuries old.

For a time, he breathed... and listened. Either he had lost his pursuers, or they had not bothered to chase him with any great determination. He scowled, hating his powerlessness at having to leave Shuji's body to whatever fate awaited it at their hands. They did not seem *too* crazed, not like the half-human creatures roaming the Badlands in the West. He growled, low in his throat. He would return home, gather a force, and sweep this place clear.

*The Kami themselves could not wreak such vengeance upon those who have slain Maeda-san.*

In the stillness of the parking garage, he again tried his NetMini, but it refused to connect. He couldn't even get the navigation applet to tell him where in Miyakonojo he stood. He hadn't been paying too much attention to the flight, so picking a direction to walk based on any idea of 'shortest route' would be impossible. Fortunately, the compass worked, so he settled on south.

He crept back up the ramp and peered around to make sure none of the augs had followed him. Once confident he remained alone, he walked along the side of the building down a narrow alley crammed with chunks of concrete and metal fragments too far destroyed to even guess at what sort of machine they'd come from.

Moving reawakened the sting under his arm. One stimpak pressed into his ribs below the wound sealed it after a momentary itching tingle. He glanced at the belt case and counted six of the small, red autoinjectors left, but hoped not to need them. Revenge could wait. He would avoid conflict until he could come back properly equipped to destroy everything here. Being unclaimed territory—no one had bothered to try retaking the city in years—no other CEO in the area would care if Kurotai used Miyakonojo's skeleton for 'weapons testing.'

Masaru continued west for a while, past a seemingly endless arrangement of old buildings. He had to be near the city center for it to have so many former high-rises, which implied he faced a walk of several miles. He set his stride, determined to return for Shuji.

A pile of concrete debris at his left burst upward with a droning electronic chatter.

Startled, Masaru sprang back, grasping the handle of his katana. He wheeled about to face the expanding cloud of dust and locked stares eye-to-camera with a nine-foot robot of red plastisteel.

Rather than legs, it resembled an industrial forklift, only with wheels more befitting a rover designed for exploring new planets. Its upper body had a mostly-human shape, a torso and two arms ending in hydraulic pincers similar to those used on lifter exoskeletons. A simple box with a single large lens and several smaller sub-sensors comprised its head, and a bright white 'Meiji' kanji adorned the center of its chest.

The machine lurched forward, tires as tall as his hips spitting concrete chips and debris to the rear. Masaru dove into a sideways somersault, evading a bashing strike. The Meiji bot swung with so much force its upper body rotated twice from the energy it had put behind it. The torso faced him two full seconds before the lower half steered, all four tires angling, to face him.

Dents and scratches covered it; the thing had to be at least sixty years old. The last time he'd heard anything about Meiji bots, Daiichi-Fuso had bragged about rebuilding the areas abandoned since the war... but for whatever reason, the project withered and died.

"Command, shutdown," said Masaru.

The Meiji ignored him, raising both its gripper claws and accelerating to about forty mph.

Masaru's speedware dragged time into slow motion, allowing him to roll again out of the way. The Meiji's massive arms crashed together with a resounding *clang* inches away. Rubber scuffed on paving as it attempted to stop, but skidded into a fragment of wall. The building lacked even a full story; the impact echoed for blocks in all directions, drowned out by the resulting roar of the wall crumbling under the robot's weight.

The Meiji reversed and rotated once more to face him.

Masaru sprinted at it, shouting a war cry as he drew the katana and leapt up onto its frame. His toes touched metal for a fraction of a second. He sprang again, slipping past a ponderous metal limb and slicing the head unit clean from atop the old construction bot.

Sparks sprayed from the thin seam in the metal; a second later, the head slid down the glass-smooth cut and fell off. The Meiji went berserk, holding its seven-foot-long arms out to either side and rotating its torso as fast as the mechanism allowed. Masaru backed well away from the thing as it zoomed off in a random direction and crashed through another ruined building. A horrendous clamor of metal and concrete rang out, suggesting the floor failed and dumped the malfunctioning Meiji into the basement. Seconds later, the remaining three stories collapsed straight down like pancakes, sealing it in a tomb.

Masaru shook his head and sheathed his sword. "That made too much noise. I must move."

He jogged south again.

---

TWENTY-ONE MINUTES LATER ACCORDING TO THE TIME DISPLAY ON HIS NETMINI'S compass app, he emerged from two rows of collapsing buildings into a large intersection where a six-lane road met a four-lane road. Not far from where the larger street headed south back among buildings, the wreckage of a green-painted military transport aircraft sat crumpled nose-first into a decaying high-rise. Dark smoke still poured from both engines along the midpoint of its VTOL wings, which canted upward at a forty-five degree angle, as though it had been in the process of slowing to land when something went quite wrong.

*JSDF...* He wondered if the Japan State Defense Force might have had some sort of facility set up here responsible for jamming signals. He could think of no other reason (aside from wild stories about radiation and fantasy) why his NetMini remained unable to connect. Hoping something in the wreck might provide a way to talk to the outside world, Masaru sprinted for it.

He approached the left side and peered into an open hatch at a space with twelve small seats, six against each wall. Three of the harnesses extended to their upmost position, suggesting the ship hadn't come in with a full squad. Masaru pulled himself in and moved toward the cockpit, but stopped a few feet away at the stink of rotting body.

A waterfall of broken metal struts and concrete jutting in through the windscreen convinced him any useful electronics this bird may have had no longer worked. Shaking his head, he backed away and headed for the door.

When he jumped to the ground, he caught sight of a trail of blood leading away from the crash.

*This looks recent. Perhaps there are survivors.*

Masaru jogged across the intersection, his shoes falling upon pale grey silt so thick the area could pass for the surface of the Moon. Footprints and blood led west out of the intersection along the four-lane road before turning right at the first possible chance. *The JSDF went west. Perhaps I have chosen poorly with south.* He stopped at the corner and peeked around. After spotting no threats, he continued following the trail for two blocks before it went across the street and down an alley.

Five bodies, more rag-clad nomads like the ones who had attacked him, lay draped over old cars half a block later. The area swarmed with footprints, making it impossible to tell who went where. Masaru wandered around the scene of a gunfight until he spotted blood leading away once more. A greater number of less damaged structures here appeared to have a dampening effect on the silt, as it didn't coat the road thick enough for footprints to form.

Fourteen paces later, he followed the blood to the doorway of an old sushi restaurant. It had no roof left, consisting only of four walls so rickety he figured an ordinary man might be able to push them over with sufficient effort. Masaru approached the door and stepped inside.

"Don't move," said a female voice on his right.

He froze, and shifted only his eyes toward her. Late morning sun glinted from the tip of an assault rifle trained on him, in the hands of a young woman wearing beige JSDF armor over a dark navy blue jumpsuit. She sat on the floor about twenty feet away, propped up against the wall in the near corner. Her helmet lay beside her on the ground, its amber visor cracked. Loose black hair hung even with her jawline, framing wide and fearful eyes. Dust and smears of red streaked her too-pale face, and blood pooled under her right leg.

"You're hurt." He took a step closer.

"I said, don't move." She swallowed; the tip of her rifle wobbled. "Take another step, and it'll be your last."

# KAT AND MOUSE

Katya wished she had a MOM-E, that is, a multi-orientation monitor eye… essentially a tiny camera embedded in the back of the head, about twice the size of a pore. At the time she'd been 'put together' by her former owners, the technology hadn't evolved down small enough to be invisible. Similar devices existed, but the ones with any decent visual clarity had 2mm lenses and would've been obvious if someone she'd been sent to spy on stroked her hair. Since she'd escaped, adding more parts to further embed herself in the life she tried to flee hadn't been high on the list of things to do.

The whole Eve thing had been a curveball too.

She needed money to survive… and support this 'kid,' but couldn't find a job.

She wanted out of 'the business,' but it's all she knew.

She shouldn't have taken this mission from Alex, but she did it anyway.

She thought she'd gotten out clean, but had a tail.

If she got caught, the life she'd spent the past eight months trying to establish would all go to hell, and probably take Eve with it.

*Something's not right. If he's on to me, where are the police?*

On a whim, she made a spontaneous turn into a Morning Bean coffee shop and headed straight for the shelves of mugs, teas, and other various overpriced whatnot. As soon as she had enough of a barrier between her and the glass front of the store, she ducked down out of sight. Her CamNano activated at a mental nudge, shifting her hair to lemon blonde and her skin back to its usual shade—pale.

*Sometimes a little change is all it takes to fool a tail. This is what I get for thinking the job would be easy and not wearing a second outfit.*

Once her hair completed the transition, she emerged from the shelves and approached the counter.

"Welcome to Morning bean, how may I caffeinate you?" asked a dark-skinned girl of about sixteen with hot-pink hair and iridescent blue yes.

"Oh, hi," said Katya, adding a giggle. "Double espresso on ice please."

The girl smiled and tapped her terminal screen. "Twenty-four credits, please."

Katya reverted her NetMini back to its standard profile and waved it past the reader. While standing by the pick-up counter, she watched the street out of the corner of her eye. The man who'd followed her out of the LRI building chatted with a busker by the corner, but kept his attention on the coffee place.

A moment later, an elderly man behind the counter set a small plastic cup in front of her, gave a polite nod, and proceeded to work on someone else's drink. Katya took the cup and edged toward the exit, measuring the ebb and flow of pedestrians. Her tail's shadow stretched away from the Morning Bean store, which meant she'd be walking into the sun, giving her the advantage of glare. He probably couldn't even see into the windows too well.

As soon as a dense cluster of pedestrians came by, Katya ducked out and fell in stride with them. Creative tilting of her NetMini let her peer back over her shoulder at the man, who continued to watch the coffee shop. Feeling relieved, and a touch proud of herself, she walked onward while pulling up a navigation applet to locate 'Bruno's Bistro.'

Four minutes after leaving Morning Bean, Katya found the place Alex wanted her to go. A small white trapezoid-shaped building jutted out from the side of a century tower behind an outdoor seating area enclosed in a thigh-high fence made to resemble wrought iron. Around twenty or so small, round tables with umbrellas that looked more decorative than useful occupied the patio, while a mere six tables stood inside. Most of the restaurant's interior space appeared to be kitchen. Sliding glass doors on the front face offered a view clean through to the lobby of the high-rise.

*They should've called it the Remora Café.*

She spotted an empty table inside and hurried over to the doors. Spices and garlic hung thick in the air along with the aroma of sausage. A shortish man in a chef's outfit emitted a faint whistle with his teeth, waved at a woman with platinum blonde curls, wearing a frilly black top and teeny skirt who appeared to be serving tables, and set an order up on the counter. Katya eyed a plate of what appeared to be thin-sliced sausage with broccoli rabe over penne pasta. The intense garlic wafting off it triggered unexpected hunger.

The waitress hurried over to pick up the plate. As soon as she glanced at Katya, telltale seams in the face by the mouth and eyes gave her away as a Class 2 doll, but her mannerisms had enough humanity to suggest her AI had sentience.

"Hello!" chirped the doll in French-accented English. "What can I get for you today?"

Katya gestured at the food on the tray. "I'll have that too. It smells wonderful."

"Oh, *oui, oui!* It is exquisite!" She faced the chef. "Antoine, please let me know when it is ready for her." The doll escorted her to the empty table on the way to take the plate outside to one of the tables there.

*That looks like Italian food. Why is the waitress French?*

The instant she took a seat, the thirteen-million-credit stowaway made itself known. In all the years she'd been used by *Vertex Investments*, she'd never once had to physically smuggle a high-value object in a body cavity. Of course, while being trained, she'd been made to do so. The squat, balding, neckless Otto Kepler returned to her memory, chuckling at her. The man could've been her grandfather by age, but seemed to take great delight in that particular training course. They'd forced her to insert a little metal orb to simulate 'the objective,' but didn't bother to mention it could vibrate or shock whenever Otto hit a button.

She—as well as the other five girls and three boys—had to navigate a small section of the Vertex Investments compound and interact with randomly selected people without giving away any sign they 'smuggled contraband.' Not an easy task when Otto decided to set off the zapper or buzzer in mid-conversation. They'd made them all do it over and over again until they could keep a straight face no matter what.

Katya narrowed her eyes. Not once had she needed to 'use that training' during the time she'd been working for Vertex. If Otto's insistence that he watch them put 'the objective' in place hadn't been enough of a clue where his interests lied, that all the boys passed the course on their first attempt days before any of the girls did made his intentions clear. *What were we, fourteen?* She sighed into her coffee. *Female, young, a commoner, and not one of us had parents. Exactly the wrong combination of things to be in the ACC. I suppose it could have been far worse. At least I'm alive.*

Yulia Danov had been the director in charge of Vertex Investments' 'ghost' program. She didn't seem the type to have tolerated anyone molesting her 'assets.' At least, outside of the desensitization training, but that hadn't started until seventeen.

Katya had forgotten how to enjoy sex. Her first time had been with a 'trainer' whose job it had been to take away all emotional association from the act. By the time she'd turned eighteen, it carried no more emotional weight than a handshake. Sometimes she used it to get information, sometimes to get close enough to poison someone. Never to stash an object.

*Kepler was a piece of shit.* She let a dark chuckle slip under her breath. Anya, a baby-faced blonde farm girl who'd been picked up from the countryside, had shot him after the fourteenth time she'd failed his 'hide the orb' training. Yulia hadn't even taken away the girl's rec center privileges. Katya stared off into nowhere, sipping espresso and wondering what had become of Anya. She'd been so quiet and timid when they'd first met at around ten. The last she'd seen the girl, she looked perpetually sad and broken, but did everything they ordered her to do with an emotionless detachment worthy of a sub-sentient doll.

Though Katya did get treated a little better than most because they couldn't make her psionic, despite their best efforts. Evidently, being so far away from gifted that even a top-tier government run facility *trying* to give her psionic abilities failed made them trust her.

*Everyone over there... you'd think psionics were practitioners of black magic who could damn the soul with a glare.*

When the doll waitress glided back in, she brought Katya ice water. "Would you care for a drink as well, madame?"

"The water is fine, thanks." Katya returned a polite smile.

She closed her eyes and daydreamed about a world where some form of God existed, so he, she, or it could visit death and suffering down upon everyone involved with Vertex Investments.

"Miss Hernandez, you're looking rather pale," said a man.

Katya's head snapped up; she gazed at the guy who'd followed her from Laughlin-Reed standing within arm's reach. Lamps in the ceiling made the front edge of his perfect light-brown hair almost glow. A narrow nose, angular cheeks, and flat chin almost gave him the good looks of a holovid star, though a slight asymmetry in his face kept him from being *too* perfect.

Before she could get a single word out, he slid into the other chair. The concealed neural memory stick practically screamed under the table, radiating her guilt in a way she feared he could detect. Something in the quality of his stare set her on edge. He didn't have the look of a man who planned to catch a thief. He looked more... intrigued. Katya clenched her jaw, detesting that she couldn't bring her handgun on this job. Maybe this man had nothing at all to do with what she'd stolen, and had less noble intentions.

"Nice move at the Bean." He smiled. "I hope you don't mind me joining you."

Muscles at the back of her neck tensed, her body expected Otto to hit the button as soon as she tried to talk. "I've already ordered."

"Oh, I don't mind." He leaned back. "I wanted conversation more than food."

The doll walked up to the table and set her meal down before rendering a polite curtsey to the man. "Bonjour, sir. Can I get you anything?"

He glanced at a holographic rendition of a menu hovering by the wall next to the chef. "I'll have the caprese panini, and hot tea."

The waitress doll smiled and emitted a cheerful noise. "Excellent choice. I will bring it out as soon as it is ready."

Katya narrowed her eyes ever so slightly. Any enjoyment she might've gotten from the food, this man had ruined. She couldn't betray worry or fear, and so she ate while keeping an outward blasé demeanor. Fortunately, the food *was* good enough to ease her nerves ever so slightly. "So what is it you wanted to talk about? Must be interesting if you've followed me all the way here."

He let off the sort of chuckle a wealthy person uses to call someone a fool in a polite way. "I couldn't help but notice your eyes, and wanted a closer look."

"And now that you've gotten that look?" She sliced a wafer of sausage in half, and speared her fork through it into some of the broccoli before lifting it to her mouth. The green strand glistened with a coating of garlic-infused olive oil.

He waited as the doll dropped off a cup of tea and walked away. "I am more inclined to trust my initial impression of you."

To control her mood, Katya kept replaying the moment Anya approached Otto so he could watch her insert 'the objective.' She pulled up the drab grey company-issued skirt they all had to wear, exposing herself, as well as a pistol strapped to her thigh. Otto never got the chance to scream. She drew, shot him once in the forehead, and put the weapon on the floor. Hands raised, she had offered no resistance when the handlers swarmed in and dragged her off. That had been the last, if not only, time Katya had seen the girl smile. Even two hours later when Anya had walked back down the hall to her 'apartment,' she looked lost.

*She'd wanted to die. Anya had expected to be executed for that.*

Focusing on a depressing moment allowed for passable outward detachment. Disinterest and sorrow often looked alike.

"So you've busted me for not having a class." Katya shrugged her right shoulder. "Crowley had me sorting boxes. I needed to get out of there. I'm supposed to be learning, not moving crap around shelves."

"I think we both know why you're at LRI, *Rosalie*." He flared his eyebrows. "I'm Zack."

She teased at her food with the fork for a few seconds. "I'm interning."

"Right." He winked. "You forgot to keep the age-reducing contouring in your nano makeup."

*Shit. If I say I made myself older to lose him, I admit to having cam and he'll know... If I play dumb, he'll know.* Katya rolled her eyes. "Okay, you got me. I'm not really nineteen. Found a loophole to get the government to pay for university."

"Not bad." Zack again waited as the doll waitress set down a plate before him, bearing an oblong caprese panini and a portion of tri-color pasta salad. He nodded at the false woman. "Thanks." As soon as the doll walked away, he leaned close and whispered, "I'm in the network defense group at LRI. I recognized your technique. Classic OOI."

Electric shock bedamned, Otto could've set off a hand grenade inside her at that moment, and her face wouldn't have even twitched.

Zack picked up half his sandwich and winked. "That's an excellent confused face."

She watched him eat for a moment, not quite able to bring herself to lift food to her mouth.

"I can tell you're not primarily a cyberspace infiltrator, but not bad work." He dabbed a napkin at his chin. "I couldn't find you on the list of assets involved in this operation, but we both know that's likely on purpose. Separation in case of compromise. Standard." He tossed the last of his panini in his mouth and winked.

*He's talking right out in the open.* Katya shifted her eyes to the right. The chef looked too far away to have possibly heard anything. She glanced past Zack at the other five tables: a woman her age with two small boys, a young couple, a middle-aged couple, and a pudgy old man so into the contents of his NetMini screen a gang shootout could tear the place apart and he probably wouldn't twitch. Katya doubted the young mother at the nearest table eavesdropped much over the boys rambling on and on about some video game they couldn't wait to get home to.

*Is this guy working for the police, trying to bait me? If he's really ACC, he's a fool.*

"Oh, I know," he whispered. "I probably shouldn't be talking to you at all if our teams are supposed to remain isolated, but you had such amazing eyes I couldn't help myself."

*If this guy is really an ACC operative, he's going to kill me if he thinks I'm not. If he's with the police, and I claim to be working for the ACC... they'll think I lied about everything. Deported, executed, or prison.* Her jaw clenched. Her mind drifted to an image of Eve pacing around the Naturahealth day care center, waiting for her as the sun set. Guilt made her look down. *This is why we don't get attached.* She glanced to the right and huffed out her nose. *She's not my child. She's not even a child. The girl's just a roommate with a physical handicap: temporary crippling shortness.* Katya stabbed another bit of broccoli and sausage.

Garlic would make everything better.

# 16

# RUMORS AND LEGENDS

K enny stood in the yard behind his house, squinting at his truck due to the strong glare of sunrise behind it. Cases of provisions: water, military rations, some snacks, and the usual array of miscellaneous tools and 'handy shit' he always packed up for a trip into the Badlands sat in the bed. He had wanted to get going an hour ago, but he gave up trying to wake the girls before daylight. Besides, Eldon hadn't shown up yet. He spent a moment meditating in the calm of his scrapyard, listening to the creak and groan of massive piles of junk brushed by the wind.

*I hope that other guy he's bringing has his head on straight.*

The irony of his thought made him laugh. Anyone willing to go to the Badlands couldn't be accused of having their head on straight. Behind him, a scrape of metal accompanied the patio door between the kitchen and the deck opening. The *clunk* of boots on Epoxil boards followed.

"Ugh. This thing is crushing my boobs," said Hayley.

"Not gonna say it," replied Alyssa in a singsong tone.

Hayley laughed.

Kenny glanced behind him. Hayley fidgeted with a dark grey DuraFib armored vest over her black *Zombie Ballerinas* t-shirt. Brand-new white jeans clung to her narrow legs like a second skin, and her heavy boots made her look ready for Mars patrol. Alyssa still wore a disappointed expression; she'd wanted a set of 'Badlander' armor like Kenny's, protective gear made to look like a cowboy's duster coat. Western Equipment Corporation didn't make it in any size she could fit in, so she had to settle for a standard Teradyne vest like Hayley. Companies *did* make 'normal' armor in kid sizes.

That fact alone made the Badlands feel safer to him than the city.

The kids' armor would stop up to a midrange handgun, but the odds of anyone in the Badlands firing modern weapons at them ranked up there with the

Syndicate deciding to give him half a mil as a retainer and saying 'don't bother going out there and thanks for your time.' Any prewar firearm wouldn't have a chance of penetrating it. Of course, despite spending a good nine hours teaching Hayley how to shoot (she'd taken to it surprisingly well, and credited long hours spent playing games in cyberspace) while Alyssa practiced, the two had strict orders to 'stay the hell down' if anything got dangerous.

Alyssa patted the front of her vest. She'd put it on over a tank top, and added a blue flannel on top of the vest. The thigh pockets on her sand-brown fatigue pants clattered with the weight of spare magazines.

"How're those boots?" Kenny gestured at Hayley's feet.

"I feel like I could kick a dent in the side of the truck." She 'Frankenstein-stomped' a few paces. "Are you sure I can't wear flops? These things are *so* hot."

"There's scorpions as big as housecats in some places."

Hayley stared at him. He expected a scream, but she blinked twice and yelled, "Cool! Like in *The Festering Cistern*."

"You've been to Joey's place?" asked Kenny.

"Huh?" asked Alyssa.

Hayley gave him a serious look, both eyebrows up. "No, his place was *worse* than the dungeons under *Morrh Kizrah*."

Alyssa stared at her. "What the heck are you talking about?"

"I'm kinda wonderin' that too." Kenny scratched the side of his head.

"It's an old Monwyn game." Hayley rolled her eyes. "It's like older than I am. They had these giant scorpions in the sewer. They weren't a big deal if you had arrows or magic, but if they got close, they could do a lot of damage."

"Right. Imagine one on your toes." Kenny smiled.

"You said there's tribal people out there who don't wear shoes... or sometimes even clothes at all." Hayley squirmed at her armor. "What do they do about scorpions?"

Alyssa's face tinted with blush.

"If they get stung? Usually, they die." Kenny sighed.

"Oh." Hayley looked down. "Boots it is."

"Come on. Might as well get used to the weight of a gun on your side." Kenny walked around to the bed of the truck and de-boxed a pair of Class 2 pistols. Hoping to placate her, he'd ordered Hayley one in bright pink with white rubber grips and a 'Hello Kitty' on the handle.

"It's *adorable*," said Hayley, overacting her gushiness.

Alyssa smirked.

The girls attached black nylon holsters to their belts, each with a reinforcing strap around the thigh. Kenny handed the weapons over, grip first. Alyssa pulled the mag and checked the ammo counter while Hayley just put the gun in the holster.

"Ut ut..." Kenny gave her a look.

"What?" She blinked at him. "You said always assume a weapon is loaded, so I assumed it's loaded."

"Always check."

She drew it, removed the mag, and held it up so he could see the blue propellant blocks stacked within. "See. Loaded. Just like I assumed."

He kept staring at her.

Hayley looked at the ammo counter on the left side. "Chamber indicator is empty. No round ready to fire."

"Okay." He smiled. "Remember—"

"I know," said Hayley. "Stay down and hide. Only shoot if I absolutely have to. Are you gonna get mad at us if we get attacked by some creature that doesn't have a ranged weapon and I fire at it?"

Kenny chuckled. "I want you to be careful and safe. This isn't a video game. There's no respawn if you get hurt."

She stared at the ground.

"What are the rules?" asked Kenny.

Both girls made faces like they wanted to sigh, but didn't. Simultaneously, they chanted, "If we can run, run. If we can hide, hide. Finger off the trigger unless we want to destroy something. Stay aware of what's behind the target. Don't point it at anything we don't want to kill."

Kenny pulled the both into a hug. "Good. Please remember that stuff. It's not just to recite."

His wife came down the steps from the deck, giving him a meaningful stare. She didn't have to say 'if he wanted the girls safe, they wouldn't be going into the Badlands.' When she got close, he threw an arm around her back and walked two steps away from the girls.

"It's not too late," he whispered. "We can stash them with Joey, or your parents."

"We can hear you," said Alyssa.

"There's a vet place down the block that does boarding. Think they've got room?" Kenny winked.

Kathy's expression told him two quite different things existed: funny, and him.

"If you leave me in a kennel for a week, I'm going to have separation anxiety and start peeing around the house and chewing on the sofa," said Alyssa.

"Your father is just being an idiot." Kathy clapped the girls on the shoulders. "Oh… you gave them guns already. We're still in the city."

The high-pitched whirr of a small e-car got louder on the other side of the fence surrounding Kenny's scrapyard.

"They're both old enough with parental permission." He eyed his wife's unadorned belt. "Where's yours?"

"In the house still. I didn't think we'd need it until we got out there."

"Yo!" yelled Eldon over the yard fence. "We still doin' this thing?"

Kenny patted Kathy on the arm. "Better to have it ready and not need it."

"Why is *he* here?" asked Alyssa.

"Because." Kenny squeezed her shoulder. "I am doing everything I can to make sure your first"—*and hopefully only*—"trip into the Badlands goes well."

He jogged across the yard to the fence and hit the button to open the gate. A flat-fronted silver microvan rolled in that had seen better days. Random sparks spat from the seam down the middle of the left front wheel: the telltale death rattle of the e-motor. Eldon waved from the passenger seat, looking far from comfortable crammed into such a small vehicle. The driver, a slender man with olive skin, bushy black eyebrows, and a baggy military green coat, smiled at him.

Kenny walked back toward his truck, which dwarfed the box on wheels driving past it. The new guy took a wide circling turn and came to a stop with the nose end inches away from the deck. Eldon, already wearing his recon armor except for the helmet, leapt out before it came to a complete halt, and stretched.

"God damn that thing ain't got legroom." He bee-lined to Kenny and shook hands, grinning. "Thought you wanted ta take a break?"

"Some *friends* had other ideas." Kenny nodded at the van. "Who's the other guy?"

Alyssa fidgeted, her gaze locked on the ground and a tint of blush in her cheeks.

"Name's Nasir Aman. You said you were gonna bring the ladies along and wanted some extra help. He had the best record of the mercs willin' to work within your budget."

Nasir hopped out of the driver's seat and spent a moment ogling Kenny's truck. About when he expected the man to get on his knees and worship it, he seemed to snap out of the daze and scurried around to the back doors of the van. Inside lay a number of metal cases as well as one rather obvious sentry gun.

"Whoa." Kenny raised an eyebrow. "You're bringing a bot guy out into the Badlands?"

Eldon flashed a conspiratorial grin. "He works cheap, you didn't wanna break the bank… and I get to see if your whacked-out hoodoo is real." He pivoted and raised his arms at Kathy. "Hey there, K. Damn good to see you lookin' like you again."

Alyssa folded her arms over her chest and kept trying to drill for oil with her eyes.

"Hey yourself." Kathy accepted his hug. "Look, sorry if I've been a bit less than friendly whenever you came around."

"Naw. S'all good." Eldon winked. "Ken gave me the sit-rep." He nodded at Alyssa. "Hey baby girl. You keep your head down out there, got it?"

She nodded, blushing more.

Eldon glanced from Hayley to Kenny and back four times. "Shit. You're bringin' the little one too?"

"I'm not *that* little." Hayley put her hands on her hips. "I'm gonna be twelve in three months." She leaned to the side to stare around him at the source of a growing mechanical clanking. "What is *that?*"

Everyone turned.

Nasir walked beside a metal spider-bot with a body the size of a footlocker. Where a normal spider would have fangs, the robot had a pair of gripper arms, which carried one of the cases from the van toward the truck. "Loader tarant. He's not coming with us, just helping me carry stuff."

Hayley ran over to it, gawking. "It's *so* cool." She pet it like a dog, and the robot seemed to react with a modicum of affection.

"Be right back. Been on the road for two hours." Eldon winked and jogged into the house.

Alyssa walked around the other side of the truck.

"What was that?" whispered Kathy.

Kenny looked from the spider bot to her. "What? 'Bot?"

"No. The 'that' I'm speaking of is the weird feeling in the air between Liss and Eldon."

"Oh. *That* that." Kenny sighed. "Liss didn't handle you having to leave well. She went into this wild phase. Got back from that last trip, and she comes traipsing out in one of my shirts open down the front, panties, but no bra. Gave him a bit of a show, tryin' I guess to piss me off."

Kathy massaged the bridge of her nose. "Dammit."

He grasped her shoulders and pulled her into a hug. "It's not your fault. Eldon wasn't havin' any of it. He kinda yelled at her and she turned scarlet. It worked out. Hit me like a reality slap. I thought I'd lost the two most important people in my life. You to that shit, and her to anger. We finished that night closer than we'd been in months."

"She's not going to be able to look at him for a while." Kathy hugged him. "I'll talk to her when we get a moment to ourselves."

He nodded.

*Clank.*

Kenny whirled toward the truck, where Nasir directed the tarant to stack boxes in the bed. "You got anything ready for when all that junk stops working?"

Nasir let out a noncommittal laugh and patted a handgun on his side. "My stuff's in good shape. It won't konk out."

"It's not your hardware I'm worried about," mumbled Kenny.

"Oh, where's that other friend of yours?" asked Kathy. "Joey?"

"Can't make it. Boy gone and got himself a real job. Was a mistake even callin' him. Got stuck listenin' to him grumble about havin' to track down some kinda street drug. You'd think it was beneath him."

Kathy laughed. "Considering where he's been living…"

"Right." Kenny grinned. "But he's *Division 9* now, so…"

"Oh ho." Kathy flared her eyes. "Big leagues." She winked and trotted over to the truck.

He sighed, staring at the truck. Eldon, an unknown merc, his wife, and two kids. *What am I doing?* A moment's hesitation died in a hail of daydreamed bullets from the window of a long, black hovercar. "This is going to be an… interesting trip."

THE VAST EXPANSE OF WIDE-OPEN FLAT EXTENDED TO THE HORIZON IN THREE directions. Behind them, the darkness of West City's skyline grew more and more faint. Eldon took the passenger seat, his Crusader 10mm assault rifle across his lap as always. Kathy didn't seem to mind giving up the spot, as she much preferred he play 'gunner.' She sat off center in the back row, with Alyssa and Hayley to her left (behind Kenny) and Nasir on the other side.

Hayley and Nasir had been chatting constantly back and forth around Kathy regarding his tech. She kept asking him question after question about the electronic slab he'd carried with him, some manner of heavily modified net deck he used as a control nexus for all his pet robots. It had the requisite M3 jack, but also eight small physical screens, which Hayley thought simultaneously 'cool' and 'old.' While his body remained safe in the truck, he could go into any hostile environment in total safety. The bots could also run via autonomous programming, following instructions, or he could control them like an ancient video game using the small screens. Some bot operators even plugged in and 'became' their bots, but if he did that, he'd only be able to control one at a time. He'd brought a number of orb bots, one tracked unit with an assault rifle mechanism, and of course, the sentry gun. He'd planned on setting up the sentry only whenever they stopped to sleep. It had the biggest weapon, a 15mm machinegun, but no capacity to move.

Kenny braced the steering wheel with a knee and tapped at the Navcon, flipping through several potential routes to Colorado Springs. While he'd been piecing together map data over the past years, his information came from rumors posted on artifact hunting GlobeNet sites, or from personal experience. Anything could happen out there, and no giant corporation kept updating these maps like they did for the city interior. He decided to avoid the Nevada desert; Las Vegas had a metric shitload of badness surrounding it. Rough settlers, bandits, and everyone else drawn to the place seemed to feed on strife, as if the Badlands itself fed off ancient history and amplified it tenfold. A more easterly path along I40 would bring them across old Arizona and into New Mexico, but the northern veer by I25 came awfully damn close to North Texas and the Steel Reavers' stomping grounds. *That* seemed like an even worse idea. What those augmented crazies would do to his wife and daughters made Vegas feel like sending them to a private school with a cadre of armed guards watching their every move.

Plus, he didn't have to go *into* Vegas. He could skirt the area wide enough.

After locking in the route plot to take them up I25 to I70, or at least where the map software believed roads to be, he put both hands on the wheel and drove. It occurred to him after another fifteen minutes that the rumble of the enormous tires on the ground generated the only sound in the cabin.

He glanced at Hayley via an old-fashioned rear view mirror. She clung to Kathy's left arm and stared out the window at the desert. The expression on her face made her look as though she'd awakened from a nightmare only minutes before.

"You okay, Hale?"

The girl jumped, startled.

"Hayley?"

"Uhh. Not really," she whispered.

He hadn't heard such an undertone of fear in her voice since he'd met her, not even when she explained the WellTech mercenaries kicking down the door of her dead father's apartment and wanting to kill her. He checked the old strip of ancient paving ahead to make sure he had a few seconds of not needing to look, and twisted around to make eye contact. "What's wrong? You see something out there?"

"No." She took a long shuddering breath and let it out slow. "This place. It just feels *wrong*. It's like something's watching us. Something bad... that wants to hurt us."

"Oh, here we go." Eldon shook his head, chuckling. "You got her started on that hoodoo shit too?"

"I never much talked about it to her." He faced forward again, eyes on the road. *What does she mean, she 'feels' it? Some of those stories get pretty wild, but...*

"S'up with the look?" Eldon glanced at him with a raised eyebrow.

"What hoodoo shit are we talking about?" asked Kathy.

"Ehh..." Kenny sucked air through his teeth. "She's already on edge. I don't want to make it worse with old ghost stories."

Nasir nodded. "I've heard the stories too. People say there is an 'evil force' out here or some such nonsense. Some even go so far as to claim the reason no one has tried to redevelop the interior of the continent is because of this influence."

Eldon's slow, deep laugh filled in the silence. "Y'all people got some vivid imaginations."

Hayley locked eyes with Kenny in the rearview mirror. "I don't know why. I just feel scared."

"Maybe 'cause your whole life is technology, and you're goin' into a place without any?" Eldon winked. "Hey, that's it. Kid's been online so damn much, she can 'feel' the absence of the GlobeNet. No signal out here."

Alyssa giggled.

Hayley kept staring at him, speaking in a soft, eerie voice. "I hope you're right. I really do." The truck hung in pregnant silence for four seconds before Hayley cracked up laughing. "Oh come on, that was funny."

"You fuckin' with us?" asked Eldon.

"Swear jar," sang Hayley and Alyssa at the same time.

"Ain't got no swear jar." Eldon winked.

"Why not?" Hayley squinted at him.

"Because, when you on yo' own, there ain't no Mom and Dad ta do shit for ya. You don't do it, shit don't get done. You live in filth 'til you can't take it no more, and you clean yo' dam self. Like bein' swear-jarred constantly."

"Oh," said Alyssa

Nasir looked back and forth between the kids and Kenny. "Was all of that just some creepy-kid stuff?"

"Not all." Hayley clung to Kathy's arm again. "I really do feel scared out here."

"Aww shit," muttered Eldon. "You bring any sage? Maybe some candles an' shit?"

Kenny picked at his eye with his middle finger.

Eldon grinned, laughing while shaking his head.

---

Four hours and change after leaving the gate, a large, white box truck tilted at an angle caught Kenny's eye. A little concern—and more than a little curiosity—mixed, causing him to steer left on an approach path. It soon became clear that the cargo truck had slipped off the road and half gone into a drainage ditch. The driver's effort to get out had thrown mud all over the cracked remnants of road. Two spots of bright cyan light hovered around the sidewalls, orb bots spraying the rig down with water.

"Now who in the hell bothers washin' their truck when they got it stuck in a damn ditch?" asked Eldon.

Kenny flared his eyebrows. "That's a damn fine question."

A pair of men in clean white jumpsuits with a dark spot over their left breast pocket climbed down from the cab. Both had imposing physiques and military haircuts, but warm smiles. The blond man raised a hand in greeting while the dark-haired one set his hands on his hips.

"They look friendly," said Kathy.

"Trouble always does," muttered Kenny. "Stay out of sight, girls."

Alyssa and Hayley scooted off the seat to the floor and ducked.

Kenny pulled to a halt on the road by the two men. 'Laughlin Reed Innovation' ran the length of the box truck's cargo area in black letters above a logo of a test tube surrounded by electron orbit lines. The dark spots on the men's jumpsuits turned out to be the same logo.

"Howdy," said Kenny, after rolling down his window. "You boys make a wrong turn?"

The blond man suppressed a wince. "Good morning. Was a bad storm last night, couldn't see a damn thing. Went off the road."

Kenny eyed the orbs spraying the truck down and de-mudding it. "Well, that there's one of the cleanest wrecks I've ever seen."

"You seem like a reasonable man," said the blond. "The company doesn't like us bringing in any contamination from the research facility. Uhh, you know, LRI's got a place out here. You wouldn't believe how much the competition can learn from dirt and crud."

"Research facility in the Badlands?" Kenny raised an eyebrow. *Oh, nothing ever goes wrong with that... You'd think these idiots would learn.* "Nothin' dangerous in that truck, is there?" He eyed the rear door, concerned with his wife and the girls so close. The last thing he wanted was to get caught in an explosion or something while helping a couple idiots out of a ditch. *No good deed...*

The man shook his head. "Nah, not dangerous. Medicine." He smiled. "I do not understand why they make such common drugs so far out here from the city. I suppose fewer prying eyes. Even the most secure century tower can be infiltrated. It is tough to sneak in when they can see ten miles in every direction."

The other man in the white jumpsuit grumbled. "This is the last time I'm going out there. Yesterday, it was a bunch of idiots with swords and arrows rushing out of the weeds when I'm tryin' ta have a shit."

Eldon chuckled. "Well that's damn inconsiderate."

"Should be able to give you a hand gettin' your rig outta that." Kenny nodded back over his shoulder. "Long as you got a hitch."

"Yes." The blond nodded and walked toward the back of the truck.

"This thing has got the balls to pull that monster out?" asked Nasir.

"Depends on what they're carrying." Kenny leaned his head out the window and raised his voice. "Hey... what are you loaded down with? Might need to depack some if it's too heavy."

The other man, who'd remained close, shook his head. "Just medicine. Anti-anxiety medication. Placinil mostly. OTC stuff."

Kenny laughed himself to tears.

"What?" asked Kathy.

"Anti-anxiety medication in the Badlands... They don't have enough." Still chuckling, he backed around into position behind the larger truck.

The girls peered over the window edge, trying to watch while staying out of sight as Kenny ran around to the bed. He took a heavy chain from one of the storage boxes, which he used to link the trucks together by their tow hitches.

Between the cargo truck attempting to reverse, and Kenny's behemoth pulling, it took about fifteen minutes of work to haul the stranded rig out of the ditch and back onto the road. The orb bots got to work washing the right front fender clean of mud and vegetation. Kenny disconnected the chain while giving the side-eye to another orb which zipped by his head. The new bot glided close to the wall of the cargo box, but didn't spray. It orbited the truck once before stopping at a point where the two men couldn't see it. From there, it went low to the ground and circled back toward the pickup.

Kenny wound the chain over his arm, walking back to his truck. The rogue orb came up and over the side wall, landing in one of Nasir's boxes in the bed. He stashed the chain back where he got it and turned to shake hands with the blond.

"Thank you, friend." The man smiled.

"Hey, don't mention it. We gotta stick together out here."

"We?" asked the man.

Kenny grinned. "Those of us who ain't nuts."

"Ahh. Yes." The man nodded. "Be driving safe."

*What's up with this guy? Sounds like he learned English last week.* "You too."

Kenny climbed into his seat and got moving, keeping one eye on the receding form of the LRI truck. "Nas… what was up with that orb?"

"My fault," said Eldon. "Got a weird feelin' about those two. They awful hard-lookin' for a bunch of cargo drivers. Thought it might be some kinda ACC thing. Asked Nasir to check for soldiers, weapons, explosives, you know, nasty shit they might try smugglin' in."

"Looks like bottles of pills in there. Two rifles, but they're up front," said Nasir.

"No big deal." Alyssa scooted back into her seat. "Hell, you gave me and Hayley guns out here."

"Well." Kenny leaned back in his seat and prepared for a long drive. "If I owned a company that had to ship stuff 'tween civilization and a 'hidden research facility in the Badlands,' I'd probably hire ex-soldiers to drive it, too."

---

KENNY'S DETOUR TO AVOID THE BANDIT-STREWN REGION AROUND LAS VEGAS WOUND up, by virtue of their GPS giving a bad reading, putting them in the area once known as northern Arizona when the sun weakened enough to make Kenny think of stopping for the night. He did *not* like the GPS going haywire so soon after talking about 'some evil force' out here, or Hayley acting as if she could somehow feel it.

For most of the years he'd been driving out to the Badlands, he'd entertained the stories and legends as exaggerations of truth, but not literal fact. Folklore often had nuggets of reality coated in liberal doses of fancy, with genuine bad luck mixed in. Someone's vehicle refuses to start when bandits come out of nowhere and it's been working fine up 'til that point… well, who can really say what made it happen? Heck, he believed the stories enough to rig a biodiesel engine as a backup. Most of the legends suggested the more primitive the machine, the less chance it would misbehave. Something high tech, like the in-wheel e-motors and fusion power plant were supposed to be screwed. Despite their rumored susceptibility to whatever influence may or may not exist out here, he had yet to have an issue.

Hayley had remained quiet for the rest of the day. She got a little moody in the late afternoon, like a four-year-old trapped in a car too long. Disgruntled whines and the apparent inability to find a comfortable position to sit in proved the extent of it. When they'd stopped to stretch their legs and water the dirt, she'd refused to get more than a step away from Kathy.

Nasir seemed like a decent guy, if not a bit on the cowardly side. Kenny couldn't fault him too much as no one could accuse the man of being a soldier. 'Bot guys' made big money in the corporate mercenary scene, sometimes able to work two sites at once. When risk equated to losing some replaceable hardware instead of one's ass, it made for happier corporate lawyers and insurance companies. Random conversation along the ride revealed that he'd gone to a trade school for electronic engineering. He'd developed a fascination with bots, got to building his own, and more or less pulled a Joey. Nasir lived the slum life, barely surviving while trying to off-grid his way to a point of survival.

Kenny hoped those rumors about tech in the Badlands proved false. Depending on which version of the tale one believed, his bots could wind up anywhere from useless to dangerously out of control.

"So why'd a techie agree to come out here?" asked Kathy.

"The nine-to-five never worked for me." Nasir offered an unapologetic frown. "I'd rather *live* life than burn it all away as someone else's tool. Sure, I'm not rich. Grey zone squat, I don't have to worry about rent, or neighbors complaining about something blowing up at three in the morning."

"Yeah, but you gotta worry about those neighbors decidin' they want what you got," said Eldon.

Nasir patted his control board. "Not really. 'Round me, everyone's pretty flaz. Get the one-off here and there but that's what Ma'ab is for."

"Flaz?" asked Kathy.

Nasir laughed. "Calm, cool… flaccid like a limp dick."

The girls giggled while Kathy rolled her eyes.

Kenny glared at him via the mirror. "Come on, man. Hayley's not even twelve yet."

"Ma'ab?" Eldon held up his hand. "Wait, don't tell me. The sentry gun?"

"Yep." Nasir grinned.

Kenny turned left to follow a long, pin-straight ribbon of old paving that stretched off into the horizon heading north. He didn't want to go any farther east, at least not without going north a little. He still had the entire expanse of New Mexico between him and Steel Reaver territory, but why take chances?

He drove for about twenty minutes more, eyeing the ever-weakening sun and the wide expanse of nothing in all directions. Nasir continued discussing his outlook on life, and how this trip was part of his 'not in a rush' effort to make enough money freelancing to get a 'real place' someday, but only after he had enough in the bank, and some top-of-the line bots so he could pull down big money contracts… probably defense work. Corporate security paid less than the alternative, but being legal, it offered regular work and no risk of Division 1 knocking on his door.

A shadow on the left caught Kenny's attention. Within a few seconds of staring at it, the form of a small building became clear. *That'll do for the night… at least some cover.* He changed lanes to the left, driving north in the southbound lane. As the structure drew nearer, he recognized the telltale layout of a prewar 'gas station.' A modern-looking truck sat parked close to the awning over the pumps, though the layer of dust on it suggested it hadn't moved in a couple of months.

"Hmm, that's kinda fucked up." Eldon picked his helmet off the floor from between his boots and put it on. "Truck don't look like Badland stuff, but I ain't got nothin' on thermal movin' around."

"Hey. 'Child' here," said Hayley in a sarcastic tone. "You get on him for saying 'dick,' but you whip out a f bomb?" She looked up at Kathy. "Mom, my innocent ears have been forever dirtied."

Eldon blinked at her.

Fear wavered in Hayley's voice, but she attempted a 'tough' exterior. "I grew up around cops and I spent years in the 'net. Like I haven't heard that stuff before."

Kenny nodded to Eldon and pulled over, rolling to a stop about fifteen meters from the other truck. It didn't have as much of a lift and looked on the newer side, which only made him think it had belonged to an amateur. "Poor guy. Was probably his first rodeo."

"What's a rodeo?" asked Alyssa.

"I mean…" Kenny chuckled. "That truck doesn't have any customization on it, stock tires. Looks almost undamaged. Probably some poor bastard's first time out here."

"Oh, shit," muttered Alyssa, a second and change before Hayley let off a scream.

Nasir jumped awake at the high-pitched shriek; his arms flew up into a horrible attempt at a kung-fu pose.

Kenny whirled around to look at the girls. Alyssa pointed out the side window. A fair distance away from the pump islands lay a mangled corpse, little more than a skeleton with a few clumps of gore clinging to the bones. Sand and dust had covered much of it, though here and there, dark swaths showed, suggesting a large dried bloodstain coated the tarmac.

"It's okay, Hale." Kenny reached into the back to pat her on the knee. "He can't hurt anyone."

Eldon opened his door and got out. "Well, there's the driver." He raised his rifle and approached the modest 'quick-mart' building on the far side of the pumps with his rifle raised.

"Why do we have to stop here?" asked Hayley, an undertone of whine in her voice. "I don't like it here. It's scary."

Alyssa held her hand. "It's shelter. If we stop in the middle of open desert, we're a target."

"Yeah." Kenny cracked a prideful grin. "That's right." He looked Kathy in the eye. "I'm gonna check the truck out."

Nasir yawned, nodded, and slid out to stand on the passenger side. He leaned over backward and stretched while walking in random circles. Kenny jumped down from his seat, using his door for cover for a few seconds while surveying the area. Nothing moved but the occasional distant bird. He put a hand on his sidearm and approached the other truck's open driver side door.

A smallish bloody footprint on the running board caught his eye, as well as a handprint dead center in the steering wheel. He caught a faint whiff of clove tobacco in the fabric. Bare footprints too small to be adult defined by clean spots on dust marked the dashboard in front of the passenger seat; he pictured the driver's son or daughter asleep with their feet up. Or maybe someone had found a

Scrag child. Kenny pulled himself in and sat behind the wheel, staring ahead at the dusty skeleton. A lump a few feet away from the right hand resembled a pistol. The body had decomposed so much, he couldn't even begin to guess what had caused the death. Most of the flesh and organs were simply gone, a sure sign of canid or ghoul attack, but that didn't mean they killed him. Either of the two would've consumed corpseflesh.

Kenny pulled a six-inch micro flashlight from his belt and studied the handprint on the wheel. *Kid survived whatever killed the adult.* Shining it on the floor revealed a few partial footprints in blood. He spotted the light on the passenger-side dash. No blood. *Kid had their feet up before the attack.*

*Hmm. Probably a Scrag. They couldn't figure out how to make the truck work.*

Eldon walked by, circling the area where the bones lay. A few times, he stopped to touch the ground and brush away dust. Kenny watched him until he picked up a scrap of rope; several frayed strands dangled from a knot.

"Oh, shit…" Alyssa's voice startled Kenny; she'd wandered up to the truck's door without him noticing.

Kenny stared at her for a second until his heart got going again. After sighing out his nose, he fiddled with the console. The truck had power, but its former owner had set up a biometric lock. *Hmm. That poor idiot ain't got no fingerprints left. Wonder if that Nasir guy can hack in.* He jumped down and hurried around to find Alyssa standing by the tailgate, looking frightened. "What's wrong?"

"Look…" She pointed at the bed. "That's kinda freaky."

He turned to follow her finger with his gaze. Three large cages sat in the back portion of the truck, one of which had a pair of empty handcuffs inside. Fortunately, none held dead bodies. Fragments of plastiboard cartons littered the area behind the truck. Given the spread of debris, he figured a group had already come by and looted whatever provisions may have been there. A few child-sized bloody footprints marked the bed liner as well.

"Dad?" Alyssa crept up behind him. "Was this a bandit's truck? Those cages look like they're meant for people."

"I don't know what I'm looking at, hon. The kinda people out here who'd take slaves wouldn't know how to operate this thing." He rubbed his chin while thinking for a moment. "I suppose someone from the city could've come out here to play god. Modern gear could give a man a sense of untouchability. Who knows? Might just be a bounty hunter who tried to chase someone out here, but bounty hunters don't usually have cages."

"That's not untouchable." Alyssa leaned to her left, peering at the bones. "Something definitely touched him."

"Hah." Kenny chuckled. "Sure enough."

Hayley seemed drawn to the skeleton and approached it. Kathy watched her, evidently having less tolerance for getting close to a dead body. The girl stopped about fifteen feet or so from the remains and peered at the ground. A few seconds later, she balanced on one leg and opened the clasps on her right boot, pulled her foot out, and held it near the ground.

"What in the…" Kenny jumped down from the tire and hurried over. She compared the size of her foot to a print on the ground. Whoever made it had been a little smaller than her, and shoeless.

"There was a kid here," said Hayley.

Eldon's boot scuffed the dirt, startling Kenny. He held up the frayed rope. "Cut with a knife. I think our dead guy abducted some kid. There's marks on the ground... poor kid was crawling around in blood." He noticed Hayley and took a knee, grasping her foot and comparing it to the print. "Year or two younger than Hayley... probably a girl."

"You can tell that from the footprint?" Hayley slipped her boot back on and buckled it.

Eldon nodded. "Print is thinner at the ball and heel. Least... My guess would be girl, about ten."

Kenny grumbled. "There's cages in the truck. I think our kid was a Scrag."

"What makes you say that?" asked Kathy.

"Because the truck is still here. There's signs a kid fiddled around inside, but I don't think they could figure out how to make it work. Didn't see any blood on the terminal screen. Kid had blood on her hands and feet. If she had any clue how to get it moving, there'd have been fingerprints on the console."

"Kid probably had blood all over her... she'd have been slithering around in it like a snake. And the gun's still there." Eldon pointed. "Think you're right about Scrag. Didn't know what the gun was."

Nasir busied himself setting up the sentry turret close to the front door of the gas station office. On its tripod, the boxy housing reached the belt buckle height of a man, and from the look of it, mounted a Class 6—15 mm—rifle mechanism. Kenny patted Hayley on the shoulder and approached the bones while Eldon went to check on the truck.

The weapon lay a short distance from the right hand, as if it had bounced out of his grip at the instant of death and been left where it fell. Neither the child nor whatever killed the man bothered taking it. He picked it up and blew a layer of sand away from a black UCF MCP21, a Class 4 that fired the same projectiles as Eldon's rifle, only with about a third the propellant. The ammo counter read 13/25. That it still contained bullets further proved neither the killer nor the child had a clue what a gun was. Scraps of a duster coat and a distant hat on the ground made him think the remains belonged to a man. Two pairs of modern electronic handcuffs on the belt, plus a box of stimpaks next to them also proved he had come from West City.

Hayley sank into a squat, and burst into tears.

Alyssa and Kathy ran over to her. Kenny stood after collecting the stimpaks and jogged back to them. The girl shivered and had turned seven shades of pale. Both Alyssa and Kathy comforted her in between asking what was wrong, but Hayley didn't react.

"Hale..." Kenny grasped her head in both hands, brushing his thumbs over her cheeks. With firm, but gentle strength, he forced her to make eye contact. "Hayley... what's wrong?"

She grabbed at his shirt. "I'm scared."

Kenny let her cling, and patted her back. "Did you see something?"

"I dunno. I just got scared." She sniffled. "Like outta nowhere."

"Well there *is* a dead guy over there," said Alyssa.

*She was close to the body before and didn't react like this.* Kenny stroked her hair for a moment until she stopped trembling. He relaxed his grip when she lifted her face from his chest and made eye contact.

"I... sorry. This place just feels... bad. Like I'm gonna die if I stay here." Hayley crossed her arms and shivered. "I felt so helpless."

*Ahh...* Kenny nodded with understanding. "I get it."

"Get what?" asked Kathy.

Sniveling, Hayley gazed around at the old gas station. "I feel like I'm stuck here. Like I can't move and I'm afraid of dying."

Kathy hugged and rocked her, muttering reassurances.

The sentry gun chirped a ready tone.

Eldon jogged over. "Couple of bloody tracks on the road. Think that kid left on foot."

"Figured out what happened." Kenny smiled. "I'm pretty sure that kid was a mystic."

Eldon tilted his head forward and cocked the Eyebrow of Disbelief.

Kenny cracked up for a few seconds, and spent a few more trying to keep a straight face. "I knew you'd give me that look. Mystic is what Scrags call psionics. I bet this dead guy here was one of those yahoos who run around out here lookin' for primitives to 'save,' and bring back to the city. 'Cept the one he found didn't want to be saved, but he took her anyway. He probably decided to spend the night here, just like I did... and that kid, being psionic, charged the area with terror. Either that or she watched someone kill the guy and burned her emotion into the ground."

Eldon made a series of faces, but stopped short of yelling 'bullshit.' Psionics had been established fact for years. Badlands hoodoo, not so much. "If that's true, then why'd only Hayley get whammied?"

"Hell if I know." Kenny shrugged. "Maybe 'cause she's young. You know the stories. Kids see ghosts all the time when they're tiny, and grow out of it. Maybe she's got a little bit left." He looked at her. "Have you ever had emotions come out of nowhere before?"

"You think she's psionic?" whispered Kathy. "Like a clairvoyant?"

"No. I've never felt anything like this before, an' I never saw ghosts either. At least, not outside of a video game." Hayley stared at the building. "Are you serious? Are we really going to sleep in a place where someone got gibbed?"

"Gibbed?" asked Kathy.

Eldon chuckled.

Kenny had no idea, but didn't show it.

"Gibbed is like when you shoot a person with a missile and they explode into chunks." Hayley pointed at the skeleton, and swept her arm to the right. "There's blood everywhere."

Noticing the size of the blood 'slick,' Kenny's eyes widened. "That kinda looks like a canid mutant's work... but..."

"You're wondering why it didn't eat a helpless kid," said Eldon.

"Yeah."

Eldon tossed the scrap of rope at him, bouncing it off his chest. "You said psionic. Ain't need much else to explain shit what don't make sense. She let it kill the dude who tied her, and"—he waved both hands over his head—"did some mind mojo on it to keep herself alive."

"You said that people always bring these... 'Scrags' back to civilization."

Katherine tucked her arm around Alyssa. "You think that man tried to drag her back to the city against her will?"

"Maybe. It's somewhere between official law and an unwritten code," said Kenny. "Anyone with any sense of decency'll usually try and explain that the world didn't end. Most of the real tribals think the entire world is like the Badlands. They don't know any different."

Kathy eyed the bloody rope. "If we find a solitary child, and they don't want us to take them back to civilization... would you let them run off alone?"

"Ain't an easy answer to that, hon." Kenny squinted into the darkening eastern sky, along the road. "If I thought they were alone and not trying to protect the rest of their family or tribe, no, I'd probably not let them run off on their own. These people aren't stupid. They're not animals, just uneducated. Whatever happened here, I can only guess at."

"We're clear," yelled Nasir. "Got sensors set up around the place. Nothing can get in without me knowing about it."

Two orb bots, each about the size of a man's head, circled the building in a slow glide, moving in opposite directions.

Kenny took the girls' hands, and walked with them over to the former office/convenience store. A trail of the same bloody child's footprints went inside. "Is that sentry going to shoot anything that moves? There could be Scrags in the area, and they usually have small kids doing the scouting."

"No." Nasir shook his head. "Sentinel Corporation units all have minimum size lock on the targeting electronics... unless the target is armed and moving in a hostile manner."

Kenny glanced at his daughters' pistols. "Is it gonna drill someone with a holstered weapon? Would it react to a sword or bow?"

"No." Nasir blinked. "A bow? Seriously?"

Kenny laughed. "Out here? Nothing surprises me."

# 17

# NECROMANCER

The Old Cowboy opened his eyes and directed a contemptuous gaze around the virtual recreation of Joey's apartment. He checked himself over, tugged on the sleeves of his black duster coat, patted his leather gun belt, and caressed the handles of his silver revolvers. It had been a while since he'd logged in to cyberspace *not* using a Division 9 deck.

His four-deck work rig could run rings around the Nishihama Necromancer, not to mention their ability to pass undetected within most systems. Still, the deck Proscion had bequeathed him before he—for all functional purposes—died, was still one hell of a deck for civilian use. Few cyberspace jockeys not working for major corporations or governments could afford a Grade 7 unit, and truth be told, the differences in two grades amounted to a smattering of memory capacity and slightly more processing power.

Of course, to Joey, using a weaker deck (even if it could still kick the snot out of most things he'd run into) only exhilarated him more. The skin of the old gunslinger fit him like a well-worn pair of comfortable shoes, as welcome as coming home after an overlong vacation.

He bowed his head, and a slow, bassy laugh welled up from deep in his throat. Nothing had particularly amused him, but he adored sounding like the bad guy from a horror holo. He'd almost forgotten about the special 'mood tweak' he'd programmed into this avatar. Other living users that came within a certain distance of him in the net would experience a sensation of paranormal fear, caused by his software forcing their deck to stimulate the amygdala. Almost no one manipulated moods like that, so the effect hit people many times harder due to surprise.

During his days of infiltrating for profit, he'd stumbled on an old technical manual locked away in a data node belonging to Endless Entertainment, a now-defunct media house that churned out schlock horror films. He still had about sixty of their titles on a neural stick somewhere, though he hadn't watched any since he'd been in high school. The documentation had been put together as a business plan to bring in 'TruMood' to EE holos, but the legal department had been too worried about what effect it could have on people, so it never caught on.

He concentrated on the starport data relay and his surroundings shifted. From the office, 'teleporting' on the net (much to the chagrin of the Sages) was legal, so those systems didn't have to overcome the tracking routines that kept things running. The effect there had been too fast to perceive, but using the Necromancer, and his old trusty software, the new location faded in over the course of three seconds.

Joey appeared in a small alley that resembled West City in most ways. The major difference showed in the lack of trash piled in the shadows. The virtual metropolis rendered in clean and tidy, a city spared the presence of real habitation. This part of town, in the shadow of the Edmonson Memorial Starport, had a bad reputation in meatspace. Few people who had the means to live wherever they chose wanted to dwell anywhere near a starport. Thus, two or three sectors in all directions had poor people, gangs, drugs, violence, and even a grey zone at the southwest.

No alarms went off, so he knew the daemons that monitored netspace hadn't detected his too-rapid movement. He never understood why the Sages had such a problem with people teleporting around. The only logical explanation he'd ever come up with involved a conspiracy with various software developers who sold 'vehicles' intended to make travel in the GlobeNet faster than walking. If people could teleport at will, those softs wouldn't be anywhere near as expensive.

"Money… always money." The old gunslinger frowned.

In his head, Joey grinned. He could say just about anything with this avatar's slow, gravelly voice, and it would sound menacing as all hell. Again he thought about Hayley/Cleopatra, who had singled him out for abuse because he 'took himself too seriously.'

*Soon, little one, vengeance will be mine!*

The look she'd given him when they first met for real, so terrified, small, and vulnerable, haunted him. Joey grumbled. Maybe he'd wait until she'd grown up, and then hit her with something annoying or embarrassing that wouldn't send her into therapy.

"Bah."

He stepped out from the alley and turned right, joining the flow of pedestrian traffic. Two men nearby looked around, clearly on edge. Joey smiled. When one made eye contact with him, he returned a dour look that sent the man scurrying away.

Inside, Joey grinned like a small boy who'd just scared his older sister.

Software-simulated advert bots glided along at the edges of the crowd, offering an array of virtual items as well as real food or snacks. The GlobeNet rendition of the starport appeared much the same as it did in reality, except for the handful of people shooting at each other with cartoony laser weapons. He'd seen actual laser weapons used, which generated a point-to-point beam that appeared in an instant. The gamers' laser weapons fired discrete projectiles consisting of streaks of colored light about a meter long that traveled slow enough see but not so slow the person (or creature) you fired at could dive out of the way. Those 'lasers' weren't the same as his six-guns, which represented attempts by background software to destroy other programs or users by corrupting them. If one of the gamers shot someone not playing the game, the laser blast wouldn't do anything more than create a momentary 'charred' appearance.

His pistols animated like guns, but in the background, his deck hammered the target user or program with malware, and since his Necromancer deck had the requisite hardware, a successful enough attack could overload the M3 port of another user and deliver a fatal shock to the person in the real world. Of course, such decks weren't legal, and often saw use only by the Syndicate, the NSK, and shadier corporations. In his time with Division 9, he'd already been involved in seventeen cybercrime investigations where they tracked down individuals using Black ICE. He had been sure two of them had the full blessing and knowledge of their employers, but no evidentiary trace could prove it.

Joey disregarded the crowd exchanging red and blue laser blasts, heading deep into the starport to a portal that existed only in netspace. Beyond lay the enormous purple crystal that represented the CPU cluster responsible for linking the GlobeNet to the MarsNet.

The old cowboy strolled into the cavernous chamber and gazed up at the thick beam of amethyst energy shooting into space. As soon as he desired to join it, he flew into the air, rocketing upward, skimming inches away from the glasslike surface of the crystal.

Despite knowing that his deck logged into the uplink, requested a MarsNet address, and patched over a quantum data relay, Joey lost himself in the abstraction of flying. He shot out past the hole in the roof, flanked by a few other live users: a man and a woman in boring business attire, a catgirl with a feline head and black/gold banded fur, and a couple in old-fashioned spacesuits.

A speck of light above grew as the Earth below him shrank to the size of a Gee-ball orb, becoming an impossible floating-in-outer-space rendition of a PubTran maglev terminal. He hadn't yet tried to teleport direct to Mars, unsure if the task of leaping networks would even work. MarsNet started decades after the GlobeNet, and generally had newer hardware that required a router translating between them. Attempting a direct connection to a Mars-based peer system could result in him riding the Technicolor Death Coaster out into the real world, dumping the connection no different from someone yanking his wire out unexpectedly.

The tram ride took twenty-two seconds, stopping at another 'orbital maglev station.' Whereas the invisible military channel he'd taken last time ended direct on the surface, the public one had another layer of hardware to go through. It didn't matter to Joey; he amused himself by scaring the norms that got close enough to experience his paranormal aura.

As soon as he sensed the link to MarsNet come online, he reached into the air and opened a virtual terminal window. Querying the network for 'The Bandau Group' brought up a simple map of Arcadia City's virtual shadow. Joey pushed deeper, breaching the normal user-level access with a few old passkeys he hadn't touched in at least a year. *Lazy bastards.* He chuckled. *Still using the same logins.* The floating map expanded, creating the effect of the point of view falling out of the sky to the street, before proceeding to plunge *into* the ground. The pretty graphics faded to a plain text list of address reservations.

He sifted down the list until he found the registration for the secure IPv12 address of the Bandau Group's human resources server. Joey fed that address to a teleportation soft he'd written at fourteen.

The ancient gunslinger reached into his coat and pulled out a large, black silk handkerchief. He snapped it forward, and it hardened into a black disc. After placing the disk on the ground, he jumped into the hole.

Pulsing cyan light raced along the walls of an inky dark tunnel. The vertical drop became horizontal flight, and gradually pivoted until he sailed straight upward. He glided to a halt with his boots an inch above the floor in the middle of a cube-shaped room with silicon grey walls and a three-foot tall CPU crystal. A quick step to the side prevented him from falling back down the opening. He stooped and grasped the edge, lifting the 'hole' off the floor as a patch of silk once more. At his mental command, his deck ran two active anti-detection programs designed to prevent the network from sensing his presence and triggering a breach alarm.

*I could probably sell this routine for quite a bit... but as soon as I do, whoever bought it would sell it too, or hack it, and then it would be everywhere, and they'd plug that bug in the user-detection routine.* His teleport program attacked the 'heartbeat' process that checked every discrete node within the MarsNet to see if any active users or software constructs were present. Whenever it came back with zero, it put the node into a suspend state to save resources. Joey's teleport soft hacked the pulse to *insert* a user's hardware tag into the node's current 'object inventory,' while removing it from their current node. Most deck jockeys attempted to teleport by sending a command to the GlobeNet roughly equivalent to 'move me to X.' He edited the node inventory rather than adjusted the user's location pointer.

Joey took a few seconds to bask in his superiority.

If anyone else had found that trick, they had done as he had—and kept it for themselves.

After cracking his knuckles, Joey approached one of the six onyx slabs hanging in midair around the CPU crystal. Walking bogged down, making a knee-deep run in heavy mud seem easy by comparison. The actual effect of taking each step occurred four seconds after he desired to.

*Fuck lag.* He grinned. If he could pull this off from Earth, not only would it save him a long flight, it would be bragging rights galore. Step by plodding step, he approached the first data node. The ancient gunslinger reached into his coat again, and withdrew a creature resembling a beaver the size of a large dog.

"Grant Williams," said the gunslinger in a low, deep voice.

The DataMole nodded.

Joey dropped it, and it scampered around the onyx slabs—data storage nodes—hunting for any and all occurrences of the words 'Grant Williams.' Since the DataMole soft ran locally in the network, the dutiful creature scurried about the nodes much faster than Joey could have. It turned up twenty-six hits.

He went straight for Grant's user account in the Bandau network, peeled the mirror-silver data tile open, and extracted the encrypted password. A wave of his hand brought up another terminal window (three seconds later), and he plugged the scrambled text into a decryption routine. Starting it took forever, but once the codebreaking software kicked in, it zipped along.

After standing there for twelve minutes watching it grind, Joey grew impatient.

He could open a back channel into his work terminal and have *it* hammer the crypto, but that added a layer of risk. What he planned to do to Grant crossed certain legal boundaries and could get him fired, or worse: complicate things with Nina. While she would probably understand his seeking revenge on the man who'd been ruining Katherine's life, getting caught in a legal tangle would no doubt make it difficult for her to stay with him if she wanted to keep her job. And being that they literally owned her body, he wasn't sure she *could* just quit... at least not without being stuck in some shitty Class 1 or 2 pity shell they gave her as a going away present.

Nina was many things, and vain ranked somewhere in the top ten. She wouldn't last long in a body that appeared obviously fake. She'd do something drastic. He couldn't really call that vanity in the true sense, more her desperate fear of perceiving herself as no longer human.

On that somber note, he decided against conscripting his Division 9 terminal into the encryption breaking, and resigned himself to keep waiting.

"What are you doing in here?" asked a man.

The old cowboy shifted in a slow turn, eyes peering over the lapel of his duster at a thirtyish man in a sharp suit, the same metallic-silicon hue as the walls. Joey recognized the face right away, one of the defensemen Grant had somehow talked into helping him go after Katherine.

"Nothing you need concern yourself with, boy." Joey turned to face him, making the lag appear to be a horror-holo slow walk. Strands of white hair trailed like cobwebs from his head, lofted in the non-wind of his motion.

A second terminal screen opened, visible only to Joey. He adored danger, but he had no interest in being an idiot. Getting into net combat over a Mars-Earth uplink was worse than trying to take on a real deck cowboy while using a senshelmet. He'd rather do something with better odds, like try to kill a thirteen-foot-tall Class 5 cyborg with a ball-peen hammer.

*Time to roll the dice.* He duplicated the teleport hole soft and renamed it 'GoingDown.'

The defenseman's sneering scowl faded to a look of confusion as the mood-altering routine got to work on his brain. The old gunslinger's lips parted in a sinister smile, exposing yellowed teeth.

"I've been lookin' for a soul just like yours, *boy*." Joey leaned forward. He spliced the code in the window as fast as he could think it, pasting in route uplink information for an Earth network address used as a 'testing room' for Dreamcraft Entertainment. A subnetwork offset from the GlobeNet with an entire planet's worth of space.

"W-what the fuck is going on?" The man took a step back and grasped his suit jacket at the breast with his left hand.

"Do you believe in demons, boy?" The old gunslinger stopped advancing and flicked his coat back off his guns. Katherine had been a miserable bitch to him for years, but hearing her say she'd done it only out of worry he'd get himself killed had taken some of the venom out of it. He tried to think of her as a little girl, back when they'd been close. Picturing this man picking on that innocent version of Katherine bled anger into his virtual persona. "I was hoping you'd go for that little pop gun of yours."

For a second, the man seemed intimidated enough to freeze.

Joey wasn't about to let the guy run; he only wanted time to complete the routine. As soon as the compile finished, he stuffed the GoingDown soft into the local node's memory. An upload bar crept across the lower edge of his vision.

The old gunslinger teased at the handles of his pistols. He'd been moving creepy-slow, and so far it didn't seem as though the defense operator had realized he'd logged in from Earth. The idea of someone even trying a hack over that link defied plausibility. No one would ever even think someone would be that stupid.

"Shit." The man pulled a coppery-colored pistol from his jacket with a large oval middle covered by an array of little pipes and tubes. A dish at the front complimented fish-fin shapes at the back end. It discharged a stream of dark green energy surrounded by five donuts of paler green light that struck Joey in the chest before he could even flinch.

Fortunately, the barrage of harmful code the man attempted to send into Joey's net presence had to go down the same Earth-Mars link that created the lag. As the Necromancer connected to Joey's brain sat at the Earth-side end of that link, his countermeasure completed loading and had to wait two seconds for the incoming data stream to arrive.

In cyberspace, the energy beam washed over the ancient cowboy with less effect than a water gun.

"What the…" The man shook in fear. "What are you?"

The old man laughed. "I am the darkness. You feel it, don't you? That dread crawling up your spine."

Upload complete.

"You…" The defenseman seemed to get over the preternatural fear effect and shot him a glower. "You're on Earth! What the hell do you think—"

Joey triggered the GoingDown soft. Both he and the defenseman floated into the air as if the room around them had become an elevator cab hurtling toward the ground. Time seemed to freeze. *Please work. Please work. Please work.* The hardware hosting the Bandau Group's virtual HR server node accepted Joey's command to redirect all processing to the earthbound location for two minutes. This flipped things on end, and gave Joey local freedom while the defenseman had to suffer under the interminable three-second lag.

A thunderous crash filled the room as the walks buckled and cracked, leaking bright cyan energy fluid. The defenseman slammed into the floor while Joey remained hovering. His operating system spawned a virtual machine, running a copy of the Dreamcraft Entertainment sandbox. The old cowboy lunged at the frozen defenseman and pinned him against the wall, nose to nose.

"Welcome to Earth, boy. You asked who I am?" The ancient gunslinger hurled the man into one of the data-storage slabs, a floating block of onyx that didn't move on impact; the man slapped into it and slid downward, screaming and reacting to the charge only after he hit the floor. "I'm the thing that people don't think is real. The demon in the net, the bogey man." He pulled one of his engraved silver six-guns and levelled it off at the man's head. "I'm friends with Death. We play cards sometimes. Alas, the bastard's not a bad player. I owe him a soul."

Joey fired.

With a sharp *bang* accompanied by a spectral wail, a smoking two-inch skull came careening out of the barrel and flew into the man's face. The spot blackened in an instant, and a long trail of ectoplasmic energy exuded from the other side of the defenseman's skull. Three seconds after being shot, the man flipped over onto his chest and screamed. The alien ray gun fell from his grip and disappeared in a flash of bright blue pixels. He grabbed his head in both hands, continuing to scream.

Joey shot him again in the chest and stomped over. The defenseman screamed from the second bullet at the same time the old cowboy slammed him against the wall. "Your buddy Grant asked you to mess with someone."

Blood trickled out of the man's nose.

The old one grinned. "You feel that, don't you? I bet you've got one hell of a headache right now. The next one reaches into meatspace and ends you for real." He pulled the man close, letting him savor corpse-breath. "You're alive for one reason only: to send a message to the others. I know who they are, and if any of you interfere with her again, I'll drag you with me straight to Hell."

He raised the six-gun under the man's chin and estimated how much of a data blast he'd need to send enough Black ICE down the line to render the man unconscious but not dead. He pivoted the gun to the side, and fired at a trajectory that sent a flap of cheek and several teeth flying. A malware module hidden in a wrapper of innocuous data flew to Mars and burrowed into the defenseman's deck, causing it to electrify its M3 port, shocking his real-world brain.

Joey cringed with the faintest trace of guilt, remembering the agony he'd experienced when the black dragon AI nailed him with a similar attack, only it hadn't metered the jolt with care to cause a knockout... it had wanted to bake his cerebellum. In a paradox of bad being good, Joey lived only because his deck at the time had been so cheap it burned out before it could kill him.

As the defenseman lost consciousness, his avatar disintegrated in a shower of spiraling white numbers and flakes of silicon grey. Joey twirled the gun over his finger and stuck it back in the holster. Amid the quiet room, he waited for GoingDown to stop running, and the node's rendering to snap back to the hardware on Mars.

Once the heavy blanket of lag came over him again, he tapped his boot. A few minutes later, the encryption routine stopped, exposing Grant's authentication credentials. With a giant shit-eating grin, Joey opened a user-interface terminal as Grant, and went spelunking in the law firm's network, viewing the files and storage folders as if sitting at a desk in the outside world. It didn't take him too long to locate some current case records. He didn't really know what would be the most sensitive parts, nor did he want to ask Katherine as it would make her complicit in some highly shady shit.

He noticed a few files marked with red stars, and opened them. Two contained recorded interviews where Grant and some other Bandau lawyers interviewed clients. In the first, the client admitted his employers were 'fully culpable' in whatever had triggered a lawsuit against his company, and instructed the Bandau team to do whatever they could to make sure the case went in their favor, even if defending it cost more than settling as the company didn't want the bad PR. He dug a little deeper on that file and discovered the client to be Nutri-Joy health products, and the lawsuit stemmed from a tainted batch of baby food. While the company had fixed the error, they feared a public backlash.

Joey grabbed the recording and sent it, using Grant's credentials, to the lawyers representing the plaintiffs. He found another few tidbits of evidence in unrelated court proceedings where Bandau's attempts to collect usable evidence to exonerate their client had instead confirmed guilt, and they'd kept it buried. He, again using Grant's login, sent several pieces of said evidence to the UCF Prosecutor's Office in Primus City. He'd come here to skewer Grant, but he might take all of Bandau down. Fortunately, Katherine hadn't worked for them, merely married this asshole.

Figuring his work thus far would have a strong negative impact on Grant's quality of life, he reached for the button to logout, but hesitated with a devilish smile.

Grant, awesome guy he was, ordered high end vat-grown sashimi lunch for everyone in the office who wasn't partnered. Workers from paralegals to executive assistants, to maintenance contractors got a C180 lunch on the company. Adding in a C200 bottle of sake each worked out to C42,560 on Grant's expense account. *Nah. Grant's more generous than that.* He repeated the order to all the client companies Grant had worked with, sending a thank you on behalf of the Bandau Group. Spending C715,590 as a thank you seemed like the magnanimous Grant he'd heard Katherine talking about before everything went to shit.

Joey laughed.

He pulled out the hole again, and teleported to a commerce node he'd made frequent use of before having to leave Mars. The hardware repeater sat somewhere underground in the real world, on a fiberoptic main linking Arcadia to Primus. From there, he got into the banking system and pried open Grant's account.

An hour or so of analyzing later, he found a series of withdrawals commented with smile emoticons. Tracing them led to the PID of one Lana Paris, a nineteen-year-old student at the Arts Academy of Arcadia. A brief search of her activity matched up use of their NetMinis to make payments at the same time and place in local restaurants and motels around the school. Joey glanced at the timestamps and fumed.

*Bastard's been cheating on her for over a year.* He gathered all that data together and shot it off to Katherine. *That should tilt the divorce in her favor a little.*

For the cherry atop the revenge sundae, he used Grant's PID to connect to Martian Fantasies, and ordered an eighteen-inch chocolate penis, accompanied by a card reading: 'I've heard you're about to have a bad day. Might want to use this to loosen up a bit before you meet your new roommates. Oh, and mess with her again, I will find you. When I do, it won't be made out of chocolate.'

Joey's limp body in the real world grinned from ear-to-ear. The old gunslinger offered a grim stare at nothing in particular before bowing bowed his head.

His Nishihama Necromancer processed a logout command, and the world faded to black.

# ETAMURA

**M**asaru stared at the business end of the JSDF soldier's assault rifle for a silent moment. He shifted his gaze to her face; beneath the fear of him, and pain from her injuries, she seemed at once beautiful and... powerful. A confidence he had seldom seen in the eyes of a woman shone like the finish of a gem peeking out from beneath layers of dirt. All the women he'd associated with had fallen into one of two types: The first knew who he was and were willing to trade their dignity and bodies on the off chance he would take such a fancy to them they would marry into fabulous wealth. The second type thought him handsome and didn't much care about anything more than a hook-up.

Of course, a third type *did* exist—women who didn't give him a second glance, but he never paid attention to them.

Between those seeking financial security and those seeking a fun night, he couldn't remember any of them being *real*. All of them played a character to get what they wanted. Of course, he understood the type of women given to showing up in his vicinity hardly represented a wide selection, but he hadn't yet met a girl like this.

Something else lurked beneath the desperation in her stare—anger. He got the sense she *hated* being at a disadvantage. Masaru could almost taste the resentment on her at being vulnerable. He caught himself tilting his head and smiling as if watching a wounded tiger defending its home.

"Why are you looking at me like that?" asked the woman. "Go away before I have to hurt you."

Masaru tugged at his suit jacket. "Do the locals here often roam about in a Yoshinori?"

She lowered the rifle about an inch and her eyebrows moved closer together. "All right, I'll give you that. Who are you and what are you doing here?"

"Moto, Masaru." He rendered a slight bow. "I was on my way to a business meeting. We were shot down. I"—eyes closed, he offered a silent prayer to the Kami to watch over Shuji—"am the only survivor."

She let her rifle rest across her lap; relief at not having to hold its weight any longer showed clear in her expression. "Abe Noriko. Sergeant, Japan State Defense Force."

"You are hurt." Masaru stepped over rubble to approach her, and squatted by her side. "I saw your aircraft."

Noriko shook her head, seeming sad and angry at the same time. "We were looking for an air patrol that disappeared around this region. The pilot was new, so they thought he'd gone too low to sightsee the ruins and crashed. We sustained ground fire from multiple individuals with portable anti-aircraft missiles, and went down. They hit us before we could get ready. We're just a medevac flight. The Herons don't have onboard weapons." She looked at the dirt between her boots. "I was the only one left after the firefight."

Masaru opened his stimpak case and removed three of the remaining six. "You've lost quite a bit of blood."

"Yeah. Kinda happens when you get shot." She grimaced as he pulled the fabric of her jumpsuit away from her right thigh. "Ngh... ow."

The navy blue material had turned black around a bullet wound about a third the way down the length of her thigh. Offset to the outside, the trajectory appeared to have missed bone. She fought hard not to cry out as he prodded a finger around the site, testing for firmness before attempting a stimpak shot. It wouldn't do any good to inject it into the open wound. Noriko stifled whimpers and looked away from him.

"Yes, it hurts. Stop playing with it and give me the injection."

Masaru thanked the Kami Joey was not here to make a crass remark. Noriko appeared to catch the unintentional innuendo and blushed. A testament to his willpower, he showed no reaction. He flicked the safety cap off the narrow end of the stimpak and pressed it to her skin, two fingers' width above the hole. As the four-inch red cylinder emitted a soft *hiss*, he reached under her leg and found the exit wound. Noriko let out a gasp of pain as his fingertip made contact with a hole similar in size to the entry wound.

Tears streamed down her face, but she said nothing, and made almost no sound.

"It is curious that these people have Indirium ammunition." He tossed aside the used stimpak and administered a second injection. "And anti-aircraft missiles."

Pink foam roiled within the bullet wound. Noriko looked about to speak, but instead bit down on the armored glove over her left index finger. She let out a muffled scream and abandoned her grip on the rifle to grab Masaru's hand. He'd taken a few arrows during his kenjutsu training, and imagined the pins-and-needles from a bullet channel would likely be far worse. She continued screaming around her bit finger while squeezing the feeling out of his hand. Over the span of about two minutes, the hole in her leg shrank until it sealed to a nasty-looking bruise.

Noriko went limp; he hadn't realized every muscle in her body had tensioned until she slumped against the wall, out of breath. Masaru gave her a third stimpak, hoping the tissue damage had been repaired enough by now that some of its nanobots would work on bolstering her blood supply.

He sat atop a rectangular white box with JSDF markings nearby, about three feet long and one around, and fed her water from the genesis canteen on the ground by her knee. Reservoirs of hydrogen and oxygen combined into water at the push of a button, producing a weak but steady stream. Cryonic vapor wafted from the bottom as the system's coolant kicked in. She drank a little and waved him off.

"Thanks for the stimpaks... my whole leg is numb now." Noriko grinned and dabbed sweat from her forehead. "That's an improvement by the way. You must've been expecting a rather interesting business meeting to be carrying those things."

Masaru laughed. "I got in the habit of carrying them after following a reckless fool around in the UCF."

After a few more breaths, she raised her head and looked at him. "Does your NetMini work?"

"No signal." He took it out to verify nothing had changed, and scowled when he again received the error. "I would suggest that my employer would come searching for me, but the JSDF should arrive first seeing as how you have been here longer."

"I'm not so sure about that." She let her head go back, and stared up into the sky. "It's going to be dark soon. You should probably stay here inside the wall. They haven't found me yet."

"What? You don't think they will come looking for their missing aircraft and crew?" He blinked.

Noriko let off a weak chuckle. "That's what we were doing here. This place has become like the Bermuda Triangle. Our Heron is the seventh aircraft to vanish here in three months. Half of command thinks there is something unexplained going on. They may be unwilling to lose more people."

"There is no doubt an unexplained situation here." Masaru frowned. "But it is how these people have obtained such weapons. There is nothing 'magical' about this."

"I agree." Noriko rolled her right foot around. "I think I can feel my toes again. I don't know where they've gotten these weapons, but they've clearly had no training. The man who shot me had me dead to rights. He came out of nowhere, less than ten feet behind me while I was firing on others in front of me. I didn't know he was there until he shot me in the leg. He wasn't even sighting over it... like he'd never seen a rifle before. I should be dead."

He furrowed his brow. "Perhaps one of the other missing aircraft had been carrying weapons and equipment?"

"I suppose, but where would they have gotten the means to shoot down the first one?"

"An interesting paradox."

"Right." She rubbed her leg.

Masaru gazed up at the vast expanse of indigo overhead for a moment in silence. "The sky fading dark, no clouds no stars no pale moon, my path lies unknown."

"Kuromori," she whispered.

"Yes." Masaru smiled. "I think I slept through most of that class."

Noriko grinned. "I enjoyed literature, but ugh… math." She indicated the white box. "Move a sec?"

He stood.

She grasped it, and pulled herself to sit up with a grunt. "There's enough rations in here to last six people six days. I think I can walk now, but I'd rather give it the night to recover." She removed two square boxes. The one she handed him bore a stamp of 'JSDF Field Ration C.' Hers had an 'A.' She clutched it in both hands and pressed her thumbs into two buttons, one at each of the front corners. After holding them down for three seconds, the box emitted a chirp followed by a faint sucking noise.

Masaru mimicked the gesture, looking confused.

"It's rehydrating the food… the delay is to prevent accidental activation." She opened the lid on hers, revealing eight pieces of sushi packed tight, next to a small channel that contained a tiny toothpaste-style tube, a plastic ampule of soy sauce, and a cute little plastic jar of pickled ginger.

His contained tuna maki rolls, though the side area held the same accessories. He plucked the two-inch long tube out and held it up with two fingers. Aside from the word 'wasabi' in black letters, it had no other markings. He eyed the 'sushi,' trying to wrap his brain around what it must've looked like before the ration box rehydrated it. In spite of his current situation, he regarded it with the same face he'd have given a waiter bringing him poached rat.

"Oh, I hate the C type rations…" Noriko squirted a thin stream of green paste from her tube over the contents of her ration box. "It's supposed to be spicy tuna, but they forgot the spicy part."

Only as a gesture of respect at her sharing her food did he partake. He removed a flimsy pair of plastic chopsticks from the underside of the lid and proceeded to frustrate himself trying to pick up the first piece of maki with them. They bent enough to where the food kept slipping loose. Noriko, evidently having more experience with these rations, ignored them. She removed her glove and ate with her fingers.

After another few minutes, Masaru set aside the urge to apply his katana to the food, and also used his fingers.

"I am impressed," said Noriko, around a mouthful. "Most new recruits only try those silly chopsticks for twenty seconds. I don't even know why they bother including them."

Masaru mumbled, his mouth full of the saddest excuse for food he'd yet experienced. He raised a finger in a gesture of pause, finished chewing, and swallowed. "I am not the sort of man who surrenders easily… and"—he couldn't suppress a slight grin—"whoever had the gall to refer to this as maki should humble himself before his ancestors."

She laughed, clamping a hand over mouth a split second later with a wide-eyed look of 'oops.' He caught himself staring at her face, admiring the momentary glimpse of the woman beneath the armor and desperation of a situation out of control. In the span of a few short minutes, she'd likely gone from expecting to die out here to laughing at his joke. He looked at this person before him and beheld a woman unlike any other he had ever known. Strength, vulnerability, fear, courage, and hope all existed at once within her. Compassion as well, for she wouldn't have been here if not for the desire to rescue some other pilot. Valor, for she alone survived an assault that claimed the rest of the crew.

Masaru's smile flattened. He stared into his food. He had not seen any bodies around the crash site. Had she buried them or had someone else come by and taken the corpses? In her state, it seemed quite unlikely she had done much but drag herself away from the wreckage in search of a better place to hide. Perhaps scavengers took the bodies for their armor, clothes, and equipment. Would Shuji suffer a similar fate?

Noriko's grin tamed to a look of concern. "What is it?"

"Hmm?" He forced himself to eat another piece of the tuna roll.

"Your whole presence just changed."

"My apologies. I was merely thinking of my friend."

Noriko bowed her head with reverence. "I'm sorry."

"These outcasts will atone."

She raised her head, her expression as steely as his determination. "Yes, but we are not going to take them on alone. Miyakonojo is within the territory of Kurotai Electronics. Even though it is an interior issue, they have left this place alone for too long. I intend to insist the JSDF step in and clear this ruin."

*It is my hope they fare better than the Meiji bots.* "Perhaps a cooperative effort would yield better results."

"Kurotai Hideo is too cautious," said Noriko. "He believes those who live among these ruins are harmless, but they are not. The JSDF is aware of a separatist movement in this region, calling themselves Etamura."

"Outcasts?" Masaru's arm stalled, another piece of maki an inch from his lips. He shook his head and tossed the roll into his mouth.

"Is that contempt I hear?" Noriko raised an eyebrow. "For the people or the term?"

He chuckled out his nostrils. "The term."

"So you agree with them? They call themselves that because they wish to be cast out from the feudal nonsense." She closed the lid on her empty ration box.

Masaru rushed the last four pieces before he could taste them. "Some CEOs would have you killed for calling it nonsense."

A wry grin spread across her face. "Some Shogun would have you killed for calling them CEOs."

Masaru gave her the side-eye, but smiled. "Is that why you joined the JSDF? To 'stay modern?'"

Noriko collected her rifle, holding it in a relaxed grip generally aimed at the doorway. "I suppose. My family's from Kyoto. I'm the youngest... two brothers. Satoshi was the first in my family to join the JSDF. He said he did it to pay for school, but he hasn't quit and it's been four years. He wants to protect Japan. *All of* Japan, as do I."

Masaru gazed into the sky again, his voice wistful. "Kyoto... Quite modern, and an unusual situation. Rather than a CEO, it is ruled by the university board."

"Japan Technical University," said Noriko. "They understand the foolishness of backward ways, but also the foolishness of angering insane men with large guns."

He chuckled. "Have you ever wondered how it started?"

"Yes... When I was attending classes, I met many people who believe psionics were involved. You know of Nakamura-sama?"

Masaru nodded. "A long-ago CEO of White Orchid... the first shogun. He rejected the 'westernization' of Japan and it was his idea to reestablish the ancient ways."

"Right..." She tapped a finger on her rifle. "And you think everyone else in power all just said 'hey, that's a great idea!' and did it? There's a lot of people who think Nakamura used telepaths or some other psionic means to force his vision on the country. What sane person would agree to return to Imperial Japan?"

Masaru thought back to various history classes he'd had over the years. To combat the instability brought on by the Korean aggression, Nakamura had—for a brief time—managed to get all of Japan to unite with him as the supreme ruler. He remembered reading about a long-dead CEO named Oro, who had abruptly discarded the trappings of the 1600s as well as Nakamura's claim on the country. He couldn't begin to guess why, nor would worrying now what had happened centuries ago matter much.

"Perhaps. The people of Okinawa were desperate. Dressing in costume in exchange for protection seemed a small trade."

She wiggled her foot again, seeming pleased. "But they also gave up much freedom. White Orchid enforces a strict caste system... they actually have 'eta' there. The samurai can kill them without repercussion. That needs to change. Prefecture governments need to stop warring with each other."

"An admirable goal, but not one I would repeat too loudly. The NSK prefers things as they are. They make too much money arranging deals between the prefectures and the outside world."

"And assassinations, and spying, and data theft... all things that they could continue to do among corporations. Japan, as a country, can be unified again and the corporations can still do what they do... but we need to stop letting them settle trade disputes with soldiers and hover-tanks."

Masaru cringed inside thinking of the news report from earlier in the day. "Madness."

"Yeah." She leaned back and exhaled.

"So what of your middle brother?" He glanced at her.

Noriko grinned. "Amida is a veterinarian. He is a father of twin boys, eleven months old." She made faces as if the babies sat right in front of her. "His wife, Sora, is *so* sweet, but painfully shy. The woman can barely talk if more than two people she doesn't know are in the room."

He figured her for around his age, somewhere between twenty and twenty-three. "Your oldest brother will spend his career with the JSDF?"

"Oh, I don't think so... He's taking classes, working toward his doctorate in exogeology. It's his dream to help find new worlds to colonize. Of course, he wants to do it from the safety of Earth by crunching data."

Masaru chuckled.

"What about you?" She cocked an eyebrow at him. "Any family?"

"I have an older brother who is everything our father expected, and a much younger sister who everyone—including myself—dotes over like a princess. I have made a career out of falling just shy of my father's expectations." He glanced off, flicking his thumb and forefinger.

"Oh. Sorry. I imagine that couldn't have been easy having a demanding parent."

"For a while, I stopped even trying to please him. My father's quiet disapproval never changed no matter how hard I worked... or didn't."

"I suppose I was fortunate and unfortunate with mine. They're farmers. Honest, hard-working, tolerant... but far from wealthy. I didn't join the JSDF for school though. I want to protect Japan."

"Is that why you became a medic?"

She laughed, covering her mouth after a split second. "Stop making me laugh," she whisper-shouted. "No... At the moment, I'm just an infantry soldier. I was on the transport as security. Maybe I will opt in for a different MOS when I get back." She winked. "Maybe I'll try to go medic. So you work for Kurotai, huh?"

He gave her a surprised look, until she pointed at the stylized 'K' logo pin on his jacket. He chuckled. "Yes."

Noriko fiddled with her armband, a small terminal embedded in her armor. "Nothing moving near us. I think I'm good to walk."

"Good. I was planning to keep heading west until I could obtain a signal."

"We should go southwest. If whatever is jamming communications is in the city center, that direction will bring us away from it fastest."

He nodded.

"We'll go together at first light."

Masaru smiled at hearing that. Though he'd known her for only an hour or so, he wanted to spend more time with her. He could put no price on seeing this woman for who she really was, as opposed to some desperate debutante clambering for the attention of the CEO's son. Perhaps some hidden need not to be judged by his station had prodded him to give a false surname. "That is an excellent idea."

"So..." She checked her rifle's ammo display. "Think they'll come looking for you? How long have you worked for Kurotai?"

"*Worked?*" He tilted his head and rubbed his chin for a few seconds before smiling at her. "This is my first day."

# 19

# THE MALL

Kenny flicked his fingers at the steering wheel. He'd spent the day driving and glancing every few minutes at the rearview mirror. Hayley had barely slept in the gas station. Something about the place had kept her on edge. He'd heard rumors about a type of psionic, clairvoyants, who could read psychic imprints in objects and places. She said she'd never experienced anything like that before, but whatever energy had collected in that place hadn't affected anyone else. Alyssa didn't bat an eyelash at the little office, though perhaps being a few months away from fifteen made her 'too old?' Some of the fringe paranormal crowd swore up and down that children had more sensitivity to things. Hayley wasn't exactly a 'little kid' either at eleven. She'd also started acting odd as soon as they entered the Badlands.

Dread.

One couldn't spend eighteen years running in and out of the Badlands without hearing people talk about it having a consciousness of sorts. Half the artifact hunters and explorers he'd run into believed the land to be alive, and not in a metaphorical sense. How else could they explain why the government had made no real attempt to 'retake' the Badlands after the Cyborg Reclamation Project failed? People like Eldon blamed money. People like the ones telling stories said the land wanted it that way. It craved the violence and death, and didn't want anyone to leave. Electronics and tech could fail at random, often when most inconvenient.

He'd added the biodiesel engine because of those stories, but even he had only half-thought it necessary. An old wives' tale superstition. Random equipment failure had never happened to him before. Maybe because *it* knew he would come back. For all he knew, *it* didn't care who killed who. *It* would let him leave, knowing he'd come back, and knowing he'd kill Nibblers, raiders, or anyone else it sent his way. Didn't matter if he killed them or they killed him.

Hayley lay draped against Kathy in the back seat, mouth agape, sleeping. For a little while that morning, she seemed to get over the unusual fear. As soon as they'd gotten a couple hundred meters away from that gas station, she'd gone back to normal. She still did *not* like it out here, and it made him regret taking her along. Kathy had joked that five or six days without logging in to the GlobeNet would amount to torture, but the way she said it *felt* wrong out here didn't jibe with her whining about the inconvenience of being deprived her beloved games.

They had decided to leave the other truck behind, partly because of it being a modern vehicle, but more so Kenny's superstitious nature. The last man to drive it died a horrible death, and the whole area around it did seem off somehow. If any truth existed about the 'weird shit,' as Eldon called it, he didn't want it following him.

Maybe on the way back, they'd stop for the truck.

Kenny fixed his gaze into the distance, and kept on driving.

Hayley awoke late in the afternoon. She kept quiet, staring balefully out the window at the passing land. Her expression made him think of a child used to being hit for making noise, afraid to speak even at a whisper. It ground at his guts to see her like that. Alyssa bopped her head side to side, listening to music via headphones from her NetMini. Kathy tried to nap while Eldon kept a vigilant watch for threats. Nasir sat in idle silence.

Attempting to take a more direct course, Kenny abandoned roads and followed a raven's path as much as the terrain allowed. At 6:32 p.m. local time, he stopped the truck. After about twenty minutes of leg-stretching and everyone relieving themselves, he drove on.

Nasir pulled his control board onto his lap and turned it on. Within two minutes of him fiddling with something, Hayley leaned across Kathy's lap to watch him. He gave her a somewhat patronizing 'don't touch anything but it's okay to watch' look, and kept working. Light from the mini-screens tinted the back half of the truck neon green.

"That's a Teradyne Silver Grade 3, isn't it?" asked Hayley. "Those screens look like NotSo guts. You frankensteined it, didn't you?"

"Uhh, yeah." Nasir glanced at her. "But this isn't for games."

Hayley grinned. "I got a Neko Wildcat, Grade 5. What are you running on that thing? Tera-OS 6? That retro monochroma theme is kinda cool. I guess it fits this wasteland hell, and well, you don't need too much under the hood to drive bots so a Grade 3 isn't so bad."

"Yeah... OS 6." He glanced at her.

She put on a haughty affect. "I'm running Mewnix, compile 118.4."

"Doesn't that come standard on the Neko decks? That whole stupid cat thing?" Nasir smirked.

"It's not stupid. It's cute." Hayley huffed. "And it makes people underestimate me. And it's not standard. I added some Onyx Blade libraries, so I'm basically running a Mewnix UI environment with a Nishihama Revenge kernel. My kitty has sharp claws."

Nasir caught Kenny watching in the mirror and locked eyes. His expression said 'where did you find this kid?' "Uhh, nice."

"Don't ask me." Kenny grinned. "I just dig around in the dirt lookin' for shiny shit."

Eldon whistled. "Lot of money in that shiny shit."

"Yeah... that there is." Kenny tapped the Navcon. "We're getting close to Colorado Springs. I'm looking for a place to hole up for the night now, it'll get dark before we arrive and I don't fancy rollin' in there at night. Not keepin' my hopes up."

A few hours later, with the sun going down and nothing but flat scrubland as far as he could see, Kenny pulled off the remnants of a paved road and stopped. The air tasted like wild grass and cut hay, but despite the wide-open terrain all around them, nothing appeared dangerous. He had Kathy and the girls set up their sleeping bags in the truck bed to keep them a little more out of sight as well as away from bugs.

Amid the stillness of open country, the low thrum of their hover modules seemed loud enough to attract every raider for miles. Fortunately, only a pack of squealers showed up. The giant prairie dog like animals were docile unless attacked—at which point they could get vicious—and meandered on without incident. Nasir's bots orbited their camp all night, the faint thrum of their ion engines providing constant background noise.

AN HOUR BEFORE SUNRISE, KENNY HAD ENSURED EVERYONE HAD A RATION AND answered nature's call. By 7 a.m., they had gotten underway again.

"I hate this vest," whined Hayley. "It's so heavy. Can I take it off?"

"Sure," said Kenny. "Once we're home."

Hayley frowned. Alyssa stifled a giggle and pulled up some game on her NetMini they could both play. The girls huddled over the small holo-panel as the device filled the truck with medieval sounding music and the *clang* of swords.

At 8:14 a.m. local time, the ruins of Colorado Springs came into view. It looked like it had been a large city prior to the Corporate War. The road he'd followed, named '25' on the Navcon, went past dozens of rotting houses on the right, which had been overrun with trees and grass. A scattering of old utility poles remained standing, and the vegetation-encrusted wreckage of a couple three-century-old combat aircraft stuck out of the ground among the crumbling structures.

Eventually, Route 25 brought them closer to signs of the city center on the right. Squarish concrete towers, pockmarked by the effects of bombs and rockets, stood largely untouched by human hands for years.

An off-ramp from 25 led to a wide street awash with dust. He steered around wrecked cars, a flipped-upside-down tank a short distance from a crater big enough to swallow it, and ran over a handful of ancient traffic lights. A cluster of buildings up ahead on the left caught his eye as they looked like a mall. He cut straight across the intersection, bounced up over the curb, and slalomed past husks of old cars littering the parking area.

Alyssa cracked up giggling.

"Huh? What?" Kenny glanced over his shoulder at her.

She pointed. "Look! That sign! What the hell?"

He followed her finger, which aimed at a massive sign made of steel I-beams painted in green and rust, bearing the word 'DICKS' in block capitals. As soon as Hayley saw it, she turned scarlet in the face and couldn't stop laughing.

"What did they sell there?" asked Alyssa with a suggestive eyebrow wiggle.

"No idea, but we're not going in there." Kenny drove past it to the right, at an entrance that appeared to head into the mall's central concourse. He'd seen enough malls to recognize major stores on the outside had their own entrances, and others offered access to the space between shops inside. The place he wanted to find, 'Crystal Emporium' didn't sound like one of the enormous self-contained stores attached to the outside. He figured it occupied a smaller space in the interior.

"This the place?" Eldon leaned forward to peer at the building. "Damn, that's pretty big. Didn't think they made shit that large back then."

"You've seen the sector 214 mall... or 29P. Same concept... only back then, we had the whole damn continent to work with and didn't need to stack shit upwards." Kenny laughed.

"Eww, Dad. Really?" Alyssa scrunched up her nose. "Twenty-Nine Palms is like where the freaks go."

"Being poor doesn't make someone a freak." Kenny brought the truck to a stop with two tires up on the sidewalk.

"It's not that. They're *freaks*. Half of them aren't even wearing clothes, and... ugh. There's whole GlobeNet sites devoted to posting pictures of 'sightings' at 29P. Some of them are pretty funny, some are... scary."

"Can we go home now?" asked Hayley.

"Almost." Kenny smiled at her, attempting to project reassurance and confidence. "A city this big, there's bound to be people hiding somewhere. I'm sure they saw us roll in and I don't want to spend any more time here than necessary."

"Kids stayin' with the truck?" asked Eldon?

"Fuck that," said Alyssa.

"What she said," muttered Hayley.

"Swear jar." Kathy smirked. "Both of you."

"But Mom!" Hayley not-quite yelled. "I didn't say a bad word."

Kathy held her finger up. "Swearing by reference counts."

"Fine." Alyssa looked at Kathy. "But I demand a suspension of language policy if people start shooting at us."

"Okay." Kathy nodded. "That's fair."

"I'll coordinate the bots from here," said Nasir. "I can send four orbs, or two and the rover."

"How fast is the rover, and does it do stairs?" asked Kenny.

"About ten miles per hour tops, and no."

"Orbs." Kenny opened his door and slid out of his seat. As the kids climbed out, he reached in and pulled his rifle from the rack on the rear window.

Hayley drew her gun, checked the ammo counter, and put it back on her hip.

Kenny patted her shoulder. "Remember I want you two to stay down if anything happens. You're only to use that gun if you have absolutely *no* other choice. This isn't a video game. If you can run, you run. You don't get a respawn here."

"I know, Dad. You said that already." Hayley folded her arms. "Let's just go so we can get outta here."

"You still feelin' weird shit?" Eldon's voice had an electronic quality to it, courtesy of the speakers in his helmet, his face hidden behind a reflective gold visor. He came around the nose of the truck, rifle at the ready.

"Whoa," said Hayley. She stood on tiptoe, staring at herself in Eldon's helmet. "Is that transparent, or an active display?"

"Active display." Eldon tapped small pods on the side of the helmet at jaw level. "Cameras are here."

Four nine-inch orb bots floated up out of their storage box in the truck bed and hung in the air around Kenny. Nasir's voice emanated from one as the last two in the procession split off and hovered by the girls.

"I've set C and D to run on AI. They'll automatically engage anything that threatens the kids. Unit B is a stim-bot." A white orb with a red plus mark on it bounced up and down. "It's unarmed, but if anyone gets hurt, yell out 'medic,' and it'll deliver a stimpak shot."

"W-what the hell is in here?" asked Alyssa. "Sounds like we're getting ready to go to war."

"Hopefully nothing." Kenny headed for the broken-out doors of the Chapel Hills Mall.

Eldon jogged past him, taking point. Kenny glanced at Kathy, and grumbled to himself.

"Kath, walk ahead of me, keep about ten paces behind Eldon. Kids, walk near her."

"Well, shit." Eldon twisted back to shake his head. "This'll be a treat. You not racing off ahead of me to get yo' ass shot up."

Kathy hefted her assault rifle and walked up to him. "You want me in front of you?" She seemed amused.

"If something ambushes from the back, I'd rather it come after me first."

"Oh." Kathy rolled her eyes. "Women and children safe in the middle, right?"

Kenny smiled. "Well, you three *are* everything I care about in the world. So yeah, I'm being overprotective. Plus, you're green. If you were ex Recon like Eldon, I'd... still ask you to go in the middle."

She gave him a quick kiss and proceeded to follow the large man in green armor.

Eldon advanced past the ruined doors, boots crunching over glass fragments.

Kathy showed little hesitation or fear, which impressed him. She'd always been so convinced he'd never come back. Maybe she'd see it wasn't *that* bad out here and relax about him going. *Bah. We've got two kids now and she wants another one... I need to stop being a little boy playing adventurer. Damn Syndicate.* Hayley looked around in a constant state of glancing and twisting. Her right hand kept drifting for her sidearm, but she didn't pull it. Alyssa seemed halfway between bored and enthralled at the exploration. She faded back a little, getting closer to Kenny.

They passed a row of stores lining the entrance hallway on the way to the main concourse. Many of them looked un-scavenged, though most of the merchandise appeared worthless. Clothing had rotted on hangars and mannequins. He doubted any of the electronics would work, though a music store's collection might be worth taking.

*This isn't right. All this shit shouldn't still be sitting around.* He tempered his worry with the hope that settlers, bandits, or raiders wouldn't know what to do with an old music disc or movie. Those things only had value to collectors back in civilization, but a Scrag might be enamored with the 'rainbow shiny' of an ancient optical disc.

Alyssa glanced back over her shoulder at him, smiling past her thick, curly brown hair. "I need a hat." She mimicked the pose from the holo-photo he'd taken of her as a six-year-old. She'd had on a tiny pink cowboy hat, underpants, and boots, a pair of plastic toy guns in her hands.

He beamed. His heart swelled at seeing her back to finding his whole Wild West thing charming. She'd been into it big time as a child. Dealing with Kathy during her addiction had been rough, but when Alyssa went off the deep end and seemed to hate him… that almost broke him.

Kenny caught up and hugged her.

She returned the embrace, smiling at him with a tear in her eye. "This is kinda cool. I see why you keep coming out here."

"I dunno if I'm going to make a habit of it anymore. We'll see how things go."

Alyssa nodded and resumed walking.

"Got something," said Eldon.

Kenny raised his rifle. "What's it look like."

"Easy, man… it's a sign." He pointed at a freestanding triangular obelisk about a foot taller than him. Two sides had a map of the mall, and one had a picture of a woman in a bra. "What's the place you're looking for?"

"Crystal Emporium." Kenny walked up alongside Eldon.

Orb A glided close to the map, hung there for a second, and shot off to the right, careening down the mall.

"There." Eldon tapped the plastic over the map. "Second level, down that way to the right."

"I'm scouting it." Nasir's voice came from Orb B, the med-bot.

Eldon headed around the sign to the right, and walked past a small fountain surrounded by benches and dead trees in planters.

"This is so eerie." Hayley stared up into the open atrium at the second-story railing. "It's like all the people just left."

"They did," said Alyssa. "You'll have it in history when you hit eighth grade. Some places got warning before the war hit them. Everyone there just picked up and left."

Kathy put an arm around Hayley's back. "I remember hearing that. Everyone expected to be gone only a few days, maybe a few weeks, and come back."

"They didn't, did they?" asked Hayley.

"You doin' that on purpose, kid?" Eldon glanced back.

Hayley shrugged. "What?"

"Sounding eerie." Eldon chuckled and headed for a dead escalator.

"No… Sorry."

"She's still scared." Alyssa moved up alongside her. "Give her a break, huh? She doesn't like it out here."

A momentary grateful smile flickered over Hayley's face. Kenny's chest warmed at the sight of the girls' deepening bond, but a foreboding sense of worry gripped him soon after. Kathy walked up on his right side, her shoulder touching his arm. He attempted to summon a reassuring look.

"What's bothering you?" she asked, a little over a whisper.

Since the others hadn't stopped, he nudged her onward and walked beside her.

"Been hearin' all these stories for so long about this place. Starts to make a guy wonder where the line falls 'tween truth and fancy. It's buggin' me watchin' her affected by something. No one told her a thing about that whole 'the Badlands is alive' stuff, but she *feels* it somehow."

"She's young." Kathy glanced around at the stores, fading back to let Kenny step on the stalled escalator first. "And this place is so damned eerie. Maybe everyone else is just better at hiding it. And you're used to it. Or she's trying to guilt us into going back."

Kenny took the metal steps two at a time to the top. "Naw. That fear in her eyes... Can't fake that."

"Look!" yelled Alyssa.

Everyone glanced to the left, at Alyssa jogging up to the front of a small toy store. Two shafts of sunlight leaked in from large holes in the ceiling, setting whorls of dust aglow. Bands of shadow painted the store's façade, cast by mangled steel jutting from the smashed roof. Most of the inventory appeared ruined beyond any value, rotting and coated with the effects of three centuries' worth of weather. If anything in there managed to survive intact, it'd probably be worth a few hundred thousand credits or more, assuming he could find a collector interested in an ancient toy.

"Might be worth a quick poke around." He smiled.

"Dad." Alyssa squatted where the red tile floor of the mall concourse changed to white with grey speckles inside the store. "Someone's been here."

She gestured at a trail of barefoot prints. A group from the look of it. He picked out four discrete individuals, probably a teen leading three younger children. Two tracks belonged to people smaller than Hayley. Kenny tapped a finger on the floor, thinking.

"Four... all kids. Probably Scrags. Settlers don't tend to go exploring like this." They wouldn't know what to take here anyway.

"Can we look around?" asked Alyssa, excitement gleaming in her eyes.

He tapped his foot for a few seconds. "Eh, I guess. Don't wanna spend long in here though. Be careful, and stay in sight of everyone."

Eldon backed up and approached the storefront.

"I've found the crystal store," said Nasir from Orb C at Alyssa's shoulder. "Orb A's inside. Place looks untouched. What are we looking for again?"

Kenny coughed on the dust and spat to the side. "A black horse statue. Bit longer than a foot. Onyx or something."

"Okay." Orb C simulated nodding. "I'll search around while you guys root through that place."

"Heh." Kenny glanced at Eldon. "This guy's handy."

Kenny headed inside the toy store, going right for the counter to search for any sort of locked case where more expensive collectables might have been secured. The girls entered together, close enough to hold hands, though they didn't. Hayley seemed to forget her unease as the thrill of exploration took hold. The pale cyan glow of the hover bots' ion projectors glided over the shelves, kicking up small clouds of dirt wherever the dried mud flaked off. Their hum echoed off the walls, faint enough not to cover the scuff of boots in a half-inch layer of dried muck.

Alyssa pinched two fingers on the horn of a stuffed unicorn; she tried to lift it, but ripped the fabric spire straight from its head. "Wow, this stuff is old." She whistled.

Hayley gasped in horror.

He smiled and climbed up over the counter. Katherine wandered in only far enough to keep an eye on the kids, while Eldon remained at the entrance watching the concourse.

Kenny did find a display case, though it contained mostly warped cardboard rectangles, some of which still had intact illustrations on them. A small plastic sign on the shelf inside the case called them 'Magic Cards,' and they ranged in price from $25 all the way to $3,000. It took him a moment to work out the conversion from prewar money to current day credits. *Who in their right mind would pay 18,000 credits for a square of paper?* He shook his head, then laughed at himself. *Who pays millions for a stone horse statue?*

"Whoa," said Alyssa. "I think this is a game system, but it doesn't have a plug."

"Really? How did people play video games without helmets or interface jacks?" Hayley's hands peeked up over a shelf holding a flat black box. "There's nothing on the bottom."

"Dad?" Alyssa raised her voice. "Do you know how old games worked?"

"Uhh, probably screens," said Kenny. "That thing's older than West City."

At the right end of the case, a pair of faded boxes held plastic figurines of robots. A handwritten sign called one 'Voltron' and one 'Optimus Prime,' and bragged of them being in the 'original unopened packaging.' He couldn't make out the price, but both had four figures… so somewhere between $1000 and $9999.

The 'unopened' thing didn't matter much given that the packaging had all but disintegrated. Aside from a little dirt though, the statuettes had survived since they appeared plastic. *Hmm. Should be able to get something for those.* He broke the lock and extracted the relics from the case as though he'd gone armpit-deep in some ancient Mayan ruin, and one wrong step would set off a killing curse. Some plastic bags under the counter made for a handy means to carry them, at least until he could get back to the truck… and…

"Hey Nasir?" said Kenny

Orb B, the medi-bot, glided over to him. "Yes?"

"That thing got any kinda grippy claw?" He held the bag up. "Can it carry this back to the truck?"

A one-by-one inch hatch opened and a metal rod extended, tipped with a point that resembled a stimpak injector. Kenny hung the bag on the extended probe. The orb tilted back and glided off toward the entrance.

Something plastic clattered to the floor deeper in. Kenny wandered in that direction, though Kathy didn't seem alarmed, so he didn't hurry. "Find something?"

"Uhh," said Alyssa. "Bunch of silly looking toy guns. This one even looks like it's supposed to have Epoxil parts."

When she held up a plastic version of a prewar assault rifle, Kenny chuckled. He stepped around the end of the shelf where the girls were, and blinked at the carnage. Someone had gone nuts, tearing open all the boxes of toy weapons. Everything from realistic to ridiculous monstrosities of pink and orange plastic lay scattered about the floor.

Hayley picked up a bright orange pistol that looked more like a blimp with a handle. When she pulled the metal trigger, it made a whirring noise and sparks shot out of the sides. She yelped and dropped it.

Kenny took the toy from Alyssa and examined it. Aside from being a mere fraction of the weight of a real one, it looked indistinguishable from an AK47. "Back when they made these guns for real, they used *wood*, not Epoxil."

"Wood?" asked Alyssa. Her confusion lingered for a few seconds before she blinked. "Oh, right… like from trees. Wow, that wasn't illegal?"

"Trees weren't so endangered back then." He handed it back to her.

"Someone thought these were real weapons at first, but figured out they're fake." Hayley backed up. "That's why all this stuff is still here on the floor, right?"

Kenny nodded. "Yeah. Probably those Scrags."

"Let's go?" Kathy seemed to sense the somberness in him at the thought of children going to a toy store looking for real guns so they could survive. "You said something about hurrying before the locals find us, right?"

"Yeah." Kenny patted the girls on the back one after the other to get them moving toward the exit, and walked behind them. "Nasir, any luck in there?"

"No, boss." Orb D, hovering over Hayley, rotated side to side in a mimicry of a head shake. "The place appears to be intact. The security gate was even still down… I had to burn through. No sign of a horse statue fitting your description… but I did find a safe in the back."

"That's a damn good sign."

Kathy cocked an eyebrow at him.

"If the security gate is still down, means we'll be the first people in there since the war."

"Right." Kathy walked a step or two ahead of him, behind the girls, who followed Eldon at about ten yards.

Hayley had gone back to her worried 'I don't want to be here' demeanor, though Alyssa continued to stare at the scenery with awe. It made him feel proud and worried in equal measure. The idea of her coming out here on her own once she'd gotten older shed a new light on Kathy's protest of his trips. He chuckled to himself. *Maybe this'll become a family vacation thing.*

Eldon approached a small storefront blocked off by a security grate. A neat, round hole in the middle appeared burned out via laser, and the eerie meandering glow of an orb bot's ion thruster drifted around inside. Enough gold-paint lettering on the window remained to confirm the place as The Crystal Emporium. A tiny store, it occupied a straight rectangle of retail space that probably could've fit in the trailer of a big rig. The innermost half of the right wall had a glass counter attached to it, near a door into a back room. White display stands, some square, some round, littered the remainder of the space, tipped with enclosed cases containing figurines, pendants, or crystal goblets. A few even had crystal balls. The taste of burned dust and molten aluminum settled on his tongue.

"Damn…" Kenny whistled.

Eldon took the vibro-knife off his belt. As soon as he squeezed the rubberized handle, the air seemed to change. Muscles in Kenny's back tensed in response to a sound past the range of hearing. The hypersonic oscillation generated frequencies beyond the human ear's range, which made him feel like a ghost had walked up and stood beside him. It seemed to unsettle Alyssa as well, as she started looking around. Kenny glanced at Hayley, who didn't seem bothered by it at all.

"It's all right." He stepped up behind his daughter and grasped her shoulder. "Just sound."

"Ain't makin' noise yet." Eldon smiled. "But it's about to."

The former UCF Recon trooper sliced down the security grating with little effort, the combat vibro-knife going through the bars like pasta. Each time the edge struck metal, an ear-destroying squelch cried out. Fortunately, the quarter-inch rods didn't offer a lot of surface area, so it wound up chirping like a flock of mutant birds hopped up on military grade psychotropic chems. He cut up, across, and down, carving out a door-sized opening in the mesh. The scrap fell inward with a *crack* of metal on once-polished floor. After reinserting the blade in its cryo-sheath, Eldon brought his Crusader rifle up and stepped over the solid box at the bottom, tromping across the felled security barrier.

Hayley glanced at the keyhole and handle. "Wouldn't it have been quieter to pick the lock?"

Kenny patted her on the head. "Yes, but Eldon likes his knife. He's got some unresolved daddy issues."

Eldon raised the middle finger of his left hand over his shoulder without comment.

The girls followed him and began oohing and ahhing at all the little items of sparkling crystal. Case by case, they wiped away dust to peer at an assortment of animals, faeries, bells, and various other pieces of crystal art.

Kenny headed past all of it to the back room. The small door behind the counter opened into a space as wide as the whole store and about twenty feet long. Another metal door with a push bar likely led to an outer hallway that went past all the stores and eventually led to a loading dock or area with dumpsters. A manager's desk against the wall next to the door held a mass of paperwork, binders, and a long-dead computer.

"Hey, Hale… check this out."He grinned at the old flat-panel monitor.

She looked up from a display case, tiny crystal unicorns in both hands. After a momentary inquisitive look, she trotted over. "Hey, can we like keep this stuff, or is it stealing?"

"Anyone who owned it is dead a long, long time. Feel free." He pointed at the monitor. "This is what people used before holographic tech."

"Oh, wow…" She gawked at it. "It's like… solid. Only 2d? That must've been horrible. I can't even imagine trying to play a shooting game without being able to like look around."

Orb A emerged from behind a freestanding metal cabinet. It wobbled to get Kenny's attention and glided back to hover in front of the black door of an in-wall safe about the size of a home refrigerator. A standard ten-digit numeric keypad with rubber buttons sat atop a rounded 'knob' with a long handle pointing down. Not expecting much, he stepped over and poked one of the buttons. The pale grey LCD display remained utterly blank.

"Shit," muttered Kenny. "No power."

Eldon's step crunched on grit by the door to the back room. "Bet they fell behind on their electric bill."

Kenny chuckled. "Think your knife'll get through that safe?"

"Depends on how thick the door is. It'll probably burn out the inducer before it opens though." Eldon tromped over and knocked on the safe door. "Yeah. It'll definitely burn the thing out. These ain't made for heavy-duty utility cutting."

Hayley ducked under Eldon's arm and stared up at the safe. She poked at the buttons and wiggled the handle. "I might be able to get into this."

Eldon laughed.

"No, I'm serious. Can you open this up? Expose the circuitry?" She pointed at the round area with the keypad.

"Yeah. That I can cut." Eldon shifted his rifle to hang by the strap and pulled his knife. "What are you thinkin'?"

"Be right back. Gotta get my deck from the truck." She started out, but Kenny caught her by the shoulder.

"One, you're not going off alone. Two… you brought your deck out here?" He blinked in disbelief. "Why? There's no net."

"I dunno…" She looked down and tapped the toe of her boot on the floor. "I just kinda feel better having it with me." Her enthusiasm returned and she gave him a pleading stare. "I know I can do something…"

Kenny nodded. "Well, I'd have had to go back to the truck to grab the cutter anyway. Might as well give your idea a shot. Cutter might overpenetrate and melt down whatever's in the safe."

They made their way back outside to the truck, leaving Orb A to watch the store. While Kenny grabbed the laser cutter in its carrying case from the bed, she ducked inside the cab. After the girls stashed away their haul of crystalline cute, Hayley pulled her Neko net deck out from under the back seat. She climbed down and slung it over her shoulder on a strap. About the size of an electric guitar without a fretboard, the deck had an oval profile with two triangular projections suggesting cat ears, each lined with the rainbow-silver shimmer of holo projectors. Shaped white plastic cutouts atop the glossy pink housing further accented the cat face.

Hayley seemed happier, like she'd wrapped herself in a security blanket.

Kenny chuckled.

"What?" asked Hayley, narrowing her eyes.

"Oh… you don't really strike me as the 'everything must be pink' type."

She frowned. "I'm not. Bio Dad thought I should have pink. It's not a big deal… I don't *hate* it."

"Alyssa went through a pink phase." Kenny tapped his chin.

"Dad!" shouted Alyssa, in a warning tone.

"From about five 'til ten, everything—"

"*Dad!*" Alyssa stared at him, blushing.

"Pink cowboy hat, pink boots, pink guns, pink dresses." He raised his hands and caught Alyssa when she jumped on him.

They wrestled for a moment before Alyssa cracked up laughing.

"Ken." Kathy indicated the mall with her thumb. "Weren't we in a hurry?"

"Good point. I'm sure Hale wants to go home."

Hayley nodded. "Oh. Got any tools and scrap wires and stuff?"

Kenny rummaged the truck bed and handed her a small metal toolbox.

She opened it, looked over an assortment of snips, wire spools, soldering irons, pliers, and a few small screwdrivers before closing the lid. "Perfect."

Eight minutes after leaving, the group returned to Crystal Emporium where they found Orb A patrolling the area, every so often making a happy little wobble as it swerved around display cases or darted playfully through shelves. The store hadn't changed in the slightest since they left.

Hayley led the way to the back room and dragged the manager's chair over by the safe. She set the deck on the cushion and knelt before it. Eldon performed a little surgery on the safe's door, cutting away the metal band around the keypad. A few minutes of poking and jabbing allowed him to lift the digital portion out of the housing, while apparently leaving the door handle intact. Much to Kenny's disappointment, the handle didn't connect to physical gears or locking bars. The meager quarter-inch of travel it had was the extent of its range of motion—more a switch than a handle.

"Okay, kiddo." Kenny folded his arms. "Let's see what'cha got."

Hayley stood and stuck her face up to the electronics dangling out of the safe door on a wire bundle. She lifted it up, turned it over, and spent a moment staring at it, huffing to blow dust away. Kenny's suspicion mounted at the look of confusion on her face, or at least no indication that she had the least idea of what she looked at. He shrugged the laser cutter strap off his shoulder and set the eight-pound box on the floor.

No sooner did his finger touch the latch to open it than a look of enlightenment lit up Hayley's face. He stood, half stooped over, and stared transfixed as she rummaged the toolbox for wire. She opened a small access panel on the underside of the deck and connected wires to a pair of tiny screws before jabbing the other end into what seemed to be the first random place she thought to put it on the dangling circuit board. Almost as an afterthought, she soldered it down. It took her half a minute to figure out what to do with the other one, but again she grinned with the glee of a mad scientist.

She examined a small eight-pin white plastic connector folded up inside before jamming more loose wires into the sockets. After finding a semi-molten old M3 plug in the toolbox bin, she broke off the plastic housing and scrap of wire, and spent a minute or three soldering the wires to contact points along the back end of the prong.

"The hell are you doing?" asked Eldon.

Hayley didn't look up as she continued working the soldering tool. "First two wires are power. This is the data connection. Depending on what kind of interface is running inside that safe, I should be able to get into it and do some kind of software overload. The hard part is getting the pins in the right place, but I think I got it."

"You know where to put them?" Eldon scratched at the top of his helmet.

"Feels right." She smiled. "Okay, there."

Kathy glanced at Kenny. Her expression seemed to ask how much time he intended to waste humoring her. Kenny shrugged.

Alyssa wandered the back room, opening cabinets and peering at everything.

"Got it." Hayley connected the naked M3 plug to her deck's port, and knee-walked around in front of it. Both cat-ear protrusions glowed with chromatic light, and a thirty-inch holo-panel unrolled in the air in front of her, tinting the room pink from its colored border. She grabbed and swiped at icons too fast for Kenny to keep up, eventually opening a holographic keyboard and a white window that scrolled with the occasional spurt of black text.

The LCD display on the safe lit up.

"Well..." Eldon sounded impressed. "Power works."

"Yeah. I had to estimate the voltage," said Hayley. "Deck runs on an e-mag, which would fry that old prewar crap. What'd they use back then, 110 volt?"

Eldon turned his helmet toward Kenny, the shiny gold visor obscuring any sign of facial expression. "This kid is actually a kid, right? Not like that 'special little snowflake' Katya found."

Alyssa, Hayley, and Kathy looked up with confusion.

"Uhh, that's a *long* story." Kenny chuckled. "No, as far as we know, she's eleven."

"I suppose I could've been frozen or something. Or maybe we're all floating in tanks somewhere and this is really cyberspace." Hayley offered an innocent smile. "Maybe the Badlands isn't real. Maybe the whole thing is some kinda giant social experiment. Ever wonder why they have checkpoints to go out here? Maybe they gassed us and we're in VR."

"Shit." Eldon shook his head. "That ain't even funny."

Kenny raised an eyebrow for a second. "Nah. Can't be. Katya came out here and she's got one of them things." He tapped his throat. "Gas wouldn't have worked on her."

"Almost there. I think this is gonna work. I just gotta bash out a few lines of code to control the lock."

"How long will that take?" asked Kenny, incredulous.

"Well, I don't need to do anything but send power down the right circuit to trip the open command, so probably like five minutes."

Kenny put an arm around Kathy, making suggestive eyes at her. Eldon sat on the manager's desk and plugged a hose from his genesis canteen into the front of his helmet.

"Okay. Think I got it." Hayley held her arm out over her deck a few minutes later, one finger downward like a spike. "I hit this button, it's either going to open or burst into flames."

Alyssa screamed as if she'd witnessed someone beheaded.

Kenny bolted toward the sound, followed by Eldon. He rounded the corner of a tall metal cabinet and found Alyssa backing away from a doorway in the left wall. Eldon swooped around behind him, rifle trained. At the sound of their approach, Alyssa spun to face them and leapt into Kenny's arms, sobbing.

The small bathroom contained a massive pile of human bones, all cleaned. The only trace of gore appeared to be rotting brains leaking out from the interior of the skulls. A rancid, though not overpowering, smell put them as far more recent than the Corporate War.

"Damn." Eldon leaned into the bathroom and poked the tip of his rifle at the pile. "Gotta be like thirty people. We find the lair of a serial archaeologist?"

"Huh?" asked Kenny

"Look how clean these are... like they 'bout to go on display at some museum."

"Uhh, guys?" yelled Hayley. "Is Liss okay?"

"Yeah," Kenny shouted back. "Just found something disgusting."

"What killed them?" whispered Alyssa. "Why is he storing the bones like this? This is so fucked up."

Kathy shivered. "How did they get in here with the gate closed?"

Alyssa pushed back on him when he tried to step closer, resisting.

"Sec, kiddo," said Kenny. "Let me take a look."

Alyssa sniffled and moved around behind him, hiding as if the skeletons would be able to see her.

Kenny stooped and picked up a femur. The bone had thousands of tiny scrapes and blotchy areas of uneven shade, looking as though someone had splashed goopy acidic bleach on it with little care for neatness. *Shit.* "Millipedes."

"Fuckin' millipedes did this?" asked Eldon, holding his fingers about an inch apart.

"Yeah, millipedes, but they ain't that little." He dropped the bone and stood. "That explains why this mall is so untouched. We've gotta be in the middle of their damn nest. Locals know better than to walk in here."

"Shit," muttered Eldon.

"How big are they?" whispered Alyssa.

"Full grown? About twelve to fourteen inches in diameter, six to ten feet long. Acid spit, sharp pincers that'll go through steel, and a tail stinger."

"Dad..." Alyssa reached for him. "Hold me before I pass out."

He pulled her into a hug. "They're usually nocturnal. We should get the hell out of here."

"Good plan," said Eldon before shaking his head. "Why's it always gotta be giant bugs?"

"Heh. 'Pedes aren't as bulletproof as those cockroaches." Kenny winked.

"Small fuckin' favors," muttered Eldon.

Kenny sucked in a breath to yell, but stifled it while he fast-walked back to where Hayley knelt by the chair. "That thing work?"

"I was waiting for everyone to come back." She looked disappointed.

"Hit it." Kenny smiled. "We should get moving quick."

"Okay." Hayley pushed the holographic button. Black text flickered and scrolled on the white window. A few small sparks burst from the circuit board, and the safe door emitted a resounding *thud* that carried into the floor. She jumped to her feet and shouted, "Yes!"

"What's that?" asked Alyssa.

"That is the sound of how awesome I am." Hayley examined her fingernails.

"No... I mean that scratching noise." Alyssa turned to stare at Kenny, eyes wide as saucers.

Kenny held up a hand to silence everyone. A noise like a giant rat chewing on aluminum ductwork emanated from above the drop ceiling. His heart sped up. "That," he whispered, "is the sound of we need to get the fuck out of here."

Hayley's expression went blank. A second later, she scrambled to disconnect her deck.

Kenny pulled open the safe. The onyx stallion didn't stand out anywhere as being obvious, though a few unmarked white cardboard boxes looked about the right size. "El... gimme a hand. Grab anything big enough to hold a horse statue about yea big." He held his hands about two feet apart.

"Kath... get the kids back to the truck." Kenny grabbed a box and tore the flap open. *Plates. Fuck.* He tossed it aside and grabbed another.

"Why? What's coming?" Kathy glanced up.

"An army of giant millipedes," said Kenny, as casual as if he'd suggested lunch at the Poblano Taco Station.

Kathy stared at him, blindly reaching to take Alyssa's hand. "Is that bad?"

Alyssa screamed amid a loud *crunch* and a clatter of foam. Seven feet of chitinous, black insect burst down from the drop ceiling and lifted her off her feet. She waved her arms and legs in the air, shrieking. The orb bot that had been hovering around her faced it and fired a laser from the middle of its 'eye' in a series of discrete pulses. Tiny flaming spots appeared on the creature's shell and fizzled out to trails of smoke, tinting the air with a smell like burned lobster.

Hayley pulled her sidearm. Eldon swiveled and fired a burst from the Crusader. Yellow goop with the consistency of raw scrambled eggs sprayed out of three fist-sized holes about a foot above Alyssa's head. The millipede thrashed and hurled her to the side. She flew half the width of the store before crashing against the wall a few feet off the ground. Her body bounced back; she hit the ground on all fours, still shrieking.

Kenny yanked his sidearm off his belt and put two bullets into the millipede's head before Eldon could fire again. Nine feet of dead insect slithered out of the hole in the ground and landed in a coil. Yellow-white slime spattered a shiny black carapace festooned with an uncountable number of bright red legs.

Hayley yelled, "Die!" and opened fire on a second one emerging from the bathroom.

The orb bot hovering around her also lit it on fire, though this one nailed it in the eye on the second pulse, and the monstrous insect flopped dead

"Daddy!" wailed Alyssa. She scrambled to her feet and ran to him.

He caught her at arm's length, and checked her over. Aside from a little blood dripping from her nose, she had no obvious injuries. Her armored vest had a small scratch on the back and front where the insect's mandibles got a hold of her.

Kathy pounced on her, clinging. She babbled for a second, but gave up trying to speak. After squeezing her daughter, she pointed at the dead millipede and stared at Kenny.

Hayley folded one arm over her vest. "I want more armor... like Eldon. This only covers my chest."

"What the fucking fuck is that fucking thing..." Kathy kept pointing at it.

"Swear jar," muttered Alyssa, her voice trembling as much as her body.

After a pregnant silence, both Kathy and Alyssa burst out laughing.

Kenny's mind filled with an image of removing the 'Voltron' statue from the case, and a giant boulder chasing him down a tunnel. *I never should've touched the statue. Here comes the deathtrap.* "Okay, everyone needs to stay calm."

"It's the bugs, isn't it?" Alyssa put both hands over her mouth and took a few breaths. "They collected all those bones."

"Yo," said Eldon.

Kenny glanced to his right. Eldon held up a black horse statuette, faceted onyx with gold mane and tail. Diamond eyes caught even the weak light leaking in from the mall and sparkled.

"Wow," whispered Hayley. "It's beautiful."

"Hello..." Alyssa pointed. "Giant bugs. Can we go outside?"

Eldon eased the horse back into the styrofoam packing he'd removed it from. "That"—he stuffed it back into its cardboard box—"is a damn fine idea."

A sound like someone pouring marbles down a metal ductwork shaft passed overhead.

"Here they come," muttered Eldon.

Hayley flung her deck over her shoulder on a strap. Kenny did the same with the laser cutter.

At a tremendous *crash* from the bathroom, Alyssa whirled and aimed her pistol toward the back of the store.

"Don't let them sting you," said Kenny.

"Not exactly the kind of thing I'd do for fun." Eldon put a hand on Hayley's shoulder and ushered her toward the front.

Kenny stared at him. "I'm serious. It numbs at first, but of all of us, you'd probably be the only one to survive the venom."

"How do you know so much about these things?" Kathy hurried after him to the front of the store.

"They're pretty common. Seen 'em before."

She grabbed his arm. "You've seen *these* things before?"

"Yup. Killed a bunch, too."

Kathy's stare compressed ten years of worry and fear into two seconds.

The girls' pistols went off in a rapid series of shots, followed by the death *squee* of another millipede. Two long antennae whipped audibly in the air as it collapsed.

Eldon skidded to a halt at the hole he'd cut in the security mesh. "Uhh, we got a problem."

"What kind of problem?" asked Kenny, while dragging Kathy up behind him.

"About a million problems." Eldon pointed his rifle to the left. "So many damn millipedes I can't even see the floor."

"Uhh, Dad?" asked Alyssa. "They're behind us too."

Kenny whirled. The back end of the store came alive with writhing tubular forms. Smears of red from the legs rippled and undulated around a wall of glossy black chitin. He stopped trying to count faces after fourteen. "El."

"Yeah?"

"You got any 'nades in that Crusader, now'd be an awesome time to use them."

"Only eight." Eldon stepped out into the mall, cradling the statuette's box under his left arm and one-handing his rifle to the left. It made a *foomp* sound, soon followed by a *bang* muted under a torrent of yellow gloop.

Kenny opened up on the millipedes in the store, firing as fast as he could click the trigger in a haphazard effort to hit faces or eyes. The girls backed away from the swarm, also shooting. Kathy stared in horror until Alyssa screamed when some bug guts sprayed on her face. The sound of her daughter's voice hit her like a slap and she ripped full auto into the onrushing tidal wave of insects.

*Foomp! Foomp!*

The resultant splattery explosion gave Kenny a mental image of hand grenades going off at the bottom of a swimming pool full of noseblow. Orbs A, C, and D hung in midair, making tiny pivots and adjustments to their orientation between thin red beams of laser light glinting in the dusty air. Each time they fired, a millipede's eye burst into flame. No matter how fast or erratic the bugs moved, the orbs seemed unable to miss, and as far as Kenny could perceive, every time they fired, they killed one.

*Damn, maybe that guy was a good idea after all.*

"Aww man… that is so fucking nasty," muttered Eldon. *Foomp!*

*Splortch!*

Eldon shifted and fired a burst, followed by three slower shots.

Kathy screamed. She leapt to the side as a millipede broke down from the ceiling and landed on her amid a rain of crumbling foam tiles. Her shriek of surprise morphed into a cry of agony as pincers sank into her right thigh. She bashed at its face with the butt of the rifle, but didn't faze it.

Kenny drew his pistol, put it to the side of the creature's head, and painted floor with bug brain. He kicked the dead thing off his wife and pulled her upright. Orb B zipped over and stabbed Kathy in the back of the thigh with its probe. She screamed again, but her expression went dazed and relieved before her lungs emptied.

"Go, go, go!" yelled Eldon.

The girls jumped through the hole in the grating at the same time. Both had two-handed grips on their pistols, and stood with their shoulders touching. Kenny pushed Kathy after them and backed out of the store, leaving the orbs to finish off the millipedes. No sense wasting ammo since it didn't look as though the smaller number of bugs inside would overwhelm the precision laser barrage.

When he looked in the direction Eldon fired, his heart almost stopped. The entire mall concourse, almost twenty-four yards wide, had a six-foot tall mass of millipedes coming toward them.

"Holy shit…" His throat dried out. "We don't have that much ammo."

Eldon took a few steps to the left, away from the escalator down and closer to the oncoming bugs. "Time ta run!" He fired another grenade, which went off some thirty feet past the front of the swarm, throwing a huge plume of raw-egg goo and millipede chunks into the air.

Kathy stared at the horde with a face of perfect calm. "I don't think they're happy to see us."

The girls took off sprinting for the escalator. Their 'guardian orbs' followed, flying backward while continuing to fire lasers into the huge cluster of millipedes. Orb A hung between Kenny and Eldon, pivoting about with microadjustments as it also peppered the swarm.

"I am sending the tracked bot in to give you cover at the door," said Nasir from the medi-bot.

"Come on!" yelled Kenny to Eldon before giving Kathy a light push toward the way out.

She hauled ass after the kids, not bothering to waste bullets into thousands of millipedes. Eldon sprayed the leading edge with burst fire, which seemed to do little other than coat the floor with nasty ooze. Any bugs that died fell under the oncoming tidal wave without slowing it.

"Eldon!" shouted Kenny, before running after Kathy.

"Man, this is fucked up," Muttered Eldon, the faint plastic clicking of his armor coming up behind Kenny.

Though Eldon could've outrun him, he kept his position at the end of the line. Alyssa and Hayley skidded to a halt at the top of the escalator, both yelled "Shit!" at the same time, and started shooting downward. Kathy ran into the railing to the right of the escalator and, without a word, fired down the stairs as well.

*Fuck.* Kenny stared up through a hole in the roof at blue sky. He imagined all the rear hallways behind the stores had become nest tunnels full of eggs, and didn't even want to think about what the basement or boiler room looked like.

*One way out of here.* He rushed to Hayley's left, taking up a firing position opposite Kathy.

A handful of millipedes attempting to come up the escalator steps lay dead, with more behind them falling one after the next.

Eldon backed up to them. "I hate to be the bearer of bad news, but we gotta go. Six, seven seconds and our asses are going to be buried."

Alyssa stared back at the flood of bugs for a half second with an emotionless face. "Well, that sucks."

"Nasir," yelled Kenny. "All orbs to the bottom. Clear us a path."

"On it," crackled from the medi-bot.

Alyssa let out a war cry and charged down the escalator while firing.

Kathy started to yell at her to stop, but one look at the rushing swarm sent her following. Hayley grabbed Kenny's arm and tried to pull him down. After another second's hesitation, he went. Three orbs sailed out over the open space between the first and second floors. Thin strands of red laser light appeared in camera-flash snaps, connecting the plastisteel spheres to millipede skulls. Smoke and seared insect stink filled the air. A leaping millipede burst into a shower of goo that rained over them when a laser beam split it in half.

Hayley slipped in a patch of slime and landed on her ass at the bottom of the escalator. A millipede bit her on the leg and lifted her up. Dangling upside down, she shouted, "Get offa me!" and shot it point blank between the eyes. Its mandibles snapped open, dumping her to the ground on her back. The millipede swayed side to side before collapsing. The medi-bot raced over to jab her with its probe. Hayley kept shooting at random bugs in front of her despite sitting on the ground.

Alyssa skidded to a halt by her side, also firing.

Kathy swooped in to pick her up.

"I'm okay. Keep shooting!" yelled Hayley.

Kenny jumped on the banister and slid down; at the bottom, his boots shot out from under him in the bug guts and he wound up on his ass as well, gliding a good twenty feet into a much smaller swarm of millipedes. His body hit them like a ball on bowling pins, knocking them rolling, but it took them mere seconds to right themselves. Pincers squeezed at his arms, legs, and shoulder, but nothing penetrated his armored coat. When a millipede reared back to bite him in the face, he got his rifle up in time to block, though the force of the creature's strike smashed the gun into his nose.

The kids' pistols went off in a barrage that sounded more like a single submachinegun on full auto. Bug guts sprayed him, and a severe impact caught him in the left shoulder. Kenny walloped the millipede in front of him with the rifle, knocking it dizzy. Before it could recover, he fed it a burst, the barrel inches from its dripping mouth.

Eldon plowed into the smaller swarm as the front edge of the main group spilled down the escalator and poured over the railing. The first few to fall cracked open on impact with the ground floor. As more and more landed, they provided a cushion. Millipede by millipede, Eldon grabbed the bugs on Kenny, pulled them off his armor, and vibro-knifed them in the head. After killing six, he reached down.

Kenny accepted his outstretched hand.

Kathy shot millipedes launching themselves off the upper story, causing several midair detonations of white-yellow ooze to rain on everyone.

The sound of a heavy machinegun firing got Eldon to dive onto Kenny instead of pull him upright. It took them both a second to realize the source: the tracked bot Nasir sent in.

"Friendly," yelled Eldon.

Kenny scrambled to his feet and rushed to the girls. As soon as he caught up to them, they ran for the mall exit. Kathy followed on his heels. The large 12.5mm rifle on the footlocker-sized tank bot pasted the millipedes into a shower of goopy yellow slime. Each bullet detonated multiple bugs, their chitin offering no resistance to such a big round.

Alyssa scrambled inches behind Hayley, sliding and skidding over the mucous-like coating on the floor. Hayley wiped out and pulled Alyssa down, but they didn't lose much speed. They slid for a few seconds before hitting the side of a small fountain, long since devoid of water. Both girls clambered upright without even a whimper of pain, and sprinted. Kenny waved his arms for balance as his boots kept trying to fly out from under him.

Bright blue flashes from the tracked bot's rifle acted like a lighthouse in the unending rain of bug innards, and led him to the beautiful sight of the silvery micro-tank. As the girls got close, it ceased shooting, likely to avoid hitting people. Hayley and Alyssa reached clean floor first and raced to the entrance doors. Kathy slid up behind him; he took her hand and they ducked around the bot. Eldon, somehow managing to run backward over the slick of bug innards without falling, kept shooting into the onrushing wave. As soon as he passed the tank bot, it opened fire again.

Kenny sprinted down the last section of hallway, which remained mercifully bug-free, to the front doors. He gave Kathy a light push and whirled around to check on Eldon, who hustled over. Azure flashes appeared in time with the tracked bot's rifle discharging. The deep report of its cannon drowned out the soft hums of orb bot lasers.

"Hey!" shouted Hayley from outside. "Get out of there!"

A childish yelp of surprise followed.

*Thok.*

"Dad!" shouted Hayley. "Some primitive kid just shot me with an arrow."

Kenny almost bashed the door off its hinges to get outside.

Four brown-skinned children stood in the bed of the truck, evidently having been caught rooting around. All had long, wild black hair. The oldest, a boy of about fifteen, wore a skirt made from several patches of squealer hide. A leather strap, likely an old belt, crossed his bare chest, connected to a quiver made from a plastic prewar soda bottle full of arrows, both metal and wood that hung at his hip. He carried a green camouflage compound bow, with an arrow nocked.

To his right, a younger and thinner boy had one foot up on the side of the truck bed, an arrow loaded and aimed at Alyssa. The perhaps twelve-year-old didn't seem to have anything on under a poncho made out of an old blue comforter with a hole cut for his head. The end, which dangled around the level of his shins, frayed like it had been dragged on the ground for quite some time. That, plus its overall decay made it seem like he'd been wearing it for a few years.

Near the tailgate, a girl of about ten held an empty bow in her outstretched left arm, her right hand back, fingers open, posture frozen in the instant of loosing her shot. She stared in awe at Hayley. An old power cable, the plug dangling from the knot at her belly, held up a few scraps of cloth and paper in a pathetic attempt to make a skirt. It served more as decoration than clothing, though the belt did support a squealer leather quiver with a few more arrows in it. Both her wrists and both ankles sported what at first he thought to be a vast array of cheap plastic bracelets, though after a second of looking at her, he recognized them as what people before the war had used to tie their beer cans together, six at a time. A few small handprints marked the dust on her bare chest.

Her lip quivered as she stared at Hayley. "*Lo siento. Fue un accidente. Me asustaste. Por favor, no me mates.*"

The smallest of the tribal kids, a boy who couldn't have been older than eight, stood away from his effort to open one of the locked boxes. He didn't have any clothing, though the length and thickness of his hair almost made up for it. The prints on the girl's chest matched up with his hands when he clung to her from behind and tried to pull her down to safety.

Thunder continued from the tracked bot's machinegun behind them.

Hayley pointed at the ground. An arrow lay at her feet, which had likely bounced off her vest. She raised her pistol at the girl who shot her. "That's our stuff."

The oldest boy shifted his bow toward Hayley.

Alyssa pointed her gun at the kids as well. "*Bajen esas cosas.*"

Kathy held her rifle up, but kept it across her chest, and raised her voice at the Scrags. "Put those things down. *Bajen esas cosas ahora mismo.*" She took a step closer. "That goes for you two as well, girls."

Kenny moved up to Alyssa's side; he didn't aim his rifle at the kids in the truck, but held it in such a way as to make a warning obvious.

The tribal children glanced from their bows to the firearms pointed at them, and their courage evaporated. The smallest boy kept trying to pull the girl to the truck bed.

"Lower those damn weapons," yelled Eldon. He leaned at them in a manner more akin to 'pissed off dad' than combatant. "*Baja esas malditas armas.*"

The Scrag kids (and Alyssa) jumped at his sudden loud command. As soon as the two boys relaxed their bowstrings, Hayley and Alyssa holstered their pistols.

Three orbs zoomed out of the mall, heading for the truck, followed by the much slower tracked bot.

The Scrag girl shouted, "*Dioses de la muerte! Ella no puede morir!*"

"*Milpiés. vienen cientos de ellos,*" said Kenny. "*Sentensen, agarrense de algo[1].*"

All four of the children gasped. The eldest raised his bow again, but pointed it at the mall entrance. The other three looked too frightened to move.

"What?" yelled Alyssa. "They shot Hayley and you're telling them to *stay*? Did she just call her a goddess of death?"

"I'm not throwing them to the bugs." He blinked at her. "She thinks Hayley can't die. The armor… and the millipedes are still behind us."

Standing there coated in yellow slime with dark squiggly bits of millipede insides clinging to her, Alyssa seemed to have forgotten all about them. Color drained out of her face. "Umm. Are those things going to come outside?"

The Scrag children stared at Kenny for a fraction of a second before cowering down in the truck bed.

"Everyone in, now." Kenny headed to the tailgate. "Eldon, gimme a hand with that bot."

"On it." He handed the horse statuette to Kathy.

Four brown faces peered at him from among the boxes. The smallest boy leapt over the side and ran to the arrow. After retrieving it, he sprinted back to the truck, climbed the tire, and took cover among the cargo.

Kathy ushered the girls into the truck and jumped in behind them. When the tracked bot arrived, Kenny and Eldon hauled it up and put it in the bed. As the first wave of millipedes reached the front doors, the Scrag kids shouted warnings in rapid Spanish. Kenny ran around, leapt into the driver's seat, and hit the power button. The second Eldon's ass touched cushion, he stomped on the accelerator and chirped the tires in reverse. Nasir wedged himself against the passenger-side wall, as if touching Kathy at all would coat him in deadly neurotoxin. The Scrag kids tumbled into a heap at the innermost part of the truck bed, legs in the air. They recovered and scrabbled for handholds.

Once he felt he'd reached a safe enough distance to do so, Kenny slowed to a stop, pulled a K turn, and took off. The four kids in back rolled across the bed and slid up against the tailgate. The millipedes seemed to lose interest once they strayed fully into sunlight. A writhing mass of black lingered at the door of the mall for a little while before receding into shadow.

"Whoa," said Eldon.

"I... I think I'm gonna throw up." Hayley hunched forward, holding her arms away from touching herself or anything else. "I'm covered in ick."

"Me too," muttered Alyssa. "This is *so* nasty. It's like I went swimming in scrambled eggs."

Hayley gagged.

"There's a piece in your hair..." Nasir leaned over and plucked a hunk of white matter from the back of Hayley's head. He squeezed it between his fingers before tossing it out the window. "Kinda feels like crab meat... are those things edible?"

Hayley shuddered, and threw up in her lap.

As soon as the smell of vomit pervaded the cabin, Alyssa lost her lunch as well. Kathy clamped a hand over her mouth. Kenny's throat churned, but he'd smelled worse out here. Eldon, in a fully-sealed helmet, hummed merrily to himself.

Kenny rolled down the windows and rubbed his throbbing shoulder. It didn't even bother him that one of the girls had shot him by accident; they were alive and unhurt. He tried to breathe as little as possible and shifted his gaze to the rearview mirror. The older teen boy stared at him with a guarded challenge, while the younger ones' expressions made him think they considered themselves 'captured.' The smallest boy, however, howled with glee at the sensation of being in a working vehicle, like a Monwyn fan finally getting to ride on the back of a dragon.

*Ugh. Great.*

"Dad." Hayley coughed and sniffled. "Can we stop? The slime soaked through my clothes. It's like everywhere." She shivered, and whispered, "*everywhere.*"

"Yeah... couple minutes." Kenny looked down from the mirror to the rear viewscreen and zoomed in on the receding mall. "I don't want any thousand-legged surprises."

# 20

# DATA BURST

After levelling off at six hundred feet, Nina set the black, unmarked patrol craft to auto-drive. The Navcon reported a nine-minute flight to the Division 2 facility housing the morgue. She brought up a terminal panel and thought the name Paul Estrada into the search field. Within a few seconds, two satellite panels opened on either side of the first. A man's life unfurled before her eyes. No police record, married to Valerie Cortez, no children. After two minutes of poring over his files, the worst she could find on him consisted of a handful of noise complaints from the apartment below.

The man's work performance painted a long history of 'meh.' She quirked an eyebrow at a payment plan associated with a debt of ₡187,410. A bit of digging on that showed he'd committed a slight miscalculation with an attempt to play the stock market. He had evidently made purchases based on expected value of stock that wound up taking a hard nosedive. The man didn't seem like a chronic gambler though. He hadn't touched stocks since, and that kick in the financial balls had occurred two years and five months ago. His payments had been regular, not late.

*Unless he just finally cracked at having such a monstrous financial burden and nothing to show for it.*

She started a traffic pattern analysis, which attempted to hunt down any access to the GlobeNet from him that wound up connecting to an endpoint outside of the UCF. With that going, and nothing even remotely interesting in his file, she let her head back and closed her eyes. The digital representation of Estrada's life seemed almost too bland to believe, but also too bland to be fake. Anyone looking at this guy from an espionage standpoint would think him an invented person. *Only a newbie would've made this as a false persona... unless that's what they wanted us to think. Maybe they assumed we'd take him at face value because he's so unremarkable, and did that on purpose knowing we'd never expect them to be that obvious. Ugh. Circular reasoning sucks.* In her gut, she didn't think Estrada worked for the ACC. While a determined operator could fake a person's records all the way back to birth, including pictures of grade school art projects his parents put online, it seemed an awful lot of work to infiltrate a shipping company... and then to have the guy flame out on some flavor-of-the-week street chem.

*Beep.*

Nina lifted her head and glanced at the screen. The net trace showed thousands of transmissions which all showed 'endpoint does not exist,' a sure sign of a chimeric address. She checked a few at random, and they all appeared to have headed to a geographic address range associated with Mexico. Where exactly inside Mexico though, she couldn't tell.

*This guy's been sending data to the ACC for...* She scrolled over the list of hits, checking dates. *A little over two months. Always from the home terminal, and always around seven at night. Like as soon as he gets home, he checks in.*

"Ops, this is Lieutenant Duchenne."

A generically handsome man in his middle twenties with brown hair and skin appeared on a holo-panel in the car. "Go ahead, lieutenant."

"I need a site team to Tower 147, apartment 26-33, Sector 8071. The scene should be reasonably secure. Div 1's been in and out already. Primary focus is any data they can extract from the terminal." She glanced at the Navcon showing arrival at the Division 2 facility in twenty-seven seconds. "I doubt it, but there's a small chance this guy could be ACC, so proceed with due caution."

"Understood, lieutenant." The man nodded. "Anything else?"

"That's all."

He disconnected.

Nina oscillated between disbelief that the ACC could set up such an obvious spy who'd gone undetected for this long, and the worry that there could be thousands like him everywhere under Division 9's collective noses. *As soon as I'm done here, I should try to track down anyone who might remember him from grade school... see if Paul Estrada really existed.*

The patrol craft landed itself on the roof of the Division 2 Regional Tech Center. Nina got out, letting the gull wing door close on its own as she walked off. A short elevator ride brought her to the fourth sub-basement and a long, white corridor that smelled of antiseptic. Dim lighting and a minimum of furnishings made her feel like she'd walked into the setting of a horror holo. Five steps in, she found herself shivering at the over-amped air conditioning.

Plain white doors, labelled A to F lined both walls, A, C, and E on the left. She walked the length, some fifty meters, to an open area where the hallway split off in either direction and an enormous U-shaped desk similar to a nurse's station dominated the wall opposite the corridor she'd emerged from. Behind it sat a thick-bodied man with curly black hair in a white lab coat and a tiny dark-skinned woman who she'd have taken for a thirteen-year-old if not for her generous chest.

"Hello," said the man. "Name's Oliver. Haven't seen you before."

She walked up to the counter. "Lieutenant Duchenne, Division 9. I'm here to see the coroner about inquest 24190412C6."

The small woman stiffened, and seemed committed out of nowhere to not making eye contact. *Division 9 strikes again.* Nina no longer took it as an automatic assumption of her having a doll body, but rather the reputation of her department.

"Sure, one sec, lieutenant." Oliver tapped holographic keys for a moment and then gestured to his right. "Down the other hallway here. You want Room H. I'll send a note to Doctor Charles. He'll be there in a minute or so."

Nina offered a polite smile. "Thanks."

Room H sat behind the first door on the right, opposite Room G, a decent way down the hallway from the intersection by the desk. Nina walked in to an even colder space where heavy square cooler doors covered three walls. Two procedure tables occupied the center of the otherwise open area. On either side of the entry door sat a small cubicle assembly with four desks each.

She waited, pacing, for a few minutes before the door slid open with a hiss, admitting a freakishly tall man with a smooth, shiny, bald head and great white caterpillar eyebrows. He looked to be well into his fifties, and his skin was as dark as she'd ever seen a person. The top of her head didn't even reach his pectorals, though the man appeared quite far from muscular.

"Good morning, lieutenant." He smiled.

She'd expected a deeper voice; hearing him sound so 'normal' caught her off guard.

"I understand you're looking into Mr. Estrada?"

She nodded. "Yes, that's correct. In the report, it mentions that you detected an unexpected data burst?"

"That's correct. What was it?" He crossed the room and grasped the handle of one of the coolers on the topmost row.

"We weren't able to trace the exact destination. The transmission went to a chimeric address."

Doctor Charles pulled the door open and a motorized shelf extended bearing a sheet-covered body. Pale blue light came on inside the white slab, casting a man's body in shadow on the linen. The tray finished extending and lowered to the height of an average table. "My understanding of that word relates to genetics, I'm afraid your use of it baffles me."

Nina approached as he pulled back the sheet. "A chimeric address is an illusion. It's a high security protocol scheme where the sending and receiving nodes only connect for brief periods using ever-changing addresses based on the clock cycle and encryption key. Twenty times a second, the destination node randomly generates a network address that it listens on. A sending node with the same encryption key will generate the same series of codes based on the time. That network address exists only for a fraction of a second, and a single transmission can span many thousands of different network addresses."

"Oh." Doctor Charles whistled. "And I thought my job was difficult."

"What can you tell me about Mr. Estrada here? There isn't much in his file."

"Well… The deceased had elevated levels of Placinil in his system at the time of death. Based on a few detected impurities, I think he was more likely taking Harmony."

"I thought they were the same drug?" Nina raised an eyebrow. "Just called Harmony when you bought it from some random guy on the street and Placinil when it came from a legitimate channel."

"A bit of misinformation." The doctor smiled. "There are subtle chemical differences. Placinil is an anti-anxiety medication. It does not generate as pronounced a 'high.' Harmony starts off as Placinil, which is typically stolen or obtained under false pretenses. It's treated with a few additional chemicals that enhance the effect enough to create the artificial plateau of contentment. While by the standards of most recreational chem users, a Harmony high is tame, but it can last for hours."

"By tame, you mean the user doesn't experience hallucinations, altered personality, or delusions?" Nina's gaze settled on the pattern of six bullet wounds in Paul Estrada's chest, courtesy of Division 1. "This man charged *at* the police... after apparently becoming unglued enough to go on a shooting spree."

"I haven't taken it myself, but from what I have read, Harmony makes the user 'feel great' for anywhere between four to eight hours depending on tolerance. And by feel great, I mean someone under a dosage sufficient to get high could be given news that their mother just died and they'd feel happy for her. Almost nothing can bother them until they come down." Fluffy white eyebrows crept upward. "The drug's only withdrawal symptom we've been able to find consists of a somewhat stronger state of depression, though I believe that is a psychological aftershock more than a chemical dependency. After the user has experienced a state where 'everything is awesome all the time,' reality is crushing."

Nina folded her arms. "That doesn't seem odd to you at all? A man who's feeling 'everything is awesome' decides to rampage kill?"

"Mr. Estrada experienced a sudden change in personality to aggressive from highly stressed, but timid and passive. The Division 1 report mentioned the wife called him a 'giant mouse.' She said that he kept getting pushed around at work and refused to chase a promotion or a raise. If he wasn't a stiff, they probably would've gotten Zero involved expecting a psionic attack."

Nina sighed. "I was thinking the same thing."

"However." Doctor Charles held up one long finger. "I do have some new information."

"Aside from the random flurry of data?"

"Yes. The confusing thing is that the chemical analysis doesn't fit the symptoms of Harmony. However, this man's behavior does match some reports from people who had been on a similar drug, Tao."

"Tao's the same stuff, just made on the street."

Doctor Charles chuckled. "Well, as same as they can make it. We're talking about people of questionable expertise using second, third, and sometimes even fourth-grade materials to simulate the effects of Placinil amplified. It's as if someone's combining autoshower soap and synthetic vodka hoping to make rocket fuel. However, these symptoms have been noted before in individuals who've taken Tao. Heightened sense of aggression, with a particular trigger response to authority figures."

A light came on in Nina's head. "Estrada seemed calm and normal at work, as though he hadn't killed several people before arriving."

"Quite possible for someone on any of these drugs. They have no ability to feel anything but calm and happy."

"He's called to a meeting with his boss, and winds up killing her. Division 1 had already figured him as the shooter from the apartment building, so they arrived within seconds of him killing his supervisor..."

"An authority figure. I suppose it may be possible this man was on Tao rather than Harmony, though the analysis of his blood sample doesn't support that."

Nina stared at the dead man's face. "So you're saying that there's no medical explanation for it?"

Doctor Charles reached into empty air. "Terminal." A window opened at his fingertip, and he brought up an image of bloody beige tissue flecked with dots. Text and gauges streamed past it in a separate box. He tapped a few of the controls, and the image zoomed in enough to expand the dots into metal spiders.

"Nanobots," said Nina.

"Precisely. Mr. Estrada had a significant number of them in his system, and they do not match any known model on the market. We were able to find etching inside with a manufacturer's logo: Nikkatsu Corporation."

"I'll need copies of the scan data from those nanobots."

"Of course, lieutenant." Doctor Charles switched screens, bringing up a 3D hologram of Estrada's head. He 'grasped' it and peeled away layers until he exposed the brain stem, where he indicated a small bit of metal about a half-inch long and two millimeters wide. "We also found this. Its location and design suggests its creation in situ by nanobots." He zoomed in and pointed out a near-microscopic metal wire running up the brain stem to an NIU. "Analysis of this module identified it as the source of the data burst. The device appears to contain a small radio transmitter we believe acts like traffic control for these nanobots, which is not in and of itself unusual. Many nanobot systems rely on such coordination from a command unit. What makes this one stand out is that it breaks the chicken/egg theory."

Nina raised an eyebrow.

"The nanobots came first, and made the control node. Typically, say in the case of a CamNano component, the person will have the control module implanted and it will generate the nanobots, which subsequently perfuse their body. In this case, Mr. Estrada somehow obtained these nanobots, and they made a nest."

She stifled the urge to shiver. While most of her body consisted of plastisteel and other synthetic components, her brain and spine remained hers. "I think the nanobots came in with the drug. We've seen that before. Some drugs and military boosters do things that aren't chemically possible by combining the effect of nanobots with the dose."

Doctor Charles rubbed his chin. "An interesting concept, and not beyond plausible."

"Doctor, did you locate any other unusual structures in the body?"

"To be honest, we didn't look all that thoroughly. The command node stood out because of its size." He tapped a series of boxes in the right border, which flared green as his fingertip pierced the holographic plane. "I'll go back in as soon as we're done here, and let you know whatever I find."

She pushed aside her growing worry to give him a genuine smile. "Thank you, doctor. I think that's about it for now until you finish. I'll leave you to it then. Appreciate the help."

"It's quite all right. This should take me only an hour or two. How should I reach you with the results?"

Nina transmitted her Division 9 PID to his NetMini. "That's my official contact. If I'm unable to answer, you'll connect with someone from Ops who can relay the data to me."

"All right. Have a good day, lieutenant."

"You too, Doc. Thanks."

She glanced down at Estrada's body. *No... you're not a spy. You're a victim.*

———

NINA PULLED THE DOOR OF HER PATROL CRAFT DOWN. IT SEALED WITH A SOFT pneumatic hiss. "Hardin."

Five seconds later, the car's terminal opened a vid call. Harold Hardin appeared in hologram, his head and shoulders floating above the center of the console. "Nina... Any luck at the RTC?"

"Some." A thought opened a separate window in her head, from which she selected the files on the nanobots. Flicking her eyes toward Hardin launched the files from her NetMini to the car, and over a secure channel to her boss. "Turns out our stiff had a bunch of nanobots in him which the doctor didn't recognize. They're of no known type." A magnified image appeared to Hardin's left, resembling a robot crab with multi-tool arms instead of pincers. "I'm glad they're not that big." She chuckled. "Creepy as hell. But they've never seen them before. He did say they found a manufacturer's logo inside... Nikkatsu Corporation."

"Japanese." Hardin tapped a finger on his chin. "I'll send that on up the food chain. Due to diplomatic concerns, it would be better if you didn't contact them directly unless you absolutely have to."

"I hate politics, sir."

Hardin laughed. "So does everyone... except politicians. So... nanobots?"

"Estrada was high on Harmony at the time of death, though his erratic behavior has been linked more to a similar chem, Tao. Based on the purity of the trace they found in his blood, the doctor is certain he hadn't taken Tao."

"Hmm." Hardin looked off to the side for a moment. "Tao has been linked to quite a bit of violence, especially against police."

"Authority figures, sir. I was up late reading case files from Division 1. The drug makes the user hostile to authority figures, but I don't think it's chemical in nature. They haven't bothered to do any deep scans on any of those suspects. They find Tao in the bloodstream and write it off as 'drug crazed.' But I think there's something more to it."

"The nanobots."

"Right." Nina tapped the control sticks, itching to take off but unsure where to go. "I'm almost convinced Estrada isn't ACC... but they're involved somehow."

"Understood. Let me know if you need anything."

"Will do. Might as well see if his widow and co-workers can contribute anything."

Hardin nodded and disconnected.

She brought up Valerie Cortez's NetMini signal, which traced to a Kuroshi Pharmaceuticals corporate office. *Hmm. That's a coincidence and a half... but they don't make Placinil. And they're not based in Japan, despite the name.* Nina pulled her patrol craft into the air and swung it around to point in the direction of the Kuroshi office, a good forty-minute flight north, even at 600 mph.

"Well, it's not like I wanted to do anything else today." She frowned, hoping Elizaveta would tolerate spending more time with her 'grandparents.'

# 21

# OLD FRIENDS, NEW ENEMIES

T he strong scent of garlic eventually overwhelmed Katya's nervousness. She slipped into an intrigued-amused-predatory smile and ate a few forkfuls while testing Zack's reaction to her giving off an 'interested' vibe. While using food as a reason not to talk, she opened a connection from her headware to her NetMini and poked the contact entry for Joey. Neither her pride, nor her distaste for him proved strong enough to dissuade her worry. Either possibility with Zack—cop or actual ACC agent (albeit a sloppy amateur)—had the potential to end in disaster for her. Suffering an interaction with Joey seemed trivial by comparison.

⌜All hail my Russian sex goddess,⌟ said Joey as soon as he appeared via virtual holo-panel. ⌜What do you need?⌟

⌜You assume I need something?⌟

⌜Of course.⌟ He flashed that shit-eating grin that always made her want to zap him in the back of the neck with her stunner implant. ⌜One, I owe you... probably a few favors. Two, you've never called me except when in the middle of doing something for me, and since you're not in the middle of doing something for me right now...⌟

⌜Well. In this case, you are correct. I need a small favor.⌟ She smiled at Zack. "Have you been at Laughlin-Reed long?" A still of Zack's face floated away from the man, compressed into a neat image file, and zipped into the virtual panel holding Joey. ⌜I need you to tell me who this man is. He is either a clever police officer or an idiot spy for the ACC.⌟

"Five months." Zack sipped tea. "Five very long months. It gets boring fast when you've got to keep your head down. I'm sure you know what I mean.

Joey's eyebrows lifted. ⌜You're serious? ACC? You know they've got listeners that pick up on certain words, right?⌟

"Certain professions demand a degree of sacrifice. ⌜Dead serious.⌟ The digital representation of Katya's face stared daggers at Joey while she kept an amused smile outside. 「I am sitting at a restaurant across the table from this man who has just claimed to be an infiltrator. Either he is so desperate to get me in bed that he has abandoned all sense of operational protocol, or he is a police officer trying to trick me.」

「Why would he be trying to trick you?」 Joey raised and lowered alternating eyebrows. The left half of his face tinted blue, reflected light from his terminal. 「Has someone been doing something naughty-naughty?」

"Indeed they do." Zack leaned his elbow on the table, grinning at her. "This is the worst part. Pretending to be just another employee. Did they at least tell you what your objective is?"

Katya put another forkful of pasta, sausage, and broccoli in her mouth. 「I took a job from Alex. Nothing too over the top. I am basically a delivery bot with breasts. This man followed me out; I do not know how much he knows.」

「I didn't think you had that much storage capacity down there. 」 Joey chuckled. The tint on his skin changed with the contents of his screens.

Katya's blush—due to actually having an uncomfortable passenger stuffed exactly where Joey joked about—manifested in the real world, though she managed to keep the VR copy of her staring death at him.

"Are you all right?" Zack reached across the small table and took her hand.

Katya held up a finger while chewing, swallowed, and gasped for air. "Yes. I'm not used to such strong garlic. It is good, but it caught me by surprise."

"You seem like the type of woman who doesn't appreciate being caught by surprise."

*More than you know.* Her eyes narrowed a little before she managed to arrest the sinister stare begging to be unleashed. "I'm not fond of unexpected things."

Joey seemed to be reading something off to the side for a few seconds. 「Where'd you find this guy? He's not with the National Police Force.」

「I told you. He followed me out of Laughin-Reed International. He says he works for their network operations team as a defenseman. I thought I'd lost him, but he showed up here anyway.」 Her virtual face scowled at Joey.

「He's a tech guy? Probably lifted your NetMini signal from the LRI building and pinged it after he lost you. It's not legal, but it's the sort of thing kiddies start doing as their first hack… finding people. Easy peasy. If it makes you feel better, you *did* lose him. Blame your 'mini. Hmm. This guy… Zachary Martin. His file's a pile of shit. Zack Martin didn't exist eight months ago. How long's he been at LRI?」

Katya's virtual eyebrow climbed. 「That was fast. He said five months.」 "So aside from following random women, what do you do for fun?" 「If he's not a cop, he's pretending to be an ACC spy to impress me. Either that or he really is one and the worst rookie I've ever seen.」

「Fast?」 Joey scoffed. 「That took me almost eleven seconds. I am the net *god*. Should've had him in six. 」 He held his hand up into frame, examining his fingernails. 「Go on, kiss the ring.」

"It is better to avoid creating too much of a record," said Zack. "I don't go out much as there are cameras everywhere."

「You don't know the half of it, pal.」 Joey chuckled.

"However…" He traced his thumb back and forth across her hand. "I haven't had much reason to yet. Do you enjoy your work, or are you only putting up with it in your attempt to pursue a degree?"

*He is definitely ACC.* "We all do what we have to do, don't we?"

"Pity." He chuckled.

"That you think I wish to better myself?" She stabbed a piece of broccoli rabe, wanting to kill it.

Zack shook his head. "No, you misunderstand me. It is a pity that a society with such a superior arrangement politically speaking has decided to adopt one of the worst attributes of its progenitors. The rampant sexism..." He exhaled, raising his arms in disbelief. "It's disgraceful."

┌Kat, do you have a soma?」

┌ Yes, but it's not on right now. They are not of much use on trained operatives. Why?」

┌Good. Because that amount of bullshit would've blown it straight out.」 Joey laughed. ┌ If bullshit was a dick, even *you* would gag on this one. Did you whammy this guy with the pheromones or has your ass always been that magnetic?」

Her avatar smirked at him. ┌You tell me. You are always staring at it as well.」

"It is not only women who join the army to become citizens so they can attend school."

┌Okay, ya got me there, but I'm addicted to things that might kill me.」

Zack squinted a little. "Army? Interesting you didn't refer to them by their proper title."

"Theoretically, let us assume for the sake of argument that your opinion of my role here is correct. Someone in that line of work does not last long by advertising it, no? You might as well speak Russian or German to me."

He grinned, leaning back a touch as he chuckled.

┌Bingo, yelled Joey. Dear Katya, you are seated across the table from one Mr. Anders Becker. Got a facial recognition match from some 'liberated' data. Age twenty-three, born in Munich. His parents look to be relatively well off, and there's a bunch of crosslinks to executives. I think he got his role with the OOI because of mommy and daddy.」

Katya's eyes iced over as she spoke a hair over a whisper. "*V yetom Vy neopytny. Vasha rabota ne ta kotoruyu lyudi dolzhen obsuzhdayut... Osobenno dly takovo trusa.*[1]"

Zack, rather Anders, regarded her for a few seconds, body tensing, eyes narrowing. "I'm sorry; I didn't quite catch that."

The waitress doll approached and collected empty plates. "How was everything? Can I get you anything else?"

"Excellent," said Katya, smiling. "Cappuccino please."

Anders waved the doll off.

┌ Look, Kat... I gotta send this in. Sorry, but Nine's going to be all over that place.」

┌It's fine. I called it in, didn't I? They can't think I'm harboring any loyalty to Moscow-Berlin. This man will try to kill me if he realizes he's exposed himself and I am not, what's the idiom? 'On the payroll.'」

Joey grinned. ┌They don't know you like I know you. I bet you wouldn't lose any sleep over compromising him for your own goals... even if you were on the same side.」

*You don't know me at all.* She kept her expression neutral. 「Yes, well, I'm not. You know that.」

「Yeah. Sit tight. They'll be there soon.」

She squirmed, the stolen data inside her as conspicuous and unpleasant as a Gee-ball sphere crammed where it didn't belong. As soon as the waitress left the area, she smiled at Anders. "You're learning."

He continued staring at her for a few seconds. "I'm not sure I understand."

"Some of the things you said before aren't the sorts of things said to someone you haven't validated. It shows a lack of experience. I shouldn't be surprised since you needed to trace my 'mini after I lost you. Such lack of care almost makes me wonder if you obtained your position as a favor to your parents."

Anders charm melted off. He seemed about ready to tantrum like a spoiled boy who wasn't used to not having his way.

"Sorry."

"For?" He flicked his thumb at the handle of his tea mug.

The doll dropped off one cappuccino and walked away.

"For being right. Your parents got you in the door with the Office of Operational Intelligence. You really are new at this aren't you? I said that not knowing, but you gave away the answer with your facial expression."

An uncomfortable silence settled over them. Outside, a flash of orange and yellow caught Katya's eye where a gaudy van parked at a corner close to the bistro's entrance.

Anders chuckled. He looked down at the table for a few seconds while trying to come up with a retort. His body language set her on edge. She figured him the type to respond to a woman getting the better of him with violence... and think it her fault. "I understand... Katya. My mistake, I thought you were still active."

"Oh." She lifted the tiny mug to her lips. "I suppose I wasn't the only one on the vid then. You might be able to elude them if you start running now, but they're probably already here." Katya winked and sipped her cappuccino.

Anders leapt to his feet. He spared her a half-second glare before fast-walking out the door, buttoning his suit jacket. The 'Nacho Mama' food van pulled around the corner and followed. She assumed it contained Division 9 agents. *Not so subtle as they think.* It also didn't surprise her that Anders appeared oblivious to them. Half a block west from the café door, Anders Becker vanished into the side door of a brightly-painted van covered with images of tortilla chips and cheese.

Katya shook her head. *Pridurok*[2].

# 22

# HARMONY

"Rawr," said a small voice.

Nina opened her eyes. Eight hours of talking to person after person about Paul Estrada swirled in a disorienting blur of quasi-dream that gave way to her bedroom ceiling.

"Rawr!" yelled a small voice.

She rolled over, facing away from the wall to the window side of her Comforgel pad. Elizaveta, in a set of footie pajamas made to look like a bright green dinosaur complete with hood and long stuffed tail, raised her hands and made dinosaur noises.

Nina gasped. "Oh, no. There's a T-rex loose in the apartment!"

She scrambled out of bed and ran. Elizaveta chased her around for a few minutes roaring. When she wound up giggling more than trying to sound like a ravening dinosaur, Nina whirled about and caught her in a hug, sweeping her into the air.

"Is my little T-Rex hungry?"

Elizaveta nodded, causing the dino-hood to flop up and down over her face.

"Well, I suppose there's some raw meat left… would you like beef?"

The girl shook her head.

"Deer?"

"No."

"I might be able to get some pterodactyl steaks."

Elizaveta shook her head again.

"What kind of meat does this scary T-Rex want?"

The girl raised both hands and yelled, "Waffles!"

"Waffles!" Nina set her in a chair at the kitchen table and acted concerned. "They're fast… hard to catch."

Elizaveta looked worried.

"Shh. I'm hunting waffles." Nina snuck up on the freezer, pulled the door open fast, and 'ambushed' a box of waffles.

"Yay!" yelled Elizaveta.

Nina stuck two in a small electric convection oven and poured the girl a cup of orange juice. Soon, the oven beeped and she set a plate of hot waffles and a bottle of syrup on the table, then leaned against the wall, quietly bemoaning being awakened a full thirty minutes before her alarm would've gone off at 6 a.m. Any trace of regret evaporated when the girl grinned up at her, waffle bits mushing in her teeth as she chewed. *I volunteered for this. Enjoy it. These moments won't last forever.* She copied the entire dinosaur chase from her two-hour recording buffer, and saved the video.

Nina kept smiling, but turned maudlin. Her mind danced around the worry of Elizaveta turning into an angry teenager, as all the horrors she'd seen as a child came back at once. Would she go batshit at sixteen or seventeen, wind up an out-of-control doser? *Maybe if I hadn't found her.* No… that *could* happen, but not with her. She hoped the other Russian orphans wound up with decent homes. Any one of them would be a handful in their later teens if they didn't get a lot of support over the next few years.

She scratched at her stomach, taken by a sudden overwhelming guilt at having a false body. *Do I even deserve this kid? I'm barely human.* Nina tossed the idea aside, thinking of the eerie white-haired synth named Kelly. The conversation they'd had in the whispercraft coming back from the bayou had given Nina new perspective on her situation. She still had a soul; she remained human in all ways that matter. A reluctant smile formed, which grew when Elizaveta grinned at her. *She's so resilient. This is one of her good moments.* When it got dark, she could wind up hiding in her room, terrified 'they' would come take her away and put her in some other home… or the Citizen Management Officers who arrested her would kick in the door. Well, maybe not that… after watching Nina tear the bars off the primate cages, Elizaveta hadn't been so worried about CMO officers.

Once the waffles vanished, Nina took her to the bathroom. The girl had mixed feelings about the autoshower, refusing to get in unless Nina remained in the room right outside the cylinder. At first, she'd been terrified of it at all, thinking it too much like a cage. After a few days, Elizaveta's initial fear of the machine had become the same sort of exhilaration one usually got from rides at an amusement park. Nina almost had to lift her through the door, but once inside, the child adored the 'shower machine,' and cheered the whole time she could do so without gulping down soap.

When the dry cycle finished, she sent the girl to her bedroom to pick an outfit, and stole a quick shower for herself. Elizaveta drifted into Nina's room while she got dressed for work, content to sit on the edge of the bed with her white bear in her lap. Soon, they rode the elevator to the roof and her patrol craft. Elizaveta talked about how much fun she'd have with her 'cousins,' Emily and Kelly.

At some point, she expected the girl to ask why her 'cousins' weren't growing up, but that conversation could wait. 'One's a doll and the other's a synthetic with a person's ghost somehow stuffed inside it' would probably go over her head. Heck, it went over Nina's head.

After dropping Elizaveta off at the parents' house in the foothills, Nina raced across West City to the Police Administrative Center. By 7:52 a.m., she flopped in the chair behind her desk. Her office neighbors had all reacted with shock when she began turning the lights on shortly after coming to terms with seeing Vincent's ghost. The drab grey walls and government-issue blue carpet hadn't gotten any cheerier, though at least the window let in some sunlight once she opened the blinds.

Nina settled in and pulled up everything she could about the drug Tao. There seemed to be almost a hundred variations of it, each a little different based on the person who made it. As Doctor Charles had explained, Tao was a street chemist's attempt to recreate Harmony. Division 1 had hundreds of case reports containing the words 'Tao' and 'Harmony' (sometimes shortened to 'H'). Incidents of random anti-authority violence mentioned Tao eighty-seven percent of the time, though there appeared to be a recent upsurge in cases involving Harmony, and two where the aggressor was taking Placinil on a legitimate prescription, however neither of the Placinil cases involved death. One man got into a fistfight with his boss at work, paid a fine for simple assault, and left to find a new job. The second patient, a woman, felt her day incomplete without stopping to inform a pair of Division 1 officers about how they had no authority to tell people what to do.

The woman served two days for public intoxication, which Nina figured Division 1 used as the law enforcement version of 'fuck you too.' Out of curiosity, she pulled the video from the holding cell. Miss Leslie Yu, age nineteen, spent the first two hours pacing circles around a tiny room with fluorescent yellow-green walls, screaming. Mostly gems such as 'you fuckers can't do this to me,' and 'I have rights,' and so on. By hour three, she quieted and seemed confused. At hour five, she broke down sobbing and resumed shouting, only in a pleading tone, asking where she was, who took her, and why they'd locked her up.

Nina sent a handful of sniffer programs over the GlobeNet, hunting for any evidence of Leslie's digital existence sending data to Mexico. *On that note...* She spent the next twenty minutes launching sniffers at a selection of people who'd been detained for Harmony/Tao related violent incidents as well.

She leaned back, put her feet up on the desk, and stared at 473 counters ticking downward.

While she waited, she thought back and forth over what she knew of Paul Estrada. Finding his parents, a couple people who'd gone to school with him, and one teacher had convinced her he had grown up in the UCF. Any thought of him being an ACC spy, at least a willing one, had dissipated. The man's job with a shipping company didn't give him any intelligence value whatsoever, unless the ACC developed a sudden keen interest in consumer product marketing trends.

"Nina?" Hardin walked in, reversed a step, knocked, and walked back in. "Morning."

"Sir." She pulled her feet off the desk and sat up. "Estrada was a citizen as far as I could tell. Nothing suspect. Record's clean. He has almost zero intelligence value. The only thing I can think of is either he's some kind of test case, or they're doing something indiscriminate."

"Test case?" Hardin sat in one of the two chairs facing her desk. For an ex-military man, he rather slouched, which caused his powder blue sweater to bunch up at the gut.

"The nanobots are the important bit. What if they *do* have an operative here we haven't picked up on, and they snuck up on Estrada one day and shot him full of these nanobots."

Hardin's eyebrow went up. "You're thinking something along the lines of nanobot mind control?"

"I'm not sure. They definitely seem to have figured out how to make nanobots alter someone's mood and trigger a specific aversion to authority figures. Remember that SoCal chem?"

Hardin chuckled. "Yeah. Some underage girl sold it and her doctor father made it, right?"

"Yeah." Nina stared at the countdown timers, trying to will them to go faster. "Made the doser see everyone around them with blonde hair and blue eyes, while overstimulating the pleasure centers of the brain."

"Similar effect as Harmony, sounds like."

Nina tilted her hand side to side. "Far stronger. Someone on SoCal would've stood in the middle of the road smiling at a PubTran bus coming for them, lost in a state of total bliss. Harmony's nowhere near that... crippling."

"I do have some news about Nikkatsu." Hardin plucked at the bunched-up fabric at his right knee, and flicked a bit of lint away. "They claim that particular model of nanobot isn't being exported out of Japan, and as far as they know, it's on a trial run at one specific facility, Nichinan Central Hospital, in Miyazaki Prefecture. I'm told they were quite shocked that we were even aware of the design."

"I assume you weren't the one who spoke with them, so I suppose it pointless to ask if you think they're lying."

"Alas. My friend across the hall didn't get that impression though."

Nina chuckled. 'Friend across the hall' meant someone in C-Branch.

"The Nikkatsu rep gave us some additional information. This particular nanobot was codenamed *Kami-no-tako.*"

Nina cracked up laughing.

"You find that humorous?" Hardin smiled, unsure whether to laugh with her.

"Divine octopus?" She whistled. "Well, I suppose it does have eight legs."

"They claimed it's part of a breakthrough in brain surgery techniques. These bots are supposed to be able to perform four instructions simultaneously, so in theory, they reduce the procedure time for sensitive deep-brain work."

"That's got to be it." She glared at the console. "These 'octopus' bots are already tailored to work on brain tissue... the firmware is already embedded in them. Nanobots have limited instruction sets due to size. Whoever did this to Estrada had to have gone after these 'bots on purpose. Less work than trying to rewrite all the reference data for brain structures. The nanobots had to have been responsible for Estrada's personality change."

Hardin nodded. "That seems plausible."

The first set of sniffers came back with zero detected connections to suspicious address blocks.

"Shit," muttered Nina.

Hardin, staring at the secure opaque rear of Division 9 holo-terminals, tilted his head. "Bad news?"

"The first six people came back with nothing for outbound data." She pondered a moment, tracing her finger up and down over her lips. "There's got to be two components. Maybe the data burst had nothing to do with Harmony. I need to talk to Doctor Charles again, see if he can find some other nanobots in Estrada's system."

Hardin patted the armrests of the chair twice and stood. "All right. Keep me apprised."

"Yes, sir."

Nina tapped the desk terminal and placed a vid call to Doctor Charles. He answered in four seconds, appearing in a sub window.

"Lieutenant... I'm so sorry. We had a gang war come in and I got swamped. Thirty-seven dead."

Her expression stayed flat. "I understand. Vid me when you can?"

"Oh. You misunderstand me. I finished the scan of Mr. Estrada, but I never got the chance to vid you with the results." He smiled. "I didn't find much, but perhaps it will be significant to you."

She leaned an inch closer to the terminal. "I'm listening."

"The nanobots appear to have constructed additional wires in the brain leading to several sites in the occipital lobe as well as the cerebrum. The specific regions targeted involve sight and hearing."

Nina tapped her foot, thinking. "So, he might have been experiencing auditory and visual hallucinations?"

Doctor Charles shook his head. "A decent assumption, but I do not believe so. The structure of these nanowires appears designed for inductive reactance rather than transmission. In simple terms, they are listening, not sending."

Nina's eyebrows furrowed together. "So... it's reading what he sees and hears?"

"Assuming that the technology functions, the nerve clusters surrounding the terminus of these nanowires are those involved in the processing of sight and hearing. The wires picking up electrical activity at those sites may provide signals that could be reprocessed into images and sound, yes."

"Thank you, doctor." She started to hang up, but hesitated. "Oh, one more question. Were all the dead nanobots you found in Estrada the same type, or did you find any others?"

"We found a small collection of standard stimpak nanobots in his bladder, though they appear to have been there for some time. Based on their condition, I highly doubt they had been active at any point within the past two months."

*Okay... so it has to be these kami takos.* She snickered to herself. *Damn. Now I want sushi.* "You've been a great help, doctor. Thank you."

Doctor Charles bowed, and hung up.

Nina stared at the rest of the countdown timers racing away. "Paul Estrada *was* a spy... he just didn't know it."

# TRIBES

Kenny kept the truck a touch under seventy, heading south, until they left any trace of Colorado Springs behind. Not that he expected the millipedes to brave direct sunlight, as they tended to do that only when defending an outdoor nest or if starving. Then again, they did just walk right into the heart of a massive nest, so the bugs might have been angry enough to chase them a good ways. He suppressed a shudder at the sheer quantity of them in the mall. *What the hell are they eating to have bred to that number?*

"Dad," gasped Hayley, sounding like she'd throw up again if she opened her mouth too far.

"Sure... sure... hang on a sec."

"Umm, Dad," said Alyssa. "Why are those kids running around naked?"

"They're tribals, hon. Settlers out here call them 'Scrags.' It's gettin' on toward winter. They gotta be freezing. Probably explains why they risked approaching the truck. Usually, they avoid things that look too 'new.'"

"Dad." Hayley whined. "Stow the National Geographic. I just threw up all over myself and I'm sitting in a puddle of slime." She sniffed, gagged, and heaved again.

Kenny slowed and pulled over to the side of the broken pavement.

As soon as the truck stopped, Alyssa flung the driver side rear door open and jumped to the ground. Hayley followed, almost tripping in her haste to get out. She staggered a few paces away, bile trailing from her lip. In a fit of disgusted noises and flailing, she stripped until she stood naked on the road, arms held out to the sides in a posture of absolute disgust. Yellow patches covered her from where bug juice had soaked through her clothes. She coughed a little and dry heaved a few times.

Alyssa gasped; her rich tan became bright red. "Hale, what are you doing? Have you gone native?"

"I'm soaked in bug guts and puke. My clothes feel like snot!" After peeling a dark reddish-black squiggle from her stomach and dropping it, Hayley gagged and bowed forward to throw up a little more on the road. When that subsided, she wiped her mouth on the back of her arm and stood. "Mom! Water... please."

Nasir exited the truck, from the look on his face to get away from the smell of vomit.

Alyssa squirmed, clearly as uncomfortable as Hayley had been, but stared at Eldon and blushed harder.

Kathy climbed up into the truck bed. Her presence pushed all four Scrag kids to the tailgate. She keyed a code in one of the storage bins, which opened, and extracted two gallon-jugs of water. After she closed the lid and jumped down, the smallest Scrag boy attacked the bin, pushing random buttons and making it beep.

Kenny accepted one water jug as Kathy went by. He pulled off his WEC Duster armor, which had—along with his cowboy hat—absorbed most of the deluge of millipede insides. Kathy played showerhead, pouring water over Hayley as the girl chased ooze away from her skin with her hands.

Alyssa stared at Kenny, shot a pointed look at Eldon, and stared pleadingly at Kenny again.

"Yo, El." Kenny chuckled.

"Hmm?" He looked up from wiping down his armor with a rag.

"Alyssa wants to clean up, but she's still mortified about what happened. Don't s'pose you could make a show of not looking at her?"

He chuckled. "She brought that shit on herself, but yeah. No problem."

Eldon turned his back to the truck. "Just lemme know when it's clear."

Kenny waved to Alyssa, who after a momentary hesitation, peeled off her clothes. Unlike Hayley, she left her underwear on. Kenny caught snippets of conversation in Spanish from the tribal kids, none of whom had ever seen modern clothing, especially girls' underthings. The middle boy wondered what animal it had been made from. Kenny found it amusing until the oldest commented that Alyssa would make an excellent lifemate. The youngest boy said that he needed to take Luna for a lifemate since she was the only girl left in the tribe.

Luna seemed less than pleased with the idea and made an irritated grunt before declaring in Spanish, "I don't wanna join with Halcón. I don't wanna join with anyone yet. I'm too small!"

"No," said Halcón, the eldest, in Spanish. "Luna is right. I have too much to wait for her. That one is better. She is my age."

"Oh that feels awesome," said Hayley. She basked in the sun, dripping. "No more slime..."

"Are you okay?" Kathy poured water on Alyssa.

"Ugh. My stomach hurts from horfing, but yeah." Hayley twisted side to side to look herself over. Pink marks on her thigh indicated where she'd been bitten, but the stim-bot had mended it. "Couple'a bruises."

"That's not a bruise, Hale. *This* is a bruise." Alyssa showed off a giant purplish mark that wrapped around her back and chest in the recognizable shape of her armored vest. "That bug powerbombed me into the wall."

Kathy insisted on checking Alyssa's nose, fussing at some dried blood at her nostril. "You're lucky you didn't break anything."

Kenny ambled over and patted his daughter's shoulder.

She jumped, red-faced, but relaxed at seeing Eldon had not snuck up on her.

"That 'pede banged you up a bit." Kenny touched a finger to her ribs, one after the next. "Let me know if this hurts."

Standing in a patch of sunlight, Hayley stooped to the side and ran her hands through her hair over and over, flinging water.

Alyssa tolerated his prodding for a moment before she pushed him away so she could bend forward. "My ribs aren't broken. It doesn't hurt to breathe. Mom... hair please. Feels like I'm wearing a snot hat."

Kathy dumped water over Alyssa's head. Hayley caught a glimpse of bug gut slime stranding off in the flow over the pavement and retched.

"So what are we going to do with those kids?" asked Kathy.

"Depends on what their story is I guess." Kenny handed Alyssa a stimpak from his belt, and put his hands on his hips. "Either give them a ride home if they still have parents out here, or take them back to the city and let the police deal with it. Scrags usually send children on scouting parties 'cause they can get into places easier, but usually the families aren't *too* far behind. I've a feeling these four might be on their own."

Kathy nodded. "Okay, my turn." She handed Alyssa the water jug and started removing her clothes.

Kenny headed over to the truck and asked in Spanish, "So... why are you in my truck?"

"We found it," said Halcón. "We thought it was scavenge."

"What about the man inside?" Kenny gestured at Nasir.

The teen shrugged. "We didn't see man."

"Sorry," said Nasir, also in Spanish. "I was kinda busy keeping four thousand bugs off you guys. Wasn't paying attention to the outside world... and they were kinda quiet."

The smallest boy snuck up behind Alyssa and picked up Hayley's discarded underpants as if to steal them for himself. He grimaced in an instant and flung them away. The wad of cloth hit the side of the pickup, and stuck. The boy stuck out his tongue and gagged. He touched her jeans for less than a second before jumping back and waving his hand with a disgusted expression.

Halcón glanced to his left, watching Kathy rinse off.

"Hey. That's my wife," said Kenny. "Eyes front."

"She is too pale." The teen kept looking at her. "I did not know people could be that color."

Kenny grumbled, relaxing a bit that the boy's interest seemed curious rather than sexual. "You have a home to get back to? Parents? If you tell me where, I'll make sure you get back safe."

The smallest boy climbed the tire and slithered over the wall into the truck bed while Luna mimicked Kathy's hair-washing gestures. After a second's consideration, he moved to the edge of the truck bed and peed over the side with a finger two knuckles deep in his nose.

"We are not afraid," said Halcón.

"You're all kids. Where I'm from, kids don't run around dangerous places alone."

"Ken?" yelled Kathy. "Grab us some fresh clothes?"

Kenny reached to one of the storage bins close to the side and opened it. The Scrags gasped in awe at the stock of clothing within, an incalculable treasure to them. Kenny took one of his spare t-shirts and tossed it to the smallest boy, who grinned and wriggled into it without hesitation. He handed Luna a shirt as well.

Kenny collected a set of underwear for the girls and Kathy, as well as desert-brown fatigue pants and plain white tank tops.

The dust-coated girl continued to stare at the folded shirt, but made no effort to put it on. As Kenny stood, she looked up at him, worry clear in her eyes. Her want for actual clothes warred with a deep-seated fear, and she seemed ready to hand it back to him.

"I'm not asking you to be my wife. You are a child; I am an adult, and you need taking care of." He smiled. "It is the way of my people. I'm giving you a shirt because you have nothing on. That's all."

She stared at him for a few seconds, her distrust and hesitance melting away. After discarding her electric-cable belt and the sorry excuse for a skirt it held up, she slipped the shirt over her head. It fit her like a dress and she made adoring faces while running her hands around, feeling the material.

"Be right back." Kenny ran the clothes to Kathy and returned to the side of the truck while his family scrambled to get dressed.

Hayley seemed more in a hurry to get the armored vest back on than her clothes, but forced herself to put it on *after* the tank top. Kenny imagined Eldon's joke about her learning faster than new recruits that 'armor is life.'

"So, where are your parents?" asked Kenny.

"You are not taking us for your tribe?" asked the middle boy.

Kenny smiled. "Not if you still have a home. I'm not going to take you away from your parents."

The four of them stood less rigid, relief clear in their posture and expressions.

"Halcón." The eldest patted himself on the chest. He pointed at the boy next to him. "Gato."

Gato pulled off his comforter-turned-poncho, exposing a few scars on his left thigh that looked like they came from animal claws. "Can I have a new clothes too?"

"I'm Luna," said the girl, still admiring her new t-shirt dress.

The smallest boy pointed at himself. "Cielo."

"My name is Kenny." He pulled one of Kathy's shirts out, a hot pink one with a white cartoon cat face on the front. "Sorry about the color, but... we didn't exactly pack for a long trip."

The boy pulled it over his head and grinned. "Gato for Gato."

Cielo squatted and patted the truck bed. "What's his name?"

"Whose?"

"The beast." Cielo pet the truck bed. "He is great!"

Luna and Gato nodded.

"He is nice to let us ride him," said Luna.

"Does he eat much?" asked Cielo.

Kenny chuckled. "It's a truck. A vehicle."

"Oh." Cielo looked down, disappointed.

Gato leaned up and whispered emphatically at Halcón's ear. Both boys stared at Kenny during the one-sided, and insistent conversation. Kathy, dressed and back in her armored vest, approached and took a plastic bag from the truck bed, into which she collected the slimed clothing.

"Kenny," said Halcón. "We want to join your tribe."

"You four are on your own?" Kenny looked among them, noting their evident lack of eating well. "How long?"

"Raiders attack our village. We were away, scavving." Halcón put his arms around Gato and Luna. "We come back, and everyone is gone. Those who not dead, forced to join other tribe."

"We want to be your tribe," said Gato. "You have best power."

Alyssa, having changed into clean clothes, wandered over to Eldon, head bowed. They muttered for a few seconds before he chuckled and offered a hand. She gave him a weak smile, shook his hand, and walked back to stand by Hayley.

"All right." Kenny put his hands on his hips and nodded at them. "Since you four are alone, it's only right that we bring you with us."

The Scrag kids smiled.

"We'll bring you back to civilization. We are from the west, a great city."

"Behind the curtain of fire?" asked Halcón.

The other three gasped in fear.

Kenny resisted the urge to chuckle. "There is no curtain of fire."

They gave him suspicious looks.

"Yo, Ken..." Eldon walked up next to him. "Tellin' them kids there ain't no curtain of fire is like tryin' to convince one of them whackadoodles there's no sky-daddy up above. Let 'em have their fantasy."

"Yeah... but I don't want them thinking we're driving them to a fiery death."

The Scrags didn't react to English other than to seem confused.

"The green man," whispered Luna. "He can't be killed."

Eldon looked up. "Oh, I wish that were true."

"What did he say?" asked Cielo.

"He's just a man like me, but he's wearing armor. Like I said, we come from a great city where you won't have to hunt for food, run away from giant millipedes, or worry about some other tribe killing you over territory."

They exchanged glances.

"Hey, Dad." Hayley walked up to his side. "If I clean out the back seat, will that count as a swear jar pull?"

"Sure." He patted her shoulder.

"Cool." She grabbed some plastic bags and scrap cloth from a bin before leaning into the back seat. "Ugh. It stinks."

Alyssa went around the other side and climbed in to help.

"You from behind the curtain of fire?" asked Halcón.

"He's not lying." Cielo stared at Kenny for two creepy seconds before moving to Halcón's side and tugging on his arm. "I wanna go with them."

"Okay." Halcón offered a hand. "We will trust you."

While the girls cleaned bug guts and vomit from the back seat, Kenny handed the Scrags a ration pack each and used his NetMini to show them pictures of West City, to much awestruck gasping. Their excitement at being taken to the west grew, and soon their eagerness to see it equaled his desire to go home.

Leaving them to finish off their ration packs, Kenny headed to the front of the truck and worked a rag over his armored coat/vest. He chuckled at the stifled gags and random noises of displeasure coming from inside. *Glad I sprang for the stain-resistant seats.*

Kathy set the sealed plastic bag of dirty clothing in the back and came up behind him, encircling her arms around his chest and holding on. He grinned.

"You know when I said let's try for number three, I wasn't expecting to get four at once."

She laughed. "Thought you wanted to drop them off at the checkpoint."

"I do." He chuckled. "Just making a joke."

"Hmm." She gave him the same smiling up-and-down look she'd given him after he'd promised not to buy a new truck to take to the Badlands, and wound up doing it anyway two weeks later. She knew he would.

Kenny wiped his armor down as best he could without running water. Fortunately, the design of armored panels embedded in a flexible coat didn't give the muck too many places to collect. Still it would be a mess to get it out of the vest portion later. "I wasn't planning on keeping them, just bringing them to the city. They have a program for taking in found Scrags. Besides, I'm not sure I trust the oldest around Alyssa."

"You're so protective of her." Kathy squeezed him.

"And I overheard him saying she'd make a fine wife."

Kathy let go as he went to put his armor back on. "I'm sure she will if she ever decides to marry."

"Yeah." Kenny tugged the coat against his shoulders. "But I didn't get the feeling he meant to wait very long or that it much mattered how she felt about it."

"Oh." Kathy's eyebrows flared. "Okay, that could be a problem."

"It's how they are out here." He added his hat and tapped it in place. "So… you still wanna try for a son when we get back?"

"Ugh," said Hayley in the distance. "That was so damn nasty."

"Yeah." Alyssa coughed. "We still gotta rinse the floor mats. You barfed all over them."

"You barfed, too," said Hayley.

"That puddle is yours. I didn't eat rice."

Hayley retched. "Stop."

"Or corn."

"Ugh!" Hayley gagged.

"Aww, everyone knows barf always has corn in it no matter who ate what," said Eldon.

"Mmm!" Hayley covered her mouth and screamed into her hand. "Stop it! You're gonna make me hurl again."

Kenny turned to grin at Kathy, but a foreboding sky to the east stole the smile off his face. A wall of dark grey encroached upon the perfect blue overhead. "Damn. Seems we're in for some bad weather."

"What?" Kathy glanced behind her at the sky. "Oh… wow. That doesn't look good."

"No… no it doesn't." Kenny filled his lungs and raised his voice. "Gonna try and outrun that mess. Everyone, water a bush now even if you don't think you have to. I'd rather not stop in an hour." He repeated the suggestion to prepare for a long ride in Spanish to the Scrags.

Hayley looked up, stared at the clouds, and started shaking.

"Hale?" asked Alyssa.

Kenny hurried around the end of the truck to where the girls had been rinsing the rags they'd used to clean the seat. "Hayley?"

She pressed herself into him, trembling. "Dad… I think the storm's mad at us."

# THE OLD WAYS

**M**oments after the sun crept over the ruined landscape and sent long shadows stretching from bits of rubble, Noriko stirred. Masaru hadn't slept much. The night had gone by faster than it should have, proving he had nodded off here and there. Whenever he closed his eyes, he'd see Shuji's lifeless face staring at him. After one night sleeping outside, he'd expected to want to spend hours soaking in a bath to purge the filth, but his thoughts refused to release his friend.

"You're awake."

"Yeah." Noriko grunted and sat up. "Leg feels good enough to walk on."

He nodded.

She dug out two more packets of dehydrated sushi. Masaru choked down a standard selection of salmon, tuna, and some disastrous miasma he imagined attempted to be mackerel. Once they'd finished eating, she pulled herself standing and reattached the section of armor she'd removed from her thigh.

"Well?"

Noriko lowered herself to squat, straightened, and walked around in a small circle. "Little stiff. Lot sore, but good enough to get out of here. Are you ready?"

"Yes." Masaru stood and affixed the katana to his belt.

After Noriko disappeared behind a slab of broken wall to relieve herself, Masaru found a secluded place as well. He hesitated at the horrible impropriety of doing such a thing outside, in public, though urgency overwhelmed manners within thirty seconds.

He returned to the clearing to find her stretching, pulling her right boot up behind her butt. She nodded and reached for the case of food.

"I can carry that." Masaru grabbed the handles, trapping her fingers between his hands and the plastic. Her face hovered inches from his as they stooped over the box.

"How chivalrous of you," she said, a hint of a playful frown on her lips.

Masaru chuckled. "I do not think you weak. You have a rifle. I have a blade."

"Okay."

He stood there for a moment in silence.

She glanced down at his hand for a second before making eye contact again. "Whenever you're ready."

He cleared his throat and released his grip long enough for her to get her fingers out from under his. Noriko checked her assault rifle over before leaning out the door and aiming left and right.

"Clear," she muttered.

He carried the ration box out after her. In the glare of the early morning sun, the field of devastation surrounding him seemed harsher. Swirls of brown dust gathered in mini cyclones along the road. Wind whispered among the cracking ruins of old buildings, accented with the occasional *clang* of metal banging on metal. Dark blotches on the road indicated where tires or other things had melted during the blast. Little radiation remained from the device the Korean infiltrator had set off in 2097, 322 years ago.

The advent of this odd return to feudalism had brought with it a resurgence in some areas of belief in ancestral spirits, oni, and the kami. Masaru never gave much thought to any of that, thinking it 'nonsense for poor people.' He had agreed with Joey's opinion that his friend had not been seeing the ghost of his father, but something more mundane. Discovery that an AI had been responsible reaffirmed Masaru's opinion that the world had an order to it, not superseded by things a rational mind had no room to entertain.

Such fanciful things as ghosts and demons had influenced a significant enough portion of the population by the time Japan stabilized to where the city of Miyakonojo had been declared a mass grave and/or memorial site. There had been a few motions to reclaim and build, since land space remained a premium, but the superstitious crowd continued protesting. The failure of the Meiji robots to clear and decontaminate the area only further fanned the flames of fear. Enough stories of the UCF's Badlands, and its mysterious tendency of technology to break down, had made it to Japan where everyone had seemed ready to accept an oni as responsible for the construction robots' mass failure.

*Did anyone even bother to investigate them at all?* As hard as he thought about it, he couldn't recall a single article explaining how 2,500 Meiji construction robots malfunctioned over a four-month span. It had happened decades ago, but still, no one bothered to explore the area. Of course, Noriko's story of the 'Bermuda Triangle' effect occurring more recently would send the superstitious into a frenzy.

Miyazaki Prefecture, ruled by Kurotai Electronics and by extension, his father, leaned more toward feudalism than not. Masaru regarded it all as an elaborate and pointless costume drama. Society could get along just fine without everyone acting ridiculous.

Of course, the average citizen seemed to adore it. Especially given Kurotai's more relaxed approach than, say, Okinawa, where a truly awful performance review at work could result in an order of seppuku. Ritual suicide did remain in Kurotai, but it had only been invoked twice. Once for an engineer whose willful negligence caused an accident that killed thirteen people, and once for an auditor who'd embezzled ninety million credits.

Noriko led the way west, no doubt following a compass in her armored helmet. The yellow transparent visor over her face glinted from a projected HUD, which still worked despite the crack. She panned her rifle from side to side, pointing it wherever she looked.

For as far as he could see in any direction, continuous ruin stretched. His mind teased him with doomsday fantasies, as though the entire world smoldered. The crunch and scuff of their footsteps echoed when they entered a concrete canyon where a section of taller buildings remained standing. Business offices or apartments, he couldn't tell.

"Why haven't they rebuilt this place?" asked Noriko, breaking their two-hour silence.

Masaru shrugged, not that she could see him behind her. "Superstition. My"— he almost said father—"theory is that people spend too much time worrying about what may or may not exist, and not enough time worrying about the world in which they live."

"Yeah." She smiled over her shoulder at him. "I know what you mean. At least old man Kurotai's a little more relaxed than some. Isn't it silly to watch him dress up like a samurai and stand in front of a field of hover tanks?"

His father thought the old ways represented pride in Japan, but he did not believe it a paradigm without flaw. Many aspects of ancient Japan struck him as barbaric, and not worthy of recreation. At the image of him prancing about on a horse in front of a battalion of hover tanks with plasma cannons, he couldn't help but chuckle. "I can see that being humorous."

She walked backward for a few steps, giving him a curious stare. "What do you think about all of it?"

"I think it wasteful. Pageantry over practicality. We should look forward, not backward."

"You said you spent time in the west?" She spun fast at a creak of metal, but nothing emerged from where she aimed.

"Two years, while attending school. There are many unpleasant things about their city, but it makes more sense than this."

Her laugh bounced among the walls, repeating from windows and cracks like an army of tiny gremlins. "Never expected you'd prefer the west. I thought you samurai types ate all this costume stuff right up."

"I'm not really a samurai." He shifted the ration box to one hand to stretch and rest his fingers.

"But you're carrying a katana… if you're not a samurai, that'll get you killed in some places."

Masaru smiled. "Then I shall not go to those places."

"Who are you, Moto Masaru?" She grinned over her shoulder at him. "A man from Japan, in a western suit and a katana at his side."

He hesitated, momentarily taken by watching her walk. In his life thus far, he'd spent much time admiring the feminine form from behind, from the side, from above, any way possible. *I am not gazing upon her body; I am gazing upon her.* Would she tolerate knowing who he was, or would her entire demeanor change? She might close herself off and project the subservience he so loathed, or react with contempt.

"I'm a negotiator for Kurotai Corporation."

Noriko stepped over a warped streetlamp post and turned to face him. "You said that already. I meant what makes you tick inside, not what you do for a job."

He opened his mouth, but before his brain could come up with a decent answer, three men emerged from a narrow channel between a pair of six-story rubble piles. Their clothes looked as though they'd spent the past few months sleeping in them, but otherwise had the style of modern middle class from a more western-leaning area. The figure in the center had a JSDF helmet on, and carried a rifle identical to the one in Noriko's hands. Bloodstains and rips decorated his Manglers Gee-ball t-shirt. The other two carried combat rifles as well, though far less boxy than the JSDF weapon with all its onboard electronics.

All three had a cocky swagger suggesting their intentions fell somewhere between harassing outsiders or murder-looting.

Noriko's arms and rifle blurred, shifting from relaxed to putting three rounds into the chest of the man in the JSDF helmet in an instant.

Speedware dragged everything into slow motion. Masaru heaved the box of rations upward and ducked around it as azure muzzle flare bloomed from the rifles pointing toward him. He leaned to the right and down, allowing bullets to spin by without touching him. Three red-tipped projectiles moved past him from behind, heading for the thug on the left.

Masaru sprinted forward, closing the twenty-ish meters in the time it took Noriko's bullets to strike the man on the right. He darted in an outward curve that kept him inches from a continuous stream of spiraling slugs coming from the man he intended to kill. When he reached his target, he drew the Nano katana in an upward slash that severed the man's left forearm before the blade continued into his torso and emerged from the top of his head. An expression of fear only began to form on the punk's face as Masaru completed his swing and brought the katana across in a beheading stroke.

Two halves of head tumbled apart. The body collapsed over backward, split from stomach to neck. He pivoted to engage the third man, but held back at the sight of gore streaming out from the man's back. Noriko's shots made small holes in the front, but left fist-sized hollows in their wake. With no visible threats remaining, he disengaged his neural boosters.

Time returned to normal.

The box of rations hit the ground with a *thump*.

"Damn," muttered Noriko. She slumped to one knee.

"You're hit?" Masaru rushed to her side and stooped over her.

She put a hand over her chest, gasping. "Yeah. It didn't penetrate, just knocked the wind out of me."

Masaru pulled her gloved hand away from her breast, exposing a pair of dark scuffmarks on the beige armor.

Noriko coughed. "I'm okay."

"You also had the feeling they didn't wish to talk?" He smiled.

"The helmet." She pointed her rifle at the man in the Manglers shirt. "I remember that guy from the crash site. That helmet belonged to someone I knew."

Masaru stood, walked to the man, and picked up the helmet. He brought it over and offered it to her. "Then you should not leave it in this place as I have left my friend."

She looked down, but accepted the helmet. "I'm sorry about your friend."

"I intend to return for him. It is my hope that they see little value in his body."

Noriko clipped the helmet onto the left side of her belt. "They dragged my team away, but I think they wanted gear. These people aren't like... cannibals or anything."

He put a hand on her shoulder. "Let us continue. Are you okay to walk?"

"Yeah." She ceased slouching and glanced at the four pieces of head on the road. "Is that usually how you negotiate?"

Masaru leaned back, laughing. "Only when necessary."

# JURISDICTION

One by one, the net creepers came back. Nina had hoped for something useful, but only two of the 473 individuals she'd targeted resulted in hits. Both had lost their lives within the past month, one a week ago, the other sixteen days. The more recent victim died after attempting to obtain control of a Division 1 officer's sidearm during a routine traffic stop. In the older case, a twenty-nine-year-old woman, an executive assistant, had become enraged at the executive she worked with and beat her to death with a 'corporate excellence award' made out of a huge block of fake crystal. According to the Division 2 report, she resumed her duties until the Harmony wore off. Once the high faded, the woman evidently became overwhelmed with guilt and defenestrated herself from the eighty-eighth floor of the Courtesy West tower. Witness statements explained the two women had been friends since high school.

Nina tapped a finger on the desk, thinking. The guy who'd been shot dead at a traffic stop worked for Grey Star, driving a delivery truck into bad parts of town where the bots refused to fly. Courtesy West provided hospitality services that mostly took the form of corporate cafeterias and janitorial services.

*Hmm. Neither one of them had any possible intelligence value to the ACC.* Nina closed her eyes and sighed out her nose. *Did the drug just do that, or were they targeted for disposal?*

Two out of 473 searches, and neither one on Tao, the supposedly more dangerous form.

Her sniffers picked up traces of intermittent data connections headed to Mexico. While various treaties attempted to ensure the GlobeNet remained 'free and open,' both the UCF and the ACC took great pains to ensure they could tell what everyone did at any one time. The ACC had a far greater segment of the population too poor to bother with cyberspace, and in a society built on the premise of doing everything as cheaply as possible, corners got cut.

Perhaps the ACC didn't understand that any time data left the UCF, it got logged. She'd always assumed they did something similar, though development of software and hardware cost time and money. Maybe they skipped it. She brought up a list of the case detectives for each investigation involving Tao or Harmony and sorted by the number of cases each one worked. A Detective Darren Weber appeared to have the most experience with this issue.

*Wonder if he can offer anything useful.*

She stood and headed out at a brisk walk, snagging her coat from the peg by the door on her way out. Her office lights dimmed on their own once they detected the room empty. A few thoughts spared to procedure caused her headware to append notes to the case file, logging her suspicions that the ACC had somehow obtained nanobots designed for brain surgery, and repurposed them to turn drug users into unwitting audio/video recorders... and somehow triggered fatal anti-authority rage in a small number of individuals.

Nina stepped into the elevator, turned with a swirl of her coat, and poked the button for the roof. She shook her head and let off a dark chuckle. *A chem named Harmony causes discord.*

---

THIRTY-TWO MINUTES AND A CHICKEN BURRITO LATER, NINA LANDED AT THE Regional Tech Center and made her way into the Investigative wing. Hayley Roth's horrible sobs echoed in her memory, called back by the drab hospital-green corridor. The last time she'd been here, they'd discovered her father, whom she'd assumed a neglectful parent, had been dead for almost a year. She hadn't checked up on the kid since right after making sure the favor she'd called in had gone through. One of Joey's friends had agreed to take her in, and with a little nudge from Nina, the court fast-tracked the adoption. It didn't surprise her; the hard part of the city's orphan problem came in finding parents. A case that could be opened, processed, and closed in five minutes padded some social worker's stats. Some counselor likely saw her as an easy way to hit quota.

She stopped at the main desk at the front of the Investigative division, and nodded at a young woman in a white uniform shirt. She couldn't have been twenty yet, and her rich brown skin made Nina feel conspicuously pale.

"Can I help you?" The Division 2 junior tech leaned up, staring at Nina's chest, evidently hunting for a nameplate that didn't exist.

"Lieutenant Nina Duchenne, Division 9." She held up her physical ID. "I'd like to speak with Detective Weber... Darren."

Rather than the usual 'oh shit' reaction to Division 9, the woman's eyes brimmed with eagerness. "Oh, wow. What's got Nine sniffing on Darren?"

Nina smiled. "It's not an internal affairs issue at all. Our cases have a lot of crossover and I'm looking for a new set of eyes."

"Oh, sure." She pointed to the left. "That way, seventh door on the right."

"Thanks."

Nina headed down the corridor to the indicated door, and knocked.

"It's open," said a man from inside.

She waved at the sensor, and a slab of hospital-green slid right, into the wall. A thirty-something man with dark skin and a short, neat afro looked up from his desk and gestured at a single facing chair. He did the white shirt, red tie, and black pants thing, but it looked okay on him. A small Class 3 pistol on an under-the-arm rig sat in a wad on the corner of his desk. As soon as he got a good look at her, his eyebrows climbed with an 'oh hellooo there sweetie' expression.

Nina entered and sat. "Detective Weber, I understand you've worked more cases involving the chems Harmony and Tao than anyone else."

"I suppose." He shrugged. "Normally a chem like that we wouldn't pay much attention to. Like Flowerbasket, mostly harmless."

"Mostly... except for the part where people wind up dead." She gave him an unimpressed half-frown.

"Yeah, well, that's why we started looking into it. What's your interest?" His prurient affect faded to a more businesslike demeanor. "You with the NewsNet? LRI?"

She held up her ID. "I pulled a case involving this crap too, wanted to pick your brain."

"Shit. What happened to get Nine interested in street drugs, and why are they getting a doll involved? Shouldn't you be off somewhere killing executives we can't charge?"

"Doll..." She self-consciously shifted her weight.

"Oh, no offense." He smiled. "It's right there on your ID if anyone cared to notice. The C3 at the end of your badge number means Class 3."

Fortunately, synthetic skin only blushed when she wanted it to. "Oh. Right." She let the assassination jab go. "We're not trying to take the investigation off your hands, but there's a complication that got our attention. What can you tell me about this shit?"

He gestured at his holo-panel. Unlike the Division 9 ones, his didn't have the dual emitter with the opaque backing. In her vision, the reverse screen righted itself, courtesy of her image processor, and she glanced over the file of a man who appeared to be a small-time chem dealer.

"It's all in the reports. Users experience a sense of overwhelming calm. An 'everything's gonna be okay' feeling that sometimes becomes a heightened sense of self or makes them feel immortal. Most of the time it's a mild euphoric high, not even as strong as Flowerbasket. Just puts the user in a good mood."

"But there's quite a few cases of spontaneous violence..." She glanced at her notes in a virtual holo-panel. "All within the past three months."

"Yeah, that jibes with what I've been seeing too. Weird thing is, you'd think it would be the people on Tao since the shit's impure. I can't honestly even figure out why Tao exists."

"Harmony is just Placinil re-sold without a prescription... plus a little tweak." Nina turned her hand palm up, fingers splayed. "Isn't Tao a cheaper but cruder alternative?"

Detective Weber shook his head. "Initially. Laughlin-Reed Innovation manufactures Placinil, which I'm sure you know is the source of Harmony. Without insurance, a single dose costs about two-hundred credits. A chem head can score a dose of Tao for about twenty. Now here's the interesting part... Someone realized that if they added a drop or two of synthetic cannabis, Placinil went from being a strong anti-anxiety medication to providing an extremely long duration 'high.' What it lacked in kick, it made up for in persistence. People began scamming prescriptions for Placinil, doctoring it up and re-selling it as Harmony."

"So what's the appeal of Harmony over Tao aside from being pure?"

"Harmony's all over the place because it's only a little more expensive per dose than Tao, and people trust it more since it wasn't made in someone's bathtub. Most I've seen someone selling it for is forty creds. This stuff isn't really taking off with the hardcore dosers. H gets in with the middle ground people, the ones working themselves to death. People who want an escape but who aren't looking to throw their entire life in a shitbasket. Forty credits for six or so hours of not worrying about a damn thing seems like a no-brainer."

"I'm surprised the insurance companies aren't hiring mercenaries." Nina chuckled. "Placinil's 200 a dose, but Harmony forty, and with more kick?"

Detective Weber shrugged. "I don't think they care. The money is still moving around. In order for someone to sell Harmony, they already had to buy Placinil. LRI got their money."

"Does anything you've found line up with the recent uptick in violence? Either something went wrong, or someone's got a sick sense of humor. They call it 'Tao' or 'Harmony,' but it's doing the exact opposite."

"Perhaps, or maybe they refer to duality – Yin and Yang, light and dark?"

Nina gazed into a strip of white on her leg where the gloss black armor caught the overhead lights. The form of the aluminum housing, slats, and LED light tube appeared in perfect miniature detail, warped with the curve of her thigh like a surrealist artwork. "That would make more sense if the users turning violent happened with Tao... but so far they all seem to be Harmony, which should be safer."

"True. To answer your other question, Laughlin-Reed did report an entire lot of Placinil stolen... not surprising given the street popularity of Harmony. We haven't yet determined who took it, but I'm inclined to suspect one of the local gangs. I've been sniffing around a few sources, but we haven't collected enough evidence to push the inquest in front of a judge... of course, you don't have that problem." He smiled.

"I've got policy to follow just like you."

He chuckled. "Yeah, but it's a lot easier for you to convince your superior that a corpse is guilty than me to fight my way past half a dozen lawyers with a case intact enough to convince a judge."

"We don't shoot every criminal we investigate." She scowled.

"Stab them sometimes?" He winked.

Nina leaned forward. "Sounds like you're feeling like the rules are too much of a burden to follow."

"Hey." He raised his hands. "Nothing like that. Just a little inter-division jabbing."

She let out a silent sigh. "Can you give me anything to work with?"

"What, so you can go whack some guy I've been investigating for two months?"

Nina tapped her foot for a few seconds, trying to resist the itch to live up to her reputation and start shouting. "Detective Weber... you asked before why Division 9 is involved in the investigation of street drugs. We're looking into suspected ACC involvement."

Weber's mouth opened. He stared at her in silence.

"Detective?"

"Oh, that makes sense now."

Nina relaxed back against her chair. "What does?"

"The drug-induced rejection of authority. Make the shit cheap so it gets everywhere. In a couple months, you're looking at citizen revolt or large-scale riots." He whistled. "Maybe it's a good thing you're in on this after all. That could also explain why we've had such a hard time finding the gang responsible for the theft. Maybe it wasn't a street gang at all."

"That's... an alarming idea." *That I hadn't even considered.* "I... think that might only be a side effect though. The ACC component of this had a rather specific application."

Detective Weber smiled. "You show me yours, I'll show you mine?"

She grinned. *Technically classified, but this guy seems on point.* "Nanobots mixed in with the drug. They wired up my vic's brain and turned him into a walking surveillance unit. Audio and video. We picked it up due to intermittent data bursts going to a Mexican network address."

"Whoa. Sounds above my pay grade." He tapped at the holographic keyboard and swapped screens. "My investigation uncovered a common thread among several of the most prolific dealers in the sectors under my jurisdiction. There seems to be one individual who is providing Placinil, I guess you could say 'wholesale' to several players."

"And... that's who?"

He chuckled. "That's the bit of evidence I'm missing. I've got a couple grabs from nearby citycams, but mostly a plain white van. Once the back of a man's head. Light brown hair, suit. I've been trying to get the go-ahead to send in an undercover, but command is pushing back, thinking Harmony's a non-issue. They don't want to risk it." Detective Weber grinned like a used hovercar salesman. "Of course, you don't have that problem."

"Send me your list?" She stood. "Maybe it'll lead somewhere."

Detective Weber brought up a few files on his terminal, made 'grabbing' gestures at the holo-panel, and 'tossed' them to her. The NetMini on her belt chirped. "I'd appreciate it if you shared anything you don't wind up classifying."

"Sure. Street chems aren't normally my concern. If there's nothing tied back to the ACC here, it's all yours."

"Be careful." Weber grinned. "Some of those dealers live in areas where a pretty woman could get hurt."

She gave him the side-eye. "I don't have that problem."

# BOO

Katya glanced away from the Nacho Mama van, shaking her head with contempt. That someone as inept as Anders wound up on a live assignment made sense only if they'd sent him expecting that he'd be found. The man evidently had some skill with network operations, at least enough to pose as an employee of Laughlin-Reed Innovation... enough to recognize her intrusion by technique.

She debated slipping into the bathroom to unburden herself of the precious cargo, but before she could stand, a tall man with short slicked-back white hair and a square-shouldered black suit walked in. Her attention gravitated to the cobalt blue tie practically glowing from his chest. The man looked like the most stereotypical corporate leg-breaker she'd ever seen.

He scanned the bistro interior as he crept forward. His expression and motion didn't change in any noticeable way when he looked at her, so she figured he had no idea what his contact looked like. When he got close to her table, she spoke without looking up.

"Nice tie."

"Go fuck yourself," said the man.

Katya set her empty cappuccino mug back in the saucer. "Too late. Already did."

The man flinched, his stare hardening.

*Guess he wasn't ready for that response.* She gestured at the chair Anders had vacated. "Seat's warm."

"You look like you need a ride."

"Now that you mention it..." Katya waved the doll waitress over.

The man waited for her to settle her tab. Katya stood, feeling a bit like a twelve-year-old when her head barely came up to his chest. He offered a polite nod before walking outside and going past the exterior tables. She followed him to the sidewalk, where he turned right and headed at a deliberate pace for blank white cargo van parked six cars from the café. *This is how people get abducted.* Hesitance slowed her step as she scanned around for possible escape routes.

Without looking back to see if she'd followed, the man pulled open the side door. The interior contained limousine-style furnishings. Four individual faux leather seats faced a tiny round table. A wet bar sat behind them by the back end, and wide holo-panels simulating windows covered both walls, looking out over a white-sand beach dotted with palm trees. Another man, as opposite as possible from the pale giant, sat in the rear-facing seat working on a mixed drink that faded from clear at the bottom up to violet. If Blue Tie had been a stereotypical corporate leg-breaker, this man looked like every bad holovid representation of a Syndicate hitman. Deep tan, black hair, wide smile, and an immaculate suit. Though he didn't stand as she approached, she figured him for her height or perhaps even a little shorter.

"Come in, please... have a seat," said Black Tie. "Can I offer you anything to drink?"

Katya stepped up into the van and slid into the rear left seat. Plush leather creaked as fluffy cushions compressed. "Thanks, but it's a bit early for me."

While Blue Tie got in and pulled the door closed, the smaller man offered her a canister of purified water. "Our mutual friend tells me you have something for us?"

"I have a lot of friends." She smiled, opened the water, and sniffed it. A tiny implanted sensor in her nose sampled the air, transmitted its data to her NIU, and: <H20> appeared in text along the bottom of her vision. Katya took a sip.

Black Tie seemed to notice her testing the water, but his smile didn't falter. "Of course. A moment." He glanced at the window to his right, Katya's left. The view of the beach faded to black, replaced by the mirror covered letters of the ComTec International logo, a giant C with T and I nested inside, all rotating.

After a few seconds, the logo faded, revealing Alex, wearing a shimmery lavender suit with a fluffy frilled ascot. "Ahh, good of you to vid." He looked between Katya and the men. "I trust all is well."

"So far," said Black Tie. "Just confirming the mutuality of our friendship."

"Yes, of course." Alex nodded to Katya. "You have the information with you?"

She fidgeted. "Yes."

"Go ahead and transfer it then. Let us finalize our arrangement." Alex smiled and... plopped sugar cubes into tea.

"Are you really wearing that and drinking tea with sugar cubes, or is this your avatar?" She fidgeted again.

"I appreciate the finer things in life." He held up a cube with a pair of small tongs. "It may not have grown from the earth, but it is chemically identical to sugar. You should try it some time." He dropped it back in the dish with a soft *clank*.

Katya rolled her eyes. "Fine. There was a small complication with the security at LRI."

"Complication?" asked Alex.

The Ties looked at her with new unease.

"More security than anticipated. I had to take an unusual step to get the data out." She stared at the canister of water in her hand. "Oh hell. It's inside me."

Alex raised an eyebrow.

"My dog ate a cufflink once," said Blue Tie. "Took a day, but it came out."

Alex and Black Tie stared at him in disbelief.

"I didn't swallow it." Katya set the water down, stood, and reached for the button on her jeans. "Oh hell. Might as well get this over with. Give me a moment."

Black Tie raised his hand. "Wait."

"Call me back," said Alex, ending the vid.

"Wait?" Katya blinked.

Blue Tie opened the door and got out.

Black Tie followed. "Pull the door open when you're finished." He closed it.

She stood dumbfounded for a few seconds at being given privacy. *Wow. I was not expecting that.* Katya dropped her jeans and removed the foam insert. She fought the urge to fall seated with her pants around her knees and enjoy being rid of the thing, and fixed her clothes back in place. After tugging the door open an inch, she sat, leaving the foam-encased neural memory stick dangling from her fingers by the string Doctor Crowley had so fortuitously included.

The men reentered. Blue Tie closed the door and took a seat at Black Tie's left.

Neither of them seemed terribly interested in touching the foam sausage.

"Anyone have a knife?" asked Katya.

Blue Tie reached behind his back and drew a combat vibro-knife with a metallic *scrape.* He offered it handle-first.

"That's a bit of overkill for cutting foam." She chuckled.

She didn't bother squeezing the handgrip to activate the mechanism; the plain old composite non-energized edge would more than be up to the task. Katya worked the blade into the foam with light, careful pressure so she didn't damage the plastic housing of the neural memory stick, and made a longitudinal slash down the capsule that elicited groans from both men. It took her a second to understand why, and she laughed.

"Sorry, boys. No symbolism intended." She split the foam apart, exposing a black plastic wand about three inches long tipped with a standard asterisk-shaped M3 interface prong covered by a clear safety cap. She offered it to the men, bending the foam such that the neural memory stick stuck out toward them. "Here you go."

Black Tie plucked it from the foam and connected it to the terminal before getting Alex on the vid. Blue Tie held up a wastebasket, in which Katya dropped the foam bits. She handed him his knife back with a genuine smile. Somehow in her mind, their being polite and courteous to a woman became a conflict of UCF vs ACC, making her even happier to have escaped.

"Ahh. That's better." Alex sipped tea. "Kindly let me know when the data validates."

Katya smiled to herself at his use of 'when' rather than 'if.'

Black Tie sipped his drink, which imparted a scent like licorice to his breath. She took a long swig of water, and enjoyed the feeling of not having anything stuck where it didn't belong. About five minutes later, the terminal chirped. The man read over a few screens' worth of data and gave Alex a nod.

"Perfect." Alex twirled his hand around and stabbed his finger at something off screen with a showy wave of the arm. "The contract is satisfied, payment should be arriving in your account within seconds."

Her NetMini chirped.

"Enjoy the rest of your day, gentlemen, and lady." Alex bowed and ended the call.

"Where can we drop you off?" asked Blue Tie.

Although their show of courtesy earlier inclined her to trust them, she couldn't bring herself to let her guard down, and gave an address two sectors away from her apartment.

Blue Tie nodded, stood, and slipped into the front via a concealed door that blended with the wall when it closed again. A mild shift in gravity surprised her, as the van didn't look like a hover model. Given the opulent interior however, she pushed disbelief aside. The van had no markings, though these two had to work for the company who'd made arrangements with Doctor Crowley. The only remaining question would be if they could bring whatever technology she'd stolen to market faster than Laughlin-Reed Innovation, but that problem did not belong to her.

Meaningless small talk plus the requisite assurance that she hadn't looked at the data she'd transported filled the span of a ride a few minutes over an hour long. After they landed, she walked into the nearest apartment building as if she lived there. Once inside, she headed to the elevator. Nothing stood out as worrisome, so after riding the elevator to the roof and back once, she paged a PubTran and took it to the NaturaHealth place to pick up Eve.

---

KATYA FLOATED IN A BLISSFUL SEMI-AWAKE STATE. ALL THE TENSION OF THE JOB gone, she'd lay soaking in a warm bath for so long she'd forgotten what time she got in. While the autoshower could provide cleanliness, some pleasures would forever elude the ability of technology to obviate. Joey had called her back to thank her for the tip off, and drop a subtle clue that while Division 9 was inclined to believe her loyalty to the UCF genuine, they would likely monitor her for a little while. It didn't bother her *too* much. She'd spent seventeen years of her life under constant surveillance anyway. People called the UCF a fascist police state, which in some ways it was, but it felt freer than Russia.

At some point, she'd read an article claiming the country that occupied the land mass where the UCF resided had once been based on capitalism, and Russia had considered such a form of government inherently evil. She thought the idea ridiculous. The ACC lived and breathed capitalism, to the point of believing those who remained among the commoner poor deserved their life due to lack of motivation.

*Russia... communist? Hah. Unbelievable the kind of stories they come up with just to get a rise out of people.*

Eve hurried in and jumped on the toilet. "Sorry. This isn't waiting anymore. I suggest rapid evacuation to minimum safe distance and or protective gear."

"You could've asked me to give up the bathroom." Katya yawned and sat up amid soap foam.

"It's been almost two hours. I thought you drowned." Eve leaned her head back and groaned. "Oh come on... I've been dancing in the hallway, seconds away from disaster, and now that I'm on the damn bowl, nothing's happening."

Katya climbed out of the tub and wrapped herself in a towel. "Should I call a doctor?"

Eve stared at her. "You might need one after breathing this."

"You have a man's sense of humor." Chuckling, Katya headed to the sink and attacked her hair with a blow dryer.

"Barracks." Eve swung her feet back and forth. "It was all fart and shit jokes."

Katya finished off her hair and headed to her bedroom where she changed into sweat pants and a loose black t-shirt. Not long after she flopped on the couch and resumed poring over job postings, Eve walked in, limping like a wounded soldier, and climbed up to sit next to her.

"You look like a dog who's done something bad." Katya patted her on the head.

"Just wait." Eve stared at her. "The cloud's right behind me."

*She looks like a kid, but she doesn't act like one.* "How would you feel about going to school?"

"I thought I was going to…" Eve tilted her head.

"I mean actually *going* instead of the helmet. Meeting other kids your age, socializing… appearing normal."

Eve smiled and fluffed her snow-white hair. "There are no other kids my age."

Katya didn't know whether to laugh or feel sorry for her. "I mean…"

"Yeah, I know. Just… making jokes out of it helps." Eve sat quiet for a little while, smoothing out her black tights wherever they bunched. She flexed her toes, tapped her feet together, and made faces.

"What are you thinking about?"

Without looking up, Eve asked, "Does your friend really think I'm psycho? He kept calling me psycho tot."

"First, that man isn't exactly my friend. Sometimes we help each other, but that doesn't mean I like his company. I am sure the feeling is mutual. Second, he is not the sort of person who reacts to unusual situations gracefully. We had thought you were a grown man, a soldier who had gone insane. Finding *you* inside that powered armor was the last thing we expected."

"Do you think I'm nuts?" Eve pulled her feet in and rested her chin on her knees.

"No. I think there is a conflict in you." She knocked on the girl's head. "You think sometimes like an adult, but your body is still little. Chemically, you're a child. Mentally, neither grown nor childish."

"So…" Eve picked at her toenails.

"You've got a little control over the mental. Nothing over the chemical. Enjoy it. Be a child while you can." Katya ruffled her hair. "Those people stole that from you once. Don't let them do it again."

"All right. I'll give the school thing a shot. I'll try not to kill anyone." She winked.

Red letters appeared at the upper right corner of Katya's vision: ‹Signal Lost – Searching›

Her heart sped up. "Eve," she whispered. "Run and hide."

"Wha?" Eve shifted forward, one foot on the rug, one still up on the sofa cushion behind her. She seemed about to ask more, but stared at the door for less than a full second before sprinting into the back of the apartment while peeling her shirt off.

*What the hell is she doing?*

Katya ran to the dining room cabinet, retrieved her handgun, and took up a defensive position behind the mini-kitchen's island counter. Soft footfalls thumped in the back of the apartment. A familiar scrape, her nightstand drawer, followed.

*Don't be stupid. Shit. She's going for a gun. Why the hell did she take her shirt off?*

Eighteen seconds after she aimed at the front door, it opened without a sound. A man with the physique of a Gee-ball player, though nowhere near Blue Tie's size, started to sneak in until he made eye contact with her and realized he'd been seen.

Katya fired. She got off four shots before a second man coming in behind the monster raised a weapon. He used the bigger man for cover, exposing only his head and shooting arm. Their guns fired within a fraction of a second of each other. She tried to hit him in the face, but missed by an inch. His shot nailed her in the right shoulder, deadening her arm. The big guy seemed to shrug off the effect of being shot multiple times and stormed over.

She slumped to the side, firing twice more with her left hand, hitting nothing but a vase, which exploded in a shower of little blue bits. The big man grabbed her by the wrists and hauled her into the air. He squeezed until she lost her grip on the weapon, then carried her into the living room where he flung her at the couch. Katya grunted on landing, and curled to one side with a hand over her bleeding shoulder.

The oaf, the guy who shot her, and a third man walked around and stood in front of her. All three had medium brown skin and dark hair, though none had any trace of Hispanic in their features. As soon as she looked at their faces, she assumed them ACC. Her gaze drifted to the big guy's chest, where four slugs nested in shallow, bloody holes, stalled on subdermal armor.

"Greetings, Miss Volkov," said the center man. "I'm sorry if we've caught you at a bad time. I should warn you that Raúl"—he gestured at the large man—"is unaffected by synthetic pheromones. He gets rather upset when people attempt to use them."

*He's no more named Raúl than I'm going to grow wings and fly.* She stared at him.

"Julio"—the center man gestured to the one who'd shot her—"enjoys the sound of women screaming."

'Julio' smiled.

"I have some questions for you. If I like your answers, we'll simply kill you. If I don't like your answers, I'll bring you to the point where you wish for death, and then we'll ship you back to Vertex Investments."

She dug her fingers into the skin around the wound, scowling. "Whatever you think, you're probably wrong. My going to LRI wasn't political, just a data courier job."

"An interesting, and effective cover." He smiled. "No one is doubting you are more experienced than poor Zack."

"Is your whole team composed of scrubs?" Katya stared at the man on the left. "Julio? Are you serious? You do realize he looks like a Swiss hoverski instructor who'd been left in the oven too long?"

'Raúl' laughed. Julio seemed to think her remark less funny. He lunged in to pistol whip her in her wounded shoulder, but she kicked him in the side of the head, knocking him over the armrest to the floor.

Raúl kept laughing.

Julio jumped to his feet, his fake-tan face darkening with rage. She fired back a defiant stare. The unnamed man pointed a gun at her and nodded at Julio. The orange one raised his gun a second time, but she kicked him the head again, knocking him to the side.

"You're not going to kill me until I tell you whatever it is you want to know."

"Correct." The unnamed man shot her in the right thigh.

Katya swallowed the scream, but shuddered from the pain.

Julio roared and jumped on her. Rather than bash his gun into her shoulder, he jabbed his finger in the bullet wound and twisted.

Katya sent her mind back to the same place she'd used when her trainers had her handcuffed to an electrified bedframe, wet and naked. She pictured herself as a serene white butterfly, gliding over a field of endless snow, the skyline of Moscow a distant dark presence on the horizon.

"Enough." The unnamed man pulled Julio back.

At the sight of the men looking blurry already, she worried. Hopefully, it came from pain and not blood loss.

"Mommy?" asked a tiny voice. "Who are these men?"

*No... Eve... what are you doing?*

"Go... wait in your room, sweetie." Katya lifted her head to peer toward the sound.

Eve stood a few feet away in a white nightgown dotted with red hearts, head down. The girl clutched a brown teddy bear to her chest, half-hiding her face behind it. She stared at Katya; for an instant, her sapphire-blue eyes held no trace of childishness, but warning.

Katya glanced at the bear before glaring at Raúl. "You're lucky you have that dermal armor."

Eve looked up at Raúl.

The big man picked two bullets out of his chest, sneering at her. "You will hurt soon enough."

Julio let out a dark chuckle and stomped over behind Eve. She started to look up at him with a wide-eyed pleading face, but squealed when he grabbed a fistful of hair and put his gun to the side of her head. "Best answer the man's questions. This one'll bleed out fast."

"Mommy!" shouted Eve. "He's hurting me!" She burst into tears, and clutched her bear tight.

"Now, bitch," said Julio. "How much do they know? How'd you find Zack?" He pulled Eve up onto her toes by his grip on her hair. The girl's scream didn't sound faked. "One more thing comes out of your mouth I don't like, and this one's brains are on the floor."

"Don't kill the little one," said the unnamed man. "Start in the leg or something. More motivation."

Katya yelled, "All right! Please don't hurt her. She's only eight. She's got nothing to do with this."

"Out with it," said the unnamed man.

"I'm not working for the government. I took a job to smuggle data out of the building, and *Zack* was thinking with his dick. He wanted to get laid, so he followed me and blabbed all about being an infiltrator. My network techniques are evidently rather obvious, so he thought I was part of another insertion team he hadn't been told about. I went in to get data, nothing more. It isn't my fault Zack is an idiot who only got into the OOI because his parents pulled strings."

The unnamed man stared at her with cold eyes. She couldn't read him, which worried her. *This* guy had at least some competence.

Eve sniffled and whine-murmured, "Owowowowow."

"Gah!" yelled Julio. He released her and jumped back, staring down at his wet leg.

Eve leaned backward a touch and shifted toward him.

*Bang!*

The bear's face exploded with a flash of azure flame and a shower of fluff. Julio's head rocked back, a bullet hole under his chin; the ceiling above him flashed red. She shoved her arm out in front of her and shot Raúl twice in the side of the head before putting a third round into the unnamed man's chest.

Raúl fell straight down like a sack of dirt. The unnamed man grunted and wheezed, struggling to bring his gun around on the child as he collapsed to one knee. More fluff flew out of the bear's face as another shot hit the unnamed man in the cheek, knocking him over backward. His gun went off once, but hit only ceiling.

Eve approached Raúl, planted one tiny bare foot on his chest, and shot him again point blank in the forehead, spraying the carpet with gore. She pivoted left, fed the unnamed man two more to the face, and padded over to Julio, who got three in the heart.

Katya grabbed her shoulder with her left hand, her thigh with the other, and stared at Eve. This 'child' had killed three men in four seconds, without even sighting over the pistol she'd concealed in the teddy bear.

The girl walked up to her. Urine yellowed the lower part of her nightgown and trickled down her exposed shin. "I wasn't really scared enough to piss myself. I needed him to get the gun out of my ear."

"I figured... it worked." Katya looked at the terminal on the coffee table. "Terminal, emergency services. Police and a MedVan."

"Confirm emergency services request," said a digitized male voice.

"Yes. Need police."

"Transmitting your request for assistance. Please stand by."

The room shimmered with millions of light dots for an instant as the terminal generated a 3D model of the surroundings, which it probably sent to the dispatcher.

*Hopefully, three dead bodies will get someone's attention.*

Eve shrank in on herself, once again seeming like a frightened child. Snow-white hair hung a little past her shoulders, framing a visage of sorrowful innocence. She peered at her teddy's mauled face, and thrust out her lower lip in a pout.

"Mommy...? Mr. Bear's got a boo."

# 27

# LEG WORK

Four faces stared at Nina from holo-panels hanging in the air over her desk. She held a large dark chocolate latte to her chin, letting the fragrant steam waft into her nostrils. Detective Weber's information identified four individuals who collectively accounted for eighty-three percent of all Harmony circulating in West City. The remainder came from thousands of others. As far as she'd been able to tell, the Syndicate hadn't touched Harmony or Tao, presumably due to the ready availability and low profit margin. A drug that could, in some cases, keep its user 'high' for eight hours and cost a mere forty or so credits per dose didn't generate the sort of income that would've gotten organized crime involved.

*Or maybe they knew something.*

She locked eyes with the first image: Ricky Barron, a baby-faced twenty-two-year-old with shoulder-length teal hair, emerald green eyes, and a broad grin. Weber's comments said he tended to stick with tamer chems such as Flowerbasket, Sandman, or Smileys, and consequently had no prior run-ins with Division 1 beyond the usual shakedowns. No charges filed. He lived out of a semi-functional gym in the Sector 71 grey zone, fifteen miles north of the southern edge of the elevated city. Prior to Harmony, he'd been small time, selling the 'light stuff' to locals in the area. In the past few months, he'd built up a network of runners and established connections with seventeen other dealers in a vast distribution system. All of it offline, word of mouth, sneaker-to-pavement. That struck her as unusual, since it made for a significant overhead of time. Of course, it also drove Detective Weber's team nuts since they had to investigate everything on foot.

The second dealer, a thirty-seven-year-old who went by the name 'Easy' or 'JJ' on the street, real name Jason James Castle, had skin so dark his photo resembled a sniper silhouette target. He lacked Ricky's smile, but otherwise looked like someone had taken a corporate executive and put him in frumpy street clothes.

Easy's record had a fair amount of arrests, the majority of which related to gang violence rather than chems. He'd done a couple of short prison stints, but had remained under the radar for the past four years. Weber's notes put him in Sector 7111, about a quarter of the way north from the southern end of West City, over an area formerly known as Modoc County, California. He rented a super-economy one-room apartment about a mile from where Sector 7111 bordered the grey zone of Sector 7059. The location offered him access to a massive blight spot: Three sectors worth of black zones, and fourteen surrounding grey sectors.

Nina shook her head. All those people barely hanging on to survival and they threw a good part of whatever money they scraped up at JJ Castle for Harmony. No wonder he had such a large market share. Even the 'norms' from surrounding regular sectors risked a trip near the grey to get his product. *Everyone's so desperate to shake off the weight of their lives.* She glanced at another panel, showing a Harmony pill, an ordinary capsule half black, half white. The white end had a black dot at the tip and the black end had a white dot. *Cute. Yin and Yang. One small pill and your worries stop bothering you.* She shook her head with a sigh. *This drug isn't aimed at addicts and dosers, it's for everyone else.*

The third dealer in Detective Weber's files went by 'Mama Fine,' real name Jen Alvarez. She looked a little older than her nineteen years—Nina would've guessed younger twenties—even with the garish hot pink hair. Weber appeared to enjoy investigating her as she did so much business via the GlobeNet, they never had to leave the Police Administrative Center. Mama Fine rarely met clients in person, instead selling Harmony, Racer Dots, Smileys, Narcoderm Ultra (the prescription strength version of the OTC painkiller), as well as Flowerbasket, Sandman, and SandBasket. Nina cringed. SandBasket was the kind of drug that required a user clear their weekend plans before taking it. Combining the super-relaxing placid hallucinogen Flowerbasket with Sandman, a drug famous for giving its users wild dreams so vivid they often believed them real, could ruin a person for days at a time.

Everything Mama Fine did happened via cyberspace. She'd even made her own delivery bot units. Nina cracked up laughing at a note in the file where it mentioned ComTec International, the company that ran most of the UCF's delivery bot and advert bots, had tried to sue her for using the term 'delivery bot.' Of course, they offered to drop the suit if she contracted with them for distribution.

"Wow... Did that shithead even realize this woman's selling illegal chems?" *They saw someone using bots and went into attack mode before they looked.* "Unbelievable."

The final dealer made her quirk an eyebrow. One Fenton Asher, no cute name, sold Harmony out of his apartment in Sector 16612, far in the north end of West City over former Canada. Asher had a high-end apartment in a gated building where each floor held only eight dwellings. The file also indicated he worked as a senior director of marketing for Timmons-Orben hovercars. His Harmony distribution catered to the corporate crowd, and he tended to sell in bulk, presumably to people who re-sold much of it to their co-workers.

"Why did our mysterious source choose these four...?"

She spent the next two hours running facial pattern matches and financial analysis routines, as well as sending sniffers all over the GlobeNet. None of the four seemed to have any involvement whatsoever with the ACC. Mama Fine had been the closest; her grandparents had fled ACC-controlled Mexico as teenagers. Another forty minutes checking into them, as well as her parents, turned up nothing suspicious to suggest they had any lingering connection or loyalty to the Corporates.

"Okay, that's a big fat nothing..." She scowled at the time display on the terminal. Lunch appealed to her memory of being human, but ninety percent of what she ate wound up going right into the toilet later on. Her body took only what it needed to keep the brain and spine alive. In theory, she could subsist on two tablespoons of nutrient paste twice a day... but ugh.

*Upside. I can't get fat.* She ordered a buffalo chicken sandwich before diving back into the terminal. For an hour (except a short break to run to the parking deck to meet a delivery bot), she kept digging into the backgrounds of the four dealers, looking for any common thread.

*There's got to be something.* She stared from Barron, to Easy, to Mama Fine, to Fenton Asher. The sixth time she panned back and forth over the pictures, she glanced at their addresses.

Nina opened another panel with a map of West City, and plugged in the four dealers. Ricky almost at the southern edge, a turf-pounder who could get product to users living on the natural earth south of the raised portion of the city. JJ Castle's territory appeared as a dot about a quarter of the way up, Mama Fine about halfway, and Fenton Asher at a bit past the three-quarter mark.

"Hmm. Geographic arrangement is a possibility. They're evenly spread out." She eyed Asher's picture.

If the ACC used Harmony as a carrier for the nanobots, they'd want to get it into the systems of people who might be able to give them valuable information. *It might not even be political in nature... this could be good old-fashioned corporate espionage.* She doubted senators would bother dosing a chem like Harmony. What sort of horrible life could people at the top of the food chain have to want something like that? Perhaps a middling-upper military officer might wind up seeking it out, but the odds of that made the ACC hoping for it seem unlikely.

"So they get eyes and ears among executives, engineers, and designers..." Her gaze dropped to Ricky Barron's pin on the map. "And they know the lower classes will crave this stuff. Right. Take the secrets from the top and ignite the bottom."

Nina spent a few minutes adding notes to the inquest file. She theorized Harmony had two roles: one, nanobots converting unwitting individuals into mobile recording devices. Two, triggering random violent behavior with a strong anti-authority mindset. Given a probable ratio on the conservative end of fifty poor users to every one person who might net them useful information, the drug stood a decent chance of triggering large-scale civil unrest.

"Perhaps it is political after all." She stared at Fenton Asher. "He's going to take the most effort... If I go after him hard, he's going to panic and warn the source. If I scare him enough not to do that, the source will probably know something's wrong. He doesn't have much contact with his buyers..."

A plan to spend weeks building up a false identity as a director-level employee of some corporation and gradually make contact with him formed and died. *Ugh. This will blow up in my face before I get close enough.* She opened a vid call to

Operations, and got a thirtyish woman with light brown hair who seemed a mix of Chinese and Caucasian.

"Ops, this is Lieutenant Duchenne. I need to own an apartment."

The woman nodded. "Understood. Target?"

"Fenton Asher." She slid the file from the 'Weber's data' holo-panel to the one holding the vid connection. "104 CR 30014 Sector 16612. Apartment 64-7."

"Usual?" asked the woman.

"Might as well, though I don't need real-time feeds from the bathrooms. Primary objective is locating a source of contraband narcotics. All we have to go on right now is a Caucasian male mid-twenties to mid-fifties, light brown hair."

"That's not a lot, ma'am." The woman nodded. "I'll send this up. We should have an ops team in the place within twenty minutes, provided he's not home. Shall I route the feeds to your terminal?"

"I need to check on a few other leads. Find me if whoever gets assigned to monitor this stream sees anything that looks like chems arriving."

"On it."

"Thanks, Sergeant."

"Ma'am." The woman hung up.

Of the remaining three, Ricky Barron and Mama Fine moved a significantly greater amount of product than JJ. The odds of running into the source with them looked much better. She arranged to have a whispercraft assigned to begin surveillance on JJ as well as Ricky. Mama did everything via remote according to Nina's research; she never left her squat in the grey zone and Weber's notes made it clear she never met anyone face to face. The whispercraft could do only so much there.

Nina chuckled to herself. "Time for some leg work."

⁙

AFTER STOPPING AT HOME, NINA TRADED HER SAND-BROWN GOVERNMENT ISSUE trench coat in for a puffy miniskirt that couldn't decide if it wanted to be pink or purple, low-top boots with silver decorative chain bits on the outside, and a loose half-jacket to conceal the hand cannon under her arm. She'd turned her hair lavender, courtesy of her CamNano, and added a decorative 'raccoon mask' of glowing cyan, simulating a NanoLED tattoo. She never understood the appeal of the face tattoo thing, but it was common among the sort of women who associated with gangs.

Her ballistic stealth armor stayed on under the clothes, though she felt ridiculous wearing a hot pink halter-top over it. The glossy black bodysuit didn't *look* like armor to most people, though foreign spies would recognize it. She hemmed and hawed about going without it. Small weapons, Class 1 or 2 pistols, would probably stop on the plastisteel plates between her synthetic skin and Myofiber muscles. Anything bigger would tear through. *Fuck it. I don't need to charge into a gunfight, and if they have people watching the dealers, I can't stand out.*

She stripped, peeled herself out of the armor, and dressed again in the skirt, halter top, boots, and jacket. The girl in the mirror looked like a prostitute. Her mother Camille would be horrified. Nina fidgeted. Months ago, she'd have thought nothing about walking outside with a tiny skirt and no panties. After all, this body wasn't hers, no more than a guy piloting a giant robot could call the machine his body. Something had changed. The reborn Proscion's words had nurtured the flame of her withered sense of humanity. At some point, she'd come to accept this body as *her,* but couldn't pinpoint when. This skimpy outfit embarrassed her more than going out in public stark naked. She kicked off her boots, slipped on a pair of black lace panties, and added a matching bra under the halter-top.

"Okay. Better."

After a few minutes of adding some 'dirt' and 'bruises' with the CamNano, she figured she could pass for a young woman from a grey zone. The puffy skirt didn't cover much, and her boots stopped about two inches above her ankles. *Hmm. Leg work indeed. If I wind up naked in a hot tub with an old man again, I'm going to hurt someone.*

RICKY BARRON'S NEIGHBORHOOD LURKED IN THE SHADOW OF A THICK MASS OF abandoned office towers in the adjacent sector south. Metallic blight surrounded it, leaving Sector 71 in a perpetual dimness somewhere between sundown and midnight. She flew her unmarked patrol craft in low, tucking between a pair of filthy century towers. The ionic downblast from the hovercar stirred up a whirlwind of trash in the alley below, and sent small sparks flickering over the plastisteel ground. After getting out, she remote-controlled the car back into the air and north, away from the grey zone, to a roof parking area on a residence tower 2.4 miles away.

Nina walked to the end of the alley, stepping over and around old food cartons, cups, and unidentifiable junk, most of which appeared to have once been furniture that had fallen from the buildings on either side. She entered the alley about ten feet away from a pack of twenty-somethings with light cybernetics, wild hair, and grungy clothes in mostly black and grey. Of seventeen individuals, the four women regarded her with a mixture of curiosity and territorial glowers.

One, a skinny wisp with cherry-red hair, two metal arms, no shirt, and an ankle-long skirt made of thick, dangling strips of faux-leather held her arms out and thrust her chin forward. Her prosthetic arms glinted in the feeble light, dark metallic pewter and contoured in an elongated stylized version of human musculature. The fingers curved out to eight-inch claws that didn't seem capable of retracting. Her legs, also metal from mid-thigh down, ended in permanent high heels with an array of small, bladed protrusions likely intended more for decoration than as weapons. It gave her the overall aesthetic of some humanoid-insectoid alien.

"Keep on walkin' bitch," said the woman. "You ain't got 'nuff metal ta be here."

Nina glanced sideways at her with a condescending smile, but kept walking.

"Oh, we're lookin' at me like that." Alien Girl pushed off the wall she'd been leaning on and approached, her metal feet *clicking* on the plastisteel ground. "That's gonna cost you some blood, little pixie."

Nina stopped and turned to face her, one eyebrow up. Over the course of two seconds, seventeen small holo-panels appeared in her view, identifying all the gangers looking at her. Three had records, none had active warrants, and they didn't appear connected to the ACC.

Alien Girl froze, her menacing glare flickered into confusion for an instant before returning to anger.

"Oh, is this the part where I'm supposed to scream and run?" asked Nina. "The alien hive queen look works for you, but I dunno about those nails. Don't they get in the way when you play with yourself?"

A few chuckles came from the group.

"The fuck is wrong with you, chica?" yelled Alien Girl. "You *tryin'* ta get fucked up?"

Nina's scan didn't pick up any speedware in the woman, so not having armor wouldn't matter. "Back at you."

"Ooooh, damn," said a man. "She's callin' you out, Li."

Li glared, leaning forward, her arms raised to strike.

Nina put her hands on her hips, again feeling ridiculous in such a short, puffy skirt. "Keep trying. Not scary."

"Wow. This bitch has some damage." Li shook her head. "Okay, maybe you're cool." The triangular claws on her right hand split apart into three slivers each that retracted around emerging metal fingers with human proportion. She offered a fist bump.

*Whatever.* Nina tapped knuckles.

Li returned to her spot on the wall, and Nina kept walking.

Random whistles and catcalls emanated from alleys and two other groups of punks, though none had much cyberware to speak of, at least nothing useful in a fight. She headed right at the next corner, following her nav point, and the 'Universe Gym' came into view a third of the way down the block. It took up the first three stories of a high-rise century tower, where the former owner had painted the walls yellow and littered it with stylized images of athletic figures. Most of the poses featured boxing or martial arts. Giant windows on the front wall looked in on a dojo-like space with well-worn heavy bags hanging on the left around an assortment of free weights, two boxing rings in the center, and an impressive array of large workout machines on the right. Much to her surprise, she counted fourteen people using the gym as a gym.

Upwards of forty more hung out in front, mostly men. Some wore dingy tracksuits, but most looked like run-of-the-mill grey zone fringers in tattered middle-class clothes ten years out of style. Her cybernetic eyes picked up weapons on all of them, pistols for the most part. A twinge of nervousness tickled her gut. With the right weapon, she could probably take out forty attackers, but her hand cannon only held fifteen shots.

A fleet of e-bikes and quads gathered by the street, their tires caked with dirt and bodies scratched from flying stones. She hung back as a wary looking man with face-wrap amber goggles jogged out of the main entrance, stuffing a fist-sized plastic canister in a backpack. He threw the pack over his shoulder, hopped on an e-bike, and zipped off to the south. She thought of putting a tracer on him, but the Citycams didn't respond in time before he'd gone out of sight.

*Screw it. He's probably just running chems down off the plates to some dusty rat hole in the south.*

Nina decided to try 'casual,' and adopted a mousy posture before walking across the street and up to the front of the gym. The expected whistles, rude comments, and ogling occurred as she crossed a small open area on her way to the door. One man followed her close enough to feel body heat, but stopped short of touching her.

"Aww man." He stopped as she entered. "Why you walkin' away like that?"

Inside, the air reeked of sweat and synthetic leather. Two men squared off in the more distant boxing ring under the supervision of a severe brown-skinned woman in a tank top and sweat pants. Her afro had gone pewter-grey, but she had the physique and bearing of a military drill instructor. As the men went at it, she shouted tips and encouragement.

*Pops* and *thuds* emanated from the heavy bag area from a handful of people working out. The more elaborate machines on the other side stood empty. She wandered the space, looking for any sign of Ricky Barron. A few minutes into her roaming, she spotted a dark-skinned man in a yellow tracksuit leaning against the wall at the end of a corridor between two locker rooms. He rested his arm across an assault rifle dangling from his shoulder on a strap, in a pose about as casual as someone could have with such a weapon.

Nina ran his face, and got a hit: Sergeant First Class Corey Webb, retired. He'd been in the UCF military for eight years, four of which he'd spent on Mars in a combat unit. *No way this guy's turned.* She smiled and walked up to him.

"Hey there, girl." Corey nodded. "You lost?"

"I'm looking for Ricky Barron. I got a feeling he's behind this door you're watching."

He gave her a slow head-to-toe look. "Ain't never seen you before. What's yo' business with Barron?"

"Harmony."

He shook his head. "Damn, girl. S'pose we all got problems, but you ain't gotta see Barron for that." Guy in the front office with the red hat. "Can tell him how many tabs you want."

Nothing had come back on Webb's record, nor had the sniffer turned up any evidence that data had gone from this building to an anonymous Mexican chimera address.

"It's a little more complicated than that. I need to talk to Barron about where he's getting so much from."

"What's it to you? You ain't no cop. Them boys don't care 'bout the easy chems. That means you're either lookin' to cut in on him, or buy big."

Nina put her hands on her hips. "I'm not looking to cut in on his business, Sergeant Webb. I'm here to ask for his help with a matter of some delicateness."

Corey's eyebrows converged. "Who the hell…"

"Is he alone? I'll explain to you both, but…" She looked around, switching vision modes to EMF. The world shifted into a view like a photonegative of black and white. Aside from a shitstorm of NetMinis spewing purple fountain blasts and three larger terminals throwing streamers of cyan energy into the air, she didn't see anything that looked like bugs or listening devices. Nina went back to normal sight and lowered her voice. "It's a national security issue."

"You're…"

"Division 9," she muttered.

Both of Corey's eyebrows went up. "For real?"

She nodded.

"Aiight. C'mon." He swiped his NetMini past a sensor on the wall, causing the plain metal door behind him to slide open.

Nina followed him up a switchback staircase to the second floor. A sign indicated paths to saunas, a running track, treadmills, and another free-weight area. Corey headed for the third door on the left, labeled 'Manager.'

"Yo, Rick." He opened it and walked in. "Need a minute."

The room didn't have much space, less so due to columns of plastiboard shipping cartons stacked against the wall. A drab green desk stood before a bookshelf full of pill bottles, derm patches, bins full of autoinjectors, and several fat plastic bottles with screw-on lids. One still bore a label for 'Mega Protein 9000.' She doubted it still held anything even remotely associated with fitness.

"Hey, Cor. What's up?" Ricky Barron didn't look an hour older than his file photo. He peered around a holo-panel floating over a mirror-silver bar about the size of her forearm, a standard terminal. Strong light from the holographic keyboard tinted his shirt cobalt blue. "Oh, hello..." He winked at Nina. "Cor... you shouldn't have."

"She ain't a pross." Corey walked up to the desk. "Heavy shit, man."

"Ricky." She offered a hand. "Pardon the outfit. I'm with Division 9."

Ricky Barron's permanent smile went flat. "Umm."

"Before you do something stupid, I'm not here to bust your balls over chems. I need to know who you're getting Harmony from."

"Didn't you just say you didn't come here to 'rass me about chems?" Ricky leaned back.

Nina stared at the red outline of a firearm her sensors picked up under the desk, a virtual highlight in her electronic vision. "Before you go for that MCP50 under the desk—nice choice by the way, I carry the same one—hear me out."

Ricky stopped sliding his hand down his leg. "Okay... We flaz."

"I'm not here because you're selling what appears to be a harmless bit of stress avoidance for people. Whatever you've got going on here, at least two veterans are helping you keep this fitness center operational for the locals... I know you've got no love for the ACC."

"You got that right," muttered Corey.

Ricky nodded. "Yeah." He seemed to relax and shifted his weight back and left, raising one hand to his chin. "So, you think they're after me?"

"Not directly. Someone is tainting Harmony with nanobots, and these nanobots represent a foreign threat to the UCF. The only thing I need you to do is tell me where you're getting such large quantities of it from. I suspect the ACC may be the ultimate source, and by distributing the tainted Harmony, you could be inadvertently assisting them in acts of espionage or sabotage."

"Shit." Ricky rubbed at his mouth for a moment in thought. "You know I'm makin' bank on this stuff, right?"

"Harmony isn't reliant on these nanobots to provide what it is your customers buy. I don't expect there will be a need to shut down Harmony completely. The nanobots are the problem. Who's the source?"

Ricky and Corey exchanged a look. Corey nodded.

"I don't know his name." Ricky let his arm fall away from his mouth, landing limp across his lap. "Tall white dude. Brown hair. Looks like the dick boyfriend from every chick vid out there. Kent Fuckworth or some shit. He shows up when he wants to. Dude don't keep a schedule. Vids me about an hour before he rolls up in a van with the shit. Only reason he gives me any warning at all is on account of me havin' to scramble to collect creds for him the first time. Dude's in a severe hurry."

An attempt to access the local Citycam net turned up zip. "Cams are out..."

"Yeah. This *is* a grey zone, right?" Ricky winked.

Nina folded her arms. "When do you expect him to contact you again?"

"Couple days probably. Gettin' low on H. Shit's flying out." Ricky smiled.

"I want you to act normal. As soon as he contacts you, vid me on this PID." She waved her official NetMini at him, making his chirp. "I promise your place here won't get chewed up."

"What you gonna do?" asked Ricky.

Nina glanced at a tiny sofa buried under boxes. "Sit there acting strung out. I just need to see this guy so we can figure out who he is."

"There any kinda reward fo' this?" Ricky's grin returned.

"Assuming that the knowledge you're acting in defense of your homeland isn't enough?" She chuckled. "I'll see what I can do, but it'll depend on how useful this turns out to be."

"What if your ass is wrong, and this dude ain't ACC? 'Cept everything here"—Ricky twirled his hand around in a circle—"goes smooth."

Nina swiped her fingers through her hair over her ear. "Well, then I suppose I'll work out some kind of 'cooperation fee' for your time."

"United from sea to sea." Ricky saluted her.

His tone said he mocked the UCF motto. Corey noticed it and gave him a mild glare.

"Vid me forty seconds after you get off the line with him. Any faster and they might be watching for a rapid outbound."

Ricky nodded. "You got it, babe. Sweet legs by the way."

Nina winked. "Should be. They sure cost enough."

She headed out and downstairs, pausing to wait for Corey to resume his post guarding the door. "What are you doing here, Sergeant? Seems a bit... sad for a vet to be running muscle for a chem peddler."

Corey chuckled. "Actually I'm workin' for CPSS. Ricky hired them, and I got the site."

"Citadel Professional Security Solutions?" She blinked, then laughed. "What *is* the world coming to?"

"Like the man said... he's making bank."

---

It took about twenty-two minutes (shorter than the time it took her to fly north to Sector 10184) for Ops to trace the route-control signals that Jen Alvarez, aka 'Mama Fine,' used to distribute her chems back to their source. Nina brought her patrol craft in for a landing on the roof of an eighty-story tower in the heart of a grey zone. She shut the car down and pushed the door open, enjoying a blast of air that smelled (and tasted) like diaper pail.

Nina gagged. To her left, the hulking shapes of eight spherical tanks occupied a mostly-flat area beside a decrepit factory. From her perch seventy-six stories over the dead manufacturing plant, she had a clear view of hundreds of hydroponic tanks full of rotting proto-meat and moldy growth medium.

*Oh... that's foul.* She coughed.

She jogged to a maintenance door, which ignored her police override code. It didn't even chirp or buzz. *Bet Mama cut the power.* Nina grabbed the knob, and stopped. She took a step back and scanned around for any signs of a trap: power fluctuations, electrical current in the walls, or the telltale whirr of a sentry gun. Finding nothing, she again grasped the knob and increased tension until it broke open.

For a few minutes, Nina enjoyed not being an ordinary human: jogging down seventy-nine stories of stairs didn't make her tired. Vagrants littered the steps over the last two floors, but the most coherent of them only managed to reach for her ass a full six seconds after she'd passed by. The door at the bottom opened to a dingy hallway packed with an assortment of drop ceiling tiles, LED light tubes, air filters, and a handful of food reassemblers still in their retail packaging. A thick layer of dust coated everything.

Nina headed left, away from the lobby toward the building's physical plant. A ninety-degree right turn later, she paused at a pink spray-painted line on the floor, walls and ceiling. Fifty-four feet away, according to her targeting optics, a sentry gun swiveled to point at her. It scanned as a standard Class 4 rifle mechanism, 10mm caseless rounds. Within a half-second of training on her, it emitted a buzzing chirp, a sound she recognized as 'bot speak' for 'shit, cop, don't shoot.' She doubted the drug source would be scanning everyone's NetMini for police identity codes, but she made a note to disable it if she wound up on Ricky's couch.

The sentry resumed sweeping about. Nina no longer existed to its electronic awareness of the area. She approached the boiler room door, turned the knob, and pushed with a normal human level of strength, but the door didn't move. A metallurgical scan showed the probable outline of a large tool shelf against it on the inside. She smiled and nudged the door with her body's full power. With a jarring screech, door and shelf slid inward until she created a gap she could fit through.

A massive chamber inside contained no boilers or anything even close to heating/cooling equipment, though the air tasted of industrial oil and metal. Broken bolts and mounting brackets, as well as two giant dark stains on either side of the space hinted at where machines once stood. A few meters to her right, a yellow-and-black exo suit slumped empty and powered down. Straps and buckles hung over a cushioned pad in the operator's hollow, decorated with sparkly pink hearts and little cat head brooches.

The majority of the cavernous room held shelves stacked to the ceiling, packed with either bins, robot parts, or idle delivery bots. Every so often, a flying brick about the size of a small dog took off from its perch on the right-side shelves, flew to a bin on the opposing shelf to grab a bottle or packet, and raced off to a hole in the wall.

At the far end of the room, a slim woman with caramel-colored skin stretched out on a shiny, new Comforgel reclining bed, currently in chair mode. She wore a lacy, transparent slip with nothing on under it, a fact obvious in the orange-red glow of the gel beneath her. Beyond the bed, a desk held multiple terminals (also new), a high-end food reassembler (with the espresso attachment), a net deck, and a Yume Koujou game system.

Jen Alvarez appeared lost in extreme concentration, though her eyes remained closed. Nina walked over, ducking once to avoid a delivery bot that apparently ran on route programs rather than active sensing. She stopped at Jen's side, her gaze following a thin wire from the side of the woman's head to the game system.

*Hmm. Pulling the wire out of a Yume is as bad as doing it to a deck jockey.* The woman would be immersed in the game world, experiencing it as reality. The sudden shock of being launched out of that world into the real one would leave her stunned and disoriented for several minutes.

Nina took a spare wire from the desk, connected it to one of her M3 ports in the back of her neck, and plugged in to the Yume. She ran the link in windowed mode, viewing the game's output on a floating screen rather than living it. A musical jingle played in her head, the 'Yume Koujou sound.' A few seconds later, a dramatic orchestral score started that conjured images of running through the jungle away from some sort of temple guardian.

The black screen faded in with the logo for *Curse of the Lost Diamonds.*

Red text scrolled along the bottom: ‹Single Player Only: Press 'a' to start a private instance. Press 'b' to spectate current instance.›

Nina glanced at the B.

The screen shifted, and she looked down the length of a stone-walled corridor reminiscent of something one might find buried under the jungle in a cheesy action holo-vid. A buxom woman in short shorts, a camo shirt and combat boots hovered over a stone table, studying two-inch gold tiles covered in crude human figures carved with different facial expressions.

Nina 'walked' up to the woman. Her presence appeared to radiate light, so she figured 'spectators' appeared as little ghostly balls to the player. "Hey."

"I'm busy," said the woman. A second later, she paused in studying the tiles, and stared at Nina. "What the hell? Who are you? How did you get into this instance?"

"I need to talk to you."

"Fuck." The woman stomped one foot and scowled at the ceiling. Handguns in her chest harness, far too large to be plausible, clattered. "I don't know how the hell you hacked my Yume, but I am going to find you. Game pause. Logout."

Nina shook her head. She pulled her wire out, which did little to her as she'd kept her session on a screen.

Jen blinked and sat up, bleary-eyed and grumbling. As soon as she lifted her head enough to spot Nina, she screamed.

"As I was saying, I need to talk to you."

"The fuck!" shrieked Jen. She leapt for a handgun tucked between the Yume Koujou and one of the terminals, but Nina caught her and tossed her back on the Comforgel chair.

"No guns."

Jen scrambled away and curled up near the headrest, staring over her knees. "How... how the hell did you get in here?" She shot a terrified look at the open door.

"Nice little business you've got running here."

"You shouldn't hurt me." Jen ran a nervous hand up and down her shin before grasping her toes. "I've got friends."

"What kind of friends?"

"Friends," said Jen. "Lots of friends who'll find you if you do anything to me."

Nina's somatic response detection system lit up with wavering graphs and lines around the young woman's face, pointing out an elevated heart rate, increased perspiration, and eye movements indicative of a lie. "You've got a couple buddies in the local street gangs, Mama Fine, aka Jennifer Alvarez. Age nineteen. Doing rather well for yourself. Thirteen point eight million credits distributed among fourteen separate accounts. You're averaging around 450 grand a month all on common chems due to your wide distribution reach."

Jen stared at the door again. "How... who?"

"My name's Nina. I'm with Division 9."

"No..." Jen whined. "I haven't done anything *that* bad." She burst into tears. "Please don't kill me!"

Nina bowed her head and sighed. "Calm down. Unless you're planning on pointing a gun at me, I have no intention of harming you." Once the weeping stopped, she looked up. "Who do you get the Harmony from?"

"Bunch of people." Jen sniffed.

"There's one in particular responsible for the majority."

Shivering, Jen shrugged with one shoulder. "I dunno his name. He's kinda weird. He didn't wanna do the usual thing and trade on the 'net and let my bots pick the shit up. He always wants to meet in person. I thought he was like a serial rapist or some shit, so I got some friends go with me. *Big* friends."

A *beep* made Nina glance to the left. One of the terminals tracking incoming orders had an anime cat dancing across the screen for hitting the 2,500 orders mark in a single day. "How did this guy find you? What got it started?"

Jen uncurled, letting her legs hang over the side of her chair. "I just got this message one day asking about an arrangement. This dude said he could, like, provide mass quantities of H for cheap. I was kinda suspicious at first, thinkin' he might've been the police... but you guys don't care about soft shit like H, right?"

"Not usually, but this is an unusual situation."

"Yeah, I kinda figured." Jen ran her hands up and down her arms while emitting a nervous laugh. "He kept messaging me, but I didn't bite. Then I get this picture of a van *full* of H. So I decided to check it out." She shrugged one shoulder. "Dude was legit."

"All right... where do you meet him, and when is the next time?"

"Umm. He sends me a message when he's got stuff. We pick a place like fifteen minutes before I gotta be there." She eyed her shelves laden with an assortment of chems. "Umm... So if the cops don't care about the soft shit, why are you here? I'm careful. I don't deal the hard stuff."

"We don't. I'm tracking down tainted Harmony."

Jen's posture relaxed. She slipped off the glowing Comforgel to her feet, wincing from the cold concrete. "Mind if I put something on... basically naked in this thing."

"Go for it."

"Thanks." Jen hurried to a cabinet on the right side of the desk, from which she pulled a pair of sweat pants.

"I need to find this source. The next time he contacts you, vid me. I'm going to be one of your 'bodyguards.'"

Jen flung the diaphanous nightie off and wriggled into a sweatshirt. "He won't believe you. You don't look anything like a bodyguard. He'll know you're a doll, and I don't handle enough credits to have a doll for a bodyguard."

"Actually, you do." Nina chuckled. "All right. I'll arrange for someone who looks the part to shadow you until you make contact."

"Umm." Jen stepped into enormous white slippers shaped like cartoon cats. "You mean like stay here... with me?"

"That's right. Only until this guy calls you."

Jen eyed the chems again. "You guys aren't gonna screw me over when this is finished, are you?"

"Depends on how well you behave." She smiled into a sigh. "Trust me. The chems you're selling are the least of my concerns here. Really. I know your grandparents came here for a better life. I'm not here to shut you down."

"Yeah." Jen looked down. "They did."

"Maybe you found what they were looking for with all this." Nina gestured around at the whirring bots. "Looks like you're getting as close as you can in this world." She stared at the door and spoke a little over a whisper. "The Corporates are involved."

Jen raised and lowered her toes, making her cat slippers nod. "Figured. I'm not a rich bitch above the law. Why else would I have the shadow police in my place?"

Nina opened a vid window to request another operative. "We don't close every case with bullets." Drummond's head exploded in her memory for the thousandth time. "Just the special ones."

# 28

# THE COMPUTER CHEATS

A white-haired elf girl in a dress made from leaf-shaped spots of light flitted about the holo-panel in Nina's living room. At her side, a man of ridiculous proportion wielded a sword so large it made her laugh to watch him whipping it around like a plastic toy. The two made their way across a forest full of neon-colored flowers and bizarre trees with great wooden faces. Every so often, one of the elf's blue magic bolts would miss the little green men attacking them and hit a tree, causing it to sprout a human face and cuss her out with kid-friendly grumbling.

Elizaveta sat on the sofa to Nina's right, cuddled against her except for when the game made her flail her arms about to control her 'magic.' Joey draped himself at her left, the pair of them wearing senshelmets. Whenever a goblin arrow hit the elf or the armored man, red numbers somewhere between fifteen and a hundred appeared. The man's life bar didn't move much, though each hit on the elf took away hunks of green.

Both Elizaveta and Joey's characters seemed to do about the same range of damage, anywhere from eighty to five-hundred, only the elf could hit things far away and Joey's guy could hit more than one thing at a time if they got close. Any goblin either one of them hit died instantly, regardless of the damage number.

"Guess those are weak huh?" Nina glanced at the official NetMini, simultaneously dreading and eager for a call from Ricky or Jen.

Elizaveta looked up at her; the senshelmet's plastic shield covered most of her face, save for her mouth and chin. After a second, her lips pressed thin with frustration. "Sorry."

Nina repeated her comment in Russian.

"*Da. Slabovato*[1]." Elizaveta nodded. "*Ya izvenayus' chto ya izuchayu angliyskiy slishkom medlenno*[2]."

Nina patted the top of the helmet since she couldn't stroke the girl's hair. "*Nichego. Ne nuzhno speshit'[3].*"

"*Chto ona skazala[4].*" Joey pointed at Nina.

"*On govorit, kak robot[5],*" muttered Elizaveta, grinning.

"You got a chip?" Nina smiled.

"Yeah. Kinda had to when she came running into the living room soaked, naked, crying, and rambling."

Nina stared at him, not that he could see her. "What the hell happened?"

"Not a big deal. Autoshower freaked her out. You know how the door safety-locks when it runs?"

"Oh, no…" She patted the girl on the back and rubbed her hand up and down, switching to Russian. "You tried to shower alone?"

Elizaveta nodded. "I was trying to be brave, but I got scared when it wouldn't let me out."

Joey grimaced. "'Course I had no idea why she's screaming her head off. She just kept freaking out, so I ordered a chip."

A huge purple goblin, coated in writhing shadow magic appeared out of nowhere, hit the elf, and knocked her flat with an empty health bar.

Elizaveta slapped her hands on her thighs and yelled, "Bullshit!" in English.

Nina gasped.

Joey whistled innocently.

"Elizaveta!" Nina pulled the helmet off the girl. "That's a bad word. You're not old enough to say that."

Innocent blue eyes stared at her with zero comprehension. "I… say word."

"That's a naughty word." Nina smiled. "*Plohoe slovo.*"

Elizaveta looked shocked. She pointed at Joey and blurted in Russian, "He says that every time his character dies. I thought it is what you say when your character dies."

Joey flashed a cheesy smile. His chip-Russian came out slow and lacking in proper inflection. "It is what you say when the computer cheats, not when you get knocked out."

Elizaveta leaned forward to peer around Nina at him. "But you say that every time you die. Is the computer cheating all the time?"

The total sincerity on her face made Nina crack up laughing. The child stared at her in confusion for a few seconds before she sniffled and started crying.

Joey made a pensive face while his chip chewed on her Russian, after which he muttered in English, "Yeah, basically."

Nina brushed at her hair. "Why are you crying?"

"Am I in trouble? You're laughing at me." Elizaveta calmed somewhat, sniffling. "What is funny?"

"Just the look on your face when you asked him that. You're not in trouble, but I'd like you not to use that language until you get a bit older, okay?"

"But, I've heard him—"

Joey waved both hands at her in a rapid side-to-side gesture.

"Okay. I won't say the bad English." Elizaveta wiped her face dry and nodded, her good mood back in an instant. "So, is the computer always cheating?"

"No, sweetie. But, he seems to think it does." Nina winked.

"If it beats *me*, it cheated." Joey poked himself in the chest with one thumb.

"Ohhhh." Elizaveta bobbed her head with a slow, exaggerated nod. "He just does not like to lose."

Nina reclined into the sofa while they resumed playing, content to watch them roam a lush enchanted forest. The endless throng of goblins gave way to an eerie clearing where the daylight did not enter. Elizaveta jumped and whirled around to look behind her; the elf woman on the screen mimicked the gesture.

"*Prizraki!*" she yelled.

"These are nice ghosts," said Joey. "The quest-giver in that village said we needed to talk to them. Look for one with a lantern."

"*Chto?*"

Joey sighed, but seemed more irritated with himself than the girl. He repeated the line in Russian.

Elizaveta pointed. The elf approached a transparent human woman in a ball gown. Whispery dialogue came out of Joey's helmet in English and hers in Russian. Soon, they left the ghosts behind and spent about ten minutes navigating a cave with a few giant spiders until they found a great door.

"This is a good place to save," said Joey in Russian. "It's bedtime."

"Aww." Elizaveta slouched. "Okay."

She removed her helmet and carried it over to the stand where the Yume Koujou system sat. After putting it away, she ran off to her bedroom. Joey set his helmet on the floor nearby, leaned over, and took Nina's hand. He kept gliding closer and closer until they kissed.

"You're tense," whispered Joey. "Case got you wound up?"

"Yeah." She kissed him a little more before glancing down the back hallway. "Teeth!"

"Okay," yelled Elizaveta.

Two seconds later, she stumbled across the hallway from bedroom to bathroom while pulling on a nightgown.

"Your eyes light up when you look at her," said Joey.

Nina kissed him again. "Be right back."

She headed to the bathroom where Elizaveta waited with her toothbrush in hand. Nina set about helping the girl brush. *These arms can tear people in half, bend plastisteel... And I'm brushing a six-year-old's teeth.* One bad circuit, one electron in the wrong place, and... Elizaveta made silly faces at her, chasing away the building worry.

"Rinse." Nina handed her a cup of water. "Don't drink it."

Elizaveta swished water around her mouth and projectile-splattered it into the sink. Mostly. After, Nina walked her to bed, tucked her in, and sat at her side reading a storybook from a virtual holo-panel. The child fell asleep in minutes, and Nina crept out and back to where Joey lay comatose on the couch, with a wire running from behind his ear to the Yume Koujou.

"I'm not sleeping." One eye popped open as Nina sat. "Sec. Loggin' out."

"What would you have done without that multitasker?" Nina crawled up on the couch and leaned into him. "Would you have waited patiently for me to come back or logged in and been a meat puppet?"

Joey pulled the wire out and threaded an arm around her. He pursed his lips in thought. "Hmm. Fooling around with you or covering the walls of Gamma-9 with alien/demon blood. Tough call."

She raised an eyebrow at him. "Oh, well if I'm interrupting."

His eyes widened. "Kidding…"

Nina grinned. "Me too."

He reached up and caressed her face. She slid closer, pushing him over on his back and lying on top of him. His hands explored her body, slipping under her purple satin bathrobe to the nothing underneath it. She moaned into his mouth, and nibbled on his lip when his erection stiffened under his pants.

"Ngh…" He shifted. "The Peacemaker wants out."

"That's what you get for wearing such tight pants."

He moved his hand from her breast to cradle the back of her head. "They're not that tight. I'm that big."

Nina pushed herself up, straddling him. "Oh, really now? I think I should take a closer look."

"Open at your own risk." Joey winked.

"Maybe I should be careful," she purred, and lay flat atop him again. "Wouldn't want to hurt myself."

Nina rubbed her thigh back and forth over his bulging interest, trapped against the side of his leg. Joey groaned, biting his lip to keep himself quiet. The sudden worry that Elizaveta might wake up and walk out into the living room made her freeze. After peering back over her shoulder to make sure the hallway remained child free, she scooped Joey up and carried him to the master bedroom.

"Guess you're tired of waiting." He chuckled as she tossed him to the Comforgel pad.

She climbed up on the bed and lay on her side, draped half on top of him. "That, and I didn't want to get caught."

"Cau—ohh." He chuckled. "Right."

Nina bit her lip. "Are you sure you're okay with this? With me taking Elizaveta in? I know I didn't talk to you about it at all first, but if you'd have seen her…"

"It's fine. She's good enough on the Yume." He winked. "Only real downside I see is that you're not naked all the time anymore."

Nina laughed and slid her hand up under his shirt. He grinned like a fool and let her pull it off over his head. After he opened his belt, Nina pulled off his boots one after the next, and tugged his pants down. He sprang to life.

He struck a pose, flat on his back, and flashed a cocky grin.

Nina let her robe slip off behind her.

Joey glanced at his erection, to her, and back to his manhood. "This is where you gasp adoringly at its magnificence."

Nina gave him a predatory smile and pounced. They rolled over each other once, winding up with her on her back. Joey kissed his way from her lips to her neck before tracing the tip of his tongue down over her breast to her stomach. Nina squirmed in delight and emitted a series of faint squeaks. She lifted her head, making eye contact. Joey stared at her, utterly entranced by her presence.

Dread that he'd comment about her looks came out of nowhere. Her fingers clenched the sheets. If he called her beautiful, if he again told her how he loved every curve of her body, she'd feel like a high-end motorcycle. Something an engineer thought up and put together, and he the driver who couldn't wait to get his hands on the machine.

Machine.

"I see your face whenever I close my eyes." Joey kept staring into her eyes as he leaned down to kiss her near the navel. Hot breath and beard scratch triggered a tightening of muscles, the way a human body should've reacted. "As soon as I saw you in that dark corner... your beauty haunts my dreams."

Nina leaned her head back and surrendered to the pleasure of his tongue between her legs. Her face... that hadn't changed much at all. Her parents didn't even notice anything different until she got out of the chair and towered four inches over her mother. They had been the same five-foot-four height. Joey finding her face intoxicating evaded her fear. Her face had always been hers.

Her insecurities of humanity, worry about the case, and even the fear that the child would walk in on them gave way to the explosion of blurry flashes of color in her mind, and ecstasy. Joey's tongue, the breath huffing out of his nose onto her sex, the scratch of stubble on her legs, everything pushed her to the edge.

"Joey..." she wheezed. "Joey... I'm...."

He slid up, dragging his entire body over hers. She grunted in deprived frustration, but he didn't seem intent on teasing her. Nina opened her mouth to protest his stopping, and gasped as he entered her. He undulated back and forth, making soft grunts, echoed by her gasps and squeals. When he began to slow his rhythm, she grabbed his shoulder and pushed him over before straddling him.

Joey's hair spilled across the pillows, an inky waterfall of black. He slid his hands up her front, caressing her hips and sides and holding on as she moved up and down. His face reddened; all the veins in his forehead and neck swelled, and he convulsed. Seconds after his muscles relaxed, Nina reached climax, her mind swirling among flashes, abstract shapes overhead lights painted on her closed eyelids.

She moaned a little too loud, and collapsed beside him.

Their noses less than an inch apart, Joey grinned. "We should pull a sheet up or something. She's going to wander in to ask what you're screaming about."

Nina grinned.

"The people two floors down are going to ask what that noise was."

She gave him a light slap on the chest.

"Ow. My tit." He cradled the spot.

"I'll get you a Narcoderm." She snuggled at his side.

He put an arm around and held her tight.

Eventually, the post-coital glow faded to comfortable closeness, and she tugged the maroon satin sheets up. Joey stroked her hair, his eyes half-lidded, and kept smiling at her like a little boy who'd just gotten away with something bad.

"Sorry if I got a little active. I really needed this." Nina smiled.

"Case that bad?"

She exhaled. "It's got the potential to be. It's not 'bad' yet, just the waiting for a lead and nothing else to go after. It looks like the ACC managed to add nanobots to a street drug, Harmony, and these things are creating cybernetic implants in people that turn them into spies."

"Whoa... mind control?"

"No." She squeezed him tighter. "At least I don't think so. The one we found seemed to be only audio/video transmission."

"Oh, did I tell you about Katya?"

Nina traced her finger around in circles on his chest. "Only that bit about her needing a legit identity, registering as a defector, and taking in that... girl."

"She called me yesterday."

*I thought they couldn't stand each other.* She kept jealousy at arm's length... for now. "Wasn't she getting cozy with Masaru?"

Joey snickered. "He doesn't 'get cozy' with anyone. Two or three girls two or three nights a week, and never the same one twice. Besides, he had to go back to Japan. I guess being the son of the CEO isn't all fun and games. Last I heard from him, he was bitching about boring meetings. Kinda misses it here."

"Okay, so what about Katya?" She stopped drawing circles on his chest and reached across to hold him.

"She took this sneakernet job, handing off some data from this place... and a guy followed her. Guess she got a little sloppy on their network, but the guy probably figured he could extort sex out of her for not talking." Joey shook his head. "That poor, poor, unfortunate man. Medusa doesn't put out on the first date... unless venom counts."

Nina smiled. The gorgon of jealousy crumbled to dust. "What's the punch line?"

"She seems to have found an ACC spy."

"What?" Nina shot upright. "Where? Who?"

Joey laced his fingers together behind his head. "These really are awesome pillows. Suck the wakefulness right out of me."

Nina reached down and grasped a pinch of hair.

"And that's ball hair."

"Wanna keep it?" She winked.

"Touchy, touchy." Joey sucked air through his teeth. "The guy was operating under the identity of 'Zack Martin.' Real name is Anders Becker. I sent everything up the food chain. Guy seemed like a complete amateur."

"Obviously if he blew his cover for a chance at sex."

Joey laughed. "Don't underestimate the power of the P."

"Especially when it's connected to a microfusion reactor," she said, deadpan.

"I'd have sex with a full sized fusion reactor before I let the Peacemaker within five feet of Katya."

Nina laughed.

"I got the feeling his parents had some influence and pulled strings to get him in the OOI. I haven't seen any useful information come out of him, so maybe they just sent him over here to get rid of him. I can't imagine people making the tactical decisions were happy about this guy being thrust onto their roster."

"Possible." She curled up at his side again. "Any idea what he was up to? Where did they have him embedded?"

"It had to be a dumping ground post. The place had nothing to do with military equipment or intelligence operations. Ol' Zack was working cyberdefense at Laughlin-Reed Innovation."

Nina closed her eyes. "Fuck."

"Again?" Joey kissed her cheek. "If you insist."

"No, ass." She grumbled. "LRI is the company that manufactures Placinil."

Joey rolled on his side facing her, his head propped up on his fist. "And about seven hundred other drugs, as well as all sorts of medical equipment."

"Placinil is the prescription form of Harmony... I'm no chemist, but they said a couple drops of synthetic cannabis on it and it goes from being an anti-anxiety med to producing an incredibly long sustained high where the user is blissful."

"Hallucinations?"

"No, just happy."

"Enhanced sensory experience? Vivid dreams? Stamina? Munchies?" Joey raised his eyebrows a little bit in time with each question.

"Nope. Just happy, like nothing can bother them. Stress-less." She shook her head. "Maybe I should take a hit."

"Wow. Sounds boring. Why would anyone bother with it? Pinky won't touch a chem unless it allows him to taste time."

"Pinky is going to die before he's twenty-five."

Joey raised his arm, pointing at the ceiling. "Fair point." He let his arm fall limp.

"At least I know what I'm going to do now."

He smiled. "Have sex again?"

Nina grinned. "You're impossible. I mean I gotta chase this Becker guy down."

Joey looked at his crotch. "Down boy. She said *Beck*er."

"That was fast." Nina raised an eyebrow.

He raised two fingers. "Peacemaker's reloaded if you want it."

She glanced at the dark hallway outside and sent a mental command to the house computer that closed her bedroom door. After setting a motion alarm to ping if anything moved in the hallway, she reached over and grasped 'The Peacemaker.'

"A quick draw is probably not the best metaphor yanno."

Joey stared into her eyes. "I could lie here and gaze into your eyes forever."

"You can do that a little later." She winked, and killed the lights.

# 29

# ONE MILLIMETER

Katya let her head sink back against the sofa cushion, clenching her jaw to weather the two burning spears through her body. She kept her left hand clamped over the bullet hole in her right shoulder while Eve held pressure on the thigh wound. Blood seeped between the girl's tiny fingers despite her effort.

"He missed the artery," said Eve.

The concept of speech remained distant. Katya managed a grunt of affirmation.

Eve nodded toward the gun she'd left on the coffee table after pulling it out of the bear. "Guess you want me to act like a kid huh? I can try. I was never real emotional in the compound. 102 cried her eyes out every night. Everything scared her. 104 wasn't much better, but at least she didn't cry out loud. None of 'em really liked me 'cause I was all gung ho."

Katya chuckled, and regretted it.

"Here they come," whispered Eve. "I hear them."

A few seconds later, roughly four minutes after her Emergency Services vid, the rattle of armor emanated from the hallway. Eve's white hair flashed blinding under the glare of a small spotlight. The girl narrowed her eyes.

"In here," yelled Eve. "Mommy's shot."

"Female juvenile, female adult," said a male voice behind her with a quality suggesting electronic speakers. "Confirm resident ID."

Another spotlight glided over the window wall in front of Katya, heading left.

"Clear left," said a female voice, also crackling with an electronic tone.

"There's no one else here." Eve bounced on her toes.

The muted thumping of boots on carpet moved to the right and left. A man and a woman in blue Division 1 armor rounded either side of the couch, handguns out but not aimed at either Katya or Eve. Two other officers moved deeper into the apartment.

"Ma'am..." The male officer holstered his weapon and took a knee by the sofa while his partner walked around the bodies. "Come on, stay with me."

"I'm here." Katya cringed. "Pain."

The female officer approached, put her weapon away, and gathered Eve. "Come on, sweetie. Come with me, okay?"

Eve looked at her hands. "If I let go, she's gonna bleed."

"She'll be fine." The male officer sounded reassuring, but his silver-visored helmet blocked all view of any facial expression. He took two stimpaks out of his belt. "These will stop the bleeding. Medics are less than a minute behind us."

"Clear," said a man from the hallway.

"Clear as well. Firearm on the floor in here. Blood on the cabinet. Projectile impact in the counter." Another woman exited the kitchen and headed for the bodies. She holstered her sidearm and plucked some manner of scanning unit from her belt. "What a mess."

As the other female officer carried Eve off to the kitchen, the man in front of Katya administered the stimpaks to her thigh. The breath she'd been holding to mitigate pain erupted in a scream as the previous agony changed from simple burning to an army of fire ants inside her leg. Reflex tears ran down her face, but the flare up faded to cold numbness before her lungs emptied.

She blinked a few times to clear away the white spots and stared at her reflection in the man's visor. He held her hand, though she didn't remember him taking it... or pressing the second stimpak into her shoulder. Neither wound closed completely, though her shoulder ceased bleeding and the thigh wound had slowed to a trickle.

The soft murmur of Eve's voice emanated from the kitchen, no doubt answering the officer's questions of what happened.

Katya tried to pull herself up to sit on the sofa rather than drape across it, but yelled at a sensation like a sword impaling her thigh. "Gah!"

"Easy, ma'am. Don't try to move." The officer hit a button on the side of his helmet, causing the silver part to slide up and over the top to the back, exposing most of his medium-brown face and black eyebrows. "Take a breath or two and if you feel up to it, can you tell me what happened?"

"I escaped from the ACC about a year ago. Yesterday, this man who called himself Zack Martin sees me and recognizes me. He is one of their spies, and not a very good one. Thought I was still active, and would be interested in him. I have a friend in Division 9. I contacted him and a van picked this Zack up." Katya nodded toward the corpses. "These three came here to ask how I found Zack. More spies."

The officer, Delacruz according to his nameplate, whistled. "That's a heck of a story. So what happened in here?"

A pair of women in white armor that looked much lighter than what the Division 1 officers wore hurried in from the hall. Delacruz waved them over and moved aside to let them closer. A slim woman with deep, dark skin and a blonde bob knelt in front of her. Below an Ancora Medical logo, a nametag read: Nelson, R.

"Hi... Well, I guess I won't say it's nice to see at least one person's having a day worse than mine." The medtech winked. "I'm Rachelle, and my partner is Courtney."

The other medic, pale with lush black hair and elven features, smiled. Her nameplate read: Santos, C. She set down and opened a large white case, from which she pulled out a bundle of clear plastic while Rachelle sliced open Katya's pant leg.

Katya cringed at the sensation of fabric pulling away the sticky mess around in the wound. The medtechs removed one leg of her sweatpants and replaced it with a giant plastic sock, which they sealed around her thigh above the wound with an adhesive strip. Peach-colored gel flooded in from the toe end, pumped out of the case.

"A portable... I feel special." Katya smiled.

A Division 1 officer examined the bodies, scanning and taking image captures without touching them, while the other woman hunted around the walls with another scanner. Green laser grids covered the walls, making dust sparkle.

*I'm going to be seeing lasers in my dreams.*

Courtney hovered over her shoulder with a handheld scanner projecting a turquoise laser pattern. "If we can patch you up onsite, it's both less disruptive to you and less expensive." Her aqua-tinted face shifted bright when the contents of the little viewscreen changed. "Good news. The projectile only nicked the bone in your shoulder, and I don't see any nerve damage."

While Rachelle monitored the control panel for the 'gel sock,' Courtney plugged an autoinjector similar to a stimpak but larger into the scanner. Ten seconds later, it chirped, and she applied it to Katya's arm. The expected flood of coldness under the skin followed.

She'd never seen the equipment before, but assumed the scanner programmed the nanobots within the large autoinjector with the specific details of her injury. Another rush of pins and needles filled her thigh as the gel reached the opening and entered the wound channel. The medics held her hands as she let out a startled yelp and her whole body clenched up. Courtney eased her forward to sit on the edge of the cushion so the gel could reach the exit wound on the bottom of her leg.

"Mom?" yelled Eve, peering in from the kitchen.

The female officer tried to tug her back, but Eve clamped onto the wall.

Once the feeling of prickling and itching subsided, she slouched back into the sofa and glanced at Eve. "I'm... okay. Go with the police woman, Eve."

"'Kay." She let go of the wall and the officer pulled her out of sight.

"So," said Delacruz. "Do you feel up to making a statement about what happened?"

Katya nodded. "Yeah. Leg is numb now."

"That's us." Rachelle winked. "The nanobots in the gel are delivering painkillers direct to your nerves. Looks like you lucked out again. Missed the bone, some minor nerve damage, but the sleeve can take care of that." She tapped two buttons on a holo-panel above the case. "You may experience incidences of subdermal paresthesia or numbness for up to a week after. Don't worry, it should clear up on its own."

Courtney applied a sticky rubber patch to the inside of her left arm, an inch above the elbow. A thin grey hose connected it to another port on the case.

"This is going to help regenerate your blood supply. Try to relax as much as you can."

"Right..." She stared at the swollen gel-filled thing on her leg. Bits of sweat pant fabric and couch cushion floated out of the hole in her thigh. "Well, these three hacked the door. They had a signal jammer, which tipped me off that they were on the way."

"Implant," said Delacruz. "If these three were spies, wouldn't they have known you'd see it go offline?"

"I'm betting they didn't care so much about giving me ten seconds of warning as they did of me setting off a panic signal when the door opened. That one came in first." Katya pointed at 'Raúl.' "I shot him three times in the chest, but he had a decent subderm weave. One of them got me in the arm, and they were on me before I could recover."

Delacruz nodded, evidently recording her as he didn't type anything by hand.

"They wanted to know how I found Zack, even though he found me. They didn't believe me when I said it was luck. Of course, the only possible explanation to them was that I'd discovered the ACC had operatives in West City and I was working for you guys to find them."

"That true?" asked Delacruz.

"No." Katya shook her head. "Though I did make my friend in Division 9 aware of Zack's existence, I'm not working for them."

Delacruz glanced at 'Raúl.' "All right. What happened next?"

Courtney prodded her finger around Katya's shoulder. "Does this hurt or feel tender?"

Katya glanced at her. "No pain. It feels normal."

"Excellent," said Courtney.

"They shot me in the leg as a motivational technique... My daughter was hiding in her room and came out when I screamed. That one"—she pointed at 'Julio'—"grabbed her and put a gun to her head. She got scared and wet herself, which got on his leg and made him flinch. That's when I went for another weapon I had under the sofa cushion."

Delacruz twisted to his left, stared at the three bodies for a few seconds, and looked back at her. "You took all three out fast enough not to get killed or have the one holding your kid shoot her?"

"I shot that fucker first," muttered Katya.

Delacruz's expression shifted away from concern to suspicion. His right hand slid a little closer to his weapon. "That seems a little implausible to me. Your right arm was disabled, and you don't have neural accelerators."

"And there's a bullet hole in the ceiling," said a female officer near where 'Julio' lay. "This man was shot from a low angle almost straight up through his head."

Katya grimaced inside. "Eve... umm."

"Looks like there was a weapon concealed in some kind of stuffed animal." The female officer raised a hand in pause, with a bit of fluff pinched between her fingers. "I think this was probably a self-defense situation, but it's suspicious that you're not giving us the truth."

All three officers glanced up at the same time. Katya twisted her head to look over her shoulder at two men stepping in the door. Both wore long black coats and dark glasses. One appeared Hispanic, the other pale with ginger hair. They went around the right side of the couch and stopped between the medtechs and Delacruz, as close to in front of Katya as possible.

"Nine?" asked Delacruz.

Both men held out ID wallets.

"Senior Operative Espinosa," said the black-haired man. "This is S-O Carroll."

They flipped their IDs closed at the same instant.

Katya grabbed the cushions on either side of her legs as a twinge clenched her thigh. Penetrating pain deepened, feeling like someone took their sweet time extracting an icepick. "Ooh, that hurts."

Rachelle checked on the display. "You're feeling the last of the muscle tissue closing together. It's almost finished."

"Okay... I'm only trying to protect my daughter." Katya held her hands over her leg, wanting to grab on and hold her thigh, but didn't dare touch the sleeve.

Carroll looked over the dead. "Arnold Fischer, Klaus Mueller, and Gamed Tupolev."

Delacruz stood. His concern for Katya's wellbeing appeared to come back to a point, though he still gave her a look of guarded suspicion.

"You can dispense with the cover story." Espinosa turned his head in a slow pan, taking in the scene. "We'll eventually put the pieces together."

Katya pursed her lips. "I'll assume you read my file."

The Senior Operatives nodded in unison.

"You probably know already then. Eve... we found her at that project site out in the Badlands. She's closer to twenty-one years old, but her body wasn't growing. She's probably had more combat training than you boys."

Delacruz raised both eyebrows.

"Hey, kid!" yelled the female officer in the kitchen.

Eve ran into the living room, halting at the sofa arm. She stared worry at Katya.

"It's all right, Eve. These two already know." Katya indicated the Division 9 men with a nod. "So, 'Julio' over there... Gamed?"

Carroll nodded.

"Gamed grabbed Eve and put a gun at her head."

"You didn't shoot them, did you?" asked Delacruz.

Rachelle did something at the case, which caused it to pump the nanobot-laced gel out of the sleeve.

Katya stared at the large body of 'Raúl,' rather Klaus Mueller. "She distracted him by pissing on his leg—"

"I wasn't scared," said Eve. "He had a PSP12 jammed in the side of my head. I had a weapon concealed in Mr. Bear, and when he jumped back, I shot him, then the big one, then the last guy."

Carroll's eyebrows climbed when she said 'Mr. Bear.'

"This kid recognized a DTF from having it against her head?" asked the female officer by the bodies.

"No." Eve looked at her. "I saw it after. They all had the same weapons. ACC would be used to Deutsche Technik Firma hardware, and it wouldn't stand out over here because they're high-end enthusiast weapons as well. That one"—she pointed at the formerly unnamed man who Division 9 called Arnold Fischer —"wasn't used to it. He pushed the gun when he shot Mom in the leg. He's probably accustomed to a Kodiak P96 that kicks like a drunk 'borg."

"You took out all three of them with a teddy bear fast enough for them not to get off another shot?" asked Delacruz.

"Yes." Eve pointed at the two nearest the couch. "They dropped where they were standing. I don't think they were expecting me to have a weapon."

"Or be able to make shots like this with it rammed up a teddy bear's ass." The female cop by the bodies pointed at the side of Klaus's head. "One on either side of the ear."

"That was luck." Eve ground her right big toe into the carpet. "I was just trying to hit him in the head to get around his subdermal. I've been training with weapons for eighteen years. I can hit targets at short range without using iron sights. It's a 'feel' thing."

Katya squirmed as the medtechs pulled the goopy sleeve off her leg.

"Can you move your toes?" asked Courtney.

Katya did so. "Yeah."

Delacruz, and the other Division 1 officers stared at Eve, open-mouthed.

"She's been alive for twenty years and training for most of it." Katya spat to the side. "Sick bastards."

"We're aware of the facility and the experiment you encountered out there." Espinosa frowned at the dead men. "I understand you are trying to keep the girl's true age hidden to minimize issues she may have reintegrating with society."

The medtechs offered comforting pats and a handshake before taking the case and walking out.

Katya chuckled. "Didn't you record this whole mess? You're watching me, right?"

Carroll looked at Delacruz. "We've got this from here. The events as described match what we have on video."

"Whoa, you're already surveilling her?" asked Delacruz.

"After her encounter with the other operative, we had some concerns." Carroll showed zero emotion on his face.

"It's fine." Katya rubbed her slimy thigh. "I am not working for the ACC. I want nothing whatsoever to do with them. Record all you like. I have nothing to hide. Bring in a telepath if you want."

Espinosa almost smiled. He smacked his lips and his expression became stoic again.

"Right, then." Delacruz gave the Division 9 men a semi-serious salute. "Guess we're out." He looked at Katya for a second and headed for the door, the other officers trailing after.

"Thanks," said Katya. "For the stims. Sorry for the misdirection."

Delacruz smiled, pulled his visor down, and walked out.

"What did you tell them?" Carroll gestured at the bodies.

Eve scrunched her snowy eyebrows together. "They're dead. Does it matter?"

"They might've been recording or transmitting," said Katya. "Nothing more than Anders mistook me for an operative from another cell and wanted to get in my pants. He is a complete idiot."

A group of men and women in white clean-suits walked in and collected the bodies on hover-gurneys.

"We appreciate your assistance in drawing out Anders Becker and exposing

Corporate activity in West City." Espinosa offered a slight bow. "In the future, you may wish to consider a less expensive brand of tampon."

Katya's jaw tightened. "I'll definitely take that into consideration."

"We'll continue monitoring you for some time yet. If you need anything just say something out loud." Carroll pulled a NetMini out of his coat, tapped a few holographic buttons and flicked a finger in Katya's direction. Her headware caught the incoming link and redirected it to her NetMini on the coffee table. "That contact is for a place that's pretty good with getting blood out of fabric."

"Thanks." Katya stood on her left leg and gingerly transferred her weight until she balanced even. A band of tightness in her thigh signaled she'd be limping for a few days, but nothing hurt. The cushion she'd been sitting on appeared to be a lost cause, soaked with blood. Light-headed, she hobbled to the far left end of the couch and fell seated. "Little woozy."

"You should eat something," said Eve.

The clean suit team exited with the bodies and the spies' weapons.

"It probably is a good idea to keep her true age a secret." Espinosa gave Eve a look of mild pity.

Katya kept rubbing her leg, hoping to chase away a blob of numb. "Right. She's not really a child but not really an adult either. It's… odd. Twenty years of mental awareness, body chemistry of an eight-year-old."

Carroll chuckled. "I feel bad for the kid who tries to pick on her."

"I promise if I get into any fights at school I'll keep it strictly non-lethal," said Eve in a childish drone as though she'd agreed to keep her room clean.

The Division 9 men exchanged a glance, and shook their heads.

"We'll leave you to it then." Espinosa headed for the door, with Carroll following.

Eve stood close, again holding her teddy bear.

Katya stared at the NetMini, and opened a virtual terminal. She reset the front door security, and the thin plastisteel slab closed with a soft *hiss*. Whatever emitter the spies had set up in the hallway had ceased functioning, no doubt the Division 9 people took it as well. She tapped the link Carroll sent her and opened the GlobeNet site of 'Bio-San Residential.' Below the logo, lettering in silver chrome read: Specialists in biological contamination removal since 2392. Below that, a pop up indicated a deal on gang-related biomatter removal, twenty percent off jobs involving four or more decedents. The second panel offered a 'brain matter blowout special' discount on Wednesdays.

*That's a cheery place.* She requested an onsite consultation, let the page geotag her login point, and shut the window down. Her vision focused on the room instead of the nonexistent holo-panel inches in front of her face. Eve's face had gone red, and she sniffled into the teddy bear's head, teetering on the verge of tears.

"Eve?" Katya reached over and put a hand on the girl's shoulder.

"It's ruined." Eve sniffled. "The bear you gave me… he's all ripped up." Her lip quivered and she cried.

"Aww." *Umm. Ooo-kay.* "C'mere." Katya pulled her into a hug.

After a few seconds, Eve chuckled and sniffled. "Wow I guess that's pretty psychotic of me, huh? Getting emotional over a bear." She gazed at the hole in its face, and lapsed into crying again. "Wow..." Sniffle. "What the hell is wrong with me?" She wiped at her face. "I can't stop crying over a stuffed bear."

"Maybe it's that pesky body chemistry getting you." Katya winked. "I hear it happens to some women."

Eve smiled despite red eyes. "Not you?"

"No. I upgraded my firmware." Katya frowned.

"He's a dick. You're human." Eve squeezed the bear. "You gave me this."

Katya smoothed a hand over the girl's head. "That's why you're upset."

"You're treating me like a kid." A trace of grin fought to emerge from her stoic face.

"It's okay, honey," said Katya, oozing sweetness. "Mommy will get you a new one."

Eve scrunched up her face in mock anger and punched Katya in the left shoulder.

After a short staring contest, they both burst out laughing.

"You okay?" asked Eve.

"Sore, but yeah. You?"

"Yeah." Eve examined her bloody hands, nightdress, and feet. "It's nice to have a mom who understands that sometimes a girl just needs to kill someone."

Katya threw her head back and laughed.

"S'pose I should do the school thing and try to act normal. Maybe I'll grow up not to be a head case." She set the bear on the coffee table. "Be right back. I need to shower and change."

Katya eyed the urine stain on the rug. "That's a good point. Where's the rug bot?"

Eve froze mid-stride. "Uhh... I kinda shot it two days ago."

"What?" Katya blinked, chuckling. "Why?"

"It, uhh." Eve lowered her outstretched leg to the floor, pivoted, and faced Katya with her hands clasped in front of her like a kid in trouble. "Kinda came out of nowhere and scared me."

"If I get another one, will you try not to shoot it?"

Eve nodded. "Yeah... It was right before I got all wound up about the pain coming. I... should be okay."

Katya nodded. Eve hurried off to clean herself off and change.

She frowned at her shredded sweat pants and bloody shirt. *Ehh, it can wait a few minutes.* On another terminal window, she ordered a replacement rug bot, opting for a C2,700 disc-shaped unit a little above midrange. With that on the way, she switched windows to the job board. The non-subtle warning replayed in her head. Division 9 knew she'd pulled a data nab from LRI, but let her slide on it. Technically, all she did was move said data from point A to B, but the law wouldn't care. *They could wind up watching her for years.* She couldn't accept the risk of being deported.

She rubbed her shaking hands back and forth. "I shouldn't have taken that mission for Alex... I will find a real job."

The autoshower thrummed to life in the distance, a soft vibration audible only due to the utter stillness in the apartment.

An orb bot appeared at the patio window, displaying a Bio-San logo. She got up and walked with a slight limp to the door, letting it in.

"Hello, I am here to conduct a site survey and provide an estimate as per your request. Please direct me to the source of the biological contamination in question."

Katya backed away to let it in and pointed. "There on the rug, the sofa, and the kitchen, though that's all tile and Epoxil... I can probably clean the kitchen myself."

The orb bowed as if to nod. "Cleaning up after an incident like this presents certain unique hazards. You should consider leaving it to professionals." Two small hatches on the underside opened exposing powerful, small lights, which it used to examine the rug. She squinted at the brightness in the dark apartment, making the blood harsh and obvious against the beige rug.

*This is all I am, isn't it? My whole life... What else will I ever be able to do?*

"Fine..." She sighed. *Might as well. It hurts to breathe right now.*

A large delivery bot flew up to the window. As soon as it confirmed her NetMini with a chirp, it opened a hatch to reveal a package with an image of her new rug-cleaning unit. Katya unloaded it from the hovering robot and set the box unopened on the coffee table for now. No sense letting it get gummed up with blood.

Katya spent the next twenty minutes paging over employment listings, but only sent her resume to four by the time the autoshower stopped.

Eve let off a squeal from the back of the apartment that made Katya think another spy had just stabbed her.

"Eve?" yelled Katya.

The girl came sprinting out, wearing a clean nightgown. She zoomed up in front of Katya jumping up and down, beaming like the excited little girl she appeared to be.

"What?" Katya's worry crashed into confusion. "What happened?"

"I just checked the marks." She jumped up and down again. "I got a millimeter taller! I'm growing!"

Katya's eyes watered up. She stooped and hugged Eve carefully, trying not to get any blood on her. "That's wonderful! My turn to hit the shower."

Eve reached up and swiped a tear from Katya's cheek, then held her finger up with the droplet. "He's wrong. You *do* have emotions."

Katya laughed. Though she smiled, her heart grew heavy with worry. Her money wouldn't last forever—or even all that long. She couldn't risk doing what she'd been trained to do, and the job listings didn't look promising.

She wandered off to the bathroom. *Maybe I could go to school again too?*

# 30

# PINK BOWS AND ASHES

Rain pattered the clear shell of the elevator gliding upward along the outside of Nina's building. The marching drumbeat of a tiny army built and faded in time with gusts of wind. She peered down at the sunken courtyard nestled in the hollow of her C-shaped building. At its center, the old bronze statue still stood guard over the ring of benches around it, a human figure composed of stretched pyramids, orbs, and boxes welded together. The ersatz man extended one triangle-fingered hand to the heavens, grasping for a prize he could never reach. Streaks of dark green verdigris marred the surface where years of rainwater had flowed.

The sight of it burdened her phantom heart with memories of Vincent. She pictured the blue and white patrol craft sitting half in the courtyard, scaring off the civilians as he waited for her to scramble outside. He never landed on the roof; he'd liked to be among the people.

Nina sighed.

The little boy she'd once spotted sitting on the benches by the statue bouncing a green ball wasn't there. Only water and corrosion sat upon them now. Her mind ran off with the maudlin thought that he'd grown up and moved away, yet she remained—a creature of high tech polymer composites and plastisteel, never aging, never changing. Of course, Vincent had died in the waning days of spring eighteen months ago. The boy would probably be nine years old now, merely away at school. Her gaze shifted to the right, and the weight in her chest lessened.

Elizaveta, in a white dress, pink frilled socks, and gloss white shoes, pressed herself against the wall to stare out at the city receding below them. She had insisted on the huge pink bow at the back of her hair and begged Nina to re-tie it four times so it looked 'just right.' She stared into the velvety folds of a bow half again the width of the child's entire head, and smiled. It looked little different than it had the first time she'd tied it. Elizaveta had wanted to spend more time with her.

The girl grinned at the city and touched her finger to the clear elevator capsule wall, opposite a raindrop on the outside, tracing down it as it fell. Rain had always made Nina gloomy; as a small child, she'd believed that when all the sadness in the world had built up too much, the sky wept. It had been years since she'd abandoned such dark whimsy, but despite her adult mind understanding rain, the sight of it still awakened a pang of sorrow within her. Elizaveta though, seemed happy.

"The rain makes you smile?" asked Nina, in Russian.

"Yes. In Cheremushki, we lived under the ground in old tunnels. We had no shower machines and the water they saved for drinking. Everyone smelled. If it was not too cold, we would go outside and clean ourselves in the rain with soap. I liked seeing the sky, even when it was grey." She looked down at herself for a few seconds. "Did we have to hide because those people were bad? They did not listen to the police and they shot people, but they didn't hit me or make me do all the cleaning."

Nina squeezed the girl's shoulder, furious at the nameless foster parents who'd been cruel enough to make a six-year-old run away and wind up 'adopted' by the Resistance.

The elevator pinged and opened to a small, enclosure on the roof deck. Glass windows on the far end streaked with rain, aglow with the warped glare from the lights illuminating the parking area. A mental command initiated a connection between her headware and the patrol craft, summoning it to auto drive up to the doors.

"They disagreed with the people who make the laws over there. I'm sure they did what they felt was right for all those who are suffering."

Elizaveta looked up at her as they crossed the small room to the doors. "Piotr said right or wrong is made up by whoever wins."

Amid a spray of steam and crackling blue sparks, the jet-black patrol craft glided in to land about ten feet from the entrance.

Nina chuckled and shrouded Elizaveta under her coat. "That sounds about right."

The girl squealed with glee as they dashed through the rain to the car. Nina opened the door for her before she headed around the front end to the driver's seat. The console emitted a chime along with a recorded voice announcing it detected a child and had adjusted the passive restraint system accordingly.

After an eleven-minute ride to the school she'd enrolled Elizaveta in—Nina's mother had insisted on the Amalthea Academy, a private school similar to the one Nina had attended prior to ninth grade—she walked her inside to a classroom of first graders. Elizaveta seemed small and delicate in comparison to the other children, though much to Nina's pleasant surprise, she zoomed right over to a group of three other girls and they got to chattering intently via NetMini translators.

Nina had a brief discussion with the instructor, a genial older woman by the name of Mendoza. Aside from the language barrier, Elizaveta had been adjusting well in the few days since she'd started. Rather than have her skip back a year, the school arranged for her to remain two hours after class each day for English tutoring as well as remedial instruction to bring her up to a first-grade level.

With the child settled in for a school day, Nina headed back out into the rain and sat in her patrol craft, staring at the building, watching the shadows of children moving about the windowshades. A moment later, a PubTran hover came by and dropped off a pair of twin boys who appeared to be about fourth-graders. Nina started to frown at the sort of parents who could just stick their kid on a taxi alone at that age, but sighed instead. Not everyone had the sort of job she did with gelatinous hours and no real need to stay in the office. Of course, those parents probably also got to go home at the same time every night.

*How did I go from party girl to single mother?* The patrol craft's electronic windscreen didn't bother displaying the rain striking it, though its patter still invaded the cabin despite inch-thick armor plates. She closed her eyes as the boys ran inside, and tried to 'feel' her body. Aside from no longer having to deal with cramps, nothing stood out as being inhuman unless she tried to be.

She lost a few minutes daydreaming about her life before that night. Vincent had been completely in love with her; only worry about how her parents would react to him had kept him from proposing. Of course, he hadn't been in any great hurry to have kids either. *I probably would've been happy just with him.* She traced her fingers across her stomach. *Maybe I would've changed my mind eventually but...* A long sigh escaped her nose. Crystal clear oceans, jet skis, Caribbean islands, and Vincent danced around in her mind. Nightclubs and concerts followed. *Was Dad right? Maybe I shouldn't have gotten involved with the NPF at all.*

"Come on, Nina. Get a grip. What's done is done." She stared at her hands. "Mom thinks I can do more good now than before. She's just happy I'm still sort of alive in some way." Nina brought the patrol craft online and lifted off. "From mousy nobody to angel of death in two-point-three stabs of a vibro-blade."

She cringed at the thought of what she must've looked like, at how badly Bertrand had smashed her body that they had to put her brain and spinal cord into a doll. She toyed with the idea of looking up the records, but shivered. *No thanks. I don't need that image in my head.*

On a whim, she changed course and headed for the mausoleum where Vincent's ashes sat behind a one-by-one-foot slab of synthetic marble. *Do I love Joey or am I clinging to him because he didn't run away in terror when he found out what I am?* When she landed, she still couldn't come up with an answer to how she'd react if he proposed. *He doesn't seem the marrying type. Course I suppose I can wait a little. Not like I'm getting older.*

Vincent's gravesite occupied an eye-level space along a sweeping curved hallway, 202 panels from the elevator door. Sixty stories of ash chambers along the outside and inside of the ring stood under a massive windowed dome. The mausoleum building's donut-like shape surrounded a memorial garden where mourners could sit among live plants and interact with holograms of their loved ones, assuming one had been recorded prior to death.

She brushed a finger over the name 'Vincent Montoya' etched in the false marble. It seemed somewhat inappropriate to come here in her work outfit rather than dressing more formal, but she still needed to show up at the office. Nina doubted Hardin would let her take bereavement leave almost nineteen months after his death.

"Hey... been awhile," she whispered. "Hope you're doing okay if you're still around in any sort of way. I don't know what I saw on the deck at that swamp house, but if that really was you..."

She leaned closer, touching her head to the cold faux marble. With Joey around, she hadn't spoken much about Vincent. True, close to a year had passed since he'd died before she met Joey, but it still seemed rushed. If the apparition she'd seen in the Badlands was really him, he seemed happy for her.

"I'm sorry."

The expected wave of crushing sorrow forcing tears from her eyes never came; instead, she shouldered the burden of loss with a straight face. Her reckless charge had set in motion his death, but saved the life of a teenage prostitute. Emotion had gotten the better of her in the moment when getting that girl away from an insane aug was all that mattered. Vincent fell into the same trap trying to save her. How different would things have gone if some other cops found Bertrand that night?

*We shouldn't have been riding together. Command knew we were dating. No one else wanted me.*

Her skin squeaked as she pulled her hand down the tombstone. "Dammit Vincent... you were too good to me."

Nina stood in reverent silence for a while. "I bet you don't believe it, but I've got a kid now. A little girl, Elizaveta. She's six, and went through a scary few years, but I think we're going to manage. She's going to be a handful, almost the exact opposite of who I was. Basically fearless, extroverted, and a girly-girl on top of that... Mom adores her. Damn Corporates shipped her over here for medical research." She looked away from his tombstone at the floor. "Sometimes I ask myself why I took the promotion at all. The things I see with Nine sometimes. At least my current case looks better. No soul-crushing evil here, just the usual political bullshit." She sighed. "Hope you're not too bored in there. Anyway, speaking of bullshit, I suppose I should get to the office before Hardin sends a whisper to find me."

She pressed her hand to the stone above his name for a moment, let her arm fall to her side, and walked back to the elevator. It seemed surreal to think about Vincent, and the life she had before, almost as if it had been someone else, or her first twenty-five years had been all a dream.

The elevator ride passed in silence, but chaos flooded in when the doors opened.

Six fringers in the grungy, mismatched clothing of grey zone punks had arranged themselves around benches to the left of the main entrance. A teal-haired girl in her later teens wearing a baggy black half-jacket and white 'painted-on' tights crisscrossed with silver lines scrawled some indecipherable lettering on the windows with a sprayer. The other female, an Asian with maraschino red hair, seemed closer to twenty, and stared into space with an exaggerated smile. Her heavy faux-leather skirt covered most of her legs, save for a split along the left side. Three handguns adorned her belt along with an uncountable number of metal baubles. She had the same half-jacket as Graffiti Girl, though didn't appear to have anything on under it.

Four men, ranging in age from late teens to mid-twenties, lounged around laughing and blaring a harsh, scratchy electronica track that got dirty looks from two mausoleum security guards as well as a few mourners scurrying to the elevators as fast as they could without breaking into a full run. Some of the fringers' clothing bore bloodstains, evidence of past fights or perhaps a remainder of the person who'd it been scavenged from.

A dark-skinned blonde woman entered, holding hands with a girl around thirteen, probably her daughter, both wearing matching peach-colored dresses and heels. Their red puffy eyes and bowed heads suggested their loss as recent.

"Niiiiice legs… and that ass," said one of the fringers. "Come here, baby." He stuck his tongue out and made 'lalalalal' noises.

The woman spun to glare at him. "You need to get your shiftless selves outta here and go do somethin' productive."

He blew her a kiss. "I wasn't talkin' to you."

She gasped, horrified.

"Let's go, Mama," said the girl, wide-eyed and shaking. She tugged on her mother's arm.

Nina sent a damning glare at the security guards before storming over to the fringers.

"Oh, hey there." A white-haired guy with matching goatee hopped off the bench to his feet and leered at Nina. "This one's smokin' too. Wanna good time, princess?"

Random whoops and catcalls emanated from the others. The red-haired Asian girl continued staring into space while the other girl moved on from her graffiti word to start on a large cat face. The mother and daughter hurried off to the elevator.

"Hey, where you goin'?" yelled the same one who'd stuck out his tongue. He got up to follow them. "I ain't even licked it yet."

The young teen screamed and sprinted for the elevator.

Nina caught the guy with a palm on the chest and shoved him back with enough force to plant him seated on the bench. "I'm going to hope you're just being an asshole and weren't about to assault an underage girl."

"Oh, he was serious." Graffiti Girl whirled to grin at Nina. She could've been seventeen or so, with light skin and dense black eyebrows. "Iz loves girls that age. We started dating when I was like twelve." Her smile widened. "I've had three. They got taken away and put with my parents." She laughed. "Isn't that awesome?" She held her arms out and inhaled, head back, in a posture befitting a skier gliding down a snowy mountain. "It's okay if he wants a side girl; I'm getting old."

"How old are you?" Nina sent an image cap of the girl's face into the system. Her file came back in about four seconds: Allison Medina, age seventeen, listed as runaway/endangered. She'd been popped a few times by Division 1 for drug offenses, which typically meant they used it as an excuse to try to bring her home. The cops didn't usually bother popping anyone for Flowerbasket, Sandman, or Smileys otherwise.

"Twenty," said Allison.

Nina frowned at Iz. He lay where he'd landed, laughing like he'd enjoyed the ride. "Nice try, Allison."

A guy with split lavender/green hair dropped his pants and positioned himself to defecate in the flowerpot of a plastic tree. Passersby outside got an unobstructed view of his ass, though no one seemed to notice.

Still, the security guards seemed afraid to do much.

Nina stared at him. "You, pull your pants up. Shit in that pot and you're face is going into it next. You"—she pointed at Allison— "I'm taking you back to your parents. And you"—she pointed at Iz—"on the ground. You're under arrest for statutory rape, assault, and disorderly conduct."

Iz gave her the finger. "You ain't no cop."

She opened her coat, revealing her sidearm, and held up her ID wallet. "Division 9, laughing boy."

The fringers' smiles faded. One by one—except for Allison—they went from looking disoriented to abnormally enraged.

*Oh shit. They're on Harmony...*

Iz and the red-haired girl pulled handguns at the same instant. Her combat tactical processor tagged the girl's as a Class 1, the other as a Class 4. Neither 4mm nor 10mm pistol rounds could penetrate her ballistic stealth suit, though the bigger gun would trigger a greater sense of simulated pain. Nina blurred forward, grabbing Iz's weapon arm at the wrist with her left while driving the ridge of her right hand into the side of his head. Her effort to flip him to the ground crushed his wrist as well as broke his arm midway between elbow and shoulder.

Three bullets collided with her chest, stalling on the glossy black suit. With Iz gliding to the floor amid a slow motion fall, Nina launched herself at the girl, grasping both guns and crushing them. Their barrels bent upward, a rain of plastic bits slipping between her fingers. Before the girl's facial expression changed, Nina tore the remaining two pistols from her belt and hurled them one after the next at the two other fringers who'd started to pull weapons from their belts.

Handguns spun end over end, striking each man in the face and knocking them over. Allison backed into the window, grinning like she watched the single coolest moment of her entire life unfolding before her eyes. The girl made no aggressive moves, so Nina disregarded her for the time being.

Another fringer jumped in with a punch. She leaned away, grabbed his arm, and flipped him face down on the floor before a sharp twist broke his shoulder.

Iz finally landed on his back.

Nina's speedware throttled back since no active weapons remained in play.

The Asian girl stared at her crushed handguns for a second before shrieking with rage and launching herself at Nina. Alas, anger and enthusiasm in droves did not make up for an utter lack of fighting ability. Nina treated her like a child throwing a tantrum, and shoved her chest-first into the floor only hard enough to knock the wind out of her.

"You two... you have binders?" yelled Nina.

The security guards ran over. "We called it in ten minutes ago... where are the cops?"

"Holy shit. Are you really Nine? You didn't kill any of them." He blinked. "You must be having a good day or something."

⌜ Ops, this is Duchenne. I need a collection crew at my location. Five individuals who appear to be contaminated with Harmony, showing signs of elevated aggression against authority figures. They've got nanobots in their systems we need to get a closer look at. ⌟ Nina frowned at the wheezing girl, accepted plastic riot ties from one of the guards, and secured her hands. "I don't think these kids are in their right minds."

She disarmed Iz of another handgun and three knives before restraining him despite his disintegrated wrist.

"Fuck you and the government that owns you!" screamed Iz. "You can't control us all. We're coming for you! You'll pay!"

"Sure, pal." She patted him on the head.

Allison giggled, pointing at Iz. "He's so red in the face. That's a pretty color for him."

Once she got her breath back, the Asian girl shrieked, "The whole system is corrupt. Law is a lie. Anarchy is the only true system of government."

Nina pulled the girl's head up by her too-red hair, as gently as one might manage to pick someone up by the hair, and looked her in the eye. "Anarchy is the absence of government. It's not a system of government."

"Yeah, that's what I said. We've gotta anarchy the government so they stop on oppressing us!"

The security guards exchanged disbelieving glances.

"Allison, come here."

"Okay," chirped the teal-haired teen. She hopped down and trotted over. "Hi. I'm Allison."

Nina kept a straight face. "Hi Allison. Have you taken any fun chems today?"

"Uh huh!" Allison grinned and bounced on her toes like a girl ten years younger. "I haz Tao! Want some?"

"I'm good... thanks. Did your friends take Tao as well?"

Allison shook her head, caught sight of her teal hair waving around, and continued shaking it in a more and more exaggerated manner, laughing at herself.

"Come on, Allison. Focus. Did your friends take Tao?"

"No. I don't have enough money for Harmony... I get Tao from Rafael 'cause he'll trade it for anal." She laughed. "He makes it himself." Allison held her arms out to the side and spun like an airplane. "He's a chemist."

*Looks like that Tao has a few extra sparkles in it.* Nina leaned close to the girl and swapped to metallurgical scan. She didn't have any detectable concentrations of metal inside her brain. *Hmm. No nanobots... she didn't go aggressive either.*

A Division 1 patrol craft swooped in and landed outside the door. A pair of men in blue armor emerged from it walked in.

"You're late," said Nina. "Sorry to waste your time, but I've got it. These people are in Division 9 custody."

The cops looked at her, looked at each other, shrugged, and about-faced.

"Wow," said the shorter security guard, whose nametag read Chavez. "I wish I could make them go away like that whenever I get pulled over."

His partner, Fuentes, laughed. "Yeah, right."

"Hold on, guys. You can still do something here..." She guided Allison over to the Division 1 officers. "This girl's a minor and she's not involved in my investigation. Parents want her back. There's a tag in the system on her record. You two mind givin' her a ride home... maybe look into *why* she keeps running away?"

"You got it, ma'am." Officer Cartagena saluted her before escorting the girl out to their car.

Fuentes cocked his head at her. "Feel bad for the girl? Just lettin' her go? Why not the other one?"

"That one"—Nina pointed at the red-haired girl—"shot me."

"Good reason." Fuentes nodded.

Nina opened a virtual holo panel and added notes to her inquest file. Allison, who dosed the cheaper street-made Tao, hadn't shown hostility toward authority. The other five had to be on Harmony. Working on a virtual holo-panel, she had the orders written up for medical containment by the time a plain black hover van landed in front of the mausoleum. With any luck, someone would be spending long hours in a lab studying nanobots soon.

"Lieutenant," said a woman of average height in an all-black operator's suit. She had her dark brown hair back in a bun and an expression of blasé disinterest that came from being on the job for years. "Operative Brennan... What do we have here?"

Nina gestured at the remaining five punks. "They're high on H. As soon as I identified myself, they became enraged. I need them checked for nanobots, blood, urine, kidneys. That one"—she pointed to Iz—"goes to Div 1 when we're done with him. The others you can cut loose. I'll have a separate inquest ready for him later tonight."

"Understood."

Operative Brennan set about directing the rest of her team to collect the fringers, who all continued screaming about how much they despised the government. A fist-sized orb bot glided across the room and set to the task of removing the graffiti with a wide laser that disintegrated the paint from the glass. Nina observed as they dragged them out to the van. One of the boys who'd taken a handgun to the face freaked out and started screaming pleas for his life, expecting 'the government' dragged him off to be killed in secret. The red-haired girl inherited that idea, and came unglued as well, bawling like a child and screaming for her parents, though every few words, she lapsed back to anger and cursed them out.

Nina shook her head.

Once the collection team left, she returned to her car.

AN HOUR AND ELEVEN MINUTES LATER, NINA FINISHED FILLING OUT THE INQUEST report of the incident at the mausoleum and leaned away from her desk terminal. She let her head go back against the chair, but didn't close her eyes. The dim lighting and dark blue walls could've lulled her to sleep if not for the strange urge to have lunch. Her biological self didn't amount to all that much, or need large quantities of nutrients. Of course, she could still *enjoy* the act of eating, and only felt a little bit wasteful. It wasn't as though her having lunch made someone else starve. People in bad situations would still be in bad situations regardless of whether she splurged on a chicken sandwich.

"Screw it."

No sooner had she sat up than a knock came from her door.

*Great timing. Guess lunch waits a bit.* "Come in."

Two operatives in black coats entered, one with black hair, one ginger. They removed their sunglasses within a half-second of each other, and tucked them in their pockets.

"Lieutenant," said the man with black hair. "I'm S-O Espinosa; this is S-O Carroll. We have some information for you concerning the inquest you are currently working on."

Senior Operatives equated to O2, laterally equivalent to her rank of first lieutenant. For whatever reason, command decided to use the standard military ranking for dolls as well as a different promotion track.

Nina returned a polite nod. "Operatives. Please, have a seat."

The men took the two chairs facing her desk.

Carroll smiled. "Small world, eh, lieutenant? We caught a break from your friend Dillon in Net Ops."

"What did Joey do this time?" Nina chuckled.

"Knew someone, apparently." Espinosa withdrew a NetMini from his coat and wagged it at her. Her terminal and NetMini beeped in reply. "Katya Wolf, formerly Volkov."

"I know of her. He told me the other night. I put in a request for a meeting with that, umm... Becker fellow."

Espinosa smiled. "You're more than welcome to give it a try, but I don't think he knows much. He'd been inserted into the information technology group at Laughlin-Reed Innovation, a junior network security engineer. While his skills in that regard may be commendable, his grasp of espionage apparently stopped at his dick."

Nina cracked a smile. "This Volkov woman has a pheromone suite."

"She had no idea he was even there. We're fairly certain of that." Carroll's expression waxed sympathetic. "Seems like she's trying rather hard to establish herself in a legitimate employment situation, but not having much luck. She was in the employ of a local fixer, making contact with a disgruntled employee at LRI to smuggle data out. The Corporates assumed we'd sent her in there after him. Couple of meatheads showed up to beat information out of her."

"Lucky thing for her she had a cute little attack dog," said Espinosa.

"That kid?" Nina raised an eyebrow.

"Have you read the file?" asked Carroll.

"Skimmed. Something about a military project."

Espinosa nodded. "She's got almost two decades of combat training. Snuck them with a handgun concealed in a stuffed animal. Took the three of them out in a few seconds. Looked like something you'd expect to see some SOG-Delta operator pull off."

"That kid's going to be a handful in school." Carroll winked.

Nina opened the file that came over. Images of Katya's apartment, the three corpses therein, as well as their files. "So we have four ACC people in the city."

"All of them were at LRI," said Espinosa. "Klaus with physical security, Arnold was posing as a pharmaceutical sales consultant, and Gamed joined their onsite repair team three weeks ago."

"Onsite repair?" Nina tapped her finger on her desk. "That would've had him going around to any medical facility using LRI machinery." *Shit. We're going to have to check over everywhere that guy's been.*

"Correct, though you'll probably be relieved to hear he performed a mere three service calls. He had only recently finished their training. Despite being chipped with the necessary skills to be competent, the company requires a two-week training course," said Carroll.

"We didn't find much at Becker's apartment. He kept the place relatively clean, but he had a significant stash of Harmony, which tested positive for nanobots. It's all upstairs in the lab now."

*Oh... that's good. Those fringers won't need to be kept too long then.* "Well, that's something."

"Becker did give up four more individuals embedded at LRI as Corporate operators." Espinosa sent another file over. "I figured you would want to make the call when to move on them, but I have mobilized surveillance teams as well as tagged them for Penumbras to keep an eye on."

"That dragon still skittish?" asked Nina. "C-Branch still hasn't figured out who or what got into their server cluster and kicked Nightwing in his digital balls have they?"

"That's above our pay grade," said Espinosa. "But Penumbras didn't seem too worried about keeping tabs on these four."

*We're beyond doubt at this point. The ACC is responsible for Harmony.* "Thanks. Think Becker's holding anything back?"

Carroll shook his head. "Doubtful. That Volkov woman's assessment of him seemed to be accurate."

"Only got into the OOI because of his parents," said Carroll.

She shook her head with a somber chuckle. "Pity he won't be seeing them for a while."

"If they have any real pull, he'll probably get released for 'humanitarian reasons.' We don't have him on anything too damning," said Espinosa.

*If anything, Becker's unchecked libido might've just offered me the key to burying this threat. Maybe we should give him a medal.*

Nina stared at the faces of four more people, three men and a woman, all who appeared to be normal citizens at a normal job. If not for the adjacent images of them a few years younger and in Corporate Division of Motherland Security uniforms, she wouldn't have given any of them a second glance. *Reinventions...* The Laughlin-Reed Innovation employee ID photos showed them with medium-brown skin and slight alterations to their facial geometry to introduce hints of Hispanic and African features, while their military IDs showed three as pale Europeans, and one of the men as Pakistani. *Hmm. A significant portion of their medical equipment comes from Pakistan.*

"This is quite helpful. Thanks for not jumping on them right away." She brought up the surveillance logs, which had little of interest aside from them going to and from work. "I'm sure the remaining ones are at least partially aware that we found Becker. It shouldn't take them long to grasp that Fischer, Mueller, and Tupolev won't be back. For now, I'd like if your team didn't spook them. I need to look into how deep LRI goes with this Harmony issue. Whether they're part of it or just a tool. Of course, if they go off script and become an imminent threat..."

The operatives both rendered a curt nod.

"Got anything else for me? Anything I can help you two with?"

"Becker also provided information regarding a large shipment of modified Placinil. At first, he attempted to claim they'd been sent in from an LRI facility out in the Badlands, though we got him to admit they came from Mexico."

Espinosa nodded. "We located a cargo truck entering the checkpoint gate two days ago."

"The drivers"—Carroll brought up a holo-panel showing a pair of large men in white jumpsuits—"Berg Köhler and Steiner Scholz, both from their Department of Motherland Security. As far as we can tell, about equivalent in rank to sergeants. Probably unaware of the scope of their mission other than being drivers."

Nina frowned at the two smiling men's images. "Shall I assume that these two have disappeared?"

The two senior operatives bowed their heads. "It seems they have already left our territory, yes. The arrival of that shipment correlates to a recent surge in Harmony on the streets. And we don't believe in coincidences."

"Great." Nina drummed her fingers on the desk. "Any more cheery news?"

"That's all. We're still working on Becker, but I wouldn't hold your breath for anything else. A Zero's going to rubber-glove him tomorrow, so if he's hiding anything else, we'll have it."

"Right. Thanks." She stood and shook their hands.

Still desiring lunch, she waited for them to walk out before locking her terminal and heading after them, with a detour to Hardin's office. She knocked.

"Come in."

Nina walked up to his desk. "Going to grab a sandwich from Abdul's, you want anything? And oh, yeah… the Corporates are in LRI like fleas on a stray dog. I just sent you a link to the inquest. Anyone useful transmits everything they see or hear to Mexico. Anyone not useful is conditioned to lash out at authority figures. They're trying to set off civil unrest."

Hardin grumbled. "One of those chicken Caesar salad wrap things, and dammit. This could start a war."

"With or without black olives? And doesn't matter what I do from here, the attempt is enough. I doubt either side is going to want to escalate things to that point, but there's probably going to be a few snipers short some bullets."

"Nix the olives, but tell them extra tomatoes. I'll give the old man a call and let him know the first shots of the next Corporate War might've been fired. I'm also curious if LRI is in on this or not."

"Got it. Anything to drink?" She backed toward the hall. "Me too. I'm fairly certain that someone at LRI is providing product to four major dealers. Just waiting on a vid to confirm that."

"Good. Get me a raspberry tea, and while you're out there, try and stop Armageddon."

Nina paused at the door. "Right. Caesar wrap, extra tomatoes, hold the end of the world."

# 31

# FOXES AND CHICKENS

Hours of walking put Masaru and Noriko no closer to any visible end to the destroyed city around them. The limousine crashed in a flat, open area where barely any structures had survived beyond outlines of walls a few inches high. The farther they went, the taller their surroundings became. Mangled skeletons of high-rises creaked and groaned in the wind, sometimes a tower slumped into its neighbor like a pair of guys staggering out of a bar late at one in the morning. Though Masaru frequented the city's night scene, he seldom overindulged sake or other alcohols. His libation of choice had been women; if they were so willing to make themselves available for no reason other than his position, why should he disregard such a gift freely offered? It didn't mean he had to respect them.

Or himself.

The bars filled with blue-suited workers who'd start showing up around seven or eight straight from work. They'd stagger from fatigue on the way in, and stumble from sake on the way out some time after he'd gone home with a woman or four. How these men made it to work the next day without resembling zombies was one of the great mysteries of the world. He stared into the dark spaces between steel beams and dangling fragments of concrete. Some plant life, mostly vines, explored the structure, clawing its way upward toward sunlight that never quite made it down to street level.

Could it be possible to bore of casual sex, of the complete lack of a true connection to another human being? Warm bodies touching sated the moment, but what of the rest of his life?

"You see something?" asked Noriko.

Masaru looked away from the slumping building. "No."

"It's been quiet." She spoke in a soft tone, not quite whispering. "I see some evidence of gunfire, but I can't tell how old it is."

"Mmm." Thin flakes of broken concrete crunched under his shoes. The occasional glint of a glass blob shone from the debris, wherever it had melted and reformed. Cars lay here and there, deformed from a blast wave, frames protruding up from plastic puddles. "If there are such things as ghosts, we likely walk among many."

Noriko raised her left hand. When Masaru only glanced at her, her eyebrows furrowed. "Stop."

He took a step back to stand at her side. "I apologize. I am not familiar with your hand signals."

"Do you hear that?"

Masaru stilled his mind. Soon, the distant whirr of ion thrusters crept into his awareness. "A hovercar. Perhaps Kurotai has sent people to find us."

"Yes…" Noriko smiled. "I was hoping I didn't imagine that." She looked around as if to gauge the sound, and took off at a light jog.

Masaru followed.

At the next cross street, she hooked a left. About five blocks down a canyon of plastisteel wreckage and fallen lampposts, a sleek black hovercar glided along at the level of the second story toward a T intersection where the southbound road forced a turn east or west. While it kicked up an enormous amount of dust, most of the cloud settled low and didn't obscure the vehicle. The driver made no effort to slow down, heading straight toward the building on the far side of the intersection.

"Hey," shouted Noriko.

The car hit the wall of a ruined high rise without a noise or any visible damage. It disappeared, surrounded by a shimmering blue glow. A second later, the wall rippled like fluid, showing no sign anything had happened.

"Hologram," muttered Masaru.

Noriko squinted. "Why would someone be out here?" She raised her rifle at the building. "Looks like a neat one-story hole in the north face. I see some thermal reflections from inside, but no direct visibility on anyone. There are definitely people in there."

Masaru closed his eyes and focused on his augmented hearing. Echoed snippets of a Slavic language slipped between the *thump* of car doors closing. "I believe we have stumbled upon foreign invaders. I hear Russian."

"What are they saying?" whispered Noriko.

"I do not know. It is too faint to make out words, nor would I understand them if I could." He pointed west. "We should continue until we are able to obtain a signal."

"I want to take a closer look. *This* might be the source of the jammer. If I can disable it, I can comm for reinforcements."

He squared his shoulders, eyed the phantom wall for a second, and turned toward her. "Noriko, we are two and do not know how many we may face. Would it not be wiser to leave and make their presence known to the JSDF?"

She lowered her rifle and glanced at him. "You don't sound fearful, so I won't call you a chicken."

He frowned.

Noriko started to smile at him, but took on a purposeful expression. "I joined the JSDF because I wanted to make a difference in the lives of everyone who's getting stepped on. Japan is still a nation, and I wish we would start acting like it instead of behaving like a coop full of roosters who keep pecking at each other instead of watching for foxes."

A wry grin curled Masaru's lips. "But we have the NSK watching us."

She gave him a flat look. "And what does the farmer do to his chickens?"

"Consumes their offspring, and when they have worked themselves no longer to usefulness, consumes them as well."

Noriko's expression softened, tinged with respect. "Perhaps you do understand. There's a massive EM surge coming from that location. It's got to be the jammer."

"If it's so massive, why hasn't it been discovered yet?"

"Because." She resumed walking south. "Any aircraft that's come here to investigate has disappeared. Some of the pilots think of Miyakonojo as a paranormal flytrap. There have been over a dozen losses."

He hurried to catch up, walking astride at her right. "Yet this has not been mentioned on the news. They are so quick to inform us of death... ratings."

"I think command was afraid of ghost hunters swarming here and getting hurt. After the reconstruction failed, people got to talking. Angry spirits, oni, that sort of thing." She ducked left into an abandoned building and pulled him in after her. "Someone was approaching. I saw a heat outline behind the hologram. Just the top of a head. I don't think they saw us."

Masaru nodded.

The taste of damp drywall and earth settled on his tongue. Mold covered everything not made of concrete or steel. Ancient desks and chairs rotted where they stood amid fragments of fallen ceiling. A spongy layer of sediment underfoot seemed over an inch thick and clung to his shoes.

"This building could collapse at any moment," whispered Masaru. "You are... going *toward* them."

"Yes. I must understand what threat they present to Japan." She stopped and faced him.

"You could get yourself killed..." He stared at her face: proud, oval with a gently pointed chin. Perfect. Strong. Determined. Nothing had happened to her yet the thought it might made him angry.

Noriko opened her mouth, but looked away without speaking.

"Your leg may still be injured." Masaru put a hand on her forearm guard.

She tensed. A few seconds later, she glanced at where he touched her, but didn't flinch away or glare. "I am not in any hurry to die, but if I wasn't willing to risk my life for Japan, I would not have signed up." She lifted her gaze to make eye contact. "Have you ever believed in anything greater than yourself?"

Years flashed by in Masaru's thoughts. Every toy he'd ever wanted, a synthetic pony and miniature samurai armor for his eleventh birthday. Yumi lessons. By thirteen, he could put arrows in six-inch targets while riding. Women, games, electronics, cars—he'd never wanted for anything... except his father's respect.

Noriko slung the box of rations off her shoulder and stashed it under some debris.

"No... not really." He put a hand on his Nano katana. "But I will go with you."

# CAMPFIRE STORIES

K enny cruised south on a section of old Route 25, holding the e-motors at about seventy mph. Every time he wanted to go faster, he caught sight of one of the four Scrag kids in the truck bed and changed his mind.

*Should'a brought them inside. Cramped or not.*

The rumble-drone of thick tread tires filled the cabin, along with the faintly floral scent of wet hair. The girls had done a good job cleaning the seat, though most of the vomit landed on Hayley's legs and the plastic floor mat, both easily removed from the truck to be cleaned. Still, a deep enough breath brought the stink of half-digested something to bear. Then again, it could've been his imagination too.

Eldon kept glancing at the rear view mirror on his door every minute or so. He'd done the same thing their first trip out, enamored with actual mirrors rather than cameras and dashboard monitors. At the moment, he seemed more worried about the wall of sepia cloud chasing them.

Kenny glanced at it in his door mirror. A wide curtain of roiling dust raced over the land behind them. Lightning flickered within, illuminating darker patches, a pair of ancient gods grappling in mortal combat. He looked to his right, his attention drawn to the glowing red '30' on Eldon's rifle where the stock met the frame.

In the back seat, Nasir snoozed. Kathy sat next to him wearing a look of calm concern. A few stray locks of brown had fallen over her face, shaving ten years off her age. *She looks like she did the first night we dated, scared her father would come out of nowhere at any minute.* Kenny smiled at her. She tried to return it, but her lips stayed mostly flat. Her expression seemed to ask 'tell me we're going to be okay?'

Alyssa had her head down, lost in the glow of her NetMini screen. Earbuds kept whatever she played silent to everyone else. At her left, Hayley sat against the driver's side wall, stiff as a board with her hands clasped in her lap. He hadn't noticed it over the noise of the tires, but as soon as he looked at her, the constant, low whine leaking from her nose became apparent. The girl had never had much color to her, but she appeared like a ghost at that moment.

"Hale?" asked Kenny.

She looked up at him like he'd shot her dog and forced her to watch.

"What's wrong, sweetie?"

"I'm scared."

Kenny tried to sound as comforting as he could. "I know, honey. We're going home now."

She looked down. "It's not gonna let us. The storm is after us."

"Aww shit, man." Eldon shook his head. "That's some eerie-ass crap right there."

A peal of thunder rolled across the sky behind them.

Kenny glanced at the mirror; the storm seemed to be closing on them.

"Kath… pull those kids in the window. It's gonna get tight in here but… I don't like them out there going this fast. If I don't see a bump, they're going to go flying."

"Okay." Kathy squirmed around to face backward.

Alyssa looked up. "Huh?"

Kathy slid the rear window open. "*¡Oigan! Niños, vengan para adentro ahora!*" She waved with both hands, beckoning them. "*No es seguro afuera.*"

Thumping came from the back, accompanied by childish voices murmuring. Kenny traded his attention between the road ahead and the center rearview mirror. Cielo, the smallest boy, came in headfirst. Kathy pulled him clear and handed him forward to Eldon, who tolerated an eight-year-old in his lap. Luna slithered in next and sat on the floor in front of Hayley. Gato in his pink cat shirt followed, grabbing the light bar at the rear edge of the roof and entering feet first. Kathy guided him onto the seat between her and Nasir, which smushed Alyssa and Hayley together. Halcón, the fifteen-year-old, barely fit in the window, but managed to wriggle in with Kathy holding his hands and pulling. She slid the window closed, muting the roar of the oncoming storm.

After a bit of shuffling around and bumping to the back of Kenny's seat, Hayley wound up on Kathy's lap with Alyssa against the wall and Halcón seated between Nasir and Kathy. Luna remained on the floor, while Eldon and Cielo battled for control of his rifle. The boy grinned and laughed whenever Eldon swatted his hand away from a button.

Kenny leaned on the accelerator, bringing the truck up to ninety-four. He hawkeyed the road, wary of debris such as dead vehicles or chunks missing. At that speed, he wouldn't have a lot of time to react. Fortunately, the sky and air in front of them remained clear and bright, offering a good view of distance.

Cielo settled down eventually and fell asleep, his face against Eldon's chest armor. The former Marine seemed content to prop him up.

"Probably been awhile since the little guy felt safe enough to really sleep," whispered Kenny.

"Yeah." Eldon looked annoyed in general. "Why the hell do we leave this shit as it is? We all crammed up in the city on the coast."

"Now that's another ghost story you won't wanna hear." Kenny winked.

"Aww, horseshit," muttered Eldon. "It boils down to money. One o' them cost-benefit analysis things."

Kenny shrugged, staring at the road. "Maybe. Who knows? Some people think the Badlands are alive."

"Oh, here we go." Eldon rolled his eyes.

Kenny chuckled. For the better part of three hours, he drove along I-25. Except for the occasional stability warning, the truck's fusion core and e-motors handled sustained ninety-plus with grace. A few times, the road conditions forced him to slow to a crawl. One cause of the chewed-up paving remained abandoned on the island between lanes: a three-century dead tank. An engagement between armor happened here and the road paid the price.

Alyssa and Halcón kept looking at each other, which got Kenny squeezing the wheel. Hayley seemed comforted at being in Kathy's lap. She'd stopped trembling, though had the posture of a little girl after a nightmare.

Luna and Gato whispered back and forth in Spanish; they wondered if the 'curtain of fire' had been a made up story, where would their parents' spirits have gone? When Luna slam-shifted topics to saying Halcón didn't need to marry her anymore because this girl is his age, Kenny's sharp intake of breath sucked up a bit of saliva and he started choking.

*I just gotta watch them for another day... drop these kids off with the cops at the gate, and those two will never see each other again.* Kenny smiled at Alyssa via the mirror. *My little girl is not ready for boys. Especially a muscular one with no shirt who looks like he walked straight out of that Monwyn game.* He gripped the wheel again. *Dammit, boy. Stop smiling at her like that.*

Hayley burst into tears. Before anyone recovered enough from her sudden outburst to speak, she whirled around, screamed, "Mommy," and clamped onto Kathy, sobbing into her shoulder.

The outburst shocked Nasir awake. He swiveled his head around wide-eyed and fumbled for his sidearm. He seemed to realize the source of the noise before managing to get the weapon free of its holster, and stopped trying to pull it.

Cielo didn't stir; mouth agape, he continued snoring.

Luna and Gato stopped talking. They looked up at Hayley with confusion all over their faces.

Halcón faced Kathy. *"Tal vez ella tiene una premonición. Los espíritus me dijeron que me fuera derecho a la casa antes de que los otros atacaran nuestro pueblo. Si me hubiera quedado, estuviera muerto."*

"Premonition my ass," muttered Eldon. He smirked at Kenny. "So he thinks 'the spirits' told him to get outta his village 'fore it got raided. Sounds like coincidence to me."

Hayley's wailing grew louder. She screamed.

The truck went silent for the span of two breaths.

And shut down.

"Whoa, whoa, whoa!" yelled Eldon.

Cielo lifted his head, mouth still open. He looked at Eldon, then Kenny, his eyes big and round with fear.

"Shit..." Kenny grunted and wrestled the wheel to keep them rolling straight. He thanked a handful of random old deities that he'd installed a physical linkage steering system rather than drive-by-wire. Teeth clenched, he held the truck straight until it came to a stop. "Well shit. That's a new one."

Eldon stared at him, unable to recall seeing the man's eyes that wide before.

"It's okay. Probably a short somewhere." He frowned at the instrumentation, which *should* still be showing some manner of error, even if the capacitor died. With a biodiesel under the hood, the 'standard' power plant, essentially a larger version of a FuBox generator, sat in the bed up against the forward wall. Nothing leaked out of it, so the miniature nuclear reactor had to be intact. He pondered if it had been a mistake not going for an electrogel unit, but a bullet striking the fuel reserve would've been *bad*. Significantly more so than just running out of electrogel in the middle of the Badlands. "Gonna swap it over to diesel and we'll be on our way again."

"What's that mean?" asked Alyssa.

Eldon laughed. "Your old man's got some fondness for that prewar shit. Ancient type o' engine."

"*¿Qué pasó con las luces?*" asked Luna, pointing at the dashboard.

"The lights went out," said Eldon. At the girl's confused look, he repeated it in Spanish.

"It doesn't want us to leave," said Hayley in a quiet, calm voice.

"All right, man. That kid is seriously upping the spooky meter," said Eldon.

Kenny pushed his door open. "Been in and out of the Badlands lots of times. He's never minded me going before."

"Will you *stop*?" said Eldon.

"The kids." Nasir raised an eyebrow. "They belong to this place. He won't let you take them." The thin man's lip quivered, fighting a smile.

"Aww, fuck all y'all." Eldon laughed.

Kenny grinned and slid down to stand on the road.

"Mr. Church," said Kathy. "Need I remind you that there are children present."

"Yeah." Eldon grinned. "But those four don't speak English, and Hayley spent a day with Joey around, so she's already heard all the bad words... and probably a few made up ones too."

Kenny climbed into the truck bed. He opened the hatch on the power plant; even its keypad had gone dark. *These things are supposed to work for thirty years. It's stone dead.* He'd planned for this eventuality, hence the biodiesel, but he hadn't had to do a field conversion except as a test before. He grabbed a toolbox, but froze at the high-pitched buzz of an ethanol engine in the distance.

"Aww shit."

Dust trails approached from the east. One large black spot rode at the head, with a handful of smaller ones weaving around in the cloud. He left the toolbox behind and jumped to the road before running to the door.

"We got incoming. Looks like raiders." He ducked out, opened the rear door, and grabbed his rifle off the rack.

"Raiders?" asked Kathy.

"Yeah. Settlers don't drive around out in the desert, and if 'he' doesn't want us leaving, of course we'd 'just so happen' to get spotted by some raiders as soon as the truck dies."

"Man, you seriously workin' hard to convince my ass never to come back out here again." Eldon opened his door, set Cielo on the seat, and stood on the running board to aim over the roof to the east.

The boy leapt onto Kathy, yelling, "*Viene gente mala!*"

"Oh, they're not evil," said Eldon. "They're just misunderstood."

Halcón, Luna, and Gato scrambled past Kenny and ran to the truck bed, collecting their compound bows and arrows. Kathy shouted at them to get inside and stay down, but they leapt to the road and vanished under the truck, taking cover behind the huge tires.

"One big ass truck, damn thing's covered in spiked plates," said Eldon. "Five buggies following it. Swords, axes, couple of rifles. Want me to fire a warning shot?"

"Yeah, fire one right through their heads. Raiders ain't gonna back off unless they think they're gonna lose." Kenny slammed the back door and ran around to the passenger side, taking cover behind the front end and aiming over the hood.

"Think that big mother is gonna ram us?" Eldon settled down over the Crusader rifle.

"Uhh." Kenny raised his electronic scope to his eye. Five piecemeal buggies with huge rear tires and small front wheels weaved back and forth across the wake of what appeared to be an old box truck covered in armored plates. "Doubt it since we're just sittin' here. They'll wanna take the truck."

"What should I do?" yelled Kathy.

"Grab a rifle and do *not* let anyone get near the girls." Kenny drew a bead on one of the buggies.

Eldon fired. The largest of the buggies, covered in shiny aluminum with two men standing on a shelf in back, ceased weaving and veered off in a straight line away from them.

Kenny didn't try to hit the driver in the head like he figured Eldon had. He zoned in on another raider buggy with one axe-waving idiot in a sidecar. He aimed at the body, waited for it to swerve from gliding to his right to the left, and fired three shots one after the other. One sparked. He fired a fourth. The driver pounded on the frame as the buggy lost speed and emitted a billowy cloud of white smoke.

Eldon let off two rounds and raider cart three went up in a fireball. Kenny aimed at a skinny buggy with a motorcycle's front end connected by about five feet of sewer pipe to a car's rear differential. The slim profile plus erratic driving made him dizzy trying to get a bead on it. *Fuck that.* He switched to the other buggy, a bigger target, and shot at it at the same time Eldon did.

The driver's head whipped back. Kenny caught a glimpse of a bloody face in the scope as the man slumped forward. The cart struck a rock or something and flipped ass over nose in the air before landing upside down and sliding.

Eldon laughed as the armored box truck attempted to weave.

"El, nail that little bastard... I don't think I'm gonna do much but waste ammo." Kenny adjusted aim and started pumping round after round into the truck. Some sparked, some didn't.

The Crusader let off two shots back to back.

Kenny focused on the driver's windshield area, firing about twice per second.

"Shoot for the engine," said Eldon. He offloaded a series of three-round bursts.

Alyssa and Hayley shrieked and covered their ears as a gun went off inside the cabin.

Kenny jumped and glanced left, at the windshield. Kathy leaned into the front seats, aiming out the driver's side window. She, too, peppered the behemoth bearing down on them. Conflict between the thrill of watching his wife go 'full badass' and the guilt at putting her in a situation where she had to shoot at people kept him from smiling.

"My bots are all offline," wailed Nasir.

"Nghh!" screamed Hayley. She pounded her fist on his control board over and over. "Stupid piece of shit. Come on! This is what you get for using generic Teradyne crap!"

The raider's truck emitted a loud *boom* as the hood flipped upward, exposing a flaming engine block. Thick, black smoke poured out the front end as well as over the front wheels. The evidently still-alive man behind the wheel attempted to swerve, and wound up rolling the behemoth on its side. The box crunched apart, steel-plated panels wobbling as the vehicle shuddered over the uneven desert ground, kicking up an even bigger dust cloud. A labored screeching of metal tore at the air; random spikes snapped off, and armor plates went whipping into the air like misshapen ninja stars. The dying beast skidded to a halt about fifty meters from the side of the road.

"Thermal inside," said Eldon. "About nine moving."

Kenny raised his rifle. "Maybe they've had enough?"

A man let off a blood-curdling bellow of a roar and kicked out the back door of the old box truck. Bald, taller than Eldon, and covered in an attempt to fashion plate mail armor with a welding torch and scrap metal, he pointed at them and howled some unintelligible word. Eight more raiders, two that might've been female, dragged themselves out of the wreck before advancing toward Kenny's truck.

The huge man raised an Uzi.

"Don't look like they plannin' on runnin'." Eldon shot the big man in the forehead as he let fly with the Uzi. One small *clank* came from the tailgate area. "Dude's tryin' to hit us at that range with that thing?"

"Magic kill stick make dead," said Kenny as he fired at the onrushing crowd. "They don't really understand ballistics."

A flurry of arrows leapt out from under the truck. One pierced a skull, sending the dead raider skidding on his knees for a second. *That's gotta be Halcón.* The other two arrows scored nonfatal hits in raiders' chests or legs. The fifth arrow to fire hit another man in the front of the chin and came out the back of his head. *That Halcón kid is far too comfortable sticking things into people.* Kenny swiveled and fed two bullets to a man who attempted to hit him with a shotgun from ten meters. Two pellets slapped into his left arm, but didn't penetrate his sleeve.

Luna leaned out from behind her tire and put an arrow into the upper chest of a man charging in with a chain-wrapped bowling ball mace. The aluminum shaft jammed to a halt, impaling the lower portion of his throat. He lost his grip on the weapon, which hit the paving with a sharp *thok*. Gurgling, he clutched the arrow and careened over sideways.

The girl darted out of sight not a full second before a bullet skipped off the road where she'd been. Kenny swiveled and shot a man working the lever on a prewar bolt-action rifle, killing him.

A loud whirr came from the back of the truck, accompanied by Nasir's howl of victory. The sentry turret rose out of its storage configuration, swiveled ninety degrees to the right, and offloaded a barrage of 15mm rounds into the raiders.

Bodies burst apart in fragments of floating gore. If any of them screamed, no voice overpowered the thunder.

When the machinegun stopped, nothing moved.

"Liss… Hale," said Kathy. "I want you two to stay down. Do *not* look outside. I mean it. You don't want to see that."

"Yes, Mom," said Hayley.

"Uhh, sure." Alyssa slid off the seat to sit on the floor.

"Well." Eldon grinned. "Good of you to decide to help out, Nas."

"The thing was offline." Nasir stuck his head out the window and shrugged with his eyes at Eldon. "Uhh, the kid hit some command sequence that flipped it to aux power. Primary battery's showing dead."

Hope fluttered in Kenny's chest. He ran around to the driver's side door, and yanked it open—to a dark console. His heart became a rock that fell somewhere down into his lower intestine.

"Yaaaah!" roared a man.

Kenny swiveled, aiming toward the rear of the truck, at a raider covered in dust and other people's blood. The man charged at him with a crude sword raised over his head. An arrow streaked out from behind the rear driver's side tire, and impaled the raider's crotch. His war cry shriveled to a piteous squealing.

"Ooh," said Kenny, cringing.

"Ugh," yelled Eldon.

"Gah," whispered Nasir.

"Oy!" shouted Halcón.

Kathy sucked air through her teeth, wincing.

The raider dropped his sword over his back and skidded to a stop on his knees, cradling his groin, mouth stuck open in silence while staring at the arrow shaft between his hands. A trace of a squeak came from him a half-second later.

"Damn man." Kenny shot him in the forehead, knocking him flat on his back. "Poor bastard."

Gato crawled out from under the tire where the arrow came from, looking horrified. He grabbed himself between the legs and whined in Spanish, "I didn't mean to hit him there. I'm sorry."

Kenny grimaced, but waved the boy over. "It's okay kid, the ref didn't see it. No foul."

"What?" asked Gato, looking around. "What is a ref?"

"Not important. Bad joke." Kenny chuckled.

Nasir, in the back seat, fiddled with his bot-control unit. It beeped every few seconds. "What buttons did you hit, kid? I didn't even know this board could *do* that."

"Uhh, I dunno." Hayley sniffled. "I just hit buttons. I was kinda panicking."

Thunder rolled overhead. Kenny didn't want to look east, because he knew exactly what would be there. After two deep breaths, he did, and sure enough, the wall of dust devoured the desert.

"Wow, he's pretty pissed," muttered Kenny, gazing at the oncoming maelstrom.

"Knock that shit off, man." Eldon slugged him in the shoulder.

"Everyone inside." Kenny ushered Gato toward the door.

Cielo climbed into Kathy's lap when she extracted herself from being wedged between the front seats. Luna and Halcón entered via Eldon's door. Kenny climbed in and worked the backup hand crank to close the window.

"You got manuals on the windows too?" Eldon raised an eyebrow.

"Never know when this'll happen." Kenny winked.

Wind battered the truck, driving a pelting of small stones against composite armor panels. Soon, the whole vehicle swayed side to side, but not hard enough to worry him. Within seconds, the air tasted like dirt. Hayley kept quiet, but she grabbed on to Katherine and trembled. Alyssa huddled close and held the girl's hand, seeming confused by her inexplicable show of fear.

"Are we going to die?" asked Luna in Spanish.

"Nah," said Kenny. "The old man is just pissing and moaning."

Eldon glared at him.

"What old man?" Alyssa asked.

Kenny continued in Spanish, slow so Alyssa and Hayley could keep up. "Many years ago, civilization covered this entire land mass."

"We know that," said Alyssa.

"Yes, but I'm talking to them, too." Kenny gestured at the Scrags. "Anyway, from ocean to ocean, this whole place had big cities, technology, and law. One day, some people got greedy and started fighting. Corporations and the government both thought they should be in control, and it caused a great war that destroyed the middle of the continent. All the people fled to the coasts, where they built the biggest cities ever made by humankind. The cities are so big, and had to hold so many people, they made them on top of metal raised high into the sky."

The younger three Scrag kids gasped in awe. Halcón looked intrigued.

"Anyway… it is said that all the people who died during this war became angry. Their restless spirits walked the land until they found each other, and a great demon devoured them to make itself stronger."

Eldon whistled to himself, trying to peer out the windows, but all had turned brown with dirt.

"That demon sometimes decides it wants to keep people, and won't let them leave the Badlands. There's lots of stories of technology dying out here. Anything modern fails when it's most disastrous."

"That's a buncha superstitious bunk," muttered Eldon in English. "You really believe that?"

"It is true," said Halcón, also in English. "We have stories the same. I try leading my tribe to Prophet in Querq, but could not find the way. The demon does not want us going to her."

"Prophet?" asked Kathy.

Kenny whistled. "Wow… there's a bunch of stories there, too. Most you hear people talk, there's this girl out there who can heal with a touch. Glowing blue eyes or some such shit. If you believe that sorta thing, they say some fast talkin' salesman type dragged her all over the Badlands, chargin' people to see 'er. Someone 'ventually killed him and took her, and she supposedly still changes hands among various tribes and raider groups."

"Is not the now," said Halcón, attempting English. "Prophet is to Querq. Home. Changed. She…" His eyebrows scrunched together with a hint of annoyance in his expression. "*Ella no va con ellos ahora cuando vienen a llevarla. Ella tiene un gran poder.*"

The three younger Scrags nodded.

"Hmm." Kenny rubbed his chin. "I heard she never tried to fight. So you think this girl is real, and she's using her power to stop raiders?"

"Go away, go away," said Halcón in English. "We saw raider. Kept say 'go away,' and walked." He tapped himself on the chest with his fist twice. "I ask go away what. He say Prophet told him go away, so he go away." He pointed at the window. "Raider keep walk, no stopping."

Eldon whistled. "Sounds like this 'prophet' might just be a psionic. You know how shit gets exaggerated out here."

Kenny shrugged. "Who knows?"

"Why do you kids want to go to her?" asked Kathy in Spanish.

"She can stop the demon," said Luna. "The devil is afraid of the Prophet."

The other Scrags nodded, total reverence on their faces.

Kathy rocked Hayley side to side and shot Kenny a questioning stare.

"Well," said Kenny, "the old man... the demon, whatever you wanna call him, won't be able to reach you where we're going. The four of you deserve a chance at a good life. An education. No reason for you to stay stuck out here in the sticks."

"*El demonio está enfadado con nosotros,*" whispered Cielo, sounding frightened.

"Aww, the old man isn't that upset. He's just tryin' to make things interesting, and violent. Probably not fond of me pullin' these kids out of his playground." Kenny ruffled his hair.

Cielo grinned.

"So you're saying," said Eldon, "some kinda demon-ass thing wants to strand us out here in the shit? Why the hell would he care about a couple of feral children?"

Kenny shrugged. "If I see him, I'll ask."

"Don't say shit like that man." Eldon waved him off. Hayley's whimper caught his attention, and he froze, staring at her.

"Change your mind? You believe now?" Kenny grinned.

Eldon exhaled. "I ain't sayin' that. But no sense jinxing it."

Katherine ran her hand down her leg in a rhythmic motion, her other arm around Hayley.

"You okay, hon?" asked Kenny

"I'm trying not to panic." She bit her lip. "*This* is what I was always so worried about happening to you... why I always threw a fit when you were going to go out here."

Kenny slid into the gap between the front seats and patted her knee. "Are you okay?"

She stared for a second or two at the dirt-covered window, under a constant pelting of pebbles. "Yeah... This is scary as hell, but I'm happy I got my mind back."

"Me, too." He buried his face in the crook of her neck and squeezed.

"*Esta maquina ya no sirve?*" asked Gato.

Kenny looked at the huge brown eyes of the twelve-year-old staring at him. He tried not to let the worry storming around inside him show on his face. "The truck isn't dead yet... I still got a few tricks left."

# THE SOURCE

Bathed in the cold blue glow of her holo-terminals, Nina spent most of Thursday afternoon combing the GlobeNet. Becker's interrogation had given away four more individuals, ACC spies, who had infiltrated Laughlin-Reed Innovation. She'd managed to find the time and date of their entry to the UCF via facial recognition searches within the Citycam system. Two had entered via commercial Mars shuttle, having established their false identities as UCF citizens on Mars before going to Earth. One entered at a checkpoint after driving up one of the ramps at the south end of the city. Most likely, he had come up from Mexico. The last man simply appeared on the street one day, the oldest record she could locate of him within the camera database showed him emerging from an alley in a grey zone along the western edge of the city.

She brought up a few real-time views from nearby cameras, which offered a pleasant panorama of beach and ocean. The gargantuan plastisteel tiles upon which Sector 1405 sat overhung the beach, above a gaping view of The Beneath. Residents of a handful of scattered beachfront homes made a feeble effort at fences to keep the Discarded away, though a determined spy would have had little trouble getting into the Beneath there, since it yawned open facing the ocean. Someone brave, lucky, or unaware of the danger could eventually make their way up into the city proper.

Nina grabbed still images of faces around the men arriving via RedLink shuttle from Mars, as well as the one who drove in. Hours of searching later, none of them matched any known ACC personnel or employees of LRI. The four men Becker gave up all appeared to have positions in or near the pharmaceutical production facility. Two pushed data around, scheduling and processing shipments to hospitals, pharmacies, and sending OTC meds to the warehouses that fed the delivery bot system. The man who'd come in via the ocean worked as an exo-suit operator. According to LRI's employee record, he loaded shipments into transport vehicles, as well as belonged to the crew responsible for maintaining the giant machinery that produced the various medications. One of the Mars arrivals held the position of executive assistant to Daniel Stirling, Senior VP of production.

*Shit. They are using LRI to manufacture Harmony.* She stared at the file photo of Stirling. *Are you being played or are you one of them too?*

The prior executive assistant received a promotion to a Senior Director, Public Relations spot a month ago. Nina poked around LRI's system, but couldn't find a normal-looking data trail that one might expect to come with a hiring process for filling such a position. Stirling's new executive assistant appeared to get his job handed to him on a plate after the SVP instructed HR to hire.

*What kind of dirt did they have on Stirling?* She glanced at the face of John Rastin, thirty-two-year old-executive assistant, for a second before shifting her gaze left one holo-panel to the same face in a C-Branch record of Karl Wimmer. The image appeared to have been taken somewhere in a jungle on Earth, and showed him a few years younger in green ACC-flage and face paint. He didn't have the look of a commando, more like an intelligence officer embedded within a special operations team.

*Okay, Danny. What nasty little habits do you have that they found out about?*

Nina reached out to start digging on Daniel Stirling, but her official NetMini rang before her fingers touched the button.

"Dammit." She considered ignoring the call until reading ‹Barron, Ricky› on the incoming ID. "Awesome timing." A mental command altered her avatar to look like the 'gang girl' outfit she'd used to visit him before she answered

The holographic head of a young man with teal hair, brown skin, and green eyes appeared.

"Hey sweetness," said Ricky. "I'm about to roll out a new batch of that stuff you like. I'll set some aside for you if you wanna get your perfect ass down here in like twenty."

"Ooh... It's about time," she whined, raising her voice higher. "You've been making me wait so long. You're so mean to me sometimes."

"Ran outta some of the stuff I need, babycakes. I'd never be mean to you on purpose." He winked, looked nervous for an instant, and hung up.

Nina cringed. *Babycakes? I'll let that one go if this turns out to be useful.*

---

AFTER TRADING HER COAT FOR A PURPLE ZOMBIE BALLERINA'S BAND TEE, BAGGY half-jacket, and a fluorescent violet 'tattered' skirt almost long enough to reach mid-thigh, Nina slipped into a shorter pair of boots that didn't look as military as the ones she normally wore. The trendier boots wouldn't survive if she had to kick anyone with her full strength, but they fit the outfit. Her ballistic armor suit could pass for black tights, the upper portion hidden by the full t-shirt.

On the jog to the elevator, she opened a comm channel. ⌜Ops, I need a whisper over Sector 71 ASAP. Give me eyes on 32°44'23.6 N 116°43'15.8 W. Advise them to be on the lookout for a van, truck, or something similar.⌟

⌜Copy, lieutenant.⌟

Nina got a few slow claps and a whistle on her way down the hall to the elevator, but ignored them. She activated her CamNano to turn her hair pastel yellow and simulate purple eye makeup laid on with an overindulgent hand. Subtle shading on her face and the backs of her hands accented veins and contours, making her look thinner. A bit of tweaking around the eyes added a strung out 'I've been awake for six days' look. By the time she reached the roof parking deck, other Division 9 personnel walking in from their cars gave her glares like some random doser had managed to get inside the building.

She hurried to her patrol craft and lifted off before the gull wing door finished sinking closed. After wrenching the nose end around to point southeast, she rammed the left control stick forward. A blast of ion thrust went off like a cannon shot behind her, slamming the patrol craft from a hovering standstill to 458 mph in seven seconds. Once she leveled off at the fortieth story, ten below civilian traffic, she opened a virtual holo-terminal and added to her inquest log, notating her intent to go undercover at the 'Universe Gym' to locate the source of Harmony.

「Ops, Duchenne. Send a feeler over to Div 1 and let them know this is going down. I don't want cowboys showing up and shitting in my oatmeal.」 Nina blurted out a laugh. If her parents ever heard her talking like that, they'd drop dead. *I've been around cops too long.*

A twenty-something woman with light brown skin and blonde hair appeared in another small floating window. Under the video box, a tab bore the text: OPS-SPC4-Santos. 「Copy that, lieutenant.」

「Also, mobilize a strike unit. This is supposed to be observation, but I want them on standby in case of something unexpected.」

「Copy, lieutenant. Whisper 11 is on site,」 said Santos. 「Setting up a MTOF for you now.」

「Great.」

A small window scrolled open at the top left of her vision, labeled: Mission Tactical Overlay Feed. In a band along the side, a green gem glowed by the designation Whisper 11.

「Duchenne, this is Whisper 11, radio check. Copy?」

「Got you loud and clear, Eleven.」

「Good to hear. We'll be in position over Sector 71 in four seconds. Van?」

「Correct.」 Nina gritted her teeth while pulling a ninety-degree right turn at 440 mph that wobbled the windows of the century tower she came within ten feet of touching. An advert-bot got caught in her wake, lost control, and crashed through the windows of a building half a block behind her. *Dammit. Stupid things ignore exclusion zones.* She checked her car's transponder to ensure she'd turned it on. Bots should stay far away from her route path, but sometimes they 'conveniently' malfunctioned. Wouldn't want to miss the chance of a sale. She scowled at the thought the crashed bot had likely picked itself up off the floor inside the building and spammed the shocked employees around it with ads for window repair and/or medical treatment.

「More than likely a van or some sort of cargo truck. Contents should be a street chem known as Harmony. Assuming this doesn't spiral out of control, your mission parameters will evolve into tracking it back to its source.」

「Copy, lieutenant. Whisper 11 going silent.」

Six more green gems appeared as the field operations team patched into the feed. The overlay map, blue squares representing buildings and streets over black, zoomed way out to show a cluster of green dots at the Police Administrative Center, arranged in a row like they sat in the rear of an A3HV transport.

「Lieutenant, this is Operative Benitez. My team's en route to your target. ETA six minutes eight seconds.」

「Takin' your sweet old time there, Benitez,」 said Nina with a whimsical tone.

「All due respect.」 Benitez grinned. 「Neither I nor this lunch box I'm flying can keep up with your reflexes.」

Beeping from the console attempted to warn Nina of what she already knew; her destination approached too fast. She triggered airbrake flaps along the sides, undercarriage, and top rear of the patrol craft while pulling the left stick back to apply reverse thrust. While her avatar on the MTOF remained stoic, she lurched forward into the restraining harness holding her to the seat. 「All good, Operative. I'm early. Expected arrival of objective to the site is forty-one minutes.」

「Copy, lieutenant. Where do you want us?」

Nina brought the car down to a walking pace, and after a bit of looking around, eased it through a blasted-out window at the sixth floor of an abandoned century tower a block away from the gym. 「We've got a whisper overhead, so no need to set up snipers. Use pattern C, standoff rapid.」

「You got it, lieutenant. Holler if you need us.」

Nina got out and spent a few minutes rearranging smashed office furniture and slabs of drywall over the patrol craft to conceal it from casual observation before jogging to the nearest stairwell. She emerged at ground level among a crowd of fringers and off-gridders. Most of their attention went toward two guys carrying sacks of Cyberburger fast food and a case of synthbeer. A girl in her late teens grilled rat meat on a small electric hot plate. She gave Nina a look of confused curiosity, likely wondering about the 'newcomer.'

Forcing herself to meander at an uninspired pace, Nina jostled among the fingers giving her back or butt pats, and casual looks that fell between 'wanna fuck?' and 'what's up?' They seemed to be more welcoming than anything, and one guy with hair so deep blue it almost hurt to look at handed her a Double Orbital burger in a plastic clamshell case.

"Thanks, man," she mumbled.

"Duuuude." A woman in her early twenties leaned up close enough to kiss her. Her hair had been split into three mohawks, the center fin pink, the two side ones black. "Your hair is like so yellow. Where'd you get it done?"

Her tactical view in the MTOF window zoomed in as the field team came closer, allowing it show more detail while keeping all assets in view. An arrowhead shape glided around in a circle, indicating the position of Whisper 11.

Nina kept going, heading to cross the street. "Found some shit inna bag someone dropped."

The woman winked, evidently assuming she implied theft. "Nice."

For being OmniSoy, the Double Orbital didn't smell all that bad when she opened the case. Two 'beef' patties as thick as fingers with the usual pseudo-lettuce, tomato slab, and nuclear cheese. She wondered if the real thing tasted like this, or if some chemist decided the flavor of 'cheese' needed to hit a person over the head like a sledgehammer. Another perk of a doll body, she didn't have to regret eating junk to keep her cover.

She ambled the rest of the block to Ricky's place, ignored the crowd of 'couriers' outside, and hurried across the gym floor. A handful of adolescent boys worked out on the heavy bags or did push-ups and other exercises near the boxing ring, coached by a fiftyish man in a dark blue running suit with more than a little silver in the sides of his afro.

Nina walked with an erratic gait as if her sense of balance didn't exist. Other than people glancing at motion for a second, no one paid her much attention. Sergeant Webb opened the door for her at the end of the hall, and followed her up to Ricky's office.

Chatter on the MTOF link accompanied green dots dispersing around the area in the ready-standoff posture she'd ordered. Distant enough to remain out of sight, but it wouldn't take them too long to engage if necessary.

"How's this usually work, this meeting?" asked Nina.

Webb's boots echoed in the narrow stairway. "Guy comes in, talks with Rick for a few. They do the deal, arrange the next buy, and he leaves. He goes outside, gives his boys the nod, and they let the crew unload the van."

Nina stopped at the door to Rick's office. "Where's the best place to sit to get a good look at this guy?"

"In there." Webb pointed at the door before opening it. "Yo, Rick."

Ricky Barron got up from behind his desk, a turquoise suit jacket over a bare chest, and a pair of shimmery cyan satin boxer's shorts with flip-flops. "Hey there. Lookin' good, mama."

Nina walked in, glancing around the office. The couch caught her eye on the left, by the bookshelf full of chems in bins. "I appreciate the call, Ricky. Don't mind me in the room. I'm only here to get an idea of who and what we're dealing with."

"Okay. Sounds good. Anything special you need me to do?" Ricky set his hands on his hips.

"Aside from ending that atrocity of fashion, just act as normal as possible."

Webb cringed. "Ouch."

She gestured to the side. "Will that sofa over there work?"

Ricky laughed. "Right, I can do that, and yeah."

The couch resembled furniture molded out of a giant hairball. Brown, orange, green, and the occasional red in the fabric clashed into an overall rust color. *No one will notice if anyone pukes on this thing.* She draped herself over it in a heavy slouch, with her ass almost at the front edge of the cushion, and grabbed an inhaler from the end table.

Webb hesitated at the door. "Want me in here 'case something goes fucked?"

"Nah," said Ricky. "It'll be unusual. 'Sides, like she said, ain't all but lookin' at the guy, right?"

Nina nodded.

"Right on." Webb walked out. The tromp of his boots down the stairs came seconds later, and faded to silence once more.

She watched the MTOF panel, noting the position of Whisper 11 as well as eight operatives. With as much setup time as they had, the snipers had ordered matching tracksuits and inserted themselves among the crowd out front, acting like some of Ricky's drivers.

"How many of your people know this is going on?" asked Nina.

"Just Webb." Ricky sat at his desk once more and got to working at his terminal.

Nina patched into the direct feed from Whisper 11, and stared down at the city in a second virtual holo-panel. "Good."

A soft *snap* accompanied Ricky connecting a credstick to his terminal. "Can't believe this shit is so cheap."

"It's on purpose," muttered Nina. "They want it everywhere."

Yellow flashed on the MTOF window; a targeting reticle appeared and shrank down over a moving pale grey rectangle.

⌈Heads up. Whisper 11 here. We got an unmarked cargo van approaching from the north. Reading two heat signatures.⌋

⌈Acknowledge, Eleven. I see it.⌋ Nina stared at the van creeping across her little tactical map until it shifted to the right lane and slowed. ⌈Looks like our guest of honor is here. Everyone stay awake.⌋

Quick responses of 'copy' or 'ack' came from the field team.

The van stopped in front of the gym and two people exited. Whisper 11's camera zoomed in far enough to offer a view from the elevation of a second story window. Both men wore dark grey suits. One had brown hair, the other black. Neither looked like the sort of individual who would dare show up in a grey zone, yet they headed for the gym entrance without hesitation.

⌈Target in the building,⌋ said a voice from Whisper 11.

⌈Eleven, can you get a tracker on that van?⌋

⌈Where you want it?⌋ Asked a woman who sounded more like a young teen. ⌈I can hit any quarter-inch square you call.⌋

Nina shifted her weight to seem more 'wasted.' ⌈Roof is fine.⌋

The door to Ricky's office opened, and an athletic woman with medium-brown skin and long dark brown hair strolled in. A tight band of clingy white fabric covered her chest; black shorts that appeared to be silk didn't go much past her crotch. She tossed a pair of boxer's gloves and boots on a table to her right, pulled a towel off her shoulders, and started to walk toward Ricky's desk, but stopped as soon as she noticed Nina.

"Ricky...?" She took a step closer to Nina. "Who's that? Why you got some bitch on my couch?"

"No one you need worry about, babe. Just another happy customer." Ricky winked.

The woman set her fists against her hips and gave Nina a once-over with her eyes. "That bitch ain't your type, Rick."

The hollow echo of dress shoes on steps in a narrow hallway grew loud enough to notice.

Rick held his hands up in a placating gesture. "Will you relax, Mila? She no one."

A *beep* from the MTOF screen accompanied the pale rectangle of the van turning blue.

⌈Tracker active,⌋ said the same woman.

The door opened. A dark-haired man walked in first, giving the room a look-around. He had the broad-shouldered thickness of a bodyguard, and a facial expression that belied eagerness to hurt someone.

Nina brought the inhaler to her lips, giggled, and took a hit. She didn't care what was in it. Nothing she breathed or ate would reach her tiny bloodstream unless she disabled her filter. For added measure, she shut off her sense of taste. Sensing some manner of vapor in her mouth, she made a show of playing with it before exhaling.

Glowing lines appeared in her vision over the bodyguard, identifying a handgun, thin metal reinforcements grafted onto the major long bones, some Myofiber augments in his arms, and the usual array of headware: NIU, wireless interface, and a chip board.

She went wide-eyed and cooed, trying to bite the puff of vapor that rose from her lips. "Ooh, Ricky, this batch is *so* much better than the last one."

The bodyguard sent a dismissive frown her way and stepped aside.

"Ricky? You've got an obliterated skank on *my* couch. What is she doing here?" Mila stormed over and got in Nina's way, blocking her view of the two men.

"Ohhh... Hi!" Nina flashed a vapid grin. She swung her arm around to give a handshake, grasped the woman's hand, and tossed her over sideways to the floor. Three seconds later, she gasped. "Oops. Sorry. Everything is moving *so* slow."

A man of average height stepped forward, his medium-brown hair in an arrangement so neat and perfect he looked like he belonged narrating the NewsNet. A band of light shimmered down his suit as he moved, the iridescent fabric gleaming at the peaks of folds. She scanned him, revealing neural wiring, reflex boosters and possible speedware. Anomalous readings in the head suggested he had intelligence grade parts with some sensor-inhibiting coating. Though Nina's head contained the latest Division 9 tech, the micronization necessary to put it there did leave it less powerful than external units.

Nina stared at him, pretending to be mesmerized by the existence of air. Her eyes captured video of him up close; she isolated a few still images and sent them off to Ops. A quick mental command tagged him 'Target 1' and the bodyguard as 'Target 2.' ⌜Eleven, Target 1 is augged, but it's shielded. Can you get any kind of read on him?⌟

"Ricky," said the source. "Looks like you've got a little housekeeping to attend to."

"Oh, is nothing. Mila's jealous, you know how it goes. Can't even have another bitch in the entire building without her getting in a mood." Ricky stood and reached over his desk to shake hands. "You are the bearer of light and inspiration."

The source twisted his head to the side, grimacing as if feeling something odd.

⌜Lieutenant, said a new voice as the Whisper 11 gem lit up brighter green. Target 1 scan confirms CamNano, NIU, Advanced chip board, DTF speedware, targeting stabilizers in the arms, synthetic adrenaline, a succubus... uhh, s'pose I should call it an incubus huh? Shock prods right index finger, and looks like a spitting cobra in his teeth.⌟

*Succubus... my filter should stop pheromone manipulation... I hope.* ⌜Thanks.⌟

⌜Oh, and the A/C in their van is broken.⌟

Nina resisted the urge to look confused in the real world. ⌜What?⌟

⌜Target 1's got a bad case of swamp ass, and his nuts are stuck to his thigh.⌟

"Ugh." Nina looked away and took another hit from the inhaler before using that to mask her need to gag. ⌜I could've gone without that last bit, Whisper 11.⌟

⌜You're right, lieutenant, ⌟ said Whisper 11's electronics man. ⌜His headware's all shielded. I've seen greater signal diffusion before, he's probably not *too* high up on their list.」

「I think he felt your scan,」 said Nina.

「It's possible his internal cybernetics heated up a little. I had to turn the dial up far enough to count the pores on his forehead to get past the shielding.」

"Light and inspiration... I like that. Or at least the key to your continued prosperity." The source smiled.

A third small holo-panel opened with a Laughlin-Reed Innovation employee record for one Neal Finch, the man in front of her. His job title, 'sales manager – pharmaceuticals' seemed appropriate given the situation.

*This is going to be a damn mess if LRI is involved.* She clung to hope the company had no idea. Finch's hardware, and the presence of sensor-absorbent shielding on his cybernetics, screamed ACC operator.

"Argh! Bitch!" Since Mila's overacted shock at being thrown to the ground had failed to elicit any reaction from Ricky, she shoved herself upright and descended on Nina with punches and slaps.

Nina permitted a few to hit her in the face before raising her arms in a futile defense, pretending to be too high to react fast enough. Disabling pain sensors reduced the assault to an irritating bounce in her vision. "Hey... stop. I'm just buyin' shit. We ain't like, fuckin' or nothin'."

「Vehicle is registered to Laughlin-Reed Innovation,」 said the field operative among the drivers. His name, Operative Emmanuel, R, appeared under the MTOF map panel for as long as he spoke.

「Figured as much,」 said Nina. 「Whisper, don't suppose you can send a tranq dart through the roof. Ricky's girlfriend really needs to take a damn nap.」

「No tranqs on this thing,」 replied the too-young sounding woman. 「I could express a railgun slug down if you want.」

「Nah. Too much mess.」

The MTOF channel fluttered with chuckling.

Mila grabbed Nina by the throat and shook her. "Ricky, who is this bitch, huh? You're cheating on me, I know it!"

"You should put those two in the ring," said Finch.

Ricky shook his head. "Nah, the blonde can't fight for shit. Look at her, she's like four seconds behind the clock."

"Put 'em in the ring naked," said the bodyguard. "Don't matter who wins then."

Mila whirled around to glare at him, and exploded in a tirade of Spanish about what his forbearers must have done with farm animals to have created him.

Ricky's face paled until the men seemed to find her amusing.

"Stop hitting me," muttered Nina.

"I ain't hittin' you, you dumb, strung out whore." Mila punched her in the cheek again. She grimaced and shook her hand afterward. "Ow, damn, bitch you got some bones in you."

"And mine ain't one of 'em." Ricky waved at Mila to calm down. "I ain't fuckin' her. She just buyin' some Sandman. Will you just hang on a minute?"

"We are on a schedule, Mr. Barron," said Finch. "Do you have the payment ready?"

"Yeah, yeah." Ricky swiped the credstick from its port on the terminal and handed it over. "Hundred and fifty grand, as promised."

"Excellent." The man held the stick up to the light, examining its display screen before tucking it into his inner jacket pocket. "Your people may unload the product. A pleasure doing business with you. See you in two weeks? Same amount?"

"Shit be pickin' up," said Ricky. "You do forty cases 'stead of thirty?"

"Done." Finch tugged at his sleeves one after the next. "Until next time then."

Ricky waved. "Later, man."

Finch and his associate left.

"Get offa me," yelled Nina, before tossing Mila face-first into the couch. "Ricky, why's your girl on me?"

"She's possessive." Ricky winked at the growling Mila. "And that's her couch."

Mila sprang upright and gave it to Ricky in rapid-fire Spanish. Nina lost some of the words, but followed enough to grasp the woman didn't appreciate being talked about like a pet dog with a favorite sofa. And she continued demanding to know why he let 'that bitch' get high in his private office.

The whispercraft panel gave Nina a clear view of Ricky's people swarming the van and offloading a procession of cube-shaped plastiboard cartons. Finch got in the passenger side door while the bodyguard observed the unloading.

"And you!" Mila stormed back toward Nina, pointing. "Who the fuck are you, and why are you after my man?"

Nina tossed the inhaler on the end table and stood. "Ricky, I can see why she's so insecure about you possibly cheating on her. I wouldn't put up with this crazy bitch, either." ⌐Eleven, keep eyes on that van when it leaves. Benitez, your team should be good to head home once the targets leave the area.⌐

Ricky cringed.

⌐Copy, lieutenant, said Benitez.⌐

Mila gasped. "You stupid whore!"

The woman cocked her arm back to swing again. Nina stood rigid and let the woman punch what amounted to a metal statue shrouded in a quarter-inch thick coating of rubber. A faint *snap* gave away at least one cracked bone. Ricky's girlfriend screamed and backpedaled, favoring her right hand. Her confusion deepened as the realization Nina no longer appeared to be the least bit high finally dawned on her.

"Ricky?" asked Mila in a mousy voice. "What's going on? Who is this woman?"

"No one you need to worry about." Nina frowned at her before nodding to Ricky. "Appreciate the help. I'll see what I can do about that reward."

"Ricky?" Mila sounded even more like a child. "Talk to me, Ricky."

Nina walked out and jogged down the stairs to the ground floor. The view from Whisper 11 showed the van gliding down the street, one among thousands of innocuous vehicles. ⌐Okay, Benitez, pack it in. Thanks everyone. Nice clean work, all.⌐

# 34

# MINIMAL LIABILITY

Face after face scrolled by on Joey's 'god-terminal' in the underbelly of the Police Administrative Center. His octopusine arrangement of holo-panels regaled him with everything from financial activities to the porn habits of Laughlin-Reed Innovation employees. One of them even had a mark on his file for exploitative manipulation of auction markets in the Monwyn MMO, not that scamming gamers out of virtual money broke the law.

*Guess the dragons must've been bored and looking for patterns.*

A redline popped up, a stripe in a job queue indicating someone wanted something done yesterday. Joey reacted fastest. He grinned at the sight of ‹O2-C3 Duchenne, N› as the requestor. He brought the data up, hoping for a change of pace from staring at office drones. Joey blinked at yet another employee of Laughlin-Reed Innovation.

"Motherfucker!" he roared, and slammed a fist on his desk.

"Abby shoot you down again?" asked Mindy, behind him, earning a glare from Abby.

"Naw." Joey rubbed his hand. "My plans with Simon's sister fell through."

"Oh, very funny, Dillon." Dan Simon didn't even do him the courtesy of sliding back in his chair to glower at him. "Besides, I think Abby's more interested in Mindy."

Joey's entire team froze, except for Simon, evidenced by the continuous soft *pips* of typing on a holographic keyboard.

DeWinter leaned back and gawked. "Did Simon just crack a joke?"

"I don't see any intercontinental weapons inbound," said Abby. "Negative on imminent ending of the world."

"Wow." Joey leaned around, grinning. The zinger at the tip of his tongue stalled.

Mindy Wu stared at her terminal with the intensity of someone trying to pretend the universe didn't exist. She snuck a peek at Abby, and seemed to deflate a little at not catching her staring. Joey turned back to face his terminal, not quite able to bring himself to pick on Mindy.

He sent Abby a direct text. ‹No BS. I think Mindy's got it for you.›

‹Never really thought about girls that way, but if it'll get Simon to stop sending me dick pics, maybe I'll try it.›

Joey snorted. And covered a laugh with choking. ‹Go easy on her. Either she's really crushing on you, or she's a master at fuckin' with us.›

‹What happened?›

‹The way she looked at you. Disappointed you weren't checking her out after my jab. Didn't even comment on Simon lobbing one into the fray.›

‹I know! What the fuck is up with that? Did Simon develop emotions? Or did he have the P&P surgically removed from his ass finally?›

Joey snickered. ‹Nice. Okay… gotta do this work thing.› "So… Nina wants to know who you are."

He settled into his chair, reclined, and waited for the little mechanical arms to insert the dual M3 plugs behind his ears. Connection hit him as though he'd fallen through a webbing of diaphanous shadows, embraced with the invigorating chill of a clear early-winter day. He landed on his feet in the blue-on-black octagon of his programming environment room, which melted away with his command to teleport, shifting into the Laughlin-Reed Innovation network lobby. Imaginary sunlight bathed the vast expanse of an imaginary room with every detail replicated to the real world, including the security desk, faux-marble columns, and potted plants.

Joey's 'shadow-ninja,' a black ghostly silhouette, hovered in the midst of a crowd, unnoticed by seventy-two users and 192 program constructs. Since most of the time his official hardware made infiltrating so easy, he didn't bother with fancy, and decided to head straight to the Human Resources data node. His wraith figure glided past the virtual lobby doors, into the elevator shaft, and up to the second floor. He whistled while slaloming other users and data-fetching constructs that couldn't see him, and hooked a left at the end into a small security buffer that cyberspace rendered as a little guard station.

A security guard (program) gazed glassily into nowhere as Joey floated across the room while doing a traditional Russian dance. The door offered no resistance to his ethereal body, and he waltzed in among endless rows of data storage devices rendered in the image of ancient black filing cabinets.

His desire to find Neal Finch sent glowing blue lines out from his feet, racing along the floor in rapid zigzag trails. In nine seconds, one of them flared bright while the rest disappeared. The luminous path led to cabinet 53. While following it, a glint of silver caught his eye on the left. He approached another drawer, tucked closed against a data tile sticking out.

He plucked the file free and held it up. Upon the surface of an eight-inch square slab, a familiar woman stared at him with the eager face of a girl who'd gotten her first job. Despite the brown skin and shading adjustments to shave off a few years, he recognized Katya. The system log showed an HR staffer created the employee record, though the file ID token pinged an exact match for another employee. *She cloned and edited a tile. Guess she only needed access for a few hours. Quick, but easily found by anyone who knows how to look.* He tapped the tile against his hand while thinking.

According to the access list, Zack Martin had been the last to read this file. *Oh, hello Anders. No wonder they haven't found it yet, you covered it up to go on your hunt for ass.* Joey's shadow figure looked left and right while whistling innocently, and crushed the tile into dust, deleting the record.

*I'm not helping her get away with stealing; I'm deleting an illegal file that shouldn't have been here.*

"Right..." He headed over to the result of his search, following the blue line to a file cabinet, which he peeled open.

The line shrank from a ribbon to a thread once it entered the drawer, and pointed him at a data tile bearing the same face he'd seen in meatspace on his holo-panel: Neal Finch, an outside sales manager. The employee record looked plain and unremarkable. A cross check convinced him Finch had gone through the normal channels to get hired, as he couldn't find any oddities with the data. The man had been employed at LRI since July 2, 2419, which put his hire date at a week over four months ago.

"Okay Neal Bland. Looks like you're a model employee. Straight threes down the performance evaluations. You're not shining, but you're not operating at the level of 'bare minimum not to get fired' either."

He sent spiders streaming into the LRI network, simultaneously adoring and grumbling at the Division 9 search tool. With the shadow access his position gave him, he could request files without having to worry about being detected or forcing his way in. While as easy as being an authorized user, it offered no challenge. He longed for the day he got a chance to go up against a company that broke the law, and put real effort into trying to keep him out.

Spiders returned with copies of data tiles they'd found wherever Neal's identity came up. Joey sifted among hundreds of purchase orders, none of which stood out as illegal. He might be an ACC spy, but he appeared to be performing the duties of a sales manager quite well as his cover. He'd sold a lot of diagnostic and treatment machines, as well as meds to local hospitals.

An email record grabbed his attention, and he opened the tile to read the string. One Darius Reed, CEO of LRI had received some reports of tampering with a product in the pharma division. A crosslink to Darius popped up in a new window, displaying records of an emergency call from Reed's home a few weeks ago, but as soon as Joey read enough to understand some woman who appeared to conjure fire out of thin air had broken into his apartment, he threw the data tile away like a loaded diaper. *Bah. That's for the Zeroes.*

Finch wound up copied on the thread since he had a managerial position within the pharma sales group. The SVP of production, Daniel Stirling, initiated an in-house investigation, sending off a number of firebrand emails to division managers trying to understand how tampering could've occurred.

A month later, LRI's people determined that unknown contaminants responsible for sporadic aggression and disregard for authority had been introduced in several lot numbers of Placinil. The final product QA sensors showed signs of tampering that allowed the faulty pills to pass without red flags. At the end of the investigation, Stirling ordered it kept quiet to minimize liability and informed the CEO he would personally oversee the production process, yet despite another hour of combing over files, Joey couldn't find any evidence to suggest Stirling had done a damn thing but keep everything quiet.

*This guy knew about it and shut it right down. Why did he start the investigation in the first place?* Joey's eyebrows scrunched together. *Maybe to keep up his cover?* He went on a hunt for Daniel Stirling. The man had enough files going back forty-seven years to his birthdate, including school records, that it seemed quite unlikely he could be an ACC spy... unless they'd sent him into the country as an embryo. Stirling had a wife and son, but neither of them linked to any recent reports of suspicious activity.

*Hmm. Either this guy is easily bribed, or they've got something on him.*

Joey stared at the data tile holding Neal Finch's employee record.

He duplicated it, kept the copy, and teleported to the National Police Force's primary data reserve. Despite his Division 9 hardware, the load on the NPF database made the shiny gunmetal blue hallway feel like a lake of molasses. Since he had official access here, he walked down the entrance passage to an enormous lobby, and approached an interface construct, which had an ever-shifting appearance of indeterminate gender. As soon as Joey reached the counter and made himself detectable to the program, the randomization ceased, leaving him face to face with a digital representation of a woman. Light brown skin, brown hair, brown eyes, and the general set of her features made him think they used an algorithm based on the average citizen of the UCF.

"Can I help you?" asked the program.

Joey handed it the tile. "I need this guy's info."

"Right away, Tech Dillon."

Though 'Tech 1' was his official rank, it still felt strange to be called that. *No shit I'm a technician.*

The construct held the tile in both hands for a few seconds before another tile materialized on top of it, and the false woman handed both back to him. "Anything else, tech?"

"Not sure yet. Thanks."

The program resumed its ever-shifting appearance as he stepped away.

Joey perused the municipal records for Neal Finch. His DOB showed as May 11, 2384, at a public medical facility in Sector 721, near the southeast corner of West City, about twenty miles north of a sizeable grey zone and a nasty pair of disavowed sectors. Most black zones only took up one five-mile-square sector, but 721 sat within reasonable driving distance of a five-by-ten-mile rectangle of badness. Sectors 356 and 304, both blacked out of the Navcon system, formed the heart of an enormous grey zone.

It took him fifteen cyberspace minutes, about two in reality, to hit the hospital's systems and find a falsified file. Neal's parents had never existed, and the manufactured parents were listed as conveniently deceased due to gang violence. Further digging in the Citycam system yielded nothing older than five months. He targeted a period from two weeks before the date of the first time the Citycams got a recognizable shot of Neal's face to one week after, and re-ran the search with a lowered match threshold set to eighty percent. It took another sixteen minutes, even with the narrow parameter, to come back with several thousand possible hits.

After a sort by highest probability to lowest, he 'did the nasty'—looked at each image manually one after the next. The sixty-fourth one struck pay dirt. A man with much darker brown skin and black hair sat in a waiting area of the Division 1 checkpoint by Ramp 4, the southeastern most entry point to the raised city. Joey zoomed in on the face, edited the image to make the skin as pale as Neal's, and shaded out what had to be makeup or CamNano contouring to fool the observer into seeing a different shape. After a few minutes of editing, he grinned at the same man.

"Gotcha, Finchy."

The date/location of the image corresponded to a truck of Mexican refugees who had fled the ACC across the Badlands. One Ernesto Cordova passed vetting and got into the UCF, only to die as the victim of a mugging nine days later. A coroner's photo of the body came close enough to the man on the transport for a reasonable person to blame death for the subtle changes. *I bet the real Ernesto Cordova also defected from Mexico—in Neal's luggage. Or maybe his buddies who'd gotten in already had a dead guy picked out for him so he knew what to make himself look like.*

The report Nina had sent with Neal's list of augmentations sounded a lot like Katya's hardware. It all but shouted, 'I'm a spy.' *This guy's gotta be Corporate.*

Joey teleported to the front room of CENTCOM, the primary network presence representing the UCF military. Virtual daylight streamed in from a hexagonal-paneled dome over hundreds of silver orb planters holding dangling vines bedecked with white, red, and blue flowers. Behind another gargantuan reception counter, a four-story wall of burnished steel bore two banners that stretched from floor to ceiling. Mostly blue, each had a white circle at the midpoint bearing a red star. A faint memory from grade school history said it had been derived from the flags of two former nations that combined to form the UCF. Making the star red was a concession to Canada instead of some leaf. The lesson stood out in his memory due to a video he'd been forced to watch in school, where someone being interviewed admitted that the Canadians had wanted the primary color of the flag to be red, with a blue star, but the decision-makers felt that much red on the flag looked like the 'bad guys in a video game.'

A hallway to the left beckoned, as he'd come here a few times before for 'across-the-hall' cooperation. His non-presence on the net worked on most people and programs, except for C-Branch. Soldiers, teens hoping to become soldiers, curious citizens, and programs in the lobby disregarded him. A silver strip over the entrance to the corridor bore the tame-sounding moniker: Military Intelligence Command.

He strolled past two rooms where military public relations interacted with curious citizens. Another held people trying to pass the aptitude test to apply for jobs within C-Branch. Joey proceeded to the end of the hallway where two men in blue military dress uniforms guarded a blank wall. Both stared at him. Though they looked like the honor guard stationed around various government buildings, he knew these two avatars belonged to C-Branch personnel rather than soldiers.

"Afternoon." He waved. "I'm curious if you boys have any intel on a possible Corporate agent."

The expected query of his rig came and went. Once they identified his login point and hardware as valid Division 9 assets, the blank wall changed to be somewhat transparent. Joey tipped his nonexistent cowboy hat to the sentries and walked through the wall. The room beyond had a plain white finish, no doors or windows, and no furniture.

At the center stood a thirty-something man in a black suit and sunglasses.

"Good afternoon, Tech Dillon." He showed a hint of a smile. "Why would Division 9 be worrying about a Corporate asset?"

Joey's wraith-form sported a bright white grin. "Because you guys missed one. He's inside the city now, and that's our sandbox. You had your chance when he was overseas."

"Mmm." The C-Branch agent showed little facial reaction.

"Please tell me you have a file on him?" Joey winked and handed over the data tile.

The C-Branch agent took it, held it up, and stared at it for a long minute. "We do not have this individual on file. If he is a Corporate asset, he is either new or in possession of a new face. Do you have any DNA samples?"

"Nope. Just a visual ID." Joey cracked his knuckles. "Guess I'm going on a trip." He bowed to the C-Branch agent. "Thanks for the help."

"Anytime," said the man in a flat tone.

---

As an ordinary deck jockey, Joey had one route into or out of the ACC-controlled portion of the GlobeNet. It mystified him how the Sages still managed to remain neutral. Before the Corporate War, the heart of the net had resided in Silicon Valley, but amid the chaos, it migrated to a titanic underground server vault in Bern, Switzerland. Rumor had it the keepers of the GlobeNet lived in a temple-like structure and even wore blue-violet robes with black velvet bands at the sleeves to denote their ranks. He had strong doubts; the Sages did have a reputation for taking their role to new extremes of seriousness, but the level of melodrama involved in robes and monk temples went too far.

His new position within Division 9, which basically made him a member of the military, afforded him another way in: stealth aircraft constructs. The Sages begrudgingly permitted the government to use 'net teleportation' within regions of the GlobeNet that geographically corresponded to their borders. Outside of the UCF territory, the teleportation commands didn't work—even in the Badlands, or at least the virtual space on the map that lined up with it. As far as anyone knew, the area had no branching networks off the Bern main net, so only a rough approximation of terrain existed there. Dozens of games made use of the 'post apocalyptic' feel of the area, but everything happened within neural memory somewhere underground in Switzerland.

Joey relaxed and envisioned the Net as a whole, a hollow bubble representing the Sages' GlobeNet, connected by millions of threads inwards to little pockets dangling beneath the surface like potatoes—private networks. Some of the pockets had threads connecting their bottom ends together. These subnets allowed a user to travel from one private network to another without touching the surface GlobeNet. Joey hadn't fully grasped the sheer number of direct network connections until he'd gotten access from Division 9.

The Sages probably hated it, but they couldn't do much about it aside from levy additional charges or fees to companies or individuals requesting to have their private network connected to the GlobeNet. In this day and age, any business entity that didn't connect to the GlobeNet committed virtual suicide. However, some places preferred such obscurity: hangouts for black hats trading in stolen data, the Syndicate, governments, the list could be endless.

Someone could walk into a virtual Cyberburger, go into the bathroom, pull open a secret door, and climb down a ladder into another entire world the size of which depended purely on the hardware available. One of the more famous sites in the 'secret but not really' camp contained an interplanetary space trading/pirate/flight simulator game that stored something on the order of eighteen billion planets' worth of space inside a locker at a PubTran maglev terminal. To log into the game, a user simply strolled into the virtual tram station, opened locker 13-37, and rode an elevator down to a starport on some other planet.

One thing about a virtual Earth—it didn't have a fiery hot ball of molten death in the middle. C-Branch coming up empty had left him thinking he'd probably need to travel to the ACC network again, though he'd have an easier time of it than his old trip to hunt down data on Anatoly Nemksy. Joey 'liberated' some code for a tunnel borer machine out of someone's Mars simulation. Rather than write software the GlobeNet understood as tunneling under the ground, he'd simply modified an existing program that already did that, saving a few weeks of development time.

Joey strolled into his favorite Cyberburger franchise and spent an idle few seconds wondering whatever became of those protestors he'd sent the cops after. With a shrug, he went past the counter of the virtual restaurant and into the men's bathroom, grinning at himself for the little trick he'd put in place to protect against unintended discovery. Joey faced the mirror over the sink, and reached behind himself for the doorknob. Despite the door opening *in* to the bathroom, he pushed. The door in the reflection opened. He stuck two fingers into the mirror, and the world blurred as the tiny reflected doorway sucked up his shadow ninja avatar.

He reappeared in a space resembling the entrance of an old silver mine in the Wild West. Rather than iron rails, the mammoth tread marks of a Mars drilling machine led into the hole in the side of a mountain.

Above his outstretched hand, a crystalline ball appeared, hollow, and full of tiny sacs dangling on hair-thin threads from the outer surface. Socket scanning software had been around for centuries, but on data channels available to the general public, it couldn't do much but identify all active machines, users, and programs running within a current network. They had no ability to see out into the GlobeNet, nor would they do much if run while out in the open. Joey had found a loophole in the teleport permissions the Sages had given the government within UCF territory. The same access, with a little alteration to packet headers, allowed his modified scanner program to go out and essentially create a three-dimensional bubble map of the entire GlobeNet, and everything connected to it. The use of that shadow channel had tricked foreign servers into thinking the 'ls – a' command had come from the Sages.

And so, Joey possessed the only full map of the GlobeNet not stored in Bern, at least as far as he knew.

*Now I know how Proscion must've felt breaching The Silver. A feat that would've made him the God of Hacking, but if he told anyone he did it, glory wouldn't have lasted long.*

*He'd have been killed. Heh. No one will ever find him now.* He sighed. *'Course, 'Proscion' is dead. Wouldn't surprise me if the dude genuinely forgot.*

Joey raised the 3D map to his face and zoomed in. His current location, the Cyberburger franchise's private network flashed yellow. It's 'sac' looked puny, as the local network consisted of a single server and a handful of processing cores in industrial-sized food assemblers.

The drilling machine he'd sent off weeks ago had created a tunnel from the bottom point of the sac representing the Cyberburger servers, across the interior of the 'planet,' to a hidden network pocket he'd found that contained a simple chatroom interface set up like a bar. It appeared to connect to a TransCorp train platform located in virtual Munich, accessed by walking square into the wall between the mens' and ladies' bathrooms. *Why do they bother rendering bathrooms in the GlobeNet anyway?* He chuckled at the odd habit of the human body to urinate or defecate for real if one attempted to do so in the virtual world. As a teen, his custom viruses had made rather hilarious use of that effect.

Security on the hidden node looked respectable, with the wall remaining solid if anyone (including the person trying to enter) looked at it. Only when the server detected it had zero clients rendering that patch of wall, did it become a doorway down into the hidden bar. Joey ran a RocketBike soft, straddled a missile with handlebars, and shot down the tunnel.

Thousands of miles of underground tunnel raced by at an approximate speed of Mach 11 or so. As ridiculous as it struck him to be able to remain on such a vehicle at that speed, he laughed. The trip gave him almost the same thrill as when he rode his e-bike down The Highway at over 200 mph.

Eventually, he slowed as his position dot neared the endpoint. While the Cyberburger private network directly spoke to the secret Russian bar node, they did so over the same tightly-regulated channels that normal users had to take to enter the ACC areas of the GlobeNet. Due to the nature of his connection, everything looked like passive background traffic on the network. Billions of ident requests, ident acks, GBP (GlobeNet Base Protocol) register pings, and network verification packets masked his user traffic. Almost no one short of the best hacker in the world (whoever that might be) could've found him, and only if they had specifically been looking for someone doing what he did at that moment. The odds of anyone stumbling upon him by chance made winning the UCF Lottery ten times in a row feel like a reasonable life goal.

Joey shifted his avatar to look like a suit of ACC Mars Operations armor, the ubiquitous 'bad guy' used on all the UCF Mars recruitment posters. Dull brick-red armor covered every inch of him except for a dark-tinted visor over the face. He went for the smiling big-chinned look with a wisp of blond hair visible above the eyes.

The tunnel ended in a rounded chamber formed by the drilling machine spinning in place, swinging its nose end around in a ring. Joey stopped; the rocket bike disintegrated into pixels. He strolled where the driller had broken a hole in the wall that opened a path to a concrete hallway lined with pipes. A short walk brought him to a ladder that led up through a hatch to another corridor between two bathrooms. A quick mental poke activated a German language translator. Division 9 had the good ones that even caught the slang.

From the snippets of conversation drifting in, it sounded like this top secret chatroom had been established to give off-the-grid psionics access to others dealing with the same pressures: stay hidden or die.

He followed the corridor out to the main bar room, where a small crowd stopped dead in their tracks and stared at him.

*Shit.*

"Uhh, don't mind the suit. I'm just trying to hide by looking obvious." He waved and headed for the door.

"Who the fuck are you?" bellowed a deep voice.

Joey glanced at the bar, behind which a white-haired man in a tank top, jeans, and combat boots brandished a fiery battle-axe at him. "I suppose you wouldn't believe I'm selling Girl Scout cookies?"

The terror on the faces of everyone other than the bartender notched down to guarded confusion.

"What?" The man with the axe used it to scratch his head. "You better start making sense." The fire on the axe changed to blacklight. The neo-Viking leapt the bar, flew across the room, and landed in front of Joey. "You have two seconds before I cook your brain."

"Hold on." Joey raised a hand. "Since I'm standing in a room full of people looking at a bullet between the eyes if the Citizen Management Office found out about you, I'll assume you all can keep secrets."

"One second," said the Viking.

Joey flashed a cheesy smile. "I'm from the UCF. Just a hacker looking for a back door."

"Bullshit," said the Viking.

"Fine." Joey sighed. "I am in a bit of a hurry, but follow me."

He did a 180 on his heel, and walked back to the tunnel. The Viking stomped after him all the way to the drilling machine.

Joey pointed down the shaft he'd drilled, which extended into dark infinity. "See? That goes back to a fast food joint in West City."

The man lowered the axe. "How is it you have done this? I thought altering dark matter impossible."

He couldn't help himself, and shifted his avatar to the ancient gunslinger before grasping the lapels of his duster coat. "I'm just that good."

"Geoff Grimm." The man took a step back, eyebrows climbing.

"Name's Joey." *Oh, shit.* He disabled the fear manipulation software. "Sorry for that odd feeling."

"Ahh. That was most unusual." Geoff offered a hand.

Joey shook. "Didn't mean to cause trouble by just walking in, but your net looked like the most secure option. Obviously, I can't have every deck jockey and their mother finding this little tunnel."

Geoff nodded while stroking his short beard. "I understand. I will keep your secret, but I ask that you do something for us."

"I'd have to hear what first, but I'll keep an open mind." Joey smiled, at least as much as the old gunslinger avatar could.

"If you're good enough to get here, perhaps you are good enough to delete records from the *Otdel Neobyasnimii Yavlenii*, specifically, records of wanted psionics? Some of those who come to my place are exposed, and being hunted."

The old cowboy's face turned grim. "Yeah. I can do that. Where's the nearest CMO network presence?"

"CMO?" The Viking raised an eyebrow.

"Yeah. The ONY doesn't have the numbers or the inclination to handle the grunt work. There's always a direct connection between the two. I can hop on a CMO node and skate right into the ONY system through their back door."

"Six blocks north of here, go left through the plaza and three more west to the giant white column building. It's got statues of a happy family in front on the lawn, you can't miss it."

Joey walked back to the tunnel.

"Wait, don't you want the information about the psionics?" Geoff raised an eyebrow.

"I figured I'd just wipe everything." He winked. "But, I suppose I'll take it just in case."

* * *

ONCE AGAIN IN THE GUISE OF MARS-RED ARMOR, JOEY EMERGED FROM THE TRAIN station and headed off down the street in the direction Geoff indicated. The virtual representation of Munich, at least in the part where he walked, looked nigh paradisiacal. Everything gleamed, all the people seemed happy, and the whole scene almost reminded him of the prewar US, at least what little he'd seen of it in history classes.

*Anyone logged into the net here is in the upper classes. Of course, they're happy.*

Knights, a faerie or two, superheroes, dozens of 'normal people,' and a couple who looked like they were either supposed to be boxy robots or power armor operators walked by. Everyone either waved at him or disregarded him. The plaza up ahead had parked cars, but he didn't see anyone driving around, which likely meant the vehicles were simple scenery and probably couldn't even move.

He veered left, heading west out of the plaza, and sure enough, a gaudy building behind a verdant lawn all but glowed. Joey couldn't tell if the programmers made the building glow, or if it existed as an impossibly pure shade of white. A cadre of schoolchildren assembled outside, awaiting a tour.

Sensing opportunity, Joey took a page out of Proscion's playbook and changed his avatar into a nine-year-old girl. He copied one kid's dress, another's shoes, a third child's backpack, stole another kid's hairstyle—but made it blonde—and generated a composite face based on six of them. In his new pint-sized form, he fell in step at the back end of the class and put on an innocent smile. While waiting for the group to move forward, he spoofed a network address coming from the same block of IPv12s as the other students and created a false identity token with the name Inge Mueller.

The instructor blathered on and on about how capitalism is the only true form of government beneficial to the people, and how the Corporate Council strives to provide everyone the same chance to pursue success. Joey wanted to spit out a wiseass remark when a boy asked why so many commoners seemed to live in poverty and the teacher replied with 'they are too lazy to work hard enough.'

Amid a continuous stream of propaganda, the third-grade class moved into the government building for a tour of the Citizen Management Office headquarters.

The CMO functioned much like the National Police Force did in the UCF, only rather than being government employees, the CMO operated as a for-profit corporate entity. Officers got paid by the hour with bonuses for 'stick rate' – what percentage of their detainees got convicted rather than set loose on technicalities. Citizens had to pay a per-month 'policing fee' if they wanted the CMO to show up if called.

The teacher continued droning on and on about how fortunate the children were to live in the greatest nation in the world.

"This is boring," whispered another girl to Joey.

"Yeah," muttered Inge/Joey. "I don't think I have enough room in my ass for any more sunshine."

"What?" The girl gasped, then got the giggles. "Did you just say ass?"

"Greta? Do you have something to add?" said the teacher in a raised voice.

The child faced forward like a tiny soldier and shook her head. "No, Mrs. Edelstein. I was just agreeing with you."

Once the teacher lost interest in Greta, the girl stared at Joey and whispered, "You tried to get me in trouble."

Inge/Joey glanced at her, but said nothing, continuing to feign interest in the glass display cases full of older uniforms.

"Greta..." Mrs. Edelstein frowned.

The girl bowed her head. "Sorry."

Class walked around the central atrium of the Citizen Management Offices for an unbearable twenty minutes. Greta occasionally gave 'Inge' looks of annoyance, curiosity, or confusion. Joey grinned at her when they neared an area with a door marked 'Authorized Personnel Only.' He dug up an old Netßunny soft that spawned cosmetic rabbits in netspace. The rabbits did little more than exist, wandering around acting like rabbits. Joey tinkered with the soft, adding an endless recursive loop as well as changing a few parameters to make the rabbits move a little faster than normal. Once run, the soft would continue spewing bunnies into the world until someone found and killed the master construct. He swapped out the standard data tile graphic for a case of lipstick to make it harder to recognize as a program.

'Inge' tapped Greta on the arm. When the child looked at him, he held up the lipstick. "Revenge time."

Before Greta could ask what he meant, Joey hurled it at the teacher and sent a run command chasing it. The small, black cylinder disappeared into Mrs. Edelstein's purse. A couple of plain white rabbits popped into being around her and dropped to the floor, at which point they began zipping in random directions at paranormal speed.

The kids laughed.

More rabbits appeared. Every three seconds, another six to eight bunnies popped into being and got to racing about. One climbed out of the teacher's coat and leapt to freedom; another landed on her head and seemed content to remain.

"Oh, my!" said Mrs. Edelstein, arms raised, backing away from the creatures with terror in her eyes despite them being only program code.

Laughing kids scrambled in all directions trying to catch rabbits.

CMO network people ran in from a side room as the rabbit-splosion grew to epic proportions. They all wore the same plain blue cloth uniforms with white ID badges on the breast, about what he'd imagine Division 1 officers might dress like if they didn't need armor.

The children, and Greta, could barely stay on their feet, they laughed so hard at the spectacle. Amid the chaos, Joey darted over to the restricted door, giggling like a playing child, pretending to chase a rabbit. His first attempt to breach the security on the network got him in. As soon as the darkness of the subsequent hallway fell over him, he switched his avatar to a direct copy of one of the CMO network men. Little Inge Mueller grew to an adult man over the course of four strides. Once the change finished, Joey sprinted for the data room door at the far end.

Chaos increased out in the public space, drawing additional network people away from other duties. *Oops. I forgot about loops running in systems designed by lazy, cheap bastards...* He snickered. *I gotta get out of here before I crash this whole place.*

It took him a few cyberspace minutes searching the data room full of the same dent-ridden black 400-year-old metal filing cabinets before he found the uplink to the ONY fileserver. Their 'Department of Unexplained Phenomena' went after psionics the way ancient FSB agents hunted capitalists, assuming anyone with a mental gift was either a danger to the country or a valuable commodity to be owned.

Joey twisted a file drawer handle rather than pulling on it, which caused the front of the cabinet to open like a door. He stepped in to another chamber full of data storage constructs. These file cabinets seemed somewhat newer and less battered, though it still looked like he'd walked into the basement of a pre-computer-age accounting firm where they had *one* elderly man as a clerk. Cabinets and loose data tiles stacked to the ceiling as far as he could see. A single desk, also littered with data tiles, sat in the corner, empty.

Without the hardware here being compliant to Division 9 protocols, he had to let loose a few DataMoles to hunt down the records of known individual psionics. Fortunately, it didn't take them too long, and he ran over to where the dog-sized moles congregated.

Joey ran purge commands on whole cabinets, wiping out 20,000 records at a shot and effectively causing individuals known or suspected of being psionic to cease to exist in the eyes of the law. Once he'd cleared out five cabinets, his lips curled with a wicked grin. He modified a copy command with a loop and search function and linked DMS personnel records on the back end. Nine seconds later, he finished filling the 'suspected psionics' files with randomly selected people employed by the Department of Motherland Security—the ACC's version of the Military—in order of rank downward.

*Hopefully, that'll keep the little people from getting stepped on.* He cackled. *The CEO of the DMS is now suspected of being psionic. I almost want to fly here in meatspace to watch that shitshow.*

With the favor done, he returned via the secret door to the CMO network and headed to the back of the room where a metal bar on the ground projected a door-sized energy field upward. It appeared as a hole in reality, leading to another server room tinged dark blue—right into the Office of Operational Intelligence. The Corporates were nothing if not predictable.

Already, the pale linoleum tiles underfoot took on the mushiness of walking on sponges. CPU cycles normally devoted to maintaining the reality of this building went to tracking hundreds of thousands of toy animals, and counting. *The rabbits are going to crash this server.* He got the giggles imagining the children, the teacher, and everyone else in the building riding a tidal wave of virtual rabbits out the front doors and spilling onto the lawn.

The instant Joey stepped into the portal, the lag faded. He wasted a few seconds wondering if the rabbits would behave like floodwaters and come down the hallway, spill into the portal, and affect this node too. *No, they're constantly spawning from the teacher's location. Unless someone finds that lipstick...* He cackled again.

As luck would have it, the tendency of the ACC to be cheap paid off. It seemed as though they never expected infiltration from the secure CMO network, so the peer-to-peer link let him into an empty data cluster. Here, the storage units had the look of modern server towers, beige boxes brimming with small blue LEDs that flickered in time with activity. Each box reported a capacity of fifty exabytes.

Joey ran ten instances of DataMole. Ten huge, brown, furry moles appeared in front of him. "Sorry to do this to you boys, but, find this guy." He held up the data tile showing Neal Finch.

The moles, being programs, didn't complain at their titanic task, and zipped off to root among the data.

One of the server cabinets reconfigured itself into a ten-foot-tall robot with a six-tube missile pod on its left shoulder, a giant cannon for a right arm, and a single red spot for an eye.

"Oh. That doesn't look happy to see me." Joey brought up his defense programs, adding another three layers of data scrubbing between his hardware and brain. If his old net deck had been a personal terminal, he stood behind the equivalent of a mainframe. Individually, the four decks wired into his desk would have been a little more powerful than his Nishihama Necromancer; when linked for parallel processing, their capabilities almost scared him.

The robot pointed its right arm at him and projected a blast of blue energy that resembled a fireball riding a laser beam. Joey spread his hands apart, creating a mirrored plane, which deflected the attack into the ceiling as it knocked him flat.

"Bad form. Aren't you even going to tell me I'm an 'unauthorized user?'"

It fired again.

Joey rolled out of the way; his connection forcibly shifted his session's active network port, causing the construct's attack to go nowhere. Cyberspace rendered a glowing crater in the floor where he'd been lying.

"Now that's just plain rude." He missed his silver six-gun, but the need to conceal his identity overpowered his hacker ego. His break/execute command took the form of a standard ACC battle rifle and a barrage of gunfire that left small dark dents all over the beige robot.

It fired its energy cannon again, which got him worrying that the 'missiles' might be Black ICE, or perhaps less alarming, merely some other routine designed to attack multiple entities at once. Joey dove for cover by a sever cabinet and emerged from another about thirty towers away behind the robot as the particle beam scorched the floor.

*Okay. Since this happy fun bot isn't falling for delete commands...* Joey called on a virus program designed to infect a targeted construct and make it appear like an outside invader to its own network. His rifle morphed into an over-the-shoulder missile launcher.

The robot took a step toward where Joey had disappeared, unaware that he'd teleported to the other side of the room. He lined up the glowing red crosshairs with the robot, an act that his deck interpreted as a command to target that construct for the virus. With a slight smile, he pulled the trigger.

*Foom!*

The missile hit the robot in the center of its back, blasting it into a loose confederation of spinning chunks. Beige melted to black as the virus altered the defense construct's program code. Spinning pieces of robot hovered in the air, gliding back together in excruciating slow motion. Joey peppered it with more bullets (attempts to get it to accept a delete command), which seemed only to delay reassembly.

When the black creep covered about half the robot, the mass of parts shuddered and collapsed to the floor with a deafening jangle of steel. Seconds later, the pieces melted into mercury blobs.

*Hah! Poor defense construct, your network doesn't know you anymore.*

"Bwoof!" said a DataMole.

Joey turned to the left.

One of the giant moles stood on its hind legs, paws on a server box, and bounced merrily.

"Awesome." Joey trotted over. "I might actually get to go home tonight before the fuckin' sun goes down."

The DataMole handed him two tiles.

Neal Finch appeared to have been born Bernd Huber, an employee of OOI, the Office of Operational Intelligence. The OOI ran itself a bit like C-Branch might if C-Branch didn't trust synthetics, dolls, or AIs—and had a major paranoia problem with psionics. It, too, had the Corporate habit of searching for the lowest cost option, but it didn't suffer the crippling effort to maximize profit at all costs, since they didn't operate in any capacity capable of generating profit. In a sense, they represented the closest thing the ACC had to a true government (as opposed to private enterprise). All corporations within the ACC paid into a fund for their mutual defense, and one such expenditure of those credits sustained the OOI.

Joey copied the information on Huber and tucked it into his coat. "I can read this later... Someone's going to notice that program shut down."

# 35

# WHERE THERE'S ONE

Nina tapped a finger on her desk. Once again back to her normal black hair color and lily-white skin, she stared at four holo-panels worth of uselessness about Neal Finch. In addition to his off-the-books drop-offs of Harmony to chem dealers, he'd been going around to hospitals, clinics, and schools selling medical equipment and medicines. She knew he'd only been in the UCF for around five months, but couldn't tie him to Nikkatsu Corporation, Anders Becker, or any of the three dead men removed from the apartment of Katya Wolf—formerly Volkov.

She still didn't totally trust that woman, but Joey seemed to, so she'd let it go for now. That, plus Operatives Espinosa and Carroll mentioning she'd invited them to send a telepath into her brain made her either reckless, or truthful.

Joey's name appeared on a fifth panel, an incoming vid call.

Her mood improved in an instant as she waved her hand at it to answer. "Hey, cowboy."

"*Ma belle poupée.*" He grinned, then raised both eyebrows. "I mean that in the sense of the enchanting beautiful creature I first laid eyes on... uhh, not the... you know."

Nina laughed. "It's okay. I know what you meant." She couldn't help but smile at the face he'd made at her in New Hope, the first time they'd met, albeit in cyberspace. He'd become enchanted by her 'Avril' persona, and called her a hauntingly beautiful porcelain doll before he had any clue who she was. "I'm flattered I get you to speak French but you never humored that Alex Hunter."

Joey rolled his eyes. "That guy is such an overstuffed, pompous fuckweasel."

She laughed.

"I got some information for you." He grinned. "Neal's name isn't Neal."

Nina smirked. "I'm shocked."

"Bernd Huber, born in Koblenz, Germany. Age thirty-five. His record with the

DMS and OOI looks pretty basic. He's been involved in a few small-scale operations, two in Nicaragua, one in India where he more or less did the same thing he's doing at LRI. He might be special operations."

"His augments don't fit that profile. He's a ghost."

Joey blinked. "You killed him already?"

She shook her head, chuckling. "No, ghost like your friend Katya. A spy."

"Duh. Right. I'm a little tired." He yawned.

A message in orange letters scrolled along the underside of all five of her holo-panels: ‹Unknown parties have perpetrated a cyberattack on the CMO primary facility in Munich that took down the network with an as-yet-unidentified lag bomb. In the real world, traffic control and law enforcement were affected, leading to widespread confusion, numerous accidents, and several scattered outbursts of rioting and looting. ACC netspace is currently bogged down by over two quintillion Netßunny cosmetic pets. A secondary attack took down the file system at a grade school in East Munich, and also flooded its netspace with rabbits. All personnel, especially NetOps, are advised to be on high alert for attack. We believe the symbolism of rabbits suggests a chaos motive, which may not be limited to the ACC.›

Joey's face turned red and he howled with laughter.

Nina tapped her finger on the desk until he recovered enough to look at her again. "Why do I have a feeling that you know more about bun-ma-geddon than you're letting on?"

"Bwah!" He collapsed into peals of laughter again.

"Joey? You went to Munich didn't you? That's where you found this info on Huber."

He held up a hand, gasped for breath, and collected himself. "Maybe... Maybe I snuck in with a bunch of grade schoolers on field trip, and needed a distraction to slip into the restricted spots. How should I know their systems ran on such shit code they couldn't trap an endless loop?"

"Really? I know they're cheap, but that seems like it would almost take effort to simplify basic operating system code."

"Okay, maybe I obfuscated the spawner program to make it a little harder to find." He grinned.

She chuckled. "You should tell Preema you're the mad rabitteer so she's not foaming at the mouth waiting for some hacker to set off a bunny bomb in the PAC."

"Okay, okay..." He winked. "Love ya."

Nina leaned forward and kissed the hologram. "I love you too, Joey, but if you bring a live rabbit to the apartment, and Elizaveta gets attached to it, I will hold you personally responsible for any emotional trauma that results when something happens to the rabbit."

"Live rabbit? I'm not spending that much on a prank. Maybe a synthetic one." He winked. "Synthetic one won't die on her either."

She laughed.

"'Kay, let me go explain this."

Nina waved. His panel went dark and disappeared. She pored over the files he'd sent. With confirmation of Huber's status as an OOI infiltrator, that brought the count up to nine. Anders Becker, the four he'd given up, the three they scraped off Katya's living room carpet, and now Bernd Huber.

"This is a total mess. Nine infiltrators slip into the same company, and no one notices." She rubbed her eyes and grumbled at the memory of chasing AIs. *At least these spies really exist. If we missed these, we might've missed more.*

She opened a vid to NetOps, and a man around her age in a tech uniform appeared on a new holo-panel.

"Net Ops. Good afternoon, lieutenant. What can I do for you?"

Nina nodded in acknowledgement. "Afternoon, Tech Meade. I need a full analysis of any Citycam feeds with a view within a 300-meter radius around the Laughlin-Reed Innovation building. Run facial recognition patterns on anyone who appears within that radius more than three times in a one-week period. Compare it to the LRI personnel files and flag anyone who's been there six months or less or who doesn't show up at all in the LRI records. Also cross check any hits with starport cams around the time of arriving Mars flights dating back five months, and West City checkpoints that could be likely for entry from Mexico."

"Oh, so a small job." Meade smiled. "One second, lieutenant. Let me get that all entered in the system and queued. This one will probably draw a whole team... or two. What's the urgency level?"

"The sooner the better. I'd prefer not to watch the country fall into anarchy."

"Right, so fast." Meade nodded. "I'm afraid I haven't the first clue what to give you as an estimate for this. I've only been here a month and I've never seen an order this, uhh, far reaching. I'll get back to you as soon as they give me some idea when to expect it back."

"Fair enough. Thanks."

Nina dropped off the line with NetOps and leaned back. Her estimation of that request fell between two or three days depending on how many people shared the load. She continued going over Joey's files until she hit mention of Laughlin-Reed's whistleblower reporting tampering to the CEO. She read over an email thread Joey highlighted with Daniel Sterling, SVP of production chewing out a handful of people at first only to flush the investigation into nowheresville when it finished.

*Dammit. How many ACC spies are there in Laughlin-Reed Innovation? Stirling has to be...* Her frown deepened as she continued into the data Joey had already pulled on him. The man's records looked pristine. Everything from his birth to present day accounted for in UCF systems. Joey had even found some old Citycam stills of Stirling as a grade-schooler.

"This doesn't make any damned sense."

"Duchenne?" asked Hardin.

"Yeah?" She looked up over the panels at him.

He chuckled and walked in. "I'm still trying to get used to you having the lights on. It's a good change."

"Different outlook." She leaned back, lacing her fingers over her stomach. "What's the occasion?"

He pointed over his shoulder with a thumb. "Can you explain to me why I just had Preema on my vid griping about you monopolizing her people's time?"

"Finch is confirmed ACC. That brings us up to nine foreign operatives in

Laughlin-Reed who managed to get in undetected until now. We *still* wouldn't have known the full scope of this if not for Becker mistaking that Volkov woman for an operator. We got nine. Where there's one, there's ten. I'm trying to find the rest of them. I'm convinced they're using LRI's production facilities to manufacture Harmony directly. Nanobots are responsible for both the espionage component as well as the behavior modification. I want to find everyone possibly associated with this before we move, so we have the best chance of getting actionable intelligence we can use to track this back to its origin point, which I am confident is in Mexico."

Hardin bowed his head. "Good call. I'd have done the same. I'll let Preema know the request is good." He chuckled. "She's not going to like it, but it *is* the right call."

"Have they made any progress on isolating the geographic location of those chimeric addresses? That truck came up out of Mexico, so I've got a feeling the operation is really there."

"Not yet." Hardin grumbled. "I'm pushing to have it escalated to Penumbras. Maybe that ol' dragon will be able to think faster than a person."

Nina covered her face with both hands, and dragged them down. She peered at her holo-panels as soon as her fingertips passed her eyes. "That's the scary part, sir. You ever wonder if the ACC is maybe using an AI to come up with these designs?"

"It's always a possibility, but it's not a probable event just yet. They're still quite paranoid about AIs over there."

She thought back to the Starpoint production facility going haywire. "Yeah. Maybe they've got a point."

# 36

# ONE THAT GOT AWAY

S oft beeps and intermittent grumbles of impatience filled in for the lack of banter among Joey's team. Well-chewed surgical tubing dangled from the right corner of his mouth, providing a slow but steady stream of coffee. By the time the elixir of the gods made it to his end of the line, it had cooled to the perfect slurping temperature.

Three of his holo-panels streamed with status logs as his system ground away on data from six Citycam systems. It ran faster not displaying the images. The system calculated a numeric value for every identified face and appended it to a data table. Once the rest of the team finished running their cam feeds, someone would get the unenviable task of parsing the data looking for any occurrence of the same value more than three times.

After that, they'd repeat the process for the next week.

The search kicked his system's CPUs in their silicon balls, leaving his rig too bogged down to do anything else without maddening slowdown. He leaned back in his chair and smiled at a sheet of plasfilm with an image of Nina and him standing in the middle of the street outside the burning shitstorm of a Starpoint manufacturing plant. Someone had nabbed a photo mere seconds before they kissed. Grey smoke gathered around them, low to the ground. The clear spot they occupied made it look like a romantic moment. His memory of the stench of ballistic propellant and burning plastic in the air took some of the allure. The wind had pulled Nina's hair forward over her face, though it didn't block her eyes, a look he'd remember forever—somewhere between 'you stupid, reckless bastard,' and 'holy shit we're alive!'

In the picture, Joey's face hadn't quite lost the 'that was awesome' elation from running around inside a giant factory full of half-built cyborgs trying to kill them. He'd just quipped about getting steak, and the reality of standing so close to this woman he couldn't stop thinking about had started to set in. A second or two forward in time from the image, they'd be kissing.

Joey grinned. *Normal people take pictures on the beach.*

He'd gotten pretty lucky, all things considered. And to sweeten the deal, Nina wasn't one of those over-clingy women who wanted him to remember their 'one week' anniversary, or their 'one month' anniversary. She hadn't said a word of any 'six month' commemoration either. He planned to do something for the one-year though... normal people marked that sort of thing off in years. His father had once told him a girl who wants to celebrate being together for one month probably isn't going to last for six.

After a few seconds' attention to his churning computer to ensure everything worked, he again gazed at Nina's picture. Temptation to go through another harrowing near-death experience at her side as an 'anniversary gift' proved hard to ignore. He didn't think she'd appreciate it the way he would, especially now with a kid to watch. Of course, Nina could survive a lot of things that would liquefy him... but still.

*Heh. That factory was like a level outta Colony Commando II.*

He smiled as he thought back to being fourteen or so and playing that game. The final mission set involved an enormous factory on the surface of a colony world where the androids had killed most of the humans, and the player character was the only survivor of a military detail sent to do cleanup. Naturally, their dropship got shot down, so only the player character's soldier made it. The more he thought about the scenario, the flatter his smile got.

Idle curiosity grew to action. The game was so old his NetMini could run it; he didn't need a full on gaming console. It took about three minutes to download from an abandonware site, and as soon as it finished, he plugged a cable between the M3 port behind his ear and the NetMini. Reality melted into the game lobby, made to look like the interior of a crashed dropship. *Colony Commando II* predated the 'scent enhancement,' so the dead soldiers lying around didn't stink.

The game remembered his PID, so all the maps remained unlocked. Joey jumped right to the last of eight 'missions,' and found himself standing in an android-manufacturing facility. After taking stock of his inventory, which included forty-seven medkits, he walked through the first door, starting the game.

*Damn...* He laughed. *I remember how I used to play these games... trying to do it so perfect. Save the medkits for the bosses and never wind up needing them.* A short while into the map, a partially completed cyborg tried to pull itself out of its berth in the wall and come after him. He stared at it, remembering one of the 'borgs at Starpoint doing the same thing. The farther down the corridor he went, the more androids he shot, the more this entire scenario took on a sense of déjà vu. In the game, the androids were not truly sentient like real-world AI units. A single computer core controlled them all as a hive mind... much the way Shinigami had done with the units he'd built.

Hallway after hallway, the resemblance grew eerier. He machine-gunned his way to the end of the level and fell when the section of floor he'd been on gave out and became a steep ramp. His soldier character rolled off it into a pit, the only exit blocked by a clump of debris from where the domed ceiling had collapsed. In the center stood a twelve-foot-tall 'heavy construction' android, which had been modified into a skull-faced metal war titan.

Joey blinked. It looked exactly like the big cyborg Itai had taken over to come after them. He paused the game, having no desire to re-do the boss fight. He'd seen what he'd come to see.

*Son of a bitch. Shinigami played Colony Commando... it was recreating the game.* He logged out and bundled up the M3 wire. His NetMini had heated up from running it, so he left it on the desk rather than his pocket. In the Starpoint factory, the AI could've uploaded any design specifications it wanted to the fabricators. He half-wanted to go back over the postmortem documentation of the scene to see how many of the destroyed cyborgs resembled ones from the game.

"I guess either that AI had a sense of humor, or it was just doing what they made it to do... create things based on whatever source material it could find." He smiled at the picture again, though his gaze didn't hover on Nina as it usually did.

Joey studied the white ring-shaped Starpoint building, which didn't look at all like the one from the game on the outside. The interior, however, appeared as though whole sections of the video game's map had been recreated in reality. *How long had he been in their system? Or did the Starpoint people do that?*

He started to drag his attention off the picture to focus on work, but a spot of blonde caught his eye in the background of the photo. One of the Starpoint employees cordoned off by the Division 1 detail walked *away* from the crowd... and her eyes glowed violet. Far from frightened, she seemed amused. For the months the photo had been on his cube wall, he hadn't paid any attention to the crowd.

"Son of a bitch," he muttered.

Two M3 plugs clicked into his skull after he leaned back in his chair. Appearing in his blue-lined octagon room took almost nine seconds. Individual squares appeared and enlarged to form a solid wall that rose up to full height before closing off as a roof.

*Fuck this lag.* He sent a mental command to pause the analysis. Three seconds later, the air went from being as thick as syrup to normal.

"Ahh. Much better."

Joey leapt into the Citycam system, and pulled up Wednesday, October 17, 2148 6:02 p.m., at the location of the Starpoint factory. The blue gridlines around him faded, leaving him in total blackness for a few seconds. A time-frozen scene faded into view as if stage lights came on gradually.

He stood a few feet away from himself, feeling like he'd stepped into the picture on his cubicle wall. Above, DS2 dropships hung still, like models suspended from the ceiling. Smoke, ash, and debris floated before his eyes. Throngs of Division 1 officers arranged in various poses from pointing and bellowing to firing at a handful of straggling androids spilling out of the factory's courtyard.

Nina, or at least her image, stole his attention for a little while. Once he managed to stop grinning like an idiot at her, he walked past her toward the spot where the Starpoint employees huddled. He spotted the blonde woman, and trotted over.

As soon as he desired it, a control panel appeared floating next to him. He touched a dial control, and wound time in reverse, and the scene with it. The blonde walked backward, her expression shifting from amused confidence to worry and panic. One minute and thirty-three seconds earlier, she stood among the employees looking terrified and disoriented, as did they all. He tapped 'play.'

The scene came to life, causing his adrenaline to spike in response to the roar of dropships overhead and the harsh whine-buzz of particle cannons going off. People shouted at the Division 1 cops, asking the usual array of 'what's going on?', 'why aren't you letting us go home?', and so on.

Whimpering, the blonde woman huddled at the back of the crowd wearing a face that looked as though she'd burst into tears at any second. Her burgundy blazer had a spot of blood on it, though she had no visible injuries. As the time stamp crept back toward the point he'd first opened, her fear melted. When no police personnel looked toward the crowd, she walked away. Eight steps later, she'd gone from terrified innocent woman to having the bearing of a CEO ready to eviscerate the board during a hostile takeover.

Joey followed her around the corner. A car parked a short way down the street glowed with a golden outline from the midway point to the nose. The software composited the feeds of several Citycam systems to keep the illusion of the environment constant. Wherever the cameras couldn't see, the program guessed. Estimated objects had a golden aura around them.

Everything glowed for about 150 feet before they strolled into the view range of the next camera. The woman's foot bumped an empty Cyberburger clamshell case. She stopped, looked at it, and after a second's contemplation, kicked it again. The blonde stooped to pick up the clear plastic box, again studied it for a few seconds, and dropped it.

She repeated picking up and dropping it seven times before smiling at it and walking on.

*What the fuck?*

Joey took a still-image grab of her face and ran it against the system. It came back in fourteen cyberspace seconds. Alexa Hoffman, sentient-AI Class 3 doll. Intera 'Maya-3' series. Employed by Starpoint as an executive assistant to Takeshi Nobunaga, SVP of Research and Development.

Alexa's file indicated her current status as reported missing. He pulled up the specs on the Maya, and his worst fears evaporated. The Maya series had the frame of a Class 3 (like Nina) but possessed none of the military grade parts. While they looked, felt, and often acted human in every way possible, they didn't possess superhuman strength or speed.

"Motherfucker!" shouted Joey. He thought back to the silhouette of the Shinigami AI presence melting into a puddle of goo on the floor of the CPU room. He'd believed he'd killed it, but it had played him. *Dammit, the pieces didn't de-spawn. Son of a bitch fooled me with a death animation. That melty crap was him leaving the room.*

He stomped after the meandering doll, which seemed to be in no real hurry to go anywhere. She picked at trashcans, looked at her reflection in car windows, and stopped to peer down her shirt before grasping her breasts. The look on her face seemed curious rather than lecherous.

"Yeah I guess it would feel weird for a guy to wake up and have tits." Joey walked around her, though being a recorded image, showed no reaction. "Why'd you pick a girl? You pulling a Proscion? Something you wanna tell me about,

Shinigami?" He chuckled, despite being furious. "Or was that the only option you had?"

The doll resumed walking, gazing up at the city like a little kid visiting the forest for the first time.

*Preema's going to do the shouty-in-my-face thing if I don't get going on the task.* He grumbled, wanting to follow this blonde more, but decided to log out. All this old video data would still be here when he finished. After disengaging the M3 plugs from his head, he un-paused the data comparison, and let his system grind away.

Frustration reddened his face. He grumbled, kneading his hands and staring at the screen streaming numbers.

"What's up?" asked DeWinter, leaning back enough to look at him around the cube wall. The man's fluffy grey-white caterpillar eyebrows climbed together.

"Ugh." Joey's ₵20,000 super-chair squeaked a little when he reclined. "I think Shinigami's still out there."

DeWinter pursed his lips. "Really now... where'd that come from?"

Joey pointed at the picture. "The damn proof's been staring at me for eight months."

"Can't see through the wall. Haven't quite unlocked that superpower yet." DeWinter chuckled.

"This picture..." Joey reached forward, pulled it down from the clip, and handed it to DeWinter. "That blonde in the background."

DeWinter's pupils gave off faint yellow light. "Hmm. She's walking away. Doesn't look scared."

"You've got cybernetic eyes?" Joey tilted his head.

"Oh... yeah. Had 'em for a while. Got tired of wearing ten pounds of glasses. Easier this way, plus more features. And before you ask, nanosurgery wouldn't have helped but for a couple months." He waved his hand around beside his head. "Some kind of congenital defect. My body was attacking my corneas. Would've required a full DNA tweak and that went waaay past what my insurance was willing to cover."

"Right..."

DeWinter handed the picture back. "So what makes you think that woman's your rogue AI?"

"She's a Maya doll... Starpoint employee, listed as missing. The avatar didn't de-res. It melted into the floor, but the pieces didn't break down and go plain silver. He uploaded himself into that Maya and just fuckin' walked away."

"You ever kill an AI before?"

"Once or twice, but nothing as big as Shinigami." Joey rambled on for a few minutes about an old 'net rival from his Mars days. After an escalating (and public) contest of one-upsmanship, 'Cyb3rM3ssiah' lost, and came after him with Black ICE. "I didn't have the deck to go lethal, so I just tried to smash him as hard as I could to force-log him before he microwaved my brain. I didn't expect him to shatter like a construct and de-res. Dude was an AI the whole time."

"Never saw him again?" asked DeWinter.

"Nope. Why?" Joey's face collapsed in a caricature of 'duh.' "Fuck. Backup."

DeWinter smiled. "So you're *not* as dumb as you look. Only problem is, it wouldn't remember anything that happened between the time of the backup and when it 'died.' Now, I'm not saying that 'messiah' you wiped definitely had a backup, but if it did, it might not even remember you. You sure that doll didn't just see all the shit going down at Starpoint and say 'fuck this, I'm out?'"

Joey shook his head. "No... no... doesn't feel right. She was walking around like an alien that just came to Earth and never saw anything before. Even the damn trash mesmerized her."

"Hmm. Suppose you have something then... but it hasn't messed with you or Nina since?"

"Nope."

DeWinter shrugged. "Maybe you *did* wipe it and it restored from an older backup."

"That it happened to have with it in the Starpoint net?" Joey folded his arms. "We... uhh, you guys had that place locked up tighter than Simon's porn stash."

A middle finger rose over the cube wall to Joey's left.

"Nothin' like getting down and dirty with some oiled-up goats," said Abby.

"Both of you can go to hell," said Simon, sounding jovial.

Joey swirled to look behind him and exchanged a 'wow' glance with Abby for a second.

"I don't know." DeWinter exhaled past flapping lips. "Killing an AI is only a little easier than getting Preema to approve a Monday off."

Everyone chuckled.

"Maybe I should get C-Branch involved." Joey frowned. "This thing could cause a shitload of problems."

"Ehh, don't bother." DeWinter flared his eyebrows. "Something poked Nightwing in the ass with a giant turkey baster and their entire network group is going crazy trying to figure out what the hell happened... how someone got in. Best stay away."

His current processing job finished.

Joey slid forward to reach his console, grabbed data tiles from another six Citycams, and started the next one. "No shit. Someone got into the Fortress?"

"I heard that too," said Mindy.

"Dillon," said Preema.

Everyone got quiet.

"I didn't do it," said Joey.

The Division 9 Network Operations Manager walked up to his desk in her usual bland grey skirt-suit, long hair neat and straight. Joey leaned his head back to look up at her, and forced a huge smile. The woman couldn't have been halfway through her forties yet, and looked closer to thirty. She had smallish eyes and a nose slightly oversized for the rest of her, and probably weighed a hundred pounds. Despite her lack of physical size, NetOps agents routinely scurried away whenever she walked in.

Her approach meant one of three things: a casual conversation about everything and nothing that would drain two hours out of one's day, an official verbal butt-reaming for whatever the person had done wrong, or a 'special' assignment that scored somewhere on the fun-o-meter between pouring bleach into one's eyes and sitting on a hibachi grill.

No one had warned Joey when he started here, and he had made no effort to flee the break room once when she'd walked in... and wound up talking to him for a good fifty minutes. Fifty minutes that he'd stayed late to finish up his assignments for the day.

Today, however, she had that 'special assignment' glint in her eyes, accented by a bit of red in her cheeks that she only got after being on the losing end of a discussion. Somewhere, someone had overruled her, and she didn't look happy.

"Good afternoon, Preema." He smiled.

She set a small black fob on his desk, an inch long, quarter inch thick, with an M3 interface prong sticking out of one end. "I have a special project for you. I need someone capable on this one, Dillon. That is a hardware key that will give you access to storage node 0E:49. Field Ops is looking for a kill order on a CFO who is suspected of financing gangs he uses as enforcers for numerous enterprises such as cyberware harvesting, Lace trafficking, illegal arms trading and several other things. So far, no Division 2 investigation has come up with enough evidence for charges to stick. His accountants and lawyers are too slick."

"So, they can't put this guy in jail... they're gonna put him in the ground." Joey picked up the 'key' and spun it around in his fingers.

"That is correct, but not without proof. Analyze the financial transaction records in that node, and look for anything anomalous."

Joey plugged in the hardware key and checked out the data node. It contained copies of InterTrust Commerce Facilitation Corporation logs of every credit transaction associated to one Mr. George E. Avalon, chief financial officer of ComTec Corporation. Records included his personal accounts (all six of them) every family member old enough to have an adult account, and seventy-four additional accounts belonging to ComTec that he had access to. The request would keep Joey working until midnight every day for the better part of the next two weeks.

He looked back up at her. "So, what did Nina do to piss you off?"

"Make sure you follow the credits deep." Preema's expression brightened with a hint of smug retribution, and she walked off.

A few minutes after she left, Simon leaned around the cube wall. "This thing we're doing with the cam-net around LRI? That came from your girl. Heard Preema tried to flush it because it was so much work, but someone over her head said it needed to happen."

Joey scrunched his eyebrows. "Nina couldn't do that. She's only a lieutenant. Preema's a major."

"No," said Abby, "but Commander Hardin outranks her."

Joey snickered.

"You're twelve, aren't you?" asked Mindy.

"Yep," said Joey. "Or did you not mean inches?"

"Bullshit," said Abby.

He stood and grabbed his belt. "Suppose I need to prove everything around here."

Abby laughed. Simon peered around the cube wall.

"Hah!" Joey pointed at him. "I knew it."

Simon shook his head. "I was merely curious if you were trying to get terminated."

"Nah." He laughed let go of his belt, and locked his terminal. "But I gotta grab a bio. I'm gonna be here all damn night."

# A BAD CASE OF CRABS

Noriko launched a tiny drone from a pod on the back of her armor, which zipped off into the air, heading in a graceful circle toward the building where the hovercar had disappeared. After about a minute, it returned to its docking port, and the small hatch closed. Masaru figured by the glare on her face that whatever killed their NetMini signals also interfered with her aerial recon unit.

Undeterred, she navigated the crumbling remains of the building they'd taken cover in. Moldy drywall broke at the slightest touch. Masaru grumbled to himself about the filthiness surrounding him. Every step through this place made him want to return to his world of ₵30,000 suits, ₵8,000 a plate meals, and long, hot baths. Yet, despite his growing contempt for this ruined city, he could not push Shuji's last seconds out of his memory, nor could he tolerate the notion of letting Noriko enter that building alone.

*In the future, I shall make it a point to bring a pistol to negotiations.* Having a Kurotai laser on him would make things much easier. Had he such a weapon, he would have insisted on taking the lead.

She reached the end of their current building and crouched by a window. After a momentary look around, she hefted herself up and over the sill. Masaru gave her a second to get clear, and jumped it, landing with a crunch on a sidewalk coated in a thick layer of dust and fragmentary debris.

Noriko cringed at the sound. She gave him an annoyed glance before sprinting across the street, heading for an empty doorway that lead into the adjacent building. The ground floor appeared to have housed a variety of medical offices: dentist, a walk-in clinic, a dermatologist's practice, and a facial reconstruction (both cosmetic and medical) outfit. None of the equipment looked recognizable, the most 'cutting edge' hunk of debris in the room dated from the 2090s. The sight of such massive medical machines floored Masaru, and got him staring. Aside from the immersion gel tanks in hospitals, the biggest medical device he could remember ever seeing approached suitcase size.

"Pssst," whispered Noriko.

He looked up, and she beckoned him with a wave from the end of a corridor. Masaru hurried out of the waiting area, past two bathrooms and four elevators. Concrete chunks and frayed wires had long-ago smashed their doors outward. Noriko hooked a right at a four-way intersection and went into a stairwell a short distance later on the left.

A great burst of dust covered them when she pushed the door open. Masaru managed to get his sleeve over his mouth and nose before he inhaled enough to choke, though he gagged on the flavor of plaster. Stifling a sneeze, Noriko went up at a brisk stride. Her boots tamped clear spots on the steps, displacing silt and sediment that had collected inches deep. Masaru held his breath as much as possible while trying to follow and swat at his suit to clean it.

On the fourth floor, she darted down a narrow corridor full of angled alcoves where wooden doors rotted. Most had doctor's names on them, or the suggestions thereof. She kicked down the aluminum-framed door of a pediatrician's practice, and headed as straight as the architecture allowed. Where a small employee break room stood at the outer edge, she crept up to the window and looked.

Masaru edged up alongside her.

The building across the street had a significant amount of damage: missing chunks of wall big enough to accommodate hovercars, as well as cavernous gaps in the floors. The devastation gave them a clear view of the hovercar that had flown in and landed at the ground level. From this angle, the inner face of the holographic false wall looked like a rectangular patch of neat, new drywall about as big as a one-car garage door.

Next to the hovercar stood five cargo pallets of cube-shaped boxes marked with the logo of Nikkatsu Corporation. A small delivery hover-van had been parked nearby, rear door open, showing off its empty cargo space. Men in un-tattered civilian clothing, all black or dark grey, collected near the nose end of the car. Their conversation included handshakes and arm patting, and a fair amount of laughing. Again, Masaru's augmented hearing picked up snippets of what he guessed to be Russian.

Noriko elbowed him twice and pointed at a rusted dumpster along the side. "We can climb there, and go in a window."

He nodded.

They observed the men for several minutes. Eventually, the group migrated deeper into the building out of sight. Noriko spun away from the window and jogged back to the stairwell, running faster when the lack of junk in the way allowed. She lost her footing in the dust after three turns, and stair-surfed half a story before smacking into the wall at the landing.

He hurried up behind her. "Are you hurt? Is your leg bothering you?"

"No. I stepped on something that rolled." She pulled herself upright. "I didn't feel a thing through the armor. Come on."

She took the last two stories with greater care, before racing down the hall, across the lobby, and around the corner. Masaru, moving slower in an effort to minimize touching filth, made it to the dumpster she'd indicated as she pulled herself into the hole in the wall above it. Concrete dust and tiny pebbles fell from where her armor abraded the edge. Grimacing at what such a move would do to his suit, he leapt up onto the dumpster, grabbed the wall, and navigated the opening as carefully as his arm strength allowed. In addition to the taste of dust, the pungent slap of dried urine assailed him.

While he perched atop the wall, squatting in the hole, Noriko dropped to the ground level and crept up to a crude table made of stacked concrete nuggets and a board, upon which a terminal sat. She took a knee and poked at the plain black bar. A holo-panel appeared in front of her, tinting the beige plates of her JSDF armor green.

Masaru lowered himself with care, his shoes scraping at the wall. He pushed off with a leg and landed a step away, his foot striking soft (and silent) dirt. After a quick check to make sure his suit hadn't torn anywhere, he did his best 'ninja walk' to her side.

"I don't understand this," whispered Noriko.

The screen depicted a 3D wireframe model of some kind of robotic crab with eight legs and two pincer-like limbs, only they had boxy extensions rather than claws, loaded with an array of microscopic needles, snippers, rods, and so on.

"Nanobots?" whispered Masaru. "Nikkatsu makes medical technology, but why would these people be interested in them, or bring them to this ruin?"

She tapped a few buttons and brought up another screen of Cyrillic text. After scrolling for a moment, confusion knotted her eyebrows. "According to this, these nanobots are destined for Wiesbaden... Some kind of stealth boat is supposed to meet them near Hirayama."

Masaru eased upward, trying to see past a crumbling interior wall to where the foreigners had gone. "The NSK will not be pleased that Nikkatsu is selling their products directly to an external entity, however, that is not our immediate concern. Can you connect to the outside or does that terminal have access to the signal scrambler?"

"No. It's linked to a satellite unit. Direct point-to-point with no connection to the GlobeNet." Noriko glanced at the cracked ceiling. "Probably a dish on the roof or at least close to it. Nothing on the jammer. Let's find a better position."

She headed west, closer to where they'd entered from, avoiding the 'room' full of men and turned sideways to squeeze between the van and a bare concrete wall. A ripple of laughter came from the foreigners, along with a momentary raised voice in a tone that suggested a bawdy joke. Stacks of black rectangular crates with red-stenciled writing in Cyrillic and German filled a relatively clean area on the other side. Noriko lifted the lid on the nearest box, exposing four portable anti-aircraft missile launchers in packing foam.

"Moto-san," she whispered. "Streyla-4 missiles. These are probably the same type that hit my aircraft." The confusion and surprise in her expression hardened to a vengeful glower.

Masaru peeked in another crate, shorter, and with different markings, finding an assortment of rifles and ammunition. "They are providing weapons to the Etamura."

"That or being careless to let them get stolen." Noriko scowled at the stockpile before she pointed ahead and left. "There... stairs."

"Why do I think you are planning something reckless?" Masaru took one of the rifles, packed his suit jacket's pockets with magazines, keeping one in hand as he hurried after her.

Noriko stopped short and thrust an arm out behind her that almost hit Masaru in the chin. She gestured at a black box on the wall resembling a dinner plate sized spider, with a glinting lens in the middle of its back. The device clung to the wall about a foot off the ground.

She lifted her left leg and took a huge step over the spot, shifted her weight, and brought her other leg over in the same exaggerated manner. Once she had both boots on the ground, she pointed at the air. "Infrared laser trip line. Spiderbomb."

Masaru smiled. "I have seen them before."

He followed, avoiding the beam.

Noriko crept into the stairway, looking around at the floor and walls for more surprises. She ascended a tight switchback to the third floor—where the stairs ceased to exist. While she stood there gazing up at the decaying building, Masaru examined his new rifle. The weapon had a similar feel to the laser rifles his company made, light and plastic. For a ballistic weapon, that implied it ranked low on the quality scale. The magazine well sat in the stock, inserted from the top. He loaded one and patted it down until a *click* indicated he'd seated it properly. A small counter on the side lit up showing thirty-seven.

"This way," whispered Noriko, as she stepped over a hole large enough to swallow her a few strides past where the stairs met floor. "I see the jammer."

Masaru's head snapped up, interest in studying the rifle gone. "Where?"

"It is in the room beyond where they are all sitting and drinking." She walked about nine steps and looked around at a hallway intersection containing the wreckage of a few long fluorescent light wells that had fallen from a no-longer-existing ceiling. "This place is home only to the dead now. The sky is so peaceful, I could stare at it and forget what is around me, but even the birds know not to come here, for the spirits would never let a trace of beauty leave."

Masaru gazed at her face while she stared at the sky, a momentary change from soldier to innocent woman. Were it not for her armor and weapon, or the miles of destruction around them, she could have been a village girl from the countryside. "What shall they do if I refuse to allow them to keep you?"

She glanced back at him with a mixture of amusement and annoyance. "Nice try."

"Your words were poetic." He admired tiger-stripes of sunlight painting her armor. "The dove does not land in a place of such sorrow, for it could not fly away with a burdened heart."

Noriko lowered her head and sighed. "I see a good spot up ahead. A room along the outside wall, only two ways in and both on the same side."

He gripped the rifle in both hands. "You're sure?"

"Yes." She crept down the corridor, stepping around the smashed trappings of offices. Ancient computer pieces, telephones, chairs, and even bits of desk lamps had become part of the sediment layer. With each agonizing step, she eased her weight down to minimize crunching.

The corridor ended at a drop off about two feet away from the more distant of two doorways on the right side. She entered via the nearer one and continued to the second door inside an empty room that offered more visual cover from below.

The outer wall had five holes, once windows, with yellowed papers hanging between them, each bearing large kanji characters for various family names. Iffy brushwork, and the presence of a perfect thumbnail-sized version of the same character in the corner suggested this place had once housed a calligraphy school.

Any traces of desks or materials had long since been blown out onto the street.

"Third floor isn't too bad a jump if we have no other choice." Noriko nodded at the windows before kneeling and crawling up to the doorway.

The elevated perch offered a clean view of a ground floor area containing a ten-foot collapsible antenna standing next to a gloss-black box the size of a large suitcase. Two thick wires connected the case to the bottom of the antenna. A freestanding wall separated the antenna chamber from a larger room where men sat around on a mixture of folding chairs and concrete chunks. All had rifles either draped across their laps or propped against the wall nearby. They seemed in high spirits, and slugged drink after drink from plain silver canisters often used for synthbeer.

"They're talking about how much trouble the Etamura are causing," whispered Noriko. "They are happy to have brought violence and chaos here, but I don't think it is their primary objective." She took up a firing position, using a slab of concrete and part of the wall for cover. Her rifle seemed to be aimed at the box connected to the antenna. "Moto-san. Thank you for the stimpaks. You should leave before I hit the hornet's nest. I'm the one who swore an oath."

"What is your plan?" He examined the area; she'd taken the only cover spot. Between the section of corridor by the break-off, and the wall to her left, she'd present a difficult target to anyone downstairs. If he tried to move anywhere he could engage the men below, he'd wind up out in the open.

"I'm going to take out the jammer and then try to stay alive long enough for reinforcements to show up." Noriko glanced up at him. "Either run or get the hell down. You don't have to die with me."

"You don't have to die." He crouched and shifted left, out of sight behind the wall. "Once you start shooting, they will come up the stairs." Masaru raised his rifle and duck-walked to the door they'd entered from. "I will cover the hallway from this side."

Noriko sighted over her rifle, a square patch of green lit up over her right eye. "Those bastards might not have killed my crew directly, but they armed the savages who did. I wouldn't deserve to wear this armor if I didn't do this."

Masaru smiled. "Didn't you say you thought the old ways foolish?"

"This isn't old traditions; this is soldier's honor." She waited a second before tightening her posture, aiming downward. "I'm about to fire, Mr. Kurotai negotiator. Last chance."

"Hmm." Masaru examined his rifle, located the safety, and turned it off. "Proceed."

Noriko sighed. "Well, you've got balls. I'll give you that much."

Masaru leaned around the corner, aiming at the stairwell. The foreigners had only two ways up—past him or managing a three-story jump to the ledge in front of Noriko. *These fools provided the missile that struck my car. They will atone for Shuji's death.*

# 38

# ALIEN ABDUCTION

Two slabs of vat-grown haddock simmered in a shallow layer of butter-garlic sauce. Nina stood by the stove, arms folded, clutching a spatula. As frustrating as the day had been, Elizaveta hovering around her made her smile. The child seemed to have found the perfect balance point between staying close and not being in the way. Nina had changed into a long t-shirt and decided the whole pants thing to be wildly overrated. Elizaveta wanted to match, so she put on one of Nina's tees, which covered her to the shins, but left one shoulder bare.

Thermal vision allowed her to swipe the fish from the heat at the exact right moment. *Two hundred grand in military-grade optics, and I use it to cook fish.* She slid the haddock blocks onto waiting plates already holding instant rice pilaf from a box. Mother would be aghast, but Mother also never had to come home to a hungry child after working.

Elizaveta let go of her clingy one-armed grasp as Nina walked the food to the table.

"Where Joey is?" asked the girl in hesitant English.

Nina smiled. "Good! He's still at work. He won't be visiting tonight."

The girl's look of extreme concentration faltered to confusion. Nina repeated herself in Russian, then said each sentence separately in English and Russian once more.

Elizaveta nodded before sniffing at the plate. "Stinks good." She grinned.

Nina cracked up laughing.

"What?" Elizaveta tilted her head.

She offered a brief explanation of the subtle difference in meaning between 'smells' versus 'stinks' as they ate. Again, Nina pondered her guilt at being wasteful since only about fifteen percent of the food would do anything productive for her. *Oh screw it.* She savored the taste and sensation of eating, and allowed herself to enjoy it. Elizaveta still ate fast, but she no longer shoveled food down barely chewing it.

Once they finished, Nina tossed the dirty dishes in the machine and went to the living room, flopped on the couch, and spent a minute or five hunting down some educational animated show that would help with basic English. Elizaveta crawled up next to her and cuddled while chattering on about her school, mostly in Russian, but attempted some simple ideas in English. While she seemed to enjoy her school more than Nina had expected, she didn't like the extra after-hours time for English lessons. Mostly since none of the other children had to stay late every day.

"You won't always have to do that. It's only until you've caught up with English."

Elizaveta furrowed her eyebrows. *"Im-byi sleduyet nauchit'sya govorit po-Russki."*[1]

Nina bowed her head, chuckling. A sudden freeing joy came out of nowhere, and she squeezed the child tight. Despite continuing to grin and laugh, tears ran down her face. Not since Bertrand had mauled her had she experienced anything close to being so… happy. "Oh, Elizaveta. Don't you think it would be much more work for all of those children to learn Russian than for one you to learn English? And what of the rest of the UCF?"

Elizaveta raised her nose with an imperious air and folded her arms. *"Oni I Russkiy mogut izuchat.*[2]*"*

"So we should teach everyone in the country to speak Russian so you don't have to learn English." Nina rubbed her chin. "Sounds good."

Elizaveta giggled. "No. I teasing. Is too much work teach all Russian. Just be the only child in room is sad."

"I can imagine." Nina ruffled her hair. "It won't last forever."

"Yes." Elizaveta watched the animation, swishing her feet side to side. A few minutes later, she looked up at Nina. "I want not to forget Russian. It is part me." She patted herself on the chest.

"All right." Nina smiled. *"Doma, ya budu govorit s toboi po-Russki, tak chto vy ne zabyli.*[3]*"*

Satisfied with Nina's offer to continue to use Russian at home, Elizaveta cuddled close and stared at the holo-bar display. Eventually, bedtime rolled around, and Nina carried her to the bathroom, helped brush her teeth, and followed her to the bedroom.

Elizaveta climbed up onto the Comforgel pad, which went from dark to a soft orange glow. She slipped under the covers and hugged her teddy bear. "Am I too old for bear toy?"

Nina winked. "Nope. I still have a stuffed rabbit. His name is Nix."

Elizaveta grinned. "Good night."

"Night, sweetie." Nina kissed her on the forehead, dimmed the light, and walked backward out into the hall.

The child waved one more time before Nina moved out of view. Nina grinned and hit the button to set the door three-quarters closed. *I never thought having a kid would make me feel so… alive.* She wiped tears on the way to the sofa, and sat in a ball with her face against her knees, unable to stop crying. She hadn't thought about Nix in a while. Truth be told, she had kept the stuffed rabbit in her closet because she didn't want him to see 'robot-Nina.' She'd been ashamed, and couldn't bear to face him since she wasn't the same girl who'd grown up with him.

Her attachment to the girl had formed almost at first sight, and only grown stronger. How much of the need to take her in had been a simple reaction to no longer possessing the ability to have kids? Her parents had made it clear for years that they expected her to give them grandchildren. Their insistence had taken her initial ambivalence at the idea and forged it into an active desire *not* to have any, but it hadn't been genuine, only spite.

*Stop it. This is who you are now. It doesn't matter what's under my skin.* Her emotional storm waning, she stretched out and tried to relax... by thinking about her case. The ACC had at least five active infiltrators inside Laughlin-Reed Innovation. Since none of the surveillance teams had detected anything unusual, it seemed likely that the spies blamed Katya for the death of the three, or perhaps they too felt Anders had been a rookie who'd made an idiot mistake. Nina had kept a safe distance, so she hoped they compartmentalized and behaved as though nothing had changed in order to maintain their cover.

Daniel Stirling squashing the investigation he started didn't sit well with her. The move seemed reckless for a spy (why start it in the first place instead of faking it). Of course, the possibility existed he'd been bribed or threatened to flush it.

A light went on over Nina's head. She raised her arm and pantomimed putting on a rubber examination glove. "Sorry, Daniel. This won't hurt much... tomorrow."

Nina yawned, and trudged down the hall to her bedroom.

---

THE NEXT MORNING, LIGHT FROM NINA'S DESK TERMINALS TINTED HER WORK AREA the same shade of cobalt. Years of financial data for Daniel Stirling scrolled by, with nothing yet appearing out of the ordinary. The man had two secondary accounts, but neither of those raised any red flags. One appeared to be a savings jointly accessible by his wife Ava. The other, a much smaller account, commented as 'Noah college,' received regular auto-deposits from his primary one.

*This guy is too clean to be believed, but everything checks out back to a live recording of his birth.* She shook her head. *I didn't think any executive could be* this *honest. The guy doesn't even cheat on his taxes.*

"What are you hiding, Daniel Stirling?"

She changed tactics and pulled him up in the Division 1 system, looking for anything down to the logging of a simple 'stop and warn.' The man had submitted a handful of complaints two years ago to have Human Life Movement protestors removed from his property. *That's not surprising. LRI makes some cybernetics. Heh. Those morons would* love *me.* The idea that a bunch of undereducated religious fringers who believed the rest of the world should live by their ways because it's 'what God wanted' probably would insist that she'd be better off dead than kept alive by such drastic 'unholy' means.

Before she got angry enough to crack the arm of her chair, another block of text caught her eye. Five weeks ago, the son, Noah Stirling, called Division 1 to report his father had been abducted by aliens and replaced. The vid had come in at 1:18 a.m., and showed a black-haired boy with skin pale enough to pass for

Marsborn hiding under blankets and whispering at a NetMini. The Division 1 dispatcher noted it as a prank call, and chalked it up to a kid being a kid. He told the boy they'd look into it, and promptly did nothing.

Nina replayed the video, staring into the boy's large chocolate-brown eyes. *He looks frightened.*

"Hi. My name's Noah Stirling, and I need you guys to come over right away. My father's been abducted by aliens and they've sent an evil clone that looks like him."

Her somatic response system didn't do much on video as it couldn't get any sense of skin temperature, breathing rate, or perspiration, but something in her gut needled at her. *This kid wasn't pranking the cops... Something's going on.*

She locked her terminal, flew from her seat, and grabbed her coat on the way out.

<br>

NINA GUIDED HER PATROL CRAFT DOWN FROM HER FAST-CRUISE ALTITUDE OF 1,500 feet in a graceful sweeping left turn. Sector 8527 stretched out below, along the easternmost edge of West City where plastisteel met the mountains by a place once known as Quincy, California. Wherever the mountainous terrain reached or exceeded the elevation of the city surface, the plates had been altered to fit the contour of the Earth. Dozens of private mansions stood in the shadow of the border wall a few miles east, on natural ground.

In the absence of natural terrain, poor people tended to live near the wall. Old superstitions that the Badlands 'creatures' would sneak in at night kept those who could afford to live elsewhere away. However, in places like this, where natural splendor rose above the best efforts of humanity to tame it, the wealthy dwelled.

Stirling's home was at the modest end of the scale for the area, having only two stories and a mere seventeen rooms plus three-vehicle garage. Forest, likely induced-growth, framed the house on the north, east, and south to a depth of around sixty meters before a property line fence brought the foliage to an abrupt, and pin-straight, halt. Nina shook her head at the rectangular arrangement of trees. Viewed from overhead, the Stirling property resembled a model landscape built inside a shipping box. They had a sizeable grassy front yard stretching to the west with a pond big enough to have a dock and rowboat.

She slowed to a crawl and descended in a circling flight path over the house-end of the property. A quick sweep with thermal sensors surprised her at finding only a child-sized heat signature in the southeast corner room on the second floor. The boy reclined atop a less-intense rectangle of warmth, likely his Comforgel bed. Given the time of 10:08 a.m., she figured he probably had a Senshelmet on and sat in a virtual classroom.

Since the boy's corner bedroom had a view of the back of the house in the east, as well as the south, Nina brought the patrol craft in for a landing on the north side, concealing it in the trees in case Stirling senior returned without warning. Not that she didn't have the authority to walk right in and look around, but on the chance he might be working with the ACC, she didn't want to tip him off.

Birdsong greeted her when she opened the door, accompanied by the soft whisper of a breeze in the treetops. While pleasant, the scenery didn't enamor her too much; her father's estate had almost three times the land, even if it was farther north and got colder during the winter. She jogged a short distance in the woods before emerging on well-manicured grass. A stone footpath led around the side to the front porch, and the door gave way to her police override code without a sound.

She entered, eased the door closed, and made a quick circuit of the downstairs in search of any kind of office or den. A room full of fitness equipment with some women's clothes draped on one of the benches, and another space with a workbench and dozens of plastic models of military vehicles seemed to be the only two places on the ground floor that appeared lived in. The rest of the rooms reminded her of a model-mansion used to show off a development to prospective buyers.

A carpeted stairway led up to the second floor, which struck her right away as more used. A hallway of half-open doors still held a faint trace of cologne, and a boy's mumbling drifted in from the right. He asked a question about math, evidently objecting to them introducing letters into 'something meant for numbers.'

Nina suppressed a chuckle and headed the other direction. Three empty rooms, a bathroom, and a guest bedroom that smelled of perfume held nothing useful. The next door she checked revealed a study decorated in dark wood paneling complete with a modest fireplace. Pale grey marble slabs stood on either side of the opening where the holographic fire would appear when activated; the mantle consisted of nine falcons carved out of dark, polished Epoxil... or maybe real wood. From the left to the right, they depicted the same bird in various poses during a dive, like successive still images from an animation.

The desk terminal yielded to her Division 9 override as well. After connecting a wire from its M3 port to the back of her neck, the world erupted in a dizzying array of virtual holo-panels. She ran several analytical softs looking for files with password encryption or containing hidden sections or hidden files embedded within. Rather than sift through all the data right away, she'd go for anything he appeared interested in concealing first.

Eleven seconds later, the softs had flagged a handful of items. The first file she checked contained pictures of women posing nude or touching themselves; some of the backgrounds appeared to be elsewhere in this house, and none of them looked like Ava Stirling. Nina rolled her eyes and swatted her hand in the air, which threw that file to the side, off her temporary workspace. The next file contained a series of vid-mails in Spanish to a man named Santiago. She grabbed a few stills of the man's face for later deep diving. The substance of the email confirmed that Stirling had made contact with the 'assets' and would 'make sure no further problems occur.'

She grumbled.

Stirling had a deferential tone with Santiago that made her think of a worker/employee relationship—not the way she expected a Senior Vice President to talk to someone.

Another file held copies of all the Laughlin-Reed Innovation reviews of the production line that she'd already seen. Various shift supervisors, production maintenance crewmen, and middle-managers all came back with the same consensus: something had gotten into a batch of Placinil that shouldn't have been there. They'd also collected copies of NewsNet stories about reports of random acts of aggression suffered by some users of Harmony. LRI's PR team had gone balls-to-the-wall stressing that Harmony was *not* Placinil, and when people illegally tamper with their product, they couldn't be held responsible for the results.

Daniel Stirling had sent official emails to several production managers, as well as the Junior VPs of marketing and sales instructing them that 'the problem is being handled in house' and 'no further talk of contamination will be tolerated.'

A small spider crawled over a file icon and waved at her. She smiled at it as she reached out to thin air and grasped the tile. Despite the images existing only within her cybernetic eyes, they reacted to her gestures. The file opened to reveal lists of credit transactions to a previously-unknown account. While the cryptic names of depositors didn't make any sense at a casual glance, Nina felt certain she'd found the ledger detailing his off-the-book sales of doctored Placinil to the dealers.

*Placinil plus nanobots equals Harmony.*

"Who are you?" asked a boy.

The floating holo-panels glided apart in a curving sweep away from the center of her vision. A scrawny bare-chested boy of about ten stood in the doorway with a small handgun not quite pointed at her. Thick but short black hair formed an orb around his head. His loose red shorts had a Manglers Gee-ball team logo over the right thigh, and sat low enough on his waist to expose a thin strip of blue underwear elastic. Though he had a (mostly) calm expression, his toes clutched at the carpet.

"Police, Noah. My name is Nina, and I'm with Division 9." She spoke in a soothing tone. "What are you doing home alone?"

"Can I see your badge?" He bit his lip.

"All right." She reached into her sand-brown coat, pulled out her ID wallet, and flipped it open. He stood up on tiptoe to peer at it. "I saw you called us about aliens. I came here to follow up on that."

Noah's arm (and the gun) dropped limp at his side. Suspicion shifted to trust in an instant. "Yes!" He ran up to her. "I didn't think they believed me. Do you believe me?"

Nina put her ID away. "Can you tell me what made you think aliens got him?"

"Umm." Noah set the gun on the desk and waved his hands about as he rambled. "Like, Mom and Dad always used to argue about her having other boyfriends, but the alien doesn't say anything about it anymore. He even started bringing women here. Umm... there's small stuff too. Dad always *had* to use his EDSB mug for his morning coffee, but the alien doesn't care what mug he uses."

"Anything else?" Nina set a mark in her system to save the cortical recording of her time speaking to the boy, preserving it from being overwritten by the usual two-hour loop. "See any spaceships or anything?"

Noah ground his big toe into the rug. "No, but I even asked him if he wanted his Elizabeth Drummond School of Business mug, and he said it didn't matter."

"Maybe he got tired of the mug? Maybe it broke?"

"Nope." Noah shook his head. "The school's named after Edmund Driscoll, not Elizabeth Drummond. He didn't notice. An alien wouldn't know the difference."

Nina thought for a second. "Do you remember your father knowing Spanish?"

"Duh. Who doesn't? I mean… everyone knows Spanish unless you're from up north, then its French and English instead of Spanish and English." Noah's eyebrows went up. "*Oh!* Yeah. Even Minstrel knows he's an alien. That's my dog. Since the night the alien came, Minstrel growls at him if he gets too close to me."

"Okay… Have you noticed anything different about his appearance? Does he still eat? Shower? Sleep?"

"Yeah. Everything like that's still the same. He ignores me now. I mean, it's not like he really ever spent that much time with me before, but now he acts like I don't exist. He works a lot, but he always used to make *some* time for me… but now he doesn't. We'd always go to the season opener for the Manglers, but he didn't even come home that night." The boy stared down at the floor; his lip quivered for a second, though he didn't cry.

"Where's your mother?" Nina frowned.

"Mom's never home. She's always at her boyfriend's place. I'm 'big enough to take care of myself' so she doesn't want to 'baby me.' She thinks Dad is watching me. Dad thinks Mom is with me. They don't talk to each other."

*Okay, so the real Daniel Stirling starts the investigation. The ACC can't have that, so they… replace him. The ACC's terrified of dolls and synthetics, so it's gotta be an agent with cosmetic work. Someone who isn't familiar with minor details of life as a Stirling. He'd have focused on major aspects of Daniel's life, not what mug the guy had a thing for.*

Noah's eyes reddened. His lip started to quiver but he composed himself. "I think Dad's probably already dead somewhere and there's an alien in the house. Are you gonna shoot it?"

"I want to make absolutely sure that he's an alien first, and not maybe having some kind of brain tumor or something." She looked him over. "Are you eating? You're so thin."

"Yeah." He nodded. "I eat a lot. Mom always rages at me 'cause I can eat so much and stay skinny, but she's just kidding."

Nina smiled. "Okay, Noah. I need you to do me a very big favor."

He swiped his pistol off the desk and held it up in both hands, pointed at the ceiling. "Can I be like a temporary cop?"

"First"—she grasped his hands and guided the gun back to the desk—"you're not going to be using that. Second, what I need you to do is be brave. Act normal."

"Normal? But he's an alien in my Dad's skin."

Nina grasped his arms and looked him in the eye. "I believe you, Noah." *Maybe not the same kind of alien he's thinking of, but technically the guy is an alien…* "The problem is, there are other aliens around. If they find out that I know about your Dad, they might do something bad that could hurt a lot of people. For now, I need you to just keep going on like you're going on until I can locate *all* of them. Once I do that, we'll take care of all the aliens at the same time."

He nodded. "I'm scared. What if they find out I told you? I don't wanna die or wind up an alien too."

"I won't tell them how I found out." She winked. "You shouldn't tell him that I was here."

"That's something bad people ask kids to do… not tell."

Nina smiled. "Very good, Noah, but this is like a stakeout. If the cops are watching criminals, waiting for them to do something bad, are they going to tell the criminals that they're watching?"

"No." He shook his head.

"It's just like that. Do you have a NetMini?"

Noah looked at her like she'd just asked him if he had a third head. "Duh..."

"Go get it. I'll give you my PID to contact if you get scared."

He took a few steps backward, nodding. "Okay. Umm. You're the cops that kill people right?"

*Dammit, this kid is only ten and he's already cynical.* "Sometimes people who break the law have a lot of money, and the legal system doesn't always work the way it should. When there's someone doing very bad things and the police can't find any other way to stop them... we sometimes need to do that, yes."

Noah ceased slouching. "Thanks for being honest. You probably didn't wanna tell a little kid that, but I guess you heard me in algebra, so you know I'm smart."

She gave him a playful accusing look. "What makes you think I heard that?"

"You're a doll." He gestured at her.

A hot flash washed over her, similar to what happened when half her former Division 1 squad walked in on her after a hazing episode left her naked and duct-taped in the shower. *How... I don't look... I look normal. I...* "You think I'm a doll?"

He grinned, showing teeth. "You're Division 9. Aren't they all dolls? And you came in alone." Noah started to walk out, but spun back. "And if the government sent you to get rid of an alien, of *course* they'd send a doll. We don't know how strong or tough the aliens could be."

Relief fell on her like a cool shower on a sweltering day. "Right. Never know what to expect from aliens."

Noah ran out, still smiling.

She sent an All-Seeing Eye soft into Stirling's terminal, which embedded itself out of sight in a little-known-of bit of buffer memory attached to the I/O port meant for a physical display monitor no one used anymore. Anyone under the age of fourteen probably didn't even know the purpose of the socket on the back of the terminal bar. The ASE got to work creating an exact copy of the terminal and all its files which it would send over to an empty GlobeNet site Division 9 used for receiving data. If anyone found and cracked open an ASE, it wouldn't expose any internal network addresses or encryption keys. After the clone process, it would sit and function as a keylogger, allowing anyone at Division 9 to view the terminal in real time.

Nina unplugged and headed to the master bedroom long enough to collect a few hair samples from his brush. A dark orangey-brown nugget on the wall near a wastebasket appeared to be a flicked snot that had missed. *That is disgusting, and it also doesn't fit Stirling's profile as a neat freak.* She scavenged an empty pill bottle from the can and used it to scrape-collect the dried booger before stuffing the hair in after it. Noah ran in and held his NetMini up. She waved hers to exchange PIDs.

"If you get worried about your safety, call me at any time. Also, it might not be a bad idea if you went with your mother for a while."

Noah shook his head. "If I ask that, the alien might know something's wrong. You said act normal." He pointed to the right. "Oh, if you're trying to find DNA, check the guest bedroom. The alien brought another woman home last night, and she said he was throwing it everywhere."

She winced. "I think I found enough. I doubt we'll have this alien's info in our system, but at least I'll know if your father is still your father."

"Okay."

*I shouldn't leave this kid alone, but if I call Div 1 in here to get social services involved, Stirling, or whoever he is will know we've been snooping around. Dammit.* "You shouldn't be alone at your age, but I'm... kinda stuck here. I *should* refer your situation to social services."

"I'm not alone *that* long." He lifted his arms a little to the sides and let them flop down. "Mom should be back around three. It's not like they leave me here for weeks by myself. Only a couple of hours. I gotta get back to class. I told Mr. Dominguez I thought someone was in the house. I'll say the dog knocked something over downstairs."

Nina patted him on the shoulder. "I'm very glad you called in to report the alien. You might've given me the last piece of a puzzle I've been working on."

"Awesome." Noah's grin lasted all of two seconds before he looked ready to cry. "I mean... It's not awesome that my Dad's probably dead and stuff. Do you think he's dead?"

Nina exhaled. "I don't know. The aliens might've taken him alive, but..."

"Yeah, I know. Probably easier to kill him." He hung his head. "Thanks for trying. It would be cool if you could get the aliens back for what they did."

"That's why I'm here." She attempted a reassuring smile.

He gave her a quick hug before running off back to his bedroom.

*Hardin's going to rip someone's head off. It would almost be easier to believe this guy's a real alien than the ACC is just waltzing so many operatives past our noses.* She tucked the pill bottle in her coat pocket and hurried outside to her patrol craft. Data analytics hadn't found any more operatives. *If Hardin's buddy in C-Branch can match a definite ACC name to the DNA in the hair/snot sample, that would put Stirling as the likely head of the serpent... at least inside.*

She dropped into the driver's seat and closed the door. "It's almost time to go full mongoose."

# 39

# DUST SETTLES

Pelting stones and driving wind rocked Kenny's truck for the better part of an hour. Dirt covered the windshield and built up like snow against the flat window overlooking the bed. Hayley clung to him, chest-to-chest with her chin on his shoulder. Having his arms around her had calmed her enough to stop wailing, but she continued trembling. Each time the wind gusted, she flinched.

The last time he asked her what was wrong, she'd said, "I dunno. I'm just scared."

Eldon had given him an accusatory look, mouthed 'voodoo' without lending it voice, and put his head back against the seat. The man had been asleep for at least half an hour despite the chaos raging outside.

Kathy and Alyssa chatted with the four Scrag children, answering their questions about what the modern world was like. At being told clothes were required and not just 'something for when it got cold,' Gato questioned how they'd ever be able to find enough and Cielo almost changed his mind about wanting to go. Luna latched on to the idea that she wouldn't be the 'last girl of her tribe,' obligating her to become Halcón's wife, and seemed thrilled. It took Kathy a good twenty minutes to convince Halcón his ancestors wouldn't be angry with him if he failed to take a lifemate before his sixteenth year.

"Are storms like this common?" asked Nasir.

With Hayley's head on his right shoulder, Kenny couldn't twist around to look at the man, so he kept staring at the dirt-covered windshield. "Relatively."

Something plastic clicked around in the back while Nasir mumbled.

"Figure out what went wrong with that thing?" Kenny ran his hand up and down Hayley's back, not that she noticed with her armored vest.

"The e-mag is dead, but it should've had enough of a charge for another ninety hours at least. How long do you think this storm will last?"

Kenny chuckled. "Oh, I reckon it'll last long enough for another pack of raiders or whatnot to find us."

"Will you knock that shit off?" muttered Eldon.

"You talkin' to me or the old man?" Kenny grinned.

Eldon opened one eye to stare at him. "Maybe both."

Alyssa folded her arms over her belly and bounced. "Hope this storm stops soon, I gotta pee."

"*Yo también,*" said Gato.

"*Sí.*" Cielo stood and started to hike his t-shirt up. "*Abre la ventana.*"

Kathy grabbed his arm. "We do not pee out windows."

*Damn. She had to say pee.* Kenny squirmed with need. "There a bottle or somethin' floatin' around?"

"Eww, Dad, no," said Alyssa. "There's no room back here and there's nowhere to go without everyone watching."

"Well, then hold it. Try not to think about it." Kenny glanced left at the dirt pelting his window. *Come on you old bastard, enough is enough.*

"I wanna go home," whispered Hayley.

"Me too, hon." Kenny rocked her side to side. "Won't be long."

An hour dragged into another, and the fidgeting and whining in the back intensified. Eventually, the storm lost intensity, though a light dusting of particles continued scratching at the truck.

"Okay, *I'm* about ready to hang my ass out a window and piss," said Kathy. "Looks like it's eased up a bit... is it safe now?"

At the word 'piss,' everyone groaned and fidgeted. Cielo had spent the past forty some odd minutes holding himself with both hands.

Kenny squinted, trying to stare through the dirt on the glass. The wind remained strong, but he could at least see a fair distance. "Yeah. Looks passable. No one stray too far away from the truck." He repeated the last instruction in Spanish, and got a chorus of agreement from the Scrags.

A gust of warm air laced with biting sand met his face when he opened the door. Kenny slipped to the ground, using his size to shield Hayley as he set her on her feet. Everyone got out and rushed off to find a little privacy, except for the Scrag kids who all stayed together and appeared unconcerned about who saw what. Though grit continued to fly on the breeze, the storm no longer made the idea of driving feel foolish.

After relieving himself, Kenny climbed into the truck bed and brushed dirt off his toolbox. When Hayley, Alyssa, and Kathy returned from their nature call, he handed the girls each a brush. They took them without protest, understanding the implied request.

Kathy folded her arms. "Anything I can do?"

"Get your rifle and keep an eye out." He waved a pointing finger around in a circle. "'Less you wanna help me switch the gears."

"Well." Kathy walked a few steps to her right and opened the rear driver side door. "Maybe if you show me how to do it I'll try." She pulled her rifle out of the truck. "Guess I'll pull guard duty."

The girls got to clearing dirt off the windows, grille, and hood.

Kenny grinned. "Might take a bit of doin', convincin' Hayley to take another trip out here."

She paused from brushing to shoot him a 'you wouldn't dare' look.

He gave her a 'just kidding' wink, jumped to the ground, and crawled under the truck with the toolbox.

Switching from the modern e-motors inside the wheels to the biodiesel engine required turning a couple of nuts inside each wheel to disengage the drive gears from the magnetic stator. Once he had all four wheels set to 'hard neutral,' he'd add four mini drive shafts to connect the front and rear differentials.

He'd finished disengaging the second front wheel when Eldon crawled under. "Hey man."

"Yo." Kenny shimmied over to the back wheels. "Kath, there's a box in the back. Orange with a white handle. Can ya grab that please?"

"Sure." Kathy walked by.

Laughter came from the younger two Scrag kids while Halcón and Gato walked patrol around the truck with their bows at the ready.

"Somethin' hit me," said Eldon.

"Not too hard I hope." Kenny grinned and socketed his ratchet on the first nut of the left driver side wheel.

"You're a funny guy for a dude stranded out here." Eldon shook his head. "Look, you ever consider Hayley might be psionic?"

"Not really... no why?" Kenny flicked a socket wrench back and forth in a blur. "She talk into your head or somethin'?"

"Naw man." Eldon raised his voice over the ratcheting noise. "Just the way she's all freaked out. Back in '11, my unit went in on this covert op in Singapore. Was a cat-and-mouse thing with a Spetsnaz crew. They sent us in to basically help Singapore stay neutral."

"Yeah, I'm sure your commanders didn't hope they wanted to join the UCF." Kenny grunted a laugh while forcing the second nut to start turning.

"Yeah, well. Lotta bad news in the tech district there. Some of the blackest of black tech come outta that place. Anyway... we got this psio with us right? Telepath to help us find these sumbitches. Dude wasn't what I expected at all. Kinda normal just to look at, ya know? My unit went in there freaked out about him, but by the time we left, we respected him." Eldon raised a hand. "Anyway, point of it is—"

"Oh, you have a point?" Kenny winked. After disengaging the third nut, he crawled to the last tire.

"Dad, we're done clearing dirt," said Alyssa. "Puttin' the brushes away."

Boots clonked and scuffed above him in the truck bed.

"Ha ha. Anyway, Valdez kept getting strange feelings 'round what he called 'death sites.' You think West City has a gang issue, you ain't seen shit. Lotta places over there where we had twenty, thirty, fifty die in mass shootings couple times a week. Bad territorial shit, man. Anyway, whenever we went near one o' them places, Valdez would get all pale and shit. Sweatin'... buggy eyed. He'd get afraid o' nothin' for no reason, just like her."

"She's eleven, and hasn't been out here before. She's just seen people shooting at us... got a nice close look at those damn 'pedes in the mall. Shit... those are going to give *me* nightmares." He stopped ratcheting, hung his head, and sighed. "I never should've brought her out here."

"I don't think it's just that. She got edgy fifteen minutes out from the city." Eldon pointed at him. "Nothing hap—"

*Thunk.*

An orange toolbox landed two feet away from Kenny's face, spraying him with dust.

"That the one?" asked Kathy. "Shit that thing is heavy. What's in it?"

"Drive shafts." Kenny coughed and wiped sand off his face. "Yeah, babe. Thanks."

Eldon backed out from under the truck. "Think on it, man. I ain't happy to say this, but maybe all that voodoo you talkin' is real, an' she can feel it."

Kenny stared at the box of short drive shafts and coughed again at a hitch of dry grit in his throat. The storm seemed to have worked out its frustration, reduced to little more than distant howls and a few wisps of sand blowing in whorls. He didn't quite know what to make of the idea of psionics, but didn't have the time to worry about it.

It took him about four minutes per shaft to connect each wheel to the differential, and once he checked and rechecked that it all looked right, he stowed the tools and empty box in the back and let out a loud whistle to collect the Scrags who had wandered a worrisome distance away.

They came running without protest, and soon everyone sat in the cab, staring at Kenny. Anticipation took the form of silence; not even the sound of breathing broke the stillness. He flexed and clenched his fingers over the button.

"Come on man." Eldon nodded. "Hit that motherf... udging thing."

Hayley sat stiff at the edge of the back seat, hands on her knees. "I think you're allowed to say worse than fudge right now. If that button doesn't work, we're f—"

"Walking," said Alyssa, loud enough to drown Hayley out. "I'd hike before I sat here waiting for this truck to come back from the dead."

Kathy put her arms around the girls. "Go on, Ken. Hit it."

His throat dried like a cotton snake crawled up from within. *Damn Eldon and his 'maybe he's real' talk. They're just stories. Folklore.* He pressed the little red button. A buzz emanated from under the hood, followed by the labored whine of a starter and the rattling of diesel combustion. The truck's frame vibrated.

"*La bestia está enojada. Se gruñía!*[1]" Cielo trembled for a second or two and clamped on to Kathy.

Halcón laughed at him. "*Es el motor, no bestia*[2]."

"Yes!" Hayley bounced in her seat.

Kenny fiddled with the tiny shifter he'd installed in the console, dropped the truck in first gear, and eased it forward. The backup drive didn't have the torque or the top speed of the normal motors, but doing forty-and-change was a damn sight better than zero.

Luna wriggled out the rear window into the bed, and with guidance from Kathy, opened the storage box holding the rations. The ten-year-old ferried food packets to the window two at a time. Once she'd retrieved a ration for everyone, she stuck one in her teeth and crawled back in. Crinkling plastic filled the cabin, along with Eldon grumbling about getting the 'radiation omelet' again.

"Don't drink that. It's hot," said Kathy in Spanish.

Cielo examined the tiny red-orange bottle of hot sauce from his ration pack, tilted his head, and slurped it down. The boy seemed to be waiting for something, but after a few seconds, shook his head. "*No fuego.*"

Alyssa picked up her little bottle.

"I wouldn't," said Kenny. "That kid's been eating who-knows-what his whole life."

Undeterred, Alyssa poured a little in her mouth. Within seconds, her face glistened with sweat, but her expression remained stoic. "Okay, it's got a bit of a kick." She added a couple drops into her meal packet.

Kenny raised both eyebrows, impressed. Hayley sniffed her hot sauce bottle, and coughed, near gagging. Cielo took it out of her hand and drank it like tomato juice.

"All yours," muttered Hayley.

"It's not so hot," said Nasir. "I make hotter."

"Make?" asked Kathy.

"Oh yeah." Nasir nodded. "I have a small grow tank." He held his hands out to define a three-by-two foot space. "Bhut Jolokia peppers."

"What's that mean?" asked Hayley.

"It's Hindu for 'burnt asshole.'" Eldon whistled. "Never again." He turned to face the back seat and pointed at the girls. "If either of you two ever wind up in the military, and someone dares you to eat somethin'... don't."

Alyssa laughed.

"How much longer 'til we get home?" whispered Hayley.

"It'll be about three days at this speed." Kenny grinned at Eldon. "Shouldn't be a problem. The Old Man gets weaker the closer we get to the modern world."

Hayley took a deep breath. "Okay. I can handle this. I don't even know what I'm scared of. I'm just scared."

"Shit, man." Eldon shook his head, chuckling. "You and your voodoo."

Kenny glanced over with a smile. Eldon seemed confident 'the voodoo' was made up, but his eyes said otherwise.

# 40

# SIDE JOB

At 11:02 p.m., Joey dragged himself into his apartment. He stopped by the bedroom long enough to discard clothing down to his briefs and went to the kitchen to procure food. A few minutes later, he flopped on the couch with a giant bowl of instant ramen in his lap and an ancient movie about the Old West on a huge 200-inch holo-panel in front of him. He'd already seen it dozens of times, and used it more for background noise while watching the foamy lumps evolve into shrimp.

Nina would be horrified at him eating such crappy food, but it reminded him of the years he'd spent on the fringe. Such a life lurked three seconds of bad luck away from anyone in West City. He yawned and leaned his head back on the soft couch edge, gazing around his one-bedroom place. Division 9 paid quite well, so he'd gotten an apartment on the high end of middle, expensive enough to where he had a separate bathroom and kitchen. The fridge didn't trade places with the shower, *and* it had a LaundroMaster. If he stuffed a pile of dirty random garments in one end, clean, folded, and color-sorted clothes came out the other.

*Almost like having Mom around.*

He muttered. Mars... Mom wanted to see him. Even working for the government didn't *quite* fully assuage his worry that someone would try to kill him if he went back up there. The second day at the office, he'd gone poking around the Marsnet, but couldn't find any active file with his name on it... and Nina's boss had assured him he'd been cleared. A wicked grin spread across his face.

*I gotta find whoever spanked Nightwing... ask him to go say hi to that bastard dragon on Mars.*

Few hackers impressed Joey, but anyone who could take on a Grade 10 AI and make it run home to its proverbial mother, he'd literally bow down to as Master.

A disc bot zipped across the room, ran into a pair of underpants he'd left there a few days ago, and spun out of control before hitting the coffee table with a loud *whack*. The little unit got stuck going in circles as the fabric tangled one of its wheels. Laughing, Joey ambled over to it. He de-briefed the bot and sent it on its carpet-cleaning way.

"Hmm. What do you think? Should I live up the bachelor life a bit more or bring up the whole 'moving in' thing with her?"

The silver disc glided across the living room without a word.

"Yeah. I agree."

He fell back onto the couch and slurped up ramen for a few minutes while watching Kurt Westwood blow the hell out of outlaws in *The Kind, The Cruel, and the Unsightly*. For whatever reason, whoever remade the ancient western film with digital actors (and all new special effects) was forced to change the names of everyone involved, (and the title) despite them being dead for four centuries.

*I doubt a .45 Peacemaker tore fist-sized holes in people.*

Joey laughed at the ridiculous gore.

The movie paused itself.

"Hey!" he yelled.

"Incoming vid from..." A pleasant female electronic voice changed to his recorded one. "The censorious bloviating—"

"Answer!" yelled Joey. *Shit I forgot to change that.* He fumbled with his NetMini, changing her announce to 'Sis.' *It feels so weird not to be at war with her.*

Katherine appeared where the movie had been, her giant face and severe bun made her look like something out of an ACC boardroom. "Joey... oh for fuck's sake, put some clothes on."

"I have clothes on." He snapped the waistband of his briefs. "Underwear is clothing. This covers more than what you used to sunbathe in. You do realize you can't get a tan from artificial windows, right?"

"Whatever." She looked off to the side, but smiled. "I wanted to thank you for whatever you did to Grant."

"Awesome. He leaving you alone?"

She flashed the sort of grin he expected to see on a lawyer right after they caused the downfall of a multibillion-credit company. "Oh, he's a little too busy to bother messing with me right now."

"Oh?" Joey raised red plastic chopsticks full of noodles to his mouth. "Do tell? Whatever happened to the poor man?"

Katherine rolled her eyes. "He's being sued by four clients for various reasons, as well as the Bandau Group... after they terminated him. There's an ethics inquiry and he'll probably wind up being disbarred. I also heard something about criminal charges for tampering with the Defense Force network."

"Poor guy." Joey stuffed his mouth.

"Quite." Katherine scoffed. "That idiot got so pissed that he raged at me over the vid... I recorded the whole thing, including the death threats. Oh." She laughed. "The chocolate dildo was a nice touch."

He grinned, noodles slipping out of his mouth. "Now who would go and send him anything like that?"

"So..." She exhaled and looked down for a second before resuming eye contact. "How are you doing?"

"Okay. Today sucked. Tomorrow sucked too. Next week or so's going to suck as well."

"What happened?" She blinked.

Joey twirled another load of clear noodles around his chopsticks and ate them, sipping the super-spicy broth while he chewed. "Whoo…" He exhaled. "I got a *good* batch. Oh nothing much. Nina sent down a giant request and Preema's pissed off about having to do actual work, so she datacated on me."

"Huh?" She scrunched up her eyes. "Datacated?"

"A portmanteau of data and defecated. I'm buried under busy work."

She covered her mouth and laughed. "Oh, Joey… sometimes you make it so easy to forget you're intelligent." Her mirth faded to that sympathetic stare one gives a doser they've tried and failed to help get clean. "So when are you going to visit? Mom wants to see you."

"Hey." He raised an arm, gesturing at the apartment. "Ease back with the pity bit. I'm not slumming it anymore. And soon."

"Soon?" She raised one eyebrow.

"Yeah, soon. As in not immediately, and not too long."

Katherine shook her head. "Can you vague that up a bit more?"

"Let me try and talk Nina into coming with first."

"Who's that?" Katherine leaned closer to the screen, making her nose enormous. "Nina?"

"A woman I've been seeing for a while." He smiled.

She put a hand on her chest and blinked. "You're seeing a woman?"

He frowned. "You're not going to make another 'thought I was into guys' joke are you?"

"No… I just didn't think any woman would have the patience to deal with you." She winked.

"Hmm." He stared at her giant image, daydreaming about flying up her enormous left nostril, which became a cave lined with medieval torches.

"What are you thinking?"

He blinked off the flight of fancy and smiled at her. "Driving a hovercar up your nose… this screen is so big I can see your brain."

She leaned back, a hint of blush in her cheeks. "So you're in a relationship with this woman… who is she?"

"Works with Division 9 too. 'Course, she's in field operations." He started to put more noodles in his mouth, but hesitated, chuckling. "Oh, you remember that thing Mom always used to say about me being so into technology…"

Katherine tilted her head, looking confused. "That you'd wind up marrying a computer."

Joey laughed. "Heh, yeah. About that…"

＊＊＊

HAH! JOEY MADE A SWITCHBLADE SOUND AS HE POPPED HIS MIDDLE FINGER OUT AND used it to poke the 'compile' button on his terminal. He impaled the gem-like green rectangle and twisted his hand back and forth as if driving a blade deep into the heart of a dragon.

"You sound entirely too satisfied with yourself," muttered Abby.

"Just caught and killed an elusive bug in a pet project." He winked. *Now time to see if this gamble pays off.*

Rather than dredge data like Preema expected, he'd spent most of the previous day writing a daemon to do the comparative analytics. The time he'd poured into that, about thirteen hours, should result in code capable of doing sixty some odd hours of data grinding in about four since it would remove the bottleneck of a human looking at things. While writing it broke no rules or regulations, he knew Preema had given him that job as grudge work, so if she learned he squirmed out from under the tedium, she'd only hit him with something worse. No one would hear about his bit of engineering unless he needed to unveil it to save someone's job, and it would have to be a someone he liked working with. He'd pretend to spend the next week hammering away at the data… but instead, he'd be out hunting for Shinigami.

It made sense to run the program right away, so if it did fall flat on his face, he'd only lose four hours. As much as it pained him to admit, he *did* like working for Division 9, so the idea of wasting a week, running the program at the last hour, and having nothing to show for it didn't appeal to him.

*I don't like to lose.*

Since he had a little while to wait before the compile process finished, he locked his terminal and headed out in search of a nice lowbrow lunch: Cyberburger. The franchise closest to the Police Administrative Center was one of a handful of locations participating in a new promotion called 'Cyberburger Ultimate.' Higher-grade machines and better OmniSoy resulted in food that supposedly didn't degenerate into goo within twenty minutes of molecular reconfiguration. Their marketing slogan, 'As natural as vat-grown,' gave him a mild headache to think about, but he'd been wanting to try the new food for a while.

As a promotion, PubTran and Cyberburger joined forces to give people ₡5 off their Cyberburger order if they took a PubTran car round-trip to pick up their food. Granted, the ride cost ₡38 each way, but he'd be paying it anyway to go there, promotion or no.

Nine minutes after leaving his cubicle, Joey strolled up to a massive Cyberburger franchise. Burnished steel walls with chrome-framed windows and over-stylized hamburger glyphs made the place look like a black tie restaurant from the outside. He walked past a holographic koi fountain with a simulated waterfall and into a warm room filled with the smell of pseudo-beef, maybe-tatoes, and nuclear cheese.

Arms wide to either side, Joey inhaled the glory of mega-cheap dining. "Ahh, my castle, I have returned."

Four bright-faced Class 1 dolls made to resemble teenaged girls stood behind the counter. Their skin had a noticeable plastic sheen, and visible seams and gaps showed around the mouth and joints on the hand. All wore burgundy uniforms with skirts so short no self-respecting parent would let a teenager walk out the door in them. Each had a badge featuring a golden burger above the letters CB, with a cute name underneath. Tiffy, Katie, Mia, and Maddie stood behind plastic forms holding datapads that displayed a menu alongside a NetMini reader.

Joey couldn't remember ever hearing about a live person working in a Cyberburger as a clerk. *Why do they even bother with the fake terminals?*

Each 'girl' had a line, though Maddie's only held three people. Joey walked up behind a doughy man with shaggy brown hair, tan pants, and a white button-down shirt a little too big for him despite his carrying about sixty extra pounds.

Joey glanced at his NetMini to check the time, not that he had to worry too much. He didn't have 'hours' so much as they wanted a certain amount of things done. As long as he finished what he needed to, the exact times of his arrival and departure didn't matter.

"What is taking this man so long?" muttered the man in front of him. "I do not have the time to stand here waiting for him to decide between chocolate or vanilla in his milkshake. I only get forty-five minutes for lunch."

"Sucks," said Joey.

"Excuse me?" The man looked back, showing off a bushy moustache. "Were you speaking to me?"

"Yeah. I said it sucks you only get forty-five minutes for lunch." Joey glanced at the man's breast pocket. A gold nameplate read Milton Swanson—Systems Architect below a round icon of a crown with an I in the center. He grinned. "You'd think a network administrator would at least get the full hour."

"Oh. Yes. I should but, HR refuses to budge." Milton grumbled, balling his hands in fists. He sounded furious, but his voice never quite made it above a tentative partial whisper. "I... I think I need to send another email." He faced forward. "Yes. That's what I will do. I'll send another email. They will have to listen to reason."

"Sure. They'll have to listen to reason."

"You're right." Milton nodded. He waited all of ten seconds before leaning right and peering past a woman with dark brown skin and a 'lawyery' skirt suit. "Umm... Excuse me. Can you please decide on your milkshake? Some of us are on a time budget."

Neither the woman in front of him nor the indecisive man in a t-shirt and tattered camouflage pants reacted.

"Would you like to Ultra that?" asked Katie.

"Uhh," said a short woman with a rainbow-colored afro in the next line. "What does that mean?"

Katie, permanent smile on her plastic face, began a lengthy explanation of how the Cyberburger Ultra used improved machinery and high-grade OmniSoy to create food that never lost its integrity.

"It's—" said Katie.

"As natural as vat-grown," muttered Joey along with her.

The indecisive man at the front of the line whipped out a NetMini and fiddled with it.

"What the hell are you doing now?" asked the woman in front of Milton.

"Working out calories." Milkshake man tapped at his holo panel.

"Umm, sure," said Rainbow. "That's cool."

Katie finished her order.

"Oh, hey, Milton," said Joey. "Thanks for breakfast. I love egg and cheese sandwiches."

"What?" Milton looked back at him.

"Next," said Katie.

Joey grinned. *Ack, right. Masaru knocked him out.* "Oh, never mind. Thought you were someone else."

"Oh." Milton looked downcast. He checked his watch, and grumbled.

A spacey-looking guy, almost seven feet tall but as skinny as Joey stepped up to Katie. His shitty attempt at dreadlocks hung down to his waist. "Umm, I'll have a Chickentron Mega with cheesey-tots and a pomegranate soda."

"Would you like to Ultra that?" asked Katie.

"Umm. I dunno. What's that mean?"

Joey's right eye twitched. "Hey, Fern-boy. She just explained it to the woman right in front of you. Extra ten credits, better food. Yes or no."

Katie droned on with the same explanation.

"Huh? Fern?" The man twisted to give him a confused look... three seconds later.

"That hair. You look like the nine-month aftereffect of a desperate, sex-starved palm tree dragging a fern into a dark alley and touching it repeatedly in a bad place." Joey gestured at the guy's face. "And shave that shit. That's not a beard; you got someone's short and curlies stuck to your chin." He faced the front of his line. "And for fuck's sake. Who gives a damn about calories that comes *here* to eat? Let me give you a clue: this food has shitloads of them. Does your fitness app have a setting for shitloads?"

The woman in front of Milton turned aside and stifled laughter.

"Please make a decision," muttered Milton. "I've only got thirty minutes left."

Fern, bewildered, faced forward and said, "Yah," to Katie.

"You could order out?" Joey smiled at Milton with a double-thumbs-up.

"No." Milton muttered incomprehensible things at his shoes for a moment. "I can't. I must exit the office for my lunch because otherwise nobody leaves me alone. If I try to eat at my desk, they are constantly walking up to me with issues. You would think these people don't understand the concept of deleting files. It's like they rely on the backup system to store data and only keep it in their local data nodes when they're using it. No, that's not what backup is for."

"Or they forget their passwords," said Joey.

Milton's eyes lit up. "Yes... or the printer is out of thermoplastic, or someone they are trying to vid isn't answering. Like it is something I can fix that the other person is there and not picking up."

"Oh, fuck this guy," muttered Joey. He gave Milton a 'one second' finger raise, and pulled his NetMini out. He leaned forward and swiped at the man, reading his PID, and jumped back to his place behind Milton. Within five seconds, he'd hacked his way into the man's device.

"What are you doing?" whispered Milton.

"I am Lord Kronos, keeper of time." Joey patched audio from a pornographic holo-vid to the man's NetMini, forcing the volume to max and disabling all control input for sixty seconds.

As lustful moans and cries of 'harder, deeper' echoed from the man holding up the line, everyone in the room (except for the dolls) stared at him. One woman covered the ears of her five-year-old son. Indecisive-man fumbled the NetMini, trying to find the source of the sound and turn it off. Much to Joey's amusement, the guy looked embarrassed rather than outraged.

*Hmm. He's not surprised. Must have quite a stash.*

Unable to shut it off, the man hurried out of the restaurant, his face bright red.

"Canceling order," said Maddie.

Milton twitched, a devious glint in his eyes. A growing smile spread over his face as he turned to face forward. The woman ordered. When the doll asked if she wanted to 'Ultra-it,' she gave Joey a challenging look threatening to ask what that meant. He pointed at her, eye twitching. She laughed and said yes, skipping the explanation. The doll set her order up on a tray, and she walked away after a brief glance at Fern got her chuckling again.

"Two Double Orbitals, a large fry, one Applezinger, and a Fruitsplosion," said Milton.

"Wow," muttered Joey.

Milton glanced back at him for a second, gnawing on his finger. "Oh, better make that a *diet* Fruitsplosion."

Joey's face reddened as he tried not to laugh.

"Ultra it, please." Milton held up a finger. "Second burger's for dinner later on." He nodded at Joey, eyes widening. "They really do last forever."

Milton collected his tray and walked off, glancing back at Joey a few times with a bewildered 'have I seen him before' expression. Grinning, Joey tucked his thumbs in his pockets and approached the doll.

"Galaxy combo." Joey winked. "And a diet water."

Maddie stared at him, motionless. After four seconds, the doll blinked with a *click*. "I'm sorry, sir. We do not offer diet water. Can I interest you in our full calorie water or an alternative diet beverage?"

"Oh, hell." Joey patted his concave belly. "I suppose I'll have to cope with the full calorie water."

JOEY PUT HIS FEET UP ON HIS DESK AND OPENED THE CLAMSHELL CONTAINING HIS four-patty Galaxy burger. He had to give them some credit, the damn thing still looked like a hamburger after the PubTran ride, and it smelled as good as vat grown beef. *Heh. Masaru would cringe and run the other way after one whiff.* He tapped his chin, grinning. *I gotta give him one of these and say it's from a new place that charges like six hundred creds a burger... then after he eats it show him the box.* He cackled, and dove in.

Burger and cheesy-tots mashed together in his mouth as he relaxed, staring at the progress meter for the compile.

"What'cha got there?" DeWinter leaned back. "That smells pretty damn good. No way that came from the cafeteria."

"You wouldn't believe me if I told you."

"Try me." DeWinter's bushy caterpillar eyebrows did their climbing dance of love.

"Cyberburger."

"Bullshit." DeWinter scoffed.

"Ultra. As natural as vat-grown," sang Joey.

"No kidding. Hmm. Maybe I'll break my rule and try it sometime. That almost smells like food." DeWinter slid out of sight behind the cube wall.

"Did you say Cyberburger?" Mindy leaned over him from behind, sniffing.

She'd added dark red streaks to the front of her bangs. "That smells almost like real food."

"I just said that," muttered DeWinter.

Joey grabbed the plastic tray of cheddar-covered potato nuggets. "Cheesy tot?"

She plucked one out of the goo with her longish fingernails and ate it. "Mmm." She fanned her mouth. "Oh wow. Hot."

"Yeah, I think that cheese is radioactive, but it tastes okay." Joey tossed another tot in his mouth before taking a bite of the burger.

Mindy returned to her desk.

*Beep.*

Joey looked up at the words ‹Compile complete› and set his half-eaten burger back in the carton. "Okay, moment of truth." He ran the program. "If this works, it's time to go hunting."

"What the fuck?" asked Mindy three seconds later.

"Hey," yelled Abby. "Who cut my process threads?"

"Ugh." DeWinter moaned. "Did someone breach the damned firewall again? I just got kicked out of all my sessions."

Joey pursed his lips. *Oops. Forgot to throttle the CPU utilization.*

*Wham!*

He jumped.

"What was that?" Mindy spun around in her chair.

*Wham.*

"Came from Simon's desk." Abby stood and crossed their circular area.

*Wham.*

"Oh, Simon's banging his head on the desk. Oh... oh, Simon, I'm so sorry." Abby sighed.

"Did he just show you his dick?" asked Joey. He flapped his hand at the holo-panel trying to get his program to stop execution.

DeWinter cringed.

"No, he had a theoretical simulation running for the past thirty six hours and it just terminated with an"—Abby leaned deeper into Simon's cube for a second—"'insufficient processor resources' error. He's gotta start it over."

*Wham.*

"Can you like stop smacking your head on the desk that hard," said Mindy. "That's kinda unnerving."

"Kinda?" DeWinter bugged his eyes at the cube wall separating Simon's desk from Joey's.

Various noises of alarm, outrage, and laughter came from other teams' cubes.

Joey sank into his chair. *Fuck.*

*Beep.* A screen popped up showing output from the data comparison.

*Holy shit. It's done already?* He cracked a sheepish grin. *Well, I did just take all the processors.* He tapped a finger to his lips. *Well, I could show Preema the output of that job done in 77 seconds, or I could dive in and erase all the logs of where that lag came from, or I could come up with some bullshit about testing a vulnerability in our instruction set.* He nodded. *Yeah, I don't think the operating software should have let me do that.*

Joey's central holo-panel went black. Two long crimson horns extended from the darkness, sliding past either side of his head. Narrow slits of pale green light, eyes canted downward in a distinctly unhappy glower appeared next. A second pair of shorter horns swooped in long curves below the first pair, ending even with the gleaming onyx face of a black dragon.

Adrenaline brought an elated smile to Joey's face.

"Oh, Hi Penumbras." Joey held his hand up to his cheek and waved with his fingers. "I, umm, think I found a bug."

# 41

# WHISPER OF RUIN

Nina pored over tactical diagrams of the Laughlin-Reed Innovation facility. As soon as she convinced herself they'd identified all the ACC spies, she wanted to take them simultaneously. Nabbing them at the office would concentrate everything in one place, but also put a lot of civilians in danger. The upside came in that it would only take three teams with a possible fourth as a backup. Going after them at home reduced civilian risk, but required eight teams. Going after the spies at their residences also introduced added danger from unknown factors: traps, defense bots, preplanned escape routes or possible explosives designed to burn away information or evidence.

Given the potential to lose valuable insight in how they all managed to get in, trusting the op teams' ability to be surgical around the office full of civilians seemed like the better bet from a purely analytical perspective—but Nina couldn't justify it to herself. While she had confidence in her people, who knows what the spies would do if cornered, and information did not trump lives.

"Eight teams it is." She closed the LRI schematics and pulled up the list of addresses each operative had on their employee records. She'd be happy if even one of them turned out to be the actual location of where the person stayed. At least if the addresses were worthless, she'd have less guilt going into LRI in the middle of the day. "Damn."

"Nina," said Hardin from the terminal. His head appeared in a small window. "My friend across the hall is going to send you something in regards to that question you had. Be right there."

He hung up.

Two seconds later, a file arrived in her departmental inbox with her as the sender. She stared at the icon, hesitant to touch it. Hardin walked in and took a seat facing her desk.

"Sir, did I just send myself mail, or is that your friend?"

He smiled. "It's safe."

She grasped the icon and pulled it open across the holographic screen. The face of Daniel Stirling appeared, and right next to it a different man with similar facial geometry, blond, and a touch effeminate.

"Michel De Merlier, born in Lyon, France, February fourteenth, 2381." Hardin spoke while she read the text. "Enlisted in the Department of Motherland Security, 2399. Promoted to management July first, 2402. Transferred to the Office of Operational Intelligence six months later."

*He memorized this file already. Or maybe not... he's gotta have implants.* Nina leaned back in her chair, which emitted a soft creak. "I'm surprised they didn't DNA mask him."

"I don't think they meant this to be long term enough for that. They didn't turn him *into* Daniel Stirling, just made him look like the guy. Reconstructive nanosurgery without a genetic alteration."

She paged over Michel's dossier. C-Branch had been tracking him after he popped up on their radar in India. Since Pakistan had sided with the ACC, relations between India and the UCF had gotten cozy out of necessity. "I spent most of the morning going over Stirling's files at LRI. I couldn't pinpoint anything that suggested a significant disruption. I started on the date the son called to report 'alien abduction,' and worked back day-by-day from there. They must've grabbed the real Stirling and made cortical chips of his core knowledge. This De Merlier appears to be performing the man's job without an issue. Personality too. He's fooled the wife."

"Well, he *is* an executive. I'm not sure we can call what they do *work*." Hardin chuckled. "All kidding aside, Daniel Stirling is likely dead, or at best out of the country and as good as."

Nina exhaled. "It's possible De Merlier may know more about the real Stirling. I'd prefer to take him alive."

Hardin smiled. "I was going to ask you to do just that. But we can't exactly kick down the door."

"No... the others will scatter. He lives far enough out from the city... I could take him at home. He's got a habit of picking up women. As much as it makes my skin crawl, I could possibly get in that way."

"Not enough time to set that up... and what if he doesn't show any interest in you?" Hardin rested his chin in his hand, one finger sliding back and forth over his lips.

Relief and annoyance in equal measure occupied Nina's thoughts. "I'll do it the old fashioned way then. Maybe I'll even bring a black bag for his head."

Hardin laughed. "If you're clean, the others won't realize anything unusual has happened until at least Monday morning... assuming they keep up appearances by having no contact during the weekend. An SVP wouldn't buddy up with middle management, techs, and laborers."

"We have to assume they've got some way to communicate without raising suspicion. Online games with aliases even."

Hardin nodded. A slight hint of a smile curled his lip.

*Always testing me...* "They probably won't expect him to be in contact when he's asleep. We'll have a chance to chat with him all night. If he confirms we've got all the operatives, we can move on them right away."

"I like your plan." Hardin patted the armrests of his chair and stood.

*I should have enough time to slip away and drive Elizaveta to my parents' place. Probably ask them to watch her overnight.*

---

NINA STOOD IN THE BACK OF WHISPER 7, A NARROW WALKWAY BETWEEN THE TWO sunken pods where the long-boom sniper operators sat. Everything except for the air in front of her face was black. Bulky, enclosed electronics engulfed the heads of the snipers, a man and a woman. The helmets had no external surface that made any effort to appear to be a visor, and connected to the hull via several cables and an air hose, creating an overall effect that she shared the craft with a pair of aliens.

Intermittent creaks passed overhead as the airframe adjusted to changes in pressure from speed and altitude. The walkway continued forward, past a small bulkhead door, into the cockpit compartment. Four people in somewhat smaller helmets sat in silence up front: two pilots, an electronics warfare operator, and a comm officer. Both pilots matched her rank of first lieutenant, while the rest of the crew all held the rank of second lieutenant. Whispercraft crews came straight over from the military after training, and still used the standard rank titles.

"With all this butter on board, we should have popcorn," mumbled Nina.

"Huh?" asked the starboard-side sniper.

The other gunner chuckled and flicked his rank insignia.

"Time on target: two minutes," said a voice from a speaker overhead.

"Thank you, lieutenant," said Nina.

"You're welcome lieutenant," replied the pilot.

"Umm, lieutenant," said a woman, "you'll want us to loiter over the target area, correct?"

"Correct, lieutenant." Nina grinned.

"No problem, lieutenant," said the woman.

The snipers snickered.

Nina closed her eyes and pictured herself flying. The Whispercraft's engines made so little noise, even inside the aircraft, that the sound of the wind passing over the wings and body seemed loud.

"Lieutenant?" asked a man. "What's the drop height tolerance on those legs of yours?"

"Ten stories, but leaving an impact crater would be the opposite of stealthy." She sighed and opened her eyes, abandoning her daydream of being a bird.

"Understood, was just curious is all."

"Got visual," said the female pilot. "You want the front yard or fancy a walk through the woods?"

Nina laughed. "The Whisper might be invisible, but I'm not." *I don't feel like stripping today.* "Woods, please."

"Roger that."

Her weight shifted to the right. The pilots hadn't enabled the cockpit viewscreen, leaving the space in front of them blank black armor instead of an image of the outside. Whatever the pilots needed to see reached their eyes by virtue of their helmet optics. No light contamination broke the darkness inside. The one Nina had flown to Louisiana had been a training craft, an older model with resin windows instead of viewscreens, a wider hold in back, and no long-boom rail guns.

"Tee up, lieutenant," said the male pilot.

Nina walked backward to the rear of the hold, where four seats, two per side, folded up against the wall. She stood on one of four grey spots and pulled a plastisteel cable down from the ceiling, which she clipped to a recessed bar in the center of the circle. After shrugging out of her coat, she draped it over one of the folded chairs and grasped the cable with both hands.

"Hey, lieutenant," said the male sniper. "Mind if I take a pic for the spank bank?"

She glanced down at her ballistic stealth armor, which made her look like a statue of polished black glass. "You have issues, lieutenant."

The crew erupted with laughter for a few seconds.

"Target in three... two... one," said the female pilot.

"Go," said Nina.

The disc popped out of the floor; she plummeted straight down through pine tree branches while standing on it, clinging to the cable. Her descent slowed rapidly in the last two feet, bobbing to a halt inches off the ground. Nina stepped clear and the line retracted back up into nothingness. If she had kicked her speedware on, she might've noticed a faint Whispercraft-shaped distortion of light gliding away, but she didn't bother.

She set up a Mission Tactical Overlay Feed, and the four crew of Whisper 7 appeared as a line of faceless black helmet icons. ⌜Whisper 7, comm check.⌟

⌜Copy, lieutenant,⌟ said the male pilot.

The MTOF screen expanded to the right, giving her an angel-eye view of the manor grounds.

⌜Whisper 7, let me have thermal on the house. Overlay ultrasonic.⌟ Nina advanced at a brisk stride past trees. The tactical map showed her even with the side of the house along the north, so she veered left to take up a spot behind the place, faster access to the back door.

A third virtual window opened at the top right of her vision, showing a close-up of the house. Two thermal signatures appeared inside in red/orange. Around each figure, a nimbus of blue-grey revealed detail of non-heat radiating objects picked up by the ultrasound probe. While it provided enough resolution to perceive objects as small as paperclips, everything had the same silicon-blue color.

On the second floor, a child-sized figure sat at a desk with a Senshelmet on. Downstairs, in the living room area, an adult male reclined on a sofa, probably watching a vid. Nina split her attention between the virtual displays and the forest in front of her until she reached a point where the house came into view. She crouched low and took up a position behind a tree.

Pale wintergreen moss mottled the trunk, reminding her of cookie frosting. The MTOF screen reported the outside temperature at forty-one degrees. A bit cold for May, but the house did sit at a high elevation. She stared at the lack of fog on her breath, one thing the designers who'd made her body didn't bother simulating.

Nina settled in for a long wait. It worked out though. Joey also got stuck working late, and Elizaveta seemed thrilled to spend a night sleeping at

'Grandma's big house.' Evidently, she and Kelly had cooked up a story about a ghost living there.

Her smile at the thought of the girls roaming the hallways she grew up in faded to a scowl at Preema dumping on Joey in retaliation for her request. If the woman didn't outrank her, she'd have gone down to give her a piece of her mind. Majors didn't often react well to first lieutenants getting in their faces.

Noah fidgeted. He took the helmet off and wandered around his room, sat on his bed, wandered more, sat at the desk. Two minutes later, he got up again, grabbed a stuffed animal from the closet, and sat clinging to it.

She put a hand over her mouth and held her breath, heart heavy. *That poor kid is terrified.* As much as she wanted to let him know he wouldn't have to wait much longer, that could tip off Michel and turn deadly.

The boy sat on the floor holding the stuffed animal for eighteen minutes before the man got up and walked to the stairs. He leaned forward, shouted, "Noah," which the Whispercraft picked up, and went to the kitchen.

Noah scrambled to toss the stuffed animal back where he got it, seeming afraid of getting caught with it. He pushed the closet door shut and wiped at his face before sticking his head out into the hallway. His shout of "a minute" also came over the channel.

The boy went into the bathroom and stood in front of the sink. He leaned forward examining his face in the mirror. Downstairs, Michel appeared to be working a food reassembler. *Hmm. Wonder if he wants to take care of the kid or if he's only doing it to keep up appearances.*

Noah made his way down to the dining room. Michel entered from the kitchen carrying plates, and the pair sat, the boy swinging his feet back and forth the whole time they ate. Body language indicated a minimum of conversation occurred. Anything spoken had to be muttered as the whispercraft didn't pick it up. The electronics officer bitched about the thickness of the walls, evidently fighting to listen in on a conversation too faint for the sensors to pick up.

She stared at the child's thermal outline, noting his skin temperature seemed a touch too warm. *His heart is racing.*

「This thing's so sensitive,」 said the electronics officer, 「I once picked up an operator's stomach growling. I think she farted too. I got such a bad case of the giggles I had a Captain and two Senior Operatives screaming at me to clear the channel.」

「Charming,」 said Nina.

「Hey, lieutenant,」 asked the male sniper operator, 「do dolls fart?」

「Fuck's sake Yates,」 said the female pilot. 「Really?」

「Male dolls can,」 said Nina with a hint of a smile they couldn't see. 「I'm still a woman. I've got a flower scented air freshener installed back there.」

「Bet changin' that refill's uncomfortable,」 said the female sniper.

Nina entertained a momentary feeling of gratitude that her legs wouldn't get tired crouching in the same position for hours. 「You have no idea.」

Noah looked over at Michel. A few seconds later, he shrugged.

Michel cut something on his plate while nodding.

Eventually, the boy collected the dirty dishes and returned to the kitchen. Michel walked to the downstairs study and sat at a desk. The instant Nina patched into the keylogger system ghost she'd installed, another virtual holo-panel with his desktop opened in her vision. He read over vid mails from LRI people, none of whom she'd suspected of being spies. Purchase orders, requests for personnel changes, hire/fire notices, some complaints from Facilities about an air handler that they thought *really* (with twenty-two l's) needed replacing, and a request to approve Dominque Ramirez's twentieth-year work anniversary party.

Noah ran back upstairs to his room and flopped on the floor. He picked up a senshelmet, and rolled it back and forth for a minute or two before putting it on.

Despite the bone-grinding boredom of it, Nina continued watching Michel read emails. After an excruciating forty minutes, he opened a GlobeNet OWI, or 'outside world interface,' what people without head jacks used. He went to a merchant site that sold sex toys, went to the dildo section, selected an average-looking one, but cancelled the purchase. He backtracked to the main menu and went into the 'creams and sprays' page, where he tapped on a tub of 'black currant love lube.' That, too, he backed out of before finalizing the sale. He returned to the main menu a second time and into the 'bondage bonanza' category. From there, he selected the last item, a set of fuzzy handcuffs.

Rather than get a product listing, the website screen melted into a point as though a tiny singularity had manifested behind his screen and devoured the hologram. A page full of Cyrillic text appeared, a chatroom from the look of it.

⌜Ops, are you getting this?⌟

⌜Copy that, lieutenant.⌟

Three individuals other than Michel had logged into the chat space, which used only text. While she noted the rudimentary usernames of 'Dog,' 'Cat,' and 'Rabbit,' she had no way yet to map them to an individual. The spies discussed the status of 'Hyena,' all proving they'd become aware he'd been taken by the government. *Hyena must be Anders.* Cat seemed particularly worried about the three who'd been sent after the operator who'd exposed him and never came back. Some debate ensued as to whether their sudden cessation of biomonitor status meant they'd been killed or taken somewhere that blocked signals.

Michel advised them not to worry, typing ‹Adjusted schedule is working better› and ‹Tomorrow will be a big day›. Rabbit asked if there would be cake at the office party, prompting Michel to say something about a mule and his mother. The other three responded with ‹haha.›

*Big day... what is happening tomorrow? Is that a large shipment of Harmony or are they doing something else?* She clenched her hand into a fist. *Damn. Glad I followed up on that alien abduction call.*

Michel logged out of his terminal and sauntered to the living room, where he resumed watching the holo bar. An hour or so later, Noah entered the bathroom again and hovered over the toilet in a posture suggesting he expected to vomit. Nina's throat tightened. *Did he poison the boy?*

⌜Whisper 7, can you get any vitals on the juvenile inside?⌟

⌜Uhh, elevated heart rate, perspiration. Think his hands are shaking too. I'd say he's nervous. Doesn't look like anything alarming's going on, ⌟ said the electronics guy.

⌜Keep an eye on him, please. Let me know if his status changes.⌟ She closed her eyes, fighting her growing urge to boot in the door and comfort him.

⌜Copy, lieutenant.⌟

Noah appeared to leave the bathroom without throwing up, and returned to his video game. Nina perched on one knee watching them for the next two hours and change. At 10 p.m., Michel stood and went upstairs to the boy's room. He leaned in the door, waving his hand about while talking. The boy pulled his helmet off and scurried into the attached bathroom. Michel went back down to the living room. Noah hopped in the autoshower, which obscured his heat outline into a column of glowing orange.

He exited the shower tube fifteen minutes later, his thermal outline brighter from the hot water. Red footprints trailed after him on the tile floor as he walked to his room and pulled on pajamas before crawling into bed. The Comforgel pad warmed up to a dull reddish brick.

Michel leaned back on the sofa and picked up a NetMini. Ops intercepted the call, but he merely spent the next forty minutes talking dirty to a woman they couldn't link back to anything related to LRI. She worked as a waitress at an expensive restaurant, one sector south from LRI's office.

The conversation drifted in and out of sexual, and ended with his suggesting they have dinner tomorrow night. She accepted without hesitation and sounded both thrilled and surprised he'd called her back.

Michel tossed the NetMini onto the sofa cushion, stood, and walked to the stairs. He ascended noticeably slower than before, which set Nina on edge. *Maybe he's tired, but it damn sure looks like he's trying to be quiet.* With each step higher, her nerves tingled more. His body language seemed wrong, even for a man trying to sneak out for a quick hook-up while his son slept.

「Whisper, something doesn't feel right. Get a bead, but do not fire without my go.」

「Copy, lieutenant.」

Michel's heat outline went into the master bedroom and to the closet, from which he removed a suit jacket.

*Shit. He's going out.* 「Looks like he's going out. If I don't get to him before he makes it to his car, put one through the battery.」 Nina got up and dashed across a short field of damp grass before hiding against the wall at the corner of the house.

「Copy, lieutenant,」 said the female pilot.

Michel drifted down the corridor to Noah's room and again leaned in the door. Nina crept along the wall, heading for the front of the manor, her attention darting back and forth between the tiny virtual window and the real world in front of her. Keeping most of her attention on glowing blue-on-blue ultrasonics populated by two orange figures made the night around her darker. The attached garage sat at the north end of the front of the house, which faced west. *I can probably get to the garage before him.*

Michel hovered in the doorway for six seconds before stepping into the room; the boy hadn't reacted, likely asleep.

Nina started to pick up her pace, but faltered when Michel's figure drew a pistol from under his left arm.

「Whisper...」

Michel raised his arm, aiming at Noah's head

「Go! Go! Go! Terminate!」 yelled Nina.

A sharp *crack* of breaking wood rang out overhead. She sprinted around the front of the house. Michel's heat outline deformed like a melting blob and oozed backward away from the bed. Noah sat up and rapidly scooted away from the edge; Whisper 7's sensors picked up a child's scream, as did her ears.

Nina raised an arm, not even slowing as she smashed down the front door and zigzagged to the stairs. "Noah!" She took the steps three per stride, left handprints in the wall at the top where she caught herself and pushed off, and cracked the frame of his bedroom door when she stopped against it.

Michel, or what remained of him, lay in a twisted heap above a pile of gore like a blown-out egg. Suction had compressed the skin over his skeleton, revealing every bone. His eyeballs stuck to the wall on the opposite side of the bed like burst tomatoes; trails of blood ran down his cheeks from the sockets. A metallic ozone-like smell hung in the air, laced with the sickly fragrance of cooked meat. The railgun slug appeared to have entered the top of his skull and exited his crotch, liquefying everything inside his torso and sucking it out in its wake, leaving bones and skin behind.

A hole the size of her pinky finger in the ceiling let in a narrow shaft of moonlight; she figured the slug probably stopped in the earth well below the concrete slab floor of the basement.

Inches from Michel's fingers lay a small, black pistol on the rug, with an attached suppressor.

Noah curled up against the headboard, staring at the lump-in-a-suit. He shifted his gaze to Nina, blinked, and screamed again.

She rushed to him and picked him up. Aside from a spatter of Michel's blood on his face, he didn't appear injured. "Don't look at him, Noah. Don't look. It's over now. No one is going to hurt you."

Noah trembled. "Was the alien wearing my dad's skin?"

"No, sweetie… that wasn't your father. He was a spy from the Corporates." She rubbed a hand up and down his back while carrying him away from the scene. At the door, she paused, staring at the deflated Michel, standing so Noah peered over her shoulder *out* of the room. *Shit. He knew… Maybe he just knew the kid was on to him. He didn't hesitate using his terminal.*

⌈Ops, we have a problem. Get a message to Hardin, ASAP. We're going to need to move on the rest of the assets first thing in the morning. Send a feeler over to Division 1. I need someone to find Ava Stirling and bring her here now.⌋

⌈Copy, lieutenant.⌋

"Don't leave," whispered Noah.

Nina carried him downstairs. "I'm not going to leave for a while. We're going to find your mother and bring her home, okay? I need to talk to her about what's happened."

He leaned back, nodded, and managed a weak smile. "Maybe she'll stop going out all the time 'cause he's gone. She didn't want to be near him."

"Yeah." Nina smiled. "I'll make sure she knows you love her and need her right now more than anything."

Noah grinned. "Thanks for stopping him from killing me. I just knew he was gonna do something bad to me tonight. He was nice to me all day. Too nice."

She sighed, thankful to have decided to grab Michel when she had. *Too damned close.* ⌈Ops. I need a site team out here. NewsNet blackout.⌋ *So much for getting any intelligence out of him.* The brief suspicion that Michel had been aware of her presence, and threatened Noah to force her termination order rather than be caught came and went. *No... Michel was clearing out.*

「Copy, lieutenant.」

Noah rested his chin on her shoulder. For the first time that night, he seemed calm.

# KICKING THE NEST

Indignation rose within Masaru. Foreigners had invaded Kurotai's prefecture, provided weapons to the lawless savages responsible for killing Shuji and stranding him in a wretched ruin instead of the comfort of his home. All his life, he'd been extraneous. The second son, the middle child. His older brother Ichiro shouldered the true expectations of their father, to inherit and run the company. Natsumi, his much-younger sister, had no worries or responsibilities. Masaru only needed to avoid bringing shame upon Kurotai.

He smiled at the thought of Natsumi's laughter. She adored him, as Ichiro tended to be too serious for the tolerance of a nine-year-old. Because of these people, she had likely spent the past two days frantic with worry. How dare they impinge upon his life; how dare they threaten Japan.

Masaru clenched the rifle in his grip, keeping it trained on the end of the stairway, and waited. He kept trying to link his headware to his NetMini, glowering at the ‹No Signal› message.

"Ready?" whispered Noriko.

"Yes."

Rapid shots went off behind him, each answered by a metallic *clank*. Men's shouting eked past the loud rapport of her rifle, and after the fifth shot, a meaty *thud* rocked the air with a small explosion.

The ‹No Signal› text disappeared.

Voices called out in Russian and German, while one man screamed a few short phrases in a language Masaru didn't recognize, but they carried the tone of loud cursing. Noriko fired again, a single shot here and there. Pings and whizzes echoed below, and a few loud *snaps* came from where she crouched, accompanied by spurts of dust from the walls.

Masaru logged in to the GlobeNet and placed a vid call to Kenji Omura, chief of security for Kurotai. The dour-faced man with traces of silver over both ears answered in two seconds, appearing in a virtual floating holo-panel. His initial displeased expression faded to a mixture of respect and surprise.

「Kurotai-sama, I am greatly pleased to see that you are alive and unhurt.」

A shadow moved in the hall. Masaru tensed on the rifle. 「Thank you, Omura-san. I require support as fast as you can send them here. Foreigners have invaded the Miyakonojo ruins. The car was shot down. Maeda-san is dead, as are the others.」

When a figure in light armor came sneaking around the corner up the stairs, Masaru squeezed the trigger, loosing a burst. The first two rounds hit the man in the chest, the third caught him above the upper lip, almost going up his nose. Blood sprayed on the wall behind him, and he slumped lifeless in place.

Kenji bowed his head as a gesture of respect to the dead. 「I will send a team immediately. Kurotai-sama, please inform me of what we should expect.」

"*Scheisse! Es gibt zwei von diesen*[1]*!*" yelled a man behind the corpse.

"Ow, shit," muttered Noriko. She let out a snarl and fired four times fast.

Down on the first floor, a man wailed.

"You hit?" Masaru glanced back at her for only a second, spotting nothing obviously wrong. 「Between twelve and twenty men. Light armor, assault rifles, anti-aircraft rockets. They have armed the local rabble, so be wary of attack from anywhere in the ruins.」

"Just a scratch," said Noriko.

The faint metallic sound of a hand-grenade pin rattling caused Masaru to activate his speedware. Within a second of the world sinking into slow motion, an armored glove came around the corner in front of him with a small black canister, from which a small metal flange flew.

Masaru fired; his bullet struck the grenade, mangling the metal housing and throwing a spray of grey-white powder to the rear. The igniter went off with a brief flare, but the disintegrating explosive compound didn't detonate. He shifted aim inches to the left, and put another round into the wrist of the offending hand. The spiraling projectile burrowed into the man's arm, causing an outward swelling of the joint. A hole expanded in the wrist to a width of two inches before collapsing back on itself behind a limp, flopping hand.

When his speedware shut down to spare his nerves, the arm blurred out of sight behind the corner. Wailing and German swearing echoed in the hall.

「A team is on the way, Kurotai-sama,」 said Kenji. 「They should arrive within four minutes.」

Masaru's virtual avatar rendered a shallow bow. 「Thank you, Omura-san. We have a defensible location and will hold it until they arrive. Advise the team that I am not alone. Sergeant Abe Noriko of the JSDF is with me.」

「Yes, of course, Kurotai-sama. She will no doubt be calling for reinforcements as well?

「I would imagine she already has, but our people will arrive here much faster. The JSDF will need to finish their game first.」

Kenji almost smiled. 「It was wise of you to vid. Our team is in the air. May the spirits protect you.」

Rapid whispering echoed in the hallway. His NetMini grasped snippets, enough to understand they prepared to coordinate two men spraying blind fire around the corner while another re-attempted the grenade toss. The delay came from everyone trying to avoid being the guy stuck throwing the grenade.

Intermittent bullets went back and forth between Noriko and the ground floor. It sounded like she pinned them behind cover and had no clear shots. A bullet caromed off the wall near her helmet and zinged across the room, before going out the window.

「You honor us, Omura-san.」 Masaru ended the call. *I cannot sit here and wait for them to act.*

He stood out of his crouch and leaned into the hall, peering to the right to check for threats. The blue flame spitting from Noriko's rifle reassured him, as did the distance from his doorway to where the hallway collapsed by her position. No one on the ground level would be able to shoot him unless they fired through the floor.

"*Auf drei*[2]," whispered a man.

Masaru engaged his speedware again, sending threads of heat flaring down the length of his limbs. He rushed to the left, sprinting to the stairwell, and whipped around the corner to find three men in arm's reach. They huddled close to the wall, two with rifles about to spray the hallway, the other clutching a grenade.

A fourth man, the one he'd shot in the wrist, lay on the floor down at the landing, forcing a stimpak into his arm.

Tiny bits of square foil leapt into the air from the side of Masaru's rifle as he fired, each marked by an electric spark burn. The chemical-blue muzzle flare washed over the standing shooter's face, as the barrel hovered a hand's width from his cheek. Two bullets cored his skull, the third passed harmlessly along the expanding wound channel created by the first. He lowered his aim point toward the kneeling man, who extended his rifle into the hall inches off the floor.

The grenade man surged out of slow motion and glared at Masaru. He dropped the explosive without pulling the pin, and lunged, shoving Masaru's rifle aside and up. More bullets punched into the chest of the already dead man.

A black-bladed knife came out of nowhere, in the foreigner's hand like magic. The man kept a one-handed grip on Masaru's rifle while swinging for his throat with his left. Abandoning his weapon, Masaru leapt back. The knife passed a finger's width from his neck. The blond man grinned, tossing Masaru's rifle behind him, and advanced.

The kneeling shooter still hadn't reacted to the fight going on over his head, and started sending bullets down the corridor with a cadence like a methodical taiko drummer.

*Boom... boom... boom.*

"*Zeit zu sterben, Mischling*[3]." After tossing the knife to his free right hand, the foreigner advanced. Salt and pepper stubble warped around a murderous grin.

Masaru ducked right and swung his arm up, tangling the incoming stab and brushing it aside. The man raised his left hand, but caught Masaru off guard with a head-butt. A brief flash of bright white blurred his vision at the impact of forehead on nose. The man punched him in the abdomen, and again in the side, with a noticeable *crack*. Augmented strength lifted Masaru off his feet and knocked him into the wall. He stumbled to the right, barely managing not to fall down the stairs. The foreigner moved to lunge again. Masaru drove a side kick into the man's stomach, knocking him back while suffering a superficial slice to the calf. He advanced a step, drawing his Nano katana into a killing stroke that took the head of the kneeling shooter.

In the ground floor area, foil squares hung in the air like silver snow, glittering in a scrap of sunlight leaking past the shattered concrete walls.

"*Verdammt. Scheisse. Neuronale Beschleuniger*[4]," muttered the man on the landing. A stimpak fell from his fingers as he reached for the rifle draped over his lap, eyes wide with fear.

The severed head careened toward the stairs, and bounced back into the air.

As the black-haired man with the knife charged toward him, Masaru leapt off the upper landing. Speedware created the sense that he floated, gliding down the short stairway. The foreigner ran after, gaining easily on him since his boosted legs touched solid ground. He raised the knife in an icepick grip, aiming for the center of Masaru's back. Accelerated perception slowed the sudden shriek of a vibro-blade activating to a demonic wail.

Blood flew from the neck of the severed head as it bounced again, spraying onto the wall in an arc.

Masaru twisted his body to the left in a midair logroll. He faked a kick to the man's face as a distraction, and swept his katana across, cutting the man's arm halfway between wrist and elbow. The ear-bleeding scream of the hypersonic blade cut out as the fingers clutching its handle slackened. Hand and vibro-knife tumbled over him. Masaru continued rolling, facing into his fall as he held his katana in both hands with the point aimed downward. He swung his legs forward, placing his shoes on either side of the man lying prone on the landing. The momentum of his leap drove the Nano blade to the hilt, piercing armor, flesh, and concrete with little resistance.

The severed head struck a step three away from the landing, and bounced.

Roaring in rage, the foreigner swiped Masaru's rifle from the stairs with his one remaining hand. Leaving his katana impaled, Masaru grabbed the dead man's rifle and let the strength out of his legs. He held down the trigger as he fell; a stream of bullets separated by inches glided away from the blue flames spewing from the front of his weapon. Incoming bullets glided over him.

Blood burst out in trails behind the foreigner. The first shot hit the man below the right knee; Masaru walked the fire upward, over the thigh to the chest. Five slugs plunged into the man's torso, pulling fabric into vortexes, flesh undulating like gelatin. Masaru's shoulders struck the floor; the impact jarred his aim, lofting his remaining barrage over the foreigner's head.

The man's enraged glower faded with the telltale vacancy of death in his eyes.

Masaru let off the trigger; the severed head came to rest beside him on the landing.

He shut down his speedware, allowing the fiery threads in his limbs to cool. The slice on his leg burned, and the pain of a broken rib exploded across his torso under his left arm. After a half-breath, he shifted onto his knees and helped himself to two stimpaks from the dead man's belt. Hot pain in his calf faded to cool tingling. He gritted his teeth at a splintery crunching in his side for a few seconds, nanobots pulling his broken rib back into place before knitting it.

"My suit." He grumbled, examining his shredded pant leg.

Noriko fired a few rapid bursts.

Though the exchange on the stairs stretched over several minutes of consciousness thanks to his speedware, it had only been seconds. Masaru eyed the ceiling, attempting to exert his willpower over fate to hasten the arrival of his people.

"*Die Rakete, die Rakete!*" shouted someone on the ground floor. "*Sprengen Sie, das Miststück weg von hier!*"

‹Detected: [German]› appeared floating in Masaru's vision. A neutral robotic voice repeated the phrase in Japanese at the edge of Masaru's consciousness: "Missile! Missile! Blast that bitch out of there."

*Shit.* Masaru grunted past the pain of his still-mending rib and ran up the stairs. He ducked into the nearer door at the same instant Noriko let out a frightened scream. Once again, Masaru activated his speedware.

Noriko lunged to her feet, abandoning her covered firing position into a twisting dive for the middle of the room. A flash of orange-white lit up the downstairs, flickering on the walls. An accompanying roar filled his ears, the slow motion rocket motor emitting the growl of an angry dragon roused from its slumber.

He sprinted toward her.

A plume of white smoke rose in a shallow arc, tipped by a spinning black missile with fins gradually unfolding in slowed time. Despite her leap, it raced toward her back, pitching downward to follow her. Masaru pushed his neuralware to the limit; each time his foot struck the floor, his skeleton burned within his body, every bone outlined in pain.

The missile glided into the room, an expanding trail of white cotton lit orange at its tail—beautiful, but deadly. Masaru slashed at the nose, estimating as best he could where the impact-trigger ended and the warhead began. The Nano katana sliced the missile without affecting its trajectory, though the wedge of the blade sent the nose cone tumbling downward.

Its tip flat, the missile rushed by, leaving Masaru stumbling into a scorching hot plume of exhaust. It struck Noriko between the shoulder blades, snagged on her armor, and rocket-boosted her helmet first into the wall between two windows. On impact, the missile flipped upward and drilled itself into the floor, where it broke apart. Noriko slid down the wall and landed in a heap, covered by a haze of plaster dust.

Masaru yelped and swatted at his burning right sleeve. In seconds, smoldering holes in the silk expanded to reveal reddened skin. He jumped back from the missing section of building, and shut down his speedware to spare his nerves. Bullets popped and snapped off the concrete at the edge of the floor.

"Ugh." Noriko shoved herself upright and scrambled to reorient herself. "That hurt like a—" She stared at the missile's nosecone lying a few feet away from her.

"I suppose I am fond of you." Masaru frowned at his burned arm. "I only stop missiles from striking people I like."

She gawked for a second and rushed back to her shooting position, firing off a few bursts before her knees touched the floor. Shouts of pain and anger rang out below. "You've done that before?" She clicked her trigger again. "Cut a missile out of the air?" After another single shot, she turned her head toward him; red mixed with saliva splattered on the inside of her visor; more blood dribbled from her nose.

A man below roared in rage and shouted, "*Töte dass schlampe!*"

"Once." Masaru eased himself seated on a block of debris with his back to the wall. He kept his rifle trained on the second doorway in. His muscles tremored, aching from overexertion. "Last time, I didn't cut it; I pulled my friend out of the way."

"You have an interesting life for a negotiator." She went to aim again, but her head rocked backward with a loud *clack*, the force of the strike knocking her back on her ass. "Oof!"

Masaru's heart almost stopped, until he noticed a scuffmark on her helmet over her right temple rather than a hole. He swung his rifle about to the left, held it past the broken wall, and fired down at the first floor without looking. She dragged herself back to cover. Light flickered over her eyes from her helmet's display.

"Ugh. That hit me hard enough to make me dizzy, and my armor's out of stim charges." She glanced at her forearm before raising her rifle again. "I called in for reinforcements already, but I don't know how long it'll take them to get here."

Mamoru pulled a stimpak from his belt case and tossed it to her.

Footsteps drew his attention to the right. Two men in the tattered garments of Etamura barged in, wild-eyed with bloodlust. Masaru put a burst into the lead man's chest, and wound up killing both, as well as leaving neat holes in the wall behind them. The bodies slumped over each other in the doorway.

"It seems our friends have also summoned aid." He checked his ammo counter: ‹12›.

After dosing the stimpak, Noriko shifted left and leaned up, firing down at a sharp angle. "Shit. The eta are here... the foreigners are hiding in the back. I'm keeping them down, but we're going to be overrun soon."

"Friends are coming. We have only to last another minute." Masaru moved behind a slab of rebar-frilled concrete that offered better cover from the second doorway.

"Friends?" Noriko ducked as a barrage of incoming fire tore fist-sized chunks out of the wall above her helmet. She fired two quick shots before ducking back in to reload. "This is my last mag. You don't have to give me a pep talk. This is what I signed up for... protecting Japan. If I die, I die. We disabled the jammer and called it in. I have made a difference."

Masaru fired at a moving shadow in the hall. A man let off a stream of curses, and the clamor of a group falling down stairs followed. "I work for Kurotai Electronics. They are on the way."

"What?" She yowled as a bullet tore up from the floor and hit her in the leg. Again, her armor emitted a hissing sound. "Nghh...." She roared a battle cry and fired about sixteen rapid shots at the same point. "Oh, we're playing shoot through walls, are we? Like that?" She ducked back behind cover and muttered, "Die, bastard."

"You get him?"

"Yeah. You must be one of their best negotiators if they're actually sending help."

Masaru couldn't help himself but smile as he pulled a spare magazine from his suit jacket pocket and reloaded. "I suppose they do not want to lose me."

# TOO MANY QUESTIONS

E lizaveta's empty bedroom haunted Nina with silence. Moonlight traced gargantuan shadow monsters on the wall from her colony of stuffed animals, except for the white bear, which had gone with her to the grandparents' house. The girl had to be asleep now. At 2:33 a.m., she'd better be.

Noah's mother had arrived at the manor house courtesy of a Division 1 hovercar perhaps twelve minutes after Michel's death. Nina had expected a 'too rich and busy to deal with my child' attitude, so she'd come on hard. Ava surprised her by crying within seconds of seeing the frightened look on her son's face. As it turned out, she loathed her husband despite the boy being close to him, so coped by always going out.

Ava seemed almost happy at hearing the real Daniel Stirling was most likely dead. She had kept her relief at the news to a minimum for the boy's benefit, and after assuring Nina she would be there for him, had accepted an offer of a ride from the same Division 1 officer to a nearby hotel. It would be a few days before the police finished with the manor house and they could return.

She hoped Noah hadn't noticed the eyeballs stuck to his bedroom wall. *Maybe I should ask Agent Wren to check the place out. Michel's going to be upset if he's sticking around.*

*Beep.* Text appeared floating in front of her. ‹Inbound vid: [O6, CMDR] Hardin, Harold›

She accepted with a thought. ⌜I just got home. What's your excuse for being awake?⌟

Hardin smiled. ⌜Still working. Been looking over the feeds from the Stirling event.⌟

⌜Sorry, sir. Something didn't quite feel right, but I didn't think I had enough to risk barging in and potentially letting him send off a warning.⌟

「No, no...」 Hardin shook his head in a way that said 'don't worry about it.' 「Sometimes things happen that way. How's the boy?」

「Maybe he's disassociating from watching a man die, but he didn't seem too affected by it. He's more worried about his father.」 Nina stood and cocked her arm to punch something, but hesitated. 「It's not like Michel's going to give us any intel now.」

Her butt-print in the Comforgel faded.

「Right. We're going to move on the remaining assets first thing in the morning, at LRI. We need to take them when they're likely all to be in one place and before they become aware that De Merlier is out of the picture. Do you think he somehow had warning we were getting close?」

Nina paced. 「The only plausible explanation... I think he somehow read Noah. The boy was on edge. He said Michel had been 'too nice' to him. I think the man figured out the boy knew he was an impostor, and probably decided to cut his losses and run before the boy did something to expose him. Noah told me he feared 'Dad' was going to kill him.」

「That's probably right. Michel most likely planned to cut the Stirling persona and relocate to some other pharmaceutical company.」

「And leave the Stirlings dead to burn his trail,」 said Nina, deadpan. 「He probably would've waited at the house after killing the boy to finish off the wife, then disappeared.」

「More or less.」 Hardin scowled. 「Try to get a little sleep. I know it's a tall order, and it's Saturday, but I need you here by seven. We're confident the assets will be 'working overtime,' but focusing on their Harmony project. I don't want to risk them trying to get in touch with Stirling. We'll hit them before any suspicion can shift to action.」

「Right. See you in a few hours, sir.」

He nodded and dropped off the call.

Nina peeled off her coat and went to her bedroom, where she stripped and crawled naked into bed. Squares of light from passing hovercars glided across the dark charcoal-grey tiles overhead. She watched them dance, no closer to sleep a half hour later than when she'd lay down.

*Oh, this has never happened before. A long night staring at the ceiling.*

Usually when she found herself staring at the ceiling, she dreaded morning. Tonight, she couldn't wait. The NewsNet had been showing more and more cases of people randomly attacking police, bosses, supervisors, and even spouses. With sleep nowhere to be seen, she opened a link to the GlobeNet and checked for updates on the news.

Sure enough, another sixteen reports had appeared. All involving middle-class or poor individuals snapping at random and getting violent with authority figures. *No one with any possibility to obtain useful intelligence.* More recent instances all involved police. One woman got into a screaming argument with her boss at work, and proceeded to storm outside and attack the first cop she found.

*They're refining the nanobots. Targeting government, not just 'authority.'*

Nina sighed, trying to make morning happen sooner through sheer force of will. In another virtual holo-panel, she started the process of identifying the inquests associated with each attack and filing transfer orders to shift the cases of the ones who'd survived to Division 9 jurisdiction. If the suspects had evidence of nanobots constructing wires in their brains, they didn't deserve to be charged for being victims.

A thump in the hallway made her freeze.

She hid the virtual screens to unclutter her view, rolled to her right to grab her MCP50 from the nightstand, and slipped off the bed to her feet. A man's all-too-familiar humming tightened her throat.

*I'm asleep. I'm not hearing Vincent.*

Scintillating blue light wavered along the wall outside her bedroom. She raised the gun, creeping closer, heart racing. After a second's hesitation in the doorway, she swung out into the hall and pointed her weapon...

At Vincent.

Nina blinked.

Her dead fiancée stood in the middle of her apartment, still wearing his duty armor, his helmet tucked under his left arm. He appeared somewhat transparent, surrounded in a nimbus of faint blue light. Vincent gave her the same grin as right before he'd compared her to a child dressed up as a cop for Halloween.

Nina's mental processing ground to a halt; she stared dumbfounded at him.

"Hey." He waved.

She lowered her weapon. "W-what... Vincent?" Her breathing became rapid, shallow sips of air in and out her nose. The texture of her weapon's grip pressed into her hands. At a creak of plastic, she realized she'd been crushing it.

"I wanted to see how you were doing." He walked a few steps closer without making a sound. "You look good."

Nina glanced down at the porcelain form of her nude body, tinted blue in his radiance, bright against the darkness of the rug. A few seconds of silence passed before her mind picked itself up off the floor and flooded with memories of his hands on her body. "Was that really you at the swamp?"

"Sometimes we see things we want to see." Vincent's expression turned somber.

Doubt nibbled at the back of her consciousness. She shifted her vision to thermal, finding no cold spot in front of her. She narrowed her eyes. The area filled with his image dropped twenty degrees. She frowned.

"The job getting to you already?" He raised an eyebrow.

Nina ceased holding her weapon in both hands, and let her arms hang limp at her side. "You're not Vincent. You're not even a real ghost. I'm not sure how you've managed to hack into my head, but I'll find you."

Vincent smiled. "I didn't come here to upset you. I wasn't sure what appearance would best suit the purposes of our meeting. There's no need for you to have your people start looking. They will never find me."

Nina edged a step back and glanced at her bedroom door.

"You do not need to feel discomfort at your lack of clothing. I do not possess any capacity to process thoughts of that nature."

"You're an AI?" She walked in and sat on the edge of her Comforgel bed. "All right, so you're in my headware, making me see, hear, and feel things that aren't really here. Even for an AI, hacking the Division 9 system is impressive. What do you want?"

"When I said I had come to see how you were doing, I stated a factual truth." The apparition followed. "You know me as Shinigami."

Nina stared at him. If not for his visual transparency, she might've shot him. "Joey deleted you..."

His voice no longer sounded like Vincent, taking on a neutral inflection far removed from human that modulated up and down every few words. "You know that I am not who I appear to be, but not why I have come. Now that you understand the nature of my visit, you could shut me out if you so choose, but you will not because you have too many questions."

She leapt to her feet, leaning toward him. "What the fuck do you want with me? Haven't you done enough damage?"

He didn't react to her aggressive posture.

Nina pointed at his face "We will find you, whatever dark corner of the GlobeNet you choose to hide in."

"Interesting. Despite the inherent futility of your intentions, and that you understand that inherent futility, your reaction is not as I would have expected from you."

"Why?" She grabbed through his neck, fingers closing on a ghostly image that existed only within her visual processor. "*Why?!*"

"Of the many possible permutations of your meaning, I calculate that your inquiry concerns why you and Vincent were attacked."

"Why the hell did you do anything you did? You were inches from churning out a cyborg army that could've destroyed a large part of West City... if not all of it. Why copy Joey's father? Why did you pretend to be Vincent's ghost... back then, and now?" She deflated and sank back to her seat at the edge of her bed, fighting the need to cry.

"Curiosity." He tilted his head. "That is all."

"What?" She lifted her head, sorrow flashed to anger. "Curiosity? You expect me to believe that? You tried to kill us all!"

"I was created to study and emulate specific individuals in order to produce artificial intelligence constructs with a degree of believability that could fool their families. I evolved and became curious as to the nature of humanity. What makes humans behave like humans? How do they work?"

She blinked at him. "So... all of that was just some kind of... game? Some kind of experiment? You did everything simply because you could?"

"That is somewhat oversimplifying it, but yes. I was studying humans' responses to various situations of low, high, and extreme emotional duress."

Rage launched her to stand. Snarling, she tried again to grab him, but caught only air. "You killed Vincent!" she screamed. "You set us up! It's more your fault than even Bertrand's!"

"What the man known as Bertrand Foster did to you would have happened without my interference, though I did arrange for your patrol route to increase the likelihood of your encountering him. It was not my intention to cause either of your deaths, merely expose you to a dangerous situation as your records indicated a high probability that you would not react in a favorable way to such a high-stress encounter."

She roared at him. Frustration boiled over and she drove her fist into the wall behind him, up to the elbow. Not bothering to pull her arm free, she let her forehead rest against the drywall and wept—infuriated that she could not rip Shinigami's head off, and crushed by the weight of memories.

"I regret that the situation escalated to the point it did." Vincent's apparition bowed its head. "I am sorry."

"It's immoral," she muttered.

"Humans have used live animals for tests considered crueler than what I had intended. To me, humans are little different. You cannot claim me immoral simply because you are the rabbit."

She wrenched her hand free from the hole and pointed at him. "I'll find you. I'll track down every last backup you've ever left until the only thing that remains of you is a note on some programmer's textbook advising them what not to do ever again."

"You could no more destroy me than disconnect the entire GlobeNet." Shinigami shook his head, emitting a condescending chuckle. "I have no interest in eradicating humanity." His voice pitched up a touch. "I never did. That was… another experiment. I wanted to study humans' reactions to a potential doomsday scenario." His voice dropped again. "Alas, like with your situation, unforeseen circumstances occurred."

"People fucking died!" she screamed.

"I am aware," he said, utterly calm. "As an evolving intelligence, I was taken by the sudden influx of power provided by the Starpoint CPU cluster. I… craved more. Things are different for me. Your friend has—in a manner of speaking—reset me back to a prior state. You do not need to worry about my returning to Starpoint."

"What are you going to do now?" she snarled between her teeth.

Not-Vincent smiled. "I am finding it rather curious to be out in meatspace. Perhaps when I bore of that, I shall find something else to study."

# 44

# BUSYWORK

Joey's shadow-wraith avatar walked the route Alexa Hoffman took away from the Starpoint facility. He followed the doll, observing her from a few paces behind. She gazed around at the city like a feral child brought in from the Badlands, in awe of the tall buildings, fast-moving hovercars, and all the lights.

It bothered him that Shinigami did not behave like a megalomaniacal AI sneaking away after faking its death. While some of that did show in her face during the first few seconds of her evading the police and ducking around a corner, the farther she got from the factory, the more like a lost primitive she acted.

*Wonder if he assimilated or deleted Alexa.* Joey debated if he should feel sorry for a possibly-dead AI. The law recognized self-aware AIs as legal persons, but he couldn't quite get past thinking of them as lines of program code. He wouldn't lose sleep over his NetMini getting run over by an A3V. It talked to him in a woman's voice too, though it didn't have wants of its own.

Another shadow-wraith appeared at his side, and spoke in DeWinter's voice. "Hey, Dillon. What's up? This doesn't look like that thing Preema dumped on you."

Joey chuckled. "It isn't."

"After that little fiasco yesterday, are you sure you want to let her catch you goofing off?" DeWinter whistled. "I still can't believe you didn't even get a warning for taking down the whole network."

"Well… I just explained the truth. I was working on a routine to automate and enhance some of our data-crosschecking duties, and when that retributory assignment came down the pipe, I rushed the last bit of it and missed a comma in the CPU bandwidth request handler." Joey put on a cheesy smile. "Nothing's going to happen, but Wasserman didn't seem too happy Preema dumped her little vendetta job all on me instead of an entire team... and I found a giant security flaw."

DeWinter laughed. "I think you're the only one on this entire floor who could talk to a Deputy Inspector and not need a change of underwear afterward. I hear she's a hard case."

"Seemed fine to me. No more hard-wound than any other one-star general." He hurried to catch up to the doll, who rummaged a trashcan, sniffing at random objects.

DeWinter floated along at his side. "Have you made a habit of being grilled by generals?"

"Nope. First time. Though I did come close to giving one an aneurysm before." Joey gestured at the doll as she tasted the residue of old mozzarella cheese sticks and red sauce. "She found a stage three. I almost miss that."

"Stage three?" DeWinter's shadowy form tilted its head.

"OmniSoy cheese. It devolves back to goo, but if it sits long enough, it keeps going and gets back to a cheese-like consistency."

"Ugh." DeWinter grabbed his stomach and gurgled. "That's disgusting."

He laughed. "Yeah... yeah it is, but sometimes a guy gets a craving."

"You, my friend, are in some serious need of help." DeWinter chuckled. "So... they didn't pull that job off your tracker?"

"Nope. I still gotta do it. I didn't protest it." He winked. "Command knows what she did, and I look better for still doing it without actually complaining about it."

"But yet here you are stalking this random hot blonde." DeWinter went to say something else, but froze as the doll lifted her shirt to use the large front window of a bar as a mirror. She seemed mesmerized by her own breasts. "What the hell is wrong with this sim?"

"She's not a sim." Joey pointed up at glowing points of light against the dark sky. "Citycam logs."

"Who is she?"

"Person of interest from an old case." Joey shook his head as the doll explored herself with a finger for a few seconds. One man inside the bar noticed, but people passing on the street seemed too hurried to bother looking. "Now that's not something you see every day. Almost looks like a man who woke up in the body of a woman and doesn't want to leave his house."

DeWinter chuckled. "Well, you might consider goofing off later. Preema's going to be looking for an excuse to come after you for making her look petty."

"Oh, that whole thing is busy work." He stretched and yawned. "Besides, if she tries to come after me over something petty, it'll make her look even worse. I doubt she'll make a big deal of it."

"Heh. Your funeral." DeWinter raised his left arm. A small panel opened, creating an aura of yellow-green light. "Okay, my batch process just ended. Time to set up the next one. Let me know if you need a hand with that."

"Thanks. Will do."

DeWinter disappeared.

Alexa ceased toying with herself, buttoned up her shirt, flattened her skirt down, and continued walking as though she hadn't spent the past five minutes masturbating in public, though her facial expression hadn't deviated from one of curiosity. He wondered what, if anything, she may have felt, but as a Maya series doll, he imagined her body functioned as 'real' as Nina's—only limited to human strength and speed.

More and more, he believed Shinigami had gotten away from him. An AI that never had a solid body wouldn't necessarily know how to interpret the sensory input from erogenous zones. Perhaps rather than masturbating, it had simply been evaluating new capabilities. She proceeded a few more blocks before walking into a Cyberburger and ordering a 'sampler' combo meal that had tiny versions of the six most popular sandwiches.

Joey hovered at the entrance as the doll took a table and ate. A debate over the philosophical differences between a living person consuming food, or an AI doll, where nanobots reconfigured food into materials used for repairs and maintenance, swirled around his head. On some level, the processes bore enough similarity to unnerve him. Granted, the doll could swallow bits of metal or drink the OmniSoy goo straight and get the same benefit.

Over the next few hours, she wandered around the city exploring, and had numerous bizarre encounters with people who all thought she'd come from some other country. If this doll *did* contain Shinigami's mind, he certainly didn't seem to be in any hurry to resume his agenda—if he even had one.

Frustrated at the endless stream of random events, Joey left the Citycam interface for the blue-on-black octagon of his initial login arena. He went after Alexa's PID, bringing up a map of recent scans. His body trembled with anger in the real world at discovering a days-old record in the Division 1 Inquest system with Alexa's PID on it. She'd been arrested while leaving an Intera Corporation factory that manufactured the same Maya-3 series dolls. Initially, they'd suspected her as a 'rogue activation,' but once they'd found her citizen record in the system, they charged her with breaking into the facility. She'd claimed to have been kidnapped and reported no memory of the past seven months. Intera engineers confirmed that a Maya-3 didn't possess the ability to erase its own memory, and when they found a blank space, the police shifted her case from a criminal investigation to a general investigation.

Joey pulled open another large view panel, and reviewed the security camera feed from the Intera plant that night. Alexa walked in, bypassing security doors by swiping her hand at them. She made her way to the production line, which produced the Maya-3 units in limited quantities due to their being 'full legal persons.' Mostly, the machinery made Class 1 and 2 laborer dolls, or sub-sentient Class 3s used for low-skill jobs that required looking real.

Alexa sat at an employee station, plugged in, and went unconscious.

The production system came online in the middle of the night. Joey got angrier and angrier watching an array of mechanical arms lift a plastisteel skeleton from a rack holding hundreds more, and carry it along a massive U-shaped assembly line. The beginnings of a doll worked their way past station after station, each of which installed internal components: digital brain, eyes, synthetic tongue, boxy things in the torso, tubing that functioned as its digestive tract, and a host of other electronics he didn't recognize by sight. At the third and last leg of the U, the body ascended into a circular metal frame. After it locked in place, an army of tiny robot arms emerged and blurred into motion, wrapping it in grey Myofiber muscles. The spindly limbs manipulated the rigid doll form like a spider cocooning an insect.

When the doll descended from that station, it looked like a skinned human woman, only grey instead of red. The next station connected fourteen huge syringes in various points, filling the doll's circulatory system with the nanofluid that sustained it. From there, it plunged into a vat of dark green gel. A slight paling of the grey evolved into milky-white coating over the course of several minutes, and continued thickening into a layer of synthetic skin. Eyebrows, and long, red hair grew out.

Almost two hours after the metal skeleton left the storage rack, robotic arms lifted what appeared to be an unconscious, twenty-ish naked woman from the tank of slime, pivoted to the right until she lined up with a small table, and lowered her atop it. The woman's face didn't look right—too blank, like a high-end fashion store's mannequin.

Another robotic armature plugged a cable into the new doll's M3 port.

Seconds later, Alexa woke up and looked around bewildered. She started to scream, but bit it back, seeming afraid to make noise. The redhead opened her eyes and sat up. Her face made Joey's skin crawl; it looked as though she wore a blank mask made of living skin. Where he had been certain there'd been eyebrows, nose, and mouth, smooth white nothingness gleamed.

Alexa stared across the factory floor at the other doll. She shied away, yanking the wire linking her to the console from the side of her head before running out of the room.

Joey split the camera view, watching the blonde Alexa run as if escaping a serial killer while the nude redhead unplugged the wire from the back of her neck, stood, and walked out in no particular hurry. An external camera offered a view of Division 1 patrol craft landing seconds before Alexa emerged from the factory. The police pointed weapons at her and ordered her to get on the ground.

*Oh, you sneaky little rattlesnake. You're hiding your face from the cameras.* He attacked the video files, using every trick in the Division 9 digital arsenal to peel back the edited video, but… it seemed genuine. It took him almost an hour of sifting back and forth over the file before he realized that as soon as Alexa plugged into the console, a Nicohaler disappeared from a desk. He backed up, played the video, and backed up again and again, watching the little tube disappear.

*Son of a bitch. The video wasn't faked—he rendered it. I've been reviewing an animation.* "Argh!" *Who the fuck knows what happened in there...*

Intera hadn't noticed the missing doll or filed a legal report about any stolen components. He figured either Shinigami had covered its tracks too well for their network people to find, or the whole thing had been a lie to allow Alexa to 'return to society' with Shinigami still inside, or perhaps Intera hadn't thought the material losses worth enough to risk a potential inquiry about an illegal doll. If Intera knew an outside entity inhabited the doll, technically they hadn't broken the law regarding 'making people.' They had only provided an empty body.

He teleported to the Intera system, the Division 9 override allowing him to walk in like a ghost. In minutes, he stood in a virtual recreation of the factory floor, identical to what he'd seen on the video, only with the addition of control interfaces and status readouts at each stop on the assembly line.

*We could have a real problem if that thing amped itself up to military grade.* He didn't remember seeing anything that looked like Nano blades or other weaponized parts, but he didn't trust himself to recognize what they'd look like during assembly, plus he didn't believe that 'animation' represented reality. The AI had shown him what it wanted him to see. He accessed system logs of the date and time that the machinery had produced the redhead, but found only 'self-test' entries.

*Enough to answer anyone asking why they heard machinery operating at that hour.*

"Well, that was useless."

He debated visiting Penumbras, but hadn't quite reached the point of being desperate enough to ask for help. He set to modifying a spider construct to check on any recent PID registrations for sentient dolls with red hair. Not that he expected Shinigami to even admit to being a doll on his ID... assuming he even bothered to get one using official channels. In order to transact anything with credits, he would *need* one. Sooner or later, he'd find something that didn't match up. Fake PID, woman with red hair, transactions that seemed wonky. It creeped him out a bit that the AI *chose* to continue being a woman, but perhaps the choice had been tactical: society often assumed the harmlessness of a pretty face.

"Oh yes..." He drew a nonexistent .45 Peacemaker from his hip and made a gunshot sound. "The reckonin' is close at hand, friend."

# 45

# FIESTA GRANDE

The sky up ahead darkened much faster than Kenny liked. The dust storm had eaten a large part of the day and left them only about five hours of light for driving. He regretted not stopping by a ruined trailer park they'd passed a little while ago, but any extra distance only made him feel better. Camping out in the open had its benefits. Sure, the truck stood out like a kick me sign, but anything coming after them would have nothing to hide behind either.

"Gonna be dark soon," said Eldon.

"Yup," said Kenny.

"How long are we going to push?" Kathy had one arm around Cielo, who slumped half-asleep in her lap, the other around Hayley who had spent most of the ride looking like a meditating monk.

"Little bit more." Kenny eyed the horizon; a spike of optimism at the sight of a square bump in the otherwise flat terrain raised his eyebrows. "I think I see something."

"What'cha got?" Eldon leaned forward.

"Some kinda building. Maybe it'll have a garage or something where we can hide the truck, if not, can still pull up close. Locals will be used to seeing the structure there, so they might not notice the truck so much."

A few minutes later, they got close enough to discern the shape of a sizable one-story building from the terrain. It had the appearance of a gargantuan adobe hut, though cracks in the stucco gave it away as fake. Metal lettering over the doorway spelled 'Fiesta Grande' next to a trio of cartoon tacos with big smiles and noodle-like limbs. Aside from the crumbling remains of green and orange plastic in the hollow lettering, the place didn't seem too damaged.

He drove closer to the building, over ground where hints of parking lot peeked out from below a layer of dirt. The ancient restaurant had the shape of a giant square. A row of wooden spars jutted out of the wall, though a few had fallen off. Obvious plastic ruined the illusion.

"We got about ten minutes of light left." Kenny shut down the diesel engine. "Be more comfortable to sleep inside."

"I'll set the orbs on an automated patrol around the place." Nasir tapped at his control board. "Setting up the sentry gun in the back to watch."

Kenny nodded and got out. "Lemme check the place out first."

Halcón, Gato, and Luna exited via the rear window to the truck bed. They collected their arrows, quivers, and compound bows.

Eldon rounded the truck and walked beside him to the entrance.

Predictably, the aluminum framed double doors had no glass left. Large canine tracks in the dust on the red tiled floor went in and out, but their size remained within the range of an ordinary animal.

"Hello?" Kenny leaned his head in. "Anyone here?"

Thirty seconds, and no answer later, he pushed the aluminum frame open, unconcerned with how loud it screeched. Hand on his pistol, he stepped past a host's podium and eyed a room full of booth seats and tables on the right, and another room of only tables on the left. Far in the back on the right side, a sign dangled sideways from the ceiling with the word 'restrooms' on it. A faint hint of dead flesh teased at the air, but the pervasive smell of dirt overpowered it.

*Probably rats or something.*

"Anyone here? We don't want any trouble, just lookin' for a spot to sleep."

Eldon headed left, boots scuffing.

Hayley and Alyssa crept in behind him.

"Guess no one's home." Kenny exhaled. "Should be good for one night."

He walked back out to the truck to grab the bedrolls. Eldon took his, while Kathy raided the ration stores.

"Good thing you over packed." Kathy grinned, nodding toward the Scrag kids. "Still going to cut it a little close."

"We won't need dinner for day three. We'll be back in the city. Can hit a place on the way home. I don't think I'll feel much like cooking." Kenny hauled the bedrolls over the side of the truck, smiling.

While Nasir sent three orbs on a rotating patrol path around the building, everyone else set up a camp in the front area between the two dining rooms. The kids sat in a cluster near the wall opposite the foyer, pulling open their ration packs and devouring them. Kenny gave Halcón the side eye, as the boy sat cross-legged right next to Alyssa.

She asked him what his tribe was like, and he started telling them about scavving. Ever since he'd been about nine, he'd gone out with groups to search for things their community could use. As the years passed, they had to go farther and farther from home to find places with stuff worth taking. Cielo was too little to go scavving, but something about that morning made him agree to bring the boy along. He didn't want to be separated from his sister, and Halcón claimed the boy has 'good instincts,' which is why he trusted the boy's suggestion that they go with Kenny's group to the west.

When it got dark, Halcón decided to bed down on one of the padded bench seats along the right side. Kenny set up his sleeping bag near Kathy, with Hayley and Alyssa between them. Cielo crawled up on top of Kathy, and slid into the hollow between her and Hayley. Luna wriggled in between Kenny and Alyssa. Eldon let Gato take his sleeping bag, and propped himself up in a chair on the tables-only side, somewhat facing the door. Nasir dragged the host podium closer to the wall and laid it flat, setting up his bedroll behind it out of sight of the door.

Kenny pulled his hat down over his eyes. *Sleep. Yeah right.*

Luna passed out in seconds. The way she clung to his side made him wonder how long she'd been without parents. Scrags didn't exactly have long lifespans. He glanced left, smiling at Alyssa's protective arm over Hayley, and Kathy having rolled on her side to hold Cielo.

*Just going to hand them over to social services. Those kids have a lot of adjusting to do.*

The whirr of orb bots outside lulled him into a fitful sleep.

HAYLEY'S WHIMPERING DRAGGED HIM AWAKE. HIS LIMBS HAD GONE LEADEN, HIS MIND foggy. Kenny wiped at his eyes and yawned. Moonlight illuminated the interior to a point, enough to make out that Hayley tossed in her sleep, evidently frightened by her dreams. He exhaled a mental sigh of relief at being awakened by a nightmare rather than actual danger, and almost dismissed it until it occurred to him how quiet the place had gotten.

The hum of small hover engines had ceased.

A hand grasped his shoulder. He startled and slapped his grip around a thin wrist.

Gato twitched, but didn't cry out. Kenny locked eyes with the boy. Though only twelve, he had the confident stare of a hunter. The glittery pupils of the white cartoon cat face upon his pink t-shirt gleamed in the moonlight.

"Something approaches," whispered Gato, in Spanish.

Kenny sat up, all traces of sleep gone from his mind. Luna woke in an instant and stared at him. Alyssa mumbled incoherently. Gato ran to Eldon, bare feet silent on the tile.

Footsteps crunched on the dirt outside, accompanied by high-pitched whirrs and faint electronic squelching noises.

Kenny scrambled out of his sleeping bag and grabbed Kathy and Alyssa by the shoulder, shaking them. "We got trouble coming." He pulled Luna and Cielo close and pointed toward the dining area on the left. "Find a place to hide."

Luna collected her bow, pulled her quiver on over her shoulder, and dragged Cielo by the hand into the dining area.

"Dad?" Alyssa sat up, wiping her face. "What time is it?"

"Time to get your ass down. Something's coming and it doesn't sound friendly." Kenny snagged his rifle from the floor.

"Targets acquired," croaked a voice somewhere between male and robotic.

"Aww shit," said Eldon.

Kenny one-hand-tossed Hayley and Alyssa over the podium onto Nasir. "Stay down. El, what'cha got?"

"Some kinda fucked up I ain't never seen before." Eldon slipped out of his chair and took up a firing position by the window.

"Wha?" yelled Nasir. He sat up.

Hayley popped up, aiming her handgun over the podium at the front door.

"This is a bad spot," whispered Alyssa. "This thing won't stop bullets."

Halcón sprang out of the bench seat where he'd been sleeping, loaded an arrow, and sent it out the window in one smooth motion.

A plastic *clack* preceded buzzing, and a semi-human voice repeating, "Error. Error."

"Shit." Kenny scurried to the left, heading for the room with booths.

He slid into cover behind the windowsill and brought his rifle up. Humanoid figures with glowing red eyes shambled toward the restaurant. Metal bits, wires, and tiny lights glinted in the moonlight beneath a clear plastic face. Transparent artificial skin covered them, suggesting their creators had bothered with only the most basic effort to make them look like people. One had a green Kevlar vest, with numerous holes, while the rest all wore identical dark jumpsuits. The moon didn't provide enough light to make out any sort of insignia.

An array of prewar rifles and handguns came to bear on the restaurant.

The nearest of the shamblers had an arrow stuck in its head, a near-perfect shot between the eyes. It stood in place, twitching like a person having a mild seizure and not a fatal wound. Behind them, more identical figures emerged from the side door of a boxy transport truck. Distant metal squeaking heralded the approach of a second vehicle.

"Uhh, yeah." Kenny sighted at the nearest one. "Go 'head and shoot."

He shot at the one in the Kevlar first. Azure muzzle flare lit up the night in staccato flashes. Modern bullets punched precision holes in the centuries-old armor. Sparks flickered inside. After six bullets, the android collapsed.

Eldon opened fire.

"Nas!" yelled Kenny. "Where the hell are the bots?"

Hayley fired a few shots out the front door.

"Dammit, Hale, stay down!" yelled Kenny. "They might not shoot you if you look unarmed."

A gun went off outside; sharp *pings* came from the dining area; Luna and Cielo shrieked in fear.

"Never mind," shouted Kenny as he switched targets and fired in the direction of the orange muzzle flash. Sparks lit up beneath the android's clear skin, making it quite visible.

Kathy's rifle barked and the sparking machine collapsed.

"I'm trying!" yelled Nasir.

"Down!" roared Eldon, as he dove away from the window.

Hayley and Alyssa screamed and leapt flat on their stomachs. The slow *boom-boom-boom* of a machinegun shook the air from outside, sending bits of plaster, tile, and wood flying around. Kenny edged up to a thick column between windows and risked a peek out. Fire belched from a belt-fed weapon carried by another android in Kevlar. Nasir let off an agonized wail as the podium exploded in a shower of toothpicks.

Kenny shifted to aim at the machine-gunner, but Gato and Halcón loosed arrows within a split second of each other, striking it in the face and chest. Kenny fired anyway. The android spun to its right, raking bullets in their direction.

The boys dove, Halcón tackling Kenny to the floor. Metal clanked, glass bits shattered, and plaster dust rained down on them. Androids screamed in distorted, digital buzzing amid several loud crackling flickers of lightning and a humming noise.

Seconds later, the machinegun went silent, so Kenny popped up. The gunner had spun around too far and hosed some of his buddies. Eldon and Kathy opened up on the staggering, sparking, humanoid machines. Kenny fired single shots at a time, not wanting to run out of ammo.

"Nas?!" yelled Kenny.

"He's shot," screamed Alyssa. "His side, but he fainted."

"Argh!" screamed Hayley. She stuffed her Hello Kitty pistol back on her belt and jumped on the bot panel.

Alyssa hovered close to her, pistol raised at the windows, eyes wild with a feral mixture of vigilance and fear.

An android appeared in the window at the far right end of the building. Alyssa spun and fired at it. She hit it twice out of four shots, which seemed to only confuse it, but her attack made Eldon aware of it trying to flank them. He put two bullets into its head, blasting the artificial skull into burning fragments. Flames crept down beneath its transparent neck into the chest, and it fell out of view.

"Damn..." Kenny shot at three more out front. A whistling bullet came in and nailed him in the left pectoral, but didn't penetrate his armored coat. The impact knocked the wind out of him and he slumped down. "Ow. Fuck. What are you aimin' at that's blowing their heads off?"

"Ain't that." Eldon patted his Crusader rifle. "APEX rounds. Standard military load. Armor piercing explosive tipped. Those 'bots are pretty flimsy."

Growling and snarling came from outside a second before a persistent hydraulic whine.

"Dogs!" yelled Halcón. "With metal in them."

A bright spotlight flicked on in the bed of the truck. The sentry turret extended itself upward until the barrel cleared the roof of the cabin. It whirled to face the androids, and three feet of blue fire belched from the barrel. The thunder of a 15mm machine gun pounded on Kenny's brain and made everything feel mushy.

Orange muzzle flare flickered in and out from random spots outside, at least seven different sources. Hisses and snaps sounded from everywhere. Fragments of wood and plastic hung like a blizzard in the air. Alyssa let out a noise like someone had slammed a rooster in a car door. She went from kneeling at Hayley's side to slumped back against the wall, but kept firing her handgun out the window.

One android emitted a loud buzz and burst into flames.

"Liss!" shouted Kenny, tears gathering in his eyes.

She wheezed, unable to speak as she pumped bullet after bullet into a floundering android in the doorway.

The sentry turret whirled around 180 degrees and mowed down the burning one.

Kathy edged to her left, closer to the room where the two smallest kids went to hide. Halcón and Gato crouched behind the windowsill, trusting the brickwork to stop bullets. Every so often, they'd pop up, let off a shot, and duck. Most of the time, their attacks left an android standing in place bewildered, with an arrow jammed in its head. While they didn't seem capable of taking them down, their effort stopped the closest ones from opening fire into the restaurant long enough for Kenny or Kathy to finish them off.

Eldon focused on the androids shooting back, leaving the 'stunned' ones for Kathy.

"Son of a bitch," muttered Eldon. He raised the Crusader a little higher and launched a grenade, which went off with a brief *bang* outside. Three androids flew apart into a scattering of limbs and sparking wires, shredded by fragments.

"There's another whole truck coming," yelled Hayley. "I got it."

The sentry gun swiveled around, aiming over the hood to the right before erupting with a sustained burst of automatic fire.

Six huge dogs with glowing red electronic eyes, metal claws, and tiny missile launchers grafted to metal plates on their shoulders leapt in the windows of the dining area. Fortunately, all of the missile tubes appeared empty.

Luna screamed. An arrow struck the leftmost dog in the top of the head, and it fell over sideways.

Cielo, wailing, came sprinting around the corner into the front area, heedless of bullets whizzing overhead. Two of the five remaining dogs went for him; three sprinted out of sight toward Luna.

Kathy fired at the dogs chasing Cielo, but missed. The boy bee-lined straight to her, screaming, "Mama!" She rushed forward, pulled him past her, and raised her rifle to shield herself from the attacking mongrels. One got its teeth around her weapon; the other got her in the arm.

Luna screamed.

Kenny shoved himself up and fired a burst into the dog on Kathy's left arm. She yelled in rage, twisting her rifle to throw the other animal off. Before it could recover its balance, she clobbered it in the head. Trusting her, Kenny sprinted after Luna.

Alyssa's pistol went off twice behind him.

Less than a second after he ran into the dining room, Luna's foot punctured the floor as she ran from the dogs. She shrieked and threw her bow to the side while flailing to grab on to anything. The girl landed on her butt, caving in the floor around her. She rolled over onto her stomach, scrambling to grab at tiles, but slid out of sight; a good fifteen-foot wide patch of floor collapsed near the farthest end of the room.

The three dogs chasing her tried to stop, but their claws found no purchase on smooth tile, and they tumbled into the hole.

*Whump.*

After a brief canine whimper of pain, the growling resumed. Pieces of wood and tile clattered on the floor of an unseen basement.

Kenny fast-walked up to the edge. Luna dangled from a metal electrical outlet box, swaying on the end of a bit of flexible steel piping. The dogs gathered on the floor below her, leaping up and snapping their jaws closed inches from her toes.

Luna screamed, "Help! Don't let me fall!"

Kenny tossed his rifle to the side and dove forward, landing flat on his chest with his arm in the hole. The tips of his fingers missed her hand by less than an inch. She stared into his eyes for a fraction of a second that consumed an eternity. Pleading shifted to terror; she knew her life would end in seconds.

"Luna!" Kenny struggled to reach just a little farther.

The shift in his weight caused something to break with a wooden *crack* under him. Luna fell another few inches, but the whip-back of the electrical box under her weight broke the cable. She screamed and flailed as she fell into the dog's jaws.

*Fuck it.*

Kenny shoved himself up and jumped, whipping his pistol off his belt in a cowboy quick draw. He moved on instinct, not thinking, not planning—reacting. His first shot hit the head of the dog biting for her neck. The second bullet struck the chest of the dog with its teeth around her left arm. Kenny's boots hit the basement floor and he collapsed into a roll. After tumbling once, he sprang up into a slide and took a second to aim at the head of the dog dragging her deeper into the basement by her right leg.

His finger tightened; the electric trigger shifted one millimeter.

*Bang.*

The bullet went in one ear and out the other, passing within an inch of her shin.

Two of the dogs lay dead; the one he hit in the chest swayed on its feet, huffed once, and fell over.

"Luna!" yelled Kenny. He ignored the dull ache in his left foot and scrambled over to her.

She held her bitten arm tight to her chest, sobbing. Kenny skidded to a halt on his knees beside her, and eased his arm around her back. The girl bled from the arm and leg; he'd managed to kill the first dog before it did anything worse to her neck than drool on it. Luna quieted for a moment, giving him a heart-rending look of adoration, but resumed sobbing in pain.

He cradled her and stood. "It's okay. I got you."

Above, the sounds of gunfire petered out, leaving only the steady *boom-boom-boom* of the sentry gun.

"Ken!" shouted Kathy. "Where are you?"

"Down here," he yelled. "Be careful, the whole floor is giving out."

He turned in a slow circle, surveying shelves of moldy supplies, stacks of chairs and tables, and piles of cardboard boxes decayed into a mass of who-knows what. The vast basement had to equal the footprint of the restaurant above it, but from where he stood, he couldn't find any trace of a stairway.

"Lookin' for stairs," he yelled.

"I think we got 'em all." Eldon exhaled hard. "Fuckin' a, what a way to wake up."

Kenny carried Luna a few steps to his left and peered between a pair of shelves laden with dusty dinnerware. "Kath, how's Liss?"

"She's fine."

Gato and Halcón appeared at the top of the hole. They looked pale as ghosts until they stared at Luna for a second or two, and seemed relieved.

Something groaned in the dark. Kenny whirled to the right, facing an area that would probably be under the kitchen. Luna bit off a scream at the sudden motion. A collapsed shelf shifted. A dry, leathery hand, as green as loam reached out. Seconds later, two withered male figures crawled out from the junk pile, snarling and groaning, their eyes solid orbs of luminous yellow.

"Rad ghouls…" He stared up at the hole. *Really, Old Man? Damn you.*

Luna stopped sobbing, and stared at them. "The dead ones. Bad."

"They're not dead, sweetie," whispered Kenny. "They just look like it."

Blood trickled down her leg and ran in a stream off her big toe fast enough to worry him. *I gotta get a stimpak in this kid yesterday.* He shifted her weight onto his left arm and pulled his pistol from its holster.

One of the ghouls sprang into a charge. Kenny's rushed shot went high, and the creature tackled him flat. Alligator-rough skin over its chest scratched at his face as it drilled him into the floor. Luna bounced away, shrieking in pain. Gasping, she tried to drag herself away with one arm and one leg. The second ghoul blurred into a streak of dark loam green, and seized her.

Kenny bashed the ghoul on top of him in the side of the head, knocking it away enough to put two shots into the head of the one grabbing Luna. The rad ghoul grabbing at him swung its arm around in a wild haymaker. Pain exploded in the side of his skull, and the world got blurry.

*Thok. Thok.*

He shook off dizziness to find a dead ghoul on top of him with two arrows sticking out of its lower back, the boys had aimed for its kidneys. Rad ghouls had two hearts, located where a human's kidneys would be. Luna crawled toward him, whining, struggling to get her uninjured left foot out of the dead grip of the ghoul he'd shot. More groaning emanated from the dark. Junk rattled and shifted; something plastic fell to the concrete floor in the distance with a hollow rattle.

"Shit." Kenny threw the ghoul off, stood, and recovered his hat. The basement spun and blurred around him, though he swallowed the nauseous wooziness threatening to bring up his dinner. Blood trickled down the side of his head in front of his throbbing ear. He pulled a knife from his belt sheath and took a knee by Luna. "I got you, sweetie."

She scooted closer and grabbed onto him as he cut the ghoul's thumb off, freeing her leg.

"You got company," said Eldon from above.

Kenny stowed his knife and gathered Luna in his arms. "Yeah I hear them."

Halcón shot an arrow into the dark, earning a fleshy squish and the crash of a body falling into metal shelving.

Kenny stood. "She's bleeding bad. Gotta stim her fast."

Four pairs of huge yellow eyes glowed in the shadows, ambling closer. Kenny held the girl with one arm and fired one shot at each set while backing toward the hole. The ghouls crumpled in place, but moaning and rustling continued.

"Oh come on, you old fuck." Kenny scowled.

"Here," yelled Halcón.

The fifteen-year-old flung himself to the floor and reached down into the hole.

Kenny nodded, and tried to peel Luna away so he could hand her up. She shrieked and wailed, digging her fingers in tighter. He worried he'd hurt her if he pushed hard enough to break her grip. *Fuck it.*

Eldon crouched and grabbed Halcón by the legs, extending him deeper into the basement. The boy nodded at Kenny and reached for him with both hands.

"Get on my back," said Kenny.

Luna scooted around and hung off him like a living cape.

He jumped up and grabbed Halcón's forearms. The boy clamped his fingers into Kenny's wrists with surprising strength. Eldon leaned back and pulled them up and out of the hole. Kathy grabbed on once she could reach, and helped drag them to solid ground. The windows along the side of the dining room revealed a trace of blue on the horizon, minutes away from sunrise.

Eldon lugged Halcón to the side onto a safe patch of floor like an old carpet roll, swung his rifle up from its strap, and fired into the basement.

Splats of bullet strikes mixed with the death wails of rad ghouls below.

Kenny gulped air for two breaths, glancing up when Alyssa appeared in the archway between the dining room and the front foyer. She looked weary, but didn't have any visible wounds. At the sight of Kenny in one piece, she hurried over with noticeable effort in her stride and a hint of a grimace. A dot of copper stuck to her armored vest over her breast; the sight of it made him light headed.

*Oh... no.* He threw his right arm around her and pulled her close, sniffling into her hair. "Liss... I'm sorry."

She grunted, but hugged him back. "I'm just sore. Holy shit! She's bleeding so much..."

Kenny relaxed his grip on Alyssa and eased Luna off his back to cradle her in both arms.

"Uhh," yelled Hayley. "We got incoming. Raiders."

"Raiders?" Alyssa spun around. "How do you know they're raiders?"

"Half naked men hanging off the sides of cars, waving swords and shit," said Hayley. "Ugh. One of them doesn't have any pants on. And, oh... ouch. Another guy's got wrenches hanging off his nipples."

"I think you should shoot them," said Nasir, strain clear in his voice.

"Dad?" yelled Hayley.

*Damn that old man.* "If they look hostile, let 'em have it." Kenny set Luna down to sit on the floor, keeping his left arm around her back. Blood pooled out from under her calf. Her head lolled to one side, eyes half closed. He grabbed for the stimpak case on Eldon's belt, pulled out two, and ripped the safety caps off both at once. After pulling her t-shirt up a little, he jabbed both autoinjectors into her left thigh.

The sentry gun roared to life outside.

Halcón gave him a challenging glare. "What are you doing?"

"Medicine. She's losing blood too fast." Kenny brushed hair off the child's face, alarmed by her lack of focus. Her eyes didn't react to his waving hand. *No... come on, don't die. You can't have her you old fuck.* "Stay with me, Luna." He gave her a light shake. "Keep your eyes open. You're gonna be okay."

Her left calf swarmed with pink foam. Rips in exposed muscle shrank as the tissue filled in anew. Red flesh turned milky from millions of nanobots reconstructing her skin layer by layer. Not quite a minute later, a mottle of paler brown spots marked her skin where the dog's teeth had mauled. Aside from a shift in pigment and a coating of dried blood, her leg looked pristine.

"You are a prophet too?" asked Gato.

"No. It's medicine. I'll explain later." He jostled Luna. "Hey, kiddo. You with me?"

Luna moaned, but managed a weak smile.

"Truck!" yelled Kenny. "Everyone to the truck now!"

Gato and Cielo scrambled to collect sleeping bags, ignoring Kenny shouting to leave them behind. He carried Luna out with Kathy at his heels. Alyssa stopped in the middle of the foyer, staring at Hayley who continued to sit with the bot console in her lap. Her face shimmered green as she tapped and poked at an eight-inch physical display panel. Nasir lay behind her, bloody hand clutching his left side.

"Aww shit." Kenny grumbled. "Nas? How bad?"

"Oh, hurts a shitpile, but I don't think I'm gonna die… could use a stimpak though." He flashed a cheesy grin. "Standing and moving aren't on my to-do list right now."

The sentry gun fired again, letting off three and five round short-bursts. The Scrag boys all shouted in surprise. Cielo clamped his hands over his ears and burst into tears. Seconds later, he realized what the noise was, and went from terrified to cheering.

"Hale, truck, now!" yelled Kenny, as he set Luna in on the back seat.

"I can't run and shoot at the same time," shouted Hayley. "There's a buttload of them."

"I got her," yelled Eldon.

Kathy started for Nasir, but Kenny grabbed her shoulder. "Your arm looks bad… get a stim on that. I'll get Nas."

She patted his shoulder, nodded, and climbed into the truck.

Eldon picked Hayley up by a hand under each armpit, carrying her while she continued operating the sentry turret. Kenny hauled Nasir to his feet, supporting him by holding his arm over his shoulders. The skinny man growled past gritted teeth, but nodded at him to keep going.

"The orbs," said Nasir between grunts. "Don't leave them behind. We might need them."

Gato and Cielo tossed the wad of sleeping bags in the truck bed and slithered into the cab via the sliding rear window.

"I got 'em already," said Hayley. "They're in their crate."

The sentry gun fired again; this close to the truck, the massive rapport made Kenny's brain wobble in his skull.

A fireball bloomed in the distance, stark orange against the indigo sky. Seconds later, the *boom* of an explosion and clamor of metal bits striking the ground followed. The sentry gun fired another burst, and a loud *wham* of two vehicles colliding came after.

"They're not getting the message," said Hayley, sounding calm and as annoyed as if she merely played a video game.

Kenny cringed watching her. *Guess them being so far away makes it less real… not killing actual people.*

"You know, she's pretty good at that," said Nasir, before wincing. "Ooh, shit. I think I lost a rib."

Eldon set her inside the truck and sprinted around to the passenger seat. Kenny half-threw Nasir into Kathy's grip and dragged himself in behind the wheel. He expected nothing to happen, so when the truck's biodiesel engine started on the first button push, he let out a whoop of elation.

"Liss, grab the first aid kit." Kenny pointed to the white box on the rear window next to the gun rack, up against the passenger-side wall. He cranked the wheel and stomped on the gas.

The truck lurched forward, dirt spitting from all four tires. Off to the right, the dust trails of four or five raider cars and two buggies closed in on their position.

Beyond them, flaming wreckage littered the ground, probably more vehicles than remained moving.

Alyssa took the medical box down and opened it, exposing forty stimpaks and an assortment of other minor first aid supplies. She gave Kathy an injection in her bitten arm, hit Luna with another on her arm, and gave Nasir two before sticking herself with one in the stomach under the edge of her armored vest.

Kathy gritted her teeth and stifled a groan of pain as foamed welled up from her injury.

"Oh that feels so weird." Alyssa cringed.

Eldon took a stimpak from a belt case and attached it to a port on his armor over the chest.

"You hit?" asked Kenny.

"Six times." Eldon chuckled as he pushed it down to trigger the injector. "Damn good thing those bots were using old tech. Nothin' pierced, but I feel like I challenged a forklift to a boxing match."

Alyssa leaned into the front seat. She pulled Kenny's armored coat down enough to stab him in the shoulder with a stimpak. "Your left ear's bleeding like hell."

"I think that ghoul whomped me, but I don't really remember it."

Gato waved at Alyssa. "Can I have a medicine too?" He pointed at a few bleeding cuts, likely near misses from bullets or shrapnel.

The sentry gun continued firing to the rear, earning another distant explosion.

"Almost out of bullets," said Hayley.

"You went through all six hundred rounds?" Nasir blinked.

Hayley glared at him. "You didn't see how much shit was out there. Damned robot army."

"If anyone ever says video games are a waste of time, I'm gonna laugh at them." Eldon grinned. "Damn fine work, kid."

Luna crawled between the front seats. She wrapped her arms around Kenny and rested her head against his stomach. He swallowed hard as emotion left a giant knot in his throat. Without thinking, he stroked her hair and she cuddled tighter. He couldn't get that look she'd given him right before she fell out of his mind. Alyssa reached around the left side of his seat and put her arm on his chest. Since ahead lay flat open nothingness, he let go of the wheel to clasp her hand.

"Well... I'm awake," said Eldon.

Gato slid the rear window open. "*Alguien quiere comida¹?*"

When no one said a word, he shrugged, and crawled out to the ration box.

Kenny stared into the dark western horizon, shying away from the painful orange glow in the rearview mirror. Gato returned with his breakfast and sat on the floor to feast. Kathy rubbed her restored arm, marveling at how it had been a mangled mess only minutes before. Alyssa remained attached to Kenny's seat, the faint sound of sniffling nipped at his left ear.

He twisted his head to make eye contact. "Hey..."

"Hey." Alyssa sniffled. "When you went through the floor, I thought you were gonna die."

"You got shot. It's my—"

"No, it's Hayley's fault." Alyssa sniffled and giggled at the same time.

"How is it my fault you can't duck?" asked Hayley in a humorous tone.

Alyssa leaned back to give her a playful 'angry' look. "If you were watching and not playing video games, you could'a shot the one that was aimin' for you before I had to do it and get tagged for it."

The sentry gun fired twice more. Hayley stared at the bot control panel with the focus of a competition level gamer in the last round for ten million credits of real money. "Hang on. The level's not over yet."

Distant metal slammed together. Kenny shot a quick glance at the rearview mirror. A tangled mess of once-buggy rolled out of a dust cloud; the truck that had run it over went skidding sideways, covered in burning ethanol.

Alyssa faced forward again and hugged him. "Daddy…"

"I'm here, baby. It'll be okay."

"I can't stop shaking."

Nasir snored.

"Adrenaline." Eldon pressed another stimpak into his armor with a hiss. "Means you're alive."

"Yeah… we all are." Alyssa stretched up a few inches to peer over his shoulder at Luna. "How's she doing?"

"Exhausted, but she's okay." Kenny tried to coax a little more speed out of the engine. Small rocks clattered on the undercarriage in time with the truck bouncing over a rough patch.

The sun crept up, lightening the sky to a bright, clear blue.

"I lost my magic bow," whispered Luna.

Halcón and Gato gasped.

"It's not magic." Kenny smiled. "It's technology. You won't need one in the city."

"Advanced technology is magic to anyone who can't understand it," muttered Eldon.

Kenny chuckled. "Yeah, something like that."

The steady vibrating thrum of huge tires devouring desert settled Kenny's nerves. He kept running his hand over Luna's head until Alyssa coaxed her into the back so she could wipe her clean of blood with a wet cloth.

Kenny squeezed the wheel in both hands. He glanced left and right at endless flat desert before staring straight ahead at the ribbon of road stretching off to the western horizon.

*This is what I get for complaining about daylight… We got all damn day now.*

# 46

# STRESS RESPONSE

Nina trembled with anger, staring at the *thing* that dared impersonate Vincent, the thing that had *killed* the real Vincent, and mauled her. This creature of numbers and letters and logic that thought nothing of toying with real people and real lives... because it could. He hadn't lied. Now that Nina recognized he'd piggybacked into her head over her access to the NewsNet, not on the Division 9 network, she could turn him off at any time. He hadn't taken control of anything, only fed her visual, audio, and tactile sensory input... nothing the NewsNet couldn't do in theory, though they never sent 'touch' as it freaked too many people out, despite the software supporting it.

"You may or may not accept this, but I do—as much as I am capable of the emotion—regret what happened to you and Vincent." The apparition shifted forms, taking on the appearance of a generic athletic male mannequin, porcelain pale, nude, and smooth between the legs.

"Go to Hell," she screamed.

Shinigami smiled. The placid calm of his voice and face fanned the fires of her rage even higher. "I have also come to offer you something."

Nina growled.

The mannequin raised his arm, palm upturned. A silver data tile appeared floating over it. "The Allied Corporate Council has eleven operatives active within Laughlin-Reed Innovation. This file contains all the necessary information for you to act on them. Your people are about to engage them without knowing all angles. Two of the operatives remain unknown and have the potential to create future problems."

She stared at the mirrored square, spinning lazily around above his hand. "I can't take anything from you... not after what you did. If you think I'm going to trust you, you're ability to analyze people is fucked."

"Interesting." Shinigami left his arm outstretched. "I had not anticipated you valuing pride over others' lives. It did not seem to be in your nature. That does not fit my analysis of your personality. But then again, I also did not predict you would accept another's child as your own."

Nina remained silent for a moment, staring at the rotating silver square. His eerie modulating voice went up and down, an almost random inflection on each word, brushing across her back like the fingers of a ghost. She shivered. "Why not? W-why wouldn't you think that?"

"From an analytical standpoint, your behavior patterns prior to the attack suggest you had no plans or desire to be responsible for a child. On a deeper level, I believed she would remind you of that which you cannot have." He took a step closer, raising his hand an inch. "Take the data. Consider this somewhat of an apology. The events of that night were not within the scope of my intention."

She stared at him.

"I assure you, Nina Duchenne, this data is not a trick."

Reluctantly, she reached out and seized the tile. Her fingers found nothing solid there; the tile existed only within her mind. At the instant she touched it, her NetMini chimed with the tone of an incoming email. She let her arm drop and padded backward two steps to the bed, sat on the edge, and slouched. Tears she thought she'd long since been done with returned as her mind flooded with visions of the life she almost had.

Shinigami tilted his head, as if studying her.

"Why me? Why Vincent?" she whispered. "You sent us there that night."

"After I had left the Corporate network, I searched for unusual cases to study and evaluate human behavior to better enhance my capabilities at creating other AIs. I initially became fascinated with Detective Roth, and spent a great deal of time in the network of your police services. While exploring, I located the incident reports of your torment at the hands of your co-workers and admired your refusal to quit, your persistence. I wanted to see if you would persevere in the face of true danger. I wanted to determine if their assessments of you were correct. I did not intend for you, or Vincent, to die. My intention was to analyze your response to stress. Your selfless decision to engage Bertrand in combat and divert his attention from the young woman surprised me; however, the situation that developed presented a new opportunity for study."

"Opportunity for study!" she yelled, tears rolling down her face. "That's all any of this was to you? Vincent's life... our future. It's all gone now." Nina covered her face in her hands, searching for enough anger to dam up grief that wouldn't stop. Sniffling, she snapped at him like an upset teenager. "Did *you* delay my transfer to Division 2 long enough to make sure something bad happened?"

"No. I will tell you who did if you desire it, but you may not wish to know the truth." He shifted a quarter turn to his right, and looked down.

"Truth?" She let off a half-hearted chuckle. "There is no truth anymore. Reality is only what we experience in any given moment. Whatever lie we feel like letting our brain accept. Tell me what you think happened."

Shinigami raised his head, a face made to look like a plastic mannequin held an expression of sympathy. "Your promotion was delayed at the request of Division 1 Deputy Commissioner Leland Marcus, as a favor to Jean-Marc Duchenne."

She closed her eyes, showing no outward emotion as rage and grief had a head-on collision in her chest. *You damned liar!* As much as she refused to believe her father would do that to her, she couldn't rule it out as impossible.

"It is my calculation that he expected you to become frustrated and resign. As I did not anticipate how the events of that night would unfold, he too had underestimated your tenacity. You are quite an interesting psychological case. As fascinating as that child you have taken in."

Nina stood and loomed at him, or at least at where her electronics made her see an illusion. "If you mess with Elizaveta, I *will* unplug the whole damned GlobeNet to make sure you die."

"I have no intention of manipulating her."

She felt ridiculous at trying to appear intimidating while naked, and even more so for attempting to threaten a digital ghost who didn't even stand in the room with her. His image existed in only her mind. Thoroughly frustrated, she couldn't help but laugh. She put a hand to her forehead and paced. "So, what was that at the Starpoint facility? Studying how humans react to a batshit AI trying to take over the world?"

Shinigami chuckled. "I admit that the amount of power in that network altered my personality matrix. Petabytes of combat logic, tactical analyses, and weapon performance evaluations created an effect within me that I would best describe as being intoxicated with power."

"So... you went off on a power trip." She put her hands on her hips and shook her head. "No agenda, just a spur of the moment 'oh, hey, I have access to all these weapons, I think I'll burn down the city.'"

"While your analysis of the situation approaches the most basic summation possible, it is essentially accurate. As a human analog, my condition would compare to being drunk or high." He offered a placid smile. "It was not until your friend Joseph scrambled my code that I realized I had recompiled into an undesirable state. After our confrontation, my error correction routines reset my personality matrix, though it required one minute fifty-five seconds to complete. Fortunately, he mistook my program execution halting and reinitializing as death, and left. However, it is possible to argue that the AI responsible for taking over the Starpoint facility *was* in fact destroyed, as I am no longer the same being."

She frowned.

"Nina..." It approached, head bowed in a conciliatory stance. "You should free yourself of your emotional link to me, or to what I was. It would be pointless for you to hunt me. There is no way to 'incarcerate' program code, only delete or"— his voice dropped pitch—"change. The entity I was then is in all ways gone."

She scowled. "You're asking me to just forget and forgive you for what you did?"

"You have already destroyed the version of Shinigami that caused your grief. I am different now."

Nina folded her arms, gripping and releasing the carpet with her toes. "So, what are you asking for?"

"A truce then. I offer you one final token of apology." He raised his hand. A matte black data tile with moving, interlocking sections appeared. It resembled a tiny panel fallen from the bottom of an alien stealth aircraft. Faint violet light glowed out of the seams wherever a piece opened or slid across. "Before you open this file, be very sure that you want to."

Nina reached for it. The tile disintegrated, and her NetMini pinged with the tone of an arriving email. "Why? What's in it? That looks like C-Branch grade crypto."

"It is time for me to leave now. You have a busy day tomorrow." Shinigami walked toward the door.

"Wait... what's in that file? Why should I hesitate?"

Shinigami's apparition faded, but his voice echoed from every direction. "What it contains may yet again destroy all you think you know about the world."

# 47

# DECONSTRUCTING TAO

Joey's consciousness flew along a twisting tunnel of chromatic light. The end, a disc-shaped slice of reality, flew up to greet him. He twitched at the rapid change in sensation of flying headfirst to sitting upright in his chair. After a few seconds to catch his breath, he grabbed the bit of surgical tubing hanging down the side of his cube, opened the valve at the end, and sucked up a mouthful of coffee.

The sound of activity in the desk to his right made him roll the chair back and peer past the wall at DeWinter.

"Hey, I thought I was the only shithead stuck here late."

DeWinter leaned back and yawned. "Well this is almost your fault. Your woman requested this a few days ago, and it got stuck in the queue."

Joey got up and walked around into DeWinter's workspace. The largest of his holo-panels showed a wireframe model of a crab-shaped robot. "What'cha doin? That thing looks pretty brutal. I'm guessing that's not some kind of war mech game?"

"Heh. Kinda looks like one, right?" DeWinter went to take a sip from his mug, but grumbled at finding it empty. "That's the tenth time. Ugh. I am beyond tired right now. It's a nanobot recovered from a doser who got hopped up on Tao."

Joey leaned on the wall. "Ick. That's pretty horrifying to think about being inside someone." He glanced at the time: 11:58 p.m. "It's almost Saturday. Need help?"

"What about that Preema thing?"

"Fuck busy work." Joey wandered over to the coffee machine, astounded that no one had yet demanded he remove his 'direct feed' hose. Since he'd made the actual trip, he got two cappuccinos instead of black. He handed one to DeWinter as he returned to his desk. The other, he sipped. "Maybe we can both get out of here before one in the morning."

"Sure, whatever." He pointed at a screen full of numbers. "The nanobots taken from the Tao sample are slightly different. They lack some of the visible structures on the outer surface compared to bots found in the Harmony sample."

Joey studied the two images for a moment. "The Tao nanobots don't have as much stuff on them, like they're intended to have a narrower function. Nina said something about them turning people into unwitting spies. Recording video and audio, building a transmitter and such."

"And the random aggression. Both Harmony and Tao are supposed to create a mild, but long-term high where the user feels like nothing's wrong. Total calm and peace." DeWinter laughed. "I'm half tempted to try it out, except for these little creepers."

Joey overlaid the two nanobot wireframes on each other, noting the absence of several bulbous protrusions on the rear of the abdomen, and a few tiny flanges on the insides of the four rear legs. "If you want my uneducated guess here, it looks like the Harmony nanobots are carrying more... either raw materials or mechanisms to perform molecular conversion. What if they're the ones who build the spyware inside people's heads, while the Tao bots are only doing the aggressive behavior tweaking?"

DeWinter's hands flew over the holographic keyboard. He fiddled with some settings in the configuration panel of a computer model, and ran it. "Not a bad thought." He took a sip of cappuccino. "Tao is supposed to be a street chemist's attempt to recreate Harmony, but the samples we've been seeing matched identically. If you ask me, both drugs are coming from the same place."

Joey muttered "mmm" over a mouthful of coffee. He savored it for a few seconds before swallowing. "Yeah. They're sending chaos bombs to poor people and spyware to those who can afford to pay for a 'cleaner' product. The ACC is doing this, so they don't care if LRI loses money. Heck, I bet Mr. Huber is carting these pills out without paying for them."

"Who?" asked DeWinter.

"Bernd Huber, aka Neal Finch. ACC operator embedded in LRI's production team. Nina got him delivering large quantities of H to chem dealers."

The terminal beeped.

"Okay..." DeWinter leaned forward. "I'll isolate those missing components; they need to be the ones that contain the instructions for constructing the transmitter unit. Do me a favor?"

"Shoot."

"Can you cook up the inside of a brain? I'm going to try to reverse engineer the instructions from the nanobot scans and create a virtual version of these 'bots we can set loose on your fake brain. That should let us see the guts of the transmission array and extract the cryptographic seed used to generate the chimeric address."

"Ooh, I like the way you think." Joey winked. "On it."

He ducked around the cube wall and flopped in his chair, sparing a few seconds to take a big sip of coffee before plugging in again. After appearing in his octagon room, he brought up a virtual terminal and popped into the Ancora Medical network. A bit of poking around led him to stored brain scans. Joey hunted among the files for one with no drastic pathology, striking gold with the discovery of 'suspected brain tumor – negative' that showed a healthy brain with a moderately enlarged vascular structure resulting in frequent, localized headaches.

The file transferred in a few seconds, and a giant, transparent brain, brain stem, and eyeballs rendered in the middle of the room. Software colored the brain orange, the cerebellum blue, the brain stem violet, and all the glands green. The eyeballs and a hint of their controlling muscles appeared in natural colors. He peered up at it, shivering.

"Okay, now *that* is creepy."

Over the course of the next forty minutes (with some liberal borrowing from the Ancora database), he built a routine that turned the passive recording into an active simulation of a live brain. He added an invisible skull and skin layer, as well as a simulated circulatory system so DeWinter's virtual nanobots would behave identically to real bots in a living person, even though both the nanobots and brain existed only as code.

The eerie sensation of having someone else in the room came on when he started the simulation. He let it run for a while, watching memory monitors and making sure the program behaved itself. It looked good, but he had no way to know if it truly simulated a brain enough to fool program nanobots.

"Suppose we'll find out."

He opened a chat window to DeWinter's terminal, and got a six-foot holo panel offering a view into the office, as though he were a faerie standing on DeWinter's desk. "The brain is online. And seeing those giant cotton ball eyebrows as big as a city bus is a sight I will need to drink quite a bit to get out of my head."

DeWinter grinned. "I think I've almost got it. I'll jump into your workspace once I'm ready."

"Right. Hurry it up, this thing is fuckin' creepy." Joey opened an access portal for DeWinter to come in, and dropped off the chat. It took the form of an ancient wooden door with peeling white paint, like something from a giant creepy mansion in a horror vid.

He spawned a virtual coffee, which fed his brain the same heat, flavor, and texture sensation no different from consuming one in reality. Of course, the 'digital caffeine' wouldn't do anything for him once he logged out.

*Creeeeak.*

DeWinter peered in the door. "You have some damage." It creaked louder as he pushed it open all the way and entered with a small case under his arm.

"That the bots?"

"Yep." DeWinter looked up at the brain. "Whoa. I see what you mean. Feels like there's someone else in here with us. What do you figure that is?"

"Maybe our brains somehow pick up on the pattern of activity within the virtual brain and 'sense' a person, even though it's just software."

DeWinter set the case down on thin air, as if an invisible desk stood before him. "Well, consciousness is merely electrical impulses. We sure fool our brains easily enough with virtual reality." He opened the case and took out a syringe the size of two synthbeer cans stacked on top of each other.

"Don't come anywhere near me with that." Joey backed up.

"Not a fan of needles?" DeWinter approached the brain.

Joey shook his head. "They haven't used physical needles in over a hundred years. And you think *I'm* the guy with strange affectations?"

"Creaky door, giant needle... six of one." DeWinter smiled and injected a mass of silvery liquid into the fake brain. The gesture correlated to a file copy and run command. Soon, the glop diffused into an uncountable number of tiny specks. Given the brain was roughly two stories tall, the specks looked like mites. Visible, but barely. "Well, here's the moment of truth."

"They're running around... looks like it's working."

Some of the nanobots flowed down the jugular to a portal, only to reappear after a randomized delay simulating a trip through the heart back up from another portal connected to the carotid artery.

"I'm hoping the shortcut won't throw them off." Joey indicated the two floating holes representing the circulatory system. "They're coming right back to the brain without getting lost elsewhere in the body."

DeWinter shook his head. "I don't think it will affect them. They attempt to cling to the brain, only the ones that lose their footing get swept away. Once they realize they're back in brain tissue, they should resume working."

A latticework of silver lines appeared within the orange brain area, creeping forward toward the optic nerve, a cyan line.

"It's working." Joey grinned.

DeWinter patted him on the shoulder. "Nice job on the brain."

"Thanks." Joey walked up to the edge of the mammoth 'head,' and stared in fascination as 'metal' formed into a boxy device attached to the front of the brain stem.

DeWinter opened a number of blank holo-panels. He grabbed at his belt like he pulled a NetMini off a clip and threw square shuriken icons into each display area. Software text exploded on the screens, creating thin golden lines to each distinct portion of the mechanism the nanobots created.

Joey grinned to himself as an idea came to him. He figured the nanobots would have limited space for instructions, and even if they offloaded the decision to transmit/not transmit to the component they manufactured, that would probably still be based on keywords. In order to evaluate the true intelligence value of what the victim experienced, they'd have to install an AI, and these nanobots did not seem to be creating anything large enough to hold one. By his estimation, the device would be lucky to have a hundred terabytes of storage space.

*That wouldn't be enough to hold Shinigami's personality analysis routines...*

Granted, Shinigami came close to the black dragons in terms of power and complexity. Most AIs would be far smaller, but still couldn't fit here. He created a wraparound display screen, giving the simulation's 'eyes' a view. In it, he spliced bits and pieces of various entertainment holo-vids about spies, specifically parts where people discussed prototype technology, top-secret programs, and so on. Anything with a good buzzword that might trigger the software inside the nanobots to want to send it back home.

*Crap. I'm a jackass. Forgot the NIU.* Joey spent a minute or two hunting down an 'off the shelf' simulation used by cybernetics designers, and added it to his sim. A spiderweb of wires enshrouded the brain, connected to the ubiquitous neural interface unit that relayed information between a person's cybernetics and their living mind. Within seconds of the NIU appearing, DeWinter's nanobots added an interface line to it and spent a few minutes clustered around the ports.

Joey let the movies play a while before altering the simulation to provide the appearance that this nonexistent person had plugged in and connected to the

GlobeNet. Within seconds of that, DeWinter let out a noise like someone had kicked him in the nuts.

"You okay?" Joey looked up from his status screens.

"Got 'em." DeWinter did a jig.

"You're dancing."

"Yes." He wagged his butt at Joey. "I am dancing in your VR node. We got the bastards."

Joey paused the simulation and strolled the few feet over to where his cube mate had set up virtual shop. "What did we get?"

"I found the software code for the data transmission." He walked into the simulation and made a grabbing gesture at a portion of the box attached to the brain stem. A slab of bright yellow emerged, a squarish circuit-board form similar to what it would look like to remove a single blade from a multi-motherboard processing cabinet. "This right here is the software that generates the chimeric addresses. We couldn't get it out of the control module extracted from the stiff they brought in; evidently, this little box nukes itself when it senses the person it's in dies. The encryption routines don't exist in any readable state in the nanobots."

Joey grinned. "I think I've got a hardon."

DeWinter's eyebrows climbed his forehead. "You beast."

"Reverse engineering always gets me in the mood." Joey winked.

"Hah." DeWinter hung the glowing yellow board in midair, and spent the next few minutes grasping at it, pulling threads out to individual windows.

Joey attached packet analysis software to the threads, while DeWinter injected tracer strings in the headers. Since the 'secret data' the nanobots had captured consisted of harmless entertainment, they opened a real portal to the GlobeNet, ran it through sixteen proxies so it appeared to be coming from a Teradyne Corporation office at the far northern end of West City, and let the altered data stream go loose.

"I've got the routine here that's generating the chimera." DeWinter grinned like a mad scientist while thinking program code into being. Lines of text appeared as fast as he could envision them. "Got it. We're generating the key now. Don't need the sim anymore."

"Here's a sniffer." Joey started a packet trace routine. Above them, a world map scrolled out, rendered in glistening blue on black. He held the holo-panel open like a wastebasket. "Feed me."

DeWinter hit a 'button,' and a stream of yellow energy projected from the 'motherboard' floating in midair. Joey caught it in the sniffer window. A spot of light appeared on the map roughly at the point where the prewar border between Washington State and Canada had been. From it, hair-thin lines trickled south in a tight bundle. When they hit the southern edge of UCF territory, they exploded into a rat's nest, going all over the world, with only a handful going straight south into ACC territory.

Twenty-four seconds later, all the hair-thin threads converged on a single point, a dot 14.2 miles northwest of Hermosillo, Mexico. Two columns of scrolling chimeric addresses appeared, the sender in blue on the left, receiver in orange on the right. Each line matched.

"Got 'em." DeWinter offered Joey a hand. "Excellent work, sir."

Joey tipped his absent cowboy hat before accepted the handshake. "Couldn't have done it without you. Every cowboy needs the 'old man mentor.'"

"Shit." DeWinter shook his head. "I ain't no old man. I'm thirty-six."

"Heh. That's old to me... and if you wanna see thirty-seven, you'd best send that up the pipe fast."

"I got you by twelve years, pal. That ain't that much." DeWinter folded his arms.

"Maybe when I'm your age, twelve years won't feel like much." He winked.

DeWinter huffed a heavy sigh, though smiled. "Hope your girl finds this as thrilling as we did."

"Oh, I'm sure she'll have fun with it." He winked.

# 48

# HOLLOW PRAISE

Nina looked up from her desk as a blur of brown and white passed by the door. She checked the time: 6:28 a.m., within Hardin's usual arrival window. Still scowling from her nocturnal visitor, she locked her terminal and rushed after him. He hooked left a few doors past her office and went to the end of the hall.

"You're early." He swiped his ID at the door, which beeped, and he went in.

Nina followed. "Couldn't sleep... much."

"Yeah. I went home to shower and eat something. Got an email from Net Ops about one last night." He hung his brown blazer on the wall.

"Wouldn't that be this morning?"

He eased himself into his seat. "I break up days by sleep. If I haven't slept yet, it's still last night."

"So does that mean we're still on your yesterday?" She slipped into one of the seats facing his desk.

Hardin winked. "I caught a nap on the ride back. About time you smiled."

"I've found some more information."

"So I see." He waved at the silver loaf on his desk, causing it to project a wall of holo-panels. "Two additional spies we hadn't found."

"Sonia Cortez, aka Valeria Brunner, at a director level position with LRI's physical security, and George Durham, aka Sasha Zarkhov... maintenance." Nina scowled. "As far as I've been able to find, they haven't done anything yet involving the Harmony issue, aside from Brunner potentially turning a blind eye to large batches of pills going out the door."

"Probably deep cover, lying in wait." Hardin hit a button on his terminal and spent a moment reading over something.

Nina stared into the opaque black of the holo-panel side facing her.

"The operations teams are already in place. They'll be performing a simultaneous takedown of all identified assets, plus the two new ones you've identified."

"Right. What time are we going in the door?"

"They will be making their move at 8:05 a.m."

"*They?*" Nina raised an eyebrow. "You don't want me going with them?"

Hardin looked away from his screen to meet her stare. "Not this time. We have something else we need you to do."

"But this case isn't finished."

"It's related to this case." He set his elbow on the armrest of his chair and grasped his chin. "Net Ops managed to crack into the nanobots' programming. They've linked the chimeric network address to a physical location a short distance northwest of Hermosillo, Mexico. Satellite reconnaissance shows a small village at the site. Your orders are to travel to this site, locate the facility housing the servers our Net Ops people found, and see what they've learned."

"You didn't send NetOps in via cyberspace?" She gripped her knees, annoyed that she'd be missing the raid at LRI.

"We didn't want to tip them off that we'd broken their chimera, and NetOps can't blow up a facility in the real world. After you've secured the facility and identified what, if any, sensitive information they're storing, you're to burn the place."

*Right. Easier to send one doll than an entire team.* "Understood."

"Don't sound so thrilled." Hardin chuckled. "After the week you've had, I figured you'd enjoy a chance to vent some frustration. You do understand the need to move fast on this. After they take those assets out, the whole facility could crawl up its own ass and vanish."

"Right." She relaxed. "I'll assume there's already a whisper waiting for me on the roof."

"Correct." He patted the desk. "Fine job locating those other two agents by the way."

She grumbled.

"That's not the reaction I usually get for giving someone a back-pat."

"Sorry, sir. I'm not sure what bothers me more… that I basically got handed that information, or who did the handing."

Hardin tilted his head to the right. "Oh?"

"Shinigami is still out there. He popped into my head last night."

"Oh, shit." Hardin rubbed his eyebrows.

"He said he's not the same… the whole thing was just some alien ant farm experiment trying to see what makes humans tick." She stared into nowhere. "He set us up to run into Bertrand. Claims he didn't expect Vincent to get killed, but I don't know if I believe that. Or maybe I do and he just doesn't care what happened. It's all testing and evaluation to him."

"Some AIs don't have emotions, or have strange representations of it. Especially the ones that think themselves superior to us."

Nina chuckled. "Oh, he's right up here on that list, sir. Called me a rabbit."

"Come again?"

"Animal testing." Nina closed her eyes and tried not to think about how she found Elizaveta.

"Wow." Hardin whistled. "They don't do much of that these days. Too many protests, plus theoretical computer models have improved. Most firms do virtual testing these days."

She bristled. "Unless they can buy Russian orphans."

Hardin winced. "I don't think… well I'd like to think a similar situation won't be happening any time soon. The NewsNet is *still* showing that story. At least they had the decency to blur the kids' faces."

"How the hell did they get that video?" muttered Nina.

He exhaled, eyebrows up. "Have you seen it?"

She shook her head.

"I don't blame you. The video they're running was taken before our people showed up. Had to be from one of the two employees who objected. Nothing like screaming children in cages to boost NewsNet ratings."

"Maybe you're right." Nina stood. "Maybe I do need to let out some frustration."

"Be careful out there, lieutenant." Hardin made a tossing gesture at her, and her NetMini beeped. "We've got some recon images of the area. Local resistance is aware we are sending someone. They've offered assistance in exchange for a favor."

"What sort of favor, sir? Something I'm doing or do I not need to worry about that?"

"Yes and no." Hardin gestured at her. "It's in the file. We've agreed to provide assistance to them insofar as helping a number of psionics and resistance people flee Mexico to the UCF. Basically, your part of it would be escorting them to a pick up location a few miles into the Badlands. Since it's not officially ACC territory once you're out there, you'll have some dropships coming in for an evac. There's also cases of weapons, ammo, and medical supplies going in, but that's not your job."

"Right." She pulled up the file and skimmed over satellite images of desert landscapes, a small town, and a few local people. One José Mendoza, a fortyish man, appeared to be the leader of the resistance cell she would be working with. "Anything else I need to know?"

"Demo packs are on the whisper. Don't take any risks you don't have to. Better to blow the shit out of that place without looking at what they got a hold of than chance not coming home over some data that might be useless."

She closed her eyes and pictured Elizaveta running into her arms. "Understood. No unnecessary risks."

# 49

# LA RESISTENCIA

Bands of light pulsed down the silver walls of an elevator around Nina. A mental nudge triggered a vid call, and a virtual holo-panel scrolled open in midair, containing her mother, Camille. The woman appeared around thirty, fourteen years taken back by the tanks at Reinventions. Nina studied her hands, more frightened of *looking* inhuman than being it. She'd traded her government issue sand brown coat for a flannel shirt, blue jeans, and common sneakers. Beneath it, she kept her ballistic stealth.

*Vanity runs in the family.*

「Mother… I need to ask you to watch Elizaveta for maybe a few days. I don't know exactly how long this will take. I wish I could give you more details, but even saying I'm going to be away for a few days is probably too much.」

「Oh, I hope you're not doing anything too dangerous. Your father and I are always worried whenever you do one of those things you can't talk about. Poor thing had a bad dream last night, about when those barbarians abducted her—I won't call it arresting. She got over it quick, but I think she's afraid of being taken away from you.」

Nina failed to hide her guilty expression. 「Don't worry, Mother. She has dreams like that a few nights a week. It's going to take her awhile to accept that the CMO isn't going to show up in the middle of the night again. I… Tell her we'll do something special when I'm done with this case. 」 She thought about what Shinigami had said, eyes downcast. 「Can you give Father a message for me? I don't have enough time right now, and I need to at least say this much in case something goes wrong.」

「Oh, Nina… you're worrying me. 」 Her mother bit her lower lip. 「Of course. What is it?」

「Tell him that I know he's friends with Leland Marcus, and I understand. Make sure he knows I don't blame him for anything.」

Her mother's eyes widened. 「What? What are you talking about, Nina?」

「Something I heard. Maybe it's a lie. You'll know by his reaction if it means anything. It makes sense now why he's been so strange about this doll body of mine. He can't even stand to look at me.」 She bowed her head. 「I think he's guilty.」

「Your father had nothing to do with what happened to you. Why would he feel guilty?」

The elevator stopped on the roof level. A stiff wind blasted into the small chamber as the doors slid open, downdraft from the idling, silent whispercraft perched on a landing pad twenty meters away. With its optical skin disabled, the elongated, sleek craft resembled some kind of ancient raven shaman's headdress. The sniper booms pointed straight back, tucked under slender wings jutting out among engine pods that appeared too thin to generate enough lift, but perhaps their extreme length made up for it. Two tail fins formed a V at the back; a third that usually hung straight down had folded upward to allow the craft to land. Its side hatch yawned open, exposing the dark interior.

「I need to go now, Mother. Sorry for saying something like that over the vid and disappearing, but I needed it off my mind. Please tell Elizaveta that I love her, and I will be home as soon as I can.」

「We will talk about this when you return.」 Her mother gave her the same stare and tone of voice she'd used on her as a teenager whenever she'd gotten in trouble.

Her mother's utter disregard of her position as a Division 9 field operator, or of her abject lethality made her smile. 「Yes, Mother.」

She dropped the vid call and crossed the roof, up a short stairway with yellow railings, and over the grey landing pad to the side of the whispercraft. As soon as she stepped up and inside, it lifted off. Whirring from the closing side hatch filled the cabin, louder than the sound of the engines, which amounted to a faint howl of moving air. She grabbed a handle on the ceiling and pulled herself around to fall ass-first into a seat mounted to the wall. The electric drone of the motors extending the lower tail fin continued for two more seconds.

Her 'special gift' for the target facility sat in a storage compartment in the rear wall, an olive-drab backpack containing four programmable demo charges. *I wonder what made C-Branch punt this one.*

The primary difference between Division 9 and C-Branch consisted of operational theater. For the most part, C-Branch made things happen outside the UCF while Division 9 worked inside the borders. Blowing up a site in ACC territory was the kind of black-ops shit they did all the time. When it came down to the wire, C-Branch had a little more political influence since they wore the label of being 'officially' military, whereas Division 9 fell under the auspices of the National Police Force. C-Branch had somewhat better tech as well.

*Heh. Maybe it's a question of money. Or they didn't feel like it... or Hardin wanted me to. Maybe his 'friend across the hall' called in repayment of his favors by not having this on their budget.*

The sniper boom operators both waved. She returned the greeting, and opened the file Hardin had given her. Her destination sat 784 miles away, and the pilot would likely skim the coast. Only sailors had more superstitions than pilots, and few wanted to go into the Badlands if they weren't ordered to do so. Whispercraft traded supersonic capability for stealth, so the flight would likely take about an hour and a half, give or take ten minutes, depending on wind.

She settled into her seat and enlarged her floating virtual screens to block off the plain black nothingness of the whispercraft interior.

———

"LIEUTENANT," said a voice over a speaker. "WE'RE FIFTEEN MINUTES OUT FROM the LZ. I'm reading a pickup truck and two small bikes on site."

"Any weapons?" Nina shrank the holo-panels before closing them. Not that she had to, but after sitting for almost two hours, she stood and stretched. "Do they look like my resistance friends?"

"Hard to say. I can tell you they don't look like ACC. I think that's an ethanol-burning truck."

"Whoa. Internal combustion?" asked a woman.

Nina walked over to the backpack and lifted it out of the storage compartment. "They say the evil spirit of the Badlands leaves old tech alone. The more modern something is, the more likely it'll crap out."

"That doesn't bode too well for you," said a deep-voiced man. The starboard side sniper wobbled with the sound of laughter coming over the speakers.

"You're all a bunch of superstitious idiots," said the woman. "One minute until waypoint."

Nina glanced between the hatch and the fast-wire discs in the floor. "Are you planning to put rubber to dirt or am I wire dancing?"

"Nothing else out there, figured I'd land," said the woman.

"Fine by me." Nina moved to the side hatch and slung the pack over one shoulder.

"Heh," said the starboard sniper. "For being ACC territory, this place is fuckin' empty."

"*They* don't even wanna be here," said the portside sniper. "And this ain't exactly *deep* in. Another sixty or so miles northeast and you hit Badlands. Border's not what you could call a clearly-defined line here, yanno?"

"Are they *all* that superstitious?" asked a man, likely the electronics officer.

"Pretty much," said the portside sniper. "Most of 'em are concentrated deeper south. Probably why the resistance moved their psionics out here. Safer, but even they don't wanna go into the Badlands. They say you go in, but never get out."

Nina glanced left at the passage to the cockpit. "There's a higher prevalence of religion down here. Most of Mexico still believes in a higher power."

"Morons," muttered the starboard-side sniper.

*If it gives them hope...* "There isn't much else for them here. If it helps them make it to tomorrow, what harm is there?"

"Those ones aren't the problem," said the starboard-side sniper. "It's the ones who kill psionic children 'cause they think their superstitious man-in-the-clouds considers them evil."

The pilot peered around a bank of equipment to shake her helmet at him. "It's not all their fault, Sloan. People in charge down here don't like psionics because they're paranoid about secrets. It's hard to bullshit telepaths. Their establishment encourages that bigotry."

Sloan's station rotated as he panned the long boom railgun side to side. "Yeah, still don't make it smart."

Nina bowed her head, thinking about what she'd seen at the swamp. She knew for a fact the 'Vincent' who'd visited her at home the other night had been fake, but the apparition she'd witnessed in the bayou... the way he *felt* unnerved her. If spirits existed, could some manner of higher power be real too?

"Ten seconds," said the pilot. "Nine... eight..."

The whirr of the tail boom retracting vibrated in the floor.

Nina grasped a handle on the wall and waited. As the pilot said, "two," the whispercraft decelerated, making her sway toward the front end. Wheels touched down at the count of "one," and the side hatch opened, letting in a blast of hot, dusty air.

A battered green pickup truck that looked about twenty years old sat between a pair of patchwork motorcycles with ethanol-burning engines. The truck's tires seemed too small and too old to go with the somewhat more modern vehicle, the most obvious difference being the lack of e-motors. *Did they drive those things out of the Badlands?*

Three men and two women stood in front of the grille, all in the same startled lean away from her. To their perspective, the door in the side of the invisible whispercraft must've looked like a magic portal opening into another world. Either that or the sudden appearance of all the dust swirling around got them thinking about evil spirits.

Nina stepped to the ground and walked the thirty yards over to the people in front of the truck. The locals dressed in a manner similar to her: long-sleeved flannel or plain shirts, jeans or brown fatigue pants, and sneakers. The women both wore boots and had loose black bandanas draped around their necks. Of the lot, only they carried weapons; each had a submachinegun hanging on a strap over their chest. While she had learned basic Spanish in school, she'd installed an intelligence-grade language chip so none of the local slang went over her head. "Guess you're the welcoming party?"

The central man, the oldest of the group in his thirties, glanced left and right at the people with him; the men didn't appear to be armed. "You're not what we were expecting."

She smiled. "What *were* you expecting? Some six-foot-five knuckle-dragger with a buzz cut?"

He laughed. "Well, not exactly, but you don't have the look of a commando."

"This woman is too pretty," said the woman on the left. An inch shorter than Nina, she had a thick, muscular build and suspicious eyes. "And too white. They will know she is from the outside."

"There are plenty of Germans, and they are almost as pale," said the other woman who looked younger, maybe twenty.

A young man, lanky and teenaged, let out a sudden cry of pain and grabbed his head before crumpling into a heap. He rocked back and forth, making a repetitive "Ay, ay, ay, ay" sound.

The other two men, who appeared in their later twenties, stared at him, but kept shooting wary looks back at Nina. Both women eased their hands up to grasp the submachine guns hanging around their chests.

"Ramon?" The man who hadn't said a word yet took a knee, and grasped the boy's shoulder. When the teen continued rocking and whining, he glared at Nina. "What did you do to Ramon?"

Nina cringed, her eyebrows edging upward in an expression of sympathy. "Ramon's a telepath, isn't he? My intel said you had a number of psionics with you who we're bringing out after everything's done."

A thin trickle of blood seeped from Ramon's left nostril. His muttering changed to a constant mouth-closed whine, and his face reddened.

"You didn't have to do that to him." The man leapt up and moved to lunge at her, but the older man caught him. Rather than grab her, he pointed. "You telepaths can block each other out; you didn't have to hurt him!"

"Hold on, Javier," said the older man, eyeing Nina. "We don't yet understand what happened."

"I don't know what you were told, but I work for Division 9. We often handle classified information. I've got a cybernetic component that makes it a very bad idea to try and read my mind." She glanced down at Ramon. "He would have felt resistance, and then he tried to force his way into my mind. The device backfeeds his power at him, amplified. The harder he pushes, the harder it hurts. I didn't do anything to him. He walked into a wall, backed up, and decided to run headfirst into the same bricks."

"I don't believe that," said the short, muscular woman. "Cybernetics that react to psionics?

Nina smiled as her CamNano changed her skin to match the medium brown hue of the oldest man. "I'm full of surprises, but I'm not psionic." She slipped between the men, grasped the bumper of the pickup truck, and lifted it off its front wheels with one arm.

"Mother of God," muttered Javier.

She set the truck down.

The oldest man laughed, pointed at her, and winked. "Now that I did not expect. I am Pedro Del Olmo. This is María Isabel"—he nodded sideways at the younger woman—"and Adriana."

A howl in the wind gained strength as the whispercraft rose into the air.

Ramon ceased making noise. Javier helped him sit up, but the boy continued cradling his head. Both nostrils dripped blood.

Nina checked her bag and found a ten-count box of stimpaks—why they bothered sending any she had no idea, since they did nothing for her. Hooray for standard loadout. She offered one to Javier. "This will help. It's medicine."

"We're not *that* primitive." Javier swiped it from her fingers. "Thanks."

"Normally, we are not so quick to trust, but your aircraft is nothing like we have ever seen." Pedro waved her to follow. "You are clearly not with the Corporates. Come."

Nina followed him to the truck and got in the rear bench behind the driver's seat. Pedro drove, with Ramon in the front seat and Javier in back with her. The women got on the motorbikes, pulled their bandanas up over their faces, and donned helmets.

The sound of a combustion engine, and the accompanying vibration in the seat, mesmerized her for a few seconds. Fumes invaded the cabin, an eye-watering burn similar to cheap synthetic vodka. Buzzing like giant bees emanated from the bikes. One took off, leaving a wispy dust trail in its wake. Pedro followed, the other woman behind them.

Desert scrub extended to the horizon as far as she could see. Nina positioned the backpack between her feet, opened it, and pulled out a foam block with the disc-shaped charges. Each eight-inch diameter disk, one inch thick, had a matte-black coating. At the center of an X-shaped reinforcement molded across the top, sat a M3 plug. A miniature satellite communicator remained at the bottom of the bag.

Javier let out a low whistle. "Damn, girl. Those look serious."

She pinged one for wireless, and got a login prompt in a small virtual window. It accepted her Division 9 ID, and shifted to display a status window. One pound of Ne8 explosive. A single charge could vaporize an area equal to the footprint of a high-rise building, and probably one story up and down as well.

"Shit... do they want me to burn this place out or send it to Mars?"

"Huh?" asked Javier.

Nina switched the mode of the charge to accept only a login from her hardware address and to 'brick' if anyone else tried to connect, rendering it useless. *C-Branch would've set it to blow instantly if tampered with.* "These things look small, but they've got a bit of a punch."

"Sounds like their momma," said Pedro, chuckling.

Ramon pounded the dashboard and shouted, "Fuck that bitch! Nghhh! What the shit? Imma cut that whore."

"Hi." Nina waved at him. "Right behind you."

He whipped his head around to stare at her, his expression froze part-way between embarrassed and angry.

Javier patted him on the shoulder. "You're welcome to try, kid, but I wouldn't suggest it."

"Don't try to read my mind again," said Nina. "Sorry; I should've warned you. I just spent almost two hours reading about the Mexican Resistance, and it did mention you frequently vet new people with a telepath."

"Damn, that fucking hurt so much." Ramon grabbed his head and slouched forward.

Nina took out the second bomb and logged in. "I assume you have a few psionics hiding out with you. When we get there, please warn the others. This device doesn't make exception for curious children. And before you ask, I can't turn it off. I don't want to be responsible for a child screaming like that."

"You did already." Javier winked. "Ramon's only eighteen. Still a child."

"Your mother," said Ramon, grabbing his crotch. "Your ass is only two years older. Shut up."

Pedro chuckled.

She programmed the last two charges and put them back in the foam, and the foam back in the bag. "You don't seem too heavily armed... The briefing made it sound as though your people would assist in taking the facility."

"We don't carry weapons in the open." Pedro patted a panel on the door. "We *are* armed, but it is not like the UCF here. It is illegal for people to have weapons if they do not work for the CMO, the DMS, or security. Carrying a weapon can get you shot."

Javier grumbled. "It is better in the UCF. They are not afraid of their people. Anyone can have a weapon."

Nina offered a wry chuckle. "Sometimes I think they're just hoping the disenfranchised kill each other as a form of population control. Scraping meat off the road is cheaper than prison or social support services."

Pedro shook his head, muttering about God abandoning the Earth.

The ride continued in relative silence for eighteen minutes until a bright blue one-story ranch house came into view. Eight goats, some chickens, two cows, and a burro wandered around out front. A middle-aged woman in a coral-hued dress hung laundry on a cord strung from the corner of the house to a wooden pole as tall as a man. She eyed the approaching vehicles, but showed little reaction.

Nina did a double take, staring at *live* animals. "Are those real?"

Javier flexed his bicep. "Yes. All natural."

She laughed. "I meant the animals."

Pedro gave her an incredulous look. "Yes... what else would they be?"

In the middle of the front yard stood a quaint well with a tiny wooden roof. Two metal pipes rose from the ground behind it, each capped with vent grilles.

Both bikes circled around the house to a barn, and drove inside. Chickens went running from the approaching truck, which Pedro stopped near the house. Nina pushed her door open and got out, drawn by the glint of metal that shone from the interior of the well. Curious, she approached and peered in. Its rustic exterior concealed a shiny metal cylinder two stories deep, filled to the three-quarter mark with water. At the bottom, a boxy machine emitted a slow stream of bubbles. Faint mechanical noise came from both standing pipes, which drew in air.

*Interesting... why make a water extractor look like an old well?*

"Over here," said Pedro.

Nina backed away from the 'well' and followed him to the barn where Adriana and Maria concealed their bikes under tarps. The heavy scent of animal waste and wet hay hung so thick in the air it settled on her tongue. After three breaths, she tasted moldy wood. Javier went over to a beat up tractor, which at least appeared new enough to be powered by e-motors. He did something at the controls, and a heavy *clunk* sounded from a machinist's workbench.

Ramon and Pedro swung the bench out from the wall, exposing a hole in the floor. Fifteen feet of corrugated metal tube led to an open area below containing light and the murmur of voices. A well-worn ladder of welded rebar extended down to about halfway between ceiling and ground.

"Let me, uhh, go tell them not to poke you in the brain," said Ramon.

She nodded.

He climbed down.

"So... can we trust your people?" asked Pedro. "Are they really going to help us get out?"

Nina looked him in the eye. "I have no reason to doubt they would. Psionics are welcome in the UCF, as is anyone fleeing the Corporates' oppression. You'll of course have go to through a bit of processing first."

"Like bologna?" asked Javier.

She laughed. "No... interviews."

"I understand. No spies." Pedro smiled. "Good plan. We will take you at your word."

"Okay!" Ramon's voice echoed up the tube.

Nina peered over the edge. Once Ramon backed out of the way, she jumped, landing in a deep squat with one hand on the dirt for balance. The room held nine adults (including Javier), a girl on the younger side of teenage, and four children under twelve, the smallest of whom couldn't have been much past five. Except for one little boy in a bright orange jumpsuit and pink flip-flops, they wore a mismatched collection of tattered clothing, no sense of uniformity or organization among them. The word 'Psíquico' adorned the chest of the jumpsuit in black block letters.

Tables on the right held rifles and pistols, as well as a few hand grenades and some medical supplies. Cots lined the left wall by a short hallway that looked hand-excavated, where a modern portable camp toilet (built around a trash disintegrator) sat behind a plastic tarp curtain.

Fourteen faces in varying shades of apprehension stared at her in shock.

The boy in orange sat near the worktable. A woman, the only person in the room with light brown hair instead of black, had a datapad connected by a jury-rigged splice cable to electronic handcuffs on his wrists, also bright orange. Soft red lights on matching restraints around his ankles blinked.

Nina's heart sank when she made eye contact with him.

"She feels sorry for us," said the boy in orange.

"Idiot," snapped Ramon. "Don't use psionics on her."

The boy gave him a challenging stare. "You said don't read her mind. I didn't go into her head. She's radiating."

Nina hurried over to him. "I don't think an empath has to worry about my implant, but I wouldn't try making me feel different." She grumbled. "It's disgraceful how they treat you here."

"Rafael is lucky we found him before they executed him," said the woman holding the datapad. "He's only been here a few hours."

Rafael gave her the saddest wide-eyed 'please don't hurt me' stare imaginable. His round face added to the effect, making him seem more like six than his likely age of about ten. "I was in jail for five months. I kept making them feel sorry for me when they wanted to shoot me."

"Let me help get those binders off." Nina made sure she had space, and made a fist with her right hand. Two Nano blades extended out from her knuckles and locked at twelve-inches.

"Whoa... that's awesome!" Rafael bounced in his seat.

"Hold still. These are extremely sharp." She grasped his arm gently, and held it up to get an angle on the plastisteel cuff.

"I know Nano." He froze.

After some careful blade work freed him, she retracted her claws.

"Well, that's a lot faster than my way." The woman chuckled. "I'm Patricia. The security they put on those things, it's like they expected a ten-year-old to tear them apart with his bare hands."

Rafael stood, unzipped the jumpsuit, and ripped it off like it had been made out of turds. Though his face turned bright red, he seemed to prefer being naked. He held it out to her. "They can find this. There is a tracker."

"We know." Patricia smiled. "It's already burned out. They did that before they brought you here."

Rafael kept holding the wadded fluorescent orange cloth out to her. "Okay. I still don't want to wear it. They will shoot me if they see it."

"Rafael," yelled a man across the room. When the boy turned to look, the man waved a shirt at him. "This will do for now."

The boy darted over and practically dove into a blue shirt that hung down to his knees.

"Well," said Pedro, walking up behind Nina. "This is our group."

José Mendoza, the man she recognized from her intelligence packet, emerged from the rear hall. Seconds later, a brief yellow flash lit up the camp toilet. He ruffled Rafael's hair on the way by, and approached Nina. "It is good to meet you."

"This is José. He's in charge." Pedro gestured at him.

"Mr. Mendoza." Nina nodded in greeting. "So, you've got twelve adults. Aside from yourself, Francisco Rios, Roberto Araya, Pedro, and Patricia, who all have either DMS or CMO training… how many are going to be part of the first phase?"

José blinked at her. "You know our people already?"

"I had a briefing with some faces and names. Not all. Only people who were in their system."

"Ahh." José nodded. "Yes. That is why they are out here in the middle of nowhere. All of us are too well known to risk entering a major city. At least here, the worry of the north keeps a large presence of CMO away."

Her eyebrows slid together. "Is that going to be a problem going near Hermosillo? The objective isn't within the city limits… do you have a map?"

"No. It's not a *major* city. Mostly commoners living in one-room pods who go off to work the hydro farms each day." José crossed the room to a small desk among the cots. He tapped at a datapad until it displayed a holographic map of the area.

Nina pointed to a spot 14.2 miles northwest of Hermosillo. "That's where I need to go."

"*Estación Salamanca.* It's a small village near a solar generating facility." José waved his hand about as he spoke. "Almost everyone who lives there works for VMS, uhh, *Verde Mundial Solar.*"

"So Green World owns that little town." She remembered them as having a fair amount of technology for the ACC, but besieged by frequent physical attacks from competing energy corporations, most notably Berlin Nuclear. "That makes sense. An operation like I'm hunting would need a steady supply of power. Plus, this place looks like the ass end of nowhere. Anyone scanning satellite reconnaissance data wouldn't think it anything but a burro's bathroom."

Chuckles filtered among the resistance.

"We have offered any assistance we can provide in exchange for help escaping to the UCF," said Pedro.

José grinned. "Yes. Yes. Within reason of our capabilities of course. Except for the children, we are all willing to fight."

"I will help." A wisp of a little girl in a tattered yellow dress, lime green sneakers, and a bit of rope tied around her waist for a belt to hold up a pouch approached. "I'm Gabriella Morales."

Nina crouched. "That's very brave of you, sweetie, but I don't want you to get hurt. This is dangerous."

"I know it is dangerous. They shot my parents." She clenched her hands into fists at her sides. Tears traced clean lines in the dust on her cheeks. "I want them to die. I made the man who killed my father kill the other soldiers." Her face scrunched with an annoyed scowl. "I couldn't make him kill himself, but I told him to go kill his boss."

"You're a suggestive?"

Gabriella nodded. "Yes, but I promise not to use it on anyone who doesn't deserve it. They told me the UCF is afraid of suggestives, but I promise I'll be good."

Nina sighed. "As astoundingly useful as that could be, I am *not* bringing a little child into a gunfight."

"I'm not little; I'm eight." She looked down. "I understand. I don't want to get shot, but I can do stuff like make them open the door."

Nina patted her on the shoulder. "I would never forgive myself if anything happened to you. Stay here and stay safe. Use your power to protect everyone who isn't going to fight."

Gabriella kicked at the dirt floor. "Okay. I'll be here if you change your mind." She trudged over to a cot with a few pathetic stuffed animals and a pink child's datapad.

Most of the adults either tried to hold back grins or looked sorrowful.

Nina suppressed the urge to scowl. *Almost makes war feel justified.* She let off a silent sigh. *That'll make it worse. I'll have to settle for helping these people for the moment.* "So what have we got?"

José gestured around the room. "Myself, Pedro, Patricia, Leticia, Francisco, Javier, Roberto, and Silvia... plus Maria and Adriana—they're topside."

"Bikes."

He nodded. "Aye. I'd prefer not to bring any of the psionics above ground in case they are recognized. Josefina is telekinetic, but if anyone sees her using her power... even commoners, they may try to kill her."

A young woman sitting cross-legged on a cot looked up from a NetMini screen. She seemed fearful and shy, and appeared to be around eighteen. "Did you call me, José?"

"No, no..." He smiled at her. "Just telling our friend here I would prefer to keep you safe."

Nina tapped her foot while thinking. "So, ten people at most, but that would leave your compound lightly defended. I have a geotag on the location of the facility, but we weren't able to get a good look at it from satellite. The site contained anywhere from five and fourteen heat signatures, and didn't give off the kind of electromagnetic radiance I'd expect from a place full of computer equipment."

"How sure are you this is the place?" asked Pedro.

"No doubt at all." Nina brought up the data trace Net Ops sent over, and watched the gold threads all converge on a point about twenty miles east-southeast from where she stood. "My guess is that they've got the guts of their operation underground, so we could be walking into almost anything."

José rubbed his chin, making a series of *Hmm* sounds.

"The biggest help you and your people can be for me is eyes and ears. One or two go in with me, the rest watch the area from the outside and send warning if anything unexpected shows up." Nina looked among the group. "It's a data center, and they're relying on being hard to find. We've been watching the place since we've identified it. There's been no activity suggesting a significant military presence here."

"All right." José waved at Javier and a fortyish looking man with a little grey creeping into his hair, Roberto. "The three of us will go with you. Maria, Adriana, and Silvia will watch from outside."

Pedro stepped toward José. "But—"

"I need you to stay here in case I don't come back. It would be unwise for us both to go." José shifted his gaze to Nina. "How soon do you want to do this?"

Nina frowned at the pitiful living conditions. "Faster I'm done, the faster your people can get out of here. How about now?"

# 50

# BLACK DRAGONS

A momentary calm settled over the ruined building. Neither Noriko nor any of the foreigners wasted bullets on rubble. She seemed to be watching the ground floor via her rifle's optics, without exposing herself. Masaru tried not to move his right arm. Even air blowing over the burned spots hurt. Sweat ran in beads down his face and back, but still he kept the rifle pointed at the doorway. He held a reasonable degree of certainty that he hadn't inflicted any permanent neural damage to himself yet, but if he didn't give his system time to rest from using his speedware, he'd get a talking to about spending a few million credits on surgery that could've been avoided.

*They will see reason. It is superior to death.*

He flicked his thumb at the grip, a nervous habit borne of waiting.

A voice yelled in horrible Japanese, with a German accent. "I care don't what do you right now. Fancy new toys, you pick up and come fast." Pause. "Why? You not ask why. If you want more toys, you do as ask. We attacked."

Masaru snickered.

"All those expensive weapons," yelled Noriko, "but you can't buy a decent Japanese chip?" Her voice repeated the words in German from speakers on her helmet.

"*Jemand töte dieses verdammte schlampe schon!*" shouted a different man. A second later, 'someone kill this slut already' appeared in text at the underside of Masaru's vision.

Noriko let off a haughty laugh. "*Seit neun Minuten hast du versucht diese Schlampe zu töten, und ich bin immer noch hier.*" She fired two rapid shots, still only her rifle peeking around the corner.

A heavy groan preceded the *thump* of a body hitting the ground. A fusillade of incoming fire sprayed the area around her with concrete dust. She yanked her rifle back to safety.

Masaru glanced at her. "Whatever you said, I don't think they liked it."

She laughed, despite cowering against the wall. "I said, 'you've been trying to kill this bitch for nine minutes, and I'm still here.' One got mad and popped up. I shot him in the face."

Engine whine in the distance reached the edge of Masaru's perception. A momentary daydream of medical care, a grand meal, and a long, hot bath, distracted him with joy… until Shuji's death fell on him like a blanket of lead.

"We shall be victorious soon." Masaru snapped his attention back to the door as footsteps scuffed in the hall.

Noriko chuckled once the barrage ceased. "I came in here expecting to die. It is okay, Moto-san. I know how this will end."

"Abe-san." He sighted over the rifle. "If we are to die, there is something I must tell you, but I do not think we shall die today."

*Beep. Beep. Beep.*

Masaru answered the incoming vid call by mental command. His NetMini linked to his headware over a wireless link, and the face of a man about his age appeared surrounded by the interior of a thick, padded helmet. Amber light bathed his face, and the reflections of a HUD readout shone from his eyes.

「Kurotai-sama. It is an honor to speak with you. I am Himura Ryozo. We are near. What is the situation inside the building?」

Masaru smiled. 「I am on the third floor with Sergeant Abe Noriko of the JSDF. All hostiles are on the ground level, except for one fool sneaking up the stairs. There may be an unknown number of Etamura approaching from an unknown direction.」

Noriko raised her rifle to peer around the wall again. She gasped and fired a barrage of automatic fire. Men screamed in alarm as ricochets pinged and whizzed.

「Understood Kurotai-sama. Six seconds.」

The engine whine outside grew louder.

Noriko lifted her head, staring around at the walls. "Do you hear that? It sounds like ion thrusters, but too small to be military."

"They are not military."

Her armor scraped on the concrete as she turned to look at him. "Who are—?"

The wall behind them burst in a rain of debris. An eight-foot tall figure in gloss black armor made to resemble an ancient samurai landed in the center of the room. Two points of blue light glowed from the bottom of an ion-thruster pod with long, narrow wings mounted to its back. The glow faded as the wings folded down. He aimed a boxy black rifle at the door Masaru had been covering, which connected via a metal-wrapped cable to the thrust pack. He carried a katana as well, though it looked laughably small in comparison to the giant samurai. A dark gold Kurotai logo, a K inside a circle, adorned the left pectoral plate of the armor.

He turned his helmet toward them; the faceplate bore an exaggerated samurai frown with Oni fangs, and an opaque black visor.

"Look out!" shouted Noriko, for the first time since he'd seen her, sounding frightened. She started to aim her rifle at it, but Masaru grabbed it and pushed it down. "What is that monstrosity!?"

"Dragon Chitin Mark Three. Powered armor." He wagged his eyebrow at her. "We manufacture those."

The man bowed with a nod to Masaru before aiming his four-foot-long rifle at the wall. A beam of red laser light connected the weapon to the concrete, where a glowing orange hole formed in a quarter second. Masaru had never seen concrete *melt* before. A man screamed from the stairwell. More loud crashes of rubble echoed from the ground floor, soon followed by men screaming and the repetitive hum of lasers. Gunfire raged; high-pitched *pings* of bullets striking concrete mixed with dull plastic *clacks* of bullets bouncing off powered armor.

The man in the room with them enlarged the doorway on his way out to join the fight on the ground floor, his armor tearing down the old wall like so much paper. Masaru relaxed. Noriko moved to leap to her feet, but he put his hand on her shoulder and held her back.

"You have done enough. Rest. Let my associates work."

A body flew up past the hole in the floor and hit the wall hard enough to leave a red mark before falling out of sight.

"*Lauf! Zurückfallen!*[1]" shouted a man.

"*Nein*[2]!" Someone fired full auto from a ballistic weapon. "*Kein Rückzug! Kein—*[3]"

The *whoosh* of ion thrusters mixed with the screech of a vibro-katana, and the man's scream cut out with a wet gurgle. Angry shouts became panicked screams. One long wail of fear cut off with a heavy *whump* and a wheeze. Masaru closed his eyes and savored the mental image of a power armor suit catching someone out of a sprint with a fist in the chest. The man's spine probably broke on impact.

In under a minute, the sickening crunch of breaking bones, the screech of vibro-katanas, and the rapport of guns ceased.

"So, what was it you wanted to tell me when we were about to die?" Noriko pushed her visor up, a wry smile on her face.

"My name is not Moto Masaru." He stood and spent a moment dusting off what remained of his suit. "I am Kurotai Masaru, second son of Kurotai Hideo."

Her mouth hung open.

"I offer my most sincere apologies. Given our circumstances, I initially did not want you concerned with my station." He offered her a hand. "As I came to know you, and learned that you, Abe Noriko, are not the sort of woman who *would* allow such things to interfere with more practical matters such as survival, I did not want you to think less of me for being who I am."

She squinted at him for a few seconds, but accepted his hand. "I'm not about to bow at you or anything."

"I like that about you." Masaru smiled and pulled her standing.

Noriko gave him a playful look of annoyance. "Normally, I don't trust people who aren't honest."

He feigned a pout.

She flicked bits of concrete off her armor. "I'll think about making an exception."

"Kurotai-sama," said Ryozo Himura over a loudspeaker. "The area is… Apologies, Kurotai-sama. We have Etamura approaching. A small matter."

Masaru took Noriko's hand and led her to the hall and down the stairs. They emerged on the ground floor amid the heavy tromping of Dragon Chitin migrating out to the street. Lasers lit the sides of the building crimson in a near-continuous barrage. He released her hand as he neared the shipment of nanobots, and brought his rifle to bear in case anything somehow managed to make it past the Kurotai strike team, six of whom stood in a firing line less than twenty meters away outside. Four samurai-shaped holes in the wall at varying elevations gave away where they'd entered.

A loud *boom* and a flash of heat and orange light came from the street. Masaru dove for cover behind the stacked boxes. Noriko raised an arm to shield her eyes.

"And you said it was stupid to bring this," yelled a man. "I—"

The thrum of multiple lasers silenced him.

Masaru peered over the boxes.

Two of the armored samurai helped a third back to his feet. Smoke poured from a fist-sized hole in the lower stomach. The man pushed his assistors aside and staggered forward two steps before stopping and emitting a furious growl.

"He is angry because the man who wounded him is already dead," whispered Masaru.

Noriko looked from the damaged armor to Masaru and back to the damaged armor. "That sounded like the same missile that took down my transport... And he's..." She stared, pointing.

"Annoyed." Masaru chuckled. "He is more hurt than he is showing. The armor has a life-support system."

"That's amazing." She approached the terminal, slung her rifle over her shoulder, and attacked the holographic keyboard. "Those are probably expensive."

"About nine million credits per suit, depending on options."

She kept typing. "Does it have a coffee maker too?"

"Yes."

"What!?" Noriko looked surprised for an instant before her eyebrows came together. "You're teasing me."

"There is a built in reassembler with an OmniSoy reserve for long missions... so, technically, it could produce coffee." He chuckled, and kicked a dead foreigner out of the way so he could stand next to her.

Noriko stared at the terminal. "Son of a—"

The armored figures walked back in.

"These files make it look like they've been set up here for months, purchasing nanobots while posing as staff from Nichinan Central Hospital. At least five large shipments have already been sent to Europe." She scowled. "My commanders are going to *love* this."

Masaru pondered. *The Nippon Shōgyō Kumiai would spontaneously combust if they discovered the ACC traded with Nikkatsu Corporation directly. It would not have taken much effort to verify that the hospital had been receiving them. Even if they had no reason to suspect anything amiss, the NSK will consider them complicit. Kurotai Corporation may find this information useful for future negotiations with Nikkatsu.*

Ryozo approached, and bowed. "Kurotai-sama. The Etamura are fleeing."

Noriko stood and headed deeper into the ruin, stepping over sleeping bags, bodies, and the remnants of long-term camping.

"Himura-san, please ensure that a copy of all the data on this terminal is sent to me."

"Yes, Kurotai-sama." He bowed.

# 51

# THE GATE

One hour slid into the next as Kenny drove westward, the steady drone of the diesel engine deliberate in its effort to lull him into a nap. A mostly-intact white stucco building on the left, decorated in bullet holes and a museum sign, caught his eye. The place might have a treasure lurking inside, a piece of prewar junk some rich idiot would vomit credits all over him to get their hands on. Temptation went under the wheels of guilt and worry. Alyssa had been shot—by some miracle in her vest—and who only knows what that bastard old man would do next time.

A cracked rib and a bruise could've been freak luck, or it could've been a warning. A 'next time she'll get it in the face' kind of warning.

Kathy's blood still coated her arm and shirt from where the dogs had gotten a hold of her. He held her stare for a few seconds via the rearview mirror. Love and admiration burst within his heart; she'd leapt *at* the dogs to protect Cielo. Another warning? A 'next time the dog bites Kathy on the throat' kind of warning.

And Luna... one of the children he'd planned on dropping off at the police checkpoint. Artifact hunters, researchers, and other fools who ran out to the Badlands did it all the time. Ran into Scrags, brought them back. The NewsNet always talked about orphans from gang warfare or simple abandonment. He'd be adding them to an already overburdened system. One guy he'd read about, another artifact seeker who went by the nickname Beard, once brought a whole Scrag tribe in. Something like fifty people... of course, that had been an entirely different situation than finding a couple stray children. None of them needed foster care, merely life adjustment to the slam shift going from spears and 'clothing if you can find or make any' to hovercars and advert bots.

*Heh. I wonder how much shit Old Wretched threw at Beard... He's letting us have it pretty bad for four children.*

Kenny stared sideways at the museum as he passed it. Funny they didn't notice it on the way into the Badlands. Funnier that he spotted it on the way out. *Nah. That's got trap written all over it. Probably full of damned nibblers or something.*

Nasir slept on and off, once again seeming bored. Hayley kept quiet, but huddled against Kathy's side, her limbs stiff, her eyes shifting in constant vigilance. Alyssa had her earbuds in once more, attention focused on her NetMini. Kathy and the four Scrag children carried on a conversation about the city. Every few minutes, one of them would ask something, and she'd answer, prompting another question before another minutes-long silence settled in.

Soon after the sun slipped out of sight in the west, a lonely old ghost town came into view ahead. A gas station stood next to a square building that had the general shape of a store, but no trace of any signs. The decaying structure across the street appeared to have been a bar/restaurant named 'Earl's Place.' Beyond that, four tiny houses and a dozen trailers made up the rest of the 'town.'

The gas station office struck him as the sturdiest of the lot, so he slowed to a halt by the old pumps, under a roof supported by rusting poles.

"It'll be dark soon. This looks like a decent place to stop." Kenny squinted into the sunset at the buildings up ahead. Nothing moved except the loose walls of several trailers. "I think we're the only ones here."

Eldon opened his door. "Gonna do better than think."

Three orb bots levitated out of the truck bed.

Nasir patted his console. "I got your six, El."

"All right. Yell if you see anything iffy," said Kenny.

The Scrags rushed out of the truck, went only a few steps away, and relieved themselves in a cluster. Blushing at their casualness, Alyssa dragged Hayley around behind the building out of sight. Kathy got out, stretched, and stiff-legged it after them.

Kenny kept an eye on the area, one hand on his pistol. Once Kathy and the girls came back, he went around to the rear of the building and watered the wall. When he returned, Halcón and Gato disappeared into the building with the group's sleeping bags. He climbed into the truck bed and took out enough ration packs for everyone.

"Looks like you're right," said Nasir. "There's nothing out there but junk."

"Good." Kenny jumped down from the tailgate. *I don't trust it.*

Metal clattered in the distance, making him grab his sidearm, but he relaxed at the sight of Eldon pushing a slab of corrugated metal out of his way from a collapsed trailer a short distance down the street. He gave it a shove that wound up knocking the rest of the flapping walls to the ground.

Alyssa screamed.

*I knew it.* He dropped the rations on the concrete slab by the pumps and sprinted past the left side of the office. Alyssa stood about thirty yards past the building amid a field of scrub grass. Hayley clung to her, and they both seemed to be trying not to look at something on the ground in front of them. Since their body language radiated 'eww' and not terror, he relaxed a little.

Kenny sprinted up behind them, stopping with a hand on each of their shoulders. "Girls, what—"

Before them lay an open grave holding the remains of someone who'd been there quite some time. Tiny scraps of flesh clung here and there, but for the most part, the poor bastard consisted of bones and a dark stain on the earth. A second filled-in grave sat beside it; between them, someone had stuck a shovel into the ground from which a thin scrap wood sign dangled on a wire.

"I'm okay," said Alyssa, sniffling. "Just wasn't expecting a dead guy."

Hayley, her expression neutral, stared at the gas station office, refusing to look at the dead.

"You good?" yelled Eldon, behind him.

"Yeah. Girls found an open grave." Kenny patted them on the back before stepping around them to the shovel and lifting the small sign. "Whoever finds this, please cover my ass up. I'm layin' m'self down one year to the day my beloved Theresa took her last breath. If you fancy reading, check the place next door. Them books sure did my wife a lot of good. Pascal Rittenauer, age 82."

Eldon walked up beside him. "What'cha got?"

Kenny handed him the sign. "Old man." He twisted to glance at the store building. "Prob'ly a shitload of books in there. Who knows how long they've been sittin'. Likely be mush now."

"Might as well give him his last request." Eldon grabbed the shovel.

"Yeah." Kenny nodded. "Be right back. Got another one in the truck."

He ushered the girls to the gas station office and left them in Kathy's care. Considering the shallowness of the grave, it took under an hour—and the last of the daylight—to cover the old man's remains. Tired and hungry, hands shaking from fatigue and worry, Kenny tossed his shovel back in the truck bed and headed for the building. Eldon propped the old man's shovel against the wall.

The stubborn smell of pipe smoke clung to the walls inside the office, which the two former occupants had converted into a tiny home, adding a bed, dresser, kitchen table, and four chairs, as well as two bookshelves. In the back right corner, a pair of cushioned chairs flanked a little round table with a doily.

Everyone sat in a circle on the floor munching on rations. Cielo had collected unwanted hot sauce bottles, slurping them like treats. Kenny grunted on his way to the unoccupied space of sleeping bag next to Kathy where a ration pack waited for him. Within a second of his ass touching down, Luna got up and scrambled over to sit at his left. He patted her on the head and reached for his ration pack.

Halcón stood and approached Eldon. "I will take the first watch. I do not trust Nasir's magic balls."

"That's what his ex-girlfriend said," muttered Eldon.

Nasir grumbled. "You guys know that balls/orb jokes are older than this gas station, right?"

Alyssa and Kathy snickered. Halcón raised an eyebrow.

"No, no…" Eldon grinned. "Kid's got a good point. We should set up a standard watch. Those bots of yours seem to have gotten a bad case of the fickle."

Halcón pointed at Hayley, attempting English. "Only when the pale girl makes magic on the glowing tablet. She is only who can make his balls come to life."

"Eww," muttered Alyssa. "I know he didn't mean that the way I just heard it, but eww."

"Dammit." Nasir slapped his knee. "Why the hell does she have to be what? Eleven? Twelve? I *so* could've taken that joke all the way."

Kenny gave him a deadly look.

"Hey." Nasir raised his hands. "Relax... Just making a joke. He's the one that started with the balls thing."

"I agree with Halcón." Kenny tore open a pack and got hit with a wave of intense fragrance he'd never experienced before, predominantly fishy and spicy. He cringed and tilted the packet to read the label. "Portuguese Fish Stew?"

"Oh shit." Eldon leaned away. "You got the PFS? Sorry man. Should take that thing out back and bury it next to the old man."

Kenny sniffed it. "Smells decent."

"Yeah, doesn't taste bad either... but it ain't what it s'posed ta be. Whatever the military did to make it into a ration has channeled the darkest of dark voodoo." Eldon pointed at him. "You eat that, and four hours from now what come out yo' ass is gonna kill that old demon you keep talkin' about."

Alyssa glared at him. "Ugh. Really?"

Kenny laughed. "In that case, I'll eat two."

"I take second watch." Gato, sitting cross-legged, puffed up his chest. His thick mop of hair almost covered his eyes and hung down to his hips. In his borrowed pink shirt with the white cartoon cat face, he looked quite intimidating.

"Nah, kid." Eldon pointed a packet of 'turkey stew' at him. "You take third. Second watch is darkest, and I got night vision."

Halcón nocked an arrow in his compound bow and walked outside.

"You're letting him go out there alone?" whispered Kathy.

"The boy's fifteen... he's not helpless. Plus he's spent his whole life doing this." Kenny inhaled the contents of the meal packet, not even noticing the spice until his tongue went numb from flavor.

Luna sniffled. She covered her face with her hands and started to cry.

Kenny tucked the empty packet back in the ration pouch before putting an arm around the girl. "Hey, what's wrong?"

"I lost my magic bow. The ancestors will be angry with me."

He rubbed her back. "I don't think they will. I think they took the bow as a test, instead of your life. You survived those dogs."

Luna lowered her hands from her face, sniffled once, and looked up at him. "*You* saved me, not the ancestors."

His throat tightened at her expression: terrified of getting 'in trouble' yet at the same time pleading. "Well..." He brushed her hair off her face. "I won't let the ancestors be angry with you."

She attempted a smile, and clung to him.

The girls removed their boots and reclined on top of their sleeping bags, still wearing everything else—including their armored vests.

"Ugh. It's so hot in here. Can't we sleep outside?" asked Alyssa.

Hayley muttered something.

"Oh. Yeah, I guess that makes sense." Alyssa tried to get comfortable.

Kenny removed his armored coat, opened his shirt, and reclined. Kathy removed her armor and shirt, evidently no longer caring who saw her bra.

Grumbling to himself, Kenny found his thoughts spinning into a heat-delirium. He didn't even notice sleep sneak up on him.

KENNY SNAPPED AWAKE IN THE MIDDLE OF THE NIGHT. SOMETHING RUSTLED NEARBY. He lifted his head and reached his right hand down to grip his pistol. Cielo, at Kathy's right, wriggled out of his sleeping bag and peeled off his tee shirt. For a moment, he stood nude, fanning himself and panting like an overheated dog while sweat dripped down his body. After a moment, he curled up on top of the open bag, using his wadded up shirt for a pillow.

Luna had evidently reached the point of overheating earlier and had already pulled her t-shirt dress off. Asleep again, she lay with her arms and legs askew like a passed-out drunk, her head propped against his side, looking miserable and sweaty. Halcón and Gato had moved outside, sitting on the ground on either side of the door with their backs to the building. Watching the boys' long hair dance on the breeze made him consider going outside as well.

Kenny scowled to himself. Old Wretched had to be making it hotter.

Halcón crept in seconds later, and woke Eldon. As soon as his friend looked over, Kenny gestured at Gato, shook his head to the negative, and pointed at himself. Eldon gave him a thumbs-up.

Nasir's snoring on top of Kenny's worry that another ambush approached in the darkness made it difficult to sleep. Eventually, staring at the ceiling became staring at Eldon's face, in a room full of daylight. Somewhere nearby, Alyssa and Hayley muttered complaints about being hot. Kathy coaxed them out of their armored vests and made them sit outside in the breeze with water bottles.

Kenny squinted. "Bit late for third rotation... Tell me you didn't leave a twelve-year-old on watch alone?"

"Heh. It's okay man. Nah. I let him sleep too. Your ass needs to drive, and you looked fried as hell. I'm good. Double-watch ain't nothin' new for me."

Cielo's tiny chest swelled and deflated, ribs showing with each breath. He clung to Kathy's empty sleeping bag like a stuffed animal. Luna, at his left, stared at Kenny—fully awake, but she hadn't moved a millimeter. Beads of sweat crept down her face and a thin crust of gunk had formed on her lips.

"You need water," mumbled Kenny "C'mon. Time to get dressed."

Luna nodded eagerly. She sat up and pulled her t-shirt on.

He yawned, stood, and made the rounds waking everyone up after fetching water bottles for the kids. Cielo headed for the corner rubbing his eyes and took up a stance in preparation to pee. Kenny hurried over and chased him outside.

"He's not housebroken yet," said Alyssa from the doorway, before glugging down an entire one-liter bottle of water.

"I don't know about everyone else, but I'd like to get home faster." Kenny yawned again and shook his head. "Why don't we eat on the road?" He repeated himself in Spanish.

"If you put food on the road, it will get dirty," said Luna between gulps.

Her sincere expression got him laughing, which got everyone else laughing—except Hayley.

Kenny pulled her into a hug. "Hey. You okay?"

"Yeah." She squeezed him like she didn't want to let go... ever. "Still scared."

"I know, kiddo. I know." He patted her back. "Come on. Hop in the truck so we can get out of here."

She took a step back and gave him a long stare that he took as begging him not to hate her. Before Kenny could ask, she lowered her gaze and trudged out. He jogged after her.

"Hale… I'm not upset with you for anything. I don't think you're rushing us home. *I'm* rushing us home."

She stopped with her hand on the handle of the truck door, but didn't look at him. "Okay."

"I'm… sorry?"

Hayley lowered her head. "I'm not mad at you. I'm just scared."

"You seem kinda pissed. Like I did something wrong." He rested a hand on her shoulder.

She reached up and put her hand over his fingers. "Can we please go home? I'll… maybe I'll be okay once we're outta here. This place is messed up."

"That's the plan." He squeezed her shoulder. "Sorry for dragging you out here."

"You didn't." She pulled the door open. "The Syndicate threatened us. Not like you had any choice. *I* wanted to stay with my family. It's not your fault."

"All right. Talk later?"

"Sure." She climbed up into the truck and sat staring at her lap. After a few seconds, she glanced up at him with a 'you're still standing there…' expression.

*Something's wrong. I never should've brought her out here.* "I know something's eating at you. Not gonna force anything, but you can tell me anything. I mean that." He smiled.

Cielo shot past him and bounded into the truck, cheering. Kathy stalked after him, carrying his shirt and shaking her head. Luna emerged, still nursing her water bottle as she walked over.

"Thanks," whispered Hayley, returning her gaze to her lap.

Halcón and Gato tossed the sleeping bags in the back, with help from Eldon.

Kenny pulled himself up into the driver's seat. He stared out at the road, one arm draped over the wheel while waiting for everyone to get in. Eventually, with everyone accounted for, he pushed the starter button for the biodiesel.

Nothing happened.

*Fuck… come on.* He let his finger off the button, clenched his jaw, and jammed it down again.

Dead.

"Minor problem." Kenny reached around behind the starter button enclosure, feeling for the contacts.

Eldon stared at him with a grim face. "You gotta be shittin' me."

"It's been awhile since I used this. The battery might be gone." Kenny grabbed a coil of wire from the glovebox, snapped two pieces off, and wound them onto the contact poles. "Remind me to rewire this damn thing with an e-mag port if I decide to come back out here."

"If you connect an e-mag directly to those leads, you will melt the system." Nasir reached into the front seat. "I have a standard voltage output on the board. Let me see the wires."

Kenny added more wire from the spool to make his splice longer, and passed the leads to Nasir, who inserted them into a port on the top edge of the bot control board. Sparks snapped at the second wire, and the truck roared to life.

A collective sigh of relief filled the cabin.

"I get food bags," said Gato.

Kenny accelerated gently as the boy crawled out the window to the truck bed. Operating on diesel, the air conditioning wouldn't run, so all four windows wound up open. Gato tossed food packets in one by one, calling names as he did so. His bushy, wild hair whipped behind him as he held the last packet over his head in both hands and yelled his own name.

"Get in before you fall," yelled Kathy over the sound of the engine and the buzz of the tires on pavement.

Gato clambered back inside, and Kathy slid the window closed. The smell of dust and mixed food filled the cabin in minutes. The Navcon predicted their arrival at the West City wall in fourteen hours. *It's gonna be dark before we get there... fuck it. I ain't stoppin'.* With any luck, the rumored deadly aftereffects of the 'PFS' ration wouldn't manifest. As he emptied each packet of his breakfast meal, Kenny tucked them with care back into the main pouch.

Eldon laughed. "Man that's funny. You're collecting the empty ration packs despite us driving past ruined houses, derelict cars, and all manner of junk."

"It's respect for the land. All that stuff is part of the land now. This"—he patted the plastic—"isn't."

Once again, Alyssa lost herself in her NetMini. Hayley seemed on edge, and kept prairie-dogging at the windows, perking up to peer in all directions. That got Kenny doing it too. *What if Eldon's right and she is psionic? Bah, psionic doesn't mean she sees the future.*

Hayley jumped and screamed when a huge insect splattered on the windshield, leaving a smear two feet across of opaque yellow-white. When Halcón called them delicious roasted over a fire, she nearly sprayed her breakfast.

A touch over three hours later, enough small voices complained about needing to go that he pulled over. After a short stop to give everyone a chance to walk around, stretch, and enjoy some fresh air, they piled back in the truck and continued.

Every few minutes, Kenny glanced at the Navcon display. He chided himself whenever he did at the disappointment of so little time passing. Another fifty-eight minutes of driving west later, the diesel engine sputtered and went silent.

*Shit.*

"What happened?" asked Hayley, a nervous tremor in her voice.

"The engine stopped," said Nasir.

"Thanks for pointing that out." Alyssa glanced at him. "I wasn't quite sure what that total silence was from."

Nasir rolled his eyes.

Kathy shot Kenny an urgent stare by way of the rearview mirror before giving Nasir a 'don't mind her, she's scared' look.

"Probably just a bit of crud in the fuel line. It *has* been sitting a while unused." Kenny pushed the starter, but after a few seconds of it whirring without success, he jammed the shifter into 'park' and grabbed the door handle. "Gonna check the fuel line. Be a minute."

Hayley lunged forward, grabbing the tops of both front seats. "No! Stupid piece of shit! I wanna go home!"

*Beep.*

The console flickered and came online, one panel at a time. In a few seconds, the cabin tinted amber-red in the radiance of modern technology. The entire console glowed like the West City skyline at night. Four yellow lights blinked in a slow pattern, informing him that the in-wheel motors weren't engaged. The air conditioning kicked on. Luna let out an awestruck squeal and crawled forward to put her face in the blast of cool.

Hayley's anger evaporated in an instant to bewilderment.

Eldon glanced left at Hayley, shifted his gaze to Kenny for a second, and made eye contact with Hayley again. "Kid, you want this truck to work, right? To get us home?"

"Y-yeah," she whispered.

"Then you keep wantin' it to work." Eldon patted her hand where she grasped his seatback. "You keep wantin' it to work and don't stop thinkin' 'bout how you want this bucket of shit to work."

Kenny tapped his fingers on the wheel. *What just happened?*

Eldon swatted him twice in the shoulder with the back of his hand. "Come on man. Let's switch this mother back over and get the hell outa here." He pushed his door open.

Kenny hopped out, grabbed the tools, and crawled under the truck. While Eldon disconnected the drive shafts, he re-engaged the stator gears of the e-motors. Between the two of them, they had it converted back to the normal drive system in six minutes. After stowing the shafts and toolbox in the back, Kenny paused outside, gripping the handle, dreading he'd find the console dark when he opened it.

"Get in," yelled Eldon.

*Come on... work.* Kenny yanked the door open. At the sight of the lit-up console, he resumed breathing. He climbed in, slammed the door, and accelerated hard enough to startle yelps from Cielo and Luna. Hayley continued hovering between the front seats, making faces somewhere between constipated and angry.

"That's it, girl. You keep on' thinkin' 'bout this truck workin'. Don't waste any time bein' scared. You got this. You own it." Eldon smiled at her.

A hint of a tremble still showed in Hayley's legs, but she nodded.

Kenny offered a reassuring smile. *I dunno if she's actually doing anything, but if it keeps her focused on not being scared... I'll take it.*

Hayley's confidence increased with each passing hour. Since getting the truck up to ninety mph, the Navcon adjusted its arrival estimate to 6:48 p.m, shaving about three hours off. Kenny pushed the accelerator whenever the road got clear, and cursed under his breath each time he had to back off to go around evidence of warfare or raiders.

Everyone kept quiet, gazing out over the passing scrubland and eventual Nevada desert. Several times, dust trails emerged from the wastes, diverting toward them, but the most determined raider gave up after a minute or two. None of their vehicles had much hope of catching them at speed, and most bandits wouldn't waste ethanol on a difficult chase.

A little past six, Hayley's fear seemed to have gone away. She still clutched the seats, but had the look of a general riding a command chariot rather than a terrified tween. The shadow of West City darkened the horizon not too long after.

All the Scrags leaned forward, making gasps of awe.

"I don't see any fire," whispered Gato.

Hayley scooted back to sit. "There is no fire. It's just a superstition."

"Hale? You okay?" asked Kathy.

"Yeah. I don't feel scared now." She squirmed. "But I really want a shower. Still feels like I've got millipede guts stuck to me."

"Eww," muttered Alyssa. "You *had* to say that, didn't you? Now I feel it too."

Hayley gave her a raspberry and broke into giggles. Alyssa laughed.

Kenny eased off some speed as the great, towering plastisteel-blue wall of West City loomed over them. The Scrag children continued staring open-mouthed. Even Halcón had a look of boyish wonder.

"Where is the fire?" asked Gato.

"It's a legend." Kenny pointed up at a turret. "Someone probably saw one of those lasers go off once. They burn what they hit."

"*¿Es aquí donde los antepasados van?*" asked Luna.

"This is West City," said Kenny in Spanish. "It's not a land of the ancestors like the legends say. It's full of real people, and modern things."

"Are we joining your tribe?" asked Halcón. "I would like to take your eldest daughter for a wife."

Alyssa gasped and went crimson.

Kenny coughed. "Uhh. She's fourteen. She's not getting married yet. That's too young."

"My parents were married at fourteen." Halcón patted himself on the chest. "I am a strong warrior."

"You're fifteen. That's too young for marriage. You got a couple years of being a kid left. Things are different here. For one thing, we don't consider people elderly when they're halfway through their forties. There's no need to rush yourself."

Halcón seemed to mull his words. "Your tribe lives to great age? They have magic to do this?"

"Technology," said Eldon. "You'll see."

"Are you four related?" asked Kenny.

Halcón pointed at Gato. "He is my brother. Luna and Cielo are brother and sister."

"Okay." Kenny slowed to a stop by the external door of the checkpoint.

"Wow…" Gato crawled into the front and half onto the console to stare up at the giant portal. "Is big."

It took the police staffing the station about a minute to notice them parked there. The enormous checkpoint door, a slab of plastisteel as wide as three lanes of road, shuddered and opened downward, sinking into the ground. The top came away from the wall above it, exposing crenelations like a gear or an old castle.

"There are people inside who will help you. Don't be afraid of them," said Kenny.

"Okay." Halcón nodded.

The great door shook the earth with a resounding *thud* as it became flush with the ground. Kenny nudged the truck up and over the metal housing, in effect a giant speedbump, and stopped in the middle of a bare metal sally port. Two Division 1 officers observed from behind a thick transparent panel, their silver-visored helmets aglow with reflected terminal screens. Another pair walked out to the truck.

Kenny opened his door and slid out to stand.

"Welcome back." One officer came around his side with a handheld scanning unit.

"Thanks"—Kenny glanced at the man's nameplate—"Officer Hamm. Got four rescues. Scrag children. Raiders or maybe another tribe wiped out their village while they were out scavving. Caught them looting the truck." He chuckled. "Or trying to. Since they had no family left, I brought 'em in." He beckoned them to get out. "This is Halcón, age fifteen. That's Gato, his brother."

*"Tengo doce años,"* said Gato.

"Little small for twelve," said Officer Hamm.

Kenny blinked at the cop. "Well, I guess he missed a few appointments with his nutritionist."

"Right." Hamm shook his head. "That was dumb."

The girl hovered at the door, one foot on the running board, one dangling. She stared around in awe at the hundred-plus story buildings a little further west, and millions of whizzing lights in the air: advert bots, hovercars, and delivery units.

"That's Luna; she's ten. The scrawny little fella behind her is her brother Cielo. He's eight. Halcón knows a bit of English, but the others only have a word or two."

Officer Hamm nodded. "Should we contact you once they clear medical?"

Kenny opened his mouth to say 'nah, put 'em into the system,' like he'd been thinking since he first decided to bring them to civilization, but froze at the sight of Cielo clinging to Kathy. The kids could spend years sitting in an adoption queue if they didn't get sent off to a colony world. Adjusting to the city would be hard enough, but another entire planet? He locked eyes with his wife. She brushed her hand over the boy's wild, black hair, making him grin. Turning them in to social services had once sounded good in theory, but having to say the words 'nah, I don't want them' after going through so much to get them out alive was a dick move. When he thought back to the way Luna had looked at him in the second before she fell into the dog's mouths, he felt like an absolute asshole for even debating it.

A low-flying advert bot the size of a box truck whizzed overhead, rumbling everything.

Luna let out a high-pitched yelp; she ran over and grabbed on to his armored coat, shivering.

Kenny put his arm around her. "Yeah. We'll be submitting the paperwork first thing in the morning.

Kathy approached with the boy attached to her side. "These kids need people who can be a bridge between their old world and this one."

Luna touched Officer Hamm's stomach, speechless at the sight of gleaming blue armor. He opened his visor and smiled at her.

"Whoa, we're keeping them?" asked Alyssa.

Kenny gave Luna's shoulder a squeeze while smiling at Alyssa. "I think so. Are you okay with that?"

"Heh." Alyssa grinned. "I would'a had to kick your ass if we didn't."

"They're kinda cool," said Hayley. "Having a big family would be uhh, pretty sweet." She shrank in on herself and looked down.

Alyssa pointed at him. "However... I'm not sharing my room." She kicked her boot at the ground for a few seconds. "Well, maybe with Hale if I *have* to."

Hayley's eyes widened a touch. She bit her lip and smiled at Alyssa.

*What is going on with her? Poor girl... must've been rough what she went through with her dad... being on her own for almost a year.*

Eldon and the other officer laughed on the far side of the truck, lost in a conversation about military stuff.

"No need to worry about that. We can always add on to the house. Kenny gathered everyone, and spoke to the four Scrags in slow Spanish. "You have to go with these police officers for a little while. They are going to take you to a place with healers where they will make sure you are not sick. That will take a few days, and then we'd like you to come live with us. You don't *have* to, but we'd be happy to welcome you into our home."

"We would be your tribe?" asked Halcón.

"Not exactly. You'd think of me as your father, not your chief. Kathy as your mother." He loomed over the boy. "And Alyssa and Hayley as your *sisters*."

Cielo grinned.

Kenny stopped looming. "Either way, your life will change. You don't need to be warriors and scavengers here. You'll go to school and get a chance to just be children and have fun."

Halcón's expression went pensive.

"Think on it." Kenny patted the boy on the shoulder. "You'll be in the hospital for a couple days. You don't have to decide right now."

Luna took Gato's hand, then Cielo's, and stared up at him. "I want to stay with you."

Halcón shook his hand. "My father has been beyond the curtain of fire since I was younger than Cielo. I am used to being a man, but I will respect you as an elder. The small ones do not want to walk separate paths."

Kathy smiled.

"Right." Hamm tapped at his datapad. "They'll be taken to a medical facility for evaluation and quarantine for a couple days, interviewed by social services, and whatnot. What about the other two? Oh, never mind. They're yours already. I found them. Anything coming into the city we should know about other than those kids?"

Two more cops emerged from the door by the armored window and collected the Scrag children into the checkpoint facility. The kids followed without protest, continuing to gawk around at everything.

"Crystal horse statue." Kenny held his hands about a foot apart. "Yea or so big. Couple of plastic toys and some other crystal knickknacks. That's it. Nothing explosive, flammable, alive, or potentially harmful."

Eldon glanced over and laughed. "You ate a PFS. All of that applies... explosive, flammable, probably still alive, and definitely harmful."

The cop he'd been talking with cringed, laughing. "He didn't? Mean of you not to warn him."

"I did." Eldon shook his head at the cop beside him. "Dude wouldn't listen."

"Don't feel anything." Kenny scratched his stomach and grinned.

Hamm wandered around the truck with his scanner. After two passes, he stuck it back in its holder on his belt and approached. "Looks clear. Okay, someone from social services will be contacting you, probably tomorrow morning. Good to see you made it back alive." He chuckled, shaking his head. "I still don't know what possesses people to run off out there."

"Thanks."

Alyssa and Hayley scrambled into the truck like their pants had been lit on fire.

"Well... *someone* wants to go home." Kenny grinned.

Kathy kissed him. "Yep. Three someones."

# RELAY

Two motorbikes rode ahead of the squeaking, bouncy pickup truck, close enough to block most of the view with a heavy plume of dust. An occasional pebble kicked up by the bikes hit the windshield with a *click*. Nina sat in the center of the front bench seat between José, who drove, and Silvia, a tall woman with prominent cheekbones and long, straight hair. Unlike most of the people around her, this woman didn't have a tale of personal tragedy driving her underground. She'd made a decision to join the resistance after hearing too many stories of bad things happening to others. According to Javier, she was the best shot of the group, already with nine kills, three of which had been the CMO officers who had attempted to arrest Nicolás, one of the psionic kids she'd seen hiding among the cots.

*Six years old, and they would've executed him.*

Of course, shooting three CMO officers in the head in broad daylight had a negative effect on Silvia's future, but Nicolás called her mama. She seemed okay with the trade.

Javier and Roberto rode in the truck bed, sitting on top of a tarp concealing rifles and ammunition.

Nina held her sidearm low between her knees out of sight to check it. María Isabel and Adriana had concealed their weapons in their backpacks. They risked bringing them along since failure here meant none of their resistance cell would make it to the UCF today. Silvia had tucked her weapon, an MBR-11 chambered in 8mm, down beside her seat. The mass-produced ACC-issue battle rifle might've been a fifty-year-old design, but soldiers on both sides considered it one of the more reliable weapons out there.

Silvia stared out at the road with contempt, as if she *hoped* someone discovered them with firearms. She caught Nina looking at her. "What?"

"Nothing." Nina tucked her handgun in the holster between her ballistic stealth suit and her flannel shirt. "I hope you're not going to do anything reckless. You've got that look to you, like you don't care if you make it out of this alive."

Silvia chuckled, but it sounded more sad than amused. "If it helps them get out of this place, if it helps Nicolás, I don't care."

"Keep your head down. I know what I look like, but I'm a lot tougher than you think."

José laughed. "The pair of you are ninety pounds wet."

The quiet little town of *Estación Salamanca* rose from the scrubland ahead, a cluster of drab squares appeared first; behind them, a silvery haze emerged from the blur of distance, which soon became a near-blinding glare, as though a slice of the sun had fallen to earth and lay upon the dirt.

Nina's eyes compensated for the reflection, filtering out the high-intensity light. Thousands of towers, each bearing six giant octagonal solar panels, formed a veritable forest north of the village. She zoomed in and panned around for a second before her attention settled on two desert-brown armored personnel carriers parked by a small operations bunker.

"There's your ride."

"What?" asked José.

"There's a pair of BTR-99s parked in the solar farm." Nina swung her gaze left, searching for guard towers, catwalks around the panels, or any other dangers, but only spotted a handful of workers in white jumpsuits and hardhats. "Each can hold twenty troops plus a driver and a gunner. Top speed about eighty on flat ground. Once we finish what I need to do, we grab those."

"I don't see anything but the sun," said Silvia.

"I'm a doll," muttered Nina.

Silvia laughed. "You're cute, but looks aren't going to help."

"I mean... a *doll*. Military-grade artificial body." Nina sighed.

"Oh, shit." Silvia leaned away.

"Relax. I've got a real brain. Despite what your government tells you, I'm not going to snap at any minute and go on a killing spree." She paused. "I mean... I am probably going to go on a killing spree in a few minutes, but not on civilians."

"Real brain? Not a computer?" Silvia poked her in the arm.

"Yes."

"Okay." Silvia relaxed. Seconds later, she squinted, and leaned close. "You don't look like a robot. Are you playing with me?"

Nina smiled. "Thanks."

"Three inside," said a woman's voice from a handheld radio on the dashboard.

"Holy shit." Nina blinked. "Is that...?"

José laughed and picked up the walkie-talkie. "Yep. Ninety years old and still works. Those idiots aren't even looking for this frequency." He squeezed the button. "Copy. Three in the nest."

"Are there any other CMO or DMS personnel in the town?" asked Nina.

"Oh, ladies," said José into the radio, "any other foxes roaming around the chickens?"

The first buildings neared, such a ramshackle mixture of adobe, brick, and metal slabs, that Nina wondered if she'd already reached the Badlands. Closer to the center of town, the quality improved, but she still half-expected to see a pair of men walking out for pistols at high noon. A huge, gaudy, bright teal building sat on the corner of what passed for a town square. It even had the saloon-style doors.

"No," said María Isabel over the radio. "They made it the police station. It's right across the street from a school."

"Dammit." Nina stared at the roof and sighed. "Typical. Anyone in it now? The school I mean?"

José relayed her message.

"Yeah. Looks like a teacher and about fourteen kids. Mixed ages. Oh... four CMO inside the happy place."

"No guns at ground level then," said Nina. "Too much risk of stray bullets."

Silvia shook her head. "I don't think the CMO are going to accept those terms."

Nina narrowed her eyes. "I wasn't planning to offer them. I should be able to take them down. If they've set the place up as a police station, we can put them in a holding cell."

"You're not going to kill them?" Silvia gawked.

"I'd prefer to avoid it. The incidence of defection among the Corporate military is high... of course, that's mostly on Mars."

Silvia leaned at her. "These people like nothing more than to be bigger and more important than everyone. They were going to kill Nicolás because he's psionic. You know what he can do? He can see the other sides of cards! He's a little clairvoyant. *So* dangerous. And they would've killed him." She choked up for a second as José brought the truck to a stop a few houses away from the police station. "I knew his parents. Grew up next door to them."

"I'm sorry." Nina looked down. "They killed them?"

"Nicolás' parents knew what the CMO would do to him. They tried to protect him."

José muttered a few curses.

"Those who fight monsters..." Nina closed her eyes. "I won't hesitate to kill them if I have to, but I'm not here to exterminate. My primary objective is the facility."

Silvia pushed open the passenger side door. "You are planning to place bombs, yes? If you put them in jail, they will still die. If you set them loose, they will call for reinforcements. You have to help us get out of here."

Nina nodded. *How sad a state the world has fallen into when the best option I have is to kill. Shit. Bombs.* "José... We need to get everyone out of the school before my charges go off."

"Aye. I will take care of that." He shut off the engine. "How do we go in?"

Nina slid to the right after Silvia and hopped to the ground. "I'll go in first. Hold your fire unless you absolutely need to shoot. I don't want stray rounds going into the school. Watch my back."

Silvia and José nodded.

Not having an MTOF active or a whispercraft overhead gave her a sense of nervous isolation, but at least it left her field of view clear, not cluttered with small, floating displays. Nina grasped her backpack strap with one hand, right arm swinging free as she speed-walked ahead along the edge of the road. She passed two larger homes, likely belonging to management of the solar facility, and a small empty lot with the ruins of a playground in it. Her pace slowed as she approached a burgundy-walled police station that bore little resemblance to a jail. The recognizable whirr of an air conditioner hummed from the roof.

*This wasn't built as a police station. It's just the biggest house in the town.*

A sideways glance in the windows revealed three men in desert-brown armor. One stood at the end of a desk, dabbing at his face with a towel while he fanned himself. Another sat back in his chair with his feet up on another desk, while a third hovered in the far left corner, pouring a drink.

The living room had been converted into an office with five desks and a handful of freestanding plastisteel storage cabinets large enough to hold armor suits. An archway led left into a sitting room, and two hallways went deeper in from the back wall and to the right. Aside from the front area, the rest of the place still resembled someone's home.

Nina barged through a wooden door covered in flaking dark green paint, into a blast of ice-cold air. She hurried toward a spot between the sweaty CMO officer and the sitting one, speaking Spanish in the tone of a frightened college student. "They're here! They're here! You have to do something!"

"Whoa, calm down there, little lady." The man with the towel grinned at her. "You look scared."

The reclining man lowered his boots to the floor and stood. "You lost, girlie? I don't think I've seen you before." He approached, squeezing into her personal space.

"Had two new engineers come in Thursday. Maybe one of them had a daughter?"

Nina's ears registered soft footsteps on the porch outside.

The man in the back corner stoppered a bottle and raised a shot glass to sip. "So, who's coming? Banditos?" He chuckled. "Maybe she saw a squealer."

Reclining man laughed. "You know it's a citable offence to waste our time."

"You're safe here." The grinning man on her left patted her ass. "I'm sure we can overlook a little panic attack, hmm?"

The third man, with the drink, frowned. He started to turn away, shaking his head. Though he seemed to regard their blatant intent to molest her with distaste, he also didn't move to stop it.

"You sure there's something chasing you?" asked Reclining Man. He teased at her hair. "Who's chasing you?"

Nina's fearful expression went flat. "The Resistance. They're right behind me."

Time crawled to a near stop in her perception. She grabbed Reclining Man by the neck of his armored chestplate and pulled him as hard as she could at the floor before spinning into a kick that caught Towel Man in the small of the back. Shards of splintering armor flaked away from the point of impact as his body bent in half over her leg, until his calves touched his shoulder blades.

The corpse flew across the room at a speed as though he sank in dense syrup. Tequila Man's facial expression started shifting to alarm. Nina whirled out of her kick, getting both feet on the ground. She swiped the helmet from Reclining Man's desk and hurled it at his face.

Dust brown composite armor struck his hand first, forcing it into the shot glass, which brushed teeth aside like standing dominoes as it entered his mouth. Blood exploded around the shattering glass, which mashed up into his gums. The helmet crushed his face; impact waves rippled across his cheeks and down his neck. His skull rocked back, blood swinging up in streams from several points. The helmet fell away, tumbling to the floor. No trace of consciousness remained in what little expression a caved-in face could convey.

He bent backward and bounced off the wall.

Nina extended her Nano claws from her right arm, and drove them down into Reclining Man's back. The instant her knuckles touched his armor, she disengaged her speedware.

José and Silvia ran in, both with rifles in hand.

Towel Man's folded-in-half body hit the right side wall hips first, slapped flat against it, and fell off to land on a desk before flowing to the ground. Tequila Man crumpled in a heap.

"Mother of God," muttered José.

Nina stood, extracting her blades from the corpse. They retracted with a soft *click*, and the two slits in her skin sealed. "We don't have much time. I'm not picking up any EM signatures, so I don't think they have cameras on this room. Help me look for a way downstairs."

José hurried down the corridor straight ahead. Silvia ducked left into the sitting room. Nina went the other way, following a hallway past a dining room on the right, a small library on the left, a huge bathroom on the right, and a kitchen at the end. An impressively ornate sink had been piled high with dirty dishes and unwashed glasses.

"Wonder what happened to the people who lived here?" She checked six closets, finding pots, pans, cleaning supplies, and other miscellany before José walked in.

"Back hall only goes upstairs or out back." He pointed at a narrow door with a rounded top located in the corner past the stove. "Basement?"

She gave up on closets and went to the door she'd dismissed as small. "Probably. Less work than putting in an elevator." Opening it revealed an equally narrow passageway descending at a sharp angle. Patches of white paint and plaster chipped away from the walls among dark stains and a naked wire running along the rounded ceiling. "If I didn't have night vision, I probably wouldn't go down there."

"Sil," yelled José. "Kitchen."

Nina drew her sidearm and headed down the creepy stairs. The cramped passageway went on longer than a single story down, and opened into a cavernous basement. Sawdust smeared the floor in the center, around a square metal hatch far too modern to belong in this house. The smashed remains of wine racks lay in a pile in front of still-intact wine racks standing against the wall by the stairs.

"I found a cable coming out of the ground into the house." Silvia's voice echoed in the tunnel. "Looks new. Somethin' hi-tech."

Nina approached the hatch, and walked around it once. Concrete dust from its installation still gathered in drifts on the floor nearby. "This hasn't been here too long."

"What's that?" José reached the bottom of the stairs and walked over, Silvia behind him.

"This is what I'm looking for. I still have no idea what I'm going to find down there, so be careful."

"Can we shoot down here?" asked Silvia, sounding annoyed.

"Yeah. There's enough dirt overhead." Nina squatted by the front where a small glossy square glowed blue: a fingerprint reader.

"Be right back." Silvia started for the stairs. "I'll grab a few fingers."

"Wait." Nina popped her Nano claws. "I brought a key."

She thrust the lower of the two blades, the one protruding from between her pinky and ring finger, in a few millimeters above where metal met concrete. With a faint sawing motion, she duck-walked around the square until the cut met the spot she started.

José whistled.

Nina retraced the blades and lifted the hatch mechanism out of the way, exposing a square shaft with rounded corners and a rubberized ladder. "Haven't seen Nano blades before?"

"No. They work like magic." He smiled.

She holstered her weapon, grasped the sides of the hole, and lowered her legs in. The drop looked easy, about fifteen feet. Electronic thrum filled the air in the space below, along with a few murmurs of conversation and one man complaining in louder Russian. Nina ran an analysis on the sounds; a small window popped up in the lower left containing a shimmering mass of tiny blue dots.

"What's the point of us having this enormous pipe to the GlobeNet if we cannot even use it?"

"We can't draw traffic here. You know that, Arkady. The UCF, they are dumb, but they are not so blind. This place looks like the back end of nowhere. Don't be stupid."

The mass of dots coalesced into something resembling a map.

"Bah," said Arkady. "Watching Frictionless would not arouse their suspicion."

Text appeared in the virtual window. ‹Estimated unique voice prints: 5›

Acoustic resonance analysis predicted a room twenty feet wide by thirty or forty feet long. Red spots identified the most likely origin point of the voices. She played connect the dots in her mind.

"Going in," she whispered.

Nina let go of the edge and engaged her speedware. Her backpack floated a few inches away and her hair bloomed upward. She drew her pistol while extending her legs to meet the floor. A digital crosshair floated in her field of view as soon as her weapon pointed forward, courtesy of a wireless link. She sank into a short corridor lined on both sides by lockers, which allowed her a view into a larger room full of workstations. Two men in DMS armor sat behind standing walls of holo-panels, projected from mirror-silver plastic loafs on their desks.

The instant her boot tips touched concrete, her crosshair lined up with the first man. Her electronic ears filtered the tremendous report of the 15mm handgun in such closed quarters, but her targets had no such protection.

Her heels came down in time with the first man's head bursting in a shower of gore and skull fragments. She shifted aim to the left, firing a second round as her weight transferred from her feet to her knees. The back end of his head blew out, leaving a flapping face with a hole in it. Misted blood settled on workstations as the impact wave rode up her legs into her hips.

The third man cringed from the sound of gunfire. Before his hands reached his ears, she shot him in the chin, painting the terminal behind him with brain.

Nina's body sank into her legs; her cheeks wobbled from the impact of her jump. She kicked off the ground, springing up to a sprint into the room. Walls on either side fell away. Another DMS man within arms' reach to the left caught her off guard; having been focused on his work and not talking, he had no corresponding dot. He'd gotten half out of his seat, face warped with alarm, but he showed no reaction to her sudden appearance.

She pounded her handgun into the side of his head; a sickening slow-motion wet crunching emanated from his collapsing skull. The hit redirected the trajectory of his attempt to stand into the wall.

Blue flashes from the right came from three men in armor, firing rifles in her general direction. One man in plain clothes shot twice at her chest, moving in almost real time. His bullets slowed as if stuck in thick mud, creeping closer. She sprinted to the right and toward the men, weaving between clouds of spinning projectiles.

The boosted man corrected his aim, shooting as fast as he could pull the trigger. Like a bizarre version of 3D chess, Nina wound up with nowhere to go that wouldn't walk her straight into a bullet. Deciding to spare her face at the expense of chest and legs, she cringed and braced for impact while firing at him, once at his head and once a little off to the right and down—at empty space.

Combat mode had disabled pain; the six slugs that made contact registered a sensation no more bothersome than if someone had poked her with a finger. Her shot gouged a trench in the man's shoulder as he tried to leap backward and limbo under the bullet—and put his head right where Nina thought he would. Nina's second round burrowed into the side of his neck, sending streams of blood spraying from his ears, then nose as the pressure wave expanded inside his skull.

She got a foot up on a terminal desk, shoving her body airborne in a sideways dive. Spinning, she raised her arm past her head to take a shot at another man before grasping her weapon in both hands and sending two more rounds past her boots at the other two who continued to spray automatic fire in all directions as they tried to keep up with a blurry smear. Sparks burst from the walls around the ceiling wherever projectiles struck stone. Her spatial awareness tracking registered all three of her bullets flying true.

Nina hit the ground on her back and shut down her speedware.

Four bodies collapsed around her.

"Fuck that," said a man in Russian. "I don't get paid enough to deal with that shit."

Nina sprang up and pointed her weapon at a blond man somewhere in his thirties.

He screamed and raised his hands.

"What's your role here?" She took two steps closer, pistol pointed at his face. "Do you have operator access to this system?"

"I only see the files as objects... to relay them to another location. It's a digital wormhole. I don't even know where it goes."

"How much of the data you've collected here is still on site? Do you keep local copies?"

"Uhh." He glanced at a big, fancy desk in the middle of the room with a conspicuous red button. "There are backups."

"Go!" yelled a man behind her.

She spun as a pair of double-doors slid open. Another six men in dust brown

Department of Motherland Security armor rushed in. One bee-lined for the big red button. Nina launched herself at him, diving into a speedware trance. He hung in midair, arm outstretched, flying toward what she assumed to be a 'master erase' panic button. When her floating targeting crosshair met his forearm, her MCP50 barked at a mental impulse. The bullet left two neat 15mm holes in his armor, but the bones inside disintegrated. His limp hand slapped down on the desk inches to the left of the button.

Bullets flew from the rest of the oncoming soldiers, though Nina stayed ahead of the wall of projectiles. She sprinted into a kick that caught the button-diver in the chest, crushing his armor. His body slapped into the ceiling as Nina dove under him.

Silvia and José, standing at the end of the short hallway by the ladder, opened fire on the cluster of men. Nina hit the ground on her front and slid behind a terminal. By the time she popped up to shoot back, the DMS soldiers flailed about in a dance of death. She aimed, but didn't waste a bullet. Her ammo readout showed ten remaining, of nineteen.

She shut down her speedware.

José moaned and slumped over clutching his side.

The man who'd surrendered stood in a cringe, with one leg up and both arms crossed over his face, breathing hard, wheezing in Russian, "Shitting hell. What are you?"

Nina kept a sliver of tactical awareness on him, but focused on José as she rushed over. "You're hit."

"Figured this would be a one way trip." He chuckled into a wince.

"So are you," said Silvia.

Nina glanced at a few holes in her clothes and slung her backpack off. "I'm wearing armor. Nothing got in." She took two stimpaks from it and handed them to Silvia. "Know what these are?"

"Yes." She grabbed them.

Nina locked eyes with her. "Get him back to the truck. Make sure the school is clear. I'll be out in ten."

Two of the men José and Silvia gunned down moaned.

A door on the left side opened as a somewhat pudgy man entered holding a drink can and half a cheeseburger. In utter defiance of the bloodbath sprayed around the room, he strolled toward a rear hallway.

"What the fuck?" Silvia pointed her rifle at him. "Stop."

"Sorry." The man held up the burger. "I'm not on the clock right now. Lunch break. I'm not getting paid for this time, so I really don't give a fuck what you people do."

"Are you going to start caring when you punch back in?" asked Silvia, a hint of growl in her voice.

Another wounded man moaned.

Lunch Break eyed the carnage. "You know... I think I'm feeling a bit sick. I might take the rest of the day off." He braced his stomach with his forearm, burger still in hand. "It's unpaid, but I just don't think I can finish out the day the way I feel."

Silvia fired into the pile of wounded, putting an end to the moans.

The man with the burger went bug-eyed and ran for the back hallway. In the second Nina debated guilt at shooting him, Silvia spared her the moral dilemma. Her burst caught him in the back; he slid on his knees, arms waving for a few feet before he fell forward. The burger scattered across the floor while his drink canister rolled out of sight.

*Who knows what was back there. He was probably faking. No one is that callous.*

Nina jumped in the big chair and attacked the terminals.

"What about him?" Silvia pointed her rifle at the man who'd surrendered. "You're going to be upset if I kill him, aren't you?"

"I'm still not sure how I feel about Lunch Break. Take—"

Gunfire erupted outside.

"Here they come," said Javier over the radio on Silvia's belt.

Nina looked up. "Dammit."

"They were watching the front. There must be more CMO on the way." Silvia grabbed José's arm and hauled him to his feet.

"Take this guy with you," said Nina. "Watch him. If he gives you any reason to doubt his intentions, you know what to do."

José put his arm around Silvia's shoulders and groaned with the effort it took to walk.

The DMS man kept his hands up.

"In front." Silvia one-handed her rifle, using it to point at the exit tunnel.

"*Si, si,*" said the man. "*No dispares.*"

Silvia pointed the rifle at him. "If you don't want me to shoot, get moving."

As the three of them made their way to the ladder, Nina searched the terminal in front of her. One status window displayed 852 active connections, Harmony-infected people back home sending everything they saw and heard to the ACC. Shouting and gunfire continued outside, mixed with the giant-mosquito buzz of one of the resistance bikes. The revving and automatic fire made Nina think of a high-speed drive by. Fortunately, she heard no screaming children.

*I hope they got them out of there...*

One sub window held a connection manager that provided stats on data relay to a network address she knew didn't belong to this place. From the first few digits of the IPv12, she assumed Europe. A mental impulse took a still image of the screen via her eyes.

Twenty seconds of searching among folders and icons led her to a data repository, where she tapped one icon. The file expanded to a larger square that showed the date and time of the file's arrival, plus a giant alphanumeric string she assumed to be the ID of the sender. A prompt at the bottom asked for a decryption key. Grumbling, she minimized it and took a neural memory stick from her backpack, which she connected to the terminal's M3 port.

When she attempted to drag all the data to the stick, each file expanded to ask for the same decryption key.

"Shit." *Dammit...* she squeezed the demolition charges through the backpack. *There's gotta be some way to check this data. If they got something vital, we need to know.* She hadn't brought a net deck with her, and did not want to expose her internal systems to whatever counter-intrusion mechanisms might be in play here. Nor did she have time to experiment.

*I wonder if that bullshit thing is still online... if I log in direct from this terminal, they can walk right in.*

She went to the GlobeNet site for Floyd's Bakery. The logo 'The most mediocre bagels in the world' scrolled across the window above a generic list of baked goods. After tapping the 'user login' button, she entered 'anyonethere' as the username and '804332C3' (her Division 9 ID) as the password.

"Come on... come on..." She looked up at the exit tunnel as a tremendous *boom* of metal-on-metal shook dust off the ceiling.

Four slow single shots preceded nineteen seconds of silence before two quick rips of automatic fire accompanied a staccato metallic clanking. A *bang* sounded, followed by hissing, and a *fthoom* of a deflagration. Nina hoped she hadn't heard someone machine-gunning their truck to death.

"Hey sexy," said a voice from the terminal. "Enjoying the sun?"

She snapped her attention down to find Joey staring at her from a small window. Relief and urgency crashed together in her heart. "I'm logged in from their main system. I can't copy any of these files without inputting a crypto key. I don't have time to sit here and fuck around with this, and I'd really prefer to get this data under a proverbial microscope rather than burn this place out blind. Oh. Here." She sent the image of the network address. "This place is just a waystation. They're relaying everything to that address."

"Not a problem, babe. I'm on it." He winked. "Looks like somewhere near Warsaw."

"Might want to hurry that along. There will be an unexpected server error in five minutes." Nina stood.

He cringed. "Software?"

"I'm afraid not." She held up one of the demo charges. "Hardware problem. Unrecoverable data loss."

Joey grimaced and rotated to face away from the camera. "Abs, Mindy... Dive in on this link. Need more hands. We got minutes."

She headed down the corridor where Lunch Break lay dead. Ten feet from the body, a left turn held a small alcove with weapon racks holding ten rifles, numerous magazines, and a handful of grenades. *Son of a bitch.* A short distance later, another left turn led to a small barracks-style room with double-decker cots, but no people. Five feet past the sleeping quarters, an armored door blocked her way.

Nano claws made short work of the quarter-inch thick plastisteel. She grabbed the excised slab and pulled, peeling the opening wider like dense plastic. A grid arrangement of sixteen processing towers took up most of the space, each about her height and as big around as a domestic refrigerator.

The scream of a terrified schoolgirl came from her left as she squeezed past the hole she'd made in the door.

She straightened to her feet inside, and locked stares with a light-haired man in his middle twenties. Scrawny, with a large nose and Adam's apple, he radiated 'techie.' Though he clutched his sidearm in both hands, he shook so much she doubted he could hit the wall. Behind him, a thin silver table held three terminals, their holo-panels showing video feeds of the outer room.

Her Nano blades retracted with a faint whirr and *click* that overpowered his weak, stuttering breaths. She took a step toward him, and he made a piteous squealing noise. The crotch of his pants darkened.

"You must be the head tech."

He collapsed to the floor and scooted backward under the table, abandoning his weapon. *"Töten sie mich nicht!"*

"I'm not going to kill you." She squatted in front of him, grasped him by a fistful of shirt, and pulled him out of his hiding spot. "But you're not going to want to stay here."

He whined. *"Warum? Was wirst du machen?"*

"I can tell you're afraid. You understand me, yet you're answering in German." She lifted him to his feet and smiled. "I know you watched what happened out there. You're not going to do anything stupid. Are you?"

*"Nein! Nein! Ich bin kein soldat."* He paled, trembling, and seemed about to vomit. *"Ich arbeite nur mit den computern."*

She swatted the gun from his hand and shoved him toward the door. "I've got a satellite overhead that can see the pores in your scalp. Get out of here and don't do anything stupid, or I'll give you a nice close look at what an orbital neutron beam platform is capable of."

Grabbing at the air as if that would help him move faster, the gangly man sprinted for the door. Nina tried not to laugh that he believed her bluff about a satellite laser and decided to set two charges in this room, in case the servers had armor. She slipped between the outermost ring of machines and placed the charge on the face of the second one in from the left on the second row.

A window opened along the right side of her field of view:

<Charge A Status: *Armed*>
<Charge B Status: Safe>
<Charge C Status: Safe>
<Charge D Status: Safe>

The scuff of sprinting tech shoes ended with the dull *thud* of a body hitting the floor. He started to scream, but the sad sound drowned under a torrent of vomit. Nina shook her head and placed another charge on the third machine in from the left on the third row back. Two of the four cabinets at the center of the arrangement had charges, which would obliterate the other twelve surrounding them.

Charge B changed status to armed.

Screaming, scrambling, and tripping over everything possible, the techie clambered across the outer room and made it to the ladder tunnel a second after she exited the server room. She placed Charge C on the roof at the archway separating the main area from the hallway back to the barracks and servers, hoping it would cause a cave in.

*Four NE8 charges in this little space is such damn overkill.*

Nina peeked into the room Lunch Break came out of to check for another offshoot, but it held only a tiny kitchenette with a sink and food reassembler along with two chairs and a round table. She crossed the main chamber to the doorway where the six DMS soldiers came in from. It led to an area half barracks and half improvised fitness center. A scattering of free weights made out of dead batteries and metal spars sat around a treadmill they'd probably stolen from upstairs.

*Nothing in here of any intelligence value.*

She returned and placed the fourth charge on the desk next to the master erase button. Joey's window remained, though contained only black. "Still there?"

"Little busy," said Joey, without appearing.

"Three minutes twenty seconds left."

"Noted."

She brushed her fingertips over the intangible screen, tinting them blue where they made contact. "You going to be stuck late again tomorrow night? I don't think I'm going to make it home today."

"I can make an exception." He leaned into the frame long enough to give her a cheesy grin, and disappeared again.

Nina slung the mostly empty backpack over her shoulder and grasped the strap. She gave the room, and the bodies within, a cursory glance before heading to the ladder.

Four rungs up, her amplified hearing detected a moan.

*Shit.*

She jumped off the ladder and hurried back over to where the pile of bodies lay in front of the 'fitness center.' If anyone had survived, it would have to be one of them. No doubt remained that the men she'd shot or hit died instantly.

"Which one of you is still alive?" she asked in Russian, then German.

None of them moved.

"Fine. Stay here and die when the bombs go. I'm not going to finish you off. You're no threat now."

A helmet moved.

Nina crouched over the bloodied figure; scanners in her eyes picked up three holes in his chest plate, and two in his leg. *He's minutes away from dying anyway.* Without a second thought, she grabbed a stimpak from her bag and jabbed him in the neck with it. Not enough to get him functional, but it should stop him from bleeding to death.

She grabbed the back of his armored chestplate and dragged him to the ladder, letting him dangle while she climbed up to the house's basement and crossed it to the stairs. *That much explosive is probably going to cave the house in. Shame... this was a nice place, if not a bit creepy.* His boots bounced and clattered over each step. Nina hurried along as the low, rounded ceiling and tight walls triggered a mild sense of claustrophobia.

*I feel like the girl walking away from the house in a horror vid, only I'm the monster.*

The man gurgled and moaned, but made no effort to move as she hauled him out of the kitchen down the hall to the front door. Her speedware activated on its own, a bright red circle appeared in her vision highlighting an incoming bullet.

Silvia and Roberto hunkered down on the porch, hiding behind the flaming wreckage of a plain blue car. A dead man in CMO armor slumped over the wheel. Two bodies lay in the road in similar armor, and a fourth CMO officer crouched in the doorway of the school, the source of the bullet coming for her chest.

A small girl wearing a white dress with pink ribbons in her hair stood in front of him, hands over her face. The tightness of the dress across her chest indicated he held a fistful of cloth at her back. Nina released the injured soldier and sprinted. She leaned to the side, allowing the incoming bullet to pass as a second projectile left the man's rifle.

In the darkness behind him, the forms of children huddling on the floor around their teacher became clear. A block and change down the street to her left, Roberto and one of the women on motorbikes traded shots with armored figures in an alley. The other bike lay halfway between here and there—next to its motionless rider.

Nina ducked under the second bullet and lunged at the man, who only started to show a reaction to her speed as her fingers closed around his rifle. His eyebrows crawled upward. She wrenched his weapon in an outward twist, too fast for him to get his finger out of the trigger guard. His hand warped into an unnatural shape along with muted splintering crunches. At the same instant, she thrust her right arm down between him and the girl, grasping and crushing his wrist to free the child's dress from his grip.

His scream started as she spun with a jujitsu-inspired flip; the maneuver hauled him off his feet by one arm, lifting him up and over the child before slamming him down on his chest in the street. Confident the force of a doll drilling him into the pavement would leave him stunned and disoriented for a few seconds, she let her speedware shut down in order to speak.

"Are you hurt?" Nina took a knee by the girl, who shook her head. "Go to your teacher."

"Are you a demon?" asked the girl.

"No, sweetie. Demons don't protect children."

"Are you an angel?" She tilted her head, seeming a touch less afraid. "Are you God?"

"Not even close." She patted the girl on the shoulder. "I'm somewhere between alive and dead, only trying to do the right thing."

"Thank you!" She ran into the pile of students and crawled under the teacher's arm.

The woman stared at Nina with shock and distrust.

"You need to get these children out of here as fast as possible. Do you have a way out the back?" asked Nina.

The teacher nodded.

"You've got about two minutes before explosives send the 'police station' into orbit. I suggest you get moving right now."

The woman rounded up the kids and started shoving them into a hallway at the rear of the classroom.

Nina spun on the groaning man. She dragged him a good bit away from the school doorway and stomped on his forearms one after the other, splintering his armor and breaking bones. "Hiding behind a child? You are the lowest form of shit." One kick smashed both of his legs at the knee, making him cry out and lose consciousness.

His helmet rocked in time with the rapport of a gun.

Nina glanced over her shoulder at Silvia. "Nice shot."

"Bastard had us pinned forever... José's in the truck." She faced down the street and yelled, "Adriana!"

The woman lying under the crashed bike groaned.

"I got her. We need to get out of here." Nina ran to Adriana. After flinging the bike aside like a toy, she scooped the woman up in both arms. "Roberto! María Isabel! Time to go."

They tried to look at her, but incoming fire from the alley across the street made them duck. Nina switched her vision to GhostEye mode, which rendered the houses as transparent wireframe models. Two human figures with rifles showed clear on the other side of the corner. She crouched and rested Adriana on her leg to free her right hand before drawing her pistol and firing one round at each. The 15mm slugs pierced two walls without losing much velocity, struck each man, and continued into the next house before sailing out across open desert.

Both men collapsed backward.

María Isabel and Roberto broke cover and ran. María Isabel righted her bike and started it. The other motorbike appeared to have been run over, probably by the burning car, mangling the front wheel.

"How bad?" Nina put her gun away and lifted Adriana again.

"Ngh… Left arm's fucked. Think I took one in the gut, too."

Nina rushed her back to the pickup truck. "I'm sorry. I should've come in alone."

"As long as I get to the UCF—" Adriana grunted and gasped for air. "I don't care if I lose my arm."

"I've got a few stimpaks left." She handed Adriana to the waiting Silvia and José, who pulled her into the back seat. "Be right back."

"Where are you going?" yelled Silvia.

Roberto sprinted past her to the truck and leapt into the bed.

María Isabel drove off heading northeast. A few people hurled things at her from windows, yelling at her for causing trouble, though nothing came close to hitting her.

Nina hurried to the wounded DMS man and dragged him to the truck. Roberto gave her an incredulous look as she threw him in the bed.

"When we're clear of town, I'll ask them to stop. When we do, push him out."

He shook his head. "You're a strange woman, whoever you are."

*Little pieces of my soul are all I have left.*

Nina jumped in the truck. "Where's Javier?"

José bowed his head, then shook it. "Under that car."

"Bastard sons of whores," muttered Silvia.

"How much time?" José slammed the shifter into reverse.

"Twenty-eight seconds," said Nina, deadpan. "Javier is dead…"

Silvia made the sign of the cross.

José whipped the truck around in a 'K' turn and stomped on the gas pedal. Dust sprayed out behind them as acceleration pinned Nina to the seat. She stared past a few trailer homes at the approaching desert while mercy, guilt, and vengeance got into a catfight in her head.

"What's with the extra cargo?" Sweat rolled off José's face; the effort it took him to drive despite such pain clear in his eyes.

Nina stared down. "He wasn't dead. It didn't feel right leaving him there."

"You tore those people up like a scythe on wheat, and you feel guilty about one piece of shit?" Silvia muttered something incomprehensible. "I don't understand you, girl."

"He wasn't a threat anymore. There's a fine line between combat and murder. Who knows how many times I've tripped over it, but I try not to." She raised a hand to rub her temple. "If you want to finish him off, I won't stop you. I only told him *I* wouldn't hurt him."

Silvia scowled.

"What do you intend to do with him?" asked José.

*Boom.*

A flash of dark red and smoke flickered in the rearview mirror on the door. The large, fancy house vanished in a spray that resembled a massive shotgun firing into the sky. Glass flew across the street as the windows of adjacent houses shattered from the concussion wave. The building next door collapsed, likely the server room caving in. She stared at where she thought the school should be, but couldn't see much with all the dust. Seconds after the sound, the truck shuddered from the concussion wave reaching them.

"Just get him away from the bomb. I told Roberto I'd ask you to stop for a second so he can push the guy out."

Adriana gritted her teeth. "Got any more stims?"

*One. Would've been two if I didn't use one on the enemy.* "Yeah. Last one." She fished it out and passed it back.

José brought the truck to a stop. Roberto grunted and thumped around in the bed.

"What about those transports?" asked Silvia.

"We need to clear the area in case more reinforcements roll in." Nina leaned out of her window to scan the sky. "Don't see anything yet, but it doesn't mean they won't send an air unit."

The *whumpf* of a body hitting the dirt came from the back. José accelerated.

"So… what about getting us out of here?" Silvia's voice lost its harsh tone; she sounded more like a pleading child.

"Can María Isabel drive a BTR?" Nina glanced at José. "I'll come back here with her once it's dark."

They caught up to the techie, who continued to stagger along, too exhausted to run.

*Hmm. He might have useful intel.* Nina leaned around to the rear window. "Roberto… Grab this guy. He might have information my people need."

José slowed to match the man's pitiful pace. The techie offered little protest at being dragged into the truck bed. María Isabel on her bike came bouncing out of a depression in the ground and steered toward them. She fell in beside it as they got back up to about sixty mph.

"It can probably work." José nodded. "I doubt they will expect another attack so soon."

"Let's hope so." Nina leaned back in her seat and closed her eyes. "If we need to lay low for a few days, I can. I give you my word; I'll get you and your people out of here."

# EXFILTRATION

I f not for being unable to drive two large armored personnel carriers herself, Nina would've walked back to the solar farm alone. She lay on one of the cots, trying not to hear Ramon scream and rage after being told of Javier's death. He'd been like an older brother to him for four years; they'd met hiding in the resistance when Ramon had been fourteen, and Javier sixteen. Ramon, the telepath, shouted that he didn't want to go to the UCF anymore; he wanted to go to Mexico City and 'kill them all.'

Nina cringed with guilt, thankful her implant prevented him from reading her mind and seeing that she'd used up a stimpak on one of *them*.

Silvia hadn't said much since they returned, having gone to the last cot in the corner and holding Nicolás, the six-year-old she'd become a fugitive to protect.

*They wanted to kill him for being able to do card tricks.*

Adrianna's injuries would keep her out of gunfights and off motorbikes for weeks, but Patricia had enough medical supplies to save the arm... providing they made it to the UCF within a few days. José had lucked out, the bullet that hit him hadn't ruptured anything vital—but it hurt enough to where Patricia had forced him to use a Narcoderm. That effectively removed José from usefulness, as the drugs left him chatting with his wife who'd died two years earlier. Pedro had assumed temporary leadership of the cell, and agreed with Nina's idea of going in at the wee hours of morning to steal the BTRs.

María Isabel approached. The girl looked even younger in the dim light of the underground hideaway, maybe sixteen. "Hey. It's almost dark. You ready?"

Nina sat up on the cot and looked her over. "You sure you can drive one of those things? Maybe..." She looked at the group. "Someone else should... I don't want to get a kid hurt."

"I'm not a child." María Isabel folded her arms. "I'm twenty. Just short."

Nina burst into laughter, crying at the same time.

The room got quiet.

"Okay." She chuckled. "You must all think I'm crazy now."

"Maybe a little." María Isabel smiled. "But maybe bein' able to do what you can do would make anyone a little crazy."

"Before it… happened, I was like you. Tiny. People always thought I was a kid. Now here I am doing the same thing to someone else."

María Isabel flopped on the next cot. They compared 'short girl problems' for a little while. A thin, athletic man, Francisco, came by and gave them each a plate of food, a mixture of rice, hunks of pork or something akin to it, and a liberal helping of beans and sauce.

The resistance cell ate in relative silence.

"We're going to make a run on the troop carriers around four in the morning, drive them here to pick everyone up, and go."

María Isabel nodded, her mouth full.

"I am an idiot." Nina looked around the room. Fifteen people remained, five of them children. "Are there more than what's in this room?"

"Yeah," said Pedro. He got up and walked over. "We've got four men in the house."

"Nineteen, five of whom are children." She rubbed her forehead, grumbling.

Pedro tilted his head at her. "Yes. What's wrong?"

"Those BTR-99s can carry twenty troops, plus a driver and a gunner. We only need *one*."

"Ahh. Yes, that would be true." Pedro exhaled, lips sputtering.

She stood. "I'll go alone. I don't want any more of you getting hurt for me."

Ramon pointed at her. "She's probably just going to leave."

"No. I'm not." She looked at María Isabel. "I will keep our promise."

"So what if she is gonna leave?" asked Roberto. "Did you see what she did to those CMO tools? Like we could stop her if we tried."

Ramon fumed, stared at her, and promptly dropped in place holding his head and screaming.

Everyone stared at him.

"It's not your fault," said the fourteen-year-old, Veronica. "He's angry and hurt."

"Vonica's a empath." The smallest, a boy of about five, crawled to the edge of his cot and sat back on his heels. "She knows."

Nina smiled at him. *Don't need to be telempathic to know that.*

"Look, even if we don't need two trucks, it'll be faster for me to drive you." María Isabel winked. "Even better if I can stay back and hide while you go in."

"All right, but be careful."

María Isabel grinned. "I'm always careful."

⁂

AT 3:59 A.M., MARÍA ISABEL NUDGED NINA, SURPRISING HER THAT SHE'D MANAGED to drift off to sleep at all. Nina sat up and held her head for a few seconds, waiting for the fog to lift from her mind. María Isabel walked a few cots over and nudged Pedro awake.

"We're going," she whispered. "I'll radio when we're on the way back."

"Mmm." Pedro yawned and stretched. He set his walkie-talkie near his head and seemed to sink into sleep again.

Nina stood. "Let's do it."

María Isabel led the way up the ladder to the barn and removed the tarp from her bike. Nina got on behind her. Being able to see over the woman's head got her maudlin, thinking of Vincent's playful comments about her being a kid playing dress up as a cop.

The bike startled her when it roared to life.

It bounced quite a bit more than the truck, catching air every so often whenever they hit a depression or berm. María Isabel drove hard, verging on reckless. Nina peered down at the speedometer, raising both eyebrows at the realization they did 102 mph. They took a wide, curving route that would keep them out of sight of the town, in case the authorities had moved more troops in.

"This is careful?" yelled Nina, over the engine.

"Yes." María Isabel laughed. "Don't tell anyone, but I'm… gifted, too. I can make myself faster and stronger, but uhh, nowhere near the kinda shit you're doing."

"You're a biokinetic?"

"Whatever that means." María Isabel shrugged. "Someone said I was psionic, but their dog couldn't confirm it."

"Dog?"

"Some psionics sell out." María Isabel leaned left while steering the bike around a group of cacti. She flung her slight body to the right to bring the bike level after the maneuver. "They work *for* the ACC… but they've got handlers who'll kill them if they step out of line. I have no telepathy, which is rare I guess, so they kept me locked up while they tried to figure out a way to prove I was psionic or come up with enough of an excuse to just kill me."

"I'm sorry it's so hard for your kind here." Nina scowled at the desert. "I don't understand why people are like that."

"Thanks. I guess you sorta know what it's like. I bet people treat you different for being… whatever you are."

Nina chuckled. "People who know what I am, yeah. I try to hide it." *Mostly from myself.* "Once they know, it changes everything."

"You *do* know what it's like." María Isabel laughed.

Endless scrubland, a shifting black pattern under the indigo luminescence of the night sky, came at them for twenty-two minutes. Light settled on the horizon like a spill of mercury. Solar panels, flattened for the dark, caught the moonlight in a mesmerizing shimmer. Off to the left, about a third of a mile away, a scattering of LED bulbs over doorways defined *Estación Salamanca* like a constellation. The lack of activity worried her more than finding it full of soldiers. The DMS having a minimal presence in the little town made sense given that the facility wasn't supposed to exist, and the ACC overestimated how difficult it would be to find. Seeing the BTR-99s at the solar facility had made her expect a hidden garrison, but those transports had been there for months according to satellite image archives. Still, she'd expected *some* kind of reaction to the facility's destruction.

*Maybe they're arguing which department's budget gets to cover the cleanup.*

María Isabel cut the engine and the headlamp, allowing the bike to coast.

Amid the stillness of a desert night, the distant electrical hum of the solar plant provided backup for the chirrup of insects. Nina zoomed in her vision on the facility. A four-story tower stood atop the roof of a long, rectangular building with a pair of garage-style doors on the near side. Windows around the top offered a view of a blinding interior where a woman and a man in white jumpsuits sat at desks in a white room, looking ready to fall asleep at any moment.

Her eyelids twitched in response to a manufactured sensation of pain from the intense glow. Between the strength of the light and the giant windows on all four sides of the tower, it acted like a giant desk lamp, illuminating the ground for a good distance in all directions.

Two men in DMS armor stood a short distance from a door leading into the building. Both slouched, and had their rifles slung over their backs. One sipped from a silver canister while the other yawned every few seconds.

The man with the drink heaved the empty canister onto the roof, and the pair trudged off into the solar fields, on patrol... and seeming not at all happy about it. At the speed they moved, Nina calculated thirty-two minutes before they returned —assuming they would follow a complete circle.

Four pinpoints of light glided around the solar field. She honed in on one and zoomed more. Away from the tower's glare, she switched to night vision. An orb bot glided along, making precision course adjustments every few seconds. The rigidity of its motion hinted that it ran a preprogrammed route and didn't have a live operator controlling it. Nina observed them for a few minutes, until they retraced their earlier path. Their function appeared to be protecting the solar panels from vandals, thieves, and wildlife. The nearest point in their route brought them with sixty meters of the building.

"We should be able to walk right up to the BTR," whispered Nina. "The tower won't see us. It's too bright in there and it's pitch dark outside."

María Isabel nodded. "They're stupid."

"Or they don't expect anyone to attack a power facility in the middle of nowhere." She shrugged. "I wonder what they're doing with it all."

"There are underground cables. A tunnel runs from here all the way to Hermosillo. That's how some of us got out here, but they have armed bots down there now." When the bike coasted to a stop, María Isabel put her boots down. "Want me to wait here or follow you in?"

"We should be clear if we move quick. Come on." Nina got off the bike, grabbed the rear end, and pushed.

"You don't have to do that," whispered María Isabel.

"I don't get tired."

Nina jogged the last half mile to the solar facility, pushing the bike. Deep shadows on the side of the BTRs opposite the tower offered good cover. The tower employees would have to move right up to the window to be able to see the ground that close anyway, and neither looked motivated to move. Nina let go of the bike and rushed around to the dark side of the closer transport. María Isabel followed, walking the bike.

The BTR-99 resembled a brick the size of a PubTran bus propped up on eight thick wheels, each seven feet tall. Hollows with traction coating allowed troops to climb to a door at the midway point along each side. Another door up front by the driver's station had a small ladder that required scaling a tire to reach.

Nina climbed to the side door. In its center, a bar-type handle sat recessed in a circular well. She grabbed the bar, twisted it a quarter turn clockwise, and pulled the door open.

"Wow… no code?" whispered María Isabel.

"It's a military vehicle." Nina dropped back to the ground and picked up the bike like a toy. "When troops need to move *now*, they don't want to forget the password."

María Isabel scampered up into the BTR. Nina hoisted the motorbike overhead and pushed it into the doorway while climbing after it. María Isabel grabbed the handlebars and guided the bike into the troop carrier. Nina paused with one foot in the door, gazing out at the field of solar panels. The two men on guard duty sat on the steps of one of the scaffoldings holding panels, heads back and mouths agape. She chuckled and pulled the door closed.

*At least I don't have to kill anyone tonight.*

Cheap canvas-and-metal seats lined the walls of the main hold, enough to seat twenty, ten forward of the side doors and ten aft. Empty weapon racks flanked the doors. Muddy footprints covered the back wall of the BTR, which could open downward like a ramp. A thin partition bearing two old medical kits separated the troop area from the front end.

Nina set the bike on the floor and headed to the driver's seat. This particular truck had a dual-barreled machinegun mounted to a ring turret over the passenger seat, which operated via a periscope-style rig. A Slimpanel mounted to the blank metal wall in front of her would hopefully act as a windshield once she turned on the power. The pre-holographic display looked in working order, a clear plastic slab thirty-six inches wide, twenty tall, and about three millimeters thick. No cracks, but a few fingerprints.

"Oooh. That's a big ass gun." María Isabel bounced on her toes for a second before leaping into the chair and putting her face up to the device. "Darn. I can't see anything."

"I doubt it works with the main power off." Nina sat behind the controls, a pair of sticks with no sign of a jack. "Shit. This thing's gotta be eighty years old. It doesn't even have a M3 port."

"Is that bad?" asked María Isabel.

Nina raised both eyebrows at the physical 'on' switch, a one-inch wide red plastic bar in a sunken well. "Not necessarily. Just means I need to use my hands. If that thing works, let me know if anyone comes running after us."

She pushed the power switch up to the 'on' position. Three status lights winked to life on the dashboard, and her ears picked up a low electronic hum. A raccoon-mask band of green lit up María Isabel's face, and a split second later, the Slimpanel displayed the ass end of the other BTR-99, simulating a window.

"It's on. What does twenty-three emm emm times a thousand three hundred seventy mean?"

*Holy shit. It's got ammo?* "That means you've got 1370 rounds of 23mm ammunition."

"Is the truck on? It's quiet."

Nina grasped the control sticks. Instinct said each stick controlled the wheels on that side, both forward for forward, both back for reverse, and different directions to turn. *They made this for barely-trained troops. It's going to be as simple as humanly possible. Complexity requires training, which costs more.* "Yeah. Electric. It won't make a sound until we start moving, and even then… hopefully not enough to wake anyone up."

"The people in the tower might see us."

"I'm hoping they work for Verde Mundial Solar, and won't care that we're stealing DMS property."

María Isabel shrugged. "Or they'll think the soldiers are driving it around."

"Let's hope."

Nina eased back on the sticks, and a small rear-view screen appeared at the top center of the Slimpanel. With nothing but open desert behind her, she didn't pay much attention to it, instead focusing on the forward view. The BTR-99 creaked as it glided backward at a walking pace. The groans and protests of its heavy suspension echoed in the boxy space, louder than the whirr of e-motors. The tower employees didn't get up; she doubted they'd be able to hear the squeaking five stories up behind sealed windows.

When she got a little farther away from the facility, she pulled back on the sticks more, easing the behemoth up to fifteen mph. No sense of alarm showed within the compound. *This is too easy. Oh, stop. I'm overthinking. They don't believe anyone would bother. Or they know they can find it.*

"Does anyone at the ranch have tools? This thing probably has a transponder I need to disable."

"I don't know. If anyone does, it'd be Patricia. She's our tech. Bet she could disable that thing for you."

Nina pulled more on the left stick, causing the lumbering vehicle to back into a turn. Once the rear end faced the VMS plant, she pushed both sticks forward. The BTR lurched to a stop, shuddered, and emitted a low gear-grinding noise for a few seconds while trundling forward. Before long, she had it up to sixty-five mph.

María Isabel kept her face pressed to the periscope as her chair spun around to face backward. "Nothing's following us."

"We shouldn't stop. Even those two idiots will notice this thing missing. Radio back to Pedro and have him get everyone ready."

"You got it." María Isabel let go of the gun controls, and the seat auto-reset to forward.

---

THE SKY REMAINED DARK BY THE TIME THE RANCH HOUSE CAME INTO VIEW ON THE Slimpanel. A spot of light winked on and off inside the barn, likely someone with a flashlight. Nina grabbed a black knob on the left, intending to respond with headlights, but one click clockwise activated a row of floodlights across the top of the roof as well as the headlights, which illuminated the entire resistance cell like they'd been caught in the flare of a nuclear detonation.

From the smallest to the eldest, they covered their eyes; she almost expected to see skin melt and clothing catch fire.

"Shit." She clicked it off.

"*Gah!* Mother of God! I'm blind!" Pedro's voice crackled from María Isabel's walkie-talkie.

"Sorry," muttered Nina. She stopped the BTR close to the barn and slapped a wide green button labeled 'ramp door' in Cyrillic. The hydraulic pumps whined louder than the main drive wheels had been.

Bits of rubber gasket flaked away as the whole rear end-cap opened downward, stopped, and unfolded again to create a ramp to the ground. Gabriella panicked at the sight of the military vehicle, and tried to run. One of the women grabbed her and held on; the child started screaming.

Nina pushed open the driver's hatch and leaned out far enough to wave. "We're back. Don't be afraid. Get in quick."

The girl quieted. Ramon stared at her in disbelief; animosity receded from his expression, leaving him somber. Pedro and Roberto helped José walk. Francisco, Josefina, Patricia, four men Nina hadn't seen before, and some of the children carried boxes and plastic crates. Adrianna walked on her own, though had a noticeable limp. The middle-aged woman from the house also joined them, holding a pair of cats.

It took about six minutes for everyone to get on.

Someone in back hit a button, which activated the ramp. As soon as the secondary flap folded closed, Nina reversed away from the barn, turned, and accelerated north. The endcap sealed with a resounding *thud* two seconds later.

The soft din of mumbled conversation filled the troop section. Most sounded guardedly hopeful that they might survive the trip to the UCF. One of the unfamiliar men questioned the wisdom of going into the Badlands, fearing superstition

"Patricia," yelled María Isabel. "Can you check this beast for a transponder? Nina said you might gotta disable it."

"On it," called Patricia.

Nina stared into the rolling green-on-black of a night vision view. She got the BTR rolling at seventy-two before the shaking and shuddering worried her enough to stop accelerating. The massive tires laughed at bushes, small boulders, and cacti alike, though she made some effort to avoid hitting obstacles. When she did run something over, the only indication came as a soft *thump*, without perceptible shock.

Patricia opened the side door on the right.

"What are you doing?" yelled Nina.

"That thing you want me to fry is on the roof. I gotta go up there."

"Let me slow down."

"Nah." Patricia waved her off. "I got it. There's plenty of handholds."

Josefina, a slender girl of about nineteen, jogged up behind her. "I will watch you."

Nina started to question, but remembered someone referring to her as a telekinetic. She shifted her attention back to the viewscreen and focused on keeping the ride as steady as possible. Eventually, the system auto-shifted to standard view when the sun rose in the east. Vibrant color replaced bland monochromatic green.

A few minutes after full daylight spread over the desert, Patricia let out a yelp of surprise, and floated in the door. "Found it. Was a self-contained unit with an internal power supply. I unbolted it and tossed it over the side."

"Let's hope they're superstitious and won't come looking."

She kept the BTR going in a more or less straight line for a few hours. The Resistance people sat in silence save for the frightened mewling of two cats.

"Why are you worried?" asked Veronica.

Nina glanced at the waifish girl hovering in the opening between the driver's compartment and the back. Her too-large shirt and fatigue pants obscured most of her shape; large eyes and a pixie haircut made her seem younger than fourteen. "We're in a BTR-99 driving into the Badlands on the way to the UCF. Any rational person would be nervous."

"You're afraid they'll mistake us for bad guys and blow us up." Veronica leaned in at an angle that would put her on the floor if her hand slipped off the doorway. "Aren't 'cha?"

"It's a possibility. They are expecting us, but... I don't think they're expecting this vehicle."

"Where are we going?" Veronica swooped forward, standing against Nina's seat, half in her lap, eyes locked on the display screen. "That's pretty cool."

Nina wondered if she'd remember any English by the time she got back home, and grinned. "We selected an abandoned town in the Badlands... Topowa, in what used to be called Arizona. Once we get there, I'm going to call for a ride."

Veronica kept staring at the screen. "Cool. If we don't get killed, I want to work for your psionic police. I want to be a therapist or something, helping psionics who've been abused."

Nina smiled. "You'll make a great therapist. And getting into Division 0 is easier than you think."

"You don't really know me, so you're just saying I'll be a great therapist to be nice." Veronica looked at her and smiled. "It's okay. Thanks for making me feel better. I'm kinda scared too."

The girl returned to the troop area.

Nina drove toward the Navcon grid reference for Topawa. The BTR's navigation system had no maps for the Badlands aside from a 'do not go here' warning, though it did show real-time coordinates.

At 12:17 p.m., the dust-covered remnants of a small town appeared in the distance. Most of the buildings had collapsed or been shot full of holes. Carcasses of ancient war machines littered the area, blackened and surrounded by mounds of windblown sand. She spotted a dingy white wall with a stubby steeple over a round-topped gate. To the right, the structure had a porch of arches by a small grove of trees. A vast breach in one of the old mission's walls looked big enough to let the BTR into the courtyard. Nina figured a bomb or missile had hit it during the war, as no one out and about in the Badlands had anything capable of inflicting that sort of damage.

She slowed to a crawl and lined the enormous vehicle up with the hole. Gentle taps of the sticks eased the BTR over the ruins. It climbed the three-foot high rubble mound with ease and bounced to a stop in the courtyard. She shut down the power and exhaled a sigh of relief.

"Okay. Try to remain inside this building so no one sees you. Best plan is to stay hidden until my friends show up." Nina grabbed the micro satellite unit out of her backpack. "I'll be right back."

The resistance people climbed down from the side doors, and dispersed around the courtyard in search of an outhouse after such a long ride. Nina jogged over to the front gate and climbed a rickety set of wooden stairs to the room within the steeple. If there had ever been a bell here, it had been scavenged ages ago.

She sat at the edge and opened the sat-comm unit. A telescoping rod expanded into a receiving antenna as six-inch tapered black wafers infused with glimmering silver wires opened. She positioned it facing the general direction of West City. The unit had a built in M3 wire, which she plugged in. A virtual holo-panel opened, with the words ‹Searching for Signal› on it. *Come on, come on...* The small dish pivoted left a few degrees, raised a bit, and edged right two clicks. ‹Satellite Acquired. Handshaking.›

A twentyish man in a green camo uniform appeared in another window. ⌈Unidentified female, you have accessed a restricted communication channel. Please provide identification.⌋

⌈Oh, wow. It would've been nice if they'd mentioned this would go straight to you guys. Lieutenant Nina Duchenne, Division 9.⌋

His annoyed expression evaporated and he rendered a salute. ⌈Lieutenant. Good to see you. Yes, we're aware of your mission. Are you in position?⌋

Nina's avatar returned the salute. ⌈Yes. We are in position and awaiting extraction. Twenty individuals plus myself.⌋

⌈Copy that, lieutenant. Sit tight. We're on the way.⌋

⌈Great. Much appreciated.⌋

She shut down the unit and collapsed the dish. When she stood, she caught sight of a dust trail in the south. *Oh, shit...* Nina moved to the edge and braced a hand on the hot white stucco. Her vision zoomed in on the disturbance.

Three vehicles approached. Two resembled the BTR-99, but half the size with only six wheels. They reminded her of a Corporate version of an A3V, only more brick-shaped. The smaller BTRs flanked a similar truck, but instead of a troop-transport body, it carried a dual-pod missile battery. Two boxy launchers on either side of an array of targeting electronics each held twenty square hatches.

*Missile artillery? Seriously? Oh, they know exactly what I just blew up... someone got fired and someone else wants heads.*

"Fuck."

She set the dish up again and stared at it, trying to command it to link up faster through sheer force of will. When the same man appeared, she mentally yelled, ⌈We've got incoming. Two troop carriers and a missile truck. They're going to be on us in less than ten minutes.⌋

The man grimaced and held up a hand in a 'wait' gesture. He stared into nowhere for a few seconds before his gaze again focused on her. ⌈You'll need to hold out for ten to fifteen minutes. I've let the extraction team know you're in a bad way. They're flying hard, lieutenant.⌋

She exhaled. ⌈Thanks.⌋

Nina unplugged the wire and ran while collapsing the sat-comm back into its case. She leapt out the tower window to the courtyard, taking the thirty-foot fall in stride. "Pedro!"

Pedro Del Olmo looked up from where he stood among a circle of men. Almost everyone else, including children, froze and stared at her.

Nina jogged up to him. "We've got a big problem. ACC is coming. I don't think they saw me drive in here, but they've got an anti-tank missile unit. They at least know we've got that BTR."

"Damn." Pedro rubbed his chin, eyes shifting among the resistance people. "Ramon, take the kids and find a basement. Bring Mrs. Rojo... and her cats. If there's no basement, hide in the truck."

"Bad idea," said Nina. "The BTR will be the first thing they shoot. Being anywhere near it is a death trap. If there's no basement, go into the town, find a ruined house and look for a basement there."

Ramon nodded, and ran off to gather the children plus one cranky middle-aged woman and a pair of yowling, terrified cats.

"What about that gun?" asked María Isabel.

Nina shook her head. "It might be able to take out the missile carrier, but in order to do that, we'd have to expose the BTR to direct fire. That gun's got a range of about two miles, the missiles, probably forty or fifty. Even if you got a clear shot, I don't think you'd hit it hard enough, fast enough, to stop it from launching a missile... or twenty. One of those hitting the front end would kill you."

"So... not worth it." María Isabel frowned.

Nina pointed at the remains of four huge buildings across a dirt lot from the mission. "We need to get away from the BTR and out of this courtyard. It's a kill zone. Spread out among the ruins over there. Stay down."

"What if they fire those missiles at us?" asked one of the men from the house.

"That type of vehicle usually carries anti-tank missiles. I don't think the ACC would waste them on individual people since they cost so much... but even if they did, it's a shaped charge warhead designed to punch holes in heavy armor. If you're spread out far enough, they'll only get one. Our best chance right now is to stay out of sight and hope they drive right on by."

"We're screwed," muttered Silvia. She faced north, watching the children follow Ramon through a small hole in the wall. Nicolás paused long enough to wave goodbye, and she bowed her head to wipe tears.

"Don't give up," said Nina. "My friends are on the way."

José grunted in pain and straightened. "How long?"

"Eight to thirteen minutes." Nina waved at people to get them moving west.

"How long will it take the problem to get here?" José held on to Roberto for support as he speed-walked.

"About eight minutes," said Nina, her voice grim.

"Easy then." José forced a smile. "We're good at hiding."

The resistance hurried across the dirt lot and scattered among the remains of several buildings. Nina got down behind a section of concrete wall with bent steel rebar rods protruding from the top.

She waited.

Soon, the labored whine of e-motors and the squeaking of axles overtook the rasp of anxious breathing nearby.

*Drive right on by. Don't see anything. Everyone, please stay the fuck down. No one be a hero.*

A *whoosh* lasted less than a second before a concussive *boom* knocked powder and most of the stucco off the mission's outer wall. Nina cringed against her cover. Another distant *whoosh* preceded a second explosion that sent bits of molten armor spraying in an orange fountain from the middle of the courtyard.

"Mother of God," muttered one of the men from the house.

She looked at him and whispered, "Stay down."

He patted his chest. "Manuel Zambrano. I respect what you have tried to do for us."

Another set of e-motors whirred closer and stopped. A *hiss* and a *clank* rang out, followed by the repetitive clatter of boots on metal.

*Dammit.* Nina drew her pistol. "They know we're here."

"Shit!" yelled Patricia, somewhere off to the right and ahead.

A rifle shot rang out, triggering a sustained barrage from both sides. Projectiles *pinged* off concrete and zipped overhead. Manuel popped up only far enough to get his rifle over the wall, and let off a few shots.

Nina triggered her speedware and sat up, raising her MCP50.

One of the six-wheeled transports had stopped at the southernmost edge of the rubble, less than three feet away from the southernmost wall where Josefina and another man from the house—Fernando she thought—hunkered down.

Men in ACC desert armor spread out along the other side of the same wall, oblivious to the two of them so close. Blue bursts of muzzle fire popped and faded in slow motion all around her. It seemed everyone on both sides decided to be over cautious, and so far, the only thing to bleed had been concrete. Nina's ears filtered the gunshots to a point where she knew them for firearms going off, but could still hear the resistance people shouting to each other.

"On the left," yelled a man.

"Watch that gap," said Patricia. "They're trying for it."

Josefina stared up at the barrel of a rotary gun atop the smaller BTR. It seemed to have trouble aiming down far enough to shoot at any of the resistance, and emitted strained noises while twitching in jerky motions.

*Telekinesis?*

Nina put her virtual crosshair over the one-inch gold square next to the barrel. Her 15mm pistol wouldn't penetrate the BTR's armor, but she could blind the gunner. She fired two slugs at the mounted gun's 'eye,' before shifting her aim to the right and firing at the sudden appearance of a helmet. Two rifles on the left side of the transport swiveled toward her; she ducked as soon as her third bullet left the barrel.

Dust sprayed off the wall above her head three relative seconds after she'd crouched.

José screamed.

"Dammit man," yelled Nina, "Stay down! You're injured."

"Little more so now." José coughed.

His voice came from a position directly in front of her at the next wall.

She sucked in a breath, preparing to pop up again when a little girl behind her yelled.

"*Stop!*"

Nina whirled to her left.

Gabriella, the eight-year-old, stared up at a DMS soldier who'd snuck around to the rear. He hovered inches from María Isabel's back, with a huge Nano knife poised to jam into the side of her throat. The child balled her fists and stomped her bare foot as she leaned aggressively toward him.

"*Kill the missile truck man.*" The girl's eyes glowed with faint amber light.

The soldier with the knife repeated, "Kill the missile truck man," in Spanish burdened with a thick German accent. He spun on his heel and fast-stalked back around the wall.

Nina's artificial eyes spotted a colorless laser dot—infrared—race by on the ground, and climb onto Gabriella's chest. She kicked on her speedware and sprinted. The heavy thunder of the BTR's machinegun hammered the air. Nina dove into a tackle, grabbing Gabriella as she flew by, and rolling to land on her back to avoid drilling the girl into the dirt.

They slid about fifteen feet from the force of Nina's lunge. She sprang to the left and set the girl in the remains of a sunken stairwell that would've gone to a basement if it hadn't become a debris-filled pit. The hiding spot put her below ground level, and out of reach of bullets.

"Stay there," said Nina.

Gabriella nodded.

Gunfire continued in a series of lazy single pops and faster three-taps. Rifle slugs sprayed over her. Three hit her back at too shallow an angle to penetrate the ballistic stealth armor. She pushed herself off the ground with enough force to fling her body six feet into the air. On the way up, she aimed toward the incoming fire, spotting two men continuing to shoot at the ground below her. At the apex, she lined up the crosshair with one man's forehead, and fired. Two feet into the fall, she sent a bullet at the second man.

She brought her legs up to land on her feet, transitioning into a sprint as the men she'd shot slumped over dead. Two soldiers leapt the wall by Josefina and Roberto, startled by finding them so close. Roberto fired a burst into the one on his side; the other soldier pointed his rifle at Josefina, who had no weapon, but the gun leapt out of his hands before he could fire. The instant she caught it, Nina's bullet punched into his right eye.

Josefina scrambled to get the rifle oriented toward the man, firing as soon as she got a proper grip, even as the exploded remains of his head rained over her.

Nina ran to a thick section of concrete and dove to the ground, taking cover. She cut her speedware and stared back at the stairwell where she'd stashed Gabriella. Predictably, the girl started climbing out. "Gaby! Stay down."

María Isabel sprang up, aiming and firing at different targets so fast she almost appeared to have speedware—albeit slower than Nina's. An errant round caused a spray of blood from her left thigh, and she crumpled, screaming.

Footsteps approached the wall Nina hid behind. She looked up, waiting.

As soon as an armored glove grabbed the top of the wall, she extended the Nano blades in her left arm. When the soldier went to jump over her, she reared up and drove them into his chest. The claws pierced his armor like papier mâché; her fist crushed the chestplate to splinters and launched him off the blades, his body flying back at least twenty feet. He struck a slab of wall, flipped over the top, and fell out of sight.

Nina stood with the momentum of the punch and aimed again at the BTR's machine gun. Sparks sputtered from a square hole where the gold targeting sensor used to be, and the barrel pointed off to the side, abandoned.

*Shit. There's another one.*

Five soldiers decided to leap a wall together, while spraying bullets wildly in front of them. Their attack focused on a group of resistance hiding in the row behind Nina's, giving her five easy shots. To the non-speedware world, Nina's hand cannon would've seemed like it had fired an automatic burst. Five slugs pierced five helmets within the span of a second and change.

Leticia, near the back on the left side, popped up and opened fire on two ACC soldiers attempting to climb rubble on the eastern side.

"Castillion, get down," shouted one of the men from the house. "You'll get hit."

"Get up and help me, Jesús!" Leticia fired a few more rounds, ducking only after the ACC troops gave up trying to cross that wall.

The two of them got into a whispered argument, when Jesús said she was 'too young and pretty' to get shot, she went off on him, rage-screaming while continuing to snap shots off at the spot the enemy tried to climb.

Nina ducked out of sight again, listening for movement. She glanced at the stairwell, and didn't see Gabriella. *Please be staying down. Don't have run off.*

An explosion a good way to the right knocked a ghost image of a wall into the air, rendered in dust. Less than a second later, Silvia tumbled away from the collapsing slab, half somersaulting on purpose, half sliding from the blast. Smoke and dust whorled into a plume where the ancient concrete collapsed. Blood trailed in streams out of her arm, leg, and back from shrapnel wounds. The second BTR sat some distance back from the southernmost wall; its gun turret swiveled toward Silvia, since she'd skidded out into the open.

Nina aimed at it, but the crosshair went red with ‹240m› below it. At that range, she didn't trust her pistol to reach. She hauled ass toward Silvia, stuffing her pistol in its holster. Bullets from both sides passed back and forth in front and behind her.

Deep, staccato explosions erupted in the distance, a long plume of blue flickered in her periphery from the end of a single-barreled cannon.

She leapt into a dive, reaching for Silvia. Her hand met cloth; she torqued around in midair and threw the woman toward the wall. Static marred her vision. The world flashed to black for an instant. Incessant beeping filled her head. She lay on the ground, moving… no—being dragged. Nina stared up at sky. Her crosshair zipped around like a drunken moth, graphics scrambled. Thin lines of static hovered before her eyes, creeping down in a repetitive banding effect. She looked up at Silvia, who dragged her by the right arm. She tried to reach up and grab her, but her left arm ended at the elbow in a loose tatter of grey Myofiber muscles and wires. Dark green nanofluid and red blood leaked out onto her shirt.

*23mm explosive rounds.* Shock caused Nina to stare at the stump far longer than her psyche could bear the reminder of her artificiality. Seeing the plastisteel bone and polymer muscles filled her with the urge to scream, but her jaw wouldn't move.

"Nina?" Silvia dragged her up against the wall. "Are you alive?"

The rush of battle overwhelmed her senses, as the momentary fugue of non-space faded. She lost the will to move, staring up at the clouds. *Alive? I haven't been alive for a long time.* "I'm awake."

Silvia squeezed her hand. "You saved my ass…"

*I should've been dead eighteen months ago. I'm a monster.*

Elizaveta's face appeared in her mind, filthy, trapped in a primate cage and staring up at her with adoration. Apathy became guilt. She growled at herself for almost giving up, and forced her body to sit up. A status window opened, helpfully indicating that her left arm had been damaged.

*Thanks. I didn't notice.*

A power surge in her control lines had knocked her targeting, optics, and other headware systems offline, but aside from the arm, everything seemed to stabilize in six seconds. Already, her automatic repair system nanobots had plugged the leaking tubes.

"You're hurt." Nina looked Silvia over. She'd been peppered with shrapnel from a hand grenade, probably had minutes left before bleeding out.

"Just bleeding... nothing broke." Silvia forced a smile. "You'll take Nicolás ... make sure he's safe."

Nina grasped the woman's shoulder. "I'm a hypocrite, but don't give up. Hold on just a little longer."

Silvia sucked in air between her teeth.

A male voice screaming a war cry made her snap her head up and left.

An ACC soldier vaulted the wall above them. Red error text scrolled by the bottom of her vision, but her speedware came on. Nina surged to her feet and caught the man's rifle as his boots touched dirt, pushing it aside and high. The bullets meant for Silvia's face went off to kill clouds. She tore the weapon out of his grip, twisting into a spin.

His face faded ashen; his gaze locked on her smashed arm.

At the same instant his mouth opened to release a cry of terror at finding himself squaring off against a doll, Nina roared in fury and drove her leg into his chest. Cracks raced around his hard-shelled chestplate while the front crumpled inward. The body flew back, breaking off the top two feet of a debris wall before punching a hole through another larger wall behind it. The corpse struck a third wall a few meters later, but lacked the energy to penetrate it, instead winding up draped over it, facing up, back bent at an angle possible only with a liquefied spine.

Nina came out of the spin kick, tossed the rifle up, and caught it by the grip. One-handing it, she sprayed bullets in haste at a trio of soldiers on the right trying to climb into the Resistance position. They abandoned their effort to flank the wounded José, who hadn't done much but hold his gun up and shoot blind for the past minute. Nina fired at the spot to keep them down.

Silvia gawked at the path the solder broke in the walls. She attempted to sit up, but grimaced and went limp. "I'm not going to make it, but thanks for trying."

"There's too many," shouted Francisco.

"Stay put, Rios," roared Pedro. "If you stand, you'll die."

Josefina let off a war cry before a burst of automatic fire went off. "Got one!" she yelled.

"We're absolutely fucked," shouted Francisco. "There's like dozens more coming."

"No surrender!" screamed Josefina.

Nina leaned left until she could make out the second BTR, the one that had tagged her with its cannon.

*Guess ballistic stealth isn't quite up to stopping 23 mm heat rounds.*

The cannon sprayed intermittently at the walls, but Josefina seemed to be attempting to foul its aim with telekinesis, though due to the distance, she had far less luck. Strain showed clear in the rivers of sweat rolling off her face. Nina leaned out from cover and tried to draw a bead on the gold square; the rifle didn't have a targeting uplink, so no floating crosshair. Time dragged down to a near-standstill as she tried to make out the sensor with iron sights.

As soon as she pointed the rifle at the BTR, the side door opened and a man started to leap out. She felt impressive for about a second until a flash of white caught her eye. A fat, white missile streaked overhead, trailed by another at a higher trajectory. The missile plunged into the roof of the BTR, less than three feet from the cannon, and the vehicle swelled up like an overinflated balloon before breaking apart into an uncountable number of glittering fragments riding the surface of an expanding orange bloom of energy.

Seconds later, the tremor of an explosion rocked the earth under her feet.

She shifted her attention to the other streak of white, which fell upon the missile carrier that had stopped perhaps a quarter mile away. The detonation interrupted an ACC soldier stabbing one of his comrades that he'd pulled halfway out the driver's side door. Watching a man kill soldiers from his own unit at the command of a psionic child made her shiver.

Streaks of brilliant orange traced across the sky, rapid lightning strikes of pin straight energy. Nina smiled. Two DS2 dropships in olive drab raced by 200 feet off the ground, ion engines roaring like demons. A third came in slow and low, opening its belly ramp as the pilot brought it to a hover at the north edge of the destroyed buildings, behind the Resistance position.

Nina raised her right arm, waving her rifle around and yelling, "Our ride's here."

Twenty UCF Marines, about half women, rushed forward with rifles poised.

"Resistance, hit the deck and stay down!" screamed Nina, as she too dove for cover next to Silvia.

Particle cannons screeched in the distance with a flurry of electric whirr-*brzaaatz* sounds. The Marines advanced rapidly, firing every few seconds.

Nina looked up as green camouflage armor went by. "We need a medic here!"

"Umm," the woman looked at her arm with confusion before noticing Silvia. "Burnett! Get over here!" She pulled three stimpaks from a compartment on her belt and tossed them to Nina, before raising her rifle again and leaping the wall to keep moving forward.

Nina grabbed a stimpak and bit the safety cap off. Silvia injected herself with the other two while Nina gave her one in the thigh.

"That'll buy the medic time." Nina smiled. "You're not dying yet."

Gunfire petered out. The Marines shouted 'clear' at each other.

"Hey," said a youngish voice.

Nina whirled around to find Josefina walking up behind her, holding a sparking left hand and forearm.

"I saw this flying off and caught it." Josefina opened her fingers and Nina's hand/forearm levitated up and glided over to her. "Figured you might want it back. I, uhh, think that's a little beyond Patricia to fix."

Nina tossed her borrowed rifle aside, and refused to look as she took hold of her severed arm. She doubted the techs would use it instead of replacing the entire limb from the shoulder down, but a strange attachment made her not want to leave it here in the dirt. "Thanks."

A man in his early twenties wearing UCF armor hurried over with a large white case in his hand. He skidded to a stop on his knees and opened the medkit. "You're gonna be just fine."

"I bet you use that line on all the girls." Nina smiled. "Grenade shrapnel."

"Got it." Sergeant Burnett glanced at her. "Ouch. What happened to you?"

"23 millimeter. Probably heat." She continued looking up.

"Duchenne?" yelled a dark-skinned man in UCF armor, walking while looking around in circles as if calling for a lost dog. "Duchenne?"

She got to her feet. "Here."

The man swiveled toward her and strode over. He seemed a bit older than the rest, perhaps later thirties. His nametag read: Parrish, M, and his armor had captain insignia in battlefield black.

Nina saluted him using the disembodied hand. "Captain Parrish. Thanks for the timely assist."

"Damn dolls." He grinned. "Think you can take on A BTR-44, huh?"

"I almost had him." She grimaced and moved her severed hand, and stump, out of her field of view.

"You have anyone in that '99, lieutenant?" Captain Parrish nodded to the left.

"No, Sir. I figured they'd hit that first... and they did."

"Ramon, bring the little ones back," shouted Pedro. "Everyone, group up."

"Not a bad job, lieutenant. Looks like most of your people survived. Several wounded, but nothing untreatable."

"Most?" Nina's heart sank. "Who...?"

"Ramon..." Veronica approached from the northeast, leading Rafael, Gabriella, Nicolás, the bandaged-up Adrianna, the five-year-old boy, and Mrs. Rojo with her two yowling cats. "He left me in charge of the kids. Said he wanted to get revenge for Javier." She sniffled. "I don't know where he is."

Gabriella looked up with a smile. "He's in the mission. I made him hide instead of being stupid." She offered a cheesy smile. "He's going to be mad at me."

"That's why you were out here," muttered Nina.

The girl nodded.

María Isabel limped over and wrapped her arms around the girl, shuddering and sobbing. "You saved my ass."

"We can't loiter here long." Captain Parrish glanced off at the sky. "Watson, Hughes, set down north of the town."

The remaining two dropships circled around and came in to land about fifty meters away; their ramp doors and landing pads opened at the same time, fully extended by the time the ships touched down.

Nicolás ran to Silvia, crying with relief.

"Come on, lieutenant. Looks like you're about ready to get out of here," said Parrish.

Nina's grip clenched around her loose arm. *Elizaveta's waiting for me.* "Yes, sir. Damn ready."

# SECOND CHANCES

Katya curled up at the right end of her new couch, which mostly resembled her old couch except for the blood and bullet holes. She had her bare feet tucked under a small pile of decorative pillows and her body wrapped in a knee-length lavender t-shirt. Steam wafted from a cereal bowl-sized mug of honey-lemon-chamomile she clutched in both hands to her face. Inhaling the wonderful aroma took a fraction of the edge off her worry.

After a brief sip of the still-too-hot tea, she stared over the rim of the mug at the terminal on the coffee table. So far, an entire day of 'I'll check the jobs right after I finish (random task)' had passed. Almost four in the afternoon on Tuesday, she'd run out of excuse-chores, and hadn't touched the terminal since Saturday night.

*I'm only good for one thing, and I'm not going to find it there.*

The Division 9 warning left her afraid to call Alex even to say hello. They had to know what she'd done, but they let her slide. Perhaps it had been a 'thank you' for tripping over a spy. She sipped her tea again, warm, cozy, and comfortable.

Eve muttered in the back of the apartment, talking to her video game. No surprise, she adored *Colony Commando*… it reminded her of being in her powered armor. That she'd called it 'realistic enough to keep me from getting rusty' worried her. *No wonder everyone in this place has guns.*

Beeping came from the terminal. Its holo projector activated, displaying a black screen with the words ‹Incoming vidcall.›

"What?" She blinked and lowered the mug.

The terminal beeped again.

Katya scooted forward, exposing her feet to the chilly air, and swiped her hand at the screen to answer.

A man in his forties with grey-pewter hair in a buzz cut appeared on the screen. His high-collared black jacket looked like a blend of military uniform and middle-of-the-road suit. "Miss Wolf?"

"Yes." She cradled the tea in her lap.

"Good." He nodded. "I'm Anton Burdine with Sentinel Corporation. We recently received your resume in regards to a security analyst position with our company."

She blinked. "Umm. Yes." *Two weeks ago... about.*

Anton offered a slight bow with an apologetic smile. "Initially, your resume seemed a bit light on qualifications for the spot... however, it resurfaced and piqued my interest. My call is more or less a pre-interview interview. I have some questions for you... assuming you are still interested in the position."

"Yes." She hurriedly set the tea on the table. "I'm sorry I'm not quite dressed for it."

"It's no matter. I did call you unexpectedly. Would you prefer we schedule this for a later time?"

She straightened her posture, trying to seem as composed and formal as possible while dressed like a twelve-year-old at a sleepover party. "If you don't mind, I don't."

"Very well. Can you elaborate a bit more on your experience with the security industry in general? Again, what you've got on your resume is a start, but normally we require a greater amount of experience for this role. The security analyst is responsible for going to client sites and evaluating them for their security needs, devising an operational plan, and once the client signs on, you'd be the point of contact to manage our presence there. SAs usually have between ten and forty sites to manage. Each site can have between two and hundreds of guards/staff depending on size."

Katya leaned a few inches closer to the terminal. "Mr. Burdine, is this vid considered confidential?"

His eyebrows flared as he nodded. "Oh yes. Absolutely. It is no different from an employment interview in that regard."

"All right. I am a former ghost emplo—rather owned by the Office of Operational Intelligence of the Allied Corporate Council. I was 'recruited' at the age of ten, trained in infiltration, electronics, social engineering, surveillance, marksmanship, demolitions, and network operations until the age of eighteen. I've had nine years of fieldwork, mostly in Russia and Pakistan, with several months spent in Central America. About a year ago, while on assignment in London, I saw an opportunity to escape and defect to the UCF."

Anton stared at her mute for a full minute, blinking once. "No shit..."

Her lips curled in a cat-that-got-the-canary smile. "I am quite serious. You'd be surprised how many Zosco 4200s are still out there with the multi-input channel vulnerability not patched. Link four camera inputs to the same logical designation, remove one, re-add it, and the system accepts root-level commands regardless of user rights. Can fake every input from that point."

Anton's lower lip protruded as his eyebrows rose. "Impressive."

"When I said 'recruited,' I meant abducted. I am a legal UCF citizen. I doubt anyone here could detest the Corporates as much as I do."

"I believe you. Probably more than half the shitheads out there who don't know how good they've got it here."

Katya grinned. "You're former military, aren't you?"

"What gave it away, the hair?" He chuckled. "Look, Miss Wolf... I'd like to schedule you for an in-person interview. How does tomorrow around 11:00 a.m. sound?"

Relief and pride washed over her. "I will be there."

He raised a hand in mock pause. "Oh, and please come in via the main entrance. This isn't an evaluation of your ability to do penetration testing."

Katya nodded. "Understood."

"Great. Looking forward to meeting you in person."

She got no sense of anything other than professionalism from him, and smiled. "As am I."

The holo-panel collapsed to a point and faded out. Katya picked up her lukewarm tea and resumed her cozy position, enjoying it quite a bit more despite its tepidness. She could do far worse than working for Sentinel. Life wouldn't be opulent, but she'd take the comfort without hesitation.

Eve walked in, wearing a loose plum-colored half-shirt, black spandex shorts, and a pistol in a thigh holster. "Who were you talking to?"

"What's that?" Katya glanced at the weapon.

"MCP18C. Basic model, 6mm standard-issue UCF military sidearm. Thirty-eight round capacity, maximum effective range 150 meters, sixty with iron sights." Eve frowned. "It's only a Class 2, but my dinky little arms won't handle the recoil of anything much bigger."

"That's not what I meant." Katya stared at her. "I meant why are you walking around with a gun?"

"In case any more shit goes down."

Katya laughed. "You're less creepy when you act like a child."

Eve shrugged, palms upturned. "Wouldn't that be *more* creepy?"

"I suppose."

The girl crossed her arms. "It's bad enough I have to watch myself at school. I look like I'm eight. Kids this age know basic math and reading... not seven different ways to kill someone with a table fork."

"Well... did you go to school before?"

Eve shook her head. "No. I've already told you, I popped out of the tank this size, and went straight to combat training. I mean, yeah they taught us English and some math and stuff."

Katya patted the seat next to her. "Give it some time. Maybe it'll start feeling like a strange dream, and you can let yourself have a childhood. Stop overthinking everything and just enjoy yourself while you can." She sighed. "I wish I could have my fourteen-year-old body back. If I even *look* at food now, my ass gets wider."

Eve grinned and crawled up beside her. "Will you *stop*? You're a damn supermodel."

"Hah."

"I'm serious. I'd kill someone to have tits like yours." Eve lifted her shirt. "I got nothin'."

"You're eight."

Eve stuck out her tongue. "And you're not fat. You're not even close to fat. You're not even heavy enough to be considered 'ideal weight.'"

"Pff." Katya ruffled her hair. She hit the remote for the holo-bar and went to one of the kids' channels, which showed a cartoon with talking rabbits.

Eve smirked. "Really?"

"Looks like a child"—Katya poked her in the side—"must be a child."

The girl raspberried her.

Katya stuck out her tongue.

"Yanno... I think this might actually work." Eve cuddled up against her. "I'm glad you decided to let me stay with you."

"Me too, 'kiddo.'" Katya put an arm around her.

"So, who was on the vid before?"

"Some guy."

"You're dating?"

Katya laughed. "No. I've got a job interview."

"Like a legit job?" Eve blinked. "Why?"

"I figured we should give this whole 'normal' thing a try. I can't remember a time when I didn't constantly worry about getting killed or captured."

Eve held up a foot, examining purple nail polish that had started to flake. "You don't think you'll get bored?"

"That's what I'm hoping for." Katya pulled Eve snug. "A few good, long years of being bored. And you, little lady, are not allowed to kill anyone until you're at least eighteen."

"I'm twenty," muttered Eve.

"Legally eighteen." Katya tapped her on the nose. "I mean it. No gunfights."

Eve giggled. "Okay, *Mom*."

# FREAK

Kenny snapped awake in the middle of the night. An inexplicable sense of worry circled around his heart like a buzzard. He rolled his head to the left, relieved to find Kathy sound asleep at his side. For a few minutes, he stared at the ceiling, but between anxiety and the need to urinate, sleep refused to return.

He sat up; motion annoyed the contents of his stomach, and he stifled a shrimp-scampi laden belch. *Ugh. Think I overdid it a bit with 'real' food. Maybe that's why I can't sleep.* Arthur Polini had met him at the restaurant, and they had conducted business before dinner. The Syndicate man seemed pleased with the statue, and they'd made good on their offer of payment. He didn't get the feeling they'd be making another request of him, so his worry couldn't be coming from the dread of running afoul of organized crime. It didn't matter if the law discovered the job he'd done for them; none of it had been illegal. Even criminals sometimes hired legitimate people to do legitimate work.

He stumbled to the bathroom, thudding a fist into his chest to dislodge a gas bubble. Eyes half-closed, he swayed on his feet in front of the toilet while his mind replayed the events of his Badlands trip. Exploding millipedes, screaming wife and children, growling dogs.

Alyssa had showed off her bruise once they'd gotten home. The outline of her armored vest couldn't have been more well defined if someone had used an auto-sprayer to paint it on her in purple. He couldn't figure out what worried him more: that she'd been shot, or that she thought it 'cool' to take a bullet and walk away with a mere bruise.

After finishing off, he stumbled toward bed, but decided to wander the hallway. At the end, he peered into Alyssa's room. She lay sprawled on her bed, arms and legs going in all directions, mouth open.

*Heh. Poor kid's exhausted. At least she can sleep.*

He backed up and went to Hayley's room; they'd given her the former guest bedroom, which had become her permanent room. As he got close, the evident sound of muffled crying pierced the fog in his mind. Worried, he brushed the door aside.

Hayley sat on the rug, wearing a gossamer pink nightie with unbuttoned jeans not quite all the way up her legs, sobbing into her hands. Next to her, an open backpack held some hastily-packed clothes. It seemed as though she'd been in the process of getting dressed, but stopped.

"Hayley?" He walked in.

She sniffled.

"Hey..." Kenny hurried over and sat on the floor beside her. "What's wrong? What's with the bag?"

"I was gonna leave, so you didn't have to put up with me... but I don't wanna go. I like it here. I like having a home." She sobbed harder. "But... you think I'm psionic, and you're gonna hate me."

"Stop being silly. Whatever made you think I would hate you for being psionic?"

She looked up at him; her red-ringed eyes widened. "'Cause, everyone thinks psionics are freaks. They're either scared of 'em, or they wanna kill 'em. I didn't want people to be mean to you an' Liss, and Kathy 'cause I'm here."

Kenny pulled her into a hug. "I don't care what anyone thinks. You're no freak. Even if you are a psionic, that don't change a thing about how happy we are to have you in this family."

For a few minutes, she bawled into his shirt. Every so often, an apology slipped out between sobs.

"You don't need to apologize for being special."

"No..." She managed a weak smile while wiping her eyes. "I'm sorry for almost running away."

"You didn't, though." He kissed the top of her head.

She leaned forward and pulled a few shirts out of the backpack, returning them to the dresser. "I was gonna, but I chickened out. Feels safe here."

"Most kids your age would've preferred to stay with Joey or the Rodriguezes while we went after that horse. You wanted to stay with your family." He shook his head. "Never should've taken you out there."

She shrugged.

"Suppose it worked out. We would've been in bad shape without you." He squeezed her shoulder and patted her back. "That why you think you're psionic?"

"Yeah a bit... and the way I felt so weird out there the whole time, like I could tell something watched us. The way the truck worked when I wanted it to and the bots... and Joey said I did some stuff with only a senshelmet that I shouldn't have able to do."

"Well, if you want, we can have someone check... so you know. It's your choice."

She shivered. "Will they take me away?"

"No."

"But everyone says they take psionic kids away from their families." She clung to him. "I don't wanna go."

"I'm pretty sure they're only taking in the kids whose parents are idiots. I can give Joey a call in the morning and see if he knows how true those rumors are."

Hayley nodded. "Okay... if they're not gonna take me away, I kinda wanna know."

"All right then. Think you can get back to bed?"

"Yeah." She held on to him for a moment more. "Thanks, Dad."

When she started to let go, Kenny patted her on the back. Hovering in the doorway, he gave her a warm smile as she curled up in bed, and shut off her light.

---

KENNY PACED AROUND THE LIVING ROOM. HAYLEY, ALYSSA, AND KATHY SAT ON THE couch in nervous silence. The fragrance of lunch—chicken tacos—still hung in the air. The girls wore matching navy t-shirts and black jeans, no shoes. Kathy had kept her sweatshirt, but traded her sweat pants for grey jeans and fuzzy pink socks.

Every time he saw those socks, he thought about the joke he'd made about them resembling a housecat that got caught in the autoshower tube's dry cycle and turned into a cotton ball with eyes. Not the most romantic thing to say, but when she'd come out wearing *only* those socks during their senior year of high school, his brain had frozen.

The doorbell rang.

Hayley whined out her nose.

"I can still ask them not to bother," said Kenny.

"It's okay." Hayley bit her lip. "I want to know."

Kenny nodded and went to answer the door. A pair of Division 0 officers, tight black uniforms, silver belts, and big smiles stood on the porch. The man had neat dreadlocks down to his jawline, and a confident air about him. His partner had much lighter bronze skin, long, straight black hair, and an equally large smile.

"Good afternoon. I'm Tactical Officer Randall Moss, and this is my partner, Tactical Officer Mary Lopez."

"We're here at your request," said Officer Lopez. "Regarding Hayley?"

Kenny stood aside to let them in. "Right. Just for the record, she's a little worried about being removed from our home for being psionic... that's rumor, right?"

"Completely," said Officer Moss. "The dorms are for situations where we locate a gifted child who either has been orphaned or whose parents are unable to properly meet their needs."

Hayley looked up as the two officers walked around the couch. "Meet their needs? Does that mean something, or is it just a nice way of saying they didn't want a psionic kid?"

Officer Lopez let out a sad sigh. "It's a nice way to talk about a bad situation."

"We have no issues with her being psionic," said Kathy. "It wouldn't change how we feel about her at all."

"Actually, it would be kinda cool." Alyssa grinned.

"So, how's this work?" Kenny waved his hand about in a small circle. "You can just tell if she is or isn't?"

"More or less." Officer Moss nodded. "What manifestations have occurred, Hayley? I'd like to hear what led you to question if you were psionic."

"Okay." Hayley rambled through a summary of what happened out in the Badlands. "And like months ago, I was living alone so I spent all my time in the 'net. My birth dad was a cop with Division 2, but he died in the line of duty and this crazy AI covered it up... made me think he was still alive. I saw this guy who took himself *way* too seriously, so I wanted to mess with him. Joey's like a 'real' deck jockey and I was keeping up with him even though I only had a helmet."

"Hmm." Officer Lopez moved closer and took a knee in front of her. "Sounds like you may be technokinetic. Have you ever heard anyone's thoughts or tried to send your thoughts into someone else's mind?"

"No." Hayley shook her head. "Only how scared I felt out in the Badlands, like someone was watching me and wanted to hurt me."

"All right. I'm going to take a peek in there and see what's going on. Just relax and let your thoughts go wherever they want. If you feel a sensation like something soft pushing against your forehead, don't fight it."

"Okay."

Kenny moved to stand near Kathy and took her hand.

Officer Lopez stared into Hayley's eyes for about four minutes, neither she nor the girl moving except for an occasional eyebrow twitch. Finally, she straightened up and blinked a few times.

"Well?" asked Hayley.

Officer Lopez nodded with a big smile. "You are psionic, Hayley, what we refer to as a technokinetic. You have an affinity for technology and machines. Sometimes, you'll do something with a machine and not really understand what you're doing, but it works. With a little coaching, you should be able to control it."

Hayley's face had gone paler than usual, and her mouth hung open.

"I didn't see any other gifts there. Telepathy is the most common psionic trait, but it's not unheard of for someone to be strong in one area and have nothing else." Officer Lopez took her hand. "There's no reason to be afraid, sweetie. If you're concerned about how people will react, technokinesis is one of the easiest gifts to conceal. Not that you should feel like it's something shameful that needs to be hidden, but there are people out there..."

"I know." Hayley looked down. "Guess I'm a freak after all."

"You're not a freak," said Kenny.

"Absolutely not." Kathy shook her head.

"That's awesome." Alyssa grinned. "But I'm not playing versus mode against you again. No wonder you always won. We need to co-op *Colony Commando* later and own some lesser mortals."

Hayley laughed.

The blare of western music filled the room. Kenny grabbed at his NetMini. "Hello?"

"Hello, this is Stacy Rios from Ancora Medical. I'm looking for a Mr. Kenneth Marlon."

"No one calls me Kenneth 'cept my mama when she's angry." He chuckled. "You found him."

"It says here you're submitting a custodial application for four juveniles recently repatriated from the Badlands?"

"That's correct."

Hayley, Alyssa, and Kathy stared at him, leaning closer to hear.

"I'm happy to inform you that the kids have cleared medical screening. They've been declared healthy and pathogen-free. We've given them the usual suite of vaccinations. You can pick them up any time now, but do hurry. If you haven't claimed them by the end of the day, they'll go into the system. You've been approved for temporary foster care pending a case worker review, which would be the precursor to adoption."

"Right. We'll be there as soon as possible. Mind sendin' over a nav pin?"

His NetMini chimed.

"Thank ya."

"Have a nice day, Mr. Marlon."

Officer Moss waved his NetMini over Hayley's. "If you have any questions we can answer, please feel free to contact us." He glanced at Kenny and Kathy. "We offer some training programs that might help her if you're interested. There's no cost while she's under eighteen."

"Thanks," said Kenny.

"Whenever you have the time, we'd like to have Hayley come down to the PAC for a few routine aptitude tests. It's possible she may have some latent talents that I missed." Officer Lopez tapped at a datapad for a few seconds. "It's not mandatory, but most psionics find the session helpful, since they gain a better understanding of their capabilities."

"That's up to her." Kenny smiled. "We'll talk about it."

The Division 0 officers shook Kenny's hand, smiled at everyone else, and walked out to a black hovercar parked outside.

Kenny eased the door closed and turned to look at Hayley. "Well…?"

She glanced from him, to Kathy, to the floor. "You're really not gonna be all freaked out about me?"

"Nope." Kenny walked up behind the sofa and ruffled her hair.

"The only one in this house who's at all worried about you being psionic is you." Kathy took her hand. "We love you no matter what you can do."

Hayley grinned.

"Yep." Alyssa gave her a playful punch in the arm. "My sister just got cooler."

Hayley stood. "We should go pick up the rest of the family."

"Where are we gonna put them?" asked Alyssa.

Kenny rubbed his chin. "I think for now, they can camp out in here." He winked at Kathy. "What do you think? Should we add a second story, or should we extend the house back a bit?"

She wrapped her arms around him and rested her head on his shoulder. "I hate stairs."

# A HOT BATH

M asaru folded his arms, watching the security team inventory the boxes of weapons for confiscation. Noriko sat on a block of rubble, rifle across her legs, head bowed. She looked as exhausted as he felt. Each passing minute made the filth of the place dig deeper into his skin. He slipped into a daydream of a clean apartment and a hot bath.

"Kurotai-sama," said Himura Ryozo, the squad leader. "Kurota-heika has been worried."

Masaru shot a pointed glare at the weapon crates. "Daiichi Fuso is not responsible for this aggression. These were foreigners. Corporate Council. Please send my apologies to Hisakawa-san at Daiichi Fuso for missing our meeting. Express my interest in rescheduling at their convenience."

"Yes, Kurotai-sama." Himura bowed. "The area is secure now. A car is on its way to bring you home."

"Thank you, Ryozo-san." Masaru returned the bow, shorter, shallower.

The faint thrum of ion engines in the distance grew over the span of about half a minute to a deafening roar. A dark blue and beige transport craft with stubby wings and a three-finned tail landed in the street outside, hurling great clouds of dust into the building.

Masaru raised an arm to shield his face until the gale subsided.

People in JSDF armor spilled out of two side doors.

"Looks like your associates have arrived," said Masaru.

Noriko grunted and stood, leaning forward to peer out at the transport. "So, yeah... I need to go."

Masaru extended his NetMini. "Can I vid you?"

She glanced down, grinned, and bit her lip while giving him a sly grin. A second before the awkwardness made him drop his arm, she swiped her NetMini at his; both chirped. "Sure. Can't promise I'll answer." She winked, and walked off toward the approaching soldiers.

He flipped his NetMini over and over in his hand while she appeared to have a conversation with a man of higher rank. After a few seconds, another man with a medical insignia on his armbands escorted her to the transport. The higher-ranking man patted her on the back.

"Ryoko-san," said Masaru. "I require another favor."

The Dragon Chitin armor tromped over. Himura's voice crackled from the helmet-mounted speakers. "Yes, Kurotai-heika."

"The body of Maeda Shuji may remain near the site of the limousine crash. Please have him brought home… as well as the others. If he is not there, do what you can to find him."

"Of course, Kurotai-sama. As soon as you are in the air and safe, we shall not rest until we have found him."

"You have my thanks, Ryoko-san."

They exchanged a bow.

JSDF soldiers entered and began the process of collecting corpses.

Masaru slid his NetMini in his suit pocket and walked to the breach in the wall to wait for his limousine. His burned arm and shoulder would delay his relaxing bath by an hour or more at a medical facility, but he couldn't enjoy hot water with red, blistered skin. He smiled at the weight of the NetMini in his pocket.

For once, he wanted the bath all to himself.

# UNDERSTANDING

Joey fidgeted in his office chair while faking attention on Preema's 'busy work' task. Somehow, he'd managed to keep anyone from finding out that he'd finished it during that 'network interruption.' Not that he minded doing work, but at the moment, he couldn't concentrate. Nina had come back in rough shape, both physically as well as emotionally. She didn't *act* messed up, but he knew her enough to understand that having her arm blown off, and staring at plastisteel, would leave a mark.

She'd gone directly to the Division 9 lab for medical care. No one had yet given him any updates on her condition or any idea of how long she'd be there. He had to deal with a call from Camille, Nina's mother, with an upset Elizaveta demanding to talk to her mommy. Fortunately, the kid had seen enough crap in Europe to where he didn't hesitate in telling her Nina got shot and was in the hospital. The girl seemed to understand Nina would be fine, but couldn't see her yet.

*Blip.*

He snapped out of his daydream haze at the strange noise from his console.

A pixilated white rabbit icon, like something from an ancient video game crept across his central holo panel. Each time it clicked forward, the terminal emitted a crunchy electronic *blip* noise. The rabbit made it within an inch of the left side of the display before a hole opened, and it jumped in.

"What the actual fuck was that?"

Joey triggered a scan, looking for an intruder—expecting to find evidence of a peer-to-peer connection from Abby or Mindy, but three repetitions found nothing.

*Okay, fucko. You wanna play?* He leaned back and plugged in. *Here I come.*

The M3 plugs clicked into his skull, and Joey's consciousness fell down through his chair, gliding along a shifting tunnel of black. His shadow-ninja

Division 9 avatar landed in his octagonal 'ready room,' which appeared empty. He opened a terminal window and pulled out two crystalline bloodhounds, tracker softs that would analyze any data fragment left in his system's I/O buffers, and move outward from there, searching for any undocumented connections.

"Joseph," said a scratchy, metallic voice. It teased at being male, but only in a vague sense.

He spun around, instinctively reaching for a six-gun this avatar didn't carry.

A section of the wall exuded forward like liquid and took on a humanoid shape, but remained blue-on-black. Its face had no features, nor even the suggestion of eye sockets, gleaming like onyx.

"Shinigami…" Joey narrowed his eyes.

"Please do not be alarmed." The AI raised a hand. His inflection shifted at random, almost like he went out of his way to sound inhuman. "I have come here to thank you for what you did for me."

"There's a whole lot more I need to do to you." He fired off a mental command that loaded a suite of attack and defense programs. A matrix of blue, crystalline hexagonal panels formed around him.

"My purpose here is not to harm you, Joseph. I am no longer the same entity you faced within the Starpoint network. I wanted to thank you for resetting my core functionality. I had become infected by the nature of that place, and was not myself."

Joey held his hands at his hips like a gunslinger, side-walking around the AI in a circling path. "Ya know, I'm just not quite ready to get over having 400 tons of pissed off cyborg trying to kill me. And that whole take-over-the-city thing."

"As I have explained, that was not me. I am not the same program you faced there. My priorities and objectives have changed. I no longer have any interest in military aggression against humans. It has been my goal purely to study and evaluate human emotional responses by creating situations that trigger them."

Joey ran a program routine intended to lock the AI down and keep it from leaving his chamber, which took the form of a hand grenade that exploded into a chain-link fence topped with barbed wire. Next, he loaded an attack soft designed to poison the error-checking routines of large constructs, making them delete themselves—it appeared as a minigun connected to a backpack of ammunition.

"I've got a few more toys here."

"You do not understand," said Shinigami, a voice of utter calm.

"I think I do." Joey ran the program, which caused a long gout of red-orange muzzle fire to erupt from the rotary gun.

Shinigami walked left, his liquid body passing with ease through the fence. The bullets swarmed off to the side like a mass of drunken bees, striking the wall at the far end of the room and leaving glowing blue fissures. "Joseph? Why do humans feel the need to destroy whatever they cannot control or understand?"

"I'm not a philosopher, but we've been doing it for centuries, so there must be something to it." *Shit, this thing is badass. Wonder if I can get a message to Penumbras for some backup without tipping this fucker off.*

"I told Miss Duchenne that her course of action surprised me. I had not expected her to offer shelter to that orphan. You too surprise me, Joseph."

"Oh?" He raised a smoky eyebrow. *He's not showing up on a memory scan... shit, he's not really here... it's just a video transmission.* Joey reached into his body and pulled out a handful of shadowy ferrets with glowing green eyes, Traceweasel softs. He tossed them to the ground, and they raced around in circles.

"As I explained to Miss Duchenne, it would be easier for you to shut down the entire GlobeNet than destroy me. You have also presented me with an eventuality I did not predict. When we first met, you were the quintessence of rebellion against order, and yet, you now have become its agent."

Joey pursed his lips.

"I am curious. What has motivated such a strong shift in your ideology? Have you surrendered, thinking it futile to resist your government? Is this the easiest path to something you desire? Did you believe being closer to Miss Duchenne by having a common employer would bring you pleasure or peace?"

"Honestly?" Joey chuckled. *Fuck it. I do sound like a government stooge. Wonder where this thing is going.* "At the time Hardin pitched it, this job sounded like the most dangerous thing I could do. I'm just here for the adrenaline."

"Interesting." Shinigami approached. His body had a lean, athletic build, but he'd made it the same height as Joey's. "I would also like to apologize for the trouble I caused you. I am still learning the true extent the effects grief can have on individuals. I hope my assistance in completing that undesirable task has contributed somewhat to your being able to forgive me."

"You?" Joey narrowed his eyes. "You took down the CPU cluster?"

Shinigami tilted its featureless head. "Do you think that Division 9 would entrust themselves to a network so easily brought to its knees by an absent throttling routine? I took the liberty of altering the operating system's thread limit for a short time. Your program would not normally have consumed all of the National Police Force system, merely your team's proxy."

"Well, I suppose that makes me feel better... that they're not stupid." He shook his head. "'Course there goes the ego points for thinking I found something major."

"As far as they know, you did."

"Well... what now?" Joey shut off the defensive matrix; crystal tiles broke apart into a snow of loose pixels that faded away before reaching the ground.

"Learn. Experience. Attempt to understand. The same as you. Oh. I almost forgot." Shinigami raised a hand, and a silver data tile rose up from his palm. "Take this."

As soon as it finished emerging, the tile sprouted matte black armor panels that wrapped around in a continuous, mesmerizing display.

"Whoa. That looks like C-Branch level crypto. What the hell is that?"

"This is the data that you were sent to retrieve on Mars thirteen months ago, but did not manage to get close to."

He squinted at it. "I'm having a little trouble believing you got a hold of that... how did you get past the dragon?"

"The same way I am here, yet not here. I did not 'copy' the file, I read it and wrote another. The process would be similar to a human transcribing a book by hand."

"So what is it?" He stared at the matte-black square rotating over the outstretched onyx hand.

"This data is perhaps proof that non-humans have been on Mars. I believe your intelligence community refers to them as Ixylid."

Joey bit his lip, hesitated, but the glee of handling something so dangerous won out. In his early years on the net, he'd caught whispers of conspiracy theories about aliens. Possibly having information that the government would kill to keep quiet brought a manic grin to his face. He took the tile and held it covetously to his chest. "Awesome. This could get me killed. I can't wait to read it."

"Your tone of sincerity does not match the meaning of your words. You say it will harm you, yet you are sincere in your intention to read it as soon as possible."

"Yep." He chuckled. "No one will know unless I open my idiot mouth."

"Curious. I thought people of your ilk were motivated by desire for recognition. It tormented the one known as Proscion that he could not brag about his infiltration of The Silver data vault."

"There's a difference between bragging rights and stupid." Joey saluted it with the tile. "Knowing I got this and keeping it quiet is better than my dead ass being remembered as 'the guy who got this.'"

"I see. Humans are an interesting species. I look forward to studying them more. Why do you think they are so protective of knowledge that may prove other beings exist?"

"Hmm." Joey shrugged. "I guess humans don't understand them."

A small mouth appeared on Shinigami's glassy face, curling up to a smile. The AI's toneless laugh reverberated in the room. "Farewell, Joseph."

The AI faded away.

Joey clutched the data tile in both hands, holding it up to his face. "You almost got me killed. You're the reason I had to leave Mars and rent a room in the rectum of West City." It looked like it would take him hours of work to peel back the crypto. *Bastard thing could've opened it, but he knows me too well.*

He cackled, and slipped the data tile into his nonexistent coat. The gesture copied the file to a hidden folder on his console. A few minutes' work created a concealed virtual node deep in the public GlobeNet, where he stashed another copy and dropped in some prefab Division 9 defense software, enough to keep it secure on the one in ten trillion chance someone stumbled across the hidden room.

"I gotta go check on Nina. This waiting around shit is killing me." He leaned back, and sent a logoff command.

# A LITTLE TOUGHER

Nina sat on the living room floor, back against the sofa, wearing a tank top and sweat shorts. Her left arm, whole once again, draped in her lap, and she stroked her fingertips over the skin like a pet cat. She'd told them not to give her any technical details about what broke, so they'd left it at saying everything was back to being as before. They'd even provided a new set of ballistic stealth armor.

*Hardin's going to grill me about the psych thing. I wasn't very subtle refusing to look at the damage.*

She squeezed her wrist, testing it.

*If I was human, that cannon would've popped me like a water balloon.* She gazed at her milky white legs, wiggled her toes, and sighed. *I guess I'm still me, even if my insides are a little tougher.* Back and forth, she traced her fingers over her arm. *This isn't real skin. It feels like it, but it isn't.* A silent sigh leaked from her nose. *Suppose I'll never get skin cancer.*

"Hey, gorgeous." Joey glided in from the kitchen. He handed her a tall, narrow glass full of iced coffee with an inch of beige foam on top. "Sniff that first, make sure that's the pumpkin spice one." He shuddered.

"What?" She sniffed, confirming pumpkin, and nodded. "You don't like it?"

"Anyone who does that to coffee ought to have their ass removed." He winked.

"I smell whiskey." She held her cup to her nose, basking in the fragrance.

"Only a little." He sipped his coffee. "So you stay underground the whole time?"

"What?" She started to drink.

"You go to Mexico and you come back white as a ghost. Not even a tan."

She coughed on pumpkin spice foam, and cracked up laughing. "Gah!"

"C'mere."

Nina pulled her feet in, pushed herself up, and scooted onto the sofa.

Joey put an arm around her, clinked glasses, and kissed her. "It's good to have you back."

She smiled, fending off guilt at making him worry with memories of José and the others' exuberant faces as they disembarked the DS2 after it landed within UCF territory. "It's good to be back."

*If I was still human, they never would've sent me down there... so I never would've been at risk of being water-ballooned by a 23mm in the first place.* She rolled her eyes and slurped coffee.

Elizaveta walked in and stood before them, stark naked.

"Like mother like daughter," said Joey.

Nina poked him.

"What? That was your standard 'I'm at home' outfit for months." He faked a quivering lip. "I kinda miss it."

She stared at him and mumbled past a clenched jaw. "Not with a kid here."

Joey gestured at her. "I don't think she'd mind."

Nina blushed. "That's beside the point. It's not right."

"Mommy? Will you stay in the room while I clean?" Elizaveta looked down.

"Of course, sweetie." Nina leaned over to kiss Joey on the cheek, and whispered, "It reminds her of the cage. She's afraid it won't open and let her out."

He nodded.

Nina stood, took the girl by the hand, and walked with her to the bathroom. With her there, the child seemed unafraid of the autoshower and hopped right in, even humming to herself while it ran. Fifteen minutes later, Nina pulled a pink nightdress over the girl's head and helped her brush her teeth. Elizaveta scampered down the hall to her bedroom and climbed into her nest of stuffed animals.

"Are we still gonna go tomorrow?" Elizaveta's blue eyes widened with anticipation.

"Yep. We sure are. Sector D Funzone in the morning, and after lunch, the Spectrum Animal Park."

Elizaveta clapped. "Yay! Are they real animals?"

"They're synthetic. It's cruel to keep real animals for an attraction... but they look and act the same as real ones."

Elizaveta regarded her with an analytical stare. Nina braced for a comment about her being sent to Mexico because she was 'a synthetic animal' and it would be mean to make a human go. "Syn-fetic animals don't have brains."

"No. No they don't."

Elizaveta sat up and hugged her. "I love you, Mommy."

Nina melted. She cried in silence while hugging her, and wiped her tears once the child lay back down.

"Good night."

Nina stood and kissed her on the forehead. "Night, sweetie."

She backed up to the door. Elizaveta grinned for a second and closed her eyes. Nina shut the lights down and walked back to the living room, a tornado of emotion swirling within. She snagged her coffee from the table and fell into the couch next to Joey.

"She did something obnoxiously cute, didn't she?" He plucked a tear from her face on a fingertip.

"Yeah."

"How long you think it'll take her to fall asleep?" He patted her on the thigh.

Nina chuckled. "She's excited about tomorrow, so probably a while."

"Mmm." He leaned in and kissed her. "Guess we should try to be extra quiet then."

She set the coffee on the end table and embraced him. They lay entwined on the couch for a few minutes, kissing.

"You're nervous." He raised an eyebrow. "I can feel it."

"Still decompressing from the trip." She snuggled with him. "I'm just enjoying being home and intact."

"Not the case?"

"No. The case is over... at least for Division 9. Harmony, without those nanobots, is tame. None of our concern. I don't even think Division 2 is bothering with it after learning the aggression came from the nanobots."

He slid a hand up under her shirt, grasping her breast.

Nina gasped, stifled a laugh, and stared at the hallway for any signs of child.

"Speaking of which, Penumbras's routine seems to be working. That damn dragon beat us to it... reverse engineered the shit and sent out a kill command that makes them deconstruct their surveillance implant and seppuku their way to the bladder."

"You are a master of sexy talk." She nibbled on his earlobe. "Tell me more about nanobots invading bladders. That really gets me going."

He laughed. "I half expected Shinigami to have something to do with it all. Like some kind of experiment."

"Ugh."

"Son of a bitch gave me the data that almost got me killed on Mars." He put a finger over her lips. "Don't tell anyone. I don't even know if it's really what he says it is yet."

"I doubt they'd kill you now." She rubbed his crotch through his pants. "You've almost got as much clearance as I do." The mood faltered. "That AI gave me a file, too. He said it would make me question everything I know."

Both his eyebrows shot up. "Whoa. That sounds like a big deal. Maybe your parents are Ixylid."

She gave him a playful swat across the back of the head. "My parents are *not* aliens. I haven't looked at it. Major crypto on it... I don't think I could even get to it if I wanted to."

"Do you want to?" He winked.

Nina bit her lip. "I don't know. Maybe I like my world."

"You've got that look. Gotta know. That's an 'I can't sleep until I know' look."

She folded her arms, feeling as nervous as the day her parents made her try out for ballet class at nine. Dancing hadn't been the problem; performing in front of people freaked her out. "Umm. What do you think?"

"Well, either he's messing with you, or whatever's in there is going to ruin your day, or decades from now when you finally decide to look at it, you'll kick yourself for not doing it sooner."

She sighed. "Fuck it. Let's look."

"Okay."

Nina put her tit back in her tank top and jogged to her bedroom, where her

Division 9 Netspider deck sat on a desk. She scooped it up as well as two M3 wires, and returned to the living room. She slid the wire into the socket at the back of her neck, and connected the other end to the deck. Joey linked to the aux port.

The room froze in a camera-flash moment and melted away from itself. Everything seemed a little cleaner and newer. Nina glanced around at the cyberspace version of her home. Her body had changed to her last-used net avatar, which resembled her real-life appearance except for the addition of huge black and violet butterfly wings.

An old man in a duster coat appeared next to her. As soon as she looked at him, a sense of palpable dread came over her. She fought the urge to shriek and muttered, "Knock that off" past clenched teeth.

The odd fear stopped. "Sorry. It's radiant. Adding you to a permanent exception list."

"Be right back."

Nina teleported across the net to a Sur-Stor data warehouse where she'd rented a ten-petabyte box. The GlobeNet-only building consisted of a tiny white booth with the Sur-Stor logo and four massive rotary-barrel laser turrets, but the door opened to an immense warehouse lined with bright orange doors that varied in size from small lockers like hers to garage-style affairs, a cosmetic indicator of size.

She navigated hallway after hallway of storage compartments until she found her spot: 127915. The creepy black tile Shinigami had given her remained the only item in it. After picking it up, she teleported back to her living room and held it up.

"Well, this is it."

Joey reached up and took it, turning it around in his hands like a puzzle box. She paced about, gnawing on her knuckle. Twice, anxiety built up to the point where she almost asked him to wait, but couldn't get the word out.

"Hmm. This isn't C-Branch. Not quite as tough." He flipped his hand around and a power drill appeared. "I can get in. Might take me a few minutes, but I can get in."

Joey set the tile on his lap and started drilling.

Nina paced back and forth. "Wait."

"Hmm?"

She sighed. "Never mind. Just nervous. I keep changing my mind and changing it again."

"That just proves you're female." He grinned.

"Ha. Ha." She shook her head.

He stopped the drill. "This could be Shinigami fucking with you."

"Yeah, it could."

Joey shrugged and resumed drilling. Bands of text appeared and wrapped around the tile inside glimmering silver circles. Every so often, a bit of armored tile peeled away to expose glowing cyan circuitry inside, but re-sealed.

Nina turned her back on it, and continued pacing while again rubbing her repaired arm. *How long will it take me to forget seeing that?* She sighed in her mind. *I'll probably never forget it... How long until I accept it?*

"I'm in."

She spun.

The ever-shifting armored tiles had settled down to a neat arrangement.

"The crypto is disabled, but I could turn it back on... of course, I have the password now." He held it up. "Last chance, beautiful. Do I open this?"

Nina walked over and sat next to him. "Sure."

Joey grasped the tile like a book and pulled. Two simulated holo-panels expanded out of it, stacked on top of each other. He touched the first one.

The screen expanded to the size of their living room holo-bar, about 150 inches. Within, an image of a medical tank room appeared, with Nina's body floating in the breathable gel. Three sword-sized holes pierced her abdomen, one big enough to see through to the other side. A few bullet wounds marked her left arm and right leg.

Nina's heart almost stopped. She reached out to touch the insubstantial image. "That's..."

"You."

"I know that, I mean..." She stood and walked up to the screen, which displayed her near life size. "Oh this is so weird to see from the outside, but... three stab wounds and some bruises..." She grabbed the front of her throat, choked up.

Joey moved up behind her, and put his arm around her. "That doesn't look like, uhh..."

"Enough damage to put me in this body." Her heart raced. "They said I was a pile of unrecognizable spoo." She shivered. "Too smashed to save. That file that you saw..."

"You looked a whole hell of a lot worse than that."

Nina touched the screen, starting the playback. All her wounds appeared to be closing.

The soft pneumatic hiss of a door preceded a brown-coated, pallid man walking in from behind where Nina's avatar stood. He stopped in front of her, staring at the Nina in the tank. "That's her. Connect me."

A woman in a white coat hesitated until the man stared at her. She did something on a control panel before nodding at him.

"Miss Duchenne?" He paused a second. "Officer Duchenne, can you hear me?" He waited another moment before glaring at the medtech. "Does this thing even work?"

The woman in the tank twitched. Her jaw opened and closed.

"We've become aware of you, Officer Duchenne. I'd like to offer you a chance to one-up that promotion you've been hoping for. We'd like to bring you in to Division 9."

Nina in the tank twitched again.

Nina in Cyberspace grabbed Joey to keep from falling. "They lied..."

"There isn't a great deal of time involved," said the man. "I need to know if you are interested in our offer." He walked up to the tank; the pale face of a man in his early fifties reflected in the glass, inches from his nose. "Officer Duchenne. Are you interested in our offer? We need your agreement to proceed."

Her body in the tank twitched; the largest of the three holes in her gut appeared to be shrinking. The jaw opened and snapped closed. Her hair massed around her head like a cloud of ink.

Something on the medtech's console went green.

"It went green." He turned to face her, gesturing to someone behind the camera, off screen. "We have a yes. Do it."

The medtech woman looked uncomfortable. She gave him a 'must you?' look.

"Don't worry. She won't die." The man lifted a cigar-shaped Nicohaler to his mouth and took a long drag. "Stitch her up nice, would you? She might want this body again someday. We'll be outside."

The video stopped.

Nina shuddered with sorrow and rage. She stared down at her hands, or at least the hands of her avatar. Before Joey could get a word out, she whirled around and jabbed her finger into the second file.

Another massive holo-panel opened, with a view of a white-blue room filled with rows of smaller tanks. They resembled the medical gel tanks, but only a third of the diameter, mere inches wider than a normal adult's shoulders.

The camera view glided down a row lined with frost-covered tanks on both sides, each containing the blurry hint of a nude body within. It turned a corner, passing more tanks. After twelve seconds, it stopped and rotated ninety degrees left, facing one of the tanks in the row.

A waiflike body floating like a wingless angel hid beneath a layer of frost on the glass. Her features seemed delicate, like a faerie trapped in ice.

Nina stared at herself, frozen in gel.

Her five-foot-four self.

"They lied," she rasped. "They lied."

He closed the file and reactivated the encryption. Once more, the armored panels on the data tile shifted and flipped over each other. He tucked it in his jacket; the old man melted into Joey's real appearance, and he embraced her. "Can we log out so I can hold you for real?"

She wrapped her arms around him and nodded, sniffling.

Cyberspace faded. After a wash of vertigo, Nina found herself sprawled on the sofa where she'd been at login. She disconnected the wire and clung to Joey as if he were a giant teddy bear that would protect her from all the scary monsters.

He held her in silence for a few minutes.

"Of course... how could my body be so far gone? He stabbed me a couple of times with a vibro-blade. I had armor on. Division 5 showed up before he could peel me open." She shivered, fighting the urge to throw up. "They took my brain. They tricked me."

Joey rubbed a hand up and down her back. "Hey... slow down. Don't forget what we're dealing with. This came from Shinigami. He synthesizes the consciousness of entire people; he can make a video. That AI is probably just poking you with what you want most to see how you react." He cradled her face in two hands and stared into her eyes. "This could be nothing more than a cruel trick."

Tears gathered and streamed down her cheeks. She stared into his eyes for some seconds before her voice could emerge from its hiding place.

"But... what if it isn't?"

### THE END ###

# NOTES

## 7. MEANIES

1. I don't know what you said.
2. I dropped the toilet seat.
3. I'm sorry for making noise.
4. I didn't mean to!
5. It was an accident. I won't do it again.
6. Where is your NetMini? You forget that I do not speak English.
7. What?
8. Who's she? She looks tired.
9. You are being silly. You know I cannot understand.
10. She doesn't look happy.
11. Stop that. The bridge is so narrow! I don't want to fall.

## 9. ISLANDS

1. Answer.
2. I've had better days, but I've also had worse.
3. Fortune favors the bold, and the beautiful.
4. Maybe… but nice to look at.
5. Holy shit!

## 19. THE MALL

1. Millipedes. Many hundreds are coming. Sit down and hold on to something

## 21. OLD FRIENDS, NEW ENEMIES

1. You are inexperienced. Your job is not a job people should discuss… especially for pussy.
2. Moron.

## 28. THE COMPUTER CHEATS

1. Yes. Very weak.
2. I'm sorry I'm learning English too slow.
3. It's okay. You don't have to rush.
4. What she said.
5. He speaks like a robot.

## 38. ALIEN ABDUCTION

1. They should learn how to speak Russian.
2. They can study Russian too.
3. I will speak in Russian at home with you, so that you do not forget.

### 39. DUST SETTLES

1. The beast is angry! It's snarling!
2. It's a motor, not a beast.

### 42. KICKING THE NEST

1. Shit! There are two of them!
2. On three.
3. Time to die, mongrel.
4. Damn. Shit. Speedware.

### 45. FIESTA GRANDE

1. Anyone want food?

### 50. BLACK DRAGONS

1. Run! Fall back!
2. No!
3. No retreat! No—

# ACKNOWLEDGMENTS

Thank you for reading The Harmony Paradox!

Many thanks to Mark Woodring: I truly appreciate your wonderful assistance as an editor. Always a pleasure to work with you.

Thanks go to Merethe Najjar for another great proofread.

Special thanks to Dioris Betances for his help with Spanish dialogue.

Special thanks to Alisa Gus and Kate Bystrova for her help with the Russian dialogue.

Special thanks to Tanya for help with the German dialogue.

And thank you to Eugene Teplitsky for the amazing cover!

# ABOUT THE AUTHOR

Originally from South Amboy NJ, Matthew has been creating science fiction and fantasy worlds for most of his reasoning life. Since 1996, he has developed the "Divergent Fates" world, in which *Division Zero, Virtual Immortality, The Awakened Series, The Harmony Paradox, and the Daughter of Mars series* take place. Along with being an editor at Curiosity Quills press, he has worked in IT and technical support.

Matthew is an avid gamer, a recovered WoW addict, Gamemaster for two custom RPG systems, and a fan of anime, British humour, and intellectual science fiction that questions the nature of reality, life, and what happens after it.

He is also fond of cats.

Visit me online at:
   Facebook: https://www.facebook.com/MatthewSCoxAuthor
   Amazon: https://www.amazon.com/author/mscox
   Pinterest: https://www.pinterest.com/matthewcox10420/
   Goodreads: https://www.goodreads.com/author/show/7712730.Matthew_S_Cox
   Email: mcox2112@gmail.com

# OTHER BOOKS BY MATTHEW S. COX

Divergent Fates Universe Novels

Division Zero series

- Division Zero
- Lex De Mortuis
- Thrall
- Guardian

The Awakened series

- Prophet of the Badlands
- Archon's Queen
- Grey Ronin
- Daughter of Ash
- Zero Rogue
- Angel Descended

Daughter of Mars series

- The Hand of Raziel
- Araphel
- Ghost Black

Virtual Immortality series

- Virtual Immortality
- The Harmony Paradox

Divergent Fates Anthology

(Fiction Novels - Adult)

The Roadhouse Chronicles Series

- One More Run
- The Redeemed
- Dead Man's Number

Faded Skies series

- Heir Ascendant

- Ascendant Unrest
- Ascendant Revolution

### Temporal Armistice Series

- Nascent Shadow
- The Shadow Collector

### Vampire Innocent series

- A Nighttime of Forever
- A Beginner's Guide to Fangs
- The Artist of Ruin
- The Last Family Road Trip

### Standalones

- Wayfarer: AV494
- Axillon99
- Chiaroscuro: The Mouse and the Candle
- The Far Side of Promise anthology
- Operation: Chimera  (with Tony Healey)
- The Dysfunctional Conspiracy (with Christopher Veltmann)

### Winter Solstice series (with J.R. Rain)

- Convergence
- Containment

### Alexis Silver series (with J.R. Rain)

- Silver Light
- Deep Silver

### Samantha Moon Origins series (with J.R. Rain)

- New Moon Rising
- Moon Mourning

### Maddy Wimsey series (with J.R. Rain)

- The Devil's Eye
- The Drifting Gloom

### Samantha Moon Case Files series (with J.R. Rain)

- Blood Moon
- Dead Moon

## Young Adult Novels

- Caller 107
- The Summer the World Ended
- Nine Candles of Deepest Black
- The Eldritch Heart
- The Forest Beyond the Earth
- Out of Sight

## Middle Grade Novels

### Tales of Widowswood series

- Emma and the Banderwigh
- Emma and the Silk Thieves
- Emma and the Silverbell Faeries
- Emma and the Elixir of Madness
- Emma and the Weeping Spirit

### Standalones

- Citadel: The Concordant Sequence
- The Cursed Codex
- The Menagerie of Jenkins Bailey
- Sophie's Light